'With his colourful characters and Boxer Rebellion setting, Adam Williams has created a scintillating adventure polished by a dash of history . . . What Williams makes of his characters is a rattling good read. Full of love and loss and guts and gore and derring-do, this is as good as an adventure story gets. Some novelists are adept at driving a story through dialogue, while others find narrative more natural. Williams is a master of both. This is his first novel, yet technically accomplished . . . Beyond a cracking story, well conceived and executed, is there more? Yes, much . . . He excels in communicating China's simultaneous similarity and strangeness . . . Entertaining, engaging and informative, this book deserves to do well.' *The Times*

'An epic historical and romantic story as well as an impressive first novel.' *Sunday Mirror*

'This is a rollicking monster of a book . . . At the same time, it's a valuable and scholarly examination of what history has come to term the Boxer Rebellion. On both levels, as a good yarn and as fascinating political detail, this is a compelling read.' *South China Morning Post*

'. . . skilfully depicts the cultural disconnect between Westerners and Chinese through a sharply drawn cast of characters who confront romance, adventure and stark moral dilemmas.' *Newsweek*

'If you like derring-do, murderous characters, interesting sexual practices and intrigue, this is for you . . . indulge in a heady, passionate drama.' *Daily Express*

'Absolutely wonderful – that very ra[...] which really draws the reader into it[...]

'Intrigue, adventure and romance av[...] knowledge of China and the comp[...] sleeping dragon that makes this a w[...]

'*The Palace of Heavenly Pleasure* is a great epic sweep of a book, driven by such a powerful cocktail of history, passion, plot and character that you will be drawn completely into the world created by Adam Williams and will not want to leave. This is a story told not only with brilliant imagination, but also with the knowledge and authority of an author steeped in the traditions and environment about which he writes. A fantastic read about the tensions and people in a forgotten corner of Britain's empire.' Humphrey Hawksley

'A thinking reader's epic, a wide-screen evocation of another culture in another time, written by a master storyteller with passion, humanity and understanding . . . a book which will sweep you away to Northern China at the turn of the last century.' Celia Brayfield, *Quicksilver*

'Storytelling of the epic kind – this 700 page tale about sinners and lovers in 1900s China will have you gripped.' *Heat*

'An epic tale pulsing with intrigue, adventure and romance.' *Live Wire*

'The blockbuster of the summer.' *Good Houskeeping*

'A sweeping, old-style historical epic set in China at the end of the 19th century . . . Romance, danger and murder are interwoven in this enthralling yarn.' *Woman & Home*

'The essential summer read.' *Choice*

'Few first novels published in the last few years have been on the same unashamedly epic scale as Adam Williams's *The Palace of Heavenly Pleasure*. This is a book of grand passion and vivid melodrama played out against the colourful backdrop of the European community in China at the time of the Boxer Rebellion . . . Heroism and martyrdom, cruelty and barbarism, love and sacrifice, madness and despair all play their part in the story that unfolds. This is a big, bold candidate for bestseller status that drags the reader instantly into the world it recreates.' *Waterstone's Books Quarterly*

ADAM WILLIAMS

The Palace of Heavenly Pleasure

FLAME
Hodder & Stoughton

First published in Great Britain in 2003 by Hodder & Stoughton
This paperback edition published in 2004 by Hodder & Stoughton
A division of Hodder Headline

A Flame paperback

1 3 5 7 9 10 8 6 4 2

A CIP catalogue record for this title is
available from the British Library

ISBN: 0340 82788 2

Typeset in Sabon by Palimpsest Book Production Limited,
Polmont, Stirlingshire

Printed and bound in Great Britain by
Mackays of Chatham Ltd, Chatham, Kent

Hodder Headline's policy is to use papers that are natural, renewable and recyclable
products and made from wood grown in sustainable forests. The logging and
manufacturing processes are expected to conform to the environmental regulations of
the country of origin.

Hodder and Stoughton
A division of Hodder Headline
338 Euston Road
London NW1 3BH

To HHA, PDLW and FR lePW

Note on Chinese Names

In transliterating the sounds of the Chinese language into English I have used where I can the modern Chinese Pinyin system rather than the Wade Giles spelling that would have been current in 1900.

For well-known place names and historical personages, however, I have used the spelling that would have been current at the time. The Chinese capital is therefore Peking rather than Beijing. I have the Boxers originating in Shantung Province rather than the modern Shandong. The reformist Chinese minister is Li Hung-chang rather than Li Hongzhang (as his name is spelt in Chinese history books today). And I have used the word Ch'ing for the name of the Chinese dynasty rather than the modern Qing.

In China the surname comes before the given names. Hence Fan Yimei is Miss Fan rather than Miss Yimei. And as in our own society a hundred years ago, even friends are more likely to use surname than forename. A title comes after the surname. For example, taking the words for Mister (Xiansheng, literally Firstborn), Miss (Xiaojie, literally little sister) or Master (of trades: Shifu), 'Mr Lu' would be 'Lu Xiansheng'. 'Mandarin Liu' would be 'Liu Da Ren' (Liu the Great One); 'Master Zhao' would be 'Zhao Shifu'; 'Auntie Ma' (Frank's housemaid) would be 'Ma Ayi'. Nicknames follow the same rules: for example, the brothel-keeper, 'Mother Liu', is 'Liu Mama' in Chinese.

Chinese also tend to show intimacy and respect through a descriptive epithet before or after the surname. The gatekeeper calls Fan Yimei 'Fan Jiejie', ie. 'Elder Sister Fan'. An older friend might call her 'Xiao Fan', or 'Little Fan'. This is not derogatory at all. Nor is its opposite: 'Lao Fan', or 'Old Fan', the term of address that might be given by a younger friend to an older one. But sometimes there can be a different meaning if the adjective is put after the surname rather than before. The Chamberlain is customarily addressed as 'Jin Lao', or literally 'Jin Old' – but put this way it actually means 'the Venerable Jin' and is a term of enormous respect, given by an inferior to a superior. To use 'Lao Jin' in this case would be over-familiar.

North East China 1899

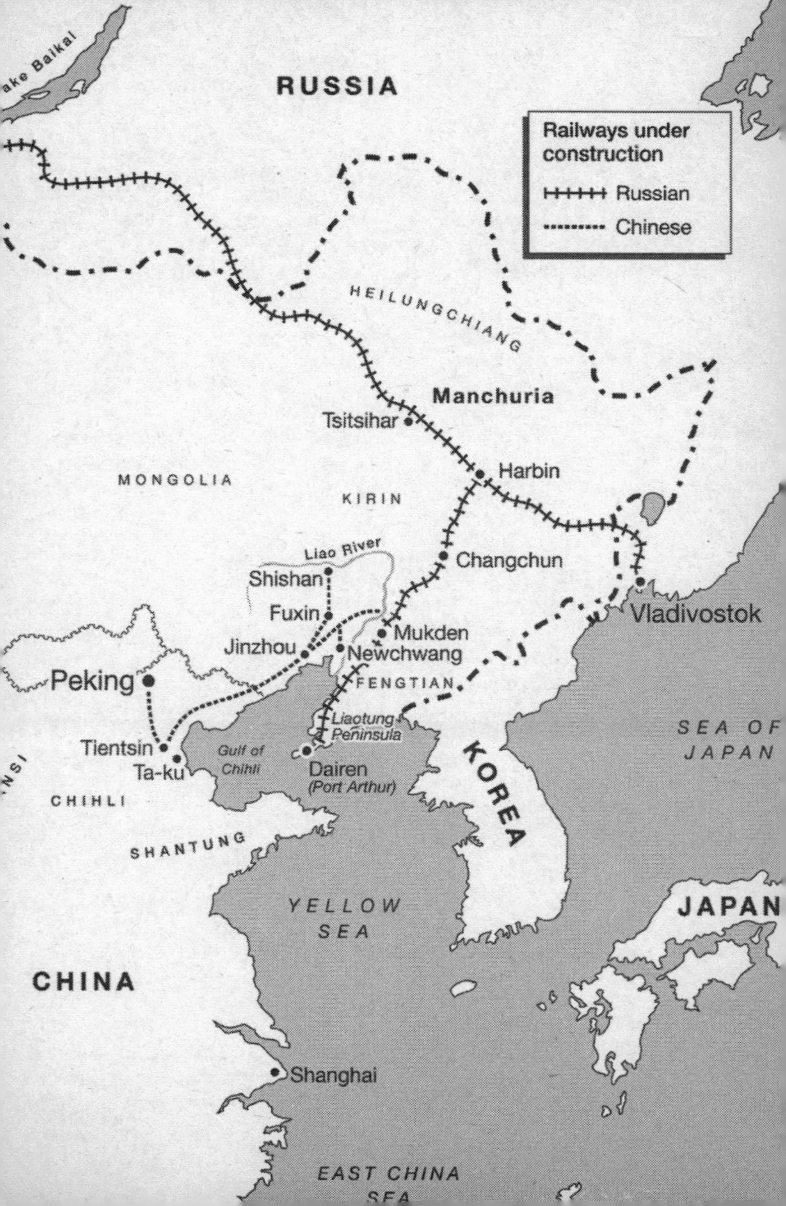

The Characters

(1) In Peking

(a) GOVERNMENT OFFICIALS

The Empress Dowager Tz'u-Hsi: The power behind the throne, effective ruler of China

Li Hung-chang: Elder statesman: 'father' of China's international diplomacy and modernization under the Ching Dynasty, in disgrace after China's defeat by Japan in 1895

Prince Tuan: Head of the xenophobic faction in the Chinese court

Prince Yi: A court official

Li Lien-ying: Tz'u Hsi's Chief Eunuch

(b) THE FOREIGN COMMUNITY

Sir Claude MacDonald: British Minister, head of the British Legation

Lady MacDonald: his wife

Douglas Pritchett: Ostensibly interpreter at the British Legation, also head of intelligence

Monsieur Pichon: French minister, head of the French Legation

Madame Pichon: his wife

Dr G. E. Morrison: *Times* correspondent, traveller, adventurer

Herbert Squiers: First secretary at the American Legation

Countess Esterhazy: European aristocratic adventuress, visiting Peking

B. L. Simpson: employee of the China Customs Service under Sir Robert Hart

Mr and Mrs Dawson: representatives of Babbit and Brenner, a chemicals company

Colonel Taro Hideyoshi: a military attaché at the Japanese Legation

(2) *In Shishan*

(a) GOVERNMENT OFFICIALS

The Mandarin, Liu Daguang: the 'Taotai', or chief magistrate of
Shishan

Jin Zhijian (called Jin Lao – Venerable Jin): the Mandarin's
chamberlain and master of his household

Major Lin Fubo: head of the Mandarin's militia

(b) THE MISSIONARY COMMUNITY

Dr Edward Airton: a Scottish Missionary Society doctor,
practising in Shishan

Nellie Airton: his wife

George and Jenny Airton: his young children

Father Adolphus: deceased head of the Catholic mission in
Shishan

Sisters Elena and Caterina: Italian nuns now working at Airton's
mission

Zhang Erhao: Dr Airton's major-domo

Ah Li and Ah Sun: Dr Airton's Cantonese servants

The Rev. Septimus Millward: American Congregationalist
missionary living in Shishan

Laetitia Millward: his wife

Hiram, Mildred, Isaiah, Miriam, Thomas, Martha, Lettie and
Hannah Millward: his children

(c) THE MERCHANT COMMUNITY

Frank Delamere: a 'soap merchant', representative of Babbit and
Brenner in Shishan

Tang Dexin, Jin Shangui, Lu Jincai: Merchants of Shishan

Mr Ding: Textile dyer from Tsitsihar, one of Frank Delamere's
customers

Hermann Fischer: Chief of the railway building project in Shishan

Zhang Dongren ('Charlie'): the westernised *compradore* at the
railway and Fischer's interpreter

Zhang Haobin: foreman of the Chinese workers on the railway

Ma Ayi: Frank Delamere's housemaid

Lao Zhao: Muleteer working for the railway company

(d) THE PALACE OF HEAVENLY PLEASURE

Mother Liu: Proprietress of the Palace of Heavenly Pleasure, a notorious brothel

Ren Ren: Her son

Fan Yimei: a courtesan in the Palace of Heavenly Pleasure, Major Lin's mistress

Shen Ping, Su Liping, Chen Meina: courtesans

Monkey: one of Ren Ren's disreputable friends

(e) IN THE BLACK HILLS

Wang Tieren (Iron Man Wang): a shadowy figure, leader of a gang of bandits in the Black Hills

(f) IN BASHU, AN OUTLYING VILLAGE

Pastor John Wang: head of the Christian community

Mother Wang: his wife

Mary and Martha: his daughters

Headman Yang: the village headman

Miller Zhang, Lao Yi: Christian villagers

Mother Yang, Xiao Hudie, Lao Dai, Wang Haotian, Zheng Fujia: non-Christian villagers

The village *bonze*: the local Buddhist priest

(3) Newcomers to Shishan

Henry Manners: formerly an officer in the British army, now working for the China Railways

Helen Frances Delamere: Frank Delamere's daughter, fresh from convent school

Tom Cabot: Frank Delamere's new assistant

The Rev. Burton Fielding: representative of the American Board of Commissioners for Missions in China

Frederick Bowers: engineer, train driver

The Boxer Priest

(4) Other Players

Orkhon Baatar: a Mongolian herdsman

Sarantuya: his wife

Lieutenant Panin, Colonel Tubaichev: Russian officers
The Rev. Richard Brown: a medical missionary
Arthur Topps: an employee of Babbit and Brenner
James Airton: Edward Airton's brother, a bookseller in Glasgow
The Gillespies: medical missionaries in Tientsin, friends of the
   Airtons
Admiral Seymour, General Chaffee, General von Waldersee:
   leaders of the Allied Expeditionary Force to Peking
Edmund and Mary Airton: Edward Airton's children at school in
   Scotland

The British Legation, Peking, July 1899

Geography books will tell you that the dust storms of summer, though rare, are generally violent.

So it was this summer.

Strong winds from Siberia, sucked into the heatbowl of a north China plain already unprotected after three years of drought, effortlessly lifted sand from the Gobi desert and powdery loess soil from the Yellow river escarpments, and deluged the cracked farmlands under an amber cloud.

The advance of the storm was like that of a barbarian horde; or one of those peasant movements that, from time to time in imperial history, have erupted from obscure beginnings and overwhelmed the decadent armies that stood futilely in their way. Like the Yellow Turbans, or the Taipings, or the White Lotus, like any of the revolts in which bandit leaders have aspired to and sometimes attained the Dragon Throne, it grew on its successes, increasing in size and fury until its armies were strong enough to escalade the high walls and tall gatehouses of the Imperial capital, bursting into the narrow streets, penetrating even the courtyards of the Forbidden City, where a weak emperor still held the Mandate of Heaven in feeble hands. So this sandstorm, on a summer night in the last year of the old century, enveloped the streets of Peking. Its myriad conquering soldiers were let loose to pillage the invested town. Dust devils howled a devastating path through the *hutongs*, whipping down the signs on the ornamented shops, splintering the gates of courtyard houses, slicing the skin of those few passers-by who had the temerity to go outside and brave the flying sand darts.

It was a day without a dusk, for the paling sun had been extinguished at its zenith. The darkness of an unnatural noon merged imperceptibly with the greater darkness of a starless night. The inhabitants of Peking, cowering in the heat of their airless homes, huddled against the shrieks and groans of the marauding wind outside; this was a night in which evil stalked abroad.

There were no parties in the Legation Quarter that evening. No chandeliers blazed in the ballrooms. Landaus and barouches were locked in the stables with the horses. Windows were battened down. Luckless marines on sentry duty wrapped up their faces and sought protection from the sand as best they could. The ministers and their ladies settled for an early night.

On summer evenings the British Legation usually presented a fairyland of lanterns in its courtyards. Lady MacDonald, chatelaine of a palace that had once belonged to Manchu nobility, liked to indulge her taste for chinoiserie. She affected not to hear the comments of the few real Orientalists in the Legation, who objected that her Mikado-esque decorations in a Chinese building were somewhat gilding the lily (or 'painting legs on a snake', as the Chinese would have it). As the premier hostess in Peking, she knew exactly what appealed to the representatives of the powers who came to her parties: it was more important to present China as it ought to be rather than the squalid reality that stank of the drains and canals outside her walls. So, if Gilbert and Sullivan could improve on three millennia of civilisation, she was all for it.

Tonight, however, all the gaudy decorations had been removed, and the Chinese pavilions and ornamental archways, with their pillars and curling roofs, lay as unprotected in the sandstorm as any other dwellings in the city. Violent spectres of wind licked over the verandas and rattled the boards that had been placed over the imported glass windows. The ginkgo trees shook their branches like demented spirits, their fan-shaped leaves flailing against the hurtling sand. The old buildings slumped against the onslaught, dark grey shadows against a darker sky. It was as if they had reverted to the decrepit state of abandonment that had existed before the English had come to renovate them. The temple-like roofs silhouetted against the howling night recalled those deserted shrines in Chinese literature popularly haunted by ghosts and devils. Lady MacDonald's garden had become a wasteland of random violence, in which the uneasy apparitions of previous occupants might well have wandered, as well as those creatures of Chinese folklore – fox spirits, snake gods, hungry ghosts – and other unmentionable creations of superstition that traditionally emerged on nights such as this.

Not that Sir Claude and Lady MacDonald noticed or cared. They were sleeping soundly in their beds under their mosquito nets in the Main Residence, formerly the Ancestral Hall.

Only one official was awake and sensitive to the perils of the night. His light burned faintly through an upper-storey window of one of the less imposing edifices on the edge of the compound, formerly a storehouse where the dukes in the past had kept their treasure. It was the room of the interpreter, a young Englishman who had only recently been appointed to the Legation. Stripped to his shirt, he was hunched over a small desk on which an oil lamp flickered. The light revealed bare wooden walls, a hospital bed and shelves loaded with books, most of them in Chinese. He was writing a despatch, out of Chancellery, out of office hours, in the middle of a stormy night – it could hardly be official Legation business; in any case, his furtive manner was enough to indicate that secrets were involved. He was sweating, his thin face pinched by tiredness, and his red-rimmed eyes widened at every noise. Occasionally he would pause, put down his pen, go to the door and peer into the dark corridors outside his room. Then he would return to his manuscript, from time to time dipping his pen into a pot of ink. He wrote hurriedly but in a neat script.

Your lordship is aware of the activities of the Germans in Shantung. We are advised that they have already established a functioning colonial government in the concession which they seized last year in Chiao-chou. There continues to be concern regarding the over-bearing conduct of their missionaries whose 'defence' of Christian communities has as often as not been supported by German troops; reparations imposed for alleged attacks on Christian property have been rapacious. This is potentially dangerous in a province with a history of rebellion and banditry, which is also the home of many of the martial-arts sects and secret societies, which colourfully thrive in poor areas such as these.

There was a crash from the floor below. He paused, staring at the door. The crash was repeated. 'Shutters. Wind. That's all it is,' he muttered to himself, and resumed writing.

More alarming are the activities of the Russians in the Northeast. Much of Manchuria is already a Russian protectorate in substance if not in name. It was evident what were their intentions as far back as 1896 when they pressured the former Foreign Minister, Li

3

Hung-chang, to sign a so-called 'defensive alliance' granting Russia the right to extend the Trans Siberian Railway eastwards across Heilungchiang. Their seizure last year of the Liaotung Peninsula was followed by demands for concessions to construct a north–south railway from Harbin to Port Arthur. Despite our protestations these were granted. It is true that since Li Hung-chang's disgrace and subsequently the conservative coup d'etat last summer a more reactionary government has shown less inclination to accede to foreign demands, but this does not alter the fact that Russian railway building is going on apace. There is already a substantial network in northern Manchuria, and once the system is linked to the sea it will be difficult to withstand Russia's economic (and de facto military) advance. The prospect of annexation becomes a practical concern.

Until recently our only recourse has been to organize financial support for the Chinese-owned Peking–Mukden Railway. The main line to Mukden is moving towards completion. The suggestion to construct a northern spur from Jinzhou to Shishan or even beyond to the Liao River, has also been greeted with favour by the board. There are sound commercial reasons for doing so: it will facilitate the transport of soy beans from the western regions of these provinces to the southern ports. There are also unspoken strategic considerations: if this can be the beginning of a line which runs parallel to the Russians' railway, it will neutralize to some degree their military advantage. We had some concern that the Honorary Chairman of this company, who happens to be the same Li Hung-chang who granted concessions to the Russians, might offer objections to this scheme, but ironically he also was supportive. Perhaps he has learned the error of his ways. Railway building in itself, however, will not be the answer to our problem. Progress so far has been slow, for all the efforts of the British and German engineers in charge of construction. It is time to . . .

A heavy bead of sweat fell from his forehead on to the manuscript, spidering the wet ink. Carefully he placed blotting paper over the page. He leaned back in his chair, and closed his eyes. He was tired, extremely tired . . . Just a moment's sleep would . . . He jerked awake and lurched to his feet. His hand reached along one of the shelves, retrieved a half-empty bottle of brandy, which he put to his lips.

There was a thump. It seemed to come from the landing. He froze. Then he went to the door. This time he stood there for a full five minutes before returning to his despatch.

It is time to consider alternative strategies. I am aware of your lordship's reluctance to commit further money or resources into a region that is not perceived to be directly an English sphere of interest. You asked me to sound out Japanese intentions, and I am pleased to report that their suspicion of Russian activities has been intensifying. There is a 'forward' party within the Imperial Army that is even now advocating aggressive steps to counter the Russians in Manchuria. Our agent with the Imperial High Command in Hokkaido – your lordship knows to whom I refer – reports that mock assaults on Port Arthur have been a regular feature of their army and navy field exercises, and he tells me that officers in the mess quite openly toast that day in the future when the Rising Sun will fly over the port of Dairen. Many believe that there will be war between the two powers within a few years, and that the victor will annex the Manchurian provinces in their entirety. In such a case it would be in our interest that the victor should be Japan and not Russia.

It was a scratch at the door that startled him, followed by a sound he could not identify: a wail that seemed to rise above the banging of the storm outside and the broken shutter downstairs. It was a thin, human sound, which could have been a moan or a cry of ecstasy. The young man reached up wildly, knocking back his chair, and grabbed, for want of anything better, a cricket bat. This he brandished above his head in striking position as he pulled open the door. 'Who's there?' he called. His voice came out in a squeak. 'Who's there?' he repeated, in a more manly tone. Dark, empty corridors stretched in either direction. The small light from the candle flickered on the polished wood. 'Come on out, if you're there,' he called. 'I'm not afraid.' He called again, this time in Chinese: '*Ni shi shei? Ni shi shei? Chulaiba! Wo bu pa.*' There was no reply, only the banging of the shutters downstairs. 'I'm *not* afraid,' he whispered. 'I'm not.' He giggled light-headedly: 'Come on, then,' he called again. 'Come out, you secret, black and midnight hags. Do you really think an Englishman's afraid of a fox fairy?' His bat dropped to his side, and with the other hand he rubbed his forehead. 'You're mad,' he whispered. 'Mad. Quite, quite mad. God, what I would give for some sleep . . .' He shut the door quietly and moved back to his desk, but it was some time and another glass of brandy before he picked up his pen again.

Between northern Manchuria and Harbin there still exists a large territory where Chinese government – albeit weak – prevails. We know that the Russians are trying by whatever means they can to win influence for themselves among local officials and army commanders, and sometimes even among powerful bandits. We suspect that weapons from the eastern Siberian supply depot at Lake Baikal are finding their way into the hands of local officials (for cash). It would be in Japan's interest to take over this 'trade in influence'. I believe that we are in a position discreetly to assist.

I have examined where best we might focus our efforts, and I favour Shishan. Your lordship will note when you glance at the map that it is strategically positioned in the border area between the Russian and Chinese centres of railway-building activity. Nestled in a bowl of hills, it is one of the few readily defensible areas in the otherwise flat plain. I am told that a well-armed force in the Black Hills could hold off an army, which is probably why, historically, Shishan was a garrison town and a safe stop-over point for caravans.

He described Shishan briefly, its population, its market economy. He added a biography (as far as he knew it) of the Mandarin. He described the foreigners living in the city: the railway engineers at the camp, the chemical merchant from Babbit and Brenner, and the eccentric medical missionary, Dr Airton, in whom he had such high hopes. Was he right to place such confidence? He recalled the strange dinner that the head of Chancellery had given Airton on one of his trips to Peking. Sir Claude made it a matter of principle never to dine with missionaries so the chore had been delegated and he had been asked along to make up numbers. He had been surprised by how much he liked the man. The common sense and dry humour. The strange obsession with penny dreadfuls and cowboy stories. An unmissionarylike missionary. Should he recommend him? Well, for the moment there was nobody else. He took the plunge: 'Airton's friendship with the Mandarin, with whom he meets regularly to discuss philosophy and politics, could be the introduction we need.'

And then he was finished, or nearly so. He could hardly keep his eyes from closing. At least the noise outside was abating a little and there had been no more strange sounds from the corridor. What on earth had he been thinking? Fox fairies! He had been warned of the danger before he left London. 'For all their apparent cultivation,' he had been told, 'these are primitive types like anybody else we have to deal with in the Empire. They've lots of weird and generally nasty beliefs behind their pretty tea ceremonies. You are to investigate the cults and the black societies along with your political work because we think they're dangerous, but you're not to go native, do you hear?' And there had been much laughter over the port while he had smiled politely, thinking he knew better than his masters because of his doctorate in Oriental languages.

I hope that your lordship will agree with what I have proposed. I am becoming more and more convinced that the Mandarin of Shishan could become the power broker of this region and our agent to stave off Russian influence. He has many qualities to recommend him: a distinguished military past, a record as a strong, independent administrator; he is ruthless and cruel, and very corrupt. And he is ambitious. He has made attempts recently to train his small garrison in modern methods of warfare. With your lordship's approval, and with the assistance of the Imperial Japanese Army and their guns, I believe that we may easily bolster his position. In which case we may discover that in His Excellency the Mandarin Liu Daguang we have the makings of our very own warlord . . .

His head dropped on to his arms and soon he was asleep. Before he lost consciousness he had an image of flowing robes, soft hair and beautiful brown eyes, red lips opening, sharp little teeth, the slow sinuous curl of a tail, and claws, fangs . . .

But a ray of sunshine was already reddening the wooden walls. The sandstorm had died with the dawn. Lady MacDonald's court-yards recovered their tranquillity. The creatures of the night – if they had ever existed – returned to the realm of the imagination from which they had been conjured. The interpreter stirred in his sleep, and the long letter – which in its way was equally fantastical, a conjuring of schemes and conspiracies from that other imagined world of the Great Game and Realpolitik – dropped, page by page, to the floor.

PART ONE

Chapter One

Bandits came in the night and stole our mule.
How will we transport the crops at harvest?

D r Airton was describing the exploits of the Hole in the Wall
Gang to the Mandarin. 'Outlaw he may be, but Mr Butch
Cassidy is not an uneducated man,' said the doctor, fumbling
in his waistcoat for a match and his briar pipe. The Mandarin,
reclining on the *kang* (he had already smoked two opium pipes
and was comfortably replete after a light luncheon and an hour
with his third, and favourite, concubine) gazed complacently at the
frock-coated foreigner sitting on a stool beside him. With a rustle
of silk and a tinkle of ornament, a maid leaned over his shoulder
and carefully poured tea into porcelain cups. In a fluid motion she
replaced the pot in a wickerwork warmer, and bowed her way out
of the study.

'Thank you, my dear,' said Dr Airton, nodding after her graceful
figure. Smoke-rings drifted round his head. 'You may be surprised
to hear that Butch Cassidy comes of a good English family,' he
continued. 'His father, though a Mormon, was born in Accrington
in Lancashire. Young Butch might not have had the fortune to be
sent to good schools on the east coast, but clearly he was educated. It
takes aptitude of mind, after all, to plan and execute such successful
train robberies.'

His last words were drowned in an altercation that erupted from
the courtyard outside the Mandarin's study, angry voices barking
and screaming through the sun-lit windowpanes. It was the cook and
the maidservant, thought the doctor, quarrelling again. It amazed
him that the minions of a magisterial household could feel free to
argue quite so loudly in front of their master; he could not imagine
such going-ons in the home of an English judge. The Mandarin
showed no rancour, but waited patiently for the noise to subside.

'It is difficult, then, to rob a train?' he murmured.

'Oh, yes,' said the doctor. 'Takes lots of planning beforehand –

knowledge of timetables, spies in the station, a convincing obstacle on the track, dynamite, skill with the lariat and a good get-away plan. And a certain amount of discipline in your gang. Unruly ruffians, cowboys.'

'I must teach my soldiers to beware of such robbers when the railway track is completed,' said the Mandarin.

Dr Airton chuckled. The idea of pigtailed Chinese wearing masks and sombreros, wielding six-guns and galloping to catch a moving train appealed to his sense of whimsy. 'I don't think you'll really ever have a problem on that score, Da Ren.' He used the courtesy title for a mandarin, literally 'Great One'. Although they were now friends, the doctor was punctilious in using the correct term of address for local officials. In return he expected to be addressed as Yisheng, 'Physician' or Daifu, 'Doctor'. He knew that he was described in a less flattering way in the town but no one had yet called him Chi Laoshu, or 'the Rat-eater' to his face. He was, however, proud of this nickname, which he had earned four years previously during the bubonic-plague epidemic that had first brought him to Shishan. Shortly after his arrival he had sent criers round the streets announcing that he would pay the princely sum of ten cash for every rat brought to him, dead or alive. This had earned him an eccentric reputation and convinced all those who did not already know it that foreigners were touched in the head; but the subsequent hunt for rodents had decimated the population of disease-bearing *Rattus rattus*, and materially assisted the elimination of plague. The Mandarin's memorial in his praise and the rumoured award of a medal from the Great Ch'ing Emperor for his work as a wondrous healer had somewhat restored his character, but the nickname had stuck, and even today he was often waylaid by peasants bearing baskets of dead mice, hoping to appeal to his gourmet tastes.

The Mandarin leaned forward and delicately sipped his tea. Relaxed in his study he was in a state of undress, his grey pigtail coiled round his neck, his loose white pyjamas rolled to the knees. His blue robe of office and jade-buttoned cap hung neatly on a wooden frame to the side. Above the *kang* were his bookshelves, stretching to the carved and painted ceiling, each shelf covered by yellow silk curtains, behind which were stacked wooden-leafed copies of the Chinese classics, as well as more popular works and an assortment of scrolls. Dr Airton knew that these included a prized collection of pornographic prints. The Mandarin had once shown him the crude pictures, laughing boisterously at the doctor's embarrassment.

A blue and white Tientsin carpet covered the stone floor below the *kang*, half lit by the sunlight, which tentatively penetrated the room. In the gloom beyond were tables and chairs in the plain Ming style, and a desk, untidily strewn with paper, ink stone and brushes in their porcelain jars. Several scrolls of calligraphy were hanging in the shadows of the back wall – gifts from teachers, painters and other officials. A grandfather clock ticked loudly in a corner. The thin rays of light by the doors and windows caught the coils of blue smoke as they twisted like dragons from the doctor's pipe, weaving through the motes of hanging dust, a thin layer of which covered every surface. The smell of the tobacco mingled with the vague scent of incense and old perfume, must and dirt. It was a small room, reminding Airton of a clipper's cabin, but he enjoyed the snug, fuggy atmosphere. It was a sign of the intimacy which had grown up between the two men that the Mandarin would invite him to drink tea with him in this private part of the mansion.

The Mandarin himself was short and inclined to fat, but his broad face and muscular physique gave him a presence that belied his size. 'Rugger-player's shoulders,' the doctor had once described to his wife, 'and butcher's hands. You can imagine him in his robe of office at the *yamen*, with a black frown on his face and his executioner with his snickersnee behind, and the poor felons in their *cangues* licking the dust in front of him, wondering if it's going to be a hundred lashes with the rod or off-with-your-head. Oh, he's a Tartar all right, my dear, quite the Tartar, with a cold, dead eye and a heart of blood. As fearsome a rogue as you'll ever meet, albeit he's amiable to me.'

'But you told me he's an old man, Edward, did you not?' Nellie had asked him nervously.

'Aye, he is. He may be sixty or eighty, for all I know, but he's remarkably preserved, and fit as a sailor for all his floppy belly and fleshy chin. A powerful man in every way. Still rides to hunt, and practises archery, and once I came early to his courtyard and saw him doing exercises with a sword. Great big cleaver, which he swung around his head as if it was a feather, moving his feet and body like an acrobat in slow motion. I suppose it was the *t'ai chi*

– you've seen the people of a morning doing their exercises by the river, but never have I seen anyone wield a monster piece of iron like that before. Showed it to me afterwards. I could hardly lift it. Told me it was the sword of a Taiping general whom he slew as a boy, beautiful jade-encrusted handle, and the cutting edge of a razor. Wonder how many heads that's lopped in its time.'

'I think you should be cautious,' his wife had said. 'I know you like to amuse yourself by saying things to frighten me and the bairns. It's your humour, which I don't pretend to understand. But this sounds a terrible man, Edward, and it can't be good that you—'

'He's my friend, Nellie,' the doctor had told her.

He seriously believed that. Both men were of a philosophical frame of mind, men of ideas and culture. Added to that, the Mandarin seemed to have an inexhaustible interest in everything to do with the outside world, and he, the doctor, was in a position to inform him about England, the empire and Europe, the balance of the powers, the developments of science and technology, and even about armaments. Surely these exchanges were to the benefit of a greater understanding and co-operation, good for China, good for Great Britain, good for all. Not to mention for the success of the hospital. And the railway too. Now he had become the appointed medical officer to the railway, he had a duty to curry the support of the local officials who could do so much to help, and also to harm, the progress of this useful project.

Dr Airton sighed. He was conscious that he had allowed his mind to wander. This often happened during the long, meditative pauses of the Mandarin's conversation. What were they discussing? The railway, of course, and he had been telling the Mandarin about the Hole in the Wall Gang, which had been the subject of one of the western shockers to which he subscribed, and which came with the monthly packet from the mission's headquarters in Edinburgh, along with his medical supplies, journals, English newspapers, *Blackwood's* magazine and domestic articles for his wife. He was pleased that the Mandarin had asked about the big continental railway schemes that were being completed in America. It gave him a lead in to the subject of bandits, which at the moment was one of his chief concerns. He felt the Mandarin's hooded eyes surveying him contemplatively.

'I am surprised that a scholar such as yourself, my dear Daifu, can speak in admiring terms of a bandit and call such a one educated. The path of learning leads towards virtue. I see no virtue in the pillaging of a train, however skilful the task might be. I cannot think much of a country that ascribes merit to its criminals, even if, as you tell me, this America is only a new country.'

'But surely in China you have legends of famous bandits and outlaws? Pirate kings? Why, last week in the marketplace I was watching with pleasure a travelling troupe putting on scenes from your great classic *The Water Margin*. Terrific costumes and stunning acrobatics, but the story was Robin Hood. Exiled heroes standing up for the common people against injustice and tyranny. Isn't that the stuff of great romance?'

'I behead bandits and pirates,' said the Mandarin, 'and it is I who protect the common people.'

'Of course, of course, we're not talking about the run of thieves and criminals,' said the doctor. 'But the ordinary man likes a bit of colour in his life and so often it is these heroes without the law who provide it. I don't suppose you've ever had the opportunity to read any of the novels by Sir Walter Scott?'

The Mandarin politely demurred.

'How I would like to translate *Rob Roy* for you.'

'It would be an exotic experience, dear Daifu – but if it is anything like *The Water Margin* I would be cautious in allowing a translation. You are correct when you say that the common man finds sensation in the exploits of heroes – this is harmless if it provides merely tales for children and vivid scenes for the opera – but it is the administrator's duty to ensure that the admiration of the common people is channelled to worthier causes. Never should anyone be encouraged to emulate a breaker of the law. I expect that the mandarins even in America are concerned about the undue praise given this herdsman who you tell me robs trains.'

'He has certainly upset Mr Harriman and the board of the Union Pacific Railroad Company,' said Airton. 'But, as you say, it is a wild, new country. I would hope that the Peking–Mukden Railway when it is extended to these parts will face no such problem, and we will have nothing to fear from the likes of Iron Man Wang and his band.'

A twitch of displeasure disturbed the Mandarin's composed features, like a ripple of wind across a smooth pond.

'I wonder, dear Daifu, why you are continually fascinated by the so-called Iron Man Wang. I have told you on many occasions that such a man – if he exists – is merely one of a rabble of petty criminals who dwell in caves and provide minor annoyance to some of our merchants, if they are foolish enough to wander the roads at night. You have nothing to fear from such a creature.'

'Of that I have no doubt, Da Ren. I only mention his name again because there is talk of him in the town, among the servants, some no doubt overblown stories . . .'

'Exaggerations of whining merchants who invent bandits' deprivations as an excuse to hide their profits from my tax collectors,' said the Mandarin.

'No doubt,' said the doctor carefully. 'But all of us were very pleased, nevertheless – our railway engineers, my friend Mr Delamere . . .'

'The soap merchant?'

'Alkali, Da Ren. He manufactures alkali crystals. All of us were very pleased to hear that Major Lin will soon be departing with his troops for what we were told would be an expedition against the bandits in the Black Hills.'

'Major Lin conducts all manner of training exercises for our Imperial soldiers. Occasionally this takes the form of marches into the Black Hills. If Major Lin and his troops were to stumble on felons in their path I am sure that they would do their duty and arrest them – but there is no question of an expedition against a bandit. I would only authorise such a thing if there was a bandit problem, which, as I have told you, we do not have.'

'The attack on Mr Delamere's mule train in April—'

'Was very unfortunate. An act of hooliganism and thievery, which embarrasses me. I caused the matter to be investigated and some criminal villagers were discovered and punished.'

'There was a beheading, yes.'

'And justice was accomplished. This was not the work of a mythical Iron Man Wang.'

The Mandarin's hooded eyes shifted and his mouth shaped itself into a wide smile. Dr Airton busied himself with his pipe. The Mandarin laughed and leaned forward to pat the doctor gently on the thigh. 'Do not worry, my dear Daifu. You and your friends are my guests, and guests of the Emperor and the great Empress Dowager. No more talk of bandits and train robbers. Tell me, what news do you bring me about the railway itself? Is the work progressing well?'

Airton felt the weight of the fat hand resting on the inside of his thigh, the coolness of a jade ring through the cloth of his trousers. He was not perturbed. He recognised physical contact as a Chinese gesture of intimacy, the mark of one gentleman's friendship with another. He thought of Lin's fierce soldiers holding hands as they walked down the street off duty, and sometimes on duty. Some of Airton's missionary colleagues were quick to condemn the most innocent display of affection as incipient lasciviousness. Not for the first time he thought that the true faith might be better transmitted if its practitioners were not so unbending. He did not believe that he was an overly sensuous man but he liked to think of himself as a tolerant humanitarian. As a physician he had sympathy with the frailty of the flesh and was disinclined to judge others harshly for their peccadilloes or habits. On the other hand, as a Scotsman, he would have preferred it if the Mandarin had kept his hands off his leg. Having treated several of the Mandarin's concubines in his professional capacity, he had an unworthy vision of some plumper and certainly more attractive thighs that this same hand might recently have squeezed. With an effort he brought himself back to the subject.

'The railway, Da Ren? Indeed. You will, of course, get a fuller report from Mr Fischer at the camp, but when I rode over to the site a few days ago it all seemed to be a hive of activity. The foundations of the bridge are being pounded into the riverbed as we speak, and I believe that one of the survey teams is examining the best location for a tunnel through the Black Hills.'

'So when will the link with the main line to Tientsin be completed?'

'Within a few months. Mr Fischer told me he is grateful for your help, and he has had very little trouble with the peasants whose fields are to be purchased for the line. I trust that they have received due compensation?'

'Your company has been very generous,' said the Mandarin.

'I'm gratified to hear it,' said the doctor. 'I'm told that peasants can sometimes be rather superstitious about aspects of all this progress we're bringing them. You know, whistling, huffing, smoking fire-wagons and strange hummings on the tracks. Evil spirits being brought in by us foreign devils. Am I not right, Da Ren?'

The Mandarin laughed – a curiously shrill cackle from a man

so bulky. He removed his hand from the doctor's leg, and fanned his face.

'First bandits, now ghosts! Poor Daifu, what a perilous world you live in! My dear doctor, do we really care what nonsense the ignorant populace believes? Drink some tea. Think of the wealth and prosperity that the wonders of your civilisation will bring.'

The doctor laughed with the Mandarin.

'Excuse me, Da Ren, but I do worry from time to time. It's the gossip. You must excuse us. We are strangers in a strange land so we are concerned when we hear of—'

'Bandits and ghosts!'

'Indeed, bandits and ghosts – but also gatherings of martial artists among the villages, secret societies, Da Ren, stirring up the superstitions of the uneducated. All nonsense, I am sure, but there have been riots in which foreigners were killed. Those nuns in Tientsin . . .'

'Twenty years ago.' The Mandarin was no longer laughing. 'And Minister Li Hung-chang and our government made reparations to your powers.' The doctor caught an uncharacteristic tone of sarcasm in the last word.

'Not everybody is as enlightened as you, Da Ren,' he said, lamely, 'and I fear that we foreigners are not always welcome in this country.'

The Mandarin leaned back on his cushion. 'Daifu, I am not one to hide the truth behind a veil of comforting platitude. These are difficult times for my country, and there are some among us who are uneasy about what the foreigners bring in their wake. You talk of superstitious fear. Even among my colleagues in the Mandarinate there are those who dislike the activities of your missionaries. I have known you for many years and I recognise you for a physician, who only has a care for my people. There are other missionaries – we have one in this town – whose motives are not so clear. The common people fear it when your missions take our children—'

'Girls who would otherwise be abandoned.'

'The abandonment of unwanted female children is an ancient custom, not a good one but our way, Daifu. I realise that your motive for gathering up these creatures is charitable, but our peasants hear stories that they are introduced into strange rites of your religion. There is talk of the eating of human flesh—'

'That is nonsense.'

'Of course it is nonsense – but you yourself are one who pays attention to rumours and stories from the uneducated. Were we not talking of bandits and ghosts? I know nothing of secret societies. Would I allow them to exist if I did? I would not. On the contrary, I have always welcomed the foreigner among us. You, Daifu, and Mr Fischer, the engineer, and even the fat soap-trader, Delamere, have many things to teach us. The Great Ch'ing Empire is weak in the face of your technology. You gave it to the barbarian dwarfs from over the sea, and five years ago they declared war on us and took our territory when they had destroyed our navy. Yes, I am talking about the Japanese. And now other foreign vultures come here to claw concessions, as you call them. The Russians in the west and the north, the Germans in Shantung, and you British everywhere. A port here. An island or a tract of earth there. There are many in our government, even at the Imperial Court, who ask, "When will this stop?" They would drive the foreign vultures away.

'Not I. I do not wish you to leave. I welcome you. If our empire is weak, then we must strengthen it. We must learn what makes a modern nation strong. It is weaponry in part. I myself fought against the foreign armies. I watched the Summer Palace of our emperors burn. That was when I was a boy. We were brave enough, and skilful with the lance and the bow – but you had better guns. Major Lin is now always asking, "Give me guns!" But it is not only guns. You have wealth. And you have technology and inventions. You have modern medicines, Daifu. You can cure as well as kill. If China is to be strong again, and if the Emperor is to sit comfortably on his throne, then we must know what you know.

'So I welcome you, Daifu, and I cast my protection over you.'

The Mandarin was laughing again, and Airton felt the hand back on his thigh.

'I will protect you from bandits, and ghosts, and secret societies.'

The Mandarin leaned forward so that Airton was looking straight into his hooded eyes. He lowered his voice to a murmur: 'And that is why I enjoy our little conversations, Daifu. They teach me what I wish to know.' Again, the high cackle of laughter, a brisk tap on his knee, and with fluid agility the Mandarin had risen to his feet and was shaking the half-rising doctor briskly by both hands. 'Until we next meet. It is always a pleasure talking to you, Daifu. Bandits and ghosts! Ha! Ha!'

The audience was over. The Mandarin, with genial courtesy, handed the doctor his hat and his cane, then ushered him to the door with an arm around his shoulder. 'I will come to the railway works one day soon to observe its progress,' said the Mandarin. 'You will pass on my regards to Mr Fischer and his crew.'

'I certainly will, Da Ren. You know that he will soon be joined by an assistant, an Englishman?'

'So I have been informed,' said the Mandarin. 'He is welcome. You are all welcome in Shishan.'

Jin Zhijian, the elderly chamberlain, was waiting by the stone lions at the bottom of the steps leading to the Mandarin's study. His hands were folded in the sleeves of his faded blue gown and he was wearing the conical white hat of a minor official. His rheumy eyes smiled, wrinkling his ascetic features.

'Jin Lao will accompany you to the gate,' said the Mandarin. 'I look forward to our next meeting.'

'Goodbye, Da Ren, and health to your family. The Lady Fan is taking her medicine, I trust?'

'Her stomach pains no longer trouble her. I thank you.'

The Mandarin watched as the doctor followed the tall figure of Jin Lao across the courtyard and through the red doors to the outer precincts of the *yamen*. What strange, heavy clothes these foreigners put on in the heat of summer. He could not imagine why they considered black tail-coats and shiny top hats the appropriate dress for an interview with a magistrate. For a moment the Mandarin luxuriated in the cool silk of his own pyjamas. His eyes lingered on the green leaves of his ginkgo tree, the black shadows of its branches creating calligraphic patterns on the white, sun-drenched flagstones. He stretched his arms till his shoulders ached and drew in deep breaths of the humid, fragrant air. From the balcony of the living quarters to the side he could hear the faint murmurs of his household. A flurry of high-pitched voices. Quarrels again? No, a squeal of laughter and the soft ripple of a musical instrument. He smiled at the memory of his little Moth, her playful white fingers emerging from the red brocade, the sharp nails lingering on his stomach, her eyes daring him to laugh as the hand moved lower . . .

What did he make of the doctor's questions? Astute, as usual. Well-informed, but also naïve. It continually surprised him that the foreigners, with their knowledge, their learning and their extraordinary practical skills, could at the same time be so inept at understanding the basic politics of life. They were like clever children at their first Lantern Festival, crowing with delight when they penetrated the first riddle in a poem, without comprehending that the poet had hidden other layers of meaning beneath the obvious puns. Did the doctor have a subtext in his talk of Iron Man Wang and secret societies? Did he suspect the Mandarin's involvement in hidden conspiracies? He doubted it. It was a curious phenomenon – and one confusing to many of his countrymen and consequently the cause of much misunderstanding – that foreigners usually spoke only what was uppermost in their minds. He who searched for subtlety in a barbarian's conversation would tie himself in a web of his own imagining. The doctor had undoubtedly heard some rumours – there were always rumours, and rumours were to be encouraged because they could obfuscate as well as reveal – but he could not know of the movements of the patriotic societies; he could not hear the silent crawling of the woodworm in the palace eaves, the stirrings of maggots in peasant dunghills; he could not know that the Mandate of Heaven was about to pass to a new dynasty. There were aspects of China that no foreigner would ever comprehend for all their mastery of the physical world. Yet the Mandarin would have to be more vigilant. It was dangerous that a foreign barbarian could identify the threads, even if he was unable to see the pattern of the great brocade.

He had told the doctor that he had witnessed the burning of the Summer Palace. Had that been too revealing? He did not think so. The doctor would appreciate the confession as another mark of the personal intimacy he seemed to value so highly. Yet he had been sincere when he told the doctor that he had been impressed by the power of the West. He recalled to this day the futile charge his banner had made on the French lines. He saw again the pennants flying, the crimson and bronze of the armour, the sunlight flashing on the ten thousand spears of their invincible army. It had not been his first battle. He had earned his horsetail a few years before, with General Tseng Kuo-fan and his Hunan Braves against the rabble of the Taipings – but this was the first time he was fighting the ocean barbarians. He smelt again the dust of the Northern Plain, the rank odour of horse, the sweet scent of sweat and fear. The enemy were entrenched on a riverbed. It would be an easy charge over the trampled millet fields. As his nervous pony twitched at the reins and the harness jingled and the line of bannermen waited for the command, he had been confident that it would be over quickly. And it was. It all ended in what seemed to him now like a moment fixed in eternity. He could not recall the noise of it today, but there must have been a deafening thunder of guns. He could not recall today that he had even moved, let alone charged and had his horse shot under him. He did remember standing still while the Chinese army died around him, horses and riders rearing and tumbling, flying earth and limbs erupting, and fires exploding in the air in a long, endless fall. And in that moment he had felt a sense of wonder and elation and invincibility that he had survived what he knew was a turning-point for his country. Nothing would ever be the same again.

He felt no animosity towards the foreign soldiers. They were men like others. He had killed one in his escape that night to the north, a young soldier looting the house in which he had been hiding. The boy had died noisily, whimpering and gurgling through a slashed throat. He had taken his rifle and his cartridges, feeling the power and beauty of the efficient weapon in his hand. He had felt no anger when, later, he hid in a thicket across the lake from the burning palace and saw the symbols of the Manchu dynasty blaze. If anything it had increased his elation. The mandate had been withdrawn and a new power was in the land, and he determined that he would be part of it.

In the hard days after the war, the vision had faded, but it had not entirely gone away. He had continued as a soldier, attaching himself to the rising new General Li Hung-chang. He had taken part in further expeditions against the Taipings and the Nien rebels, and had risen to General Li's attention. It was General Li who had arranged for him to take the imperial examinations. He had proved an efficient magistrate, an effective hatchet man for General Li, who later went on to carve a career for himself in politics at the Imperial Court. He continued to benefit by the connection. Now, in his later years, he was the sole ruler of a city and county. He had enriched himself and he was feared – but to his surprise the

Ch'ing dynasty still tottered on its throne. He knew it was only a matter of time before it would be replaced. He knew that the Ch'ing had lost their mandate on that day when their armies disintegrated on the plains of Chih-li. The foreigners were part of the process that would hasten the inevitable fall. They would snip away territories but they would never rule the Middle Kingdom. Meanwhile he who was equipped with their knowledge would benefit when the Great Ch'ing collapsed. Chaos inevitably followed collapse, and he who was powerful in his own domain would survive.

He sighed and yawned. With a last look at the ginkgo tree, he moved into the shadowy study and sat down at his table where a blank piece of paper awaited his brush strokes.

Jin Lao's smile seemed chiselled into his rice-paper features as he led the barbarian doctor into the outer courtyard. Guards and servants shuffled to their feet as they passed but Jin Lao's erect figure looked straight ahead. He did not know why Liu Da Ren spent long hours closeted in conversation with this small, whiskered, mouselike foreigner, who had the surprising ability to speak the Chinese language, but he assumed that the Mandarin had subtle reasons for doing so. Jin Lao had spent more than twenty years in the Mandarin's service and had learned not to question his wisdom. He had profited considerably from his master's generosity by keeping his silence.

The doorkeeper pushed open the great brass-studded wooden gates. Jin Lao turned to his charge and bowed. The doctor bowed back. 'Thank you, Jin Lao, as always,' he said. 'Your health? I trust that it is improving?'

'Sadly I am still troubled by my head pains.' A long white hand extended from its sleeve and moved upwards languidly to rub the the shaven temple. 'No doubt it is age.'

'I am grieved to hear it,' said the doctor. 'Perhaps these pills would be of help?'

'You are very kind,' said Jin Lao, taking the small packet that the doctor had pulled out of his waistcoat pocket. Jin's hand, with the packet, withdrew into the sleeve.

The doctor smiled. This was a ritual. He doubted whether the evil old chamberlain had ever had a headache in his life, but he knew that packets of western medicines sold for high prices in the marketplace. Not that this medicine would be effective for any serious complaint: it was merely a mixture of sodium citrate with bicarbonate, which he was in the habit of prescribing to his children for their more imaginary ailments. 'Take two in the morning and two in the evening until you are well,' he said cheerfully. 'Goodbye, my dear Jin Lao.'

Lifting his hat he turned and took a jaunty step towards the stone stairway that wound down the hill to the town. He heard the gate clang behind him. At the top of the steps he paused to take in the view. Welcome gusts of breeze brushed his face. He was already beginning to sweat in the oppressive midsummer heat. Crickets clattered in the pine trees on either side of the path.

The grey roofs of Shishan lay huddled below him. From his eminence (the *yamen* was built on a small hill on the northern edge of the town) he could make out few of the individual streets, but the main landmarks were clearly visible on this sunny afternoon.

The walls were the city's defining feature. What had once been crenellated battlements had fallen into disrepair and in parts the masonry had been stripped away leaving an eroded earth mound with trees growing from the top and artisans' houses nestled into the side, but the four great towers at each corner had survived time's depredations, and the gatehouse on the southern wall was intact. Its battlements and barbicans, topped by a curved, stacked roof, conjured visions for the doctor of medieval armies and sieges. It was manned by a small garrison, who were responsible for closing the thick wooden gates at sunset and monitoring the flow of assorted humanity, pack mules and camels that streamed in and out of the city in the daylight hours. The doctor could just make out the two antique field guns mounted on the walls at either side of the gate-house, Major Lin's pride and joy.

The scene was peaceful and picturesque, a watercolour like the plates in the big leather collection of travellers' tales he had seen as a boy in his grandfather's library. Swallows nested in the wooden eaves of the towers, cavorting and flashing in the bright sunlight. Beyond stretched the shimmering yellow Manchurian plain which continued unbroken for hundreds of miles, north to the forested borders of Russia and east to Korea. The doctor peered beyond the south-eastern tower but the railway encampment by the river was invisible today in the haze. He could make out, however, the blue line of the Black Hills to the south-west, and the pagoda of the lama monastery on a smaller outcrop closer to the town. Above him, thin bands of cirrus floated in a dome of blue sky.

The dominating landmark in the centre of the city, edging the market square, was the Confucius temple. From this distance, its orange, red and green tiles and the curving eaves looked imposing. It was less imposing at street level: on his last visit he had been struck by the peeling paint on the pillars, its air of ill-kept shabbiness, the nondescript assortment of gilt statues peering out of the smoky gloom, monks and townsmen wandering aimlessly among the burning braziers, men of all classes kneeling in haphazard prayer, or, more often, loitering, chatting and selling their wares. Moneylenders in the temple were apparently quite acceptable in the all-embracing eclecticism of casual Chinese worship – if worship it could be called. He thought fondly of the small, clean kirk he had left behind in Dumfries.

Surrounding the temple were the merchants' houses, two- or three-storeyed affairs, architecturally unremarkable like most Chinese houses but they had neat balconies decorated with flower-pots, stunted bonsai trees and birdcages, and the grey tiles on the roofs were trim and well kept. The lower storeys were shops, open to the street. Some of the fronts were beautifully decorated and carved in wooden or gilt filigree. Streets were named after a particular trade – there were cobblers' streets and pan-makers' streets, streets for clothiers and pharmacists and sellers of porcelain – the green celadon and the beautiful blue and white Jindezhen ware imported from the south. The doctor loved the ritual of shopping: the tinkle of beads as one passed through the door, the ushering to a little table and the elaborate pouring of tea, the unctuous presentation of one bolt of silk finer than the next, the bargaining, the flattery, the sighs, the groans, the beaming acceptance of a price fair to all sides. He loved to loiter in the bookshops and the curio stores. The richer merchants – the grain and salt traders: Delamere's friend, Lu Jincai, the alkali king; Tang Dexin, the tin monopolist, who owned the mines in the Black Hills; Jin Shangui, the entrepreneur – possessed luxurious courtyard villas in addition to their shops and warehouses. The doctor could see patches of green garden in the south of the town near the wall where most of these mansions were situated. Sometimes a merchant would invite members of the foreign community to his home for a banquet, on the occasion of a wedding, or if a nephew had achieved high marks in the imperial examinations. The ancestral hall would be draped in red silk, and tables would be laid out among the flowers and ornamental rock-gardens. Nellie would put on her severe, long-suffering face as she tackled sea cucumber or roast scorpion or bird's nest soup, little rice birds baked whole, the occasional bear's paw or camel hump, and all the other nameless delicacies sent to torment her. Airton smiled. Poor Nellie.

His mind returned to the conversation he had just had with the Mandarin. He had been reassuring, and Airton looked forward to telling Frank Delamere that there was little foundation to the rumours of brewing unrest. Delamere was a credulous fellow, he decided. For all their experience of the country, some of these old China hands could swallow the most transparent fictions. The truth was that Delamere kept bad company. He drank too much and spent his time carousing with the merchants in that awful house of ill-repute, the Palace of Heavenly Pleasure. It was a pity that the foreign community in Shishan was so small that there was not a decent club for a man to go to in an evening – but he would not cast stones. Delamere was a widower and no longer young. It was sad that a man of undoubted abilities and charm should end up alone in a backwater like Shishan. He thanked Providence that he himself was blessed with a wife and family. 'There but for the grace of God,' he said to himself cheerfully and, with a quick step, set off down the path to the town.

As it happened, Frank Delamere was one of the first people he met when he reached the bottom of the hill. The doctor had succumbed to temptation and was enjoying a short rest by a small bridge over the moat by the Drum Tower. It had been a hot walk down in his heavy serge suit, and his body was streaming with sweat. He had taken off his frock-coat and waistcoat, and was fanning himself with his pocket-handkerchief. It was a quiet, secluded spot and he was startled to be hailed while he was in this state of undress. It was typical of Delamere to catch him unawares, pricking his little vanities: Delamere always had an irritating knack of being able to say or do the wrong thing at any time. And as he looked up at the beaming, florid figure in blazer and white ducks lifting a straw hat, humorous brown eyes twinkling above a heavy moustache, he smelt a whiff of brandy and cigar. Delamere had had another heavy lunch, it appeared.

'Wearing your Sunday best, Airton?' boomed Delamere. 'Hardly the right weather for it. Been paying a social call on the Grand Panjandrum, have we? What had he to say?'

'Delamere,' acknowledged the doctor. 'What a surprise. I didn't expect to see you in this part of town.'

'Old Lu wanted me to have a squint at his new warehouse round the back there. I say, Airton, I've got splendid news. What do you know? My daughter's coming!'

'Daughter? Where?'

'Here! Little Helen Frances. Haven't seen her since she was this high. Now she's a blooming girl of eighteen or so. Who'd have believed it? Coming all the way to China to see her old dad! Sorry, old man, do you want a hand with that coat?'

'I can manage well enough, thank you,' said Airton primly. Then he took in what Delamere had just told him. 'But, my dear fellow, this is marvellous news. I didn't know you had a daughter.'

'Skeleton in the cupboard, eh? If she's grown up like her mother she'll be a beauty, though I say it myself. Haven't really seen much of her since her mother died of the cholera in Assam in eighty-two. Took her as a baby to her aunt in Sussex, you see. Better to grow up there than with an old reprobate like me. I never married again . . .' An unusual cloud of melancholy seemed to have descended over his features. 'Never mind all that.' He brightened. 'She's coming, Airton! My little girl's coming to Shishan! I got the letter the company forwarded to me this morning.'

Airton smiled at his companion's obvious happiness. 'This is a cause for celebration,' he said. 'Nellie will be thrilled to hear. Which way are you walking, Delamere? You must tell me more.'

The two men strolled side by side. The doctor knew a short-cut through an alley of mud-walled houses. The two of them had lived there for so long that both were used to the stink of open drains, and unconsciously adjusted their steps to avoid the offal, dung and unidentifiable pools of slime that made a stroll through the poorer quarters a navigational trial. In a few moments they were in the main street and their senses were stunned momentarily by the noise and confusion of daily life in Shishan. Mule trains, each animal loaded with huge bundles of cloth or sacks of grain, trotted down the centre of the muddy road whipped on by the muleteers, their brown padded tunics tied to their waists, though they wore their distinctive fur hats even in the summer heat. Coming the other way were wooden-wheeled peasant carts piled with vegetables, or geese with their legs tied together or pigs in pokes. The drivers of the vehicles yelled curses at each other. Coolies threaded their way through the confusion, buckets hanging from poles stretched across their backs, or straining under loads of furniture. One tottered under three heavy wooden chairs, a table and a lampstand roped in a pyramid above his bent frame. A merchant's wife, bundles of shopping on her knees, held a handkerchief to her nose to avoid the dust as she lurched in a sedan chair carried by two burly porters. Hawkers and vegetable-sellers screamed out their wares on mats by the side of the road. Ragged children were taunting a blind beggar. A barber quietly shaved the pate of a young scholar sitting on a stool, his pigtail coiled round his neck as he held a book close to his face. Like the foreign doctor and alkali merchant, absorbed in their conversation, he was oblivious of the noise and chaos around him.

Frank Delamere raised his voice above the din, explaining to the doctor that his daughter's visit could not have been more conveniently timed. His sister, who had included a note with Helen Frances's gushing letter, had told him that since the girl left school she had been pressing her aunt to take her to see her father in China. His sister had been prepared to come, despite her arthritis and *mal de mer*, but she had been relieved when she had contacted his company headquarters in London to find out that an assistant was coming out from England to join him and, having met the young man, whom she described as a steady, mature boy and a county cricketer to boot, she felt quite confident that he would be a perfect chaperon for her niece on the journey. 'So wasn't that fortunate?' said Delamere.

'A young man as a chaperon?' asked the doctor, his eyebrows raised.

'Oh, that's perfectly all right,' said Delamere. 'Can't be a stick-in-the-mud these days. End of the old century and all that. Anyway, Rosemary's a good judge of character and I've heard fine things about young Cabot. It'll be his second tour in China. He was down in Nanchang before this and old Jarvis there spoke very highly of him. Said he was one of those young chaps with a head on his shoulders, middle-aged before he was young, if you know what I mean. Quite reliable. Not the sort for any hanky-panky business or letting the side down.'

He pulled the doctor by the arm to avoid a string of unladen camels being driven at full gallop by a laughing herdsman on a pony.

'Damned maniacs,' he muttered. 'Anyway,' he gave a boisterous laugh and slapped Airton on the back, 'I'll see my little girl again!' he cried. 'After six long years!'

'Quite so,' said the doctor. 'You never told me that you would be taking on an assistant.'

'Did I not? Ah, well, age creeps up on you and it's time I started training a successor. Who knows? I might give all this up in a couple of years and get back to the old country before my liver packs up on me.'

'The state of your liver is no joking matter,' smiled Airton. 'Let me see your hands. Look at those mottled brown spots now.'

'Come on, Doctor, no scolding. Today's a happy day. She'll be here very soon, you know. The letter was dated, what?, two and a half months ago, and the P and O was due to sail within a few days of that. She must be on the Indian Ocean or even nearing China by now. I wonder what she looks like. Her mother was a beauty. Did I ever tell you?'

'Yes, just a moment ago.'

'Yes, well, Clarissa was a tea-planter's daughter, you see. I was only a lowly manager on the estate. We married in 'eighty. Don't know what she ever saw in me . . . She was so . . . so handsome and wilful and full of spirit. When her father tried to horsewhip me, she shouted him down. I'll never forget her standing on the staircase, her cheeks flushed and tossing her hair. So imperious. Her dad couldn't resist her. No one could. I couldn't. She made her pa and me shake hands and be friends. A year later we were weeping together on her deathbed . . .' He sniffed loudly. 'Excuse me, I haven't allowed myself to think about all that in a while. It wasn't a good time. Her father and mother came down with the cholera as well, and I was left in the empty great house with the babe, and the servants with their big white eyes in their darkie faces looking up at me asking what to do with the bodies. And I couldn't bear to look at the little girl, who was all that reminded me . . . Look out, old fellow, watch out for that cart! Do you mind if we don't talk about it? I get a little sentimental now and then. Doesn't mean anything . . . Why don't you tell me how you got on with the Mandarin?'

Airton had never seen Delamere so moved before. The big man was smiling down at him, eyes moist in his sunburnt face, and there was a glistening line on his cheek. For a moment he looked quite noble, and strangely gentle, standing in the crowded street with bedlam behind him.

He went through his conversation in the *yamen*, Delamere nodding, sniffing, his brow furrowed, a picture of a man demonstrating close attention.

'So the old boy denied there are such things as secret societies,' he said, after a while, 'and my caravan was attacked by some old farmer and not Iron Man Wang, and Major Lin is going into the Black Hills to gather raspberries, I suppose?'

'Well, I wouldn't put it quite as baldly as that, but the Mandarin was reassuring. Do you not believe him?'

'Lord knows. You're the man with the ear to the all-powerful round here. If you say things are all tickety-boo, then that's fine by me. I only passed on the gossip old Lu was bleating on about over his cups the other day, but he's always got his pigtail in a twist about something. Who knows what John Chinaman's up to at the best of times, eh? Anyway, I don't care. My daughter's coming.'

Dr Airton flinched. He expected another heavy slap on the back. He did not know what he preferred: Delamere ecstatic or Delamere melancholy drunk. This time he was spared further exuberance, however, because his companion suddenly paused in his stride and pointed ahead. 'Speak of the Devil.' He laughed. 'I do believe we are about to witness a march past of the Celestial Army. Major Lin and his brave grenadiers!'

'For mercy's sake, don't salute again.' The doctor's face reddened as he recalled his embarrassment the last time he had been with Delamere and Lin had ridden by, and how, afterwards, he had tried to explain away the former's behaviour to the Mandarin. The Mandarin had found the incident amusing but he doubted that Major Lin would forgive the jeering from the crowd as a drunken Delamere had strutted and performed like a colour sergeant from a Gilbertian farce. Not that a Gilbert and Sullivan operetta was far off the mark: there was indeed something ludicrous about Lin's attempts to turn his rag-tag militia into his conception of a modern army.

The muleteers were cursing and grumbling as they manoeuvred their animals to the side of the road. Major Lin led his short column riding on a white Mongolian pony. He was dressed for this occasion not in the usual bannerman's costume but in a rather gaudy uniform he had designed for himself with elaborate epaulettes and a tuft of white feathers on a peaked shako. Silver spurs glinted on shining black boots. The marching troops were uniformed in blue tunics with brass buttons and grey forage caps. The effect was offset by the traditional white Chinese leggings and cloth shoes, and the parasol that each had tied to his backpack. The first company of twenty men bore semi-modern carbines made in the Chinese arsenal of Chiangnan in Shanghai, but the rest were still armed with muskets and ancient muzzle-loaders, which might have dated from one of the Opium Wars. Despite their Ruritanian appearance the doctor found something impressive about the seriousness and enthusiasm with which they conducted their drill. The men swung their arms and kicked their legs with energy if not good timing. A corporal barked commands. '*Yi! Er! Yi! Er!* One! Two! One! Two!' Major Lin held himself erect with a fierce frown on his thin, handsome face. The doctor knew from the Mandarin that Lin had been made a prisoner on the Korean border during the recent Sino-Japanese War and had developed an admiration for the military methods and techniques of his captors. It was presumably those that he was trying to re-create here. For all the comic appearance of his troop, Lin was not playing at being a soldier.

'Just look at them,' said Delamere. 'Face it, Airton. A Celestial and a soldier are a contradiction in terms.'

'Behave,' hissed the doctor. Major Lin was now parallel with the two men. He turned his head and gave them a cold stare. The narrow eyes and high cheekbones gave him a hawk-like appearance. He was in his mid-thirties, but there was something boyish about his face, although his mouth was set in a cruel half-smile that somehow emphasised his ruthlessness. The doctor raised his hat. Lin snapped his head forward and kicked his horse with his heels. The column tramped by.

'Sinister-looking bugger, isn't he?' said Delamere, as they resumed their stroll. 'One of the girls at Mother Liu's told me he beats his woman there. Oh, sorry,' he laughed, 'you don't like me talking about the Palace of Heavenly Pleasure, do you?'

'I do not,' said the doctor, 'and with a daughter coming you should start to think about changing some of your bad habits, and I'm not just talking about your drinking.'

'Well, I won't deny you have a point. Can't have Helen Frances thinking her old man's a *roué*. Responsibilities of parenthood, and all that. Think I really can reform?'

'I doubt it,' said the doctor.

'So do I. Oh, well, I hope she hasn't inherited her mother's temper as well as her looks.'

They walked on in silence. The street had resumed its bustle. In a moment they reached the market square. A crowd was gathered round a spectacle by the temple. Artisans in blue cotton pyjamas were laughing and gesticulating. Gentlemen in brown gowns and black waistcoats were peering curiously. Over the shouts and jeers and the general racket they could hear the sound of a trombone playing the familiar notes of 'Onward Christian Soldiers'. Through the heads of the hecklers they could make out a tall blond man who was apparently conducting a woman and several children through the hymn.

Delamere groaned. 'Sorry, old boy, I'm sloping off. The last thing I want to face today is the bloody Millwards trying to convert the heathen.'

'They don't do it very effectively,' observed the doctor. 'It shames me to say it, but I rather agree with you about the Millwards – yet we must be charitable.'

'You be charitable. I think they're a disgrace to the human race.'

'To the dignity of the white man, perhaps,' said Airton, 'but they mean well. Delamere, before you go, I truly am delighted by your news, and I'm sure that Nellie will be thrilled to have the company of your daughter when she comes. There'll always be work for her in the hospital if she wants it. Let me organise a dinner for her – and Cabot, is it?'

'Yes, Tom Cabot.'

'As soon as they arrive in Shishan. Nellie can play the piano and I'll get Herr Fischer up with his violin. We'll have a merry evening, what do you say? We ought to welcome the new arrivals in a proper style.'

'Thank you, Airton. I'll look forward to it.' Delamere turned to go. Then his face lit up in a wide grin. 'I still can't believe it, you know. My daughter really is coming!' And the doctor's breath was taken away by another resounding slap on the back.

A trifle reluctantly he turned his steps in the direction of the Millwards. As a medical missionary his own focus was more on the healing of bodies than souls, but he felt some obligation to his evangelical colleagues even though they belonged to a different mission. The Millwards were American Congregationalists who had arrived fresh from New Jersey three years before without, in the doctor's opinion, the slightest training or qualification for a vocational task. He was not even certain to which actual missionary society they were attached. They were not well supported: they never seemed to receive money or mail. As far as Airton could make out they subsisted on alms from the Buddhist monastery, as embarrassing a state of affairs as one could imagine.

What they lacked in professionalism, however, they made up for in boneheaded idealism and blind faith. Septimus Millward was a tall, long-limbed man in his late thirties, with narrow, humourless features and thick pebble spectacles. Round spectacles, in fact, seemed a hallmark of the Millwards. Septimus's wife, Laetitia, and three of their eight children wore them too – the smaller the child the thicker the lenses. For the doctor, it was the uniformly thick glasses that gave the final seal to the outlandishness of their appearance. On his arrival Septimus Millward, out of some notion that they would be more acceptable to their flock if they dressed like them, had burned all their western suits, even their boots, and had clothed his whole family in patched Chinese gowns. He had also shaved the front of his head and tied his thin, yellow hair into a pigtail, which achieved the effect of incongruousness because he had preserved his full western beard.

His elder son, a sour-looking boy of fourteen or fifteen, called Hiram, also wore a pigtail. Airton saw that it was Hiram who was playing the trombone, not badly but, from his sullen expression, it looked as if he wished he were a hundred miles away. Who could blame him with such a father? He had been impressed however, by the boy's intelligence. He spoke fluent Chinese, which was more than could be said for his parents, whose indecipherable pidgin when preaching sermons was an embarrassment. On occasion the doctor had seen him playing with some of the rougher local street urchins. He wondered that the boy was not tempted to flee the nest altogether. What a nest! Airton had once made a call on the compound in which the family lived. Any Chinese peasant would have been ashamed of the squalor and poverty of their mean hovel, yet it was here that the Millwards raised their family and also brought in abandoned babies and other strays. Airton knew that this caused deep suspicion among the locals, but he could hardly prevent the Millwards saving lives. He and Nellie helped as best they could. Nellie, who was worried about the children, sometimes sent round hot meals. Septimus Millward took this charity as his due. Nellie had once asked Laetitia if she wished to have a job in the hospital. Her husband had answered for her that there was no time when doing God's work, with souls out there to be saved, to pander to the indulgences and ailments of the mere body. That had been too much even for Nellie to take and she had given him a piece of her mind. Not that it did any good: Septimus had gathered his whole family round him on their knees to pray for her.

The hymn came to a triumphant finish as Airton reached the edge of the crowd. Laetitia Millward's shrill descant echoed on a bar or two after the trombone coughed to a stop. Septimus began his sermon, and for a moment there was a bemused silence as the onlookers tried to make out what he was saying. Ordinarily Septimus had a deep, not unpleasant but commanding voice. When attempting Chinese, however, he adopted a mangled falsetto that screeched and wavered through the Mandarin tones like an out-of-tune violin. With little correct vocabulary, his grammar was arbitrary and the tones he was valiantly attempting were, in almost every case, the wrong ones. Since tones governed meaning, the most incongruous words would come out. The doctor struggled to make any sense of what he was saying.

'Jesus elder brother and little sister,' Septimus started. Presumably he meant 'Brothers and sisters in Jesus'. 'I bring good questions. You are all going to die. But Jesus has old wine for you. Yes, it is true. He will bring you to God's pigs. But you must first say sorry to your robbers. The Bible tells you you are good, so you must leave the house of ink.' With a stern frown he turned and pointed to the temple behind him, where two plump *bonze*s – Buddhist priests – in their saffron robes were smiling at him from inside the gate. 'There!' he cried. 'There is the ink house!' (*Mo Shui*? Ink? Airton was baffled. Then he realised Septimus had meant *Mo Gui* – devil.) 'But I will teach you to eat the hearts of little children,' Septimus cried, 'and Jesus will drink your wine! Beware, the robber's fees are silk!'

The majority of the crowd were smiling good-humouredly but Airton noticed hostile expressions here and there. Septimus was speaking gibberish but his intent was quite clear. His position in front of the temple and his angry gestures at the priests were expressive enough. The doctor wished, not for the first time, that the Millwards would adopt a less confrontational approach. Septimus Millward's Mandarin was comic but some of his garbled expressions could be read the wrong way. 'Eat the hearts of little children' was particularly unfortunate.

'There was a man called Samson,' Septimus was intoning. 'God made him long. He killed the king's soldiers with the teeth of a deer. He ate lion's meat with honey. They made him busy and took him to the bad temple where they tied him to a tree. Then he fell off the roof. Yes,' Septimus insisted. 'He fell off the roof. Praise be to God.'

A young artisan, stripped to the waist in the heat, his long pigtail hanging down his bare back, danced up to Septimus, and began to imitate his gestures and speech. 'Gilly gooloo gilly gooloo gilly gooloo gilly gooloo!' he shouted in his face. Septimus moved aside. The young wag moved with him. 'Gilly gooloo! Gilly gooloo!' Septimus, his brow sweating with anger, raised his voice. The comedian, winking at his friends in the crowd, shouted, 'Gilly gooloo', louder still.

The crowd was screaming with laughter. An old lady next to Airton collapsed to the ground, her eyes running with tears of mirth. He had difficulty containing his own chuckles, although another part of him looked on aghast. Laetitia Millward gathered her three smallest children protectively to her skirts. Mildred, one of the two older girls, was obviously scared, and she stared through her spectacles with big round eyes. The boy Hiram's face, on the other hand, became more pinched than ever. His shoulders were shaking. Then, unable to control himself any longer, he, too, began to laugh at his father, a breathy, high-pitched wheeze. The trombone slipped from his hands and fell with a clang to the ground.

Septimus, his eyes blazing, abandoned his doomed sermon and turned with rage on his son. 'Spawn of Satan!' he cried. 'How dare you mock your betters when they are doing the work of the Lord?' Then he slapped Hiram hard across the face, and again, hard, on the other side. 'On your knees,' he roared. 'Pray for forgiveness.' Hiram, sobbing, stood his ground. The crowd fell silent. Laetitia pulled her children down with her and, in a semi-circle round her husband, they adopted an exaggerated prayer position, heads bowed, folded hands raised to their foreheads. 'Pray, boy, pray!' called Septimus in his deep voice, then he, too, fell on his knees, his arms stretched wide. Gazing heavenwards, he began to intone the Lord's Prayer. The young comedian from the crowd loitered a moment uncertainly, then spat on the ground and sauntered back to his friends, where he was greeted with more laughs, cat-calls and slaps on the back.

'Our Father, who art in Heaven, hallowed be Thy name . . .'

'I hate you,' Hiram screamed, through his tears.

'Forgive us our trespasses and lead us not into temptation . . .'

'I'll leave you, Father.' Hiram's voice was a panicked croak. 'I'll walk out. I will. I will.'

'For Thine is the kingdom, the power and the glory . . .'

Hiram sobbed a last despairing sob. Then, pointing a thin arm at his father, he yelled, 'God damn you. I'll never, never come back,' and hurled himself away into the crowd.

'. . . for ever and ever, Amen,' chanted the Millwards.

'Hiram! Hiram!' called the doctor, but it took some moments for him to break through the stunned mass of people, some of whom were beginning to disperse in disgust. By the time he reached the open square, the boy had disappeared round a *pailou*, into an alley between two tall houses and away.

Airton felt strangely humiliated by the incident. Besides his concern for the boy and a sense of responsibility for what would now happen to him, he was incensed by Septimus Millward. The man was a menace – his eccentricities had a negative, possibly dangerous, effect on the reputation of Christianity in the town, and the standing of the foreign community as a whole. In the common people's eyes he was a buffoon but to some his unintelligible mumbo-jumbo smacked of sorcery. His cruelty to his own family was unspeakable, and his power over them unnatural. The doctor wondered whether he was clinically deranged. The Millwards were still crouched in positions of prayer. The crowd had lost interest, the spectacle over, and only one or two stragglers remained, but someone had thrown an egg at Septimus and his beard was sticky with running yolk.

'Millward,' Airton called. 'Listen to me, man.'

It was as if Septimus had not heard him.

'Millward,' he shouted, 'get a hold of yourself. What are you going to do about your boy?'

Septimus opened his blue eyes and stared expressionlessly at Airton. '"If thine eye offend thee, pluck it out, and cast it from thee",' he said coldly. 'I will pray for him.'

'For God's sake, man, consider rationally. Hiram's only a boy.'

'He has left the House of God, Dr Airton. If he comes back in repentance, I will surely kill the fatted calf and rejoice in the return of the prodigal. Until then he is no son of mine.'

'For Heaven's sake.' The man was beyond reason. 'Mrs Millward. Laetitia,' he appealed. Tears were misting her glasses, but she spoke calmly. 'My husband has spoken, Dr Airton. I will be governed by him. I also pray that the devil releases my boy.' Her last words were lost in a shaking sob. Mildred put her arms round her mother protectively and glared angrily at the doctor.

'Leave us to our sorrow, Doctor,' said Septimus. 'You can do nothing here.'

'I can at least try to find your son,' said Airton. He turned angrily on his heel. Then he faced Septimus again, began to speak, but words failed him. 'When I find him I'll take him to my hospital,' he said lamely. 'Please, reconsider your duty as parents.' He left the family at their prayers.

The young artisan who had made the original mockery of Septimus was still loitering with his friends. As the doctor passed he made a humorous face and laughed. Airton scowled at him. 'I'll have no cheek from you, you scabrous son of a bastard turtle. Get out of my way, you stinking offspring of a mule and a blind snake.' The young man grinned broadly, delighted at the fluent string of Chinese invective.

'*Ta made!*' he swore. 'One of them can speak a proper language after all!' And Airton had the humiliation of being clapped on the back for the third time that day. Furiously, he pushed the man aside and moved on, through the *pailou* at the southern end of the square, and down the main street towards the great gate of the city and his home.

The hospital and the doctor's house were located about two miles outside the city gates on a small bluff above some wheatfields.

The doctor had first acquired the compound, originally the home of a prosperous farmer, during the plague year as a makeshift recuperation centre away from the poisonous fumes in the town. It had been in constant use ever since as a mission hospital. Over the years he had converted the mud-and-wattle dwellings into modest brick cottages surrounding three interconnected courtyards in the Chinese style. He had replaced the thatched roofs with neat grey tiles, and enlarged the windows, installing clear glass panes in red wooden frames. Nellie had planted trees and flowers in the courtyards. In spring bees buzzed among the azaleas and the cherry blossom, and in summer sparrows twittered and crickets chirped in the leaves of the plane trees shading the yard. At all times it had the comforting feel of a peaceful, rural retreat. The rooms were airy and clean inside, with pinewood floors and whitewashed walls. Sister Caterina, one of the two nuns whom Airton employed, said that the little hospital reminded her of the convent in her hometown in Tuscany.

The buildings in the first courtyard consisted of a storage room and pharmacy, and the surgery where Airton treated his outpatients. Every morning at seven o'clock, his chief Chinese assistant, Zhang Erhao, would open the gate and the sick would file in to sit patiently on the benches by Nellie's favourite dwarf pine, or in winter gather around the charcoal stove in a cleared-off section of the storehouse. Not only townsfolk came, with their boils, their toothache and their sciatica, but also peasants from further afield. Often they walked all night through the countryside to get here, or were pulled on handcarts by their families if they were too ill or injured to move. These large-limbed peasants, with their broad, wind-burned northern features, would sit stolidly for hours, bearing any degree of pain, waiting for a few moments of the foreign doctor's time. Such was Airton's reputation and skill that they rarely went away unsatisfied, though the doctor himself was only too aware how little he could do with his few drugs and bandages, and that the one disease he could never hope to cure was poverty.

The main building facing the gate contained the chapel. Each evening at six thirty the little community would gather there for evening prayers, singing the hymns that had been translated into Mandarin by the Missionary Society. The courtyard beyond was the preserve of the two Italian nuns, Sisters Caterina and Elena, whose white-habited figures could be seen moving energetically between the three wards opening on to the flower garden. The Catholic sisters had early taken on themselves the responsibility of nursing the bedridden patients, and even Nellie hardly ever intervened in their little kingdom. The two women were both in their late twenties. They had originally come to Shishan to assist Father Adolphus, a saintly, grey-bearded Jesuit scholar who had lived in Shishan ever since anyone could remember – but tragically their arrival had coincided with the beginnings of the bubonic-plague epidemic, which had claimed Father Adolphus among its earliest victims. Airton had found the two nuns in one of the worst-stricken areas looking after the orphans of families whose parents had perished. He had immediately taken them on as nurses and helpers. After the epidemic, he had written to the head of their mission in Rome, praising their courage and selflessness, and requesting that until a replacement for Father Adolphus could be found the nuns stay with him in Shishan. They had been with him ever since. Once a year at Easter they would travel to Tientsin for communion and confession, but otherwise they lived with the Airtons as members of his family, sharing in all the activities of his own mission, even participating in the services in his chapel. They were both of Italian peasant stock and were simple, cheerful souls. Sister Elena's merry laugh was as much a part of the hospital as the smell of carbolic and iodine in the wards. They lived in a wing of the third courtyard, which also served as dormitory and school for the various orphans they had befriended during the epidemic; some of the older children were now grown-up enough to become willing helpers in the hospital.

Airton and Nellie and their own children, with their servants, Ah Lee and Ah Sun – a Cantonese couple who had looked after the doctor since he had first come to China fifteen years before – lived in a yellow stucco bungalow separated from the hospital compound by a short walk. It was a sprawling building, surrounded by a well-kept lawn and bounded by a wooden fence. Its sitting room and dining room would not have been out of place in his native Edinburgh. At his own expense he had shipped out furniture and family portraits, wallpaper, Sheffield cutlery, curtains, Nellie's pianoforte and, her pride and joy, a modern cast-iron stove from Birmingham, which kept the house beautifully heated in winter and allowed hot water at any hour of the day. The doctor loved this house; he loved the smell of polished wooden floors, the aroma of bacon and hot buttered toast in the morning, the chatter of his children in their nursery, the absolute quiet of his study – but for a year now the long white corridors had seemed empty. He bitterly missed the company of his elder children. His fourteen-year-old son, Edmund, and his daughter, Mary, three years younger, had been sent back to Scotland the previous summer in the care of the Gillespies, missionary friends from Tientsin, and were now at boarding-school in Dundee. Both Nellie and Airton knew that one day the younger children, Jenny and George, aged ten and eight respectively, would follow. For now, they were of an age that they could attend school in the hospital with the orphans. It was the doctor's joke, and one endlessly relayed by the two nuns, that Nellie, despite her affection for Sisters Caterina and Elena, was convinced that her children would grow up to be papists under their tutelage, and that was why she insisted on sitting in whenever they gave Bible classes. Nellie would smile along with them, but it was a wry smile: there was an element of truth behind the jest.

Jenny and George greeted Airton clamorously as he came through the door. He was tired, irritated and sticky from the heat. He longed for a bath. It had been a frustrating afternoon. As soon as he had arrived at the hospital on his return from town he had instructed Zhang Erhao and some of the other helpers to conduct a search for Hiram. Zhang had been deliberately obtuse and had only reluctantly set out after much persuasion. Sister Elena had then come to him with a hysterical complaint that moths had eaten the new shipment of cotton bandages, and it had taken him several minutes to calm her down. Then he had had to conduct complicated surgery on a wagoner whose leg had been crushed in a collision between two carts. And finally, at dusk, Zhang Erhao had returned to report that Hiram had disappeared. He had been spotted leaving the city with some of his street-urchin friends in the direction of the Black Hills. Zhang had shaken his head sadly, miming a throat being cut. 'Iron Man Wang,' he whispered. 'Very bad.' On Airton's dismissal of this preposterous conclusion, Zhang had grinned. 'Maybe it'll be a ransom demand first,' he said. '*Then* he'll cut his throat!' Airton told him to get a lantern and search through the night, if need be. Zhang had left, his shoulders shaking with silent mirth, knowing that he had successfully irritated his master; this minor malicious triumph somewhat compensated for the chore he had to perform.

Airton sank into his armchair and gratefully received a glass of whisky from Ah Lee. Nellie was sewing at her table but smiled at him, a thread between her teeth. He smiled back. What a fine-looking woman she was, with her auburn hair piled high above a wide forehead, her firm jaw and her steady blue eyes. She was beginning to show slight signs of ageing, a greying near the temple, a ruddiness of the cheeks and at the tip of her nose, perhaps a hardening of the worry lines around her mouth, but her movements were lithe and her carriage erect. With her tall height and broad shoulders she possessed a natural stateliness. He reached into his waistcoat for his watch. He had half an hour to relax before they were due in chapel. He knew he should tell Nellie about Hiram. She would be more disturbed than he – but for the moment he did not want to think about that unpleasantness. Instead he told her about his meeting with Frank Delamere and the imminent arrival of Helen Frances.

'I hope she's not going to be one of these modern young women,' said Nellie.

'Oh, do be pleased about it,' sighed the doctor. 'It's the only piece of good news I've had this whole dreadful day.'

'You poor wee dear,' said Nellie. 'I thought you enjoyed the days you go off and talk to that murderous old Mandarin.'

But Airton felt no desire to explain his bad mood. Morosely he sipped his whisky, wondering what he would say in chapel in half an hour. He thought of Septimus's dreadful sermon, his ludicrous reference to the Samson story, and then he began to chuckle. 'He fell off the roof!'

'What, dear?'

'Nothing, my love. Just thinking of what text we might use for the lesson this evening. What about a bit of Judges? The story of Samson, perhaps. "Out of the eater came forth meat, and out of the strong came forth sweetness."'

'If your mind is still on Mr Delamere and his daughter, I think it would be very inappropriate. I can't think that much sweetness could come out of a wicked old lion like him, however pretty young Helen Frances might set herself out to be.'

'Oh, Nellie, how cruel you are,' said Airton. 'And you haven't even met the girl!'

But they were both laughing. Nellie moved over and pecked her husband on the cheek. The door burst open: the children bounced in, and in a moment the whole Airton family was wrestling on the sofa, a scramble of limbs and flying cushions.

Chapter Two

*We pray in the temple for rain – but still the sun
beats down on dry fields.*

The British Legation was holding a picnic in the Western Hills.
The cavalcade of broughams, carriages, palanquins, and horse
riders had set out at six in the morning, escorted by a troop
of mounted servants. Sir Claude MacDonald, Queen Victoria's
minister to the Imperial Court, doyen of the diplomatic community
and senior spokesman of those Western nations, including Japan
and the USA, with an established and powerful presence in China,
had quietly left Peking the night before and he and his wife were
already waiting for their guests in the Taoist temple that they had
converted into a weekend villa.

Temples were rather easily adapted for diplomats' holiday homes.
There was nothing to be done about the green curlicued roofs and
complicated wooden rafters, or the inset panels complete with
carved dragons and large red pillars made of solid tree-trunks
because these were part of the structure, but a lot could be achieved
with imported wallpaper and clever lighting. A few sofas and
chaises-longues, a solid mahogany dining-table and a pianoforte,
fine paintings on the walls, a copy of Landseer's *Dying Stag* and
a portrait of Lady MacDonald's grandfather in Waterloo uniform,
blended well with the lacquer screen, lanterns and Ming dynasty
chairs; a delightful mélange of modern urban chic and tasteful
chinoiserie. The two windows, which had had to be hacked out
on either side of the original Hall of Worship, gave much-needed
light, and Lady MacDonald had chosen elegant yellow curtains to
compensate for the desecration. The foreigners were, on the whole,
observant of local sensitivities – these were, after all, places of
worship they had commandeered – and it was considered bad form
to destroy any paintings, carvings or other works of religious art
that they might find on the walls. That was where good English
wallpaper came into its own. Lady MacDonald recalled how she

had been startled on the first night she had stayed here by the faces of ancient, flaking demons and *bodhisattvas* grinning in the candlelight from a fifteenth-century painting on the back wall. A layer of William Morris had made all the difference and, what was more, the flowered design went very well with her Persian carpets.

Proud as she was of the inside of her house, she was prouder still of the garden she had fashioned out of the courtyard. She had knocked down the outer wall and one of the shrines and planted a lawn that stretched to the edge of the cliff. She had laid out flower-beds and herbaceous borders and, with the white garden chairs and tables, the swing and the roller, she was confident that if the house was still China, the garden was unquestionably Surrey.

It was here that the uniformed house-boys, their long queues hanging down their backs, were busily lining up the crystal on the sideboard and laying out the last of the silver on the four long tables neatly spaced under the shade of the willow trees. The white of the servants' jackets and the starched tablecloths blazed brilliantly against the restful background of green lawn and fir-covered hillside. They worked quietly and efficiently, but they were conscious of the scrutinising eyes of Lady MacDonald, who was making some last minor adjustments to the flower arrangements. She was dressed in a wide, feathered hat and a tight-waisted taffeta dress of a subtle and becoming violet, and the oversized pair of garden scissors were somewhat incongruous in her fashionably gloved hands. Sir Claude, on the other hand, blazered, white-bagged and straw-boatered, was a picture of ease as he smoked his long cheroot, looking idly over the drop to the yellow plain below.

Much admired by his more temperamental European colleagues for his imperturbability, the canny analysis behind his short, enigmatic observations, his understated but natural authoritativeness – a typical English pro-consul, they judged, more mandarin than the mandarins – Sir Claude was actually a shy man, whose deep reserve was often mistaken for coolness or arrogance. He was respected rather than liked by his subordinates in the British Legation. Nearing fifty he had the colouring of a younger man, a full head of sandy hair and red, bony cheeks. A blond moustache waxed to thin points stretched out way beyond his ears at either side of his narrow, freckled face. It quivered as he moved, and seemed strangely detached from his face, rather as if a yellow bat had chosen to balance on his lips. Thin eyebrows frowned above pale, searching eyes. A tall man, he walked with a slight stoop, but even in the casual clothes he was wearing today, the deliberation of his movements evoked an aura of ceremony and grandeur. Under Sir Claude, the Legation functioned with an Imperial style, which extended even to its picnics.

Sir Claude was never the man to boast about his achievements, but he had been responsible for several diplomatic successes in this posting, not least for the negotiations that had dramatically increased British territory and influence in China. He had been the moving force behind the leasing of Wei Hai Wei as a new colony and, almost as an afterthought, the acquisition of the New Territories in Hong Kong; he had also secured from the Chinese government the recognition that the Yangtse valley was a British sphere of influence. He had ably countered similar aggrandising moves from the other powers in the scramble that followed China's unexpected defeat by Japan in 1895. Sir Claude was now keeping a wary eye on the activities of the Germans in Shantung and the Russians along the whole land border. Only yesterday he had received a worrying cable from his consul in the remote outpost of Kashgar, describing suspicious troop movements in the mountain passes leading to India. He had invited the Russian minister to the picnic and would choose a moment gently to communicate a veiled warning. It was not Sir Claude's style to seek confrontation when a quiet exchange behind the scenes might defuse tension.

He had found that his method of diplomacy harmonised well with that of the Chinese. He had struck up a practical working relationship with the officials at the *Tsungli Yamen*. Together they had resolved a number of thorny issues. Sir Claude had been proud of his intervention in the autumn of last year, after the Empress Dowager Tz'u Hsi, the real power behind the throne, had deposed the Emperor in a palace coup following the young man's abortive hundred-day reform movement. A wave of executions of the Emperor's servants and advisers had followed and the Legations, knowing the reputation of the Empress Dowager, expected the worst for her nephew. The diplomats' fears seemed confirmed when the palace issued a bulletin announcing that the Emperor was ill and that 'all medical treatments had proved ineffective'. It had been then that Sir Claude had delivered a note to the *Tsungli Yamen* urging the palace that it had better find a cure, for the Emperor's death at this juncture would have an effect on the western powers that would be disastrous for China. The result was that the Emperor achieved a remarkable recovery, albeit in continued confinement in the Summer Palace. Sir Claude had been gratified, however, to see him produced at a reception that the Empress Dowager had organised in December, her way of showing the foreign community that on this occasion she had taken their advice, at least as far as the prevention of murder was concerned.

The occasion itself had been unprecedented in other ways since, for the first time ever, the old lady had requested to meet the wives of the ministers from each Legation. He did not know which had more astonished him: the sedate tea party between the mythical Dragon Empress and the respectable corseted matrons of the diplomatic community, or the repeated murmur from the old tyrant's lips, 'One family. One family.' There were different interpretations of this enigmatic remark. He personally was encouraged, believing that the Dowager, while throttling reforms, was at least convinced of the need for engagement with the powers. He tended therefore to dismiss the rumours of anti-foreign martial-arts societies gathering in the countryside, and the excitable beliefs of some of his colleagues that a xenophobic movement was being brewed by the palace. He had yet to hear an authenticated account of this 'Boxer Movement', as it was beginning to be called, which would convince him that it reflected anything more than the usual local dissatisfaction among the peasantry that anyone who had lived in China for more than a few years had come to expect. Without being complacent about the problems the country faced, Sir Claude felt justified in having said in the report he had recently sent back to the Foreign Office that there was ground for cautious optimism that Great Britain's influence and trading stake would be uncompromised in the years to come.

The dust of the cavalcade was visible at the bottom of the hill. It would take them another twenty minutes to negotiate the winding path that led to his villa. Savouring a last puff of his cheroot, Sir Claude made his way to the gate, ready to receive the select and fashionable of Peking's foreign community.

Helen Frances cautiously sipped her champagne and looked with wide eyes at her fellow guests. She had never been to a gathering where so many languages were being spoken at once and by such an imposing array of people. When Tom had told her that they had been invited to a picnic she had thought it would be something along the lines of the outings she had had with her aunt to Ashdown Forest. She had imagined a small, casual group of friends gathered round a rug on the grass, chicken drumsticks, hard-boiled eggs and sandwiches, with perhaps a canter after lunch or a tour round one of the temples that Tom had told her could be found in the Western Hills. She had not conceived that the setting itself would be a temple, transformed into a luxurious mansion filled with exotic furniture. Nor that there would be a full meal in a manicured garden, with grander placings than in the dining room of the Hôtel de Pekin or the captain's table on the liner that had brought them here. And she certainly had not expected that everyone would be in such splendid dress.

It was true that some of the men in the party, including their host, were wearing comfortable country clothes, but in the circumstances it was an exaggerated insouciance. Many of the European diplomats had come in top hats and frock-coats. The Russian minister was displaying his medals. And the quiet Japanese minister, accompanied by his tiny kimono-clad wife, appeared to be in Court dress. Even so, the men were dowdy in comparison to their wives, who might have been presenting themselves at Ascot or the Henley Regatta. Helen Frances gazed in wonder as the Countess Esterhazy, a guest at the Austrian Legation, sailed by in a shimmer of blue organdie and peacock tails, laughing at a *bon mot* from the dapper French military attaché, who was dancing attendance behind her. Wide, feathered hats fluttered like a breeze through flowering cotton or mustard fields. Some of the women were wearing riding habits, as Helen Frances herself was, but the difference was that theirs might have been designed for the Windsor Hunt, with skirts cut in elegant velvets, shining black hats trailing transparent blue silks, jackets tightened round the waist to reveal the full magnificence of the female form. Helen Frances, in her brown travelling clothes and sturdy bowler, felt as out of place as a governess at a ball.

She had begged Tom not to leave her alone but he had been whisked off almost as soon as they arrived to take part in a game of rounders that some of the younger men were playing at the end of the garden. She had watched him for a while as he fielded. She saw him leap and catch the ball, roaring, 'Howzat,' with the others, as he held his trophy high. His red face beamed with happiness, his yellow hair hung awry. She had felt warm with fondness and pride, and he had looked across the lawn at her and grinned. Then Lady MacDonald had scooped her up and taken her to meet Madame Pichon, the wife of the French minister, who had proceeded to test her schoolgirl French to its limits. After some comments about the weather, they had managed to agree that the Great Wall of China was indeed very long, and Madame Pichon was observing, a touch tartly, that that was perhaps the very reason why it was called a Great Wall, when thankfully her attention was diverted to a more interesting conversation, and a flustered Helen Frances was left to her champagne. For the moment she was happy to remain ignored.

She found herself listening to the conversation of a small group of men gathered round Dr Morrison, the famous *Times* correspondent and traveller whom Tom had pointed out to her at the hotel. Her attention was drawn to one of the younger men lounging beside him, a strikingly handsome, black-haired man, with broad shoulders and a relaxed, powerful frame, whose strong limbs were contained in a tight tweed suit of elegant cut. He reminded her of a panther she had once seen at London Zoo, lazy, somnolent, but full of energy and muscle, with a coiled strength behind the sleek skin, ever ready to spring. She had noticed him on the ride out here, cantering past her carriage. She had watched as he pivoted effortlessly in his saddle to shout a jest at one of his friends, one hand steadying the neck of his horse, his blue eyes briefly meeting hers as he turned. He had twitched the reins and the horse had broken into a gallop, disappearing in a cloud of dust. The image of his erect, military bearing had remained in her mind. In the carriage she had not dared ask Mr and Mrs Dawson, the representatives of Tom's company in Peking, who he was. For some unaccountable reason it would have seemed disloyal to Tom. She felt a sudden anxiety in case the man looked up and saw her staring at him now. Another part of her wished very strongly that he would.

'Yes, I do take the Boxers seriously,' Dr Morrison was saying, in a quiet voice that contrasted with his rough, dogged features. Helen Frances detected the slight colonial accent in his speech. Tom had told her that he was a forthright Australian.

'Oh, come off it, sir. Spirit soldiers coming out of thin air. Incantations against silver bullets and mumbo-jumbo. It's not Africa.' The speaker was a red-haired, stocky young man with a harsh, braying voice. She recalled that he had been one of the riders whom the handsome black-haired man had been racing that morning. She thought that he was probably one of the Customs crowd of whom Tom spoke so disparagingly.

'No, it's not Africa, Mr Simpson,' replied Morrison. 'This is a civilisation that had a developed history when your ancestors were dancing around in woad. Superstition's not unique to the races we so grandly dismiss as native, you know. When was the last time you stepped aside to avoid walking under a ladder, or touched a piece of wood for luck?'

'Old wives' tales, sir. Surely you don't—'

'Old wives' tales, indeed, but they go deep. I grant you, in the last hundred years or so we western nations may have climbed a few rungs on the ladder of reason and science, but in Shakespeare's time, and that's the twinkling of an eye ago as far as Chinese history's concerned, we ourselves believed in hobgoblins and fairies and jack o'lanterns. Take your Chinese farmer here. He's had no agricultural revolution, certainly no industrial revolution. He lives by the seasons and the harvests, and if Heaven's angry he'll get his crops destroyed in a flood or a thunderstorm. Damn right he believes in gods and goddesses, and magical charms. They're about the only protection he's got. Put yourself in his shoes, Mr Simpson. Imagine that you're a Chinese peasant.'

Helen Frances saw the black-haired young man smile at the discomfiture of his friend, who, feeling himself mocked, was looking sourly into his wine glass.

Morrison was relentless. 'Imagine yourself a Chinese coolie in the sticks, Mr Simpson, paddling about in your paddyfield. What would be more fantastical to you? A magic charm or a steam engine?'

Dr Morrison waited, a severe expression on his face. Simpson grinned foolishly.

'You see my point then. Superstition's real to these people and damned dangerous. I don't suppose that you've forgotten the havoc the Taipings caused in this country just fifty years ago. Can you recall what they believed in?'

'Well, Christianity, wasn't it?' Simpson rallied. 'At least, a sort of

Christianity, a bit perverted. Christ's younger brother come to earth and all that.'

'Christianity, did you say? And twenty million dead! And you're not nervous, Mr Simpson? I think that my case rests!'

The black-haired man laughed. Helen Frances saw white teeth in a brown face. She did not really understand what this conversation was about. Was Dr Morrison suggesting that Christianity was a sort of superstition too? She had heard about the Boxers but what were the Taipings? Tom never talked to her about politics. He probably wanted to protect her. She liked that in Tom, but she was still curious, and frustrated sometimes that he would reduce most things to frivolity in her presence.

A clean-shaven American diplomat, Herbert Squiers, to whom she had been briefly introduced at a stop-over on the journey, had taken up the conversation. 'I don't question the powers of superstition, Dr Morrison, but I'm afraid I'm with our friend here in doubting there's any danger from these Boxers. Sure we've had letters from missionaries with a few scare stories about midnight meetings and intemperate rabble-rousing, which we've looked into. But there's nothing solid to write home about. Peasants are all excitable one day, and next day they're happily back in the fields. Nobody's been hurt as far as I know. No mission's been torched. It's all excitable talk, midsummer madness. We're advising our people to stay calm.'

'And what happens when the first mission is put to the torch? Will you advise your people to stay calm then?'

'You really believe that that's going to happen?'

'I don't know, Squiers,' said Morrison. 'I wish I did. Maybe it is a midsummer madness. I'll tell you one thing, though, the disaffection is real enough. A lot of people had high hopes of the reform movement last year, and though the Mandarinate may be happy that Tzu Hsi's restored the status quo with her palace coup, the whole merchant class and a lot of the scholar class are very downbeat. God help us if we have a poor harvest.'

'The Boxers aren't scholars or merchants.'

'Of course they aren't. But who led on the Jacquerie in the French Revolution? Intellectuals like Robespierre and Danton. No, don't laugh. There's no proof that the Boxer movement has anything to do with the reformers, or the palace for that matter. It's just that in China there are wheels within wheels. And secret societies are just that.'

'What?'

'Secret. Take the term Boxer, what does it mean? The Fists of Righteous Harmony. Rather grand, don't you think? Don't tell me that a peasant came up with that name.'

'So who did?'

'I don't know. But secret societies are a part of the fabric of this country. Triads. Tongs. They're criminal brotherhoods, but there's something respectable about them as well. They call themselves patriotic societies. Protectors of the people against corrupt dynasties. The White Lotus were heroes who rose up against the Mongols and set up the Ming, and later they turned on the Ming when they went rotten. They still exist, as do the Eight Diagram sect, the Red Fists, the Big Swords, the Big Knives, the Black Sticks. There are hundreds of them, and who knows what tentacles they have through every class of society here? Everybody needs protection. I would bet that these Boxers are linked to one or more of these black societies.'

'I declare, Simpson,' Helen Frances was startled to hear the black-haired man's voice rise in a languid drawl, 'I never expected China to be so exciting. Am I to understand, sir,' he addressed Dr Morrison, 'that I will be endangering life and limb when I leave the safety and protection of the diplomatic community,' he waved his hand sardonically at the party around him, 'and venture into the wilds of the countryside?'

'You're Manners, aren't you?' said Morrison, looking at him coldly. 'I was told you'd be here. No, sir, for the moment I am not suggesting anything of the kind. The Boxers are a disturbing phenomenon but, up to now, they've not attacked a white man. I'm sure, from all I've heard about you, that you can look after yourself anyway.'

'My reputation obviously precedes me.'

'Adviser to the Japanese army. Yes, I've heard about you. And now I gather you've left all that and got a job with the railway. Where are they sending you?'

Helen Frances felt a rush of blood to her head when she heard him answer, 'Shishan,' but she had no chance to listen to more because, with bounding excitement, a perspiring Tom was at her side telling her that his team had won the rounders match, and, gosh, why was she standing all alone and forlorn? She must stock up on the bubbly and come and meet his chums from the Legation. As she went she turned her head and saw Manners's blue eyes looking humorously in her direction.

At luncheon, under the trees, she was placed between a quiet Legation interpreter called Pritchett and the French minister, Monsieur Pichon. After a few pleasantries, Monsieur Pichon proceeded to ignore her, speaking loudly across the Japanese minister's wife to Sir Claude, who was at the head of the table. Tom was sitting at the other end, out of conversational range. She was therefore left to Pritchett's company, and since he seemed to be a young man overwhelmed with an attack of terminal shyness, conversation was hard-going. Her eyes began to wander over to the other tables. Lady MacDonald was looking after the white-bearded Sir Robert Hart, head of the Chinese Customs Service and Peking's oldest and apparently wisest resident. Her eyes lingered on the magnificent costume of the Countess Esterhazy, who seemed to be in flirtatious and intimate conversation with the guest on her left. She could not make out who it was because he was blocked by the back of Mr Squiers' large head. Then Mr Squiers moved and she recognised Manners. Quickly she turned away.

'Mr Pritchett,' she asked sweetly, 'do you know everybody who's here?'

'Most,' he answered. 'Peking's a small community. Don't know some of the visitors. Why?'

'Oh, nothing really. I was just wondering. I saw some excellent horsemanship this morning on the way out here, some of the riders racing each other.'

'Ah, yes, that would be the Customs boys showing off. I'm sorry, I didn't mean . . .'

'But they *were* showing off. Don't worry,' laughed Helen Frances. 'There was one in particular, I'm not sure of his name. Manners, I think. He really is an excellent horseman.'

'I'm sorry, Miss Delamere, I don't really know much about riding.'

'I love riding,' said Helen Frances. 'Do you have fox hunts here?'

'Paper hunts, I think, sometimes, and there's the Jockey Club. I don't myself.'

'Mr Manners must be one of the leading lights of the Jockey Club.'

'Henry Manners? The MP's son? No, Miss Delamere, he's a visitor here. There was a cable about him at the Legation.'

'That sounds rather fascinating.'

'No, not really. A routine cable. Sir Claude is helping him to get a job with the China railways, somewhere up north. A favour to his father, Lord Beverley, who's something in the Government at home.'

'So Mr Manners is an engineer, Mr Pritchett?'

The interpreter, who had been avoiding looking into Helen Frances's face, suddenly raised his mournful eyes to glance at her directly, his eyebrows quizzical. 'I believe he was once an officer in the Royal Engineers and served in India. I understand that Mr Manners has been many things in his time. A colourful personality, Miss Delamere. Most recently he has been in Japan. May I ask why you are so interested? Apart from his horsemanship, I mean?'

Helen Frances was irritated to feel a blush to her cheeks, which she tried to hide with a playful giggle. It came out shriller than she had intended. She hoped that she had not drunk too much champagne. 'You are being very arch, Mr Pritchett. I'm not interested in Mr Manners at all. Whatever do you mean?'

Now it was Pritchett's turn to be embarrassed and he, too, blushed. 'My apologies, Miss Delamere, if I spoke clumsily.' He smiled sadly. 'I often suspect that I am more fluent in Oriental languages than in English.' Seeing that Helen Frances was smiling back at him he took courage to go on. 'Incidentally, Mr Manners is something of a linguist himself. He speaks good Japanese and has progressed well with his Chinese in the months that he's been here.'

'You seem to know him well.'

'Peking is a small town, Miss Delamere. I do not see him very often. He tends to prefer a more worldly society than the ivory tower I inhabit.'

'The Customs boys?'

Pritchett laughed softly. Their mutual embarrassment earlier seemed to have put him at his ease. 'It's what passes here for a fast set. B. L. Simpson and his colleagues, and some of the military attachés.'

'I wouldn't dare to ask what they get up to.'

'And I certainly wouldn't dare to tell you, even if I knew.'

'So am I to take it that Mr Manners is a wicked man, Mr Pritchett?'

'I think I said a colourful one, Miss Delamere.' He leaned back to allow a servant to take away the remains of his first course, his lobster half touched. 'May I ask you where you and Mr Cabot . . . ?'

'My fiancé.'

'Yes. May I ask where exactly you'll be going when you leave Peking? Your father's in the chemicals business, I believe, somewhere in the north?'

'He works in a place called Shishan. That's where we're going.'

'Ah,' said Pritchett. 'Shishan.' His eyes twinkled with sad merriment. 'And you said it was Mr Manners's horsemanship that interested you?'

This time Helen Frances found herself laughing quite naturally. 'You have discovered me, Mr Pritchett. Yes, I did hear today that Mr Manners is also going to Shishan and I was trying to sound you out about his character. Will you forgive me?'

'You were very skilful. I hope that I have not said anything to turn you against your new neighbour.'

'On the contrary. You have made him into the most intriguing personality. I'll enjoy meeting someone who is so . . . colourful.'

And attractive, she confided to herself. What a wicked thought. She really must not drink any more wine. As the waiter laid the main course in front of her – roast beef and Yorkshire pudding – she stole a glance in Manners's direction. He had his head back and was laughing loudly at a sally from Countess Esterhazy, his white teeth shining under his small moustache. She looked down at dear, honest Tom, who seemed to be replaying his rounders game with the salt and pepper cylinders on the tablecloth. One of his friends looked on, contributing to the tactics with some bread rolls. The Legation wife sitting between them appeared manifestly bored. Good old Tom, she thought fondly.

'If you are going to Shishan, Miss Delamere,' Pritchett was saying, 'can I be so bold as to give you a word of caution?'

'About Mr Manners?' she asked, surprised.

'I would hardly presume to do that,' said Pritchett. 'No, I do not wish to alarm you, but have you heard of the Boxers?'

'Nobody seems to talk about anything else,' she said, 'but Mr

Squiers was saying just now that his Legation do not consider them to be anything more than a midsummer madness.'

'That is the official position of our Legation as well. I hope we're right. But I do have Chinese friends who are inclined to a different view. Shishan is a long way from here and not yet connected to the railway. I only caution, keep an ear open and if you hear of anything disturbing, don't consider it any dishonour to leave, at once, and advise Mr Cabot and your father to do the same. I would be privileged if you would write to me to let me know what the situation in Shishan is from time to time. There. That's what I wanted to say.' He gave his sad smile.

'Why, Mr Pritchett, how very sweet of you. Of course I'll – I'll take what you say very seriously, and I'll certainly write to you. It'll be a pleasure. Indeed it will.' What a funny, mournful little man, she thought. 'But now, no more talk of these dreadful Boxers.'

After the third course, a rather ambitious lemon blancmange, the ladies left the gentlemen to their brandy. The exception was the Countess Esterhazy who, to the outrage of some of the Legation wives, not only insisted on staying with the men but even demanded a large cigar, which was lit for her with humour by Sir Claude himself, ever the perfect host. The chatter over the coffee in Lady MacDonald's living room inevitably focused on the numerous liaisons the Countess was supposed to have had with leading figures at the Austrian and Russian courts. There were rumours that during the short time she had spent in Peking she had not discouraged admirers. Madame Pichon, no doubt anxious to preserve the reputation of the French Legation's military attaché, observed that there was even a young Englishman who appeared not indifferent to her charms. Why, at lunch today . . . At which point a graceful Lady MacDonald had asked Mrs Dawson whether she and her young friend might not be tired after the exertions of the day, and Mrs Dawson, exchanging knowing looks with her hostess, had remarked that, yes, she was a trifle fatigued. Which was why Mrs Dawson and a frustrated Helen Frances were led to a small, simply furnished room at the back of the temple where they were told they could lie down for the afternoon.

As Mrs Dawson snored beside her, Helen Frances lay awake on the iron bed, thinking of the conversation about Boxers and her talk with Pritchett, and of Manners and Countess Esterhazy. Of Manners, in particular, turning in his saddle, his blue eyes and white teeth and sleek black hair. What had Dr Morrison said? Adviser to the Japanese army? And something about railways. Was he really going to be with them in Shishan? He was very different from Tom. Dearest Tom. Tom with his wide chest and strong arms. His lopsided grin and deep laugh. Imperceptibly, however, her picture of Tom began to merge with that of Manners, and suddenly, vividly, there was only Manners – his broad shoulders, his agile body, his small, fashionable moustache. Dangerous. A black panther, a prowling black panther. And what was Tom? A lion? No, a big, shaggy dog. A prowling panther and a shaggy collie, a sweet shaggy collie . . .

She woke with a headache. Serve her right, she thought, for drinking so much champagne. She followed Mrs Dawson sleepily back to the lawn. There she saw Tom standing with Henry Manners.

'Dearest, it's the most wonderful thing,' said Tom. 'Guess what? Here's a chap who's also being posted to Shishan. Henry Manners. My fiancée, Helen Frances Delamere. We can all travel together. Isn't that topping?'

'Enchanted,' said Manners, lifting her hand to his lips. She felt the brush of his moustache on her fingers. His eyes, crinkled with humour, held hers.

'Manners is going up there to build the railway. He'll be living in the camp, but it's just outside the town so we'll be able to see a lot of each other. And when I'm away up-country you and he can go riding together. It's fine riding up there, apparently, and there's even some hunting.'

'That's what they tell me,' said Manners. 'But I think it's mainly bear-hunting. Some deer.'

'I saw you on your horse this morning,' said Helen Frances. The words seemed to blurt out.

'Did you?' said Tom. 'You saw the race? Wasn't that fine? Manners and I are going to try a gallop on the way back, aren't we? If there's enough light, that is. HF, old girl, isn't this terrific? You know, I was a bit worried before – never told you, of course – about us going off to Shishan all alone, where there's no congenial company except your father and the old doctor. But having Manners with us is just the thing.'

She was spared the need to respond because Sir Claude MacDonald appeared beside them. 'Manners,' he acknowledged.

'Sir Claude. Grand picnic,' Manners replied.

'That's what we call these little affairs. It's all part of the diplomatic round. I'm very glad the three of you have met. So, you're heading off to Shishan together?'

'It appears so. It couldn't be a more fortunate coincidence, could it?'

'Aye. Well. These days I'm happier when there's a big group travelling together. As you know, I don't hold with this Boxer nonsense but there have been incidences of banditry and it's wise to take precautions. Trust you'll go well armed. Mind you, in Shishan you have an excellent man in Airton. Very sound, and he knows the Mandarin well. You should be safe enough there.'

'I look forward to meeting him, Sir Claude.'

'He's a wise head, young Henry. Listen to him, is my advice. Listen to him.' Sir Claude looked intently at Manners as if to press the point. Manners smiled and dropped his eyes. Sir Claude turned towards Tom and Helen Frances. 'I've not met your father, Miss Delamere, but Dawson tells me he is doing well by his company in those parts. Incidentally, I understand that congratulations are in order. The two of you are engaged, are you not?'

'Well, not officially yet, sir. More an understanding.'

'You have still to get the father's permission. I quite understand. Well, I'm sure he'll agree. You're a lucky fellow. You're going up there to be Mr Delamere's assistant, I believe?'

'Yes, sir. Looking forward to it.'

'Good. Good. Well, I won't detain you. You have a long ride back. Thank you all for coming. Look after yourselves in Shishan. And, Manners, mind the advice I've given you.'

'I say,' said Tom, as they made their way towards the horses and carriages, 'that was a bit like being put in front of the old headmaster again.'

'Silly old fool,' muttered Manners. 'Head in the clouds. Doesn't know what's going on.'

'What was this advice he was giving you? He seemed pretty strong about it.'

'Advice? Just the old Polonius. "Neither a borrower nor a lender be." Feels he owes it to my pater to keep me on the straight and narrow. Some nerve, actually.'

'Are you intent on becoming the black sheep of your family then, Mr Manners?' asked Helen Frances.

'HF, golly, you can't say things like that!' Tom looked anxiously at his new friend, but Manners laughed.

'I already am the black sheep of my family, Miss Delamere,' he said, swinging into his saddle. 'By the way, I saw you too this morning. The vision of you listening on the side quite enlivened Morrison's dreary homily. Cabot, Sir Claude was quite right. You're a lucky man. I'll see you on the ride.'

Helen Frances watched Manners manoeuvre his horse skilfully through the carriage park to join B. L. Simpson and several other riders who had already mounted. She and Tom walked among the shining collection of barouches, buggies, landaus and coaches, each attended by uniformed grooms in conical hats, looking for the Dawsons' carriage.

'Do you like Henry Manners, Tom?' she asked quietly, putting her hand into his.

'Why, yes, he's a terrific fellow. Great sportsman. Why do you ask?'

'He seems so different from you.'

'More worldly, you mean?' grinned Tom. 'Well, he has bashed about a bit. Done lots of interesting things.'

'That's partly what I mean,' said Helen Frances. 'He seems to have a bit of a reputation.'

'Jolly well deserved, I would think. He's been a soldier, an engineer. Lived in India, the East Indies, Japan. Probably got some good stories to tell us round the campfire on the way to Shishan. You don't mind him coming with us, do you? I'm sure he won't get in the way.'

'Of course I don't mind, Tom, if it makes you happy.' She gave him a quick hug and a peck on the cheek. 'You're a very kind man, you know that, Tom?'

'Steady on, girl, someone might see,' said Tom, but his eyes were gleaming with happiness and pride as, giggling, she kissed him again. She rested her head on his breast, and the two stood modestly embraced together, between a brougham and a landau, under the uninterested gaze of a Chinese groom. When they heard voices behind them, they quickly broke apart and turned with innocent smiles to greet Mr and Mrs Dawson, who had come to take Helen Frances into their carriage for the journey back to Peking.

*   *   *

'Who's the filly?' asked Simpson, as Manners rode up beside him.

'Helen Frances Delamere,' drawled Manners. 'It seems she's to be my travelling companion to Shishan.'

'Well, there's a piece of luck for you. Nothing like a bouncy redhead to calm the troubled brow.'

'She might be a bit of a challenge. Apparently she's engaged.'

'What, to Cricketing Tom over there? Shouldn't be any trouble to you, old man.'

'Certainly makes the prospect of Shishan more interesting. Now, what's the wager?'

'Twenty guineas I reach the city walls before you do. Or, tell you what, double the stake and I get an hour with that new Mongolian bint you've been pleasuring at Mother Zhou's.'

'She wouldn't even look at you. But all right, you're on. Make it fifty guineas. You'll owe me before sundown.'

'Ride hard, my boy, ride hard.' Simpson laughed harshly.

'I always ride hard,' said Manners, and whipped his horse to a cantering start.

Sir Claude stood at his favourite spot overlooking the plain, a cheroot between his lips, his hands clasped behind his back. In the distance he could make out puffs of dust where his guests were straggling back to the city. He could just identify the towers and the walls in the haze on the horizon. The sun was sinking behind the trees. It had been a tiring but a satisfying day. He had spent half an hour talking to the Russian minister and, as he had expected, the initial bluster had given way to smooth platitudes about harmony between their two empires and a common purpose to civilise Asia. He was confident that a cable would be despatched from the Russian Legation this evening, and that he would soon be hearing something confirmatory from Kashgar. He had also had a useful conversation with the Japanese minister and was pleased that he seemed to share the same view of the Chinese situation. One never knew with the Japanese, but he was glad on this occasion to have an ally in what promised to be another confrontation with Monsieur Pichon during the Ministers' Council on Tuesday. What was Pichon thinking about? Arming the Legations? How provocative could one get!

Behind him the servants were clearing the tables, the gardeners were sweeping up cigar ends from the lawn. His wife had drawn a bath and was resting after the party. He looked forward to a quiet evening reading a volume of Trollope, with a glass or two of good malt.

He heard a cough and was surprised to see Pritchett standing uncomfortably behind him.

'Pritchett, man, what are you doing here? Everyone's long gone home.'

'I'm sorry, sir. I rode off together with them, but then I decided that this couldn't wait until Monday, so I – I came back again.'

Sir Claude had a sincere admiration for Pritchett's professional qualities. He fulfilled his ostensible function as interpreter to perfection. He was a fine Orientalist. He was also more than competent in his other role as intelligence gatherer for the Legation. But the man was maddeningly diffident. 'You could have taken me aside at the picnic.'

'Yes, sir.'

'Well, go on, what is it?'

'We've received another letter, sir.'

'Boxers again?'

'Yes, sir.'

'Oh, Pritchett. Pritchett. You and your Boxers. What is it this time?'

'It's from our agent in Fuxin, sir. That's in Manchuria, west of Mukden. It's on the edges of Chinese cultivation, close by the Mongolian regions. There's a tomb there.'

'I know where Fuxin is. Go on.'

'Well, sir, our agent writes that there was a Boxer disturbance there, apparently after the arrival of a mendicant priest. It's not the first time we've heard of this priest, sir—'

'Or others like him. There are thousands of mountebanks in China, all rabble-rousing in one way or another.'

'Yes, sir. Whether or not it's the same priest may not be important. What distinguishes this incident was that there was a death, a murder, sir.'

'A murder? Of a missionary? Of a white man?'

'No, sir. There were missionaries there, Dr and Mrs Henderson, of the Scottish Missionary Society. They were terrorised, surrounded in their house by a mob, but not hurt in any way. They were very frightened, of course. They've left Fuxin, I gather, and are on their way back to Peking now.'

'That could start a panic. We'd better get to them before they start talking to the papers. But you said somebody was murdered?'

'Yes, sir. A Chinese Christian. A well-known merchant who had trading dealings with several of our companies. He was . . . hacked to death, sir.'

'By the Boxers?'

'Yes, sir.'

'You have that on good account? He was murdered by the Boxers because he was a Christian and consorted with foreigners?'

'It doesn't say, sir.'

'But you presume it? Your agent presumes it?'

'Yes, sir.'

'What's the situation there now? In Fuxin?'

'The local authorities sent in soldiers, and dispersed the riot. Several ringleaders were arrested, including the murderers of the merchant. The mendicant priest disappeared. Things seem to be back to normal now. There's going to be a trial at the local *yamen* and probably some executions.'

'Well, in that case it seems to be an internal Chinese affair.'

'I beg your pardon, sir?'

'A law-and-order issue, man. Townsfolk riot, whatever the reason, and the authorities reassert control. How do you know this merchant was not a corrupt, unpopular person in his town and a natural object of mob violence, maybe the cause of it?'

'He was a Christian.'

'That's no guarantee of anything. I've known some pretty corrupt Christians in my time. This merchant might have been storing grain. Anything. No, there's nothing to be read into this. It's a common riot. Happens all the time.'

'My agent talks of Boxers. And there was a killing. The first, sir.'

'Everybody talks of Boxers nowadays. No, Pritchett, it seems to me that we would be irresponsible if we overreacted to this. Forget it, man. Have your weekend. What's left of it. We'll talk about this again on Monday.'

'Sir, could we not investigate this incident further? It may be important.'

'Oh, Pritchett, you have Boxers on the brain. What are you suggesting?'

'Well, sir, Manners is passing in that direction on his way to Shishan. It's not too far out of the way, sir. Perhaps we could ask him for an independent report.'

'I don't share your trust in young Manners. He's much too much in bed with the Japanese for my liking, and anything else with two legs for that matter. He's disreputable, Pritchett. I've helped him because his father asked me to, and you seemed to think it was a good idea, but I really have my reservations. I don't approve either of this extraordinary gun-running scheme that you and London have concocted behind my back. It'll explode in your faces, you mark my words.'

'But to counter Russian influence in Manchuria . . . ?'

'Yes, yes, I've read your report. I still don't like it, and when I think that you will be relying on young Manners of all people . . .'

'We thought his Japanese connections might be particularly useful, sir.'

'Have it your own way, Pritchett, have it your own way. As for this incident in Fuxin, get him to send a report. But confidentially. The official line remains that this was a minor riot.'

'Yes, sir. Thank you, sir.'

'And make sure I see the Hendersons as soon as they arrive in Peking.'

'Yes, sir.'

'And no more scaremongering about Boxers.'

'No, sir.'

'All right, Pritchett, off you go. You have a long ride back. And, Pritchett, thank you. You're a good man.'

Sir Claude sighed. Although there were still pools of pale sunlight on the plain, dusk was settling in the hills. The first lamps had been lit in the house, and the yellow glow behind the latticed windows was warm and inviting. His cheroot had gone out. He fumbled in his pocket for matches but found that his box was empty. A mosquito was whining close to his ear. 'Damn,' he mouthed silently, and turned to go in.

The engine was belching white smoke against the pale blue sky as Tom and Helen Frances waited by their mound of trunks and parcels on the makeshift wooden platform. Henry Manners had travelled ahead of them and should by now have organised the horses, mules and escort to take them on to Shishan, but there was no sign of him. For now they seemed to be stuck in the middle of nowhere. There was a shabby clay-walled village at the bottom of a gully a hundred yards off. A thin spiral of smoke rising from a flat roof showed Helen Frances that it was inhabited, but the only other sign of life she could detect was a dog worrying at a sheep bone on the bare ground at her feet. Beyond the cooling engine, the railway bed had already been dug and the line of black-brown earth curved to the horizon as far as they could see. Neither the steel tracks nor the sleepers had been laid, however, so the railway stopped here. While Tom was pacing the platform impatiently, worried by Manners's non-appearance, Helen Frances only felt excitement. A strong wind was blowing, the scent of the grassland was fragrant in her nostrils, and she enjoyed a delightful sense of abandonment on this empty plain.

She had also enjoyed the three-day rail journey from Peking. The carriage, with its sitting room and private sleeping compartments, its kitchen and its dining room, complete with a dozen servants and cooks and attendants waiting on them, had been luxurious beyond imagination. Manners had arranged the private car for them through his position in the railway company. It had been hitched on to the end of the regular train to Tientsin. After Tientsin they had been given their own locomotive to take them to the end of the line. Helen Frances had never experienced such royal treatment in her life. She and Tom had played endless games of ludo and halma in the day room, and dined off silver plate like princes in the evening. The landscape had been largely flat and uninteresting, but there had been considerable excitement on the second day when they had slowly shunted by the Great Wall, the remains of its battlements and crenellations stretching up in inconceivable angles along the jagged mountain ranges. They had then descended to the coastline, the railway track curving round the Gulf of Chih-li. The blue sea and the small pines on the headlands had made beautiful pictures framed by the curtains of their windows as they passed.

Tom had been charming and attentive, keeping her amused with a stream of jokes and stories. This was actually the first time that she had ever really been alone with him, but he had been very sweet and proper, seeing her to the door of her sleeping compartment each evening, sealing the day with an embrace and a decorous kiss. He had not attempted anything more, which was no surprise. He took his responsibilities and her honour as seriously as life itself. She had caught herself wondering what it would have been like to travel alone in this luxury with Henry Manners. Would he have been quite such a gentleman? A young lady all alone and defenceless. The panther and its prey. She wondered why he had not chosen to travel with them on this first stage of their journey. She remembered one of the gossips in Peking speaking disapprovingly of his friends, the Customs boys, and what she called their harems of scarlet women. She knew that Manners had also taken a private company carriage. She had the wicked thought that he might not have been alone, after all. Had he spirited aboard an exotic Chinese courtesan in a blue silk gown, jade pins in her lustrous hair, with long red-painted fingernails and tiny feet? She could picture a doll-like creature sitting on Manners's knee while he contemplated her sardonically, his shirt unbuttoned, a cigar in his lips, a balloon of brandy swilling in his hand. She had blushed at her own lurid imagination, looking at Tom's open, cheerful face absorbed in an adventure in *Blackwood's* magazine, and shaken her head.

She knew that she was in love with Tom. She had been ever since that evening on the Indian Ocean, after the fancy-dress ball, when they had stood together on the top deck under the stars, the faint music of the orchestra mingling with the wash of the waves, the two of them enveloped by the blackness of the night and the phosphorescent sea. They had been told to dress as Shakespearian characters, and Helen Frances had chosen Othello and Desdemona. She had suggested daringly, and Tom had agreed, that they reverse the roles, so she had appeared in tights, doublet and shoeblack as a petite, exquisite Othello, while big Tom, draped in a stuffed dress made out of a curtain, with the end of a cleaning mop on his head as his flowing locks, and bright red lipstick daubed crookedly on his face like a French clown, had stolen the day as an outrageous parody of fair Desdemona. Naturally they had won the first prize, and somehow Tom had won her heart in the process. She had not been surprised when he had proposed, clumsily, almost apologetically, that night on the deck, and looking into his anxious eyes in the hideously painted clown's face, she had been overcome with tenderness, and accepted. He had kissed her and in doing so smeared his face with shoe black, and they had sat on the deck and laughed and laughed, holding tightly to each other's hands.

Of course, he had been overwhelmed with guilt and anxiety the next day about what her father and her aunt would think. He had agreed to escort her. Had he betrayed his trust? Had he taken advantage of his position? She had told him that certainly he had, and she was delighted by it. This had filled him with greater gloom, and she had laughed merrily at his predicament. As the weeks progressed he had recovered his cheerfulness, and now seemed quite happy at the prospect of asking her father formally for her hand. She, on the other hand, had never felt any qualms. Since the ship had left the quay in Southampton in a cloud of seagulls and spray it was as if her previous life had dwindled to the size of her aunt waving on the shore, and then vanished into memory. Reality now was the sensation that every new day brought her on this long, so far uncompleted journey. Even the first exciting weeks of the voyage, the squalls in Biscay, the strange Rock of Gibraltar looming out of the mist, the dolphins and flying fish in the Mediterranean, the lines of camels silhouetted against the desert as they passed through the cauldron of the Canal, the spice market at Aden, sights and sounds which, at the time, had electrified all her senses seemed now to belong to a vague distant past, so much had happened since. Bombay. Colombo. Penang. The spice islands in the golden setting sun. Hong Kong. Shanghai. Tientsin. Peking. She lived from day to day in a perpetual, thrilling present, and Tom was part of that present, so it seemed quite natural, almost inevitable, that she should love him. She had no fear of her father. She remembered him vaguely from when she was twelve, and he had arrived at her aunt's cottage, larger than life, showering presents. It had been the first time she had seen an adult cry. Hugging her, laughing and crying, all at the same time, big salt tears had streamed down his red face, past his swelling nose, into his thick moustache, while his booming voice roared into her ear, 'My girl. My darling girl.' After only a few days he had disappeared again. But she remembered him as a warm, loving, comfortable presence, smelling of boiled beef and tobacco, and she, too, had cried inconsolably when he was gone. She felt confident that he would like Tom, or that she could make him like him. But that was days away in the far future. Today she was happy to be standing on a wooden platform in the middle of a desert plain, waiting for Henry Manners to come with the horses. This was the exciting reality of the moment.

It was strange, though, she thought, as Tom paced up and down, and the wind roared in her ears. She had never had the sort of fantasies about Tom that she did about Henry Manners. Tom, of course, had always conducted himself entirely properly. Beyond the rare – sweet – embrace and kiss, when she loved to melt into the protection of his arms, there was never any question of a physical relationship before marriage. She knew what would happen when they were married, and she looked forward to it, or she thought she did, or would. The truth was that she had not considered it, the act, very much, if at all, until she had seen Henry Manners's muscles and sinews flowing under his tweed jacket, his thighs gripping his horse on the Peking plain. And now, especially when she was alone, she seemed to think of nothing else.

Of course she was no naïve. She had touched herself in the past, at school, and felt the intense heat and pleasure in her belly and her loins, but that sort of arousal seemed mechanical, and she had learned to resist the temptation. It seemed an improper, if not unnatural, thing to do, and she did not like to join in the whispering and giggling of the other girls in the dormitory who were doing the same and more to themselves and each other, even though she could not help but overhear them, and pulled the pillow down over her ears. Each night since the Saturday of the picnic, however, she had woken with the same heat and moistness between her legs that she remembered from her schooldays, and a new warm tingle in her belly and breasts. She told herself that it was all right. She had been dreaming about Tom. It was natural for her unconscious mind to anticipate the sensations of the wedding night; but as often as not it was Henry Manners's face she saw when she closed her eyes, and then she would lie awake in the dark, trying desperately to superimpose Tom's face on it. She told herself that she did not even like Manners. He was a bad hat, to use Tom's silly phrase. A philanderer, a man with a past. She wished she were more experienced, wiser in the ways of the world. She doubted that someone as assured as Countess Esterhazy had ever had these doubts or anxieties. But, try as she would, she could never get Manners out of her mind. 'The sooner you get married, my girl, the better,' she said to herself, in a vague imitation of what she remembered of her father's voice.

'What was that?' asked Tom.

'Nothing. Talking to myself.'

'Watch it. First sign of madness. Where the devil is he? You wouldn't have thought that a chap like Henry Manners would be unreliable.'

'Certainly not. He's a paragon, isn't he?'

'What's the matter with you, HF? Sometimes I get the feeling you don't really like Manners. We're rather dependent on him now, you know.'

'Don't worry, Tom, he'll come. Paragons always do.'

'There you go again.'

'Mr Manners is fine, Tom. I'm only sorry that the two of us won't be alone any more. I've enjoyed the last three days being with you. I'll miss you.'

'Oh, you delightful muffin,' said Tom. 'Here, let me give you a hug.'

And it was while they were hugging on the platform that Henry Manners and the mule train appeared, at a canter, in a cloud of grey dust. Helen Frances lifted her head from Tom's shoulder and looked straight into Manners's laughing blue eyes. He raised his hat ironically in the air, steadying the neck of his twitching horse with the other hand.

They adapted rapidly to the rhythm of the caravan. A string of eight pack mules carried their luggage, and the provisions for the journey. Manners had hired six mounted porters who also served as armed guards. Helen Frances thought they looked fearsome when she first saw them. They had gnarled, weatherbeaten faces, straggly moustaches and fierce, slit eyes above wide brown cheekbones. They wore knee-length padded coats, leather boots and fur hats, with long rifles strung on their backs and knives in their belts. Their queues were greasy with animal fat. They wore them coiled under their hats, or sometimes curled around their necks. She told Tom that they reminded her of Ali Baba's thieves. As she got to know them, however, she had become impressed by their gentleness and humour. Each night, round their separate campfire, she would watch them as they passed a flask of white liquor between them, smoked long pipes and sang mournful songs of haunting melody. Lao Zhao, the head man, appointed himself her personal guardian and groom. He would help her in and out of the saddle at each stop (not that she needed help: the Mongolian ponies were tiny), bring her extra helpings of noodles and mutton, unload her boxes and put up her tent, or drape a rug round her shoulders when a cold wind blew. All the time he chattered and laughed, his mobile face contorting into the oddest grimaces and humorous expressions. Of course she could not understand a word of what he was saying, but she knew he was friendly, and after the first day she became comfortable with his attentiveness.

For two days they rode over grassland and salt flats, and saw little sign of human habitation. Sometimes they would come across a shepherd with a flock of straggly sheep or a herd of goats. Lao Zhao would hail them and there would be a protracted bargaining session, from which he would come away with a sheep or a lamb for supper. Manners and Tom, riding ahead, would keep an eye open for game. Manners shot a bustard from his saddle, pulling the rifle from its holster, aiming and firing at the speck in the sky in one fluid movement. On another occasion, he spotted the spoor of wild deer. He and Tom, with one of the porters, galloped out of view, returning three hours later with a small ibex hung over Manners's saddle.

Tom and Manners were becoming firm friends. They would ride side by side, Tom listening in rapt attention as Manners described his hunting expeditions in the Deccan and the Himalayan foothills. Sometimes they would race each other, and Helen Frances would see the eager delight on Tom's face as he tried to outpace his companion. She herself was quite content to ride slowly with the baggage train, feeling the wind on her face, gazing dreamily around her at the endless expanse of grass under a cloudless sky or listening to the wild songs of the porters.

In the evenings, as they sat round the campfire, Henry Manners was surprisingly good company. Tom had been right: he had wonderful stories to tell, about the Hindu temples overrun by monkeys and creepers that he had discovered in the Indian jungles, the rock carvings of terrifying gods and the Thuggee cult, which he insisted could still be found in the more remote mountains and forests. He described the magnificent palaces in Delhi and Agra;

expeditions against the wild tribes of the North-west Frontier; the ludicrous social whirl at Simla, the modest hill station that was transformed when the Viceroy and his court ascended to escape the summer heat. He talked of his years in Japan. He would not be drawn on the details of his military advisership to the Meiji army, but he spoke of the gardens and temples, the Buddha at Kamakura, the deer park at Nara, the beauty of the coast road on the Inland Sea, Mount Fuji, and the strange rituals of the Japanese Court. He spoke with an enthusiasm and a tolerance of strange places that seemed quite at odds with the cynical, worldly manner he had displayed in Peking. Yet interspersed with his reminiscences were casual references to acquaintances whose names Helen Frances had only seen in newspapers – politicians like George Curzon and Arthur Balfour, writers like Bernard Shaw and Max Beerbohm, theatrical lights like Sarah Bernhardt, Ellen Terry and Beerbohm Tree – all of which indicated that Manners was used to moving in a racy social milieu well above her own. She even understood that he had attended levees with the Prince of Wales – Bertie, as he called him – before his mysterious transfer from the Guards to the Royal Engineers and a posting to India in the early nineties. To Helen Frances this English aristocratic world was as exotic as the bright starlight of the Asian night, and far more intimidating. Yet never once did Manners boast or show any sign of superiority. In fact, she was beginning to wonder if she had imagined the predatory flirtatiousness that had coloured her impression of him since she first met him in Peking. He was as charming and solicitous to her, and certainly as gentlemanly, as Tom. But Tom, who in age, she guessed, was only a few years younger than Manners, seemed as gauche as a schoolboy in comparison, as with eager, almost fawning, curiosity he begged more stories about Manners's colourful past, hanging on his every word.

On the afternoon of the third day the country changed from flat plain to gentle hills, and they found themselves riding through orchards of apple trees and cultivated farms. Familiar oaks and elm trees grew in clumps on the hillsides. Blue-coated peasants scythed in the millet fields, or drove donkey carts down the rutted tracks. Villages were more common, and on that night and the next, the porters elected to stay in caravanserais specially built for mule trains and travellers. The three Europeans, unwilling to sleep in the smoky rooms with the muleteers stretched together on filthy *kangs*, had their tents put up in the courtyard outside but, ever wary of stories of bandits and robbers, they were glad of the thick mud walls that gave them an illusory protection from any supposed menace in the village outside. Helen Frances found it thrilling to be sitting among the wagons under the stars, with the giant shadows of the muleteers moving across the bright oil-paper windows and the strains of a whining stringed instrument inside. It reminded her of the inn scene in *Don Quixote* or one of the medieval romances she had read as a girl.

She found herself fascinated by every detail of the ancient peasant life going on around her, and it was with some excitement that she greeted the news from Manners on the fifth day that they would soon be approaching the first walled city on their route, Fuxin. He told her that this was where the founder of the Manchu nation, Nurhachi, had set up a western outpost, and it was where one of his nephews, a grand duke, was buried. He told her that the city would not be dissimilar in appearance to their eventual destination, Shishan.

The towers on the walls loomed from some distance away. It was a small city perched on a hill. The walls were like the great edifices in Peking but on a smaller scale. On a lower outcrop to the west stood an ancient pagoda. Tom and Helen Frances talked excitedly about what they would buy in the marketplace. The road was thickening with people as they approached the great gateway, which they could see in front of them about five hundred yards away. Manners had ridden ahead that morning with Lao Zhao so that he could negotiate supplies and accommodation before the arrival of the main caravan. They were startled to see him now galloping back out of the gate, scattering people as he rode. Their attention was diverted suddenly by the loud cry of many voices to their left. There, on a smooth parade-ground, which lay between them and the approaching figure of Manners, was gathered a large crowd of people ringing an open space. From the height of their horses they could look over the heads of the throng to see the activity in the middle. Helen Frances was puzzled for a moment, could not understand what was happening. Ten or eleven men were kneeling on the ground, their arms pulled behind them by burly men stripped to the waist. Other men were standing in front of the kneeling figures pulling their pigtails forward so the bare necks were exposed. A grey-haired man in blue robes was standing prominently among a knot of robed officials reading from a scroll in a high-pitched quavering voice. Then he signalled and a group of giant men, also stripped to the waist but holding long, curved swords, stepped forward, each one taking a position by the side of one of the kneeling men.

'Oh, my God, HF, look away,' cried Tom.

But Helen Frances could not turn her eyes from the scene. The grey-haired man raised his hand and the blades wielded by the giant men rose in the air. '*Chie-e!*' screeched the man in the blue robe, and the blades came down in smooth arcs. Eleven heads seemed to bounce from the bodies, which collapsed, then rolled to a stop in the sand. There was a shout of satisfaction from the crowd. Blood was spurting in jets from the decapitated bodies. Helen Frances, stunned by what she had seen, tears of shock forming in her eyes, swung her head away from the spectacle. She saw their own porters craning in their saddles, laughing and grinning among themselves. In a panic – anything to get away – she pulled on the reins of her pony, and drove it into a wild canter down the road, ignoring the shouts of Tom behind her.

At that moment Manners reached them. He was in the act of reining in when he saw Helen Frances break away. Instead he kicked his horse on after her, reaching for her dangling reins. For a while the two horses cantered crazily together, then slowly, Manners managed to pull them both to a stop. Keeping hold of both reins he swung himself off his own horse, then with his other arm reached up and pulled Helen Frances down off hers. She was gasping with hysteria. Manners steadied her, and pulled her to his chest, stroking her hair and murmuring, 'All right. All right. You're all right. All right.'

Tom, his eyes wide in an agonised face, ran up to them, then hovered, not knowing what to do.

'Come on, man, take her,' said Manners. 'Hold her tight for a while. She's in shock.'

Gently, he passed Helen Frances to Tom. She felt herself gathered into his strong arms. Her body was shaking uncontrollably. She tried to break away. Her nails scratched Tom's back, then she slumped and her breathing gradually slowed.

'I tried to get to you to warn you. We'd better not stay here, Cabot. Press on. Foreigners aren't exactly in good odour in Fuxin at the moment.'

'Who were they, Manners? What's happening?'

'I'll tell you later. Better get going now. Can you lift her on to your own horse? Ride behind her for a while? Good. There's Lao Zhao with the provisions. We'd better head off straight away.'

The porters had turned the caravan, and steadied the horses. Manners and Lao Zhao lifted Helen Frances tenderly into Tom's saddle where he put a protective arm around her waist. The road on either side was lined with a silent crowd. The mob who had witnessed the execution had seen the foreigners and were now gathering ominously.

'All right,' said Manners. 'Quietly now. Lao Zhao, *zoule*!'

Lao Zhao jerked his reins, at the same time clouting the leading pack mule with his stick. The caravan clattered off in the direction from which it had come, leaving the silent, hostile populace of Fuxin behind them.

After a mile they turned off the road to make a detour through the millet fields in a large circle round the city. Helen Frances had calmed down enough for Manners to suggest that it would be safe for her to ride her own horse. They rode on well into dusk and that night they camped by the side of the road. Helen Frances went to her tent early, leaving Tom and Manners to smoke cigars by the fire.

'She's a plucky girl, Cabot,' said Manners. 'As I've told you before, you're a lucky man.'

'What happened back there? I've seen executions before. They're nasty affairs, but I've never known such an atmosphere.'

'There was a riot a while back. Merchant was murdered. A Christian, it seems. Authorities came down heavily. Some of the people executed were popular figures in the town. Maybe they blamed the foreigners in some way. Fault of the Christians or something.'

'My God, Manners. It wasn't Boxers, was it?'

'Boxers? Who knows? What's a Boxer? People in this country have enough to be miserable about anyway and are quite capable of rising up on their own account. Apparently this merchant who died was cheating the townsfolk by mixing his grains with animal feed. All part of the general corruption of China. Sometimes they don't get away with it.'

'My God, what are we going to tell HF?'

'Don't tell her anything. If she lives in China long enough she'll have her fill of executions. The first time is rather shocking. She'll get over it. Tell her it's a matter of law and order, as my friend, Sir Claude, so preciously likes to put it.'

'Are we safe?'

'Yes, we're safe. We have these, don't we?' Manners patted his rifle, which was leaning against his saddle by his side. 'You're always safe with Mr Remington.'

Next day it rained. The road became muddy and they made slower pace. Helen Frances was still pale from her experience but had recovered enough to put on a brave front and apologise to the two men for what she called her pathetic behaviour the previous afternoon. By the afternoon she seemed restored to her usual good humour, but the rain and the heavy clouds oppressed their spirits, and they were glad to make camp. The ground was rising. They had reached the lower slopes of the Black Hills. 'Tomorrow we should be in the forest,' said Manners, 'then it's one day's more riding and we'll arrive in Shishan.'

She had a restless night, and light rain pattered on the canvas. She had overcome the first horror of what she had seen the day before and now was trying to persuade herself that it was merely one of the adventures she had looked forward to when she left Sussex. 'What did you expect, old girl?' she said to herself in her father's voice, which she always found reassuring. She only had a dim memory of what had happened after the swords had fallen. She remembered riding away, and she also remembered a feeling of respite when Manners had held her and tried to calm her. She remembered him stroking her hair. He had been so gentle. Had he briefly kissed her forehead? She could not recall. How strange that she had panicked when he had passed her over to Tom. 'Sleep, girl, sleep,' she imagined her father saying to her. 'Get some sleep.' And eventually, fitfully, she did.

She woke early. She could hear birds singing and she saw the early-morning sun reflected on the roof of her tent. She wanted to relieve herself before the others were up so, pulling a shawl around her shoulders, she untied the flap and crawled out on to the wet grass. She looked up and screamed.

Not ten paces away from her a man was standing by the bushes. He was dressed like a priest, with a bald head and the white gaiters, staff and begging bowl she had come to recognise was the usual habit of mendicant holy men. He was not wearing the usual brown or saffron robes, however. Instead his robe was multicoloured, with stars and suns and blood-red characters woven round a general pattern of pomegranates. What shocked her, however, was his face, which was pale, fleshy, ageless, unlined. He seemed to be staring intently at her, but when she looked into his eyes, she saw that they were pupil-less, white cavities. His lips were curled in a malevolent, toothless, tongueless grin. There seemed to be nothing inside his skull. Noiselessly, he stepped behind the bushes and was gone.

Manners was out of his tent first, a revolver in his hand, followed shortly by Tom and the muleteers. They searched extensively in the bushes and in the woods behind, but could find no sign of the priest.

'I did see him, Tom. I did, you know,' she told him.

'Of course you did, old girl,' said Tom. 'Of course you did.'

'Let's get away from here,' said Manners. 'We'll have breakfast further on.'

Quickly they broke camp and headed up the dark path into the forest of the Black Hills.

Chapter Three

*Lao Tian says the firecarts have eaten up the business of
the canals and there is no haulage work left to do.*

The Tian Le Yuan, the Palace of Heavenly Pleasure, was not the
only brothel in Shishan, but it was the best one. The girls were
beautiful and cultivated in all the arts, not only the amatory ones:
they could sing, dance, recite poetry, and play the *pi'pa*, zither and
flute. The cooks were ingenious, the food was renowned; there were
baths and steam rooms and miniature gardens, even a small library;
the divan served best-quality opium; and, most important of all,
customers knew that they could count on Mother Liu's discretion.
For the merchants of Shishan it was the only place to entertain.

From the market square there was little to distinguish the establishment from any of the other houses lining the street on the
opposite side of the temple. There was a sign, three gold characters
painted on a blue plaque, but this could just as easily have referred
to the restaurant, which occupied the ground floor. Mother Liu's
son, Ren Ren, ran this as a sideline to the main family business.
It was a bustling, steaming teahouse, open to the public, serving
dumplings, pasties and other typical northern food. It was profitable
as far as it went and, more conveniently for Ren Ren, it served as
a safehouse for his streetpads to gather unobserved. It was widely
rumoured among those in the know in Shishan that Ren Ren, for all
his youth and unprepossessing manner, was in charge of collecting
street dues for the Black Stick Society. The patrons of his mother's
house were inclined therefore to treat him with respect, and a certain
amount of circumspection. A smaller circle knew of his reputation
for deviancy and sadism, and tended to avoid him altogether. That
was not a luxury afforded to the girls and boys working in the Palace
of Heavenly Pleasure.

The restaurant was sealed off from the main activity of the house.
Mother Liu's establishment, in which Ren Ren was a junior partner,
was located on the upper floors, and in the maze of buildings and

75

courtyards behind. To get there one had to go to the much more discreet entrance a block away, which was located in a dark, narrow alley between a high stone wall and shadowy artisans' shacks. A candle box gleamed faintly above a peeled red doorway and two worn lion statues. On knocking, a hatch would open to allow the doorman to scrutinise the visitor; only if he were recognised or if he gave an approved password would he be allowed in, through the small porter's lodge where two thick-set guards would invariably be hunched over a game of chess, into the courtyard beyond. There, the lucky initiate would be dazzled by a fairyland of red lanterns hanging over an ornamental bridge. A smiling servant girl would lead him along a pathway of willow trees to the paradise within.

On this occasion Mother Liu herself was waiting at the end of the bridge. She was a tall woman in her late forties, who had obviously been good-looking in her youth. She took pains to preserve her appearance now. Her hair, tied into a neat bun, was blacked to disguise any white strands, and her long, scornful face was layered with powder and makeup. She was dressed modestly in a gown of brown silk, but as she shifted on her tiny bound feet, the lantern light picked out expensive gold embroidery and glinted on her string of pearls. Shivering in the slight chill, though it was only early autumn, she pulled her black woollen shawl closer round her narrow shoulders.

She examined the garden with a critical eye, noticing the leaves that had not been swept away from the path. She had always insisted on the highest standards and punished any shortcomings severely. To run a house like hers demanded order and discipline. Only in this way could one maintain the highest reputation. It had taken her fifteen long years to build up the Palace of Heavenly Pleasure to its present prestige. It had been hard. She had been involved in the business all her life, sold at the age of thirteen to a bawdy-house in Shenyang when her father, a merchant, had been ruined. She had been raped, beaten, chained naked in a freezing loft until her spirit was tamed. She had suffered much, but she had the advantage of good looks, a strong character and the determination to survive.

At the age of twenty she had been bought out of the brothel by a moderately wealthy merchant to be his third concubine. In his household she had suffered worse than she had in the brothel. To this day she preserved her hatred for his two other wives and her mother-in-law. It was like a coal that she fanned in her heart; never would she allow herself to be humiliated again. When she had borne the merchant a son the women's jealousy and her torments had only increased, but she had had her revenge in the cholera epidemic that hit their town. They had all died, the merchant, his mother, his two wives. It had seemed strange at the time that only she, her son and two of her husband's daughters had survived, but although there had been an investigation, nothing could be proved against her. The cholera had been decimating the town and other households had suffered equal mortality. She and her son had inherited the merchant's money. She had the pleasure of selling his two daughters to the same brothel in which he had found her, then she had moved with her son to Shishan, and with her husband's money bought the house that became the Palace of Heavenly Pleasure.

At first she had tried to run a textile business, but it had failed. She found more profit in returning to the old ways, initially on her own – she had discreetly hung her portrait outside the door – and later as the madam of her own establishment. The Black Stick Society had charged her dearly for her independence but she was also grateful for the clientele they had brought her. Now she had a profitable business, a talented stable and regular clients. Her son, Ren Ren, although his own tastes did not lie in that direction, had an extraordinary ability to break in new girls. The back passage was the same for boy or girl, and the advantage was it preserved the girl's virginity, which could be sold for a premium. Nor was there any danger of Ren Ren showing leniency to any new chicken, however comely or winsome. He despised all of them. She smiled. Actually, there was no danger of Ren Ren showing leniency to anyone. She had brought him up well. Life was good, she thought. The three keystones, a prudently run business, firm discipline and modest dues to the powers that be for protection and insurance, had served her well. She determined to light an incense stick tonight in thanks to Providence. Meanwhile, her feet were aching. She wondered whether her visitor was delayed.

She had not long to wait. She heard the sound of a sedan chair being deposited outside the gate, a curt knock and a short exchange with the porter. Then a stooped, heavily cloaked figure stepped quickly out of the lodge.

'Your Excellency,' she inclined her head in a bow of formal greeting, 'we are, as ever, honoured to receive such an eminent personage into our unworthy home.'

'The pleasure is mine, Liu Mama,' the cloaked figure murmured. 'I am glad to see you in good health. But you should not be outside on a cold night. It would perhaps be better to talk inside.'

'We'll go in immediately,' said Mother Liu. 'I have prepared some refreshments.'

'You are, as always, solicitous to an old man.'

Despite her bound feet Mother Liu hobbled quickly over the bridge, the cloaked man following. She led him through another courtyard. Lights shone in a pavilion on one side and the two could hear the clear notes of a Chinese zither, a *chin*, slithering through the melody of an ancient folk tune from within.

'We are honoured to have Major Lin as a guest tonight,' said Mother Liu, looking archly at her companion.

'Ah, then, no doubt the music is being provided by the beautiful Miss Fan. She plays expertly. You are to be congratulated on her talent.'

'I fear she is only a clumsy beginner. But you are kind to say so. By the way, I have something to ask you about Major Lin and this girl.'

'Later,' said the cloaked man. 'Inside.'

They passed through another garden, then entered the larger building and climbed two flights of rickety wooden stairs. Mother Liu negotiated them with difficulty, and the cloaked man supported her arm from behind. From below they could hear laughter and male voices, one booming louder than the rest.

'Those are the merchants, Lu Jincai and Jin Shangui,' said Mother Liu, disapprovingly. 'They are banqueting the fat barbarian, De Falang.' She used Frank Delamere's Chinese name. 'They are all drunk as usual.'

'You keep a very open house,' murmured the cloaked man.

'I provide services to those who pay. Is that not the way you would want it?'

'Assuredly,' said the man.

A corridor led past a line of closed doors. From behind some they could hear sounds – a flute being played, conversation, male and female voices; from others creaks and sighs, sometimes of pleasure, sometimes of pain.

Mother Liu stopped by one of the doors, moved aside a scroll on the wall, flipped a panel, and indicated a cleverly disguised peephole. 'Would you enjoy . . .'

'Later,' said the man. 'Let us talk first.'

'Then we will go to my sitting room.'

'As you please.'

He followed her to the end of the corridor and down another, which seemed to lead to a blank wall, partially covered by a large scroll painting depicting an emperor's palace with many courtyards; in the rooms off the terraces, if one looked carefully at the detail, concubines and eunuchs could be perceived entertaining each other in a variety of ingenious ways. Mother Liu lifted the scroll, pressed a panel on the wall and a small door swung open. A short flight of steps led up to another long corridor, this time undecorated, uncarpeted, with bare wooden walls. Taking a bunch of keys from her pocket, she unlocked one of the doors, and stood aside to allow the man to enter.

It was a small room, sumptuously furnished with carpets and hangings. It was dominated by a large, curtained bed, on which a Pekinese was curled asleep. In one corner was a shrine with statues of Guan Gong and other household gods. Two candles were burning and there was a smell of incense. Laid out on a low table between two wooden chairs was a bowl of fruit, a tea basket and some wickerwork food warmers.

'I welcome you to my humble home,' she said, opening the food warmers and laying on the table saucers of sweetmeats and pickled vegetables. 'Will you drink some wine?'

'Tea will do,' said Jin Lao, the Mandarin's chamberlain, as he took off his cloak, folding it on a stool. 'You are extremely kind to offer such hospitality, which is quite unnecessary.'

'As the poet says, "A thousand cups would be too few, to drink with an intimate friend."'

'We are certainly old friends. We are also business partners of long standing,' said Jin Lao 'I believe that we have a little business to discuss tonight.'

'And some pleasure to look forward to as well. I told you that

I've prepared something for you of more than usual interest and excitement . . .'

'But business first, Liu Mama. That's the correct way, I think. I have my duty to my master.'

'The Mandarin is in good health?'

'Perfect health, Liu Mama. Perfect health, I thank you. His prosperity "like a lucky star in the ascendant rides the high tide of fortune". It is matters pertaining to his prosperity, in fact, that I would like to discuss with you. There is the small due outstanding of . . . Was it as much as four hundred *taels*? More, perhaps, this month? Your house seems very busy.'

'Certainly not more. Business has been very bad,' said Mother Liu, shaking her head.

'Business is never as good as one would wish it to be. "Boundless is the sea of troubles. Man is adrift in this world as if it were a dream."' Jin Lao smiled as he quoted the proverb. 'It is something to be thankful for that no misfortune has ever befallen this establishment. Through your own good management, of course, but also in part due to the solicitude and continued protection of your friends.'

'I am always grateful for the fatherly protection of the Mandarin,' said Mother Liu, 'who is a constant support to me in my tribulations.'

'Tribulations? Oh, surely you have no tribulations?'

'Jin Lao, you do not know. Our customers are so discerning nowadays, and always looking for something new, or different. And the only girls we can find today are swarthy, dwarfish, lumpen, devoid of any talent. A singer from Yangzhou. Or a dancer from Suzhou. Let alone a virgin! Do you know the cost to bring one here? Or to train a young one in all the arts? They are like children to me, my girls, and I lavish every attention on them. It is for the reputation of the house, Jin Lao, for our reputation. But the costs are so high.'

'I am certain that you invest wisely and well, and prudently, dear Mama. And your investment is matched by the returns. I see no shortage of customers tonight.'

'And then there are the other costs. Do you know how rapacious the Black Stick Society is becoming these days? The favours we are obliged to bestow on their thugs. I do not grudge anything to the Mandarin, who has been a father to me, but the tongs . . .'

'Isn't your son a prominent member of the Black Sticks? Not that

I really wish to know too much about what in other circumstances I might have to condemn as a criminal organisation. I am sure that you have made the necessary accommodations.'

'But there is a cost, Jin Lao. I am a poor widow and I certainly need protection – but I cannot be expected to pay equal protection to everybody.'

'Liu Da Ren is as you know, a man of infinite generosity. I am sure that he would not begrudge the matter of one or two taels in the case of an old partner in difficulties.'

'Three hundred taels,' said Mother Liu.

'Three hundred and ninety,' said Jin Lao.

'If only all our customers were good payers, then it would be easier,' said Mother Liu, 'but you cannot realise how many people – respectable people – come to my house, and wine and dine, and take their pleasure afterwards and leave without settling their bills. My debtors are too many, Jin Lao.'

'Isn't that why you pay for protection in the first place? I'd have thought that there's a matter in which the Black Sticks could easily help you out.'

'But not in every case, Jin Lao. There are some bad debtors . . . Well, there is one in particular, who seems to have his own protection.'

'Who exactly are you referring to?'

'Why, Major Lin. I told you there was something I wanted to speak to you about. I'm not saying he's not welcome. He brings honour to our house. An upstanding man. Dashing and handsome. A hero. He's very popular with all of us – but he hasn't paid me for months.'

'Have you asked him to?'

'I've hinted at it. But I'm under instructions.'

'What instructions?'

'Your instructions, Jin Lao. You told me to give him everything he wanted.'

'Major Lin's contentment is a matter of special interest to the Mandarin. Major Lin is extremely important to us. He is training our troops.'

'But free licence, Jin Lao?'

'If I were to say three hundred and eighty taels, would that be easier for you?'

'Three hundred and twenty. Let me give you three hundred and twenty. That's reasonable.'

'Three hundred and eighty is more than reasonable.'

'But then there's the problem of Fan Yimei, Major Lin's particular friend.'

'What about her? I thought he was very happy with her.'

'He is. He's almost in love with her. That's the problem. He insists on keeping her all to himself. Won't let her go with anyone else, or even play the *chin* to them at dinner. But I spent years, and a lot of money, training her. She's the phoenix in our little nest. All the clients want her and I have to make excuses every time. I can't tell them she belongs to Major Lin.'

'Why not?'

'Well, does she belong to him? I would have to charge a fortune if I were to release her from service.'

'How much?'

'Three thousand taels. At least.' She paused, looking carefully at Jin Lao for a reaction. There was none. 'Of course I'm not asking that,' she continued. 'I'm happy to do any favour for the Mandarin. But I'm losing money on her. That's all right, except there's everything else as well. Major Lin insists I reserve a whole pavilion for the two of them. Their own exclusive love nest. Think how arrogant that's made her, and how jealous the other girls are. She's getting uncontrollable. And he likes beating her. That's fine if it's his pleasure, but it marks her body and reduces her value. And Major Lin himself is sometimes unpredictable. He caused a scene the other day when he saw De Falang the barbarian here. Objects to foreigners sleeping with Chinese women. It's difficult, Jin Lao. Difficult indeed.'

'Three hundred and seventy taels,' said Jin Lao.

'At least say three hundred and fifty. It's most of my profits for the last month.'

They bargained a while longer, and eventually settled on three hundred and sixty. Mother Liu knelt by her bed and reaching underneath, pulled out a padlocked chest. It was heavy so Jin Lao helped her. Breathing heavily from her exertion she unlocked the box and raised the lid. Carefully she counted out seven silver 'shoes', which she laid on a cloth for Jin Lao to count in turn, adding to the pile ten taels in silver cash, which she took from an embroidered silk purse. Mother Liu closed the box and readjusted the padlock. While her back was turned Jin Lao quietly removed one of the shoes and slipped it through the slit in his gown into a pocket on the inside, then he quickly folded the cloth over the remaining pile and tied a knot. He had already informed the Mandarin that the taking for this month would be three hundred taels, so he had no compunction in liberating the extra fifty as his personal cumshaw. He helped Mother Liu push the heavy box back under the bed.

'The money's safe in this room until you leave,' said Mother Liu, when she had recovered her breath. 'You have the usual amount of guards for the journey back? I wouldn't like you, too, to be robbed.'

'They always called you Sharp-tongued Liu.' Jin Lao gave his wheezy laugh. 'I do so enjoy doing business with you. Tell me, before we get on to more entertaining matters, is Major Lin really a problem for you?'

'As I told you, doing a favour for the Mandarin is a pleasure for its own sake, and is its own reward.'

'Let me know if there truly is a problem. Major Lin is useful to the Mandarin, a favourite – but he has his enemies, and nobody is indispensable. I am sure that you understand me.'

Mother Liu nodded slowly.

'I would have enjoyed the scene with the foreigner,' continued Jin Lao. 'Did they come to blows?'

'Oh, no, nothing like that, but De Falang is such a roaring, drunken fool. He pays double for his pleasures and never realises we are overcharging him, and Shen Ping is the most unskilful and plainest of our girls, but he thinks she is a goddess. She's the only one who will go with him. Hairy animal.'

They both smiled. Mother Liu had once taken Jin Lao to a peephole and shown him Delamere making love. Jin Lao grimaced as he recalled the picture of the man lying on his back with the slight girl squatting between his legs and he bellowing with pleasure as she moved her mouth skilfully up and down his gigantic organ. He was like a hairy ape with a red face, all matted black coils on his arms and legs and chest and shoulders. He involuntarily shuddered at the memory. How hideous to have to rasp against such a body. He could not imagine what it would smell of. It had not been an arousing sight.

'Can you imagine?' asked Mother Liu. 'He really is in love with her. He wants to see me later in the evening to negotiate a release for Shen Ping.'

'How touching. Are you going to sell her?'

'Of course not. How can I do business if my clients start falling in love with all my girls? Tell me, Jin Lao, now we are talking of barbarians. Would you be attracted to the idea of making love with one?'

For a moment even Jin Lao's controlled features showed confusion. 'I hope very much that you are joking,' he said. 'You cannot mean De Falang?'

'Not De Falang,' said Mother Liu, sipping her tea, smiling at Jin Lao over the cup in her hand. 'Oh, no, somebody much more interesting, and attractive.'

'An attractive barbarian? That is an interesting concept. Do we have any in Shishan?'

'Come with me and I'll show you,' she said.

She locked her room as she went out, even though they were only going a few steps down the corridor. They stopped at one of the doors, and she lifted up the latch on the side to reveal the peephole. 'Have a look.' She laughed. 'I think you'll like what you see inside.'

Eagerly Jin Lao knelt down. Mother Liu smiled when she saw his eyes widen and the tip of his tongue come out slowly to lick his ascetic lips. 'Oh, yes,' he breathed. 'Oh, yes.'

It was one of the steam rooms. A charcoal fire burned in a corner, with a bucket of water and a ladle beside it. The air in the room was dense but Jin Lao could see quite clearly the two figures in the large wooden tub in the centre of the room. One was Mother Liu's son, Ren Ren. The other was a young boy in his teens. It was clearly a foreign child, although his blond hair was tied in the Chinese way. The two were apparently asleep, eyes closed, in the hot tub, the boy's head resting on Ren Ren's chest. Ren Ren's arm was draped casually round the boy's bony shoulder. His flesh was white compared to Ren Ren's. Jin Lao could see the ribs showing faintly on his thin chest.

'Can you get him to stand up?' Jin Lao whispered.

Mother Liu tapped lightly on the door. The boy did not notice the sound, but Ren Ren's eyes flashed open. He nodded in the direction of the peephole, and slowly removed his arm from the boy's shoulder. Gently he shook him awake. Jin Lao noted the startled green eyes in the thin, slightly panicked face. Ren Ren smiled and pinched the boy's cheek. The boy smiled back. Ren Ren stood up in the bath and pulled him to his feet. They were both naked.

'Your son is also an attractive man,' murmured Jin Lao, his eyes fastened to the peephole.

'I am sure that if I were to ask him he would be honoured . . .'

'No, Liu Mama, the foreign boy. The foreign boy is . . . interesting enough, as you said.'

Jin Lao saw that the boy was shivering after his immersion in the tub. Ren Ren reached into the water and produced a cake of soap. With the ladle he poured water over the boy's head then proceeded to slide the soap over the boy's chest and down his thin belly, grinning towards the peephole as he did so. The boy smiled uncertainly as the older man soaped his body, obediently opening his legs to allow Ren Ren to rub the lather around his loins and behind. Gently Ren Ren turned him so Jin Lao could have a view of his back, his narrow buttocks and haunches, then turned him round again. Ren Ren continued to rub the boy down below and Jin Lao was excited to notice the beginnings of a small erection. Mother Liu snapped the peephole shut. Jin Lao sighed.

'You must conserve your energies,' she said. 'But I hope you are satisfied.'

'I am not only satisfied, I am intrigued, Liu Mama. Only you know how to please an old man.'

'I have a room prepared for you, and Ren Ren will bring the boy to you after a short while. You may go there now to relax, or otherwise you will be welcome to drink tea with me until they are ready. Or perhaps you would like me to prepare a pipe of opium?'

'Tea would be refreshing in the circumstances. And I am burning with curiosity. Where did you find him?'

Mother Liu led him back to her room and poured him some tea. 'I really shouldn't be telling you,' she said, 'but I know I can count on your discretion. He is the son of the mad missionary.'

'I should have guessed,' sighed Jin Lao. 'Of course, of course, the boy who disappeared several weeks ago. The one the old rat-eating doctor was looking for. So it was you who had him all along. I hope you didn't kidnap him. I would have difficulty countenancing that.'

'As if I would do such a thing. It was Ren Ren who found him after he ran away. He was with one of his street gangs who brought him here for protection. As you know, Ren Ren is rather good at protection. The boy became very grateful indeed, as you saw.'

'Indeed. But weren't you worried about the consequences? The son of a foreigner. You know the old doctor went to the Mandarin about him? With a story that he had been seen going towards the Black Hills.'

'Wasn't it clever of Ren Ren to make up that story? The doctor's man, Zhang Erhao, is a Black Stick, so it was quite easy to convince him. Only the doctor was interested anyway. The boy's own family seems glad to be rid of him. I would hate for the boy really to have to disappear after all this effort, but isn't it convenient to have Iron Man Wang to blame should that unfortunate necessity arise?'

'You and your son are so very practical.' Jin Lao sipped his tea. 'I'm sure you're right. And after a while nobody will care. Especially if he is happy to work here. I assume that he is willing to become one of your catamites? It's not just a love affair with your son?'

'We'll know after tonight. You're the first paying customer, Jin Lao, and I'm sure that you will be very persuasive.'

'Paying customer?'

'A slip of the tongue. But wouldn't you agree that the experience would be worth at least ten tael?'

'It certainly would if I had ten tael to pay you. But, as you know, the *yamen*'s salaries . . .'

'I was only teasing you, Jin Lao. You are family, and there's no question of you paying me. Don't worry about the boy. I'm sure that Ren Ren has prepared him properly. He always does. And if there should be a problem? Well, there's always Iron Man Wang, isn't there?'

'That would distress me,' said Jin Lao. 'The boy is so very beautiful. A rare find. Hardly like a barbarian at all. Ah,

'Slave girls of Yueh, sleek of buttery flesh
House-boys of Hsi, bright of brow and eye . . .'

or do you remember the lines of Li He?

'The western boy with curly hair and green-irised eyes
In the high tower, when the night is quiet, quietly blows the
transverse bamboo . . .'

How generous you are to a poor old man, Liu Mama.'

'I'll always do my best to please you. If one day I could only do the same for the Mandarin himself. That would be an honour for our whole house.'

'The Mandarin has many beautiful concubines already. And as far as I am aware he is not interested in boys, even foreign boys.'

'Foreign girls?'

'Now, where would you find a foreign girl, Liu Mama?'

'I found a foreign boy.'

'Find a foreign girl first. Then we can talk.'

'He would be interested?'

'I am sure he might be. But you will not find one. Not in Shishan.'

'I might in Shanghai.'

'Find her first, then we will see.'

Ren Ren slouched into the room and sat down on the bed. 'He's ready,' he said, biting into an apple that he had picked up from the table.

Mother and son escorted the old man to the sleeping chamber that had been prepared next to the steam room. Mother Liu waited by the peephole. Ren Ren had told her that the boy would not give Jin Lao any trouble, but she wanted to make sure. Ren Ren was impatient. 'He's ready, Mama,' he told her. 'He's a natural. Didn't even have to beat him. He's doing it for me. He loves me. Anyway, I filled him with opium. He'll be fine.'

'Just wait,' she said. 'Jin Lao's important to us.'

'Jin Lao's a disgusting old cock-sucker,' said Ren Ren. 'Why do we need the Mandarin anyway? We have the Society.'

'Who do you think runs the Society?' she snapped. 'You're too low down in the order to know.'

'I don't believe you,' he said. '*Ta made*,' but he did not leave. He squatted bad-temperedly on his heels beside his mother, as she lifted the latch and frowned with her eye to the peephole.

Hiram was hunched solitarily on the end of the bed. Jin Lao had taken off his gown and was sitting in his white underclothes contemplating the boy. As Mother Liu watched, Jin Lao got off his chair and settled himself on the bed next to Hiram. His long hands stretched round the boy's shoulders and entered the folds of his green silk pyjamas, caressing his skin. Hiram gave a ghastly smile. Jin Lao, his eyes closed, moved his hands over the boy's body down to his crotch. Hiram began to shake from side to side, whimpering in his own language, 'No. No. I don't want to.' Feebly he tried to push Jin Lao away. Then, shoving harder, he rocked the old man off-balance. Jin Lao slapped his face, twice. The boy moaned, then his shoulders slumped. He recovered the ghastly smile, and Jin Lao continued the exploration of his body.

Mother Liu grunted in satisfaction. 'It'll be all right,' she said, snapping the peephole shut.

'I told you it'd be all right. When isn't it all right?' said Ren Ren sulkily. 'What else do you want me for this evening?'

'We have to see the barbarian, De Falang, about Shen Ping. He wants to buy her.'

'Tell him to fuck himself,' said Ren Ren. His eyes narrowed angrily. 'I'll beat the shit out of that slut, for one thing.'

'You'll do nothing of the kind,' said Mother Liu. 'She's the only one of the girls who'll sleep with him, and it makes us a lot of money.'

'Any of those bitches will fuck a donkey if I tell them to. Bugger the money.'

'Calm down, calm down. There's no problem. I want you there on your best behaviour, and only in case he gets troublesome. But I'm sure he'll be reasonable. We don't want to lose him as a client.'

'Wouldn't worry me. A lot of us don't like having these ocean barbarians in the house anyway. Haven't you heard? Things are happening in this country. You know what the Harmonious Fists did in Fuxin? One day we'll get rid of all these barbarians for good.'

'Well, if that happens, it happens,' said Mother Liu. 'For now De Falang's a client and I don't want you scaring him off.'

Frank Delamere was waiting patiently in the banqueting room with Shen Ping. The merchants with whom he had been dining had already left. The two were sitting decorously together on a couch, as formally as if they had met in a station waiting room. He rose as Mother Liu and her son entered, his long arms swinging nervously and his big head shaking from side to side as he tried to look ingratiating. He had been dreading this interview. 'My dear Madam Liu,' he cried. 'What a pleasure. What a pleasure.'

Mother Liu perched herself elegantly on one of the banquetting chairs. 'De Falang Xiansheng,' She smiled sweetly. 'We are always honoured when you choose to visit us. And how can I help you today? I trust that the service has not been unsatisfactory. Or that my girls have not been tiring you with their frivolous chatter.' She nodded kindly at Shen Ping, a short, round-faced girl, who gazed ahead of her in terror.

'Oh, no, Madam Liu. Certainly not. Service couldn't have been more excellent, really.'

'Then how can I assist you? Do please sit down.'

'Well. It's about Shen Ping, you see.' He put one of his heavy hands on hers. Shen Ping stiffened.

'Shen Ping has displeased you in some way? You would like another girl?'

'Oh, no. The opposite. She's a peach. In every way. I like her very much.'

'That is very good to hear.'

'Well, I think she likes me too.'

'We all of us like you, De Falang Xiansheng.'

Frank shuffled on his seat.

'Would you be more comfortable, De Falang Xiansheng, if we were to ask Xiao Shen to leave us for a while? Since it's about her that you wish to speak.'

'You know, that may not be a bad idea. Shen Ping, would you mind?'

Ren Ren, who was leaning by the door, signalled Shen Ping with a jerk of his chin, and she scurried out, her eyes avoiding him as she brushed past. Frank clasped his hands together, took a deep breath, and then, as if he had made a decision, looked Mother Liu in the eye. 'I'd like to buy her out, you see. Have her live with me.'

'I don't think I understand you. Shen Ping is employed here.'

'I know. But I did hear, if the right price can be reached – a high price, obviously – that flower girls can be bought out, released as it were. I'm happy to pay.'

'I see,' said Mother Liu. 'This is clearly very flattering for Shen Ping. She must have pleased you extremely.'

'She's a lovely girl. I know I'm not much to look at, an old man now, getting on. A bloody ocean devil, eh? Ha! But I am fond of her, and I think I can look after her, see she's all right . . .'

'This is most unfortunate.'

'Unfortunate? I don't understand you.'

'You see, Shen Ping has many other obligations. Many other clients, De Falang Xiansheng, who would be very disappointed if she were to leave us.'

'Many clients, did you say?' Frank's red face had gone a shade of purple.

'Oh, yes, she is one of our most talented girls. Much, much sought-after. I think you know how skilful she is, particularly in bed. It would be indelicate of me to remind you of all the techniques she has been able to master. She is an expert in the art of love, and is therefore very popular. She has many appointments every day.'

'Every day?'

'Oh, yes, mornings, afternoons, sometimes yourself in the evenings, sometimes others. She's always in demand. We're extremely proud of her. And often worried that she'll tire herself out. Isn't that right, Ren Ren?'

Ren Ren grunted.

'So you see, De Falang Xiansheng, my difficulty. It's not a question of money. I must think of my other clients. If she were to go away to live with you, well, she would have to return, morning and afternoon, to fulfil her obligations here. And I don't think that would be very convenient for you.'

Frank cleared his throat. 'That's not exactly what I envisaged. I had hoped for some exclusivity. I thought I had it, an under-standing.'

'Oh, no, De Falang Xiansheng. There's no exclusivity. This is a working house. Our girls serve all our customers.'

'Dammit, I've always paid you over the odds. I thought Shen Ping was—'

'Exclusively yours? Oh, no. But she is very happy to look after you when you're here. None of our girls provide exclusive services.'

'But what about Major Lin and Fan Yimei? She seems exclusively hitched to Lin.'

'Fan Yimei? Are you interested in Fan Yimei, De Falang Xiansheng? Well, I can certainly see what I can do.'

'I'm not interested in Fan Yimei. I . . . All I wanted was to take Shen Ping away from here, because I thought she . . . She told me she didn't have other lovers. Or very few. I – I know what sort of place this is. I wasn't born yesterday. But she – she said that I was . . .

special. She said I was kind to her.' Frank's voice had lowered to an embarrassed croak.

'Oh, a girl will say anything to make a man happy.' Mother Liu gave a shrill laugh. 'That's part of her job, and her skill. There's always dissimulation in the art of love. Shen Ping has many lovers. She's extremely experienced, a credit to our house. Of course, she's also a very conscientious girl. She has often told me what particularly pleases you – Flute-playing While Drinking at the Jade Fountain, the Frog Dipping Between the Pools, the Wild Ducks Flying Backwards, the Phoenix Sporting in the Cinnabar Grotto, Cicadas Cleaving, Dragons Twisting, Silkworms Entangling – need I go on on, De Falang Xiansheng? You're such a demanding, energetic man, aren't you? Naturally I urged her to practise all these things with her other clients so her technique would be even better for you . . .'

'She told you that?' Frank muttered, almost inaudibly.

'Of course. We spend a lot of time discussing how best to please you, De Falang Xiansheng. You're a most valued customer. And we discussed this lovely idea of you taking her away. I encouraged her to humour you. Don't be angry, I assure you whatever she said to you it was with the best of intentions. To increase your pleasure, and happiness.'

'I believed her. God, what a fool.'

Mother Liu knew when to keep silent. Ren Ren yawned, and spat on the floor. Frank sat miserably in his chair. He coughed, then attempted a wry smile.

'Well, I seem to have made an ass of myself, Madam Liu. I think I'd better go.'

'Would you like Shen Ping to wait in the chamber for you?'

'No, I'm a little tired tonight. Thank you all the same. I – I think I'll make my way home now, if that's all right with you. I've settled for the dinner. Good night.'

Mother Liu rose to her feet. 'It is always a pleasure, De Falang Xiansheng. I hope we will see you again soon. A servant will escort you.'

Mother Liu watched him pick up his hat from the hook and, with bowed shoulders, make his way out of the door. Ren Ren slouched to a chair. 'Well, that was brilliant, Mother,' he sneered. 'I think you've driven him away for good.'

'He'll come back,' she said. 'They always do.' She put a hand to her forehead. 'I have a headache. It's been a long day. He may not want Shen Ping again. Just in case, you'd better prepare another girl for the hairy ape.'

'Fan Yimei?'

'Fan Yimei belongs to Major Lin. You know that. Try Chen Meina, she's no good for anything.' She yawned. 'Ren Ren?' she said.

'Yes, Mother.'

'I've changed my mind. You had better give Shen Ping a good hiding, after all. And this time I don't care if you do mark her. Make her suffer, the little bitch.'

'With pleasure, Mama,' said Ren Ren. He yawned, stretched and, singing a snatch from the Peking Opera, sauntered out of the door. The raucous voice faded down the corridor. Mother Liu, left alone in the room, selected a toothpick off the table, and abstractedly began to clean her teeth.

Major Lin was sprawled on his side on the rumpled bedcovers. Fan Yimei, unable to sleep, lay on her back listening to the soft rumble of his snores. A cool breeze fluttered the silk curtains and rustled the willows outside. Fan Yimei gazed upwards at their reflections in the mirror set in the roof of the four-poster bed. Major Lin was in shadow but she was exposed to the moonlight, which drifted in through the open window illuminating the furniture and tinting her naked body an eerie ivory. The white image of herself, which appeared in the mirror, seemed strangely unreal, like a ghost hanging above her, or a corpse. The face was a shining white oval in a black pool of hair, which seeped over the pillow, lapped over the shoulders and eddied over the arms. Idly she examined the contours of this detached body floating above her, objectively noting the features most admired by her clients: the shadowy curves of the breasts and belly, the dark well of the loins between the white flesh of the thighs, the thin tapering legs ending in the silk stumps and bandages of bound feet – but the skin of this wraithly image was pallid and lifeless. She wondered if this was what she would look like if she were to die and be laid out in the House of the Dead. A hunk of inanimate flesh. A pork slab in the market. As the thought crossed her mind she saw the image of the corpse above her smile. She knew that she was also smiling. Here was a bitter joke. Perhaps the figure in the mirror was the real Fan Yimei, while whatever was lying on the bed below was only a beautiful simulacrum, trained mechanically to go through the art of making love. After all, if the heart and soul were already dead, would not the body be dead too? She had always thought that her life had really ended on the day when her father was buried and she had been brought here. Was this dead creature on the ceiling therefore conjured to remind her of the reality? Li Po's poem about Chuang Tse came into her head: 'Did Chuang Chou dream he was the butterfly, or the butterfly that it was Chuang Chou?' Was reality a long-dead Fan Yimei, now a corpse in the mirror, dreaming about a prostitute who continued to go through the motions of living in the Palace of Heavenly Pleasure? A cloud moved over the face of the moon and the image in the mirror faded. The simulacrum on the bed sighed. She also shivered. The cold was real.

She wrapped herself in a silk dressing-gown. For a moment she stood by the bed looking down on the recumbent Major Lin. He had a handsome face, she thought, but even at rest his eyebrows were fixed at a haughty angle and his mouth curved in an arrogant sneer. It made him look cruel. No doubt that expression helped him in his career as a soldier, but it was not reflective of the real man, or boy, as she sometimes thought of him. She felt sorry for him. He was so proud. Perhaps only she recognised the weakness and uncertainty within. Gently, so as not to wake him, she spread a sheet over his limbs. He stirred and muttered in his sleep. After a few moments he began to snore again. These days, he was drinking heavily. She did not mind. When he was drunk he was often violent, but his lovemaking would then be short and perfunctory, and he would fall asleep quickly afterwards. She preferred that to the nights when he insisted on showing off his manly vigour and it would be long hours before he finally achieved the clouds and rain. Sometimes the clouds and rain would not come, and then she would have to beat him with a willow rod until he was ready to try again. She wondered why Mother Liu was spreading the story that he whipped her. The other girls would laugh about this behind her back, knowing that she would hear. In fact, it was always she who wielded the rod. She wondered if the pain he wanted her to inflict on him compensated for some shame inside him. She was indifferent. She had had to do much worse with other clients, and with the unspeakable Ren Ren. Major Lin, for all his temperamental moods, was easy to handle.

She supposed that she was fortunate to have Major Lin as her protector. It was a respite from the miseries of the stable, but she had no illusions. For all his possessiveness and the affection he bestowed on her, she believed that one day he would tire of her. And then she would be defenceless against the resentments of Mother Liu and the other girls. Inevitably Ren Ren would exact his vengeance. She had heard the screams that came from the hut at the end of the furthest courtyard where he would lock the girls he had selected for particular punishment. She dreaded the torments she knew she would have to face, and when she thought about it her body would freeze with horror, but she was resigned to ill fortune, and deep inside herself she did not care. She had learned not to expect anything of life.

There were times when she was weak. Sometimes, like tonight, when she looked at the corpse in the mirror above her with envy, she longed for the oblivion of the dead. Once, after an unpleasant, drunken scene with Major Lin, when he had wept self-pitying tears, slapping her and accusing her of being unfaithful (she could not imagine why Mother Liu invented these malicious stories), she had waited until he was asleep. Then, certain that he would leave her next day and unable to face the prospect of Ren Ren's tortures, she had climbed on to a stool, flung her sash over the beam with the intention of hanging herself. Her small bound feet had slipped from the stool before she could make a noose, and she had sprawled, a tangle of naked limbs, on the floor. Major Lin had woken and sleepily called her to the bed. He had made gentle love to her, whispering endearments in her ear, and she had lain below his body, shaking with silent sobs, the little girl she had once been calling to her from the emptiness inside her soul.

She found that nowadays she would often think of her father, especially when she was alone in the pavilion. For years she had tried to bury any memory of a previous life. Mother Liu, prevented by her agreement with Major Lin from making her serve other clients, was still ingenious in finding Fan Yimei humiliating tasks to do in the daytime when Lin was away – much of the day was spent carrying the honey buckets from the latrines to bury in the pit, or sweeping the leaves, or cleaning in the kitchens – but this could not occupy all of her time, and the hours by herself in the shady pavilion, playing the *chin* and looking out of the window on to the willow garden, had become stolen moments of nostalgia. She vividly recalled the sunny afternoons when her father had patiently taught her the same musical instrument, laughing kindly when she made a mistake or proudly accompanying her on a flute when she had mastered a tune. When she was older she had played for him in his study as he stood by his table, brush in hand, painting exquisite pictures of little birds or flowers. He had always treated her like the son he did not have. She hardly remembered her mother but he had never married or taken a concubine after she died. He had taught her to read when she was six, and loved quoting the classics aloud to her, or guiding her hand through the first uneasy strokes of calligraphy. She knew that they were poor and lived off begrudging allowances from her wealthy uncles, but she had not realised how much the latter despised the gentle scholar who had failed the imperial examinations, and had never shown any aptitude for the family business. Childhood was a happy time for her in his company. He was always singing. Most mornings when she was little he would take her to the temple garden to fly kites. She remembered how he used to run down the flowered paths, the big dragonfly kite bouncing on the ground behind him. She remembered him sitting by her bed reading her stories. She remembered the humour in his eyes.

When the plague came to Shishan, they had been oblivious in their own little world. He had made light of the fever and the lump under his arm, but it had grown and one day he was delirious in his bed and did not recognise her. She had heard of the foreign doctor who had come to the town and had a reputation for miracle cures. She had been told the strange story that he received payment only in rats, so she spent a desperate morning hunting for rodents in the wainscots and under the floors. Eventually she had thought of going to the rubbish tip and there she found the corpse of a big black rat, covered in fleas. She had overcome her fear and wrapped it in a handkerchief, then run through the town looking for the doctor. It was evening by the time she found him. It was the first time she had ever seen an ocean devil. With his short stature and funny whiskers he reminded her of a wizened mouse, but his tired eyes were gentle and his smile was kindly. She had unwrapped her gift, and he had laughed. He had allowed her to lead him by the hand to her father's house. Her father was moaning on his bed, his body running with sweat. Gently the doctor had rubbed him down with a cloth dipped in hot water. After a while a strange foreign woman had arrived. She was dressed in a black robe with a white cowl, but her face was merry with red cheeks like apples although, like the doctor, her eyes were shaded with exhaustion. The doctor had left then, but the woman sat next to her father through the night, washing his body at hourly intervals, occasionally kneeling on the ground with her hands in front of her face. Fan Yimei presumed she was calling on the foreign spirits to help her. The doctor returned with the dawn but by then her father was still. The doctor had examined him briefly then turned to her sadly and embraced her in his arms. She had sobbed on his shoulder. 'But I brought you the rat,' she had cried. 'I brought you the rat.' He had stroked her hair. 'I know you did. I know. I know,' he had repeated, rhythmically stroking her hair. She had looked into his eyes and seen an infinite sadness.

The doctor asked a neighbour to fetch her uncle. He explained patiently that he had to leave her. There were many sick in the town, but the woman, Caterina, would stay with her until her uncle came for her. She hardly remembered the details of the next two days. She remembered the white robes that she and all of her uncles had worn as they followed the municipal death cart to the outside of the city gates. There were no private funerals in those terrible times. She remembered the wailing, the smoke and the stink of the lime. She had been taken straight from the burial pit to the Palace of Heavenly Pleasure. Mother Liu had been kind to her, giving her sweets as her uncle negotiated her price. That night Ren Ren had come to her room. She was four days off her sixteenth birthday.

Fan Yimei sighed and leaned on the windowsill, looking out at the willows. Lin's heavy breathing rose and fell behind her. The garden was white in the moonlight. She wished she could play the *chin*, but she dared not wake him. So instead she hummed the tunes silently in her head. She had learned popular airs for her clients, and Major Lin liked the stirring songs connected with war and conquest. When she was by herself, however, she preferred to play the haunting, melancholy poems of the Lady Li Ching'chao, the Song dynasty poetess whose life had been as lonely as her own.

> I let the incense grow cold
> In the burner. My brocade
> Bed covers are tumbled as
> The waves of the sea. Idle
> Since I got up, I neglect
> My hair. My toilet table
> Is unopened. I leave the
> Curtains down until the sun shines
> Over the curtain rings.
> This separation prostrates me.
> The distance terrifies me.
> I long to talk to him once more.
> Down the years there will be only
> Silence between us for ever now.
> I am emaciated, but
> Not with sickness, not with wine,
> Not with autumn.
> It is all over now for ever,
> I sing over and over
> The song, 'Goodbye For Ever.'
> I keep forgetting the words.
> My mind is far off in Wu Ling.
> My body is a prisoner
> In this room above the misty
> River, the jade green river,
> That is the only companion
> Of my endless days. I stare
> Down the river, far off, into
> The distance. I stare far away.
> My eyes find only my own sorrow.

She saw two figures move slowly through the garden. Mother Liu hobbling in front followed by a tall man, his features hidden by a black cloak. Some important customer satiated in the misery of one of her colleagues. She knew that she was disliked by the other girls. Most of them were jealous of her. All except Shen Ping. Plain, talkative Shen Ping who loved and was loved by a barbarian, a barbarian who was kind to her. She knew that tonight the lover would be asking for her release. She hoped passionately that Mother Liu would accept the price. There had been precedents. Shen Ping had come to her in the afternoon, her eyes gleaming with excitement. Fan Yimei had congratulated her, her heart heavy that she would lose her friend, but glad at the same time for Shen Ping's good fortune. They had wept briefly on each other's shoulders, Shen Ping tears of happiness, Fan Yimei happiness tinged with the regret of parting. Then Shen Ping had run off, fearing that she might be seen.

A cloud briefly obscured the moon. Fan Yimei yawned. She was tired. Tired.

She heard a whimpering sound and then she saw the figure of Ren Ren stride into the courtyard, pulling something behind him. It was Shen Ping. He dragged her by the hair, and she stumbled after him, sobbing with pain and fear. Fan Yimei froze. There was only one place he could be taking her at this time of night. Soon there would be the screams, but too far away for the guests to hear.

Fan Yimei stood silently by the window, a white figure in the moonlight. Her mind was numb again, her feelings buried. After an hour she turned slowly back to the bed, and laid herself softly down beside Major Lin. The moon came out of the clouds and she looked up blankly at the corpse hanging over her head.

Frank Delamere spent most of the night with a bottle of whisky, and woke in his armchair as sunlight was pouring through the windows and Ma Ayi, his maid, was dusting his rooms. Not surprisingly he had a hangover. His tongue was furry, his mouth and throat were dry and he had a stabbing pain in his temples. It took him a moment to adjust even to half consciousness. Then he focused on the clock on the windowsill and groaned. He was late for his appointment with Mr Ding, the textile dyer from Tsitsihar. He could not imagine anyone whom he wished to see less, not this morning, and he certainly did not feel up to giving a lecture on the manufacturing processes of soap crystals, but Frank had never failed yet in his duty to his company. His friend and partner Lu Jincai was convinced that Mr Ding was going to be the key to a big new expansion of his own alkali and Frank's washing-soda-crystals business into north-west Manchuria, as far up as Hailar, he promised, so there was no way out of it. For the honour of Babbit and Brenner, Frank left his vague awareness of a broken heart among the dirty ashtrays and empty bottles surrounding his chair and, like a rumpled, sleep-walking walrus, stumbled to the door, somehow managing to mutter a few polite words to a censorious Ma Ayi on the way out.

Frank had rented one courtyard of a small guesthouse, which had its own restaurant and laundry, and most of the facilities a bachelor needed. The staff had become accustomed to his habits so a mug of scalding coffee was waiting for him and a groom had been sent to get his horse from the stables. As the hot, sweet liquid suffused his body (it had taken Frank months of patient teaching to get them to make his coffee just right) his mind adjusted itself back to a semblance of normality. And as his thoughts cleared, the memory of his humiliating interview with Mother Liu came vividly back to him; he was overwhelmed by a sense of sadness and regret. The feeling stayed with him as he mounted his horse wearily and made his way through the side-streets to the main avenue and out through the city gate. The appointment had been fixed at Babbit and Brenner's godown near the proposed railhead so Mr Ding would have an opportunity to see the crystal-making processes in operation. It was a longish ride through farmland, but Frank was oblivious of the beauties of the rural scene around him, the threshing of the millet and the reddening leaves of the maple trees lining the road. He was locked in gloomy self-recriminations.

He really had convinced himself that she loved him. That was the tragedy. What a fool. What a crazed, blind fool. He knew that what he had been proposing was undignified. There was always something seedy about a middle-aged man setting up house with a young girl, a reformed prostitute at that. Well, obviously not so reformed, he thought bitterly. Of course, the whole thing would have been extremely difficult to finesse anyway, with his daughter arriving in the next month. He had identified a suitable house he could buy for Shen Ping, and his intention had been to live apart from her until he could get Helen Frances used to the idea. Exactly how he was going to achieve that he hadn't even thought. And now he wouldn't have to. Perhaps it was for the best. What a dreamer he had been. He had fantasised that Helen Frances and Shen Ping, who were nearly the same age, would become the best of friends. He had imagined them all going out on picnics together. Picnics, for Heaven's sake!

How had she managed to pull the wool so skilfully over his eyes?

Of course he should have known. What had he told Mother Liu? That he wasn't born yesterday? That was a joke. He was a babe in arms. Lu Jincai and the others must despise him as a blithering idiot. Maybe not Lu Jincai. He had been sympathetic all along. A real friend. But how humiliating! How pathetic and humiliating! What had Mother Liu said? 'There's always dissimulation in the art of love.' He had lapped up dissimulation in buckets. But he should have known. He should have known. Jin Shangui had as good as spelled it out to him before he first went to the Palace of Heavenly Pleasure. He remembered the conversation vividly to this very day.

They had been sitting in Jin's counting-house drinking tea. Jin had leaned forward, his eyes twinkling behind his spectacles, a big smile on his chubby face. 'This is a very high class establishment,' he had told him. 'It's not just a common whorehouse, you know, not like one of those places I'm told you have in Europe. You have to woo the girls. They won't sleep with you the first time, nor the second, nor even the third or fourth. It's a game, you see. They flatter you. You flatter them. You take them gifts. You have to court them.'

'But what's the point of that?' Frank had asked. 'It's a brothel, isn't it?'

'Of course it's a brothel. But where's the pleasure in just buying a piece of meat? These are flower girls. They're talented performers. Fairy spirits. They can sing, dance, play music, recite poetry.'

'A load of Chinese poetry. That really does sound thrilling.'

'You can listen to the music, then. Think about it, De Falang. If all you want to do is dip your jade stalk in the orchid boat I can take you to one of the places at the back of the temple any time. But what the flower girls give you is the illusion of love. And, like the best of love, it's hard won. So after your wooing has been successful, and the girl finally agrees to submit to you and allows you to taste the flower, imagine the height of the pleasure, the ecstasy. It's the long wait and the expectation that makes the final outcome like paradise. After that you're a couple, and she is reserved for you every time you come. Like man and wife.'

'I don't want to go there and get married,' said Frank.

'I told you, it's a game. When you tire of the girl you can talk to the Mama, and she will introduce another girl to you, and the delicious wooing process can start all over again.'

'Sounds laborious to me,' Frank had chuckled, 'but when in Rome do as the Romans. I'm game for a try.'

And, of course, he had fallen for it. Hook, line and bloody sinker. He had met Shen Ping that first night. She was shorter and plainer than the others, but she had a funny, laughing face and a river of nonsensical chatter. She and Frank had played drinking games into the evening. She had pretended to be terrified of his enormous moustache and joked about his big red nose, asking whether he was so big in all the other parts of his body. Then she had giggled behind her hands at her own temerity. Frank had been enchanted, and walked home, tipsy as a lord, chortling with pleasure at the very thought of her.

It had taken ten visits over a month. Jin Shangui had been absolutely right. The wooing game itself not only seemed natural, it had also been enjoyable. Frank felt as if the years had fallen away and he was a young, bashful-suitor again. Strangely, the expectation of bedding at the end of the wooing period had become less and less important to him. Frank found that he simply enjoyed Shen Ping's company, the sound of her husky voice as she joked with him, the way she playfully pulled his moustache or giggled as she ruffled the hairs on the back of his hand. He enjoyed trying to teach her English folk tunes on her flute, with chaotic results that caused them both to collapse in fits of laughter. He found that he could talk to her about his life, his daughter in England, even his business, easily and quite unselfconsciously, and she would listen attentively. More often he was content to smile avuncularly as she chattered away, gossiping about the other girls, or greedily describing to him her favourite dishes, or telling him about the animals on the farm where she had grown up. How skilful she had been, he thought bitterly. How she had led him along.

One night she had not been waiting in the drinking room where they normally met. Mother Liu was there instead, smiling archly and calling him a lucky devil, a powerful, attractive, irresistible man, and she had made other cruder innuendoes. With growing anticipation he had followed her up the stairs to the third floor, a part of the establishment to which he had never been before, and there she opened one of several doors in a long, gaudily decorated corridor. Shen Ping was already in bed. Her little head emerged from the sheets, her hair loose on the pillow. He had guessed that she was wearing nothing underneath. He was disturbed to see that one of her eyes was bruised as if she had been hit by a fist, but she explained that it was nothing. She had slipped on the stairs. She attempted to laugh but it sounded unusually forced. She appeared to be as nervous as he was. He worried then whether, despite their many hours together, there was a reluctance or repugnance to be in this final intimate position with a foreigner – he became suddenly aware of his own bulk and ugliness – but then she had reached out a hand and in a small voice called him to the bed. He sat on the side and entwined his fingers in hers. Her moist brown eyes, one of them stained and bruised, looked seriously up into his. There was a sad, almost questioning expression on her face. He remembered his own marriage night, so many years ago. He recalled the same nervous expression on the face of his young wife, a mixture of eagerness and trepidation. He could not believe that Shen Ping was a virgin. Not if she worked here. Yet suddenly the atmosphere really was that of the bridal chamber. That night he really did think of himself as the young husband and Shen Ping the virgin bride. Of course she was no virgin, but there had been the same sense of discovery, the magical intimacy of two lovers exploring new feelings and sensations for the first time. Now, of course, he knew better. After last night's conversation with Mother Liu he could only congratulate Shen Ping on the artful way she had managed to create this impression. On that evening he had felt only tenderness and affection, and he believed that it had been reciprocated. She had allowed him to lead her through the lovemaking, sighing quietly at the climax, then held him tightly, almost desperately until they both slept. He supposed now that that was as much of a dissimulation as all the rest.

Mother Liu had humiliated him last night, probably deliberately – he was grateful: he had needed the rude awakening – when she had listed the various lovemaking positions which, over the last year, he and Shen Ping had indeed explored together. He had believed it was mutual discovery and mutually shared delight. Their own secret world of passion. Again, he now knew better. He realised that Shen Ping had only been following the manual, in consultation with the management. That had been embarrassing to accept, but it had not been the most hurtful of the blows he had received in short succession last night. It was not the lovemaking that was important to him. It wasn't the sex that attracted him to Shen Ping. It was her friendship. And since it was clear that the dissimulation stretched even to this, he felt utterly betrayed.

What a fool. What a fool. He could not blame her. He still felt fond of her. By her lights she had treated him very well. Conscientiously, as Mother Liu had said. By God, she had been conscientious. What a professional.

They had rarely even made love on his last few visits. They had sat together holding hands and talking about the life they would lead together when Shen Ping had her release. He had talked about taking her to London, and she had asked him a hundred questions about where they would live and what they would do. They had kissed and cuddled. He had stroked her funny bound feet. He had found them strange and almost repulsive at first but he now saw them as much a part of her as the laughter lines round her eyes, which he loved. She had been so convincing. She had seemed eager and curious and excited about the world she would discover outside. Obviously this had all been as much a part of her well-learned technique as the sucking on the jade stalk and all her other tricks.

There's no fool like an old fool, he thought. Well, he would be wiser in future. Yet even now there was a part of him that only wanted to rush over there and be with her. It would take time for him to get over this, he realised. Maybe he never would.

Ahead of him he saw the sheds of Babbit and Brenner's godown. Lu Jincai and Mr Ding were standing by the gate. They were both wearing the blue gowns, black caps and black silk waistcoats of the merchant class. Mr Ding was also sporting round tinted spectacles. The two black circles made his face more skull-like than usual. Lu Jincai, a smooth, boyish-looking man in his late thirties, hailed his friend. 'De Falang Xiansheng, you're late today. I think you must have had a very enjoyable night at the Palace of Heavenly Pleasure.'

Lu Jincai and Mr Ding both laughed. They were in depressingly cheerful spirits. Frank climbed heavily off his horse. Lu patted him affectionately on the back. 'Both Mr Ding and I are very eager to hear how your interview with the Dragon Lady went. Is the beautiful Miss Shen released? Mr Ding, I told you what an irresistible lover our De Falang Xiansheng is. Now we must congratulate him on winning the most beautiful girl in Shishan!'

'I changed my mind,' said Frank, shortly. 'Thought better of it.' He was trying to think of a way to make light of it. This was the last thing he wanted to talk about, but he had to maintain face with his friends. Lu Jincai's face was already showing concern. Frank laughed as heartily as he could. 'I'm too young to get permanently hitched again. Aren't you always advising me to play the field? Well, old friend, I was on the brink. Then I decided to take your advice before it was too late. Who wants to be tied down? Ha-ha. No, it's pastures new from now on.'

Mr Ding grinned happily and Lu laughed politely. 'Miss Shen must be very disappointed,' he said, observing Frank closely.

'Well, win some, lose some,' said Frank. He felt that his heart was breaking. 'All's fair in the scales of love and war. Who wants to be tied down to a hairy old barbarian anyway? Plenty of other fish in the sea.'

'Yes,' said Mr Ding, who was enjoying this roguish conversation. He had a slight stutter. 'And wh-when you come to Tsitsihar, you must c-come fishing with me. Y-you have not b-been fishing till you've caught one of our n-nice M-Mongolian beauties.'

'Ah, that's what I want to hear!' Somehow he managed a hearty voice. 'Always knew you were a deep one, Mr Ding. Now, I'm sure our venture's going to be a success.'

'Not only a success. It will make our fortunes,' said Lu, who had the tact to change the subject. 'Mr Ding is eager to see you demonstrate your crystal-making process, De Falang Xiansheng.'

'Nothing I'd like better,' said Frank. He put his arm round the beaming Mr Ding and steered him in the direction of the godown. For the next two hours he absorbed himself in the intricacies of washing-soda manufacture, explaining the consistencies of alkali to water in the boiling pot, one picul of water to half a picul of soda ash, how to fire it, when to stir it, when to pour the dissolved mixture into the iron cooling pans full of liquor to help the crystal-forming process, how to separate the crystals from the liquid. Mr Ding followed behind him, peering into the pans laid out in the courtyard, taking copious notes. Frank then gave a cleaning demonstration, using his washing-powder crystals against ordinary untreated alkali to show the effectiveness of the new formula. Finally, over a cup of tea, they discussed the applications as they might affect Mr Ding's dyeing processes. Mr Ding seemed satisfied and in principle they discussed the prospects of shipments starting in the late autumn. Frank told him that by then he would have a young assistant who would probably be able to accompany the first mule train.

'But will you not be coming yourself, D-De Falang X-Xiansheng? R-Remember the M-Mongolian girls!'

Frank, who had managed to numb his mind over the last two hours, felt his depression return with a vengeance, but Lu Jincai, solicitous of Frank's position, already suspected that something had gone seriously wrong and managed to change the subject back to soda ash. Shortly afterwards he and Mr Ding left, to get back to town in time for lunch. Frank was left to his gloomy thoughts.

He sat in his office and tried to do some paperwork but he found that he could not concentrate. All he could see in the piles of correspondence and reports was Shen Ping's laughing face. He paced the room disconsolately, his head splitting with the pain of his hangover. He knew he had to get away, do something, or he would go mad. He made a sudden decision, strode out of his office and called for his horse. He would ride a mile down to the railway camp to check with Fischer whether he had had any word on the arrival of the party from Peking.

Of course it would never really have worked out. He must have been mad to think that Helen Frances would ever accept it. She would probably have gone right back again on the next boat and never talked to her father again. Nellie Airton certainly wouldn't have approved. He suspected that she disapproved enough of him as it was. He couldn't imagine Nellie having Shen Ping round to tea with the nuns. It would all have been very uncomfortable. He was better out of it. It had worked out for the best.

Obviously he could not see Shen Ping again. He could not bear it – not now that he knew what he did about her. It was not her fault. It was entirely his own foolishness. He hoped she would not mind losing a client, that it wouldn't be a loss of face or anything for her. He would do the right thing. Send her round some expensive gift or some extra cash. Maybe a letter. He would have to ask Lu Jincai what was best in these circumstances. From what Mother Liu had told him she was obviously not short of other customers. Mother Liu had told him she was popular. He, of all people, knew why. He doubted that her other clients were naïve idiots like him.

Or maybe she specialised in hopeless romantics. Had she despised him? Gossiped about him with the other flower girls? Laughed at him behind his back? Well, he deserved it.

He supposed that he would go back to the Palace of Heavenly Pleasure. There was no way, really, to avoid it. Every week Lu or Tang or one of the others would throw a banquet there. It was part of doing business in Shishan. There was no obligation to taste the flowers. Dr Airton was always telling him that he had to mend his behaviour. Perhaps the time had finally come for playboy Frank to tread the straight and narrow? The prospect of another liaison was not very attractive at the moment, but then again he knew his own weaknesses. Maybe there would come a day, if he ever got over Shen Ping, when he would wish to try it out with another girl. This time there would be no illusions. He would play the game as cynically as all the rest of them. At one point Mother Liu had seemed to be offering him Fan Yimei. She certainly was a beauty. Out of his league, he thought. But maybe not? Mother Liu had more or less said that all the girls were up for grabs. He didn't fancy the prospect of tangling with Major Lin, but perhaps if that arrangement were ever to break up . . .

What was he thinking of? The image of Shen Ping's face asleep on the pillow came vividly to his mind. Her little flat nose, the lips smiling even in sleep. A loose hair on her forehead. As he rode through the millet fields, Frank realised the extent of his loss. His chest heaved with despairing sobs, and hot tears funnelled down his cheeks. He had to halt his horse a short way before the railway camp to give himself time to bring his features back to some sort of order before he met Herr Fischer.

As he rode through the encampment, Frank could not fail to notice that the railway had come on a long way since he was last here. Six weeks ago only the first piles had been laid in the riverbed, but now the superstructure of the bridge was well developed, and he could observe a swarm of coolies clambering over the top works, or heaving on the pulleys to bring up the big beams and planks from the barges below. The bed of the railway line had been dug and narrowed off towards the Black Hills in the distance. He knew that another gang was tunnelling and dynamiting in the hills. Once the tunnel was through, this section would join the line that led to Tientsin on the other side of the mountain. Then it would only be a matter of laying the sleepers and tracks, and the first locomotives would come steaming into Shishan. Frank had been absorbed in all stages of the project. A railway link to Tientsin and the Taku port would considerably cut his costs and reduce his delivery schedules. Today he registered the details of the progress but he could not summon up his usual enthusiasm.

Herr Fischer's office was located in a small tent in the centre of the camp. When Frank arrived he and his young assistant, Charlie Zhang, were busy revising the plans of the tunnel in the light of new geological information from a recent survey. Hermann Fischer was a short, grizzled engineer from Berlin, a devout Lutheran, a simple man who spent most of his leisure hours reading the Bible. Frank liked him, because he was always cheerful, for all that he had a rather ponderous sense of humour. Zhang Dongren, or Charlie as he liked to be called, had studied the rudiments of engineering in Shanghai and was an appointment of the Board of Commissioners in Peking. He reported directly to the director, Mr Li Tsoi Chee, and was said to have had the patronage of Minister Li Hung-chang himself; indeed that statesman had always taken a personal interest in this project and was still honorary chairman of the board. Frank found young Zhang to be a modest, light-hearted fellow, with a cheeky manner he found appealing. He knew he was competent at his job and could win the trust of the workforce in often trying circumstances. Frank had got to know him well and agreed with Herr Fischer, who relied on him, that this was just the kind of man who would lead China into modernisation and the twentieth century. He wished he had people of the same calibre working for him at Babbit and Brenner. Charlie's hair was tied in a queue and he wore Chinese dress, but Frank often thought of him as having the mind of a European. Both Zhang and Fischer gave him a warm smile of welcome.

'My dear Mr Delamere. My dear Mr Delamere,' said Herr Fischer, leaving his charts. 'It is a happy surprise to see you. You have been forgetting us, I fear.'

'Not at all,' said Frank. 'It's you fellows who've been busy. My goodness, your bridge has come on a long way. Well done.'

'You must come one day to see the tunnel,' smiled Zhang, also speaking fluent English, with a remarkably plummy accent. 'We'll be doing the first blasting any time. Perhaps we can all celebrate with a picnic? I like your picnics, Mr Delamere. Good French wines and cheese.'

'Mr Zhang, Charlie, where are your manners?' bustled Herr Fischer. 'We must prepare for Mr Delamere some of that American coffee he likes so much. We know your fussinesses, Mr Delamere. Ah, what a pleasure to see old friends! Now sit down here and tell me what is all the news. I never go to the town now. I am too busy here.'

'Nothing much has been happening that I'm aware of,' said Frank, blocking the sad response that was uppermost in his mind. 'I might have a new business venture in north-west Manchuria. That's quite exciting.'

'Very, very exciting,' said Fischer. 'I congratulate you. See, Charlie, how these rich merchants make more and more money, while we engineers just live in our tents, working and working for nothing.'

Zhang laughed happily while he laid the coffee cups on the table. 'Mr Delamere is the king of all the merchants!' He grinned.

'Hardly that,' said Frank. 'Old dogsbody, that's me.' His spirits were beginning to lift a little in the warmth of his welcome and the banter of his friends. 'Actually, I've come here to get some news from you. Wondered if you'd heard any more about Mr Manners and his party. Jolly glad your chap is helping bring my lot up here, by the way.'

'*Ja, ja*, of course,' said Fischer. 'The China railway is naturally at the disposal of our friend Mr Delamere, especially his beautiful daughter. Charlie, what is the latest news?'

'Not much since the first letter I sent to you, Mr Delamere.' Zhang carefully poured the coffee. 'I got the message that they would all be travelling together, as I told you. They should have left Tientsin some ten days ago now. I would think they might arrive any day.'

'Any day? Well, that's something. For some reason I'd thought it would take much longer.'

'No,' said Fischer. 'Our mule trains travel very quickly. We have a picked team of good drivers. It's exciting, no? Your daughter coming? Some big changes in Shishan, *ja*? Society at last. The doctor Airton is telling me that I must practise my violin. And, Charlie, you must learn the western dances too, *ja*? The waltzes. The polkas.'

'I'm quite pleased an assistant is coming,' said Frank. 'Won't have to travel so much to the sticks as I used to.'

'We too are getting an assistant. The Honourable Henry Manners. Some sort of *Junker*, *ja*?' Frank could not help noticing a quick, meaningful glance between Zhang and Fischer. 'No doubt his experience is just what we need. He is to help us with political relations. I am sure that there are wise heads in the board who know exactly why we should need such a man for political relations.'

'Political relations? I thought Dr Airton was your go-between with the Mandarin.'

'*Ja*? Well, now we are even more fortunate. We have two such go-betweens. Even better, no? And how is your coffee? Is it – up to scratches?'

'Charlie's a master,' said Frank, sipping the ill-tasting brew. 'Delicious.'

Zhang preened. Sensing there was some sensitivity about the subject of Manners, Frank asked after the latest progress of the railway, and soon they were all absorbed in a growing pile of maps and charts, the two enthusiasts proudly elaborating on the details of their grand design. After a while Frank noticed that one of the coolies was hovering by the flap of the tent. Zhang was reluctant to be disturbed in mid-flow, but went over to talk to him, and came back with a broad grin on his face.

'Mr Delamere, it seems your timing is one of perfection,' he said. 'That was a rider from the tunnel works at the Black Hills. Your daughter and her party have arrived and are on the way here now. They should be with us within the hour.'

Frank's first feeling was one of shock. There was really too much happening to him today. He wasn't ready for Helen Frances. He hadn't prepared anything. Christ, he hadn't even shaved. He still had to negotiate more rooms in the courtyard of his hotel. There was the whole business of Shen Ping. Then he was overwhelmed by a rush of joy. His little girl would be here within the hour. Oh, God, he realised, he was going to blub again.

Helen Frances saw her father, and galloped her horse to where he was waiting. He had been eager to be the first to greet the party but he was gazing abstractedly in the wrong direction. She flung herself off the animal and into his arms. She immediately smelt the familiar aroma of boiled beef and tobacco, and felt his hot tears on her cheeks as they ran down to his bristly moustache. 'My little girl,' he was crying, 'is it really you?'

'Yes, Papa, it is. It is. I'm back,' she said incoherently. She was weeping too, and hugged him tighter.

A stunned Frank hugged her back. He was not sure whether he was dreaming. The girl in his arms who had thrown herself off her horse and was now kissing his cheeks was the image of his long-dead wife. After what seemed a happy eternity he relaxed his embrace and looked up to see two young men sitting on horses smiling down at him. One was a lithe, dark-haired man with a moustache, the other a big, blond, oaf-like fellow with a red face.

'Papa, this is Henry Manners, who brought us here. He was very brave. There were Boxers, and beheadings.' Her words were still coming out in a rush. Boxers? Beheadings? thought Frank, bewildered. 'And in the Black Hills we thought we might have had a brush with bandits but they went away when Mr Manners fired his gun.'

'Mr Delamere, happy to meet you. Your daughter is exaggerating wildly,' smiled Manners.

'And, Papa, this is Tom,' she said, pulling him towards the other man. 'Tom brought me out from England. He's come to work for you. Papa, we're engaged,' she said.

Frank was still too overwhelmed to appreciate exactly what she meant. 'Engaged?' he said stupidly. 'Engaged in what?'

'Engaged!' She laughed. 'You silly. We're engaged to be married, of course!'

'With your permission, sir,' said Tom.

Frank could have been poleaxed. His headache seemed to reverberate with renewed vigour. His mouth opened and closed. 'But I – I – you. Who . . . ?'

Herr Fischer seemed to appear from nowhere, a wild grin on his face. 'An engagement!' he was crying manically. 'This is splendid, *ja*? You never told me, you sly one, you.' He thumped Frank on the back. 'Charlie, the schnapps, the schnapps!' And next minute an idiotically beaming Charlie Zhang was thrusting glasses into everybody's hands.

Chapter Four

We dig in the fields and find only blackened husks.

The news of the young people's engagement, and of Frank Delamere's displeasure, spread quickly through Shishan. By breakfast on the second day Nellie Airton, who was concerned for the dinner party she was supposed to be arranging for the new arrivals, had become convinced that the doctor should call on Delamere's hotel to find out what was happening.

She knew that the three of them – Delamere, his daughter and the young man, Cabot – had departed for the hotel after the hysterical scene Frank had made at the railway camp two days before. They had not been seen since. Rumours, especially among the Chinese merchants and servants, had been flitting through the town. Nellie had been receiving ever more alarming bulletins: that De Falang had locked his daughter into her room; that there had been a fight between her father and her lover, and that guests in the hotel were being terrorised by a constant scream of imprecations and abuse coming from the Delamere courtyard; De Falang was drinking whisky morning, noon and night; he had taken a razor into his bath-tub and was contemplating suicide; alternatively, he had sent a man to his godown to bring him back a gun ... The latest rumour was that De Falang's red-haired daughter had hanged herself from the curtains. Frank's clerk, Liu Haowen, claimed the credit for this final sensation. He had it from one of the servants in the hotel who had spotted a brown dress and some boots dangling in the window. Liu had told Wang Puching, the secretary of Jin Shangui the merchant, whom he came across in the dawn vegetable market buying cabbages. Wang had in turn passed on the message to his friend from the hospital, Zhang Erhao, during their morning chess game in Ren Ren's dumpling shop. Zhang brought the news back to the mission, and that was how Ah Sun heard about it when she walked down from Dr Airton's house to collect the laundry from the wards. She naturally relayed the by now much-embroidered story to her husband, Ah Lee, on her return to the kitchen. It was a triumphant Ah Lee who had finally delivered a gory account to Nellie and the children as he served them scrambled eggs and bacon over the breakfast table. Jenny and George were wonderfully impressed by the details of the swollen black tongue and the staring purple eyes (Ah Lee's narrative style was dramatic: he pirouetted on his cloth shoes, one hand clutched to his throat, as he mimed the hanging victim, while miraculously balancing the tea tray in his other hand) but for Nellie this was the last straw. As soon as her husband had come in from his early-morning surgery, before he even had a chance to drink his first cup of tea, she was insisting that he go over there straight away to sort out whatever was the matter.

'They're just resting after the journey,' Airton had grumbled. 'I'm sure they don't want to be disturbed. It's not our business anyway.'

'Oh, yes, it is, if I'm to prepare a big dinner for all of you in the next two days. Anyway, who's the busybody in our family? You know you're longing to go down there and find out what's happening.'

'I resent that, Nellie.' Airton had stood on his dignity. 'I resent that utterly.'

'Does the whole of your body go blue if you're hanged, Mummy?' asked George.

'Can I go with Daddy to see the corpse?' asked Jenny.

'The two of you can go straight off to your nursery without another word,' snapped Nellie. 'I tell you, Edward, if you don't see to this, then I will. This is turning into a circus.' She noticed Ah Lee, who was smiling with rheumy eyes by the sideboard. 'And you can stop grinning like a loon, you old mischief-maker. How dare you tell such dreadful stories to my children?' Ah Lee, pretending not to understand a word, grinned and nodded happily. 'Little more bacon, Missy? Or flied blead?'

Airton finally agreed to call on Frank Delamere at lunchtime after he had finished with his outpatients.

It was with some trepidation that he made his way through the narrow streets to the hotel. The last thing he wanted was another domestic imbroglio on his hands. He had been preoccupied enough during the last few weeks over the disappearance of Hiram Millward. His several visits to the *yamen* had come to nothing. The Mandarin had been sympathetic but would not act officially unless he had a petition from the boy's father. He had explained that the extra-territorial treaty rights that missionaries had been granted tied his hands completely. Unless he had a complaint or proof that a crime had been committed by a Chinese that required his intervention, the matter remained a foreign affair, especially in this instance where, by all accounts, the boy had left his family of his own volition and with the apparent agreement of his father. Airton had argued that the boy was a minor and needed protection from himself. The Mandarin had answered that customs were different in China. At the age of fifteen he himself had left his home and was already a soldier fighting the Taipings. Age was immaterial. In any case, the final authority rested with the parent. Let the father bring him evidence of wrongdoing and he would act with the full power of the *yamen*.

Dr Airton had been equally frustrated in his attempts to reason with Septimus. At first he had thought that his words were having some effect: the man's face had crumpled with agony and worry when the doctor expressed his concerns about his son's safety. Airton had told him that all the searches in the city had proved fruitless. He was beginning to fear that the first rumours, that Hiram had gone to seek the bandits in the Black Hills, might have been true. Septimus had listened attentively. Sometimes he bowed his head, and appeared to weep. He was much diminished from the angry man who had recited gibberish in the square. He had lost weight and his pigtail and beard hung lankly from his drawn face. As he sat there, surrounded by his silent family, the atmosphere reminded the doctor of a wake. He had been affected himself by the depression in the room. Clearly, he had been wrong in his first impressions of the Millwards. They had a deep love for their son and his continued absence was a bitter loss to every one of them. Their misery was almost palpable. Yet, try as hard as he could, he could not persuade Septimus to write the petition that would bring the Mandarin's help. '"Render therefore unto Caesar the things which are Caesar's,"' Septimus had intoned at him in a wooden voice, '"and unto God the things that are God's." It is the Devil who has taken my son, Dr Airton, and only through the grace of the Lord will he be returned to us. There is nothing you or I can do.'

'But this is a case where Caesar can help you,' Airton had argued, in the patient tone that one used when talking to the slightly insane. 'And you don't have to render anything except a letter.'

Septimus's red-rimmed eyes were distracted – but he remained immovable.

'"Put not your trust in princes," Doctor, "nor in any child of man: for there is no help in them." I know that you mean well. But who am I to gainsay the will of the Lord?'

Despite the implacability of his words, his tone was almost pleading. Airton could only imagine the contradictory emotions heaving in the man's breast. 'You can't believe it's God's will for your son to be lost and in possible danger? Anyway, what about the saying "God helps those who help themselves"? What we need is a proper, well-mounted search party to go out to the Black Hills.'

'Doctor, I would give my life to have my boy, Hiram, my beloved son, back in the bosom of his family again and walking in the way of the Lord. But He is testing His servants, Doctor. The Almighty has a purpose. It's not yet revealed, but there is a purpose. "We only see through a glass darkly," as the Apostle said. But He has called us among the heathen to be foot soldiers in His service, and however the tides of battle turn we must await and obey His commands.'

'Amen,' said Laetitia, who was echoed by her children.

Mad, the doctor had thought. Mad. They're all raving mad. He had heard of the strange cults that appeared to take root so easily in the United States: the extraordinary Mormons with their harems of wives, the faith healers, the speakers in tongues. He was more than ever convinced that the Millwards were no part of any ordinary vocational establishment. He had met several representatives of the Oberlin Foundation and other American missions operating in north China. They were mostly Congregationalists, a bit fervid and evangelical for his tastes, but respectable enough, dour sort of folk with a disciplined, rational commitment to spreading the gospel, and doing good work as far as he knew. The Millwards, on the other hand, were fanatics, and quite beyond the influence of any normal persuasion. He wondered what strange, overriding impulse had brought this eccentric family across the sea to China, and to Shishan of all places. They seemed to be living in a world of their own, populated by demons and angels. He knew what answer Septimus would give him if he asked: God had called him here. Airton doubted whether divine intervention would go very far in helping him find Hiram.

He was at his wit's end. In desperation he had given some money to the Mandarin's chamberlain, Jin Lao. If the state could not help, perhaps corruption could. Last week Major Lin had finally sent off one of his lieutenants and half of his men on the long-awaited training expedition to the Black Hills. Jin Lao had told him that he might be able to persuade the troop to hunt for the boy while they were there. The doctor was not hopeful of any result. It was already six weeks since Hiram had disappeared. He had imagined any number of dreadful fates that might have befallen the lad: starvation, exposure, wolves, bears, tigers. He could hardly bring himself to think about what Iron Man Wang might do if he found him. In his heart he was beginning to give up hope.

And now Nellie was sending him to intervene in another family's problems. Frank Delamere was a trial at the best of times. His moods were unpredictable. He drank. He had an uncertain temper. Say the wrong thing and it was quite on the cards that he would be hurled into the street. Airton bit his lip in irritation. This whole affair was so typical of the man. Only with Delamere could a joyful occasion, the reunion with his daughter, become tangled in complications and degenerate into a row. It baffled Airton why other people could not live their lives in the same order and certainty with which he conducted his own.

He did not feel proud or priggish about it. He felt that his own existence, compared to some others', was humdrum in the extreme. No Jesse James or Wyatt Earp he, he thought, casting his mind to the western shockers and tales of derring-do he liked to read in his bed each evening. Yet he valued as a gift from Heaven the contentment and predictability with which his life seemed to have been blessed. Perhaps it had all been too easy for him. He had grown up in Dumfriesshire and Edinburgh in a large, loving family. Instilled in him from an early age was a simple faith and a strong sense of what was right or wrong. Living cheek by jowl in a ménage of unruly brothers and sisters he had learned out of sheer self-preservation how to value others' feelings before his own, and to make allowances for their weaknesses as they did for his. The Ten Commandments and the Beatitudes, when he considered them objectively, seemed to be the perfect Everyman's guide to living contentedly in a large, well-run household. The greatest merit of Christianity, he thought, was its simplicity and practicality. A Christian man was an orderly man.

Not that the tenets of Confucius, which he also admired, did not display the same standards of well-regulated behaviour as the Christian canon – except that they lacked the spiritual comfort that the Gospel also promised, salvation at the end of the hard day's toil. He was grateful that at an early age he had been trained in the Chinese language and had the ability to read the Chinese classics. He believed that it was his sympathy for the Sage's wisdom that suited him temperamentally to working in China. He had no doubt that one day this intelligent race would see the spiritual advantages Christianity also offered, and graft them easily on to their own fine culture. Unlike some of his evangelical colleagues, he was content to be tolerant and wait for the labours of the missions to take effect in their own good time. Patience was another of those virtues much neglected by some of his more enthusiastic brethren. It would all take time, but God's Temple had not been built in a day and in the meanwhile he felt a certainty that what he was doing was useful and right. As a fellow human being, let alone as a missionary, he had a duty to alleviate the miseries of an ancient race reduced to unspeakable horrors of poverty and disease. His childhood, his faith, his education, the years studying medicine at Edinburgh University, and his early manhood practising his profession in the fever valleys of southern China, all combined to make his present work the natural culmination of a reasoned existence. In Nellie he had the perfect wife, and no man was more blessed in his children. Actually it had all been very easy for him, a logical progression, based on firm principles he had learned in the nursery.

But Frank Delamere baffled him. Airton could not imagine what chaotic star the man was following as he lurched through existence from one confusion to the next. He had no idea how he would even broach the subject. He had little knowledge of young love, beyond a reading of Shakespeare and a score of romances. His own marriage had been to a childhood sweetheart already loved and accepted by his family. His wedding had been as predestined as his finals examinations at university, a clearly marked waypoint on the map of life. His inclination was to advise Delamere not to play the strong Capulet paterfamilias. By Delamere's own account, this Cabot was a decent, honourable young man. He and Delamere's daughter were presumably attached to each other. Common sense argued that it was unwise to resist something one could not prevent. No doubt when his own daughters, Mary and Jenny, were of a marriageable age he, like Delamere, would feel all the jealousies and passions of a father about to lose his children, but he trusted that the reason which had so far served him so well would prevail and prevent him from turning tyrant. But how to persuade a loose cannon like Frank Delamere? A lot of the success of this interview, he realised ruefully, would depend on how much liquor Delamere had consumed in the last twenty-four hours. Between mad Millward and drunken Delamere, Airton felt that he was caught between a rock and a high sea. He stepped forward gloomily through the fish market like a man on his way to execution.

It was with some surprise therefore that when he entered the courtyard of the hotel the first sound he heard was Delamere's loud laughter booming from the restaurant. It was accompanied by a high descant of female merriment. Curiously he lifted the heavy curtain in the doorway and saw him sitting at a table with a young man and woman, all of them drinking coffee and talking animatedly. He was immediately struck by the beauty of the young woman. He had an impression of flaming red hair blazing above a white, freckled face, flashing green eyes and a wide, full smile. Her head was thrown back as she laughed, and the doctor noticed a ruby locket on a white, swan-like neck. The young man, a huge fellow with untidy yellow hair, lounged contentedly in his chair, a crooked smile on his broad, honest face, his blue eyes twinkling with humour. The only odd feature about this cheerful coffee-house scene was that both Frank Delamere and the young man, whom he presumed was Tom Cabot, were sporting shining black eyes.

When he saw the doctor Delamere leaped to his feet, knocking his chair to the floor in his enthusiasm. He gave a huge welcoming grin, revealing a broken tooth in addition to his shiner. 'It's Dr Airton,' he cried. 'Marvellous. Come in. Meet my darling daughter, Helen Frances, and my prospective son-in-law, Tom.'

'This is a turn-around,' smiled the doctor. 'The story round town was that Armageddon was breaking out here.'

Delamere roared with laughter and turned to Tom who was also grinning. He pointed to their black eyes. 'Well, it did take a certain amount of earnest discussion to get me round to the idea. You know what an old stick-in-the-mud I am. But Tom put his suit very forcefully.'

'So I've noticed,' said Airton. 'You probably want some salves for those big bruises. It must have been quite a discussion indeed. My dear lady,' he said, turning to Helen Frances, 'I'm so very pleased to meet you at last. I've heard a lot about you from your father, but the reality beggars the description.'

'She's a looker, isn't she?' said proud Delamere. 'Too good for this oaf here, but what can you do?' He and Tom both laughed. Helen Frances smiled. 'Pull up a chair, Airton. Pull up a chair. Boy!' he roared. 'More coffee. *Kwai kwai kwai!*'

As the coffee arrived Airton addressed Helen Frances: 'I'm afraid, my dear, once you come to know Shishan a bit better, you'll realise that in this tiny community rumour spreads like wildfire. We were all very concerned about what we were hearing about your father and fiancé's – discussions. I'm so pleased that they appear to have had such a positive and happy outcome. May I be the first to offer my congratulations.'

Helen Frances's smile was infectious, as was her spirited laugh. 'Why, thank you, Dr Airton,' she said, in an attractive, slightly husky voice. 'Don't worry about Papa and Tom. I assure you they're quite manageable. Indeed, my only concern is how to decide which of the two boys is the bigger child – my father or my fiancé?'

'The nerve, HF!' grinned Tom. 'You can imagine what sort of marriage I'm going to have! Henpecked Tom, they'll be calling me in no time. Sir,' he said stretching out a large hand, 'I'm honoured to make your acquaintance. Sir Claude MacDonald was telling us all about you.'

'You're a very fortunate young man, sir. Have you decided on when the happy day is going to be?' Airton wrested his hand back from Tom's vice-like grip.

Delamere broke in quickly: 'Thought we'd give it a few months so we can all get to know each other better,' he said. 'Tom's got to muck down to the new job, and I'd like a few months with my little girl before handing her over for good to this bruiser. There's plenty of time. No hurry. It's not as if we won't all be together in the meanwhile. Eh, Tom?'

'Quite right, sir,' said Tom, somewhat morosely.

'Very sensible,' said the doctor, 'but surely we can celebrate the engagement? Things as momentous as this don't happen in Shishan every day. I mentioned that Nellie and I would like to throw a small welcoming party for you all. It would be an honour if we could combine it with an engagement party at the same time.'

Helen Frances looked questioningly at her fiancé. She put her hand into his. 'What do you think, Tom?'

'Fine by me. It sounds a capital idea. Very generous of you, sir.'

'Then that's settled,' said the doctor. 'What about next Friday? We'll ask all the foreigners in Shishan and have a grand party.'

'Not the bloody Millwards,' muttered Delamere. 'We don't want a prayer meeting.'

'No, perhaps not the poor Millwards. They don't get along with the nuns and they aren't cheerful company at the moment. You know they still haven't found their boy who ran away?'

Helen Frances wanted to hear all the details, so for the next half-hour the doctor chatted to the happy trio, answering Helen Frances's inexhaustible questions about life in Shishan. He was impressed and charmed by her intelligence and vivacity. He also liked Tom for all that he looked like a man who had just stepped off the rugger field.

Helen Frances was describing incidents on their journey from Peking when Delamere looked at his pocket watch. 'Sorry to have to break things up,' he interrupted, 'but Tom and I have our lunch with old Lu and the other merchants. You're welcome to come along with us, Airton. Sorry, my darling.' He turned to Helen Frances. 'Have to leave you on your own-io for an hour or two. Business. Tom, be a good fellow and bring those presents I wrapped up in my room.'

'I'll go with Tom,' said Helen Frances. 'There's still a lot of unpacking to do. Goodbye, Doctor, it was such a pleasure talking to you. I do look forward to meeting Mrs Airton on Friday.'

'Are you sure you want me at this lunch of yours?' asked Airton, when the couple had left. 'It's a business affair, isn't it?'

'No, just introducing Tom to the merchants. Makee fliendly with the Celestials, that sort of thing. What do you think of my little girl? She's a stunner, isn't she? The image of her poor mother.'

'I think she's charming,' said the doctor. 'I like Cabot too.'

'He *is* a good fellow, isn't he?' said Delamere. 'Do you know, he batted for Middlesex? In ninety-two. Was once bowled out by W.G. Grace himself. Isn't that something?'

The doctor examined the other's bloodshot eyes and haggard face. For all his apparent good humour, Airton detected a touch of melancholy. 'So you really have come round to the idea? Nellie sent me round here to be a peacemaker.'

'Thought it was something like that. You've a good woman in Mrs Airton, you know that? How do I feel about it all? Well, I'm not exactly over the moon. Getting your only daughter delivered to you with one hand and snatched away with the other. Blow to the heart, actually. A knock to the old pride, too, if one's being honest. Like someone's pulled a fast one. But I like Tom. Seems my sort of chap. Can't hold much against a man who's prepared to punch his prospective father-in-law in the eye. Shows some sort of seriousness about life, doesn't it?'

'I'm sure it wasn't Tom who struck the first blow.'

'Now you mention it, I don't think it was. Haven't behaved very well, have I, one way and another?'

'I think Herr Fischer was startled to have his schnapps bottle thrown at his head. His schnapps is somewhat sacred to him. But I'm sure he won't think worse of you. Everyone knows the news of the engagement, on top of seeing your daughter after so long, must have been a shock. He'll make allowances for the pressures on you.'

'Pressures? You can say that again. Life hasn't been much to write home about lately.'

'Oh?'

Delamere looked more than usually uncomfortable. 'Nothing. Indiscreet of me to mention it. Vicissitudes of life, that's all.'

'If it's something to do with your goings-on in that dreadful Palace of Pleasure then I don't want to know anything about it. Not unless you're consulting me in a professional capacity. It won't be the first time you've had to come to me and pull your trousers down for a dose of mercury.'

'God forbid. Nothing like that. You really know how to embarrass a fellow, don't you? There were some complications. That's all. Behaved a bit foolishly. Getting over it now. Thinking of taking the straight and narrow, in fact.'

'I'm pleased to hear it. In the nick of time, I would say, considering that your daughter's here.'

'God, Airton, you can be bloody sententious at times. But I suppose you're right. I've been doing a lot of thinking these last couple of days.'

If Delamere had been going to let the doctor have the benefit of his thoughts, it would have to be at another time, because the next minute Tom appeared with the presents under his arm, and the three set off towards the restaurant on the main street that Delamere had booked for lunch. They passed through the crowded downstairs dining hall to the second floor, where the merchants, Lu Jincai, Tang Dexin and Jin Shangui, were waiting for them in a private room.

The doctor knew all of them well. Lu Jincai he liked. Despite his boyish appearance, he was a solid, serious fellow, who radiated honesty. Straight as a die, thought Airton. For a relatively young man, he had an impressive gravity – but it was leavened by a natural tact and a sly but generous humour. Tang Dexin, the tin king, was a roguish old faddist, always going on about his diet and liable to launch into long lectures, especially in mixed company, about the benefits of a healthy sex life in maintaining longevity. He had not done badly in this respect. The doctor judged that he was in his early eighties if not older. He was a tiny, wizened man with parchment skin stretched over a humorous face cracked with wrinkles. He reminded Airton of a mischievous hobgoblin. The third member of the party, Jin Shangui, was a fat, comfortable, pasty-faced individual in his late forties, always laughing, his eyes merry slits behind his glasses, with heavily fleshed earlobes and thick wet lips that quivered when he smiled. His conversation tended towards flowery compliments, verging on the unctuous. He was a general trader with a finger in many different pies. The doctor did not trust him. He was too smooth and plausible to be entirely convincing. But today the three merchants made cheerful company, and were fulsome in their welcome of Delamere and his new assistant.

Delamere had not stinted on the menu, and soon the table was piled high with succulent northern dishes – greasy stews, pork knuckles, steamed mandarin fish, fatty bear's paw and camel's pads, accompanied by piles of dumplings and steamed bread, plates of cabbage and a sort of thick, transparent noodle floating in black vinegar sauce. As soon as he announced the news of his daughter's engagement, the merchants insisted on opening a bottle of gaoliang wine. The doctor pleaded an operation he had to conduct in the afternoon: he loathed the taste of this sour, raw spirit (he knew that if he accepted one cup he would be forced by the ritual of drinking to have more), but Delamere had no qualms about toping in the afternoon, or at any other time, and soon all in the party were exchanging a raucous round of toasts, the compliments becoming more flowery and nonsensical as the drink went down. Airton noticed that Tom held his liquor well. His Chinese was not as fluent as Delamere's or the doctor's but it was adequate for the occasion, and he established a quick rapport with Lu Jincai, who was quietly telling him about the proposed sales visit to Tsitsihar on which he hoped Tom would accompany him as soon as he was settled into his life in Shishan.

'Tom's the man, Mr Lu.' Delamere beamed. 'Knows the crystal-making process better than I do. He'll impress old Ding, no question.'

'I have told Mr Tom that we should set off as early as possible,' said Lu. 'It's a long journey and we should try to reach our destination before the first snows fall.'

'First batch should be ready in three weeks. Tom'll be ready by then, won't you, old boy?'

'Looking forward to getting on the road, sir,' said Tom.

Jin Shangui proposed a toast to the new business venture. His chin wobbled as he rose unsteadily to his feet and raised his cup. 'To De Falang Xiansheng, prince of foreign merchants, and all his business endeavours. And to Lao Lu, our old friend. May they together conquer the whole of north-east China! And bring fortune on all of their descendants for tens of thousands of years!'

'Ten tens of thousands of years!' shouted Tang Dexin, his gums cracking open in a sly grin. 'And to De Falang's assistant, this young stallion who is marrying De Falang's daughter. When their seeds mingle, may she produce the fattest of grandsons to grow up strong and prosperous like De Falang!' He patted a bony hand on Tom's knee.

'*Ganbei! Ganbei!*' Delamere emptied his cup. 'Come on, Tom. Knock it back. They're drinking to all the grandsons you're going to produce for me!'

Blushing, Tom drained his glass.

'Very strong.' Tang nodded approvingly towards Delamere as he squeezed Tom's leg. 'Your daughter will make big sons. Big sons!'

He threw back his head in a shrill giggle. Then, in the sudden manner of the very aged, his head dropped forward on his chest, his smile still fixed on his face, and he went to sleep, hunched like a shrunken sparrow on his stool.

'But are you not worried, Lao Lu?' Jin Shangui returned the conversation to the alkali shipment. 'Such rich merchandise through the Black Hills and beyond. The bandits are becoming more and more daring. If Iron Man Wang hears . . .'

'Tom's already fought off the bandits, haven't you, Tom? On the way here.' Delamere looked proudly at his prospective son-in-law. 'Tell them how you scared them off.'

'Oh, I heard about this,' said the doctor. 'This was in the Black Hills, wasn't it? The Mandarin is always telling me not to be concerned, but these incidents occur with such regularity.'

Tom smiled. 'Well, sir, HF, that's Miss Delamere, is convinced that we were set on by the Robber King himself. We were actually all a bit nervy after the executions we'd seen at Fuxin, tales of Boxers and so on, so when we came across these men ahead of us with shotguns on their backs – it was in that craggy defile with the waterfalls, in the gap between the fir forests – and these fellows, about six of them, suddenly flitted out from behind the tree-trunks, as sinister a bunch as you ever saw, well, maybe we put two and two together and made five. With the darkness and the rain coming on we were all a bit spooked. Anyway, Henry, that's Mr Manners, fired his rifle in the air. The men, whoever they were, vanished like phantoms, and we trotted our mules and horses onwards to get out of there as quickly as we could. I think they were probably quite innocent, just hunters or travellers like us. They weren't really that threatening, though Henry acted decisively, and made us keep watch all that night. That's all, really. Not much of a story to tell in the cold light of day.'

'Ah, Mr Tom is so modest,' said Jin Shangui. 'A toast, this is certainly worth a toast. To his heroic behaviour. *Ganbei!* And to that of your daughter. *Ganbei* again! What a terrifying ordeal. Terrifying. Terrifying,' he said, blinking behind his spectacles. 'What is law and order coming to when a man cannot go about his business without fear? And you still wish to travel these roads again with Lao Lu? To Tsitsihar, was it? I salute your bravery. When did you say you would be departing?'

'When are we off?' said Delamere. 'Oh, I should think—'

'No date has been fixed,' interrupted Lu calmly. 'One would not wish to encourage gossip or tempt Providence. I have noticed,' he said, looking sardonically at Delamere, 'that any attacks on merchant trains have followed a certain amount of publicity about their departure.'

'Quite so,' muttered Delamere sheepishly. 'Mum's the word. Of course.'

'Indeed you are so right,' said Jin. 'They say Iron Man Wang has his spies all over the town. This is only a conversation among friends, so it is safe to speak here, but you are right to be cautious. De Falang, you must listen to the wise advice of Mr Lu and remain silent about your intentions.'

'In this case, there should be no great concern,' said Lu, 'even if Iron Man Wang were to hear. We are only developing our business and will be carrying nothing that will be of value to him. I appreciate your concern, Lao Jin, but on this trip we are only transporting samples, a few worthless crystals, and there will be no payment even on our return.'

'That's right,' said Frank. 'No bags of money this time. Won't be until after spring that we have the big shipments. Then there'll be a tael or two in the strong box. Oh, Lord,' he said, looking at Lu who was giving him an ironic smile, 'have I been indiscreet again?'

Lu Jincai laughed and raised his cup. 'De Falang Xiansheng, you are a mountain of tact and discretion and I am proud that you are my friend and partner. Let me, too, toast the happiness of your daughter and new son-in-law who I am also honoured to meet.'

They clinked and drained their cups. Old Mr Tang woke up from his doze. His eyes narrowed shrewdly. 'Has your daughter wide hips, De Falang Xiansheng? To produce big sons she must have wide hips. And you, young man, you must not be too eager to disgorge your virile essence when making the clouds and rain. Tease out her pleasure as long as you can. The more you pleasure her the fatter the sons she will bear.'

'Thank you for the tip, sir,' said Tom. 'I'll certainly bear that in mind.'

The waitresses brought fruit – apples, persimmons and pears – and shortly afterwards the party broke up. Jin Shangui helped Tang

Dexin, slightly the worse for wear, through the door and down the stairs to his waiting sedan chair. The others followed. On the way, there were further loud congratulations; Jin Shangui offered to throw a large wedding banquet for the young couple; old Mr Tang volunteered to hire an opera troupe for the occasion; Frank was trying to offer everybody a cigar. Lu took his friend by the arm. 'May I have a quiet word with you, De Falang Xiansheng?'

'Tom and the doctor?'

'Have followed the others downstairs. They are happily engaged in conversation.'

'I know, I know. You're about to lecture me on giving away too much about our Tsitsihar deal. I truly am sorry but I did assume we were among friends today.'

'It's not wise to reveal anything even to one's friends. You do not entirely know China. There are many loyalties and conflicts that make friendship a floating commodity – although we prize it higher than anything else. I beg you, do not tell Mr Jin Shangui any more about the schedules of our mule trains.'

'Old Jin? You can't suspect that Jin would . . .'

'Is it not strange that while his caravans have been attacked on many occasions he has never actually been robbed?'

'He has good guards who drove off the bandits. As Tom did.'

'Quite so,' smiled Lu. 'And we must arm our caravans likewise, on whatever – secret – day they depart. Secret, De Falang.' Lu's eyes were twinkling with humorous affection. 'But it was not about business that I wished to talk to you.' His thick eyebrows narrowed in concern. 'I got your message about your friend in the Palace of Heavenly Pleasure, and I have prepared a letter and a gift that may be suitable for her. No, do not thank me. Instead, think, De Falang. Do you really wish to make this final break?'

Frank sighed. 'It's probably for the best,' he said, in a small voice. He raised his haggard eyes. 'Look, old man, Mother Liu spelled out the facts of life so even a dim barbarian like me can understand. There's nothing there. She's a whore and I'm a foolish old man.'

'I would advise you not always to trust the words of a woman like Mother Liu. I could not find Shen Ping when I called there last night . . .'

'Probably having it off with someone upstairs. Playing his jade flute,' said Frank bitterly.

'They told me that she was sick, indisposed. They were all rather strange about it when I asked. Anyway, I'll find out more . . . But meanwhile I think that you may be being too hard on her. I understand that she was much looking forward to leaving with you.'

'So she could whore from my lodgings? So I can pimp for her instead of Mother Liu? Come on, Lu. Leopards don't change their spots. She led me along. Fine, but now it's over.'

Lu shrugged. 'As you please. I will deliver your letter and gift, or see that she gets it.'

Frank shook Lu by both hands. 'Thanks, old friend. What would I do without you?'

'You now have your daughter again, and a fine new son-in-law. You are a lucky, happy man.'

'I suppose I am,' said Frank. 'I suppose I am.'

On Friday evening at seven o'clock the Airtons had taken their places in the sitting room ready to receive their guests. Nellie had tucked up the children, Jenny and George, half an hour earlier, but as soon as she had turned down the lamp and left the nursery, the two little night-shirted figures had crept out of their beds and down the corridor, keeping carefully to the shadows. They were now hiding behind the coat stands near the main door, tense with excitement. They were expecting to see the hanged lady who had miraculously come back to life again. Of course, their mother had insisted that Ah Lee's story had been a fib from start to finish and that Miss Delamere had been alive and well all the time. The children, however, had had enough experience of dealing with adults to know that truth was a multi-layered affair, and nothing should ever be taken at face value.

Neither Jenny nor George had much confidence in their parents' truthfulness anyway. Not since Archie, their father's chow dog's untimely death. When Archie had been run over by a cart, Ah Lee had immediately sat them down in the kitchen and given them all the gory details. He had described how their father had taken one look at the broken legs and back and, there and then, snapped the dog's neck to prevent further suffering. The children quite understood why he had done this: in the western stories the doctor liked to read to them, cowboys were always putting bullets into the heads of their brave, wounded horses. They had been shocked, however, by the story their mother and father had told them that evening over tea. In this sanitised version of events, Archie had been suffering from a terminal illness (this was strange because he had looked fine when he romped with the children that morning); God had decided to relieve his suffering; he had died quietly in his sleep, having given a last bark and a lick before rolling over on his side; and now he was in doggy heaven. It had been a soppy and unbelievable story, and the children had been embarrassed. They could only assume that the shock of the animal's death had been so great that neither their father nor their mother wanted to face the truth, and that they were somehow trying to comfort themselves with this patent lie. They were too polite to contradict their father when he began to tell them about the grave he was going to make for Archie on the hillside; they did not wish to cause him any further upset by telling him how they had seen Ah Lee take Archie's body into the kitchen and boil him into a stew.

Tonight, therefore, when judging the probability of whether Miss Delamere had or had not hanged herself, George and Jenny were inclined to give the benefit of the doubt to Ah Lee whom they saw as a forthright, hard-boiled and, above all, reliable witness. Ah Lee's description of the hanged lady had been very convincing indeed. The fact that the corpse had revived and was coming to dinner was a surprise, but they had heard of stranger things. They knew that the countryside was full of ghosts and vampires and fox spirits. Ah Lee would tell them spine-chilling stories during those afternoons when they sat with him in the kitchen watching him polish the silver or clean the shoes, and once Ah Sun had come in very agitated having seen the ghost of one of the patients in the shrubbery. They had come to accept that odd things happened outside the safety of their compound. George argued that if Miss Delamere really had hanged herself then it was only logical that she had turned into a fox spirit. That would make it perfectly possible for her to come to dinner in her former guise. Everyone knew that fox spirits were beautiful women who waited on lonely roadsides at night, luring unwary scholars to their homes in the forests where they gave them wine to drink then tore out their throats when they fell asleep. But Ah Lee had also told them that, as often as not, they were the ghosts of lonely women who had hanged themselves when rejected by their lovers. 'Just like Miss Delamere,' said George. 'QED.'

'But her lover didn't reject her,' said Jenny. 'It was her father who wouldn't let her marry.'

'Same thing,' said George. 'Still stopped the marriage and drove her to kill herself.'

'But anyway, they *are* getting married now. Isn't it an engagement party we're having here tonight? If she's getting married she can't have hanged herself, can she?'

'Yes, but is it the real Miss Delamere? Maybe they don't know she hanged herself and became a fox spirit, and the reason why Mr Delamere's now allowed the marriage is that he's been hypnotised by her magic powers.'

'Maybe,' said Jenny doubtfully. 'We'll need to look for a mark on her neck, I suppose. The rope must have left a bruise.'

The two hovered behind the coat stand, watching Ah Lee usher in the guests. The railway people appeared first – Dr Fischer and his funny assistant, Charlie Zhang, smiling and chattering in his silk gown. Jenny liked it when Mr Charlie came. He was the most unChinese Chinaman she had ever met, and she looked forward to his presents – red envelopes full of money, or sweetmeats, and once a doll dressed in peasant clothes – that he would slip into her hands with a wink and a smile when her mother wasn't looking. She knew that he probably had a present for her tonight but, like George, she preferred to stay in her hiding place until the mysterious lady appeared. Unlike George, she only half believed that Miss Delamere might be a fox spirit, but she was excited and a little scared all the same.

George tugged her hand. 'Jen. Jen. Look. She's here,' he whispered urgently. 'And, by golly – she's wearing a choker!'

A beautiful young lady was slipping off her coat. She had very white, slightly freckled arms and dark red hair, which shifted tones in the candlelight from chestnut to cherry to amber. She wore a long purple evening dress of taffeta and lace, and she had green eyes like a cat's. She reminded Jenny of one of the princesses in her book of Celtic fairy tales. Around her neck was a thick black neckband, which bore a large amethyst locket. Behind her, handing in their hats, were Mr Delamere and an enormous, yellow-haired man with a kind face.

'That proves it,' George was saying excitedly. 'She's covering up the marks on her neck.'

'But she's beautiful,' gasped Jenny.

'Of course she is. All fox spirits are. That's why they're so dangerous.'

'Well, I believe she's real and alive, and I'm going to prove it,' she said. Taking her courage in her hands, she stepped out and curtsied.

'Why, hello,' said the big young man. 'What's your name?'

'I know. You must be Jenny,' said the lady, in a sweet voice. 'I'm Helen Frances. I'm so pleased to meet you.' Jenny stiffened. How did she know her name? Was she a spirit after all? And then she smelt a whiff of perfume and a tickle of red hair brushing against her cheek as Miss Delamere leaned forward and kissed her lightly. She closed her eyes, partly in fear, partly in delight.

When she opened them again, the Delameres' party, including the beautiful lady, had already moved down the corridor to the sitting room where her father and mother were waiting to greet their guests. Another man was standing in front of her looking down at her with an amused expression. She had never seen anyone better dressed or more elegant. He wore a black dinner suit with a red cape and he was folding his white gloves into his sleeve. He had a small moustache and laughing blue eyes, and she thought that he must be a prince or a duke at the least. 'Hello,' he said. 'I'm Manners. Are you my beautiful hostess? I'll tell you what, my dear, you keep that peaches-and-cream complexion, and I guarantee that in ten years you'll be the toast of all St James's.' And he, too, leaned forward and kissed her on the brow.

Jenny was stunned. It was only when the coast was clear and she felt a tugging on her sleeve from George, who had emerged from behind the coat stand, that she dared open her eyes again.

'Did you see any scars or marks?' he asked.

'No,' said Jenny. 'She's beautiful. An angel.'

'That's what all the fox spirit's victims say,' said George. 'Nothing proven, then. I didn't like that dark man either. Do you suppose he's the lover?'

But Jenny was still bereft of words.

'Come on, Jen,' said George. 'She didn't bite you, did she? You're not in a trance? We'd better get back to our room before Mummy or Daddy catch us.'

But Jenny loitered, still enraptured, gazing at the door of the sitting room where there was a murmur of conversation. 'Oh, I wish I was a grown-up and could go in there and be with them,' she sighed, 'and hear what they're all saying. Don't you think they're the most exciting people we've ever seen?'

Exciting was not a word that would have occurred immediately to Helen Frances. Looking round the faces of these strangers she felt a sense of dislocation. When she had dreamed about joining her father, her schoolgirl fantasies had conjured an image of Shishan as a place of mystery, throbbing with dark, exotic life, full of dangers and allurements. She had not imagined that within days of her arrival she would be sitting down to dinner in the sort of middle-class English home she thought that she had left behind her (the wood-panelled dining room was not unlike her aunt's in Crowborough) or that her hosts would be as conventional as Dr and Mrs Airton.

She knew that she was being naïve. How else would English people abroad behave? Was it really surprising that long-term exiles should wish to re-create the comforting environment of the home counties? Had she expected that Dr and Mrs Airton would be living in a palace? But she could not contain a sense of disappointment. It was strangeness and new sensation that she desired above all else. She had experienced a sense of wonder on her journey. The sights and experiences had heightened her anticipation, and she had imagined that Shishan, the magical destination that had coloured her childhood dreams, would be a Xanadu of delights. Yet up to now all she had seen was a shabby, very smelly town, with dusty streets and alien, rather forbidding inhabitants. Now she found herself again in the humdrum normality from which for most of her short life she had fretted to get away.

With a sinking heart, and a growing sense of anticlimax, she listened to Mrs Airton and Herr Fischer, the man they had met at the railway camp on their arrival, discussing the weather. She had nothing against Herr Fischer, but everything about him was dreary. His head emerged like that of a reluctant seal from an old-fashioned tailcoat. With his hair cut short in the Prussian style and sunburned features, his grizzled moustache and stained, calloused hands, he carried about with him an aura of the grime and dust of the railway camp, and his pale eyes blinked like a kindly vole's as he showered her with laborious and overflowery compliments. He reminded her of one of the tradesmen on whom her aunt had called in the high street.

Admittedly the two Italian nuns in their black habits would have been a little out of place at a Sussex dinner party. And there was certainly nothing conventional about the pig-tailed, silk-robed Chinaman chattering gaily in plummy English as he spooned his soup and gulped his wine, rolling his eyes as he explained earnestly to the nuns between mouthfuls why he preferred French Camemberts and Bries to Dutch and Swiss cheeses. Yet Charlie Zhang's very outlandishness in such an ordinary setting merely confirmed for Helen Frances her disillusionment and made him for her the exception that proved the rule. He was like a parody in fancy dress of the exoticism she had hoped to discover here, the eccentric foreigner who had been invited to tea and to whom well-brought up girls such as she had been taught to be particularly polite in case they offended any sensibilities. After an hour of so of polite embarrassment a pony trap would come for him and the English household would resume its orderly ways.

As the evening progressed Helen Frances experienced a growing sense of futility and boredom. She felt that a trap was closing about her. She wanted, irrationally, to scream or make a scene, or to answer courtesies and platitudes with something so outrageous or shocking it would provoke indignant stares. When she realised that these people would be her only companions for the coming months and years she felt stirrings of panic. Even the doctor, whom she liked, appeared ridiculous to her this evening. With his pale whiskers and inquisitive eyes, his amiable and slightly bumbling manner, he might have stepped out of the pages of the *Pickwick Papers*; he certainly had no role to play in the sort of adventurous romance that Helen Frances had dreamed of discovering in China. She watched despondently as, with thumbs hooked in his waistcoat and his eyes moving round the wine glasses to make sure that none were empty, he hurried his guests to their places and on to the first course as if activity alone would somehow make the dinner party a success. As for her father – well, tonight, much as she loved him, in his unlikely and ill-fitting white tie and tails, his hair streaked with brilliantine and his moustaches curled, she saw only a bombastic caricature. He had promised to be on his best behaviour but his red face and booming laughter carried with it the atmosphere of the music-hall and the pub.

She wished she could have caught Tom's eye, as she had on the captain's table on the ship, to share with him the satire of the scene, but Tom was deep in conversation with Mrs Airton. Instead she found herself looking towards Henry Manners, whose elegance of evening attire and languid posture made him actually the most incongruous figure in the room. His whole manner smacked of a larger, more cosmopolitan world. Helen Frances imagined that he might, only a minute ago, have left a dinner at the Reform Club or White's to take his seat at this provincial table. She thought she identified a bored curl to his lip as he attended to his hostess with perfect courtesy and apparent concentration. It did not fool Helen Frances. Suddenly his blue eyes turned in her direction, and his head moved almost imperceptibly in recognition that she was observing him. Despite herself she grinned, and feeling the onset of the giggles, hastily drank a glass of water. His eyes crinkled in amusement and his teeth flashed in a wide smile. Their unspoken alliance lasted for the rest of the meal.

The doctor tapped his glass after the first course and rose to welcome the newcomers to Shishan. The two nuns clapped their hands, their eyes shining in excitement, as Airton announced the happy news of Tom and Helen Frances's engagement. If the company would forgive him, he would adopt the Chinese custom of getting the speeches over before the main course. 'Business before pleasure, as you merchant chaps say.' He nodded at her father. Helen Frances felt curiously detached. She noticed an ironic expression on Manners's face as he raised his glass in her direction, and she wanted to smile back. Instead she blushed, and Herr Fischer said something pompous about maidenly modesty. Tom rose in his clumsy manner and delivered a self-deprecatory speech in the varsity style. Her father became sentimental and talked of his little girl. Mercifully the formalities were soon over and the doctor went to the sideboard to carve the mutton.

She had to admit that everyone was being very kind to her. Herr Fischer described himself as a lifelong bachelor, but protested it was only because in his youth he had never met someone as beautiful and enchanting as her. If he had, he told her, then, by *Himmel*, he would have duelled every student in Heidelberg to win her hand.

Sister Caterina, her apple cheeks flushed with her first glass of wine, was begging to be allowed to fashion the wedding dress when the happy day came near. The darker Sister Elena wanted to hear all the details of how they had met and fallen in love, so Tom described the voyage and the fancy-dress ball, and they all laughed at the idea of him dressed as Desdemona. Sister Caterina asked Mrs Airton if one day they might have a fancy-dress party like that here, and Nellie smiled tightly and said, 'We'll see.'

Helen Frances did not know quite what to make of Nellie Airton. She admired her statuesque good looks but was a little intimidated by her severity. She pretended to be flattered when Nellie asked if she would like to work in the hospital, but feared she had offended her when she answered noncommittally. The truth was that, for the moment, no idea could have appealed to her less. She had not come all this way to work in a western hospital and to live in a house that might have been built in Surrey. The thought of being locked into a hospital ward with these cheerful nuns filled her with a sense of claustrophobia and images of the convent school she had just left. 'I do not intend to force you, my dear,' Nellie had responded, to her lame excuses. 'I was only thinking of what might be best for you. With Mr Cabot and your father away at the office or on field trips, you will certainly find time heavy on your hands. We do good work at the mission and we can always use a willing helper.'

'Let the poor girl alone, Nellie,' Airton had cried good-humouredly, from the head of the table. 'Give her time. She's got to get used to Shishan first, and her engagement, and us. What can she think, uprooted from her English home, suddenly landing in a queer place like this with a bunch of even queerer devils like us, if we force her straight away to don starch and clean bedpans?'

'I think Helen Frances would make a damn fine nurse, wouldn't you, Tom?' said her father, missing the point.

'Fräulein Delamere,' Herr Fischer was still playing the gallant, 'if ever I were to suffer illness I cannot think of an angel from heaven I would prefer to nurse me more than you.'

'It's all very well of you to say wait awhile, Edward,' said Nellie, 'but you know how short-handed we are, and Miss Delamere can hardly wish to stay in her lodgings all day by herself. It wouldn't be healthy for you, my dear, would it? You seem a spirited girl to me, and I would hate for you to be pining here for something to do.'

Helen Frances felt that she was being forced into a corner. She was relieved when Henry Manners came to her rescue. 'May I be blunt, Mrs Airton?' He smiled. 'I think your offer to Miss Delamere is most generous and neighbourly, and I'm certain that one day she'll become a veritable Florence Nightingale in your hospital. But as a newcomer myself I agree with the doctor, give it a while, and I'll tell you why. I'll say it in one word: Shishan.'

Nellie appeared puzzled and not a little suspicious of where he was leading. 'I don't think I follow you, Mr Manners. What do you mean, Shishan?'

'Well, as you may know, I've bashed about the world a bit and seen a lot of things. And I tell you that from the little I've experienced of this city it's one of the most fascinating spots I've ever been to.'

'It seems ordinary enough to me, Mr Manners.'

'You've lived in China many years, Mrs Airton. Miss Delamere and I are newcomers. May I venture that for her – as it certainly is for me – this city with its walls and towers, its temples and markets, is everything intriguing and romantic that we've ever imagined about Cathay, from the days we read stories of Marco Polo in the nursery. I confess I'm stunned and excited and I want to explore it in every detail.'

'What a romantic you are, Mr Manners – but a young lady on her own cannot go out and explore a Chinese city. It'd be dangerous.'

'Well, here's what I propose, with Mr Delamere's and Mr Cabot's approval, of course. My duties on the railroad are presently quite light and I find I have a bit of time on my hands. Is that not so, Herr Fischer?'

Fischer shrugged. '*Ja.* You have told me. You are your own master.'

'Then I propose that each afternoon for the next two or three months Miss Delamere and I become tourists together and discover Shishan. The monasteries, the rides, the temples. After that she'll decide whether she wants to work in the hospital and I'll get back to the railway.'

There was a silence around the table. Henry leaned back in his chair, a comfortable smile on his face. Helen Frances was conscious that her cheeks were burning. The doctor spoke at last. 'I'm not sure quite what to make of that suggestion, Mr Manners. In my youth it might have been considered forward, not to say shocking, for an engaged woman to gallivant alone with another man.'

'I'm talking of sightseeing, Doctor, and some rides in the countryside. We won't be alone. We'll have our *mafus*, our grooms, with us. I do not know why you should find that shocking.'

There was another silence. Helen Frances could hear the ticking of the grandfather clock in the hall.

'It's only a suggestion,' he added.

Tom, his face redder than usual, leaned forward. 'HF, if that's what you want, then I think it's a dashed good idea. I really do. I'm in your debt, Henry. I only wish I had more time myself to join the two of you. Mr Delamere, I trust you have no objection?'

'Me? No,' said her father. 'Roll on the twentieth century, say I.'

'Then it's settled,' said Tom. 'Thank you, Henry, I'm obliged to you.'

Helen Frances felt she had to contribute something to break the tension, which she seemed unwittingly to have caused. 'I'm – I'm grateful to all of you for your concern for me – and, Mrs Airton, I truly am interested in helping in the mission if you will have me. But, as Mr Manners said, I am very excited to see Shishan, and if . . . and if . . .'

Dr Airton put a hand on hers. 'Say no more, my dear. It's settled. I'm the stick-in-the-mud who should be embarrassed. Of course you must take up Mr Manners's suggestion, and later if you would like to work in the hospital a job will always be open to you. In fact . . . why don't I take you round the mission tomorrow to show you what we're doing? The first item on your tourist itinerary? Nellie, what do you say?'

'You decide, Edward,' said Nellie. 'I have to see to the third course.'

'Ah, cheese!' said Charlie Zhang, a relieved smile on his face. He had found the previous exchange rather bewildering.

'It's roly-poly pudding,' said Nellie icily.

'But there will be some cheese to come?' said the doctor, desperate to get the dinner party back on a harmonious track.

'If we have any,' said Nellie, and disappeared through the door.

But even the roly-poly pudding could not bring the conversation back to the merry note of celebration that had preceded Henry's intervention. The unspoken and vague accusation of impropriety seemed to hang over the table.

The ladies left the men to their port (and some mouldy Parmesan that Ah Lee had discovered for Charlie Zhang) and retired to the sitting room. Nellie was distant but polite to Helen Frances, and both were relieved that the two nuns took the initiative and chatted away about the patients in the wards.

In the dining room, the doctor asked Henry Manners and Tom to elaborate on the adventures of their journey. Frank told them that the news of the events in Fuxin had caused some concern to his merchant friends, but the doctor was dismissive as usual of any link to Boxers, quoting the Mandarin's assurances. Tom described Helen Frances's strange encounter with the blind priest and it was only then that Charlie Zhang, who had been concentrating on his cheese, looked up.

'He was at our camp yesterday,' he said.

The others looked at him uncomprehendingly.

'Who was, Charlie?' drawled Manners, pausing from lighting a cigar.

'The blind priest, of course.'

'You never told me,' said Herr Fischer.

'Didn't think it was important,' said Charlie. 'Anyway, I gave him the boot. Funny-looking fellow. He was disturbing the men. This cheese is so good, Doctor.'

'What was he doing?' asked Manners.

'Oh, nothing, really. He was deaf and dumb as well as blind so he couldn't say anything. Just stood there with all the work on the bridge stopped and the men staring at him. Scary, actually, as if he was casting a spell. Not like the usual mountebank who comes to make speeches about evil spirits in the railway lines. Don't know what the men were concerned about. Peasant superstition, I suppose. It's the blight of my country. Anyway, I gave him money, a Mexican silver dollar, and do you know what he did? He put it into his mouth and swallowed it.' Charlie giggled. 'I thought the men would laugh at that, but it seemed to make them more nervous than before. In the end I had to lead the priest away and see him on to the road. Men got back to work, I gave them double rations of gaoliang, and that's the end of it. Why are you so interested?'

'Someone like that was seen just before the disturbance in Fuxin,' said Manners. 'There's one view that it was he who instigated the riots.'

'A sort of Boxer priest?' asked Frank. 'That's scary, eh?'

'So some seem to believe.'

There was a chill in the air. One of the candles sputtered and hissed out in a pool of wax.

'Oh, my country is full of these crazy men,' laughed Charlie. 'We mustn't encourage this superstition. China must move forward. Are we not going to hear Herr Fischer and Mrs Airton play us some enchanting music? Now, that's the sort of magic we should be introducing to my country.'

'Hear, hear,' said Dr Airton. 'There's too much nonsense talked about these Boxers, and it upsets the digestion. Charlie here seems to be the most rational of the lot of us, for all he is a Chinaman. Come, now, the ladies are waiting. Herr Fischer, have you brought your fiddle?'

As they moved down the corridor to the sitting room, Manners murmured to Tom, 'Hope I wasn't out of court, old boy? Don't know what bee the doctor had in his bonnet. Seemed to be suggesting I was after Helen Frances's virtue or something.'

'No, I think it's a good idea, as I said,' said Tom, looking at him a little coldly. 'But next time ask me first, will you? People like the Airtons are a bit old-fashioned. Well, so am I, actually.'

'I'll drop the idea, old boy. Couldn't matter less.'

Tom stopped, sighed. His features wrinkled, then settled into his lopsided smile. 'Come on, Henry, we're friends. You take her sightseeing by all means. I'll join you on whatever day I can. Now, come on, let's face the music.' He put his arm round Manners shoulder and steered him into the sitting room.

For the next hour they listened to Nellie playing the piano while Herr Fischer accompanied her on the violin. Helen Frances was persuaded to sing an air but only Charlie Zhang was enthused by the performances, clapping and crying, 'Encore,' as if he were in a concert hall. There were no foxtrots or polkas. The guests left earlier than the doctor had hoped. He walked the last guests to leave, Herr Fischer and Charlie Zhang, down the garden path, then paused for a full minute outside his front door, steeling himself to face Nellie's inevitable bad humour. The party had clearly not been a success.

The detachment of soldiers whom Major Lin had sent to the Black Hills returned to Shishan the next day. Manacled in their train were three ragged peasants whom they had captured in the forest. They were brought to the *yamen* and tried for banditry. The Mandarin sentenced them to immediate execution, and accordingly a crowd gathered in the market square that afternoon to witness the beheadings.

The Mandarin ate a light lunch and took an opium pipe before donning his magisterial robes and stepping out of his study. Major Lin and a company of soldiers were waiting in the outer courtyard with the prisoners. They were stripped to the waist and shackled to large wooden *cangues* with holes for head and hands. Notices fluttered above their heads describing their crimes. They were slumped disconsolately by the wall of the *yamen*, bent under the weight of the *cangues* and guarded by a rifleman. They looked up when the Mandarin passed, but there was no hope in their miserable, dead eyes. The Mandarin ignored them, and walked to his palanquin where a stooping Jin Lao was obsequiously holding open the door. He nodded briefly at his chamberlain and climbed in, Jin taking a position on the seat opposite him. The palanquin wobbled slightly as the eight bearers lifted the poles to their shoulders. Major Lin mounted his white horse. His sergeant barked a command. The condemned men were pulled roughly to their feet, and to the slow beating of a drum and the wail of a horn, the procession moved solemnly down the hill towards the town.

The Mandarin leaned back in his shaking seat and closed his eyes. 'Perhaps, Jin Lao, you can now tell me what is the purpose of this charade and why it is that I am spending an afternoon using the resources of the state to execute three harmless bumpkins?'

'They are bandits, Da Ren. And kidnappers. The foreign boy. Cruelly murdered. So sad.' Jin Lao sighed.

'We went through all that at the hearing this morning,' said the Mandarin. 'I didn't believe you then and I don't now.'

Jin Lao's serene smile did not waver. 'We have proper confessions, Da Ren. And the soldiers were shown the graves in the forest.'

'Of the murdered boy and his companions?'

'Of course, Da Ren.'

The Mandarin's hooded eyes opened a fraction, then closed again. His voice was a quiet murmur when he spoke: 'Do not waste my time, Chamberlain Jin. The murdered boy is a catamite at Mother Liu's brothel. He is being kept there to be buggered by you and her degenerate son. Do not waste my time or try my intelligence.'

If Jin Lao was perturbed at the extent of the Mandarin's knowledge, he did not show it. 'You are all-knowing and all-perceiving, master, with "eyes that see a thousand miles and ears which catch the wind",' he said.

The Mandarin sighed. 'It was Iron Man Wang who supplied you with these three sacrificial victims?'

Jin Lao inclined his head.

'Presumably they are some of his debtors who are buying safety for their families with their lives.'

'That is the usual way.'

'And the bad debts of these wretches are transferred to me and deducted from my dues from the bandits?'

'As before, Da Ren.'

'Before, Chamberlain, if we staged our little executions, it was only after significant depredations had been made against my merchants and after several large shipments of treasure had been purloined. It was when the people were angry and afraid, and there was discontent in the city. It is my duty to ensure that law and order is preserved. Law and order requires retribution, and a certain amount of restitution. So through the good graces of the Society, I persuaded Iron Man Wang to provide us with a modest number of culprits. A small portion of the robbed treasure was returned to the rightful owners. Justice was done and seen to be done, all parties were satisfied, and harmony was maintained.'

'A wise and brilliant solution, worthy of such a great mandarin,' murmured Jin Lao.

'You think so? Even though the sentenced men happened to be innocent of any crimes?'

'They were common people, of the criminal class. Certainly no loss,' said Jin Lao.

'And yet I allow a greater criminal like Iron Man Wang my protection and even come to an accommodation with him. Now, why do you think I do that?'

'I imagine, Da Ren, it is because Iron Man Wang has always paid you the tribute that is due to a man of your standing and authority,' said Jin Lao.

'With you there is a venal justification for all things. Yes, Jin Lao, I am compensated well enough through our arrangements, although I might argue that I am only receiving second-hand through Iron Man Wang the unpaid taxes from my merchants that they are so skilful in hiding from me through their account books. It is nevertheless unpalatable for me to have to deal with such vermin. And these judicial murders, which you accept so casually, are distasteful to a man of honour. Has it occurred to you that there could be reasons other than self-enrichment or self-gratification that may justify such perfidy? That matters of state could be involved? That Iron Man Wang and his army of marsh brothers may be serving a higher purpose? You might call it a patriotic purpose. Do you have the slightest idea of what I am talking about? Or any inkling of what is at stake?'

The Mandarin searched his chamberlain's bland features, the enigmatic smile and the rheumy eyes. 'No, I do not expect you to understand. Greed is essentially short-sighted. And I do not hire you for your virtue.

'What I do expect you to understand is that I am not to be trifled with, and it is not for you, Chamberlain, to use my authority with Iron Man Wang or anyone else for self-indulgent machinations of your own. I do not know what grubby plot you and the brothel-keepers are cooking, or why you need to invent this fiction of the foreign boy's death. Perhaps you intend to make him disappear when you have satiated yourselves with him. Or you fear that the doctor or one of the other foreigners will discover his hiding place. That is not my concern.

'What I am telling you is that the blood money for these wretched peasants we are executing this afternoon will not come from my coffers. This time you will pay it yourself. Take it from the cumshaw you regularly steal from me, or from one of your other bribes. And never put me in this position again, or it will not be a peasant's head that rolls in the sand.

'Am I clear, my dear old friend?' He leaned forward and, grinning broadly, patted the chamberlain on the knee. 'Am I clear?'

Jin Lao avoided the snake-like eyes. His smile wavered. 'Perfectly clear, Da Ren,' he breathed. A thin hand emerged from his sleeve and wiped a bead of perspiration from his forehead.

'Good,' smiled the Mandarin. 'Then we can get on with the beheading.'

His good humour and energy seemed totally restored. 'I hope this foreign boy has been worth all your trouble, my friend. You must tell me about him one day, although I cannot say that I understand your tastes in that direction. At least you are doing me one favour. Now that his death has been established I will no longer be bothered by the doctor on this subject. His constant petitions have become tedious. By the way, you and Mother Liu had better make sure that the brat remains hidden. I don't want to have to investigate another abduction or murder.'

'No, Da Ren,' said Jin Lao.

'How comforting that I can rely on your discretion – especially where your own self-interest is so concerned. Oh, cheer up. I have never seen your face so long. Roll up the window and show me where we are. We must be getting close to the square.'

Jin Lao pulled on the string and the bamboo blind lifted to reveal the main street and the jeering crowds by the side of the road.

'Well, well, we talk of the doctor and here he is,' said the Mandarin. He recognised Airton jostling through the stream of people. His usually neat appearance was slightly ruffled and he was shooting disapproving, almost angry glances in the direction of the procession and the pathetic line of prisoners stumbling under their *cangues*. He was with a foreign woman, a young one, noticed the Mandarin. How indecorous these barbarians were: parading their women in public like equals! He assumed it must be the daughter of the soap merchant who had just arrived. The doctor had a protective arm around her shoulder, attempting to shield her from the throng rushing towards the square. The Mandarin had an impression of green eyes in a white face, and a pyre of flaming red hair. She was staring at the procession of condemned men with wonder, her mouth slightly open. Did the Mandarin detect excitement in her rapt attention?

The palanquin was quickly past. They were under a *pailou* and into the square. The crowd roared with blood lust when the prisoners appeared. The Mandarin composed his features into the bored expression of disdain suitable for a high official on such an occasion. As he did so, he caught himself wondering how even foreigners could find women of such colouring attractive. The white features of a ghost? The eyes of a civet? The fiery hair of a fox spirit? He was intrigued.

Chapter Five

*Can it be that the foreigners have poisoned all
the wells in Chih-li?*

The Mandarin's palanquin moved on, leaving the doctor struggling against the flow of the pushing crowd. He had caught
a glimpse of his old friend in the carriage window, superciliously
surveying the scene. In his present mood Airton would have quite
happily punched the haughty features. Disgusted with the Mandarin,
and himself, and temporarily with everything Chinese, he turned to
Helen Frances. 'Come, my dear, let's get you home. This is no place
for a young woman.'

But Helen Frances did not move. She was transfixed, one hand
to her open mouth, her eyes wide with fascination or horror, the
doctor could not tell which. Only a few feet away from them the
condemned men shuffled by. Two were middle-aged. One was in
his early twenties. Their heads were dragged down by the heavy
cangues, their backs and necks bending to the strain. Forced into
grovelling, cringing postures, they appeared to be cowering with
shame under the weight of the crimes that flapped in blood-red
characters on the cloth notices above their heads. The sullen eyes
in the broad peasant faces of the elder men were fixed on their
own stumbling feet and the chains dragging through the dust. Their
expressions were phlegmatic and resigned. Only the younger one
showed any curiosity about his predicament. His eyes, startling
white against the stained brown of his cheeks, flitted nervously from
side to side like those of a frightened colt. He seemed bewildered that
so many people were rushing to the square with the sole purpose
of watching him die. Two soldiers flanked each man. Their smart
uniforms and stiff, martial postures were a contrast to the abject
and broken demeanour of their charges. This juxtaposition itself
was a lesson, a living tableau asserting the dignity of the law over
society's outcasts, a morality play deliberately choreographed for
the edification of the crowd. The drum pulsed like a heartbeat

from behind. Major Lin on his white horse followed slowly with his riflemen, a picture of implacable correctness and authority.

'Come on, my dear, we must go. Let's leave the heathen to their barbarities.' Gently he pulled Helen Frances's arm. 'Do come with me now, there's a good lassie.'

'It's like Christ and the thieves on the way to Gethsemane,' murmured Helen Frances. 'Carrying their crosses.'

'Aye, very like,' said the doctor. 'Humanity hasn't improved through the ages. It's only refined its cruelty. It's a pathetic sight. Come, my dear.'

But Helen Frances still would not move. She craned her head to catch a last view of the procession as it disappeared in a cloud of dust through the *pailou*. The doctor noticed a red flush on her cheeks, and a slight trembling of her arm. 'It's all right, my dear. It's all right,' he attempted to soothe her, putting his arm clumsily round her shoulder.

Helen Frances wriggled gently out of his embrace. She turned towards him. Her green eyes contemplated him steadily, but the irises were enlarged, moist, almost shining, and she was smiling strangely. 'I'm perfectly all right, Doctor.' Her voice, though calm, was an octave higher than usual. 'I've seen an execution before. I'm not a weak woman in shock. I assure you I'm not. On the contrary, I'm ... I'm ... I'm really not sure how I feel. I – when I was a girl and read about the pirates and highwaymen being hanged at Tyburn and the crowds who flocked to see them die, I thought it was unimaginable that any person would want to see such a horrible thing, but I suppose they went because – because they found it thrilling. I think I understand now.'

'My dear, I'm not really sure what to say. I think I should be taking you home.'

The crowd on the street was thinning. The road itself was empty except for the swirl of settling dust. Most townsmen had taken their places in the square. A noise like the wash of a wave was welling from the indistinct blue and brown mass of people they could make out through the *pailou*. The desertion of this usually busy thoroughfare was ominous and menacing. Only a few stragglers could be seen and they were hurrying to get to the execution in the square. A young man in artisan's costume crashed into the doctor, knocking him off balance, cursed, then giggled foolishly when he saw it was a foreigner, before running on.

'You bloodthirsty heathen,' called the doctor after him. He stood in the dust and shook his fist. He did not know whether it was anger or despair but he felt tears of rage burning his eyes. What a day. *What* a day. He realised that he must have been holding back this emotional outburst since the late morning when he had received the Mandarin's note . . .

Everything had actually gone rather well up to then. The embarrassments of the dinner party seemed to have faded into insignificance in the light of morning, although Nellie still had a few scathing things to say about 'flibbertigibbet' young women who did not know what was good for them, and young men of doubtful morals who should have known better. She obviously still felt sensitive about the rebuff she had received. Pleading a headache, she had elected to remain in the house all morning. It was a transparent excuse to absent herself from the hospital when Miss Delamere came for her tour of the mission. Airton did not press her. There would be plenty of time for a reconciliation between the two women. No doubt it would be up to him as the 'busybody of the family' (that jibe still smarted) to arrange it.

Soon enough a cheerful Frank Delamere and Tom, on their way to a day's work at the Babbit and Brenner godown, deposited Helen Frances at the mission gates and the doctor took her straight into his surgery where he was about to remove a cataract from an old lady's eye. The equanimity with which the girl watched the whole operation impressed him, as did, later, her demeanour in the sick wards. She asked intelligent questions and was not distressed even when meeting their latest burn victim, a little boy of four who had knocked over a wok and been covered from head to foot in boiling fat. Helen Frances had sat by the disfigured boy's bed and, holding his unburned hand, whispered nonsense to him until he gave a faint squeal of delight. That convinced the doctor that Helen Frances had the pluck and sensitivity it would take one day to become a fine nurse or helper in the hospital. It was a pity that Nellie was not here to see it.

She was an appreciative visitor and a delight to show round. He enjoyed her acute questioning. Her beautiful presence brought out the gallantry in him and a desire to entertain. When they reached the opium ward – usually a depressing place where listless addicts sweated through their cures – the doctor was brimming with good humour as he described his method of treatment. 'You see, while I give them ever-decreasing injections of morphine to break down their craving, Sister Elena gives them an ever-increasing diet of Bible stories to occupy their minds. Whether it's my diluted morphine or their fear of hearing yet another story about Elijah, I can't tell,' he joked, 'but the cure seems to work. One or two have actually broken the opium habit for good.'

Helen Frances laughed politely and asked him why so many Chinese were addicted to opium in the first place, and he answered cheerfully, 'Poverty, my dear. Everything comes back to poverty. The opium dream's one illusory way of escaping the harshness of living. The opium addict's need is physical and spiritual. In our mission we try to offer medicine for both afflictions.'

'So the evangelical work goes side by side with the medical treatment?'

'In theory,' said the doctor. 'If my masters in the Scottish Missionary Society had their way I'd be spending most of my time handing out tracts. In practice I find it's all I can do to heal the body without worrying about the soul as well. And is that wrong? In my small way I'm bringing the advantages of western civilisation to the heathen. I do with my lancet and potions what Herr Fischer does with his railway, and your father with his chemicals. We're all missionaries in one way or another.'

'I never thought of my father as a missionary.'

Airton laughed. 'He's no Septimus Millward, that's for sure, but he's developing new soaps and cleaning processes. I don't know if in your school you were taught that cleanliness is next to godliness, but hygiene has as much of a part to play in the prevention of diseases as any of my medicines. And is it so foolish to suppose that if you cure the body then the cure of the soul will follow in due course?'

'And railways?'

'I tell you, my dear, railways will bring more Chinese to Jesus than any preaching by me or my colleagues. They'll transport grain to the starving, they'll bring wealth-producing industries to the poorer provinces, they'll do more than anything else to eliminate poverty and better the life of the common man. And in time this ancient

Celestial Kingdom will crumble and be replaced by a striving, modern society, like our own. And then what place will there be for the old superstitions? Bring China closer to the West and the true religion that illuminates and motivates our own world will find its natural place here.'

'Then you are an evangelist after all, Dr Airton.' Helen Frances smiled.

'Not a very successful one.' He laughed. 'Do you know how many, out of all the hundred or so Christians that there are in Shishan, I've personally converted? Two, and you've met both of them. Ah Lee and Ah Sun, my housekeeper and cook. And from the nonsense I get fed back to me through my easily corruptible children I know that they're as filled with heathen superstition and pagan idolatry as they were when I met them twenty years ago. I love them dearly, but they're Rice Christians, the both of them. I'm sure they'd die on the cross if I asked them to, but it wouldn't be for the Faith: it'd be nine parts pride and cussedness and one part loyalty to me. The truth is, my dear, that this Chinese civilisation, heathen and backward as it is, is so entrenched that all our Gospel stories are pinpricks against it.'

'But you'd have thought that they'd be grateful to be shown the Truth. Or so Mrs Airton was saying last night.'

'Yes, well, Nellie has strong views on most things. But think what we're up against, Miss Delamere. Ask any white man about a Chinaman, and he'll tell you he's a liar and deceitful. Well, so's a child until you teach it the elements of right and wrong. The trouble is, there isn't a right or wrong in this culture. There's only harmony and the golden mean. We think lying's a sin. The Chinaman thinks it bad-mannered to offend you by telling you something you don't want to hear. They don't have the absolutes we have. You say, show them the Truth. They have a complex society developed over thousands of years where truth is whatever you want it to be. Appearance not substance is what counts.

'But what a civilisation it is! Cultured, refined, with laws and government and science. Their philosophers two thousand years ago came up with the concept of the virtuous man, not Christian but honourable in every other way.'

'Except he doesn't tell the truth.'

'Ah. You're being mischievous, Miss Delamere. Well, perhaps

he isn't as scrupulous as you or I would be, but he is virtuous nevertheless. And well educated in the classics. Like the Mandarin, whom you have yet to meet. A thoroughly amiable gentleman. And, more to the point, intelligent and sophisticated, a Confucian scholar, confident in the superiority of his cultural inheritance.

'So think how our earnest missionaries go down. In we come, all smug and holier-than-thou, doling out our translations of the Bible. We know that what we're offering is the ultimate salvation. To the Chinaman, it's another book, and a rather queer one at that. Remember, this is topsy-turvy land. Black's white. Left's right. They don't think as we do. And they look in the Bible and read about the Dragon Satan. A dragon for them's a symbol of virtue. It's the emblem of the Emperor. Are we telling them the Emperor's evil? And then there are all the references to sheep and shepherds. Half the people in this country have never seen a sheep; the ones who have think a herdsman's the scum of society. And we say to them, "Come like lambs to the Good Shepherd and He'll forgive your sins". They don't even have a concept of sin: if something bad happens to them it's some god's fault not theirs.

'And then in the same breath we tell them to stop worshipping their ancestors, as if filial piety's a crime, and turn their backs on graven images because it's idolatrous. The upshot is that Christian families don't pay the temple dues any more. That's fine, as far as it goes, but in this society that's how villages fund their communal activities. So Christians immediately become antisocial elements. Others have to foot the bill for the travelling opera troupes, and what-have-you. So there's resentment against the converts. At best they're dog-in-the-manger, at worst they're seditious. Come a drought or a famine, as we have in various parts of Shantung and Chih-li, it's not surprising stories start spreading that it's Christians poisoning the wells, or it's doctors in the missions like me cutting out people's hearts for magic ceremonies, or it's telegraph wires bringing evil spirits. Resentments breed superstitions, and superstitions breed resentments. It all comes from going about things the wrong way.'

'Is that what's behind the Boxer movement? You're painting a depressing picture, Doctor.'

'Well, my view's a minority one. Most of the Protestant missionaries believe they're doing fine work and are enthused that the trickle of conversions will one day break the dam, and bring millions of souls to Jesus. It doesn't seem to worry most of them that they don't understand the first thing about the society they've come to. They don't realise how offensive their good intentions really are. They're blindly doing the Lord's work, and He will provide. End of story. Well, I believe we've got to be a bit more subtle about it. It isn't good enough to bludgeon the Chinese with the Bible, in bad Chinese to boot. We're not going to get anywhere till we get the Mandarin class on our side, and we won't do that by patronising them or criticising their customs. That's why I think it's better to open hospitals and build railways. If we can show them the advantages of our way of life, then Christianity will follow in the baggage car.'

What a splendid discussion, thought the doctor, although, now he came to think of it, he had been doing more of the talking than she. They were just about to leave the opium ward to go to the chapel when his major-domo, Zhang Erhao, brought in the messenger from the *yamen*, and the doctor's day fell apart.

To the Estimable Ai Dun Daifu, [the letter read] *On behalf of His Excellency the Mandarin Liu Daguang. Please be informed that the bandits Zhang Nankai, Xu Boren and Zhang Hongna, having confessed to the murder of the foreign youth, Hailun Meilewude, in the Black Hills, have been sentenced by the* yamen *and will be executed this afternoon in penalty for this crime and others involving banditry and robbery and sundry murders. There can be no issue of compensation because the three culprits, despite their previous record of robberies and larcenies, were discovered to be intestate and without possessions at the time of their apprehension. We trust that this satisfies your enquiries on this subject and we authorise you to inform the relatives of the murdered victim of the justice which has been meted on their behalf.*

It was stamped with the official *yamen* chop.

'Whatever is the matter, Dr Airton?' Helen Frances cried.

The doctor weakly waved out the *yamen* messenger and Zhang Erhao, and slumped on to one of the beds in the ward, tears welling his eyes. 'The poor, poor boy,' he murmured. 'It's everything I feared. What shall I tell his parents?'

And then the curt callousness of the official letter hit him. 'Monstrous,' he cried. 'It's monstrous. "We trust that this satisfies your enquiries." They're writing to me as if I'd made a complaint about lost property to the municipal council. What compensation can there be for a human life? And why wasn't I informed of the trial? This is monstrous. They're nothing but a race of savages.'

Helen Frances, the doctor's lecture on the sophistication of Chinese culture fresh in her ears, evidently knew when to keep silent.

There was no help for it. He had to go to the Millwards immediately to break the news. He offered to escort Helen Frances back to her hotel first, but she asked if she could accompany him to the Millwards. He thanked her. This was an interview he dreaded and he was glad of her companionship. So the two of them walked down the rural path leading from the mission to the south gate, down the main street and into the poorer section in the north-west of the town where the Millwards lived.

The doctor was afraid that Helen Frances would be shocked by the squalor of the Millwards' compound. If she was she did not show it, beyond pressing a small handkerchief to her nose when stepping over the open sewer that ran outside their gate. He kept a grip on the stout stick he had brought with him, but the mongrels scavenging on the rubbish tip at the other end of the lane kept their distance. He used it now to bang on the peeling wooden door. A surly child, one of the waifs whom the Millwards had 'saved', wearing ragged pyjama bottoms and no top, the prettiness of her face obscured by the dirt that caked it, opened the door. 'Thank you, my dear,' said the doctor quietly, as he entered, fumbling at the same time in his pocket for a coin to give her. She tucked it listlessly into her waistband, and led them through the courtyard.

The Millwards were eating lunch. They were seated in a semi-circle round a charcoal stove. The bowls of gruel they were holding contained more water than millet. The hopeless poverty of it all depressed Airton, and the shadowed eyes in the pale, starved faces of the children seemed to glare at him accusingly. He asked if he could speak to Septimus and Laetitia alone, but Septimus, not rising from his stool, told him to say what he had to say. So the doctor told him about the letter. Laetitia gasped and covered her face with her hands. Septimus bowed his head. The children continued to stare blankly at him, eating their gruel. A dog barked outside in the yard.

'Of course I will go to the *yamen* and find out more,' stumbled Airton. 'This isn't satisfactory. The Legations in Peking should be informed. There must be procedures, an investigation. If there is anything I can do . . .'

Septimus raised his head. The blue eyes behind his spectacles were brilliant in the shaft of sunlight that came through a hole in the roof. 'My son is not dead, Doctor,' he said.

'Of course not. Of course not,' muttered Airton. 'He is in a happier land. That must be our comfort. Yes. Eternal life is now his. Of course.'

The blue eyes did not waver. 'He has not left this world, Doctor. He still lives among men.'

'His soul. Yes. For ever. In our memories. Always.'

'You misunderstand me, Doctor. I know that my son was not murdered. The Devil has deceived you with a tissue of lies.'

Airton cleared his throat. 'But the letter?'

'Words, Doctor, words. What are the words of men in the face of the truth of God? I know that my son is alive and well. I have seen him.'

'You've seen him? I don't understand.'

'Yesterday, Doctor. The Lord revealed Hiram to me in a vision. He spoke to me, saying unto me, "Father, forgive me for the anguish I have brought upon you. Know that there is a purpose to all things. And I will come to you when it is time. As the Prodigal returned so will I. And there will be joy where there was sorrow."'

'Hallelujah,' said Laetitia, echoed by her children somewhat mutedly.

'But – but where is he, then?' said Airton.

'That the Lord did not reveal.'

'Ah,' said Airton.

Septimus stood up and put his arm round the doctor's shoulders. 'You are a good man, Doctor, and I thank you for coming to me with this important news. I know now what I must do.'

'Mr Millward. Septimus. I know how much you wish to believe that this tragedy could have been prevented—'

'It is to prevent a tragedy that the Lord is now calling me, and through your good graces, Doctor. There are innocent men to be saved and there is little time. Leave us, for we must pray.'

The doctor felt a strong arm turning him and propelling him towards the door. 'Mr Millward, I must—'

'There is little time,' said Septimus. 'Go now. The Lord is call-ing me.'

And Airton and Helen Frances found themselves in the courtyard, the door closed in their faces.

'He's mad, my dear,' said Airton.

'Obviously,' said Helen Frances.

'The tragedy's quite unhinged him. The pity of it. What are we to do?'

'Is there anything we can do?'

'I suppose not,' said Airton. 'Perhaps this madness is a godsend. The poor, poor family. I'll – I'll call again tomorrow to see how they are.'

They turned to leave. A rat ran the length of the yard. From behind them they could hear the murmur of prayers.

It was as they were walking down the main street on the way to Helen Frances's hotel that they were overtaken by the crowd hurrying to the execution. Young and old, shopkeepers and artisans, men and women, fathers carrying their sons on their shoulders, an old lady hobbling with a stick, the glee and anticipation on their faces disgusted him. They might have been rushing to the circus or a carnival. At the same time a sense of guilt and shame overpowered him. How ineffective he had been – what protection for that poor innocent boy, or succour for his sad, misguided parents had he been able to provide? For all his well-intentioned efforts, was he, as Nellie had said, only a foolish busybody? How blind he had been to trust in his friendship with the Mandarin and Chinese justice.

Here was Chinese justice about to be demonstrated. Three heads would hang in cages that evening on the city gates, and the city would go about its business as if nothing had happened. A note in the *yamen* records. Murder and summary execution. A pronouncement in the morning and three heads rolling in the afternoon. Harmony restored. The tragedy of Hiram and the execution of his murderers had become an afternoon's entertainment for the mob.

He wanted to rail against the pity of it and the waste, the lightness with which the Chinese disposed of human life – even these wretched peasants. Presumably they were guilty of the terrible crime for which they had been condemned. But why the hurry to dispense with these witnesses of Hiram's final hours? Why had the doctor not been told about their trial? Since Hiram was a foreign child, did not the laws of extra-territoriality apply? He realised, with shame, that one of the main reasons for his anger was that the Mandarin had not informed him of what was happening. He felt in some way that his friendship had been betrayed. As the dust of the procession settled, and as he raised his fist impotently after the stragglers running to catch the show, he saw in his mind the calm, cruel features of the Mandarin, who even now would be presiding over the barbarities taking place in the square. The sardonic smile seemed to be mocking him and everything he was attempting to achieve.

He was started from his gloomy reverie by a well-spoken voice above his left ear. 'Dr Airton. Miss Delamere. How interesting to find you here. Are you on your way to the execution or coming away from it? I hope that I'm not too late.'

He looked up and saw, silhouetted against the blaze of the afternoon sun, Henry Manners on his horse. He was neatly dressed in tweeds and bowler hat, and the brown leather of his boots and saddlery gleamed with soldierly perfection. His grey mare was snorting and jerking its head, but Manners held the frisky animal effortlessly in position with a tight rein.

'The doctor is taking me home, Mr Manners,' said Helen Frances. 'He says this is not a place for a young lady to be.'

'Assuredly not,' said Manners. 'Very grubby affairs, executions. I was afraid, for a moment, that after your experience in Fuxin you were developing most unladylike tastes.'

'Then you needn't be concerned. One horror was quite enough,' she replied, 'but please do not let us keep you from your own entertainments.' Airton was amazed that she was using the same bantering tone as Manners. They might have been flirting in a salon. And there was the same strange gleam in her eye that he had noticed when the procession of condemned men had passed by.

'Alas, no entertainment for me. All work, I'm afraid,' said Manners. 'Unpleasant circumstances, no doubt, but I think I might find the person I want to meet there. Executions are something in the way of being social occasions, are they not, Doctor? In a barbarous land, I suppose we must learn to adopt the heathen customs.'

'I don't understand you young people,' said Airton. 'If you must attend such a spectacle, then I suppose I can't stop you. But, Miss Delamere, I do have a responsibility to your father, and I insist we be going.'

'It was a pleasure, Doctor, no less for being so brief,' said Manners. 'A splendid dinner too last night, by the way. My thanks. And I look forward to our first tour together, Miss Delamere. Tomorrow, I believe? I'll be at your hotel at two.'

Putting his crop to the brim of his hat in salute, he spurred his horse into an easy trot, and within seconds had disappeared behind the *pailou* to the square, his erect figure melting into the dust and the crowd, which they could see dimly in the distance. As the doctor and Helen Frances turned to leave, they noticed that the murmur of voices had stilled to an ominous silence.

'Oh, goodness, they're reading the pronouncements before the sentences are carried out,' said Airton. 'Please, please, can we go now?'

The Mandarin was seated on a simple wooden platform set up close to the entrance of the temple in the market square. A servant was holding an umbrella above his head and he was sipping tea while he conversed with Major Lin. In front of them Jin Lao was reciting from a scroll to the now silent crowd, his naturally high-pitched voice wavering with literary emotion. The Mandarin doubted whether half of the mob could understand a word of what he was saying. He was certain that the three wretches suffering their last moments on earth, their faces pressed into the dust by Lin's soldiers, would not be appreciating the finer flourishes.

His eyes moved lazily over the townsmen listening to the proclamation. There was an atmosphere of tense expectation as their faces fastened with hungry attention on Jin Lao, or fixed with a furtive fascination on the miserable felons about to be executed. What brought these peaceful shopkeepers to this butcher's yard? he wondered idly. Curiosity? Blood lust? It was a crowd like this that had exploded into riot in Fuxin. He would have to pay attention that none of this Boxer madness took root here.

At the back of the crowd he noticed a foreigner on a horse. A well built, soldierly looking young man, who sat well in his saddle. He had not seen him before. It was strange that a foreigner should come to witness an execution. It was difficult to make out the man's expression at this distance, but he thought he could detect an amused smile. The man was looking in the direction of the Mandarin. It was as if he had detected the Mandarin's attention upon him, because he suddenly and deliberately raised his hat in a salute, all the time staring with the insolent eyes. For the second time that afternoon, the Mandarin was intrigued, but he allowed no change of expression on his bland features. Instead he inclined his head towards Major Lin. 'What was Iron Man Wang's answer? Has he made the contacts?' he asked. It was the first time that he had had a chance to talk to Major Lin since the troop had returned from the Black Hills.

'Lieutenant Li received further assurances, but he was not given any date for a shipment.' Major Lin's voice was languid but his body was at half attention, and he was watchful of the crowd.

'Is there going to be a shipment at all?' asked the Mandarin scornfully. 'I've paid enough for promises. When am I to see my guns?'

'Lieutenant Li was told that the guns are still at the depot near Baikal. Iron Man Wang claims that there is a new commandant at the depot who requires payment.'

'Lieutenant Li was under instructions to refuse any further demands for payment until the shipment arrives.'

'Those were his original instructions, but then he had to negotiate the acquisition of these criminals according to your new instructions, and that complicated matters. It gave Iron Man Wang a lever to bargain with.'

'New instructions?'

'The instructions transmitted by Chamberlain Jin, Da Ren. Iron Man Wang struck a hard bargain because of them.'

'I see. In future, take your instructions directly from me. It's a pity that you did not lead the troop yourself.'

'I was ill, Da Ren.'

'You were besotted by that courtesan.'

Major Lin reddened, stiffened. Then, seeing the Mandarin was smiling, grinned too. 'You remind me how honoured I am by your gift, Da Ren.'

'She pleases you?'

'More than I can say.'

'Well, don't let her take your mind off your work. Or I'll take her away from you. Give her to someone else. Perhaps I should take her to my own quarters. I've heard she's comely.' The Mandarin glanced up at his subordinate, noticing the red flush of anger. He laughed. 'Jealousy, Major? Of a whore? Come, come. I'll tell you what I'll do, get me my guns and I'll buy her out of that brothel for you for good. Then you can marry her if you're so infatuated.'

Major Lin spat on the ground. 'I don't see why we don't just apply to Peking for more guns. My troops certainly need them. It's humiliating to have to deal through a bandit with corrupt Russian barbarians, whom I don't trust anyway. I'm sorry to be critical, Da Ren, but this is what I think.'

The Mandarin closed his eyes. 'My dear patriotic Major Lin. How I value your honesty. If only our government had these guns to spare. But they don't. We are in a precarious position, as you know. Both the Russians and the Japanese want to establish spheres of influence here. The Russians have already moved their troops into great parts of Manchuria, so what can I do but deal with the enemy? We must be thankful that they are corrupt because, through them, we can acquire the weapons we need to protect ourselves against them.'

'But dealing furtively through a bandit, Da Ren? Is there no other way?'

'The Black Stick Society and Iron Man Wang have channels to the Russians. Do you have any other suggestions? If you could use your own relationships with the Japanese . . .'

'My captors were honourable men, Da Ren.'

'Of course they were, Major. Even so . . . But what is happening now?'

A man was struggling through the press of the crowd. Curses and jeers as he passed were beginning to drown the sound of Jin Lao's recitation. A murmur of anger rippled through the throng as Septimus Millward stepped into the cleared circle. His jacket was torn and a thin trickle of blood could be seen on his forehead. 'Stop,' he was yelling, in his deplorable Chinese, pointing his finger at the bewildered Jin Lao, who had ceased reading from his proclamation and was standing with his mouth open. 'Stop your bad work. God says my son lives. These men,' he cried, swinging his arm round to point at the equally amazed felons, who were staring up at him from their prostrated positions in the dust, 'these men are without drums. Without drums I say, in the sight of gods and men.'

Major Lin, quivering with anger, was shouting instructions to his men, who were hesitantly converging on the large blond man who was still screaming his nonsense at Jin Lao. The Mandarin saw him effortlessly shake off the attempts of one of the soldiers to pinion his arms. The crowd itself was showing signs of restlessness, straining against the barrier of Lin's troops. Vegetables and other missiles were being hurled indiscriminately at the condemned men, the soldiers and Millward. The Mandarin thought he heard the cry, 'Death to foreign devils!' and this was confirmed a moment later when it was repeated as a baying slogan by ever larger sections of the mob. He noticed the brothel-keeper's son, Ren Ren, and some of his cronies on the balcony of the Palace of Heavenly Pleasure on the other side of the square waving their arms and leading the chorus. The Mandarin recognised the incipient signs of a riot.

He rose to his feet pushing aside the umbrella. At the same moment one of Lin's soldiers hit Millward with the butt of his rifle. He fell, stunned, to his hands and knees. Another soldier clubbed him in the small of the back and he slumped on his face. The knot of soldiers began to beat him as he lay on the ground. The crowd howled.

'Fire your pistol,' shouted the Mandarin at Lin.

The sound of the six shots fired in rapid succession froze all activity in the square. One of the soldiers still had his rifle butt raised above Millward's body. An orange thrown a second before the shots were fired bounced off the head of one of the condemned men and rolled in the sand. The Mandarin stepped into the silence.

'This madman will receive twenty lashes for disturbing the peace,' he cried. 'Take him to the *yamen.*'

Lin barked an instruction and two soldiers dragged the groaning, bleeding body of Millward out of the square, the crowd respectfully making way.

'You've heard the proclamation. Get on with the execution,' the Mandarin shouted. The crowd roared with approbation. The executioners with their large blades, naked to the waist, their bodies oiled, stepped into the ring.

'You are fortunate, Chamberlain Jin,' said the Mandarin quietly as he passed, 'that nobody could understand the utterings of that barbarian. When he said that the condemned men were "without drums" he was trying to say that they were "innocent". You keep that boy hidden, or I will disown you.'

'*Shi*, Da Ren,' said a shaking Jin Lao.

The Mandarin sat back in his chair and reached for his tea. The executioners' assistants were pulling forward the pigtails of the condemned men to bare their necks for the cut. He saw that the other foreigner was still sitting his horse at the back of the crowd. The disturbance had not affected him: there was a sardonic, almost bored expression on his face. The Mandarin watched him all through the execution. The man's expression did not alter even when the blades fell, or when the heads were held up, then poled; there was not even a flicker of interest when the crowd rushed forward to grab souvenirs from the carcasses for their medicines. Obviously this was a man of very different mettle from his sentimental friend, the doctor.

'Ride with me in my palanquin,' he told Major Lin. 'The Chamberlain can walk back.'

The drums beat, the horn blared, and the procession moved through the now dissolving crowd out of the square heading back to the *yamen*.

'That was more interesting than usual,' said the Mandarin, when they were bouncing on their way. 'One never knows what to expect with these missionaries.'

'If I had my way, all the foreigners would be expelled,' said Lin.

'You are a patriot, which is a fine thing,' said the Mandarin. 'I am sure that in an ideal world I would share your sentiments. The problem is we need them.'

'There I cannot agree.'

'Well, you are young, my friend, and flush with all the virtues. Sadly, when you reach my age, one learns to see the world not as it should be but for what it is. And it is sometimes depressing to consider the depths of expediency one is reduced to in order to achieve an honourable aim. I satisfy myself that as long as my goal is virtuous, then any means are honourable, however wicked they appear.

'This is a view, incidentally, which my foreign interlocutor, the good Ai Dun Daifu – and he is a good man for all he is a barbarian – cannot hope ever to understand. I learn a lot from my conversations with him. He tells me about the world outside the Middle Kingdom. It is remarkable what technical skills the barbarians have developed, and therefore how apparently powerful they are – but I have also discovered that the foreigner is trained to think in absolutes of right or wrong. Now that is a great weakness in him, and the knowledge of it is immensely valuable to me, quite justifying the tedious hours I have spent in his company. You do agree, I hope, that one should always learn the weaknesses of one's enemy, for how otherwise would one ever defeat him?'

'So you do see the foreigners as our enemy?'

'They are also a means to an end.'

'I am only a soldier. I do not understand you.'

'Well, we may hope that they will supply you with guns. Is that not a means to an end? Incidentally, on this subject, you were telling me why you are not able to approach your friends among the Japanese, who, I would remind you, are also foreigners for all you seem to treat them as paragons.'

'The Japanese are different. They come from the same racial stock as us. How can you say they are like the hairy western barbarians? But I do not like to be reminded of that time.'

'Why not? It is no disgrace to be made a prisoner in war. And it seems that you learned much from your captivity. I have been impressed by the military techniques you are adopting. If you made friends among your captors, as apparently you did, then perhaps there would be no reason to treat with Iron Man Wang and the Russians. Surely, some of them are corruptible. Most people are.'

'I told you, the Japanese are honourable. He would never lower himself to smuggle—'

'He? Ah, yes, the officer who ransomed you. The mysterious captain. What was his name? You once told me of his kindness to you.'

Major Lin, for all the shaking of the palanquin, was sitting at rigid attention, his face a fiercer mask than usual. His voice was tight and formal when he spoke. 'Please, Da Ren, I do not like to be reminded of those times. I will assist you with Iron Man Wang, or obey any other commands you give me. I am a soldier and will do my duty. I am sorry if I said anything that was disrespectful, or doubted your wisdom in any way.'

The Mandarin smiled. 'Your secrets are your own, Major. But get me my guns. That is a command . . . Now what is it? One disturbance after another.'

One of Lin's soldiers was running by the palanquin, his head bobbing at the window as he kept pace. 'A foreign devil, Excellency. Foreign devil on a horse, Excellency. Wants to talk, Excellency. Sorry, Excellency.'

'The insolence.' Lin's lip curled angrily. 'Don't worry, Da Ren. I will deal with this outrage. Get me my horse,' he ordered the running man.

'No, stop the palanquin,' said the Mandarin. 'We will meet him.'

Major Lin looked as if he was about to protest, then he leaned out of the palanquin, giving the order to the bearers to stop and deposit their load. One or two bystanders looked on curiously, until Major Lin instructed his men to ring the area to allow some privacy for the meeting. After a moment the European was brought forward. The Mandarin stepped out of the palanquin. 'This is not the normal procedure for an audience,' he said. 'How can I assist you?'

'Liu Daguang, Da Ren,' said Manners, clicking his heels and holding his hat to his breast. 'And Major Lin Fubo. I hope that you will forgive my impropriety in thus interrupting your progress. I applied for an audience at the *yamen* but was rejected, and I tried to come up to you both before you left the execution ground, but the crowd was too thick. I wanted to introduce myself. I'm Henry Manners. New with the railway.'

'And?' asked the Mandarin, after a pause. 'Now you have introduced yourself. Was there anything else?'

'Well, nothing really pressing for the moment,' replied Manners, 'but I did think it important to pay my respects as early as possible after my arrival.'

'The doctor Ai Dun usually keeps me satisfactorily informed of railway affairs. Is there a reason why I should receive another railway functionary? Apart from the pleasure of your acquaintance, of course.'

'In a new environment a man is wise to seek relationships of mutual benefit, Da Ren.'

'Mutual benefit?'

'Oh, I would certainly hope so.'

His laughing eyes looked directly into the Mandarin's, who held his gaze. The two of them seemed to be weighing each other.

Major Lin could not contain himself. 'The impertinence of this barbarian, Da Ren. We should be taking this one for a whipping at the *yamen* as well.'

'I'm afraid I can't really whip the other one either, whatever I told the crowd, because of the extra-territoriality laws,' said the

Mandarin. 'But as for this one, I think I rather like his impertinence. It shows courage. You are welcome in Shishan, Ma Na Si Xiansheng. Please tell me when you believe we can be of mutual assistance. Call on my chamberlain for an audience.'

'That I will, Da Ren. Thank you.'

'There is really nothing more you have to say to me? That's all you wanted? To introduce yourself? Then I will bid you farewell.'

'There was just one thing, Da Ren.'

The Mandarin turned on the step of the palanquin.

'Yes?'

'A message for Major Lin, actually, from an old friend. Colonel Taro Hideyoshi. He's been promoted, Major. Sends his warm respects. He's posted at the Japanese Legation in Peking. Very much looking forward to seeing his old friend again. "In peace as in war," he asked me to say, and gave me a letter of introduction. Here, sir.'

'Well, take it, Major,' said the Mandarin. Lin seemed frozen to the spot. 'Indeed, Ma Na Si Xiansheng, this is most coincidental. Major Lin and I were only discussing his old friend from that regrettable war a moment ago.'

'Colonel Taro talks about Major Lin all the time, Da Ren. Speaks of him as his own brother. So much wants to restore the old relationship. And he's asked me to help Major Lin in any way I can.'

'And what sort of help would that be?'

'That would depend, Da Ren, on whatever Major Lin's requirement might be. The help could be very substantial, Colonel Taro told me, and involve only the most moderate terms.'

'I don't understand what this man is insinuating,' spat Lin.

'Oh, I think I do,' said the Mandarin. 'How strange that you and I were only just discussing how useful it would be if you renewed your contacts with your old friends.'

'If only Major Lin and I could meet in more leisurely, and perhaps less conspicuous, circumstances, I would be able to explain in much more detail what his old friend is suggesting,' said Manners.

'It is strange that he sends an Englishman as his emissary.'

'If you would like to check my records with the railway board, you will discover that I have spent many years in Japan training the Japanese officers. I, too, have been a soldier, Major Lin, and like you have lived . . . shall I say intimately? among the Japanese. I have also formed strong friendships. And is it not friendship that brings us all together today?'

'I am certain that Major Lin will be delighted to discuss these matters of friendship further with you. I would suggest tomorrow evening at the Palace of Heavenly Pleasure. Is that agreed, Major? Excellent. Well, what an interesting meeting it has been.'

Manners bowed, and the Mandarin climbed into his palanquin.

'Before you go, Englishman. I have a question for you.' The Mandarin leaned his head out of the carriage. 'When the crowd became unruly at the execution, were you not afraid?'

'Why should I fear when the Mandarin himself was there to impose order?'

'And if I chose to encourage the anti-foreign sentiments of my people?'

'Then I would trust myself to the wisdom of the Mandarin and his ability to recognise who among the foreigners are China's friends.'

'There are some who believe that none of the ocean devils can be China's friends.'

'As long as the Mandarin rules in Shishan, then I take comfort in his discernment and protection.'

'As long as I rule? Is there a suggestion that I might not continue to do so?'

'I am confident that you will rule for ten thousand years,' said Manners, with a smile.

The Mandarin laughed. Then he tapped the side of the palanquin, giving the bearers the instruction to lift the poles and continue on their way.

Major Lin was dumb with restrained fury for the rest of the ride, and the Mandarin himself was silent and thoughtful. He only broke the silence once to remark, 'I have always prided myself on my ability to identify a brigand or a corruptible man. It is intriguing to see the English version. I think you will have an interesting dinner, Major. Make sure that all the comforts of the house are provided. Let your Fan Yimei entrance him with her music.'

It was a good thing that the Mandarin closed his eyes at this point, because Major Lin's twisted and bitter expression could on no account be described as respectful.

* * *

Ever since the merchant, Lu Jincai, had given the letter to her, Fan Yimei had been in a quandary. He had slipped it to her surreptitiously, stumbling against her when the two had passed each other in the courtyard. 'Take this for Shen Ping,' he had whispered, pretending to be drunk and steadying himself by resting a hand on her shoulder. 'I know that even the trees in this place have eyes and ears. You are her friend. Read it and you will know what to do.' And, singing loudly, he had tottered on his way.

Fan Yimei, the letter burning in her bosom, had passed a suspicious Mother Liu, who was standing in the doorway watching Lu leave. 'What did that man say to you?' Mother Liu asked.

'Nothing. Only something lewd. He was drunk,' Fan Yimei had answered.

Mother Liu grunted. 'Why are you not with Major Lin?' she asked.

'He wants another pitcher of wine,' she had told her, truthfully.

'He will drink away my profits, that man,' said Mother Liu. 'Go on. Go and get it, then. Give him one of the watered pitchers. He won't know the difference at this time of night.' And mercifully she had let her pass without further questioning.

Fan Yimei dared not open the letter until Major Lin was asleep. He had been angry and brutal all evening, hunched on his chair and drinking with ferocity, barely touching his food. She had asked him what had happened today to make him so morose, but he had only grunted in reply, ordering her to refill his cup. She had attempted to play his favourite tunes on the *chin*, but he had hurled a cushion at her, and told her curtly to stop. Later, well into the second pitcher, when the drink had taken hold and his words were becoming slurred and incoherent, he began to curse the Mandarin, and the foreign devils, and Iron Man Wang and guns. Once he became violent, pulling her dress by the collar so that it restricted her neck and yelling in her face the baffling threat that if she so much as looked at an Englishman he would kill her. He had immediately become overcome by a fit of sobs, nuzzling his face in her shoulder, and repeating something over and over that sounded like 'Tarosama. Tarosama.' It had all made little sense to her. She had finally steered him towards the bed. He had clung to her like a frightened child. After a while he began the first fumblings of drunken lovemaking. She did the best she could, turning over on her stomach and offering him the dog's position, which she knew he preferred when he was in this state, but the drink had taken away his manhood. She whipped him with the willow twig but it did no good. Eventually he fell asleep.

It was only then that she had looked at the letter Lu had passed to her. It was addressed to Shen Ping with De Falang's name inscribed below. Holding it close to the candlelight she ran her eyes quickly over the neat calligraphy (she guessed it was in Lu Jincai's hand). It was elegantly composed, flatteringly written, but the message was uncompromising. A red envelope was enclosed in the folds of the letter. She did not open it. She did not want to know what price had been put on the end of her friend's hopes.

She knew that Shen Ping was not in any state yet to be shown such a letter. She had barely recognised her when, two days after her beating, she had been allowed by Mother Liu into the punishment hut to see her friend. She imagined that the only reason why she had been given such an extraordinary privilege was because Mother Liu had been afraid that this time Ren Ren had gone too far and had doubts whether Shen Ping would recover from her torture. She probably calculated that a visit by a friend might revive whatever spirits she had left.

Fan Yimei had to prise open one of the shutters to allow even a ray of light into the dark room, which stank of blood and human ordure. She noticed manacles and chains on one of the walls, and in a corner the coiled snake of a whip and various unidentifiable metal instruments. Shen Ping was curled under a blanket on a straw mat. Her face was a pulp of bruises and cuts. When Fan Yimei moved near her, she whimpered and tried to roll away. It took some time for Fan Yimei to calm her and was only sure that her friend recognised her when a broken claw of a hand emerged from the blanket and hesitantly stroked her face. Then it was all that Fan Yimei could do to restrain her own heaving sobs.

Mother Liu had allowed her to bring a bucket of water and a container of chicken soup. 'Get the bitch cleaned and fed. I'm holding you responsible,' she had instructed. Fan Yimei had to dip a handkerchief into the soup and gently squeeze the liquid through Shen Ping's torn, cracked lips, but even so her friend could only manage a few mouthfuls without choking. Fan Yimei gently lifted the blanket. She had to be careful because in parts it was glued to the body by caked blood. She nearly retched when she saw the lacerated back and the damage to the lower torso and loins. It took nearly an hour to clean her but even so Shen Ping screamed and hissed with pain. Fan Yimei wept and persisted. When it was over she cradled her friend's head in her lap. Shen Ping only spoke once. Fan Yimei had to put her ear close to the broken mouth to hear. 'He'll come?' was the rattling sound. 'De Falang will come?'

'Oh, yes, my dearest,' Fan Yimei had lied through her tears. 'Oh, yes.'

'Then that's all right,' Shen Ping had breathed, and closed her eyes and slept.

Mother Liu had been waiting outside the hut when Fan Yimei emerged.

'How is she?' she asked.

'She needs a doctor,' said Fan Yimei.

'She'll get a doctor. You'll not breathe a word about this, do you hear? Remember, this could happen to you, too, if you disobey – with or without your protector.'

That night they had moved Shen Ping to a room off one of the courtyards. Fan Yimei was allowed to visit her over the following days. Shen Ping had received some rudimentary treatment. Her wounds had been bandaged and Fan Yimei could smell the pungent odour of salves. On the second day she developed a burning fever and Fan Yimei was told to sit with her until the danger was past. She had not been impressed by the doctor, a man called Zhang Erhao who worked at the foreign doctor's hospital and whom she had once entertained before she was bound to Major Lin, a coarse, boastful man who was on good terms with Ren Ren. Mother Liu had brought him in when the fever was at its height. He had fiddled with the patient, clearly at a loss as to what to prescribe. He seemed more interested in Fan Yimei until Mother Liu had told him she belonged to Major Lin. He had then left with instructions that more blankets be piled on the patient. Fan Yimei ignored him. Remembering the night of her father's death and how the foreign woman in black had patiently sponged his burning body, she did the same for her friend through the long night, and in the morning the fever had broken.

Shen Ping now seemed to be on the road to recovery, although she was still weak, and sometimes Fan Yimei feared that her spirit and self-respect would never recover. Searching the listless eyes in the bruised face, she saw no sign of the cheerful, chattering farm-girl she had once known. The only time she ever showed any interest was when Fan Yimei talked of De Falang, and then she would hold her friend's hand tightly, and whisper, 'Has he come?' Fan Yimei, hating herself, found herself inventing stories that Shen Ping's lover had called at the brothel and asked after her, and been told by Mother Liu that she was unwell but he would be able to see her when she was better. She found herself embroidering the story, telling Shen Ping that Mother Liu had tried to offer him another girl, but that he had refused angrily and stormed off. That was the only time Shen Ping had smiled. Fan Yimei told herself that it might have been true: she had heard that De Falang's friend, Lu Jincai, had been questioning some of the girls about Shen Ping; and maybe he would one day come for her himself; but in her heart, as each day passed, she had feared the worst, and now, holding the letter in her hand, she knew the truth.

The matter lay on her mind all the next day, prevailing even over the startling news that Major Lin had flung casually over his shoulder as he was dressing. He was bad-tempered and hung-over when he woke, early as usual. As he straightened his uniform in front of the mirror he shouted commands to her to have a banquet prepared in the pavilion at sunset, expensive food, good wine, he would be bringing a guest; oh, yes, and tell Mother Liu to provide one of her better-looking floozies; he had left written instructions on the table. This in itself was unprecedented – he had never entertained before – but what he said as he left amazed her: 'And make sure you wear something modest,' he told her. 'I don't care what he does to the other trollop, but I'm not having a foreign devil ogling you.'

'A foreign devil?' she asked. 'De Falang?' She could not believe it.

'No, not that ape. Another one.'

'But you hate foreign devils.'

'Yes. So, don't talk about it. I want this kept quiet.'

'Do I tell Mother Liu?'

'No. Yes, I suppose she'll have to know. But tell her to be discreet.' And he was gone.

With a heavy heart, she sought out Mother Liu to make the arrangements. Mother Liu as usual grumbled about the expense, but surprisingly she was not angry. In fact, she smiled as she slowly read Major Lin's note then tucked it into her gown. 'He can have Su Liping,' she said, naming one of the prettier, younger girls, whom Fan Yimei knew she normally reserved for more favoured clients and who was one of her few favourites. This was perhaps due to her reputation for being one of Mother Liu's tell-tales. 'I don't think little Liping's tasted barbarian meat before but there's a first time for everyone. Only the best for Major Lin and his guests. Well, go on. What are you standing staring for? Go and see to that sick slut of yours. I want her well and back to work. All this medicine and coddling is costing me money.'

Mercifully Shen Ping was asleep when Fan Yimei reached her room, and this gave her an excuse for putting off the decision to tell her about the letter. 'When she's better,' she told herself, looking down at the sleeping head on the pillow. 'Then I'll tell her. When she's strong. It will break her if I tell her now.' But part of her wondered whether her friend would ever be able to bear the news. It was only the thought that De Falang would rescue her that was keeping her alive now. And what sort of work would Mother Liu put her to when she did get well? She had heard stories that other girls who had been punished by Ren Ren had later been sent to the squalid rooms that he was rumoured to keep behind his dumpling shop to provide cheap services for muleteers and carters, and other riff-raff of the town. If she could only get a message to De Falang and tell him the true situation. Might he reconsider? This foreigner who was coming tonight must know him. If he could deliver a letter to De Falang? She could write it today.

She sat at her desk in the afternoon, and covered a page with her neat characters. She wrote about Shen Ping's continued loyalty to De Falang through her suffering. She wrote of how it was only the thought of him that gave her the will to live. She wrote that if De Falang were to understand her true feelings then surely he would put aside whatever misunderstanding had turned him against her. She begged him, as Shen Ping's friend, to make every attempt to come to her. If only he could see her in her piteous state . . . If only . . . what? Long before she finished she realised it was useless. Sadly she put down the brush. Even if she could find a way to deliver this letter, she knew it would do no good. What did she expect of De Falang or any man? Who listened to the crying of a whore? Caged birds had more freedom. At least people loved them for their song. Who really loved a sing-song girl? De Falang had sounded sincere but he was probably only fantasising, as some men liked to do, and now he had come to himself, that was all. She had his letter. She knew that one day Major Lin would tire of her. Why was she allowing herself to dream as Shen Ping had dreamed? Oh, why did she not have the courage to finish it all? She put her head on the desk and sighed.

She heard footsteps outside, and quickly brushed the unfinished letter as well as De Falang's letter into a drawer. She had no time to lock it, but she was sure that she had not been seen and was standing composed in the centre of the room when Su Liping entered.

'Liping, it's so early. I was not expecting—'

'Oh, Elder Sister, I couldn't resist,' chattered Su Liping. 'All of us are so jealous of your wonderful fortune, and I wanted to see your beautiful pavilion. Oh, how lucky you are. Mother Liu said I could come early. I'm so excited that this evening they've chosen me. Oh, what beautiful silks and furnishings.'

She moved quickly round the room, touching a vase here, a carving there, running her hands over the strings of the *chin*, pressing her cheek against the brocade. 'Mother Liu says that if the guest wants me I can take him to the pavilion opposite. It's still being prepared but I've heard it's just like this. Oh, what a beautiful bed. And the mirror! Oh, to live here.'

'You don't mind if it's a barbarian?'

'Well, it's scary, but sort of exciting.' She giggled. 'And I've heard that foreign devils are very well endowed. Hope it doesn't hurt. Do you think I should take along a pot of grease? Anyway, Shen Ping was happy with her foreigner, wasn't she? Poor Shen Ping. So ill, I've heard.'

She moved close to Fan Yimei, and whispered, wide-eyed, 'Is it true, do you think?'

'What's true?'

'That she was punished. In that hut. Punished by Ren Ren for doing something awful?'

'I don't know,' said Fan Yimei.

'I bet you do. You're her friend and the only one allowed to see her. But never mind, I know you don't gossip. I listen to all the gossip. Strange, strange things happen here. Do you know what's the latest rumour? There's a new catamite being kept in the hidden rooms upstairs. For Ren Ren. A foreign boy. Would you believe it? I'm not sure that I do, but can you imagine?'

'You're right. I don't like to gossip. I'm sorry.'

'Oh, don't be sorry. I don't care. The interesting thing is, a foreign boy did disappear. Some people were executed yesterday for murdering him. We watched from the window. But what if it's the same boy? Quite a coincidence, don't you think?'

Fan Yimei heard a voice calling her from outside.

'Oh, Elder Sister, it sounds like Mother Liu. Quick, you'd better go. I'll be all right. Don't worry about me.'

Fan Yimei, conscious of the letters in the drawer, did not like to leave Su Liping alone in the room, but she had no choice. Mother Liu wanted to check the arrangements for the evening, and subjected Fan Yimei to an exhaustive and time-wasting catechism about the menu.

By the time she returned, Su Liping was luxuriating on the bed. 'I hope the bed in the other room has a mirror,' she said. 'Imagine being able to watch yourself doing it! You're so lucky, Elder Sister. And Major Lin's so handsome.'

'Su Liping, you're very welcome, but Major Lin may come back before the dinner . . .'

'I'm off. I'm off,' giggled the girl, jumping from the bed. 'Oh, thank you, Elder Sister, for allowing me to be with you this evening. I'm so looking forward to it.'

The drawer in which the letters had been lying was empty. Fan Yimei sat numbly on the stool looking at the space where they had been. She did not move until the servants came in to lay the dinner. Then she moved listlessly to the side room to change.

A part of her recognised that Lin's guest, for a foreigner, was handsome. He was tall and strong-limbed, with a courteous manner and blue eyes that sometimes laughed and at other times looked deeply and knowledgeably into hers, as if he was trying to read her mind. He was the same type of man as Lin, a soldier, but she detected much more strength of character, and she hoped that he was a friend of Lin because she thought he would make a formidable enemy. She thought these thoughts idly as she sat in front of her *chin*, automatically playing the music Lin liked, barely conscious of what she was doing. She was composed, almost ethereal. She was not afraid. What would come would come.

At the beginning of the evening, when Lin and the foreigner were deep in conversation, she had found a moment to ask Su Liping why she had stolen the letters from the drawer. She was not angry. She was interested only intellectually. She did not think she bore a grudge against the girl.

Su Liping had avoided her eyes, and answered sullenly, 'Mother Liu told me to search the room. She always has me spy for her. I took them because they looked unusual.'

'But why do you do it? Spy for her, I mean.'

'Oh, Elder Sister, she said that she would send me with Ren Ren to the hut. I don't want what happened to Shen Ping to happen to me.'

'Did you not think that it might happen to me?'

Su Liping looked up, momentary hatred in her eyes. 'It won't happen to you,' she hissed scornfully. 'You're protected. So beautiful. So talented. So perfect.'

'I'm sorry you hate me so,' said Fan Yimei. 'Tell me,' she said. 'Did you keep the red packet? The one with the money in it? Did you give that to Mother Liu with the letters?'

Su Liping's eyes widened with fear.

'Don't worry,' said Fan Yimei. 'I won't tell. But hide it. They *will* take you to the hut if they find it. Go on now. Don't worry. Pour the foreigner some more wine. Enjoy the evening. Drink a bit yourself. It helps.'

Major Lin was a stiff host. Fan Yimei could tell how at first he was trying to conceal his dislike of the foreigner, and how resentful he was that he was in the position that he had to hold a dinner for him. She guessed that he was under orders from his superiors, perhaps the Mandarin. The stranger, however, had the grace and charm to put even as prickly a person as Major Lin at ease. He was flattering and deferential. Over dinner he led Major Lin to talk about subjects that interested him, military matters about tactics and armaments, which Fan Yimei could barely follow. The man listened attentively as Lin expounded on his theories, and when he spoke himself it was with a knowledge and assurance that made Lin himself listen with concentration, recognising an expert in the field. Su Liping tried hard to catch the foreigner's attention using all the wiles in her meagre experience, resting a hand on his thigh and smiling archly whenever he looked in her direction. The foreigner smiled back indulgently, but largely ignored her, concentrating on Lin. There was a lot of talk about Japan, and towards the end of the meal the conversation seemed to focus on a mutual friend, called Taro. It surprised her that Lin even knew a Japanese, but then she remembered his enigmatic whimper of the night before when he was in his cups: 'Tarosama. Tarosama.' She wondered how intimately Lin had known the man. At one point, when the foreigner was speaking about 'the samurai virtues' he seemed to start and look angry, but the foreigner laughed and said he was only talking about the samurai's loyalty to a friend. What had Major Lin thought he meant? And Major Lin blushed and looked uncomfortable. The foreigner told him that he had invited this Colonel Taro to come to Shishan for a hunting trip, perhaps when the railway was completed, and this also seemed to fill Major Lin with discomfort, although he said politely that he looked forward to seeing him. They were now eating fruit at the end of the meal.

'In my country,' said the foreigner, 'we have a custom. At the end of the meal, we ask the ladies to leave us so the gentlemen can talk business. I'm ignorant of what goes on here, and I'm very conscious of the delicious attentions of this young siren on my left, but do you not think that it might be useful if the two of us were to take a leaf out of the English book and talk, as it were, unencumbered?'

'You can have Su Liping for the night if you want her. She's paid for,' said Major Lin.

'Delicately put,' said the foreigner. 'And I'm very grateful, of course, but I'm afraid I must decline. The lady is very charming but a little young for me, and I do rather like picking my own women.'

'I can get the madam to bring others if you don't like this one.'

Fan Yimei felt the stranger's eyes boring into hers. 'I see at least one exquisite one here already. If this other lady is not your own choice for the night, Major . . . ?'

Fan Yimei sensed danger and said quickly, bowing her head, 'I have the honour of being Major Lin's choice every night, Xiansheng, if he wants me. I belong to Major Lin.'

'I spoke out of ignorance, Major. Forgive me. I congratulate you on your taste, and your good fortune.'

Major Lin acknowledged the compliment. 'She is a plain woman but she serves.' Fan Yimei was pleased to hear the faint note of smugness. She had been afraid that he would have been angered. 'She plays adequately on the *chin*, Ma Na Si Xiansheng. May I suggest that if you wish to talk we can do so while she performs. She will not overhear us. The other one can leave.'

The gauche Su Liping, obviously afraid of Mother Liu's anger if she failed to secure her client, foolishly tried one last wile. 'I know many tricks, Xiansheng,' she whispered, moving her hand to Manners's groin.

'I'm sure you do, my dear.' He smiled, removing her hand.

'Get out!' hissed Lin.

Su Liping, red-faced with shame and embarrassment, ran for the door.

So Fan Yimei was left on her own, playing the mournful music that usually reflected the sadness of her own soul, but tonight left her numb, as everything did while she waited for the inevitable results of Mother Liu discovering the letters. The two men talked confidentially, the foreigner smoking a pungent tobacco rolled in a brown leaf. Occasionally she heard words and phrases, 'sphere of influence', 'guns', 'reliable shipments', 'speedy delivery', 'Japanese', 'guns', 'six to nine months', 'private arrangement', 'Taro will seal the deal', but it meant nothing to her. Nor did she care.

The two men shook hands. She had heard of this strange western custom from Shen Ping. Major Lin's face was red and excited. Whatever business they had done had pleased him. She knew that he would be full of energy tonight and her shoulders slumped at the thought. She did not care. What will come will come.

She stood up ready to bow the foreigner out. She was surprised that he took her hand and kissed it, another strange western custom. She looked up startled and saw his blue eyes, laughing and boring into hers. She looked at Lin in fear but he was smiling his crooked smile, delighted. The two men walked together across the courtyard, Lin the courteous host seeing his guest to the gate. As she stood in the doorway, she sensed a movement out of the darkness. Mother Liu. She felt a sharp pain in her arm as it was gripped by the old woman's hand, the nails pressing into her flesh. 'I should send you to the hut for what you have done,' Mother Liu spat in her ear. 'I won't. Not this time. This new development with the barbarian is much too interesting. I expect you to keep me informed of what is said, though. That stupid hussy was useless. You'll do better.

'It was that merchant who gave you the letter, wasn't it? I should have suspected something then. Lu's not the kind to get drunk. Well, why didn't you deliver it? Scared of the effect?

'Don't worry, my dear, I'm not the person to keep anyone away from their correspondence. Not me. Oh, no. Ren Ren's kindly agreed to deliver it in person. Isn't that kind of him? Little Shen Ping's probably getting to the last paragraph now as we speak . . .'

Fan Yimei felt her heart pound. 'Shen Ping!' she gasped, and twisted her arm away from Mother Liu's grasp. Stumbling on her bound feet, she ran towards the inner courtyard, her blood racing, panting with fear and exertion. She saw the light in Shen Ping's room.

Strong arms grasped her and lifted her from the ground. She struggled violently, screaming, biting, but Ren Ren held her tight to his chest, pulling her head back over his shoulder by her hair. 'Don't even attempt anything or I'll beat your teeth out,' he snarled. 'Let's give the lady time to read her letter, shall we?'

She could hear the wheezing of her own breath in the silent courtyard. Ren Ren held her close, watching the movement of a faint silhouette behind the oil-paper window. After a while, the movement ceased. He continued to wait. Then, satisfied, he dropped his burden on the courtyard pavings, and walked back to the main building, whistling. Fan Yimei lay sobbing on the ground where she had fallen.

In the room, Shen Ping let the letter fall from her broken fingers. Under the bruises there was a dreamy smile on her face. For a long while, it seemed, she lay on her back, thinking of nothing in particular. Then slowly, very slowly – she did not mind the pain any more – she lifted herself off the bed. She crawled along the floor to the chair in the middle of the room. It was with great difficulty that she pulled herself up on to it, and she fell, she could not count how many times, before eventually she stood nearly upright on the chair. At least she did not have to fling the sash over the beam and tie a noose. She giggled faintly. That was the one kindness Ren Ren had ever done her. The noose was in just the right position for her head. With her useless hands, it took her one or two attempts to tighten it round her neck. She wondered whether she should say something, one last word, to sum up her wasted life. She saw no point. It was as she kicked the chair away and as she was falling, that she thought of the one person in her life who had been kind to her, but as the words 'Fan Yimei' formed in her mind, the noose broke her neck, so no sound ever came.

Chapter Six

There is no work and little food. Lao Tian has gone to join the bandits.

———————

Nobody told Frank Delamere about Shen Ping's suicide. Lu Jincai heard the story next day from Tang Dexin, and they agreed that it would be best if the foreigner was kept in the dark about a matter so distressing and unpleasant. Quickly Lu made arrangements. If De Falang should decide to visit the brothel again and ask for the girl – an unlikely circumstance, he thought – he would be told that she was engaged with another client. A tael of silver to Mother Liu would ensure her silence and the silence of the other girls. Lu Jincai did not want De Falang disturbed before the caravan left for Tsitsihar. He knew how unpredictable his partner could be if excited, and he dared not speculate on what extravagances of guilt and remorse would be occasioned by news of the girl's death. As a further precaution, which cost him another tael, he asked Mother Liu to find a comely replacement who would be willing to entertain his friend should the need arise, but he was in no hurry to take him back to the Palace of Heavenly Pleasure, and he persuaded the other merchants, Tang and Jin, to dine De Falang elsewhere if they had to, for the time being.

So Shen Ping was forgotten. Some of the girls believed that her spirit loitered among the gardens and pavilions. In her misery Fan Yimei was convinced that one night she saw the laughing white face of her friend in the dressing-table mirror but there was only moonlight on the curtains when she turned. To Mother Liu's relief, Shen Ping did not reappear as a fox spirit to wreak vengeance on her enemies and her faithless lover (Frank was never waylaid by any apparition on the road to Babbit and Brenner, nor surprised among his pots of soda crystals by a hungry ghost.) Lighting an incense stick in her shrine for safety's sake, Mother Liu bundled up and burned Shen Ping's few belongings, then gave her cot to a new addition to the stable, a timorous twelve-year-old from Tieling who was recovering from the double agonies of having her feet broken and bound and nightly visits by Ren Ren. Shen Ping's name was never spoken again. After a while only Fan Yimei felt her presence, but as time passed it became fainter and fainter even for her. Then one evening as she was tending a bonfire of fallen leaves in a corner of the garden, she suddenly sensed that her friend was ready to leave. Fan Yimei whispered half-remembered prayers as she shovelled leaves into the flames and if anybody saw the tears in her eyes they would have attributed them to the heat and smoke of the fire, but she was at peace when she walked away, believing – or choosing to believe – that her friend's soul was now at peace among the clouds.

That evening long wisps of pink nimbus did indeed float in the heavens like the trailing sleeves of a sky fairy's dress. If the spirit of Shen Ping had been elevated to the clouds as Fan Yimei hoped, then, looking down, she would have seen a Shishan also apparently at peace. The gold of the setting sun reflected a gilded countryside. Autumn had lingered longer than usual, as if it sought to delay the coming of winter and the uncertainties of a new century. The farmyards were still carpeted with grain from the second harvest; heavy wheels of passing mule carts crushed the stalks on the roads; farmers stood silhouetted with their flails against the gold on the threshing floor. Meanwhile the acrid scent of burning haystacks hung in the chill, clear air, mingling with the smell of apples and persimmons in the orchards. Leaves swirled and blew across the fields, piling against the hedgerows and glinting in the pale sunshine, sheathing the landscape in copper. A handsome young man and a trimly dressed young woman, foreigners, were riding through the lanes, pausing to admire a ruined shrine. A man of poetic sensibility, like Herr Fischer, would have drawn parallels with some classical Arcadia or golden age.

The bucolic scene around Shishan was the only bright island, however, in an otherwise grey sea of desolation. The rainclouds that usually gathered on the peaks of the Black Hills had harvested enough moisture over the year to spare the western counties of Manchuria from the drought that was ravaging other parts of north China – but little rain had fallen elsewhere. In a dry swathe that stretched from Shantung in the east through the whole province of Chih-li, to Shansi in the west, and even to the edges of Mongolia, famine raged. Frank Delamere's merchant friends gathered in Jin Shangui's counting-house discussing the horrible rumours, brought to them by the mule trains, that over vast tracts of China families were boiling tree bark for sustenance, that the old and young were dying in hundreds, that there had been instances of cannibalism, that whole populations were deserting their villages to hunt for food, and that desperate young men were turning to the Boxers, blaming the foreigners for the disasters.

The foreigners, as usual, were largely oblivious to the threat. The consular circulars that the doctor received from the Legation in Peking were reassuring (droughts and famines were not uncommon in China, he was told), and the members of the small foreign community were busy enough anyway in their own little world not to think too much about what was happening outside it. Like picnickers on a ridge watching with unconcern the darkness of a thunderstorm brewing miles away across a plain, they contemplated the troubles in the south with equanimity.

Yet rumours of Boxer activities never quite went away; indeed, they intensified as the famine spread, and there was a week in early October when it was reported that Boxer groups from some mountain villages in Shantung had formed their own militias and attacked a town. The Boxer army, it was said, would wash like the tide over the Chih-li plain and sweep the foreigners into the sea. For a few days there was tension, even in Shishan. In the event, however, it was a nine-day wonder. The uprising, if such it could be called, was quelled easily by Imperial troops – actually it was more a police action than a battle. The victory over this rag-tag militia, however, caused great satisfaction among the Legations in Peking, and there was some noisy celebration when the news reached Babbit and Brenner's and the railway camp. The common wisdom was that this decisive action on the part of Viceroy Yu had nipped the shoots of rebellion in the bud. The Boxer menace, if it had ever existed, was now firmly squashed. Subsequent reports, however, revealed that this optimism was somewhat premature. The conservative Viceroy Yu, it appeared, not only secretly sympathized with the malcontents but had gone so far as to employ some of the most notorious of them in his *Yamen*. The *North China Herald* thundered for his removal, and it was reported that Sir Claude MacDonald had made an official protest to the *Tsungli Yamen*.

Dr Airton was much too excited to be worrying about events happening so far away. He had called at the *Yamen* a few days after the execution of Hiram's murderers, fully intending to reproach the Mandarin and give him a piece of his mind. The wind had been taken out of his sails when the Mandarin himself apologised for the inelegant way in which the doctor had been informed, blaming his clerks for their insensitive application of procedure. He explained that the personal letter, which the Mandarin himself had drafted, had not been sent and instead the doctor had received merely an official form. He regretted any disrespect that this slight might have implied. Airton hardly heard what he was saying. All his attention was focused on the large Chinese language Holy Bible that lay on the tea table between them.

'Ah, you have noticed that I am studying your Holy Book,' smiled the Mandarin. 'It is a curious work. I see many parallels with the Analects and some with Buddhist writings, particularly in the more philosophical passages. The emphasis on love is interesting, and on the sacrifice of your god. In one of the early incarnations of the Lord Buddha, he allowed himself to be eaten by some tiger cubs because they were hungry. Your Jesus's undignified crucifixion probably had some similar purpose. You can explain it to me, perhaps. I also have one or two questions that I would like you to answer on the issue of forgiveness. There seems to be a discrepancy between what Christians aspire to and how they behave. I ask this as a magistrate who has to interpret the extra-territoriality laws. Perhaps you will explain to me how the implacable penalties that the Chinese government is bound to pay after the most minor infraction of foreign terms relate to these Christian teachings of forbearance?'

Airton could hardly breathe for sheer joy. He had achieved, unexpectedly, his ambition in coming to China. Here was a member of the mandarin class – a Confucian, a pagan, but a man of enormous influence – who was reading the Bible and seeking to understand its precepts. To what might this lead? he wondered. The Mandarin's first questions were sceptical – even cynical – as was only to be expected, but it was a start. The start of which he and his fellow missionaries had always dreamed.

That first meeting was followed by another two days later, and after a time the doctor and the Mandarin had settled into a regular routine. The Mandarin liked to take a parable at a time, and in each case would apply his most rigorous logic to penetrate the message behind it. The doctor would reel out of each challenging session as exhausted in body and mind as he had been after the games of squash he had played at university as a boy. He never knew where the Mandarin's ball would come from.

By a tacit agreement, neither mentioned the death of Hiram again nor the execution that had followed it. The subject of Boxers or bandits rarely came into their conversation, and if it did it was smiled away. For the doctor, the Mandarin's questions appeared to have become more and more abstruse. He seemed fascinated by the Christian concept of goodness, asking how it differed from the virtues enunciated by Confucius. If a ruler really had the benefit of his subjects at heart, he would ask, then should it matter if he achieved his virtuous ends by foul means? Was a reward in heaven denied if a Christian strayed from the restrictive Ten Commandments? Were the certain rewards of this earth really worth sacrificing for only the promise of salvation? If Christianity was the gentle religion that the good Daifu made it out to be, then why were its precepts so fanatical and absolute? Not that he wished to offend in any way the Son of God, but was not this Jesus a little unworldly, perhaps? And please could the doctor explain how the powers of the West had managed to conquer the world if their principles consisted only of loving their neighbours and turning the other cheek.

'This rendering unto Caesar what is Caesar's and unto God what is God's,' the Mandarin would say, 'is all very well. In our system it is much simpler, since our emperor happens to be a god. Why did not your Jesus, who had, if I am to understand the other tale of His encounter with the Devil on a mountain, the power to rule the wrold, take on Himself the authority of Caesar? If He had He would not have had to worry about this untidy problem of free will.'

'Ah, but, Da Ren, don't you see? It is in the fact that He gave us free will that we have our salvation.'

'If He had worked in a *yamen* instead of strolling around the hillsides, He might have had a better understanding of ignorant human nature. In my experience, free will is only a curse, leading to the most outrageous forms of behaviour if one leaves it unchecked. I do not believe that this Jesus could have loved His people if He set them such impossibly high demands.'

'But Jesus was the God of Love,' exclaimed Airton.

'So you say,' muttered the Mandarin, biting into a peach.

But the doctor was not disheartened. On the contrary, hope gleamed in his eyes. Sometimes he even dared to wonder whether the Mandarin was at last beginning to question his own cynical principles. As soon as he detected such a thought, of course, he immediately repressed it as fanciful or over-optimistic. No, this new interest in the Christian religion was only academic; nothing in the Mandarin's manner revealed anything other than his usual bland curiosity; if there were spiritual yearnings churning behind the hooded eyes and sardonic, worldly expression, they remained concealed. Yes, yes, but on the other hand, the irrepressible voice shouted from inside, here was a high official of the mandarin class seriously asking questions about the Gospel! It hadn't happened for years! And he *must* have been reading his copy of the Holy Bible, which he, Airton, had inspired him to acquire! His natural sense of modesty struggled vainly with his ambition. He was pitifully aware of his own limitations, of course, but he could not be blind to the potential. If curiosity led to understanding, could understanding not lead to desire, and desire to conversion? Virtue lay not in himself – he was a humble Scottish doctor who practised medicine and liked cowboy books, no theologian he, certainly not, but the Lord had been known to fill the humblest vessel with His light, and work His wonders with the weakest of clay. A conversion of a mandarin could lead to the conversion of a district: St Augustine's conversion of England had begun with the baptism of a minor Saxon king; in China where Matteo Ricci and his army of Jesuits had failed, could humble Airton of Shishan not be the one . . . At which stage the doctor would chew firmly on his pipe and tell himself not to be so preposterous and vainglorious – but that did not stop him spending feverish evenings in his study with volumes of Plato, Aquinas and Boethius, which he had not looked at since his university days, and rushing out of his door to the *yamen* on the days of his appointments scarcely finishing his lunch.

The other foreign residents of Shishan were unaware of the doctor's preoccupations. Helen Frances and Henry Manners went out riding every afternoon. Frank Delamere and Tom Cabot were feverishly preparing for the great expedition that would make their fortunes.

A late October evening found them in the Babbit and Brenner godown locking up for the night. They had made a final check of the bundles of samples and provisions they were to load the following day on to the mules that would carry them to Tsitsihar and their appointment with Mr Ding. The last line of salmon pink was fading on the far horizon. A night wind started to blow. 'That's the last of it, old boy,' muttered Frank, his pipe thrust firmly under the moustache in the florid face, the kindly brown eyes watering with amusement at one of his prospective son-in-law's jokes – Tom seemed to have an inexhaustible supply of comic stories. 'One last night in the comforts of hearth and home. Then it's the wide open spaces for us. How I love this life. And what a joy it is to me that you and my little Helen Frances will soon be joining together. I'm a lucky man. A lucky man.'

'We'd better set off, sir, if we're to meet HF at the crossroads,' said Tom, bringing the horses. 'Henry said they'd get there shortly after dark.'

'Ho there!' called out Frank. 'Is that you, my dear?'

A lantern was bobbing along the road that led from the direction of the railway camp, slowly drawing nearer to where Tom and he were waiting on the crossroads. He could faintly hear the clopping of horses' hoofs. He sensed Tom reaching quietly for the rifle in the side holster. Tom was right, of course, to take precautions. One never knew nowadays who might be out there in the night.

'Ho there!' he called again. 'Manners! Helen Frances! Is that you?'

There was no answer, but a wind was blowing strongly and his voice might well have been carried away in the wrong direction.

'I'm sure it is them, Tom,' he said. 'After all, who else could it be? Dashed late, though. Wonder where they've been.'

'Apparently there's a ruined temple about six miles south of the rail camp,' said Tom.

'Oh, Lord,' groaned Frank. 'Ruined temples. Monasteries. You'd think Manners was some bloody Buddhist or something. Manners! Is that you?' he called. 'Helen Frances!'

Still no answer.

'Don't know why you ever agreed to letting her go on these damn tourist trips in the first place,' grumbled Frank. 'Mrs Airton was decent enough to offer the girl a job in the hospital, and if Manners can afford all this time away from the railway company I don't know why they sent him out here. Not having you getting any ideas, by the way, young man.' He turned to Tom. 'No half-days at Babbit and Brenner.'

'No, sir.' Tom smiled. 'Never expected it.'

'Why don't they get on with it?' muttered Frank. 'Look, tell you what I'm going to do. I'm going to light a lamp. Shouting in this gale doesn't do any damn good. Got one in my pack. Have a nip of whisky at the same time.' Heavily he dismounted from his horse.

'Want any help?' asked Tom.

'No, I'm all right. Not senile yet.'

Tom could hear the older man puffing in the darkness, the tinkling of glass and the gurgle of liquid, then more clinking of metal and glass as Frank began to fiddle with the hurricane lamp. He himself grasped his rifle stock and peered at the bobbing lantern, which he judged to be about a quarter of a mile away and moving very slowly.

'There we have it,' said Frank. 'Be ready in a tick.'

Tom blinked at the sudden blaze of light. Then he heard a cry from Frank, the lamp clattered to the ground and went out. Frank's horse reared, startling his own, which bucked. It was all he could do to stay in the saddle, and inadvertently his finger squeezed the trigger and his gun went off with a flash and a bang. It took some moments for him to bring his nervous mount under control again, then over the horses' snorts he heard Frank whisper, 'Did you see him?'

'See whom?' Tom also felt impelled to whisper.

'The priest,' said Frank. 'The blind fellow. The one who scared Helen Frances. The Boxer priest. The sinister bugger Charlie was telling us about. I saw him sitting in the middle of the road.'

'Where?'

'There. Right under our bloody feet, no eyes in his head but he still looked baleful and menacing. Sort of jumped up when the light went on and crashed into me. Felt cold and flabby when I grabbed him, and he slipped from my grasp like an eel. By then the light was out and the horses were leaping all over the place. Lucky he didn't stick a knife in my ribs, isn't it? Hold on, where's the damn hurricane? Let me get it going again.'

After more puffing and tinkling the lamp was lit. Frank held it high so its beams shone on as wide an area as possible, but the roads and the bare fields on every side were empty.

'Damn, he's got clean away,' said Frank. 'You wouldn't believe it, would you? Makes me think I imagined it.'

'You sure it wasn't some animal, sir? A wild cat? A small deer?'

'No, no, looked like a man. Felt like one. Sort of. And I won't forget the empty eyeholes. Look, Tom, no word to Helen Frances about this, all right? You and I are off to Tsitsihar for a few weeks and I don't want her frightened while we're gone.'

A clatter of hoofs and Henry Manners and Helen Frances rode into the circle of light. Lao Zhao, with the mule and the lantern, followed close behind. Manners had his rifle unslung as did Lao Zhao.

'We heard a shot,' said Manners, surveying the scene, relaxing, holstering his gun. 'What happened?'

'Oh, nothing. You know me,' said Frank heartily. 'Clumsy oaf. Going for my whisky bottle in the saddlepack. Trod on the horse's foot. He reared. One thing led to another. Tom's fingers slipped on his blunderbuss. Bloody French farce, eh? God knows how we're going to manage on the road to Tsitsihar.'

'Father, Tom, are you both all right?' asked Helen Frances, her riding hat awry, eyes wide with concern.

'Right as rain, old girl. Aren't we, Tom?'

'And anyway, we're the ones who've been worried. Where have you been?' asked Tom, leaning from his saddle to peck his fiancée on the cheek. 'HF, we really thought you must have been lost.'

'We saw this glorious temple. There was a tomb and a sort of crenellated wall around a mound. Henry helped me climb up to the top and—'

'Sounds wonderful, darling,' said Tom. 'Thank you, Henry, as always. But we've got to be going. We really must. HF, you know it's the last night in town for your father and me, and we did promise to call in at the doctor's on the way. Henry, will you be going back to the rail camp? Of course you're welcome to ride with us.'

'Don't worry about Lao Zhao and me, old boy. We'll be all right. One Miss Delamere sealed and safely delivered, that's our duty done. You really should come with us one day on these rides. You don't know how you're losing out.'

'Maybe when I get back from Tsitsihar,' said Tom. 'I am grateful, Henry, the way you're looking after her.'

'My pleasure,' said Manners. 'And don't worry about anything while you're away. You know you can trust Lao Zhao and me to continue to—'

'Thanks, Henry,' said Tom, his tone a trifle brittle. 'I know she's in good hands.'

'The very best,' murmured Manners. 'I'm talking about Lao Zhao, of course. Knows the country like a tracker. Every temple and monastery for miles.'

'You mean you're going on more rides while we're away?' asked Frank grumpily. 'How many more damn temples are there to see around this town, anyway? Don't you two get fed up with it all?'

'Oh, Papa,' said Helen Frances irritably.

'Actually, there's going to be a bit of a treat while you're away, Mr Delamere,' said Manners. 'Sorry you two won't be here for it. We'll be blowing the tunnel in the Black Hills and Charlie's arranging a weekend of picnics. I think the Airtons are coming as well.'

'If the Airtons are there, that's fine,' said Frank. 'They're in charge of Helen Frances while Tom and I are gone. That's where she's staying too, by the way. They're her chaperones – not that I trust chaperones, these days. Tom was meant to be her chaperon on the ship coming over here and look what bloody happened with him.'

'Hope you're not disappointed, sir,' said Tom.

'That's an understatement if ever there was one. Still, if I have to marry my daughter off to a gorilla, I might have picked a worse one.' He climbed heavily into his saddle. 'Come on, then, you chaps. Are we going or not? 'Bye, Manners. See you in a month or so. Enjoy your temples. *Om mani padme hom* and all that. I expect you and Helen Frances to be thoroughly enlightened by the time we get back. Living Buddhas at the least. 'Bye.'

'Thank you, Henry, for a lovely day.' Helen Frances reached out her hand and touched the flank of his horse, close to his knee.

'I'll call on you at the Airtons' in a couple of days,' said Manners. 'Have a good journey, Tom. You'll like the hunting up there. Don't worry about Helen Frances.'

Tom turned. 'Why do you keep telling me not to worry about HF, Henry?'

''Bye,' said Manners, saluting with his crop. '*Zoule*, Lao Zhao!' Turning his horse he was quickly swallowed up by the night.

'He doesn't want you to be concerned about me while you're away, that's all,' said Helen Frances, perhaps because she felt somebody had to fill the silence.

'Question is, just what am I not to be concerned about?' said Tom.

'I don't know what you mean,' said Helen Frances, after a while.

'I don't either,' said Tom, after an equal pause. 'Let's forget it, shall we? Tell me about your day with Henry.'

When the party was gone, and Frank's lamp was only a glint in the distance, a figure rose from the ditch by the side of the road. While the sightless eyes gazed expressionlessly in the direction of the vanishing party, the figure moved his right hand to his left shoulder and probed with long fingers into the hole in the flesh made by Tom's gun. A soft mewing sound came from his mouth. After a while he located the crumpled bullet and slowly withdrew it. He held it for a moment in his open palm, then placed it casually in his mouth and swallowed it. Then, picking up his bowl and staff, ignoring his wound, he began to shuffle in the direction of Shishan.

More than ever Helen Frances looked forward to the afternoons with Henry and Lao Zhao, if nothing else as a relaxation from the good behaviour she was expected to show in the presence of Mrs Airton. After the interminable lunches with Nellie and the nuns, she would plead tiredness and wait by the window of her room. Her heart would leap when she saw the horses emerge round the clump of pines and climb the hill toward the mission. By then she would be changed into boots and riding dress, and at the first sound of the doorbell, flush-cheeked, she would step out into the hall where Ah Lee would be waiting with her hat and crop.

Henry would not often come into the house. He would lounge against the porch smoking a cheroot, or squat in the yard with the children, carefully unwrapping his handkerchief to show them a grasshopper or a beetle or whatever he had found for them on his ride over from the camp. As often as not he would reach into his other pocket and produce another handkerchief, and this time unfold an orchid or other wild flower for her to pin on her lapel.

Mrs Airton, who would never fail to be present for their departure, if only to register her disapproval, would offer a sour smile when he extended a similar courtesy to her, and tell him, in her Scottish coo, what a beautiful wee bloom it was and hand it to Ah Lee to put into a jar. She never failed to ask Henry what time exactly he would be returning with Miss Delamere, reminding him that with children in the house supper times were punctual, as indeed was the daily service beforehand, not that young people nowadays observed religion with the punctiliousness that had been expected when she herself was a girl. Henry would invariably disarm her, describing the route he intended to take that day, the sights they would see on the way, assuring her that even if they were unfortunate enough to be late for prayers, he would bring back Helen Frances in time for supper, safe and sound, having worked up an appetite that could only do justice to Mrs Airton's magnificent cooking.

And then, at last, she would be galloping down the hill, wind in her face, blinding her eyes, unravelling her hair, thudding in her ears, Henry laughing and egging on her horse to go faster, wilder, racing her, daring her with his white smile and crinkling eyes, and she would cry out with the joy of being free, delighting in the rhythm of the hot, powerful muscle beneath her, the pulsing blood, the abandonment and the control, kicking with her heels and slashing with her crop. The two horses would pound past the mission and the clump of firs, into the plain and beyond, reining in by the poplars on the road, with Lao Zhao grinning in a cloud of dust as he trotted up behind.

'Well, where to today, now you're flushed and hot and unlady-like?' Henry asked her, one afternoon after one of these gallops, patting the neck of his horse.

'A temple?'

'Sorry. Run out of temples – though I'm still inventing notional ones for Mrs Dragon up there.'

'I don't care where we go, as long as it's away from the Airtons.'

'Och, noo. What a braw ungrateful thing ye are, so discourteous to your poor kind hosts.'

'The doctor's all right, I suppose. Bit of a bore. The children are sweet, funny things. It's Nellie I loathe – and those cheerful nuns.'

She giggled. 'God, those nuns. They're so damned . . . *jolly*.' And she threw back her head and laughed. A curl, loosed from her riding hat, drifted across her cheek and over her eye. Henry reached across and brushed it to the side, his fingers lightly tracing the line of her eyebrow. Startled, she pulled her head away, stiffening, her pupils dilated.

'Your hair. A strand was loose,' he said.

'Thank you,' she muttered. Her cheeks were hot and she wondered if she was blushing.

'All right,' he said, after a moment's silence. 'We'll go for a ride, shall we? I'll take you to the river. Come on.'

As she followed him she thought again, not for the first time, about the choices she might some day have to make.

The issue was much simpler for Lao Zhao, although he kept his own counsel and nobody ever asked him anyway. He was a herdsman who knew the ways of mares and stallions. It had been obvious to him from the beginning, when they had journeyed over the plains to Shishan, that Ma Na Si Xiansheng by asserting his superiority and authority over the other big Englishman, Tom, had secured the right to his red-headed woman who looked like a cat. There had never been a moment on that journey when her eyes had not hungrily followed Ma Na Si's movements, especially when he was mounted on his horse. She had already belonged to him, well before he formally claimed her in public, during those executions in Fuxin, when he had ridden after her bolting horse and taken her in his arms. The only thing that puzzled Lao Zhao was why the two of them had done nothing about it afterwards, except to talk and talk. Every day they rode together he could see the physical desire growing between them, and he would often absent himself out of tact, unnecessarily attending to the horses or pretending to sleep away the afternoon while they strolled round ruins, but as far as he could see they never took advantage of their moments alone with each other. He assumed that it was some English custom or erotic game. Abstinence heightened desire, so perhaps this deliberate delay had the object of making the ultimate lovemaking (for any fool could see that that was where this slow courtship was leading) even more passionate and delicious. He had heard of such techniques – in fact, once, in Mukden, a harlot had teased him for three whole days before finally offering her lotus, and fragrant it was after all the expectation – but he wished all the same that they would hurry up with it. Winter was coming on and he did not relish standing in the snow outside some temple while they dilly-dallied inside.

Today the weather was hot, a last burst of autumn sunshine with only a little breeze; a good day, thought Lao Zhao, picking a morsel of mutton fat from his teeth, for hunting, for riding, for any other kind of sport, and here the two of them were, just talking again. At this rate it would be spring before they got on with it. He didn't care. He was well paid and well fed and this was an easy job. Lucky the man who worked for an ocean devil: they were all pleasantly mad and never knew the value of money. '*Ta made*,' he cursed, and, lazily thwacking his mule, followed them across the fields.

'Henry,' Helen Frances was saying, in a manner she imagined was artful and fashionable, 'it's vexing for a girl – you know how silly and curious we all are – but every time I try to find out something about you you brush it away with a joke.'

'Nonsense. I'm an open book. Transparently in love with you. All adoration. And envy of Tom.'

'There you go. Being foolish. But, admit it, you are a man of mystery. You've never told me anything about yourself.'

'I spend every hour of every day telling you about myself. Answering your questions about life in London, and high so-ci-et-y. "Ooh, Henry, do, do tell me again about Lady Dartmouth's ball," for the hundred and tenth time, or is it the hundred and eleventh?"'

'All right. Laugh at me. But it's true, I don't know anything about you. Except the obvious things.'

'Which are?'

'That you're a wonderful rider. And witty. And handsome. And . . . and . . .'

'And what?'

'And good to me. Kind to me.'

'And are you kind to me in return?' he asked lightly.

'Yes,' she said. 'As a friend. As Tom's friend.'

'And if Tom were not my friend, would you still be kind? How kind would you be if neither of us had ever met Tom?'

'I am sure that we would be friends.'

'Only friends? Come, Helen Frances, tell me, if there had never been a Tom, how kind would you be then?'

'Are you flirting, Mr Manners? How kind would you want me to be?'

'Oh, I'd want you to be very kind,' said Henry quietly. His face was suddenly serious. 'But tell me, Tom's fiancée, you said you wanted to know more about me. All right. What do you want to know?'

'You promise not to make another joke? You'll really tell me?'

'Try me. Go on.'

'All right.' Her green eyes flashed defiantly. 'Why was it that you left the Horse Guards and joined an engineering regiment in India?'

Henry seemed to be concentrating on the way his horse was picking its path through the millet stubble. A straggle of thin sheep grazed in a corner of the field, the afternoon sunlight slanting on their fleeces. A kestrel and a magpie were competing for territory in the sky.

'Why don't you speak?' asked Helen Frances.

'I'm wondering whether you'll want to hear the answer.'

'Of course I would. Why shouldn't I? Is the reason . . . shameful?' She giggled nervously.

'I don't find it so. Others might. My dear pater did. That's why he cut me off. And Society – So-ci-et-y – well, Society was amused, of course, and envious, and hypocritical, and ultimately vengeful. So here I am.'

'What did you do?' Her voice had lost a little of its confidence.

'What did I do? There's an innocent little question. From such an innocent little lady too. Does Tom's trusting fiancée really want to know what I did? It might have been very wicked, you know.'

'Don't call me "little lady",' snapped Helen Frances, trotting her horse forward. 'You have no right to laugh at me. Or at Tom.' She turned in her saddle. 'Tell me,' she said. 'Tell me what you did.'

Henry trotted his horse next to her and reined it in. Leaning over, lightly touching her shoulder, he moved his mouth close to her ear. 'Do you really want to know?' he whispered, brushing her cheek with his finger. She twisted her head away angrily. 'Will it excite you, I wonder, as those executions did? All right, then.' He laughed harshly, pulling his mount away. 'I'll tell you what I was accused of. Indecent association. Adultery. Rape. Breach of promise. Is that what you wanted to hear?'

Helen Frances's startled expression showed clearly that it was not.

'According to my accusers, I debauched – you notice how I pick my words with care – the wife of my colonel, who was an earl, and later I ravished his daughter, the Lady Caroline. Terrible behaviour, indeed. You didn't know you were out riding with a twice-condemned fornicator! One who was caught in the act! *In flagrante delicto* . . . My dear Helen Frances, you've gone all red. I hope that's embarrassment pinking your cheeks and nothing else. It'd be rather immodest if you were enjoying my confession.'

Helen Frances gasped, as if she had been slapped. Henry trotted his horse back to her, and looked hard into her face. She raised her head and defiantly returned his stare, but she held the reins tightly to stop her hands shaking.

'That's better,' said Henry. 'Face me. Look at me. Be angry. You've every right to be. After all, who would have thought it? Your dear friend – oh, yes, and Tom's friend too, can't forget Tom, can we? I wonder where he is now, by the way. Fighting off bandits, no doubt, the hero . . . What a shame that dear old Henry turned out to be such a wicked bounder. Who would have thought it?'

'Why are you being cruel to me?' she asked, in a tiny but firm voice.

'Cruel? I thought you wanted to penetrate my mysteries.'

'How can you say these things to me, Henry?' she hissed.

'You asked me.'

'But those terrible vicious things you say you did, that cruel, mocking tone, it's not like you.'

'Is it not? You know me so well, do you?'

'Ravishing and debauching. Those disgusting things. No.'

'Oh, my dear sweet Helen Frances. And I thought you were so eager to listen to my stories of goings-on in high society. I thought that was what drew you to my company. I thought you wanted to be taken out of your safe little middle-class world.'

'Stop it. Please.'

She trotted away from him but he kept pace, laughing.

'Aren't you going to listen to my side of the story? I do have one, you know. I was wronged by the good earl long before I seduced his wife. Insulted. My honour impugned. My escutcheon blotted. What was a fellow to do?'

'Now you're mocking me again,' she cried. A flock of sparrows fluttered up about her horse's hoofs. 'What could this man possibly have done that deserved these terrible things you say you did to his family?

Henry laughed. 'Dear, dear Helen Frances, I hardly think that his wife considered what I was doing a terrible thing. She couldn't get enough of it. But I was telling you about the "wrong" I had suffered at the hands of her husband. If you want to be a woman of the world, Helen Frances, I'm afraid that you'll have to accept what goes on in it.'

'What could he possibly have done to you to merit such revenge?'

'I suppose he annoyed me,' said Henry, quietly.

'Annoyed you? Is that all?'

'Sometimes that's enough. You see, I was young in those days. I'd just joined the Regiment, fresh from Eton and Sandhurst. Full of martial ardour, eager for glory and renown. The good earl, my commanding officer, accused me of cheating at cards at my first mess dinner. Of course, it's a game they play with all the new officers. Each regiment has its own rite of passage. Put the raw young lieutenant in an impossible situation, test his mettle, laugh about it afterwards. The problem was that I was drunk, and – well, I didn't see the joke. I didn't like it when I was held down in my chair and the extra aces were pulled out of my pocket where they had been planted. I showed my outrage and that, of course, fuelled the humour. Upshot was I punched his lordship in the eye. And then he didn't see the joke. For a month I was on punishment drill, essentially demoted to the ranks.'

'But that's so cruel,' said Helen Frances.

'Is it?' asked Henry. 'Can't have lieutenants punching colonels. What would become of the Empire? I suppose, as a gentleman, I might have resigned my commission, but I was damned if I'd let them have that satisfaction. So I said nothing, put up with the punishment. That earned me some respect from my brother officers. No ranker was better turned out on parade. It would all have blown over – but I'm not, unfortunately, the sort of man to let things blow over. Not that easily. It so happened that the Duke of Connaught, the honorary colonel of our Regiment, was inspecting us that month. Grand day.

Great ceremony. Great crowds at Horse Guards. Our colonel, the glorious earl, of course rode beside him. Very resplendent. Unfortunately his horse started crapping the moment it left the barracks and didn't stop until everything was over. I'd dosed its feed, you see. Very embarrassing. Made him a laughing stock in the penny press, and Connaught was not amused in the slightest.'

Helen Frances giggled despite herself. 'Is that why you had to join the Engineers?' she asked.

'Oh, no,' said Henry. 'There was nothing to pin it on me. But the colonel knew. And then it was war, though nobody said anything. I won't bore you with the intricacies. He'd have got me transferred eventually, but I made sure he couldn't.'

'How did you do that?' asked Helen Frances.

'By seducing his wife, my dear,' he replied.

'What?'

'Well, he really would have been a laughing stock if he played the jealous husband, wouldn't he? Not much he could do.' He laughed bitterly. 'In those elevated circles it's not being a cuckold that is shameful but showing you care about it. You may not credit it, but the safest place I could possibly be was in his wife's bed. *C'est trop drôle, n'est-ce pas?* Of course I was foolish to underestimate him. I told you I was young. The daughter wasn't in the original plan, you see. Anyway, I was punished for my temerity. Exiled from the realm. Am I being too blunt for you, by the way? Isn't this what you wanted to hear?'

'You're not the cynical character you make yourself out to be. I don't believe it. Why are you telling me all this?' Her lip was trembling and there was moistness in her eye.

They had reached an irrigation ditch, which separated two fields. With a violent movement, she kicked her horse headlong over the lip, and lurched haphazardly down and up the steep banks, as if trying to create a distance from the conversation that was disturbing her.

Henry looked thoughtfully after her, before expertly manoeuvring his own horse obliquely down the bank and up the slope on a gentler gradient. 'Oh, I could have lied to you,' he said, when he came up to her. She had cantered a few hundred yards onwards, and had now stopped, waiting for him. 'Invented something bland and romantic. Perhaps I could have told you how I had been cheated of my inheritance by a black-hearted relation so my only recourse was to hide in the colonies to escape my debts, nursing my revenge until I could return and claim my estate – isn't that the sort of thing that happens to young heroes in all the respectable novels? But life's not like that. And you're not one to believe it is either, Helen Frances, are you? You're like me deep down, though you don't know it yet. You're no sentimentalist. You see the world for what it is. And you're hungry. Again like me. Hungry for experience.'

Helen Frances shook her head, but did not move. It was as if his speech had hypnotised her and her horse to the spot.

'Oh, I seduced the mother, all right. It wasn't as if I was sampling anything my brother officers, and I daresay the odd strapping corporal, hadn't sampled already – you haven't the faintest idea of what these Society women are like, have you? Nothing like a discreet affair with a younger man to put rose into a fading bloom – not that she was a fading bloom; she was magnificent in her way – but I was not discreet. I made sure I wasn't discreet. I wanted her husband and all the rest of Mayfair to know about it. Had to get my own back somehow. And I was toast of the season, at least in the smart clubs, and there was damn-all his lordship, the old goat, could do about it. You see, Helen Frances, sinning, as I think you probably still call it in your quaint convent vocabulary, is what gentlemen and married ladies tend to do with each other when they get the chance. We change bedrooms at house parties like swapping punts on the river, and go shooting with the cuckolded husbands next morning all smiles. It's what's known as being fashionable.'

'And his daughter?' she asked shrilly. 'You said you ravished his daughter? Did you?'

Henry looked as if he would deliver some new epigram, then he sighed. The irony dropped from his voice.

'No, Helen Frances. I ravished nobody. If anything it was the opposite. Caroline ravished me. Heart and soul. I never knew any creature so beautiful, or so vicious. It was at Leylands, and she caught me as I came out of her mother's room on a summer morning, dawn light shining through the curtains, and birds singing outside, and she was standing in her nightdress in the corridor, smiling at me like a wicked angel. I was hers from that moment, and she knew I was. She just smiled knowingly at me and slipped back into her bedroom, leaving the door ajar – and I followed her.'

*　　*　　*

Lao Zhao, reining in his mule a respectful distance away, looked curiously at the two motionless riders, rigid in their saddles, oblivious of their mounts grazing in the stubble, talking, talking, talking as usual – but this time they were being remarkably serious about it, he thought. He had never seen his master so tense, or the woman so pale and rapt in concentration.

'Of course, she'd planned it,' said Henry, after a long, wistful pause. 'She was pregnant already, though you wouldn't have known it, with her elfin body and a waist you could put your hand round. She ignored me at breakfast next day – oh, she was haughty – and that fired me all the more. All that week I lived only for the early mornings when I could be alone with her. I spent the days in a dream of her hair, her looks, her touch, her smell. Even when I was making love to her mother I only had thoughts for her – yes, she told me I had to continue my affair with her mother, I suppose it amused her, she told me it excited her. But every morning I dreaded that her door would be closed; and my heart would sing when I turned the handle, and there she would be with that wide, welcoming smile in the middle of a pool of chestnut hair on the pillow, and the thin white arms stretching out, as the sparrows and finches sang outside the window. Oh, the beauty of those mornings . . .'

'You talk as if you were in love.'

'I was in love. That was all part of their plan.'

'I don't understand.'

'On the fifth morning she waited until I was gathering my clothes again from the chair beside her bed; I was about to slip out as quietly as I had come in. And then she screamed. High-pitched, on and on, like some wounded animal. I can hear it now. Horrible. And I watched stunned as she scratched at her breasts and thighs and banged her face against the bedpost till it bruised. In his nightgown her father came charging in, brandishing a walking-stick, more like a cudgel. He'd obviously had it prepared. It must have given him some satisfaction to be able to beat me with impunity before the other house guests arrived, woken by the noise. Of course, it was all very evident to everyone what had happened, the way the father and daughter had planned it to look. The ruined girl sobbing among the rumpled sheets, the ravisher caught after the act.

'There was no scandal. I was offered the chance of marrying

her, a bit perfunctorily: my family name was good enough for them and they would have preferred the bastard legitimate if they could, though of course I was told I could never stay in the same house as Caroline and we would be divorced as soon as it was appropriate. Well, my pride raged at being used, and I refused. So I was quietly cashiered, disgraced as only the English know how, so a man's ruin never ripples the surface of Society, but everyone knows, and every door is barred. I was lucky that my father could get me a position in the Engineers, but even India was considered too close by some for the likes of me. I misled you about how welcome I was at the Viceroy's parties at Simla. My reputation accompanied me wherever I went. Mustn't moan. I was fortunate to be allowed my freedom. After all, I was now a ravisher, and that's life or a rope if convicted.'

Henry paused, then clicked his tongue, propelling his horse onward at a slow walk. Helen Frances kept pace. 'What happened to the baby?' she asked softly.

'Caroline disappeared to some spa town and after the delivery put the infant out to farm. No slur on her reputation, not that many knew anything about it, but those who did considered her to be the poor innocent victim of a philanderer who had also debauched her mother. There was every sympathy for her and eventually she was married off to some old peer.

'Who was the original father, whom presumably this whole charade was designed to protect? I don't know for sure, but Caroline had spent the best part of the season at Kensington Palace and Windsor, and Bertie was then at his most goatish. Everyone knows he has his mistresses and some know he's fathered the odd bastard – and that's all right, because his mistresses have either been actresses and chorus girls who don't matter, or married women with compliant, ambitious husbands. Having a love-child with the young, unmarried daughter of a peer would have been quite another thing. Our upper-class young ladies are supposed to be virgins till they've been to the altar, don't you know, not that many of them are. You're beginning to understand now, I take it, the mores of our polite society? Play by the rules, and you can rut to your heart's content, and Society will load you with laurels and rewards. Damnation to you if you don't.

'His lordship the colonel did well enough, honoured in the New

Year List, promoted to major-general by the spring, his reward for first pimping his daughter and then for conducting a tidy piece of housekeeping afterwards. No doubt her ladyship rapidly found some other buck to console her. And I daresay the wayward daughter, now she has her precious respectability back, is cutting a path through the Hussars in London as her mother did before her. Meanwhile I was exiled to the colonies. Why? For being indiscreet. You see, I never should have boasted in the clubs about the old girl, her mother. Laid myself open, hadn't I? Bad form.

'And there it is, Helen Frances. The whole edifying story. You asked. I answered. I suppose I should be ashamed of the follies of my youth. I'm not. But if you never want to speak to me again, I quite understand. Do you want me to take you back home now?'

'No. But I'm confused,' said Helen Frances, shaking her head. 'You're not a vicious man. I know it. And I can't bring myself to hate you. But I hate it that you've told me this.'

'You asked me.'

'I know I did. But – but you just talk about these things as if they're . . . normal. How can you?'

'Oh,' he smiled, 'you think I should be ashamed? I should be all remorseful because I've slept with various women out of wedlock? Or never admitted it to you? Lied to you? But I don't think that there is anything unnatural or shameful about a man and a woman wishing to enjoy the act of love,' said Henry, quietly. 'It's what young bodies are made to do. It's Society that tries to make us feel guilty. That's the devil of it. Whether it's stultifying middle-class morality, or the hypocrisy of the upper classes, the most natural thing in the world becomes a crime. Eastern societies don't tolerate that nonsense. There's evil in this world, of course there is. Evil is hurting others – but there's nothing evil in the love of a man and a woman, and the act that's the fulfilment of it.'

'In marriage,' said Helen Frances, eyes on her horse's mane.

'In or out,' said Henry. 'Love's love. You find it where you can.'

'I'm in love with Tom,' said Helen Frances, lifting her eyes pleadingly towards him.

'So you say. All right. You're in love with Tom. How much in love are you? Have you slept with him?'

'What?'

'I asked, have you slept with him? You said you're in love with Tom.'

'How can you ask me that? You know I haven't. How dare you?'

Henry held her gaze. Finally he shrugged. 'I'm going to the river, and I'm going to have a swim. I feel hot.'

'How dare you ask me that?' she cried. 'What sort of man are you? What sort of girl do you think I am?'

'Are you coming?' He twitched his reins.

'You're detestable,' she cried. 'Monstrous.'

'Come on,' he said, and spurred his horse towards the bank of trees that lined the river, knowing she would follow.

She followed him to the river, her thoughts and feelings jangled after the terrible story he had told her. As she cantered behind him she became aware, almost despite herself, of a welling of sympathy mingling with revulsion. She had felt hurt and bruised by his cruelty and sarcasm, the coolness of his manner, his own shocking confession of his philandering, yet another instinct told her that this violence towards her masked deep wounds. Then she remembered the quick but intense thrill she had felt when his fingers touched her cheeks, and an earlier image of him, which she had suppressed for several weeks, came back to mind: the panther with his prey, and she shivered, not unpleasantly, and that itself was alarming, for she knew that it was his freedom of spirit, his very liberation from the restraints of society, that appealed to her. Riding behind him, she became suddenly afraid of where he would lead her.

He had tied his horse to the branch of a tree that overhung the sandy bank of the river. He was unbuttoning his jacket as he looked up at her. Behind him the water swirled in deep pools divided by islands of reeds and scrub, which hid the further bank from view. Whether by accident or design they had reached a secluded spot, invisible from any prying eye.

'You have a choice,' he said. 'Lao Zhao and I will be swimming here. You can watch, join us or avert your eyes. You can be maidenly and modest, if you like, but if I were you I'd join us because the weather's warm and the water just cold enough to be exhilarating.'

'How can I swim?' she heard herself saying. 'I don't have a bathing-dress.'

'We were all of us born with one,' he said. He had pulled off his boots and stockings and now was standing in his shirt and braces. Then he started unbuttoning his shirt. Lao Zhao, more modest but with less to take off, had retired behind a bush. She heard a splash, and a shout, and saw his laughing head wash into view with the current. The fragmented glimpse of brown limbs treading the water suggested that he was naked. He was calling something in Chinese, splashing with obvious delight.

'You're wearing a shift, aren't you, under all those skirts? What are you worried about? Do what Lao Zhao did. Slip in from behind a bush. We won't spy on you.'

He had now stripped to his undershirt and long johns. She could not take her eyes away. She saw the muscles of his legs and arms swelling under the smooth cotton and the black hairs of his chest in the V of his vest. Half turning, ready to join Lao Zhao in the water, he flashed a white smile: 'Weren't you listening to my story?' he said. 'You may be prettier than most, but you haven't got anything that Lao Zhao and I haven't seen before.'

Then, laughing, he ran to the bank and flopped into the water, landing with a splash beside Lao Zhao. Her cheeks burning with anger and shame, she watched the two heads bobbing in the stream, ignoring her as they whooped and horseplayed and called boisterously to each other in a language she could not understand.

'Come on, Helen Frances,' she heard him call. 'It's lovely in here. Stop looking like Patience on a monument. Get off your horse and come and join us.'

It was anger more than anything else that made her do it. Perhaps that was what he had intended by baiting her so. She did not go behind a bush, but in front of the two of them disrobed to her shift, then, staring haughtily ahead of her, she marched into the water, the shift billowing around her. Her foot snagged on a stone and she fell and next thing she felt the icy shock of the water enveloping her as she went under. She burst to the surface with a gasp, and saw Henry's head beside her.

'It's freezing,' she managed, against chattering teeth.

'You'll warm in a minute,' he said, 'and then you'll burn with the joy of it.'

He continued to look at her admiringly. 'I must say, you're full of surprises, Miss Delamere,' he said, 'but I've never met anyone braver in my life. You know, I never bel—' But he failed to finish his sentence because at that moment Helen Frances splashed him in the face.

Laughing, the two of them climbed out of the river, Henry pulling her up behind him. Lao Zhao swam off towards his bush. Only on the bank again did she feel the immodesty of her dress, wondering if the clammy – and cold – cloth was as transparent where it wetly hugged the skin as Henry's underclothes seemed to be. She averted her eyes from the dark bulge at the top of his legs, and shyly attempted to cover her breasts and loins with her hands, but Henry hardly looked at her. 'Come on,' he was saying. 'Let's get you a towel. I packed a couple in my saddlebag in case. Here. Catch.'

Nor did he attempt to look at her until she was fully dressed.

She sat on the bank luxuriating. Her skin tingled with freshness. She felt spirited and alive. Her ears, breasts and thighs were burning with a hot glow, and her blood seemed to pound more quickly round her body. She sensed him approach as she was pulling on her second boot. He stood for a moment in front of her, contemplating her.

'Oh, Henry. That was invigorating,' she started.

'You're invigorating,' he said, and kissed her full on the lips. She felt the brush of his moustache on her nose, then the softness of his mouth, the flicker of his tongue against her teeth, and his arms around her body as he pulled her tightly to him. She felt the roughness of his tweed jacket, which gave way to a warm languor as she relaxed against him. She closed her eyes, abandoning herself to his strength and the warmth from his mouth suffusing her whole body.

'I'd better take you home,' he said, releasing her at last. 'Lao Zhao's bringing the horses.'

Early on the following Friday the Airtons and Helen Frances set out for the railway camp. The doctor and Helen Frances rode, while Nellie, Sister Elena, and the children sat in the back of a mule cart that had been borrowed for the occasion. Sister Caterina, to her disappointment, had to stay behind to look after the mission. Charlie Zhang was waiting for them at the camp, ready to guide them on the next stage of their journey to the point in the Black Hills where the tunnel was ready to be blown. Herr Fischer and Henry Manners had already ridden ahead, to supervise the construction of the tents where the party would stay for two nights. The ceremony to mark the opening of the tunnel would take place later that day, and the whole of the next would be devoted to a picnic, which Herr Fischer and Charlie had lavishly arranged.

It was an adventure for the children and a treat for Sister Elena, who had little opportunity to leave Shishan, and the chilly drive was warmed by cheerful singing and excited chatter. Their spirits were not dampened when the familiar flat countryside gave way to the dark clumps of forest and rocky defiles that marked the beginning of the Black Hills. The new railway line and the track they were using followed a river valley and they soon became used to the roar of the white torrent as it rushed over the pebbled floor of a gully to their left. Meanwhile the tall pines increased in number and size. Above them they could see the jagged peaks of the Black Hills penetrating through the low-lying cloud. The cold began to bite through their clothes. Only a few days ago, Shishan had been celebrating the last blaze of autumn. In the interval winter had come, and if it had not been for the children's chattering voices, Helen Frances would have found the landscape menacing and sombre. She still remembered her first sinister passage through the Black Hills on the journey to Shishan.

The road dipped and the tall trees arched over their heads like the vault of a Gothic cathedral, or a cave overgrown with stalactites and stalagmites. With a screech and a crash a large bird thumped off its perch and flapped into the gloom. Then they were out in the daylight again and in front of them a tall cliff loomed upwards, the top of the scarred rock face lost in trailing mists of cloud. From high above, a narrow cataract tumbled and divided itself between the ridges and cracks, a mist of spray veiling a deep pool at the bottom. Shadowed by the cliffs, the black water was seldom touched by sunlight. Among the sedge that fringed its banks runnels seeped through mossy channels into the river gully that had led them here. The whisper of the merging streams provided a restless undertow to the crash of the falls. Here, on a grey meadow, Herr Fischer had erected the tents.

Not far away, a tumble of rocks piled against the cliff face indicated where the tunnelling work had started. Charlie had told them that the dynamite was already in place and only required the lighting of a fuse to blow a hole that would connect the tunnel this side of the mountain with its twin leading from the plain. He had been immensely proud as he described the difficulties they had overcome. It had been his and Herr Fischer's idea to make this hole through the mountains. It had been hard and costly work, but the distance saved was nearly seventy miles, and probably the detour had cut six months from the schedule of the project. Herr Fischer had promised that Charlie himself would be given the honour of lighting the fuse.

'Don't be alarmed, Miss Delamere,' he had assured her. 'There will be no danger. The explosion will be deep in the heart of the mountain where the two tunnels meet. All you will hear will be a faraway pop and then, when we see the dust and smoke pouring out of the hole at our end, we will drink the champagne!'

In the event, with heavy rain thundering like artillery on the canopy where the bedraggled guests stood (they had all been caught in the downpour as they walked from the tents to the site of the ceremony and nobody had thought to bring umbrellas) none of them heard the explosion. Charlie, ignoring the rain, had pressed the plunger with flamboyant enthusiasm, beaming and bowing in his sodden robes; but afterwards it was difficult to tell if it was smoke or spray from the overhang that filmed briefly the entrance to the cave. Nevertheless Herr Fischer took the initiative and there was at least an audible pop from the champagne bottle as he cheerfully declared the tunnel open. Nellie was preoccupied with calling the children out of the wet into which they had run to dance with an ecstatic Charlie, but the doctor and Sister Elena got into the spirit of the party by clinking their glasses with all and sundry, and singing 'For He's A Jolly Good Fellow'. Helen Frances only had eyes for Henry leaning against the tent pole sipping his glass and sardonically observing the scene. He turned and smiled at her, and she felt her stomach flutter, and a rush of heat flush her cheeks. It was the first time they had seen each other since they had returned together from the river four days and so many aeons ago.

She had told herself several times over this period that she never wished to see Henry again, and sometimes she actually believed it. Then she would hold her photograph of Tom (she had forced him to pose for it in the studio on the liner: it was as she loved to think of him – he was wearing his cricket sweater and ducks, and his hair was untidy, his face ruddy from the game of deck quoits he had just left). Desperately she would try to recall the tender feelings she felt for him, and sometimes she was successful: she would breathe out a long sigh of relief and smile to herself, and recall their many shared happinesses together, their wanderings through the strange and exciting ports on the way here, his jokes and stories, his occasional endearing bashfulness. This nostalgia would last only as long as it took her to remember Henry, the ride, and everything else that had happened that afternoon.

Now as she watched him standing under the wet awning, the cheerful figures of the Airtons and Charlie and Herr Fischer merry-making around him, she relived the sensations she had felt when he had kissed her. Everything and everyone else blurred behind him. He stood out alone in vivid detail, a physical presence she felt was touching her despite the space that separated them. He moved casually towards her, his growing proximity fixing her to the spot like a captive in an enchanter's spell.

'Tomorrow,' he murmured, as he passed her. 'We'll go riding again. Tomorrow. After the picnic.'

'Tomorrow, after the picnic,' she whispered, as if she was making a response in church. Yet she knew, even as she said it, that there would be no going back.

The sense of his presence remained with her even after he had moved behind her, and for the rest of the evening; at the dinner round the campfire when his image danced behind the flames; at night in her restless dreams; all through the following morning when, somehow, she found herself managing to play with the children and even to converse for a while with Dr Airton. It was as if an automaton from inside her had detached itself to operate independently from her real self; steering her through her social functions, laughing, joking, being pleasant as usual, when in fact all her being was concentrated on the figure of Henry whom she could see reading on a campstool by his tent on the other side of the glade. She wished he would look up at her; she envied the battered copy of Virgil that was absorbing his attention – she would have liked to be one of the pages turned by his elegant fingers. 'Tomorrow, after the picnic.' His words whispered and repeated themselves over and over in her head, echoing, chattering, increasing in tempo and volume, a screaming chorus for the crashing musical symphony of the waterfall, which in turn was a counterpoint to the pulsing of her blood and the throbbing excitement coursing through her veins. Yet time seemed hardly to move.

It was this detached automaton that made bright conversation with Herr Fischer and Charlie during the picnic. She hardly noticed the spectacular venue chosen by Charlie, high on a rock above the waterfall, the peaks of the Black Hills above them, the carpet of forest below; nor appreciated the efforts the servants had made to carry the rugs and woks and the Hong Kong baskets full of food up the precipitous slope, while the picnic party clambered slowly behind. Her eyes were only on Henry couched on his side against a rock, joking with George and Jenny, being outrageously flattering to Sister Elena and even melting Nellie with his charm. She was counting the moments until they would be alone together.

She was never sure in her memory afterwards just how Henry had managed to extricate them from the activities planned by Charlie for the afternoon. She became suddenly aware of the familiar sensation of being in the saddle again, Henry's broad back in front of her, hearing the clop of Lao Zhao's mule behind, and a delicious sense of freedom and anticipation tingling her spine.

'Mind the weather now,' she heard the doctor's voice call after them. 'Don't go too far.'

Then the horses were plunging down a narrow bridlepath and they were enveloped in the gloom of the forest. She thought she saw a squirrel disappear into the branches of a tree, but there was no other sign of bird or animal life. It was a wet, silent world; even the sound of their horses' hoofs was muffled in the soggy leaves on the forest floor. Occasionally a branch of a fir tree would brush her face, sending icy droplets down the back of her neck, and she would shiver involuntarily. Henry rode silently ahead. He seemed tense and preoccupied, but turned with a warm smile when she asked nervously where they were going.

'There should be a ridge ahead where we break out of these trees and get a view,' he said. 'Then we follow an old overgrown rock scree, which winds up the side of the cliff. There's more forest at the top, and apparently there's a Taoist temple in there somewhere.'

'I don't want to go to another temple. I just want to be with you,' she said.

'And I with you,' he murmured.

'You ignored me all morning. Reading that book,' she said.

'I was looking for something, a passage I learned once at school. *Et vera incessu patuit dea.* "And in her walk it showed, in truth she was a goddess." Thought it described Dido, but in fact it was Venus. Anyway, when I saw you in the rain last night I remembered you by the river, and that line popped into my head. It's what you looked like.'

'Oh, Henry, what are we to do? How did we get into this?'

He looked upwards at the canopy of trees, the tops of which were beginning to rustle and shake in a growing wind.

'I think for a start we'd better find some shelter,' he said. 'You notice how dark it's becoming. Like night in here. I think we're in for a storm. Better get out of the trees. Before the lightning . . . That temple must be somewhere. Come on.'

He thrust his horse forward. They made a faster pace, but sometimes it was difficult to identify which narrow path, or furrow through the foliage, was the right one, and Henry and Lao Zhao would occasionally stop to discuss which fork to take. For a little time they had been hearing thunder in the distance, then there was a pattering sound and large but separated drops of rain began to fall with a rustle through the trees.

'It's on us, I'm afraid,' said Henry. 'Look, it's got to be in that direction. Keep heading upwards and we should break the treeline soon. Follow me, fast as you can.'

They cantered breakneck for about a hundred yards, rain slashing out of the darkness, stinging her cheeks, she concentrating on keeping the rump of Henry's horse in view as he twisted skilfully through the tall tree-trunks – but there was no indication of the trees thinning out, and after a while Henry had to slow his pace to a walk as the gaps between the firs narrowed. The rain was now drumming and crashing all around them, making visibility difficult enough even if they did not have to contend with the darkness. Helen Frances began to feel the weight of water on her tweed riding cape and knew that soon even that thick cloth would not be able to keep out the wet. The thunder was rumbling closer, increasing the oppression and claustrophobia.

Henry was shouting something through the noise. 'We're lost,' she made out. 'Only hope . . . keep going upwards . . . Too far to return.'

She turned, confirming that Lao Zhao was still behind her. She could barely make out his features in the darkness, but she sensed him smiling at her, encouraging her.

At that moment the forest flared with white light and in the pitch blackness that immediately followed thunder cracked above their heads. Helen Frances's horse whinnied and bucked. Another flash and she saw Henry gesticulating and pointing ahead; his face was a grimace as he yelled ineffectively against the cannonades of thunder. She kicked her frightened animal onwards and in a moment they had broken out of the forest apparently into a black nothingness. A howling wind slammed her and her mount. She felt her reins being grasped by a strong hand, and Henry's voice was shouting in her ear: 'Keep to the middle, the middle. Make for the cliff ahead. Careful. There are precipices both sides.'

The world exploded into whiteness and for a timeless moment Helen Frances felt as if she were flying. Stretched below her were the white tops of trees, mountain ranges in the far distance beyond a plain illuminated in ghostly grey. Above her, towering battlements and siege engines of tumultuous cloud warred in the heavens, hurling at each other jagged projectiles of lightning, which cracked the sky where they stabbed. Then she realised they were poised precariously on a narrow saddle of turf that linked two hills. A few paces to left or right, and she and her horse would hurtle down a bottomless gorge. Before the lightning died and she was enveloped again in the unnatural night of the storm she saw the cliff-face on the other side of the saddle to which Henry referred. She willed her horse on, inching through the wind and darkness, terrified of the void on either side, her face and body soaked and her eyes blinded by the blanketing rain. Her numbed mind clung to the image of the cliff face she had seen in the lightning flash as a place of refuge in this elemental violence. They only needed the protection of a cleft in the rocks, she told herself, a small cleft where they could huddle, and pretend that this nightmare would go away. Thunder pealed around her, shaking her, the noise exploding inside her head. She lost control of her frightened animal, which veered suddenly to the right, towards the precipice. With a despairing cry she threw herself to the side . . .

. . . Into the strong arms of Henry who caught her and supported her to the ground. 'You're over the saddle. Don't worry,' he yelled in her ear. 'You're safe. And there's a cave. Come on. Lao Zhao will bring the horses.'

A deep cleft in the rock face opened into a cavern. Within the cave Helen Frances once more sensed empty space around her. Henry left her shivering in the blackness while he and Lao Zhao busied themselves with securing the horses and exploring their new shelter. She could hear them moving in the dark. She felt cold, and tired, her teeth were chattering, her wet clothes were freezing on her body – but she did not care: the thunder was muffled now and there was no rain. That was enough. She did not care if she died here, if this cold rock hall were to become her tomb, as long as there was no more rain and lightning.

'Helen Frances, are you all right?' she heard Henry call, his voice echoing from further inside the chamber. She could not place the direction he was calling from.

She made an effort. 'I'm having a wonderful time,' she managed, her own voice echoing more faintly. 'You certainly know how to look after a girl.'

His laugh smacked from rock to rock like the sound of a racquets ball in a court. 'That's the spirit,' he called. 'Listen, it's not all bad news. Seems others have used this cave before us. There's a pile of wood here, Lao Zhao's getting a fire going now – and, yes, I can feel . . . there's a flue in the rock and a slight draught. It's a chimney of some kind so we shouldn't get smoked out.'

'How convenient,' she called. Her feet and hands were already numb, she was shaking in spasms and her teeth were chattering. She pressed the back of her wrist against her mouth to try to stop the shivering. Her face, where she touched it, was cold and smooth as marble.

'What was that? I can't really hear you,' he called. 'Never mind. Look, it's not so bad. There's even a covering of pine needles on the floor. It's dry. Probably somebody's bedding. Keep those spirits up, girl, we're going to be all right.'

She forced herself to call again, through clenched teeth: 'Sounds luxurious. Pine-needle sheets. Is there a four-poster bed as well?'

'What was that? Did you say four-poster bed?' Again the rico-cheting laugh. 'That's right. The Savoy has nothing on this. It's a royal suite at the very least. You're going to be very comfortable.'

Helen Frances closed her eyes, then her shoulders began to shake;

she could not tell whether it was humour or hysteria, or just the sheer pain of being cold. In the darkness the cold was like a succubus, caressing her, hugging her, breathing down her throat in cold gusts that stabbed her lungs. She was very tired. She wanted to lie down. The easiest thing would be to give in to the embrace, escaping into the make-believe warmth of unconsciousness. 'He's done it,' she heard Henry shout, from a long distance off. 'There's a flame.'

Then red shadows were flickering on the cave walls and she heard the crackle of burning wood. A part of her comprehended that the cave was in fact a narrow, curving tunnel. Henry and Lao Zhao had lit a fire some way inside and out of her view. She took a faltering step in the direction of the glow, then Henry was with her and lifting her into his arms, carrying her to the back of the cave.

'Welcome to the Savoy of the Black Hills,' she heard him saying, 'and here is our very own fire. Lao Zhao will light his own nearer the cave mouth.'

'Can't he share ours?' she said stupidly. It was an effort to talk and control her shivering at the same time.

'Better that he doesn't,' said Henry. 'For a start you've got to take all your wet clothes off or you'll die of pneumonia. Here, stand by the fire while I help you.'

She noticed Lao Zhao smiling as he edged past her, holding a burning brand in his hand. Then she was aware of nothing but the heat from the crackling fire, a funnel of red flame hissing up through a high pile of logs, and warmth, painful, sensual warmth, tanning her cheeks, creeping back into her dead limbs, bringing agonising feeling back to her useless fingers and toes.

Gently, he lifted off her sodden travelling cape and unbuttoned her equally wet jacket and blouse. He loosened her skirt, which slipped to the floor. She stood, half smiling, unresisting, passively allowing him to lift her arms above her head to ease up the dripping chemise, raising each leg to allow him to pull off her wet stockings. Soon she was naked.

Henry paused, a bundle of her wet clothes in his arms, and admired her. Shadows from the fire flickered over her narrow white body. Her wet tousled hair had fallen in waves over her shoulders, brilliant red in the firelight, enveloping one breast. The round swell of the other peeped out invitingly like a pear hidden in a basket of maple leaves. A slight trembling of her stomach rippled the honey sheen of her skin and the soft down on her belly and thighs, the tones shifting imperceptibly like candlelight on a satin dress. Some goose bumps mingled with her freckles, but her breathing was controlled now and the shivering had almost stopped. She stood artlessly – colt-like, virginal – resting her weight on one leg, one hand hanging loosely in front of her pubis; her eyes contemplating him calmly.

'How exquisite you are,' he murmured. 'Quite the Venus. Botticelli's, I think. You need a shell and some tritons behind you. "And in her walk it showed, in truth she was a goddess." You're lovely,' he told her.

'Are you going to seduce me now?' she asked him, in a sleepy voice. 'As you did Lady Caroline.'

'I didn't seduce Caroline. She seduced me,' he said.

'Whatever,' she said.

'No, I'm going to get you warm,' he said. 'Wrap yourself in this blanket – it's lucky I had a spare one with my oilskins, it's damp but it's not soaking – and move as close to the fire as you can. Sit down. The pine needles are quite soft. Here, let me put on another log. In a bit, you and the blanket will be dry again. It's important to get you warm and dry.'

'But you will seduce me later?' she asked.

'We'll see how it goes,' he said.

'Will you take off all your clothes?' she asked.

'I'll have to if I'm to get warm and dry too,' he said.

'I'll enjoy that,' she said. 'You're beautiful too.'

She must have nodded momentarily to sleep, because she felt a prickle of a pine needle on her cheek, and a second's disorientation. Henry was standing where he had been a moment ago, hanging her wet clothes on a line he had rigged up by the fire, his crinkled blue eyes smiling down at her. Nothing had changed – except that she was no longer in any doubt. She knew what she wanted. Henry was a rogue, and deep down she knew she could never trust him, but he was so, so beautiful. And all she had to do was to reach out and touch him.

'If you are going to seduce me now's a good time for it.' She yawned. 'A good place too. After all,' she said, 'with all those quotations from Virgil, you must have had something like this in mind. Aeneas seduced Dido in a cave after a storm, didn't he? Is that what gave you the idea? It's very romantic of you. Wonderful theatre.' She rested her head on one elbow; the blanket fell away revealing one pink nipple. 'I bet that's what you were planning this morning when you were reading your book. I'm very impressed and flattered.'

Henry had been taking off his own wet clothes as she was talking. Smiling, he knelt down beside her. Cupping her breast, he softly kissed her lips, then moving his mouth down the line of her neck, kneaded her nipple with his tongue; his hand dropped below the blanket, fingers rounding her thigh.

'Of course,' he said, 'I conjured up the storm, just for you . . . But since we do have to share the one blanket . . . and while we are waiting for the clothes to dry . . .'

'You're like Aeneas, aren't you? A wanderer, an exile.' She spoke dreamily. 'The only pity is that his Dido came to such a tragic end.'

'Hush now,' he whispered. 'There's no need to be nervous.'

Her body arched and shuddered, not with cold, as his tongue traced a snail's trail down her belly, lingering on her Mount of Venus, firing the warm wetness below. 'Oh.' She groaned, clenching her fingers in his hair. 'Kiss me again, Henry. Kiss me again, before either of us regrets this.'

As his hot lips descended on hers she felt his hands exploring her body, running over her thighs, her arms, brushing over her breasts. Their tongues touched briefly, then his mouth was over her breast again. She felt the touch of his teeth and a languorous warmth suffused her limbs. His fingers fluttered over her stomach, pausing in the groove between her loin and thigh, darting to the other thigh, alighting like a firefly, tingling where it touched, and moving again. She felt as if she was being wound in filaments of soft silk. His fingers lightly brushed the fine hairs above her mound, then his hand cupped her below and she experienced a sensation she had never felt before, not in her imaginings, as the sensitive fingers entered her most private places, pausing, exploring, tantalising, at every touch plucking a new note of pleasure in an unbearable symphony which she wanted, at the same time, to end because it was overwhelming her and to go on for ever because she could not bear it to stop.

Her own hands brushed over his chest, his shoulders. She pressed her cheek against his, and heard his deep breathing as if from inside herself. Her hand felt the hard muscle behind the soft, soft flesh of his shoulders. Hardly daring to breathe she reached below and enclosed him, gasping as she felt the hard, heavy weight in her hands. 'Yes,' he whispered, 'my darling,' brushing with his lips her forehead, her nose, her eyes. 'Oh, my love.' She felt the touch of his breath in her ears.

'Yes, yes,' she murmured. 'Oh, yes, my darling. Please. Please.'

She felt the weight of his body shift. She opened her legs, guiding him with her hand towards the fires that had been lighted by his fingers. It seemed the most natural thing to be doing in the world. She felt a pressure, then a bursting pain, which made her scream; she heard the echoes round the stone walls, but very quickly the tone of the screams changed as the pain gave way to ecstasy, and with her legs and her arms she tried to wrap this man to her and keep him inside her for ever.

Lao Zhao, squatting naked by his smaller fire at the other end of the cave, drying his quilt jacket on the end of a stick, heard the sounds and smiled.

The sharp cry of pain. For his money that was the hymen. So she had been a virgin. He was usually right about these things. Then the rhythmical movements, the grunts and the sighs; there, she was moaning again, good; screaming with pleasure, excellent. His master must have a very good technique. It was not often that a woman achieved the clouds and rain so satisfactorily on her first attempt. A fortunate coupling.

He stretched to his feet and walked naked out of the cave, squatting on his heels at the edge of the precipice, admiring the scenery. The storm was over, and he could make out traces of blue sky. There was a reddening in the west as the sun began its decline, crimsoning strands of cirrus that were sharing the sky with the few black rainclouds which were all that remained of the tempest. Now the weather was clear again, he could make out exactly where they were and how they had become lost in the storm; he even believed that he could identify the tent site far below. It would not take them long to get down again. Because of the storm the others might consider sending a search party up here – the rat-eating doctor was a fussy man – so he would remain out on guard to give the couple plenty of warning of anyone's approach.

They had more than an hour to spare. That would give them

at least one more chance to achieve the clouds and rain, maybe two.

She was an ugly woman, he thought; skinny, with odd colouring. He had observed her closely when she had worn that transparent dress by the river. Funny how the hair below was crimson-coloured like the hair above. Not for him. Barbarians were only made for other barbarians, he thought philosophically; give him a human being for choice, a big smooth-skinned northern girl for preference – but the thought of the coupling going on in the cave nevertheless made him feel lecherous. Not much he could do about it here in this cold, he decided, eyeing his shrivelled frog, even if it wasn't undignified to use his hand at his age – although, that said, he grinned at the thought, fountaining off the edge of the cliff and showering those turtles' eggs in the valley with his fragrant essence appealed. But no, he would probably stop over in the room behind Ren Ren's dumpling shop tomorrow evening on their return to Shishan. He assumed that his master would be going to the Palace of Heavenly Pleasure, as he did most evenings. He doubted whether having had his way at last with the foreign girl would change the habits of a man like Ma Na Si. He could understand why a barbarian might want to keep his hand in with a barbarian girl from time to time (one never lost one's taste for home cooking), but having been fortunate enough this last month or so to have tried a human girl – especially one of those high-class ones at the Palace of Heavenly Pleasure – Ma Na Si must even now be thinking back to more delicate meats. Then again, one never knew with ocean devils, even half-human ones like Ma Na Si. It made working for them such an intriguing pastime. One just never knew what they were going to do next.

Chapter Seven

Mother wept when we left. The wind bites through my coat;
Little Brother's feet bleed, yet we have only gone 10 li.

They arrived back at camp shortly after sunset. There had been no undue concern over their absence, despite the violent thunderstorm. The story that they had found refuge from the rains in a Taoist temple was accepted without comment. In fact, the doctor, his children and Sister Elena were far more interested in relating their own adventures in the storm. Bubbling with laughter they described their helter-skelter scramble down the mountain in a tumble of Hong Kong baskets, tables and chairs, and how Charlie, railing against the heavens for spoiling his long-planned picnic, had missed his step, rolled alarmingly off the path and ended up unhurt but shaken in the branches of a pine tree. The party had spent a sodden afternoon working out ways to bring him down from his perch. 'Can you imagine a more forlorn sight,' chortled the doctor, 'than a wailing Chinaman, in all his colourful regalia, squawking like a drenched parrot on top of a tree? It gave a new meaning to the term Celestial! I shouldn't laugh. It will be some time before poor Charlie recovers his sense of dignity. We've sent him to his tent where he's consoling himself with a bottle of claret and a Gruyère cheese!'

Helen Frances smiled politely, a little stunned that back in the world she had left a few hours before (or was it several aeons ago?), everything appeared still to be so normal, as if nothing had happened. She was amazed that nobody could perceive any change in her. How could they fail to notice that she was not the same person any more? That she was transformed? A woman now. Her body tingled; her breasts and her loins ached. How could they not be aware of the glow of happiness that was shining from the pores of her skin and radiating from her eyes? It took all her willpower not to clutch and kiss Henry's hand in full view of them, in fact to smother his whole face and body with kisses – she didn't care, she wanted to shout out her joy to the world – but he stood relaxed beside her, laughing quite naturally at the doctor's story, and winked at her as he lit a cheroot.

Only Nellie had listened to their story carefully, observing how fortunate it was that they had been able to find a small temple in the middle of nowhere that could not only give them shelter but also apparently provide a laundry service to dry their clothes.

'Yes, weren't we lucky?' said Henry calmly. 'Helen Frances was led off by the nuns to sit on a warm *kang* in their living quarters, while Lao Zhao and I had to make do huddling by a stove in the porter's lodge. But they were very kind. Very kind. And it was all a bit of an adventure, wasn't it, Helen Frances?'

Seeing Henry's eyes twinkling at her conspiratorially, Helen Frances experienced a rush of total abandonment. 'Yes, Mrs Airton,' she cried. 'It was a wonderful adventure. And educational too,' she added, smiling sweetly. Henry turned his head away to disguise a grin.

'Indeed?' said Nellie, raising her eyebrows.

The evening passed in an eternity of frustration. All Helen Frances wanted was to be with Henry, but the children pulled her arm to play with them, and when she was finally free again after Nellie had gathered them off to bed, she found that Dr Airton and Herr Fischer had already ensnared Henry in the men's talk over brandy and cigars which she knew would go on into the night. She sat on her campstool half listening to Sister Elena chattering beside her, and gazed through the fire at the flickering figure of her lover. *Her lover.* She relished the word. Occasionally he would turn his face towards her and smile, and she would feel the blood rush to her face. When it was time to sleep, she followed Elena reluctantly to their shared tent, feeling Henry's burning eyes boring into her back.

She remained awake until dawn reliving every sweet moment in the cave, and when she did sleep she dreamed that a panther was licking her body, and then she was riding him over the plains, leaving Countess Esterhazy, sitting on a donkey, far behind.

They trotted ahead of the convoy the next day, their horses close together, their knees touching, holding hands when they could. When they saw the hill leading to the mission they cantered forward, leaving the others temporarily out of sight. Henry leaned over and kissed her. She pressed her head against his chest. 'I can't bear for you to go,' she said.

'Tomorrow,' he answered. 'I'll see if I can get away. I'll get word to you. We'll ride to the ruined tombs.'

But the following morning it began to snow. Helen Frances looked out at the grey skies and the whitening lawn, and began to despair. She only relaxed when she saw Lao Zhao's smiling face outside her window holding up a letter – but even after the details of the assignation were fixed she experienced fears that he would not come, and the minutes ticked by endlessly, endlessly, and lunch was a nightmare.

'How can you possibly go out on an afternoon like this?' exploded Nellie. Helen Frances was already dressed in her riding clothes, awaiting Henry's arrival.

'Henry's *mafu* brought a message this morning,' said Helen Frances. 'There's a temple by the river . . .'

'Temples!' snorted Nellie. 'Is it really temples you're so interested in, girl? Or something else?'

'I don't know what you mean,' said Helen Frances, flushing.

'I'm not sure if I mean anything,' muttered Nellie. 'I only know I'll be glad when your father and fiancé return.'

Helen Frances glared at her angrily. 'If you would like me to pack up and return to the hotel now, Mrs Airton . . .' she began.

'Oh, get away with you,' said Nellie. 'Don't talk nonsense. These airs don't become you, young lady. And, anyway, here comes that charmer of yours. Why do I bother? There's no common sense in the pair of you. Go on out to him, then. Freeze to death, for all I care. What I'll tell your father I don't know.'

Two hours later she was lying in Henry's arms in the stele hall of an ancient tomb. Five hundred years ago it had been built for a Chinese general who had died in battle against the barbarian tribes. It had been modelled on the Imperial tombs in Peking, although on a smaller scale befitting a lower rank. In its unruined state it must have been magnificent. Even today it possessed a wild, romantic beauty. Two snow-filled courtyards led up to a tall tower. Its roof was crumbling, the tiles and rafters collapsing in a tangle of moss. Behind it was the overgrown mound covering the grave. It was ringed by a crenellated wall, which was also showing signs of dilapidation. Trees and roots were growing out of the stones. In the tower was a large oblong slab resting on a carved tortoise on which the death name and the deeds of the brave warrior were inscribed. By the side of this stele Henry had laid out his wolf furs as a makeshift bed. In their soft speckled warmth Helen Frances and he had made love, and now she was lying in the crook of his arm, gazing at the snowflakes that swirled in through the open arch. One landed on her nose, and she laughed. She snuggled against Henry, who kissed her eyes and her chin.

'I could lie here for ever,' she whispered. 'With you.'

'Not sure what the general would say about that,' said Henry.

'I think he'd be very happy,' said Helen Frances, nuzzling Henry's breast. 'If he's very good I might let him share me with you.'

'Oh, might you?' laughed Henry. 'Well, there's a minx. Thinking of other men already.'

'Only when I've tired of you,' she whispered. 'And that won't be for hundreds and hundreds of years.'

'Poor general,' said Henry. 'He'll be very frustrated.'

Helen Frances giggled. She rolled on to Henry's chest and kissed his lips. As she did so the furs slipped off her so her naked back was open to the elements. The wind flurried in and blew snow on to her behind. She squealed, and turned to pull back the wolfskins. With a shock she saw Lao Zhao's grizzled head, smoking a long-stemmed pipe, peering in through the arch. He smiled at her and nodded. With a shriek, she buried her head under the furs.

'*Ta made*, Lao Zhao, you *wangbadan*. What are you doing here?' shouted Henry.

'Sorry, Master,' said Lao Zhao. 'The horses are getting cold. Well, bugger it, so am I. And the snow's drifting up. I was wondering if you could – well – hurry up a bit with the clouds and rain, so we could get on home.'

With an oath, Henry reached for one of his boots and hurled it at Lao Zhao's head. Lao Zhao scurried away.

Helen Frances was shaking with laughter under the furs.

'The nerve of the man,' he said. 'He's got a point, though.'

'So've you,' she said, nuzzling below.

'You shameless hussy,' laughed Henry. He pulled the fur over his own head. After a while the silver skins began to rise and fall in a rhythmic motion as if the animals had come to life again.

'It won't do, you know,' said Henry, as they rode back through the white landscape, leaning into the biting wind. Lao Zhao, ahead of them, was leading Helen Frances's horse and she was sitting behind

Henry's saddle, her arms around his belly and her head resting on his shoulder.

'What won't do?' she murmured, nibbling his ear.

'Look around you. It's winter now,' he said. 'This is an unusually early fall of snow and it'll probably thaw, but Nellie's right. We can't go out riding any more.'

'I'll come to the railway camp. That'll shock Herr Fischer.' She smiled. 'And Charlie.'

He laughed. 'I've got a better idea,' he said. 'When your father and Tom are back, you'll return to the hotel, won't you? And they'll be out every day at the alkali yards.'

'We can't do it there.' She giggled. 'What about the servants? And Ma Ayi?'

'No, but you can go out shopping in the afternoon, can't you? It so happens I've been offered a place in town. A Chinese pavilion. Not far from where you live. I think it might be the ideal spot. Indeed, it's designed for it,' he said.

'Go on,' she whispered. Her mouth was on his neck, and her fingers were exploring inside his shirt.

'You'd better stop that or I'll fall off my horse,' he said.

'So where are you going to take me, then?' she breathed.

'To the Palace of Heavenly Pleasure,' he said.

Frank and Tom arrived back in Shishan, glowing after their journey, convinced that the dyeing project with Mr Ding would be a success. They collected Helen Frances from the Airtons and all of them had a big celebratory dinner with the Chinese merchants in a restaurant. Helen Frances joined in with enthusiasm, matching the men glass for glass. Tom beamed with delight as he watched her. He had rarely seen her happier, or more beautiful.

They were eager to hear all the news. When they were back in the hotel Helen Frances told them all about the expedition to the Black Hills, making them laugh at her account of the shambolic ceremony and the ridiculous accident that had happened to Charlie. Tom wanted to know more about the progress of the railway, and Helen Frances tried to recall what Herr Fischer had told her about the tunnel and when the line would be completed, but her father was already swaying on his chair.

'Well, I think that's all very fine,' he boomed. His voice was slurred with the alcohol he had consumed. 'Fischer's a damned fine fellow, and his railway line's one of the seven wonders of the known world, and we'll all make bloody fortunes when the rolling stock comes through – but what I want to know, and this is important,' he slapped his thigh, 'are you and this Manners fellow practising Living Buddhas yet?'

'I beg your pardon, Father?' said Helen Frances, startled at his question.

'What do you mean, sir?' asked Tom.

'You know what I mean,' said Frank. 'All this gallivanting about temples that you've been doing together. Are you practising Living Buddhas?'

Helen Frances took him by the hands, smiling. 'No, Father,' she said softly. 'I've stopped all that. No more riding out with Henry. No more temples.'

'Really, HF?' asked Tom. 'No more sightseeing with Henry?'

Helen Frances turned her smile on him. 'Do you want to know the truth, Tom? If I saw another temple I think I'd die of boredom. And Henry? Well, don't you think it's time he went back to his railway or whatever he's meant to be doing here?'

'I say, you haven't had a falling-out with him, old girl, have you?' asked Tom, his brows furrowed.

'No, of course not. But . . .' she took him by the hand, '. . . he's not you, Tom, is he? I've missed you and I'm glad you're back.'

She leaned over and kissed his cheek.

'Golly, HF,' he said quietly. 'It's selfish of me but I can't say that I'm sorry. You know, out there in Tsitsihar, I kept thinking of you and Henry together every day, and, well, there was something I didn't like about it. There. I've said it.'

'Oh, Tom,' said Helen Frances. 'You are sweet.'

'But hold on, old thing, what are you going to do all on your own in the afternoons? You know I have to be in the godown all day . . .'

'Damned right,' grunted Frank sleepily, rocking with his eyes closed.

'Oh, don't worry about me,' said Helen Frances gaily. 'I'll find things to do. I have my books, and my journal to keep up. And there's plenty to do and see in the town. You know how we girls like shopping.'

'You'll be all right, HF? You're sure?'

'I can't think when I've ever been happier in my life,' said Helen Frances.

She lay naked on the red sheets looking up at her reflection in the mirror. Henry, also naked, was leaning against the bedpost smoking a cheroot and smiling down at her.

Suddenly she lifted both her legs straight up into the air. Stretching out her arms she grasped her ankles and rocked on her behind, her long spine curved like a bow. She slapped her hands down on the bed sheets and rolled on to her side. Leaning on one elbow she looked up at Henry mischievously.

'You're frisky this afternoon,' he murmured.

'Mmmm.' She sighed. 'What are you going to do about it?'

'Haven't I done enough? You're insatiable.' He laughed.

She made a little *moue* with her lips, then smiled. Reaching behind her she pulled out from under the pillow a book with a red silk cover. Her brows furrowed in mock concentration as she folded over the pages, her finger running down the illustrations until she saw what she wanted. Archly she slid the book down the bed so Henry could see it, at the same time stretching out her toes to tease his groin. Her green eyes twinkled with merriment as, pushing her leg aside, he leaned over to see what she had selected. 'Humming Ape Embracing the Tree?' He guffawed. 'You must be joking. You may be that athletic but I don't think I am.'

'Please.' She pouted.

'No,' he said. 'Enough's enough. That bloody Donkeys of Spring you had me do earlier almost ruptured me. I'm beginning to regret that I showed you the damn book in the first place.'

'You didn't show it to me.' She giggled. 'I found it in that drawer next to the opium pipe. Henry, what is this place? Is it what I think it is?'

'It's the Palace of Heavenly Pleasure, my dear. As I told you.'

'Then all those girls we saw in the courtyard . . . ? That woman in the pavilion opposite . . . ? Are they . . . ?'

'Does it shock you?' he asked.

She sat back on the bed, crossing her legs. 'No,' she said thoughtfully. 'I think I'm rather excited by it. It's . . . In a funny way it's what I expected to find when I came to China. It's what I hoped to find.'

'Those nuns in your convent must teach a funny sort of geography, my dear,' murmured Henry, sitting beside her, brushing his moustache against her arm.

'You know what I mean,' she said, punching him lightly on the shoulder. 'The mysterious Orient in all its sensuality, exotic, decadent, thrilling. The corruption of centuries. This place is very you, you know,' she added.

'Me? Which am I? Sensuous, decadent, or corrupt?'

'You're all of them put together,' she said, kissing him. 'And disreputable with it . . . But that's why you're so exciting. Make love to me again,' she murmured, pulling him down on her.

'Humming apes, was it?' he smiled.

'No,' she whispered, her nails scratching his back. 'I want you to possess me. As you did in the cave. I want you inside me. To take me out of myself. To bring me oblivion. Oh, yes, yes,' and her words faded into sighs as his hands began to explore, and their tongues entwined.

'Oh, Henry,' she whispered, when they had finished, 'do you think I'm wicked?'

'No,' murmured Henry. 'You're you. And I'm me, and Mother Nature has brought us together. It'd be unnatural if we did anything else.'

'Would it? Would it? Yes, it does feel natural and right when I'm with you. I feel free. As if I could be anything, and do everything. Henry, is it wrong to want to try and do everything?'

'Shush,' he said sleepily. 'Rest.'

'Do you know? I think I'm actually going to enjoy deceiving Tom and my father. Is that shameless?'

He grunted something indecipherable. He had fallen asleep. She leaned over him, gazing softly at his face. A stray lock of hair had fallen over his brow and was covering one eye. Lightly she brushed it aside. She ran her finger gently down his cheekbone and over the thin hairs of his moustache. She laid her head on his chest and smiled. She lay quietly for a while embracing his resting body, but her blood was pounding inside her. She still felt nervous, fidgety, intoxicated. Carefully, so as not to wake him, she lifted her legs off the bed. She stood on the blue Tientsin carpet and stretched her arms above her head. Her eyes surveyed the room: the hangings, the Ming chairs, the scrolls on the walls. Her gaze rested on the red lacquer cabinet in which she had found the erotic manual. She remembered the opium pipe that had been lying beside it. Idly, she went over and picked it up. She sat on one of the wooden chairs. The smooth mahogany felt cold on her naked bottom. She examined the pipe. The long, hollow tube was like a flute, she thought. She rested it between her breasts and pretended to play it like an instrument. There was a strange, musty taste in her mouth. She sniffed. It had a sharp, bittersweet smell.

'What are you doing?' Henry was leaning on one elbow watching her.

'Henry, have you ever smoked opium?' she asked.

'Once or twice,' he said.

'Can I try?' she asked. 'There seems to be a pouch with some black paste in it in the cupboard.'

He was watching her calmly. 'Are you sure that's a good idea?' he asked. 'It can be addictive, you know.'

'You're not addicted, are you?'

'No, I'm not,' he said. 'It affects different people in different ways.'

Her green eyes were at their most kittenish. 'It can't hurt if I try it just once,' she said. 'I told you I wanted to try everything. Please.'

He laughed. 'All right,' he said. 'Just once. I may even smoke a pipe with you. It'll be more restful than that bloody sex manual of yours.'

Outside the cold wind howled. It was a bleak, hard winter. There was little more snow, for there was not much moisture in the air that year of drought in north China. Biting gales from Siberia drifted dust over bare, dry fields, and peasants made do with meagre husks in their freezing cottages.

For the foreigners in Shishan winter was a comfortable time of heavy furs and chestnuts over hot fires. For George and Jenny it was skating and sled rides over the iced-up river and ponds. Business did not stop. Work on the railway bridge continued despite the cold, and Herr Fischer and Charlie boasted that the track would be through by spring. The doctor's surgery was packed with *bona-fide* patients suffering from all the ailments brought on winter, and others who sought by his stove some respite from the intemperate weather outside. Airton himself had less leisure for his philosophical debates with the Mandarin, although he would find time to visit the Yamen if he could. Frank and Tom were absorbed with the preparations of their pots of alkali for the expedition in the spring. Each evening they would return to their warm inn, chilled after their ride, to find a smiling Helen Frances waiting for them with a tray of whisky; sometimes she would show them a piece of silk or a porcelain vase, which she told them she had acquired during her regular afternoon shopping expeditions to the antiques markets. Of course they had no idea that the pieces had usually been selected by Henry Manners' *mafu, Lao* Zhao, while Helen Frances herself was otherwise engaged in the Palace of Heavenly Pleasure.

It might have been considered remarkable, in a close-knit society where little could be concealed from prying eyes or wagging tongues, that the visits of a black-cloaked foreign woman almost every day to the most notorious house in the city could be kept secret. In the marketplace, in Ren Ren's dumpling shop, gossips chattered – but there was a tacit agreement, at least among the Chinese themselves, that some things need not be shared with the foreigners. Nor were the peccadilloes of their local ocean devils actually of much interest to a people who had been steeped in sensuality for millennia. Helen Frances's little secret was as secure as if it had been bound with chains and concealed down a well like an unwanted concubine.

There were, of course, other secrets, real secrets, which did not pass about even among the Chinese. There were few people in Shishan who knew, or even would have believed had they heard, that in the upper storeys of that same Palace of Heavenly Pleasure where the fox lady disported with her Englishman during the long afternoons, there lay another foreigner, a thin, beaten waif with a painted face blotted by tears, tied to a bed, pyjamas round his ankles, waiting in terror and despair for the turning of the door handle and the inevitable torment to follow. That was a deep, dark secret, and even those who did hear about it, whether they were over-curious sing-song girls working within the Palace of Heavenly Pleasure, or merchants who frequented it, knew that there were some things overheard that it would be expedient to forget.

In fact, that last winter of the old century was characterised by forgetfulness. It could be said that with the first scattering of snow in November a deliberate amnesia had descended on both Chinese and foreign residents of Shishan alike. They went about their business.

They made their plans. They conspired and schemed, and enjoyed themselves, in the Palace of Heavenly Pleasure or in their drawing rooms. The Boxers were no longer an item of discussion in the Airton household, whatever lurid editorials they read in the *North China Herald*. And for a while, even in the teahouses run by the Black Sticks, men no longer listened to that hypnotic music from the south, emanating from village and temple, which had briefly enticed them earlier in the year; nor were they affected by the deep magic that had been evoked from the depths of the earth and the dawn of time, mingling explosively with the piteous cries of a suffering people; the clarion call that had been sounded by the Boxers, urging the gods to leave their heavenly palaces and pleasures, to join the righteous ones below in the ever-growing and ever-invincible army gathering to drive the foreigners into the ocean. It was an attractive idea – the denizens of heaven marching in their multitudes down the rays of the setting sun, their spears and banners glinting in all the colours of the rainbow, ready to stand invisibly behind the loyal warriors of the Harmonious Fists, strengthening them with their magic, ensuring their victory – but on the whole the inhabitants of Shishan were more interested in eating their dumplings and camel's hump, and counting their taels of silver after the season's trading. And the Airtons had their Christmas decorations to put up.

It was therefore with some shock when, shortly after New Year's Day – that special and unforgettable Hogmanay when the children had been allowed to stay up until after midnight and usher in the new century – that they heard the news that a young English missionary, Sidney Brooks, had been cruelly murdered in faraway Shantung. Apparently he had been set upon while riding alone along a country road on the evening of the last day of the old year. Nobody initially mentioned Boxers – but everyone knew.

The winter's hibernation from reality was over.

A week or so afterwards, Dr Airton received a letter from a friend in Tsinan who had known Mr Brooks and who had learned the grisly details of his slaughter. The naked body had been discovered in a ditch. He had been slashed and mutilated by a thousand knife wounds. His head had been cut off. Most horrible was that his killers had made a hole in his nose, through which they had tied a string. In his last moments, the poor man had been led like a donkey by his jeering captors. The remarkable thing was that

Mr Brooks had apparently had a premonition of his fate. During Christmas he had told his sister that he had dreamed he had seen his name on a tablet of martyrs hanging in the cloisters of his old college. The letter concluded that this was indeed what Mr Brooks had become: a Christian martyr who had died joyously for his faith and the Society for the Propagation of the Gospel.

A week or so after this, the doctor received a letter from a missionary friend who had a practice near Baoding in south-western Chih-li. He was announcing his decision to return to England. The authorities in his district had turned a blind eye to Boxer activities long enough, he wrote; these were becoming daily more outrageous and menacing, with the result that he had become nervous for the safety of his wife and children. 'Weathers always was timid,' Airton had muttered to Nellie over his coffee. 'Never thought he was cut out for the missionary life in the first place.'

'At least he shows some concern for the well-being of his family,' Nellie replied. 'Which is more than can be said for some. At least Mr Weathers isn't hiding his head in the sand.'

'Whatever do you mean? Who's hiding his head in the sand, Nellie? I've taken the wisest counsel and I am assured there is nothing to fear from the Boxers. At any rate, not in Shishan.'

'So you say, dear, but I'm mindful of my bairns.'

'This isn't like you, my dearest.' He leaned across the table and took her hand. 'It's the servants' gossiping again, isn't it? You really must stop Jenny and George from tattling with Ah Lee and taking credence of his nonsense. I promise you that if I hear anything concrete, I'll put you and the children on the first boat away from China. And if it should come to that I'll follow myself. But there *is* no cause for alarm, my dear, none at all. Come, Nellie, you and I've lived in China long enough not to worry about the odd bit of rumour and scaremongering. And, anyway, I of all people will certainly be the first to hear if anything is likely to threaten us. The Mandarin will warn me. We can rely on that. You know he will.'

There were no more murders. In fact, the killers of Mr Brooks were quickly discovered and executed by the authorities. Confusingly they were discovered to have been both bandits and Boxers – or, rather, a bandit gang that had taken to wearing the costume of martial artists. 'So nothing's proved either way,' said the doctor, 'and, anyway, it all happened a long way from here.'

But the matter was not to be dropped so lightly. Jenny's godfather, Dr Wilson, like Airton a member of the Scottish Medical Mission, and his best friend in China, wrote a long letter towards the middle of February. The previous year he had become attached to a China Inland Mission hospital near Taiyuanfu. He described how just in the last two months, the Boxer craze had suddenly erupted westward over the borders of Chih-li into Shansi, and had spread like wildfire. In the villages in his district Boxers were being allowed openly to practise their martial arts in the temple squares and sometimes they were building their altars in front of the very gates of the *yamens* themselves. Tensions were brewing between the convert families and the peasants whose sons were flocking to join the Boxer bands. Even the local gentry were sponsoring martial-arts societies. Dr Wilson had not been downcast. He had heard that Peking had appointed a powerful new governor to take charge of the province. He expected that the imminent arrival of this strongman would put an end to the disorder.

'What did I tell you, Nellie?' said Airton, when he had finished reading her this letter. 'This demonstrates what the Government thinks of rebels like the Boxers. Another show of force and the Boxers will disappear back into the puff of smoke of superstition and folklore they emerged from.'

When three weeks later, Dr Wilson wrote again, however, it was to express his disappointment and surprise that the new strongman turned out to be that same Viceroy Yu who had been dismissed from his post in Shantung last year for his pro-Boxer sympathies. Far from sending his troops to bring the Boxers to order, he had enlisted a knot of martial artists as his personal guard. Nellie and the doctor exchanged few words after the reading of this letter. The clink of knives and forks on plates was the only sound breaking the oppressive silence that had descended.

The only comfort now was that these things were still happening far away.

But it was no longer a complacent foreign community that gathered at Herr Fischer's railway camp on a cold day at the end of March to greet the arrival of the first steam train from Tientsin.

Chapter Eight

We watched the martial artists in the square:
a boy broke an iron bar with his fists.

Herr Fischer, dressed in a shining top hat and an oversized tail-coat, peered uncomfortably through his binoculars. A large and curious crowd had followed the Mandarin's palanquin down the main thoroughfare of the town, out of the city gates and into the countryside beyond. Fischer could see the dust swirling above the winter hedgerows. The procession must number hundreds, he thought. Although he could not yet distinguish any human shapes he could see the tops of several banners and a score of kites, hear the bray of horns and the rising swell of voices. The prospect of the first fire-cart's arrival in Shishan had clearly aroused a good deal of excitement among the common people. He wondered if he had prepared enough space for them all to stand.

He reached into his waistcoat pocket and consulted his watch. He calculated that the procession was still some twenty minutes away from the railway camp. It was important that the Mandarin was in his seat on the raised platform under the flags and bunting a quarter of an hour before the engine steamed into view. It would be a near-run thing. He had already heard the whistle of a train. It must long ago have penetrated the tunnel and would even now be on the plain. He comforted himself that Engineer Bowers was a steady, reliable man who had been given instructions to time his arrival at Shishan at exactly twelve noon. There was still time. It was not yet ten past eleven.

He and Charlie had planned everything to the last detail. He was pleased with the dignitaries' platform, which also had the appearance of a pavilion. Despite the cold March weather outside, the heavy felt flaps and the charcoal stoves kept the inside adequately warm, so much so that the foreign guests had taken off their heavy fur coats. Refreshments were ready on the boards at the back and the servants had been well drilled. All that was needed was for the Mandarin to appear.

Nervously he ran his eyes over the notes for his speech. 'Your Honourable High Excellency,' he practised. 'It is my extreme pleasure and honour . . .' No, 'honour' was too close to 'honourable'. That was repetition. 'Your Gracious High Excellency,' he tried. 'Your Estimable High Excellency.' It was no use. He would have to swallow his pride and ask the Honourable Manners for advice. The man was arrogant and disrespectful, but he was of noble birth and should know the correct protocols of address in high society – even if he did not always choose to behave like a true gentleman himself. Even today he was not wearing the formal attire Herr Fischer thought suitable for such an occasion. He glared at the Englishman, smoking abstractedly in the seat behind him. An official of the railways, dressed in a brown suit! He suspected that this inappropriate casualness was affected only to annoy him. Herr Fischer looked beyond him at the other foreigners seated in a cheerful row on the ceremonial platform. At least the doctor, Mr Delamere and Mr Cabot had all made the effort to dress properly, although perhaps the top hat was a trifle small on Mr Cabot's large head and his frock-coat looked stretched on his broad shoulders. That did not matter. Not at all, he decided. It was the principle of it. Doing things properly.

He had no complaints about the ladies. Mrs Airton was extremely becoming in her wide, flowered hat, and the narrow-waisted blue-striped dress with the fashionable puffed sleeves. Herr Fischer had always considered her a magnificent woman. He admired her noble carriage and her striking auburn hair. Besides, he had always been impressed by the way in which, even in this barbaric country, she managed to run a neat and tidy home to make a husband proud. If she had been a German, she could not have been a greater credit to her household. He noted approvingly that her children were cleanly scrubbed and engagingly dressed in sailor costumes. They were sitting quietly, staring in wonder at the newly finished bridge bedecked with flags, the neat ranks of the coolies marshalled on either side of the track with their hammers and pickaxes sloped on their shoulders, the band tuning their instruments, and the polished silver rails, which stretched proudly from out of the far distance to the buffers in front of the grandstand. Yes, it was indeed something to stare at. A magnificent achievement, completed according to schedule. A modern railway for a modern China. His eyes misted momentarily. He and his friend Charlie had a right to be proud. Even in a small way, they were making history.

Clearing his throat, he looked beyond the Airtons and the two nuns – heavens, they seemed to be more excited than the children – to where Miss Delamere was seated next to her fiancé. As usual she radiated freshness and beauty, and a touch of modernity with her lilac gown and straw boater. How she had bloomed in the last few months. The girl had become a woman. She had always been a delight to look at, intelligent with it, but now there was a new maturity in her demeanour, a confidence that showed in her upturned chin and level, challenging gaze. Above all, there was a passion about her. It sparkled in her eyes and quivered on her lips; and there was also an impatience, a pent-up anticipation, which revealed itself in the briskness of her movements and the nervous turn of her head. Of course, she was anxious to be married. What else? Herr Fischer was a bachelor, but he could tell when love was burning in a woman's face. Oh, yes, Mr Cabot was a lucky man, a lucky man indeed. And now, like a goddess at the May Day festival, she had come to grace his ceremony. He felt honoured, truly honoured, in the friendship shown him by his fellow foreign residents of Shishan.

Only Mr Manners had let him down. Well, it was not for the first time. 'Mr Manners,' he said, 'if you please, a moment's consultation. Can you kindly tell me which is the adjective which is most proper to use before "High Excellency"? Is it "gracious"? Or "esteemed"? Or "magnificent"?'

'Why don't you try "worshipful"?' drawled Manners. 'Or "ineffable"? You can say what you like, old boy. It won't make a twopennyworth of difference to what Charlie translates.'

'Mr Manners, I owe it to the railway company to be correct in both my English and my Chinese. It is an honour that this magistrate should open our railway line for us, and we must give him all the respects that are due.'

'Only time I ever addressed a magistrate,' said Frank Delamere, 'was to say, "Sorry, your Honour, wasn't me," but he still fined me ten shillings and held me over for a session.'

'Hush, Papa,' said Helen Frances.

Disconsolately Herr Fischer marked his notes with a pencil, which he pulled from his top pocket. Then he checked his watch again. Eleven twenty-five and the Mandarin had still not arrived.

'I have been admiring your arrangements. You really are to be congratulated, Herr Fischer,' said the doctor, who had noted his nervousness. 'What a triumph. You must be very proud today.'

'You can congratulate me when the ceremony is over,' said the German. 'I am worried now that there are too many people appearing.'

'The more to give you tribute, old boy,' said Delamere. 'I say.' His features wrinkled with a sudden thought. 'Hope there are none of those Boxer types in the crowd. Aren't railways one of the things they're supposed to be upset about? Ghosts and spirits zinging down the tracks, belching monsters, that sort of thing?'

'Delamere, this is hardly the time—' The doctor tried to interrupt him.

'Don't worry, Airton, nothing to be scared about,' Delamere continued, oblivious. 'Peasant superstition's always the same. We had some trouble in Assam once. Couple of riots when someone put an electric generator down the local tin mine. The coons thought we'd woken the devil or some ancient god – but we ruled there, you see, so it didn't matter. Nothing that a few Gurkha bullets couldn't cure, eh? Shoot the ringleader, you know the drill.'

'We don't rule here,' said Manners, in the silence that followed.

'The Mandarin does. He's a reliable sort of cove, isn't he? And there's Major Lin and his Celestial guardsmen.'

'If it comes to that, can you be so certain which way Major Lin will shoot?' asked Manners.

Herr Fischer, who had been listening in growing anguish, could contain himself no longer. 'Gentlemen, gentlemen,' he cried. 'What is this talk of shooting? This is a joyous occasion. A day of progress. Of . . . of history.' He was waving the notes of his speech. 'Look, I say so in my prepared words. We are banishing superstition. We are destroying feudalism, and expelling the tyranny of poverty and want. With steam engines we are harnessing the power of the many for the progress of mankind. Here. I say so. Here. We are waking China from its sleep of ages, and stirring new forces of which Shishan was not even aware . . .'

'I think it's those new forces that Mr Delamere is afraid of.' Manners laughed sardonically. 'Boxers.'

'No, no, no!' Herr Fischer was red-faced and furious. 'I mean modern, rational forces, economic forces, not – not Boxers!'

'I suspect, old man, we'll have to deal with the one before you'll get to see the other. Don't underestimate your achievement, Herr Direktor. It's big *ju-ju* you're bringing up the line today. The bongos are beating. Witch doctors are angry. Natives are restless.'

Herr Fischer was trembling with anger. He pulled himself to his full height. 'Mr Manners, I will ask you to remember that you are an official of the Peking–Mukden Railway Company and I – I am your superior officer. Yes, sir, I am. And an engineer, sir. And I have not spent the last year making – *ju-ju*.'

Manners smiled in the face of his flustered colleague, who turned away angrily, making a pretence of tidying his papers on the speaker's rostrum.

Dr Airton, ever the peacemaker, tried to intervene. 'Mr Manners,' he said quietly, 'it's not wise to talk of Boxers when impressionable children are present.' He nodded towards a wide-eyed Jenny and George. 'And I do think you should be sensitive of Herr Fischer's feelings, especially today.'

'Yes, steady on, old boy,' muttered Delamere, who was perhaps beginning to feel guilty about the conversation that he had started. 'Maybe an apology's in order, eh? Clear the air, what?'

'Father!' hissed Helen Frances, but it was too late.

Manners was smiling dangerously. 'An apology, Mr Delamere? Very well. Can't allow the little Teuton to be upset on his big day now, can we?' And he rose from his chair.

The doctor stood up as if to stop him. 'Mr Manners, I beg you to be discreet.'

And Fischer, who had been listening to every word, turned with his eyes blazing.

'Herr Manners, I am warning you. If you say once more a disrespectful word, I am ordering you off my platform!' And he raised his fists.

At that moment, pouring into the railway yard like a colourful cocktail, the Mandarin's procession arrived, banners waving, drums beating, horns blowing. Herr Fischer turned and saw the Mandarin's palanquin lowered beside the platform. Major Lin's guards pressed back a laughing sea of curious faces. Out of the hubbub stepped the Mandarin and, without a pause in his stride, he bounded up the steps to where the westerners were waiting. A wide grin lit his face.

With horror Herr Fischer realised that his hands were still in the pugilist's position. He dropped them hurriedly to his sides. He bowed deeply. His throat was dry. Where was his interpreter, Charlie? 'Your Ineffable, Honourable Excellency,' he croaked, 'on behalf of the Peking–Mukden Railway Company, welcome to the Shishan depot.' But when he rose from his bow he saw to his mortification that the Mandarin had ignored him, had walked by him as if he did not exist, and was pumping the hateful Manners by the hand. The two were exchanging compliments in Chinese like old friends. Then the Mandarin noticed Airton and there was another intimate ritual of recognition, much laughing and exuberant patting on the back by the Mandarin. Herr Fischer began to feel like a stranger at his own ceremony.

After an age he saw the doctor gesturing the Mandarin in his own direction. The latter turned and nodded at him with a pleasant smile. At last, thought Herr Fischer, as he began to bow again, the ceremony would proceed in an orderly fashion. But when he looked up, he saw that the Mandarin was off again, this time to pet Airton's two children, who evidently interested him much more than Herr Fischer. There was ruffling of hair and pinching of cheeks, and a delighted snort of pleasure when Jenny made a greeting in recognisable Chinese.

The Mandarin exuded bonhomie. He received the curtseys of the ladies with pleasure and examined the nuns with sardonic amusement. He himself bowed elegantly to Mrs Airton, a mark of respect to his old debating companion, the *daifu*. He abstractedly passed his hand to be shaken in turn by Delamere and Cabot, and paused for a long moment in front of Helen Frances, unabashedly looking her up and down. Then he made a remark to Henry Manners, which caused the latter to bark with laughter, the doctor to smile and a red flush suddenly to burn on Tom Cabot's cheek. Helen Frances, meanwhile, the ignorant subject under discussion, looked from side to side in bewilderment. The Mandarin laughed loudly, took the embarrassed Tom by one hand and briefly squeezed his biceps with the other. Then he pulled Helen Frances gently towards her fiancé, linked their arms together, stood back like a sculptor admiring his work, and made another remark to Manners, which elicited more polite laughter all round.

'What did he say? What did he say?' whispered Fischer to Charlie, who had finally appeared by his side after seating the other Chinese dignitaries, who included Jin Lao and Major Lin.

'What he said was rather crude, I'm afraid,' replied Charlie, primly. 'I say, don't you think he's behaving rather informally?'

'Will you just translate what he said, please?' He did not mean to snap but he was at the limit of his patience.

'What he said was,' Charlie's voice dropped to a whisper, 'that Mr Cabot is built like a warhorse and no wonder Miss Delamere has chosen to marry him, and if Mr Manners wants a wife, then he'd better go into training, because however clever a rider he is all a woman wants is a powerful mount that she can control. Then there was more saucy stuff about mares and stallions. I told you he was crude.'

'This is intolerable,' muttered Fischer. 'We are planning a ceremony to mark a historical occasion and they are having a – a cocktail party. The engine will be here at any minute.'

He pulled his handkerchief from his pocket, and started to mop the perspiration from his brow. Suddenly the Mandarin was in front of him, grinning broadly. He had linked himself lightly arm in arm with the doctor and Henry Manners, and Herr Fischer had the incongruous vision of a blowsy society hostess drawing together two guests to meet a third. He hurriedly stuffed his handkerchief back into his pocket, clicked his heels and bowed for a third time. 'Welcome, Your Worship, I mean Your Excellency, to our depot,' he started, then paused in astonishment because someone was shouting in his ear. It was Charlie translating energetically.

The Mandarin surveyed him. The hooded slits of his eyes narrowed. 'So this is the great engineer,' he smiled, 'whose achievement we have come to celebrate. Ha, I thought at first that it was a mighty warrior who wanted to fight me,' and with a flurry of his hands he parodied the two-fisted position in which he had caught Herr Fischer when he first arrived. 'Ha-ha,' he cried. 'Is this how you practise your western martial arts?' And he lightly tapped a horrified Herr Fischer on the chest, with such surprising force for so gentle a movement that the engineer rocked off balance. Immediately Herr Fischer felt a strong arm around his shoulders steadying him, and then his back was being heartily thumped and, with a roar of laughter, the Mandarin led him by the hand to the front-row seat marked with a red cushion. 'Oh, worthy Engineer Xiansheng, sit down with me and tell me all about these marvels of modern science you are bringing us.'

'I – I do not know what to say. I have a speech prepared,' said Herr Fischer, looking anxiously at the notes he had left on the rostrum.

'Excellent, excellent,' said the Mandarin, settling in his chair. 'The occasion is worthy of a speech.' He yawned, and looked around as if he was missing something. 'Some refreshments would do nicely,' he murmured. 'Give me something strange and western. I have come into your world today, and I am eager to try everything new. Daifu, what is that drink you are always telling me is superior to our wines?'

'I was probably recommending whisky, Da Ren.' Airton leaned forward, smiling. 'The elixir of life, at least as far as we Scotsmen are concerned. But Herr Fischer maintains that he can do better even than that with his own German schnapps. Is that not right, my dear fellow?'

'But, Dr Airton, the schnapps is for the toast. It is for *after* the ceremony. It is not yet time. For early refreshments I have only tea biscuits and lemonade prepared. Oh, yes, and Garibaldis . . .'

'Heaven spare us,' sighed Manners, and rolled his eyes in theatrical despair. The look was caught by Helen Frances, whose shoulders immediately shook with the giggles, though she tried desperately to disguise them as a coughing fit. Tom, seated stiffly with his arms folded, glanced at her severely. 'For Heaven's sake, HF,' he whispered. 'It's embarrassing enough as it is.'

'I – I'm sorry,' she gulped, tears on her cheeks, her bosom heaving. 'I – I can't seem . . .' At which point Manners winked at her, and her paroxysms started all over again. Tom glared at him with momentary hatred.

By this time, the Mandarin was looking dubiously at a Garibaldi biscuit, which he held between the thumb and middle finger of one hand, while in the other he balanced a glass of lemonade. 'These black fillings,' the Mandarin was asking. 'They are . . . a sort of insect, perhaps?'

'Oh, no, Da Ren, certainly not. They are fruit. Raisins. Dried grapes,' said the doctor quickly.

Manners could not resist an interpolation. 'But the manufacturers do try to make them look like squashed flies, Da Ren. It's part of their appeal.'

More muffled giggles from the vicinity of Helen Frances's chair, echoed by a peal from where the children were sitting.

'How very interesting,' said the Mandarin, taking a bite. 'Delicious.'

It was a thoroughly demoralised Herr Fischer who made his way to the rostrum. He looked at his watch. It was already a minute to noon; they were way behind schedule. He hoped heartily that Bowers would be late or he wouldn't have enough time to finish his speech. He peered nervously over his spectacles at his audience, the chattering crowd, the coolies lined up by the rails, the dignitaries behind him. The Mandarin looked comfortably settled. He was peering at the plate of tea biscuits. Behind him an elderly official with a long white beard was fastidiously removing every raisin from the Garibaldi biscuits.

'Your Ineffable High Excellency,' he shouted, above the noise of the crowd, 'my lords, ladies and gentleman, this is a historic day.'

Charlie was staring at him. 'Go on, translate,' Fischer hissed. 'What's the matter, man?'

'Are you sure you mean "ineffable", Herr Fischer? Is that really appropriate? The Mandarin's not the Emperor . . . All right, all right, I'll translate it,' Charlie said, when he saw his boss's expression and raised hand. It came out as 'O divine and mysterious Da Ren, noblemen and peasants . . .'

'"Divine and mysterious"?' said the Mandarin. 'I've never been called that before. How charming.' He turned to Airton. 'You don't think of me as divine and mysterious, do you, Daifu?'

'Mysterious, perhaps, Da Ren, but not divine. I think you know my views on that score.'

The Mandarin leaned back comfortably in his chair. He liked nothing better than a philosophical debate with his friend the doctor, and he was already bored by the high-sounding phrases that were pouring out of Herr Fischer on the rostrum. In fact, none of the Chinese officials was bothering to listen to Herr Fischer's oration, and imperceptibly his voice and Charlie's rose higher and higher to be heard above the chatter behind them.

Meanwhile the Mandarin was addressing Airton's implicit challenge. 'Indeed I do know your views,' he said silkily. 'You worship the tyrannical Jesus Christ with His fearsomely absolute views on what is right and wrong. Tremble and obey. Tremble and obey. Is it not so?'

'Not so, Da Ren. My God is one of infinite mercy and love.'

'So you say, but I have read your Ten Commandments. Worship only Me. Don't steal. Don't kill. Don't sleep with anybody else's woman . . . Tell me, Daifu, do you think your Jesus enjoyed His life on our earth? Ma Na Si Xiansheng,' he turned to Henry, 'the *daifu* and I are old. You are young and therefore wise. What do you think of these Christian commandments? The virtuous *daifu* believes that it is wrong to covet another man's wife. Of course, in my magisterial capacity, so do I. But I was young once. Ma Na Si, tell an old man, is it evil to love another man's woman?'

His amiable smile seemed to embrace the whole foreign party. The doctor watched him carefully. Did he imagine it or had the hooded eyes lingered fractionally on Helen Frances and Tom? And immediately after that, did they flicker again to rest momentarily on the stiff figure of Major Lin? He could not be sure, but he knew the Mandarin of old and he sensed that he was up to something. Could there have been some undertone of meaning, or challenge, or signal, that the Mandarin was communicating to young Manners as they looked each other in the eye? He couldn't for the life of him think what it was. Unless . . . but no, he had already discounted Nellie's suspicions as unfounded prejudice. There was no love lost between the two women; they had never got on since Helen Frances spurned Nellie's offer to work in the hospital, and the relationship had become no better when Helen Frances had been a guest in their house during Frank and Tom's long absence in the north. Nellie was usually a shrewd judge of character but in this instance she seemed to have been swayed by sentiment, and was behaving no better than a gossip. On his part he had never seen anything at all reproachable in Miss Delamere's behaviour, let alone any signs of an improper relationship with Manners. She was a delightful, well-brought-up young lady. He firmly believed that the friendship between Mr Manners and Helen Frances was merely that. A friendship. One only had to look at Tom and Helen Frances together to see how much in love they were. Tom and Manners themselves were friends. Anyway, as he privately knew, young Manners's appetites lay elsewhere. Had he not seen him once of an evening leaving the alley that led to that abomination of an establishment Frank Delamere frequented? The

Palace of Heavenly Pleasure, or whatever degrading name they called it. It was not for him to judge Manners. Young men would be young men, and he had never considered him to be any better than he ought to be. But of one thing he could be sure: if Manners was seeking amusement among courtesans then there was no way he could at the same time be paying court to his friend's fiancée. Nobody could be so depraved. So what was the Mandarin insinuating? If he was insinuating anything at all. How would he know about Manners and Helen Frances anyway? And what did the glance at Major Lin betoken? Silly old fool, he told himself. You'll be chasing your own shadow next. Meanwhile Manners had summoned his laziest smile. 'I'm only a simple soldier, Da Ren, and not used to pondering such high philosophical issues.'

'Ha-ha. High philosophical issues! Is that what you call adultery? Come, come, Ma Na Si, I am raising only hypothetical questions. While the good engineer here bores the crowd with his history lessons and his paean to machinery, how better than to spend the time in gentle debate? Tell me, how do you answer?'

'As I said, Da Ren, I'm only a soldier, and my morality, if I have any – I've never really thought about it – probably comes from the Army Regulations.'

'Indeed? And what do they tell you?'

Manners's smile widened. 'Well, sir, they tell me never to pass up any opportunity to secure a tactical advantage in the field. And I believe it was Napoleon who once said that there is nothing which succeeds like audacity.'

'Ha! Audacity? Listen to him, Daifu. This is a young man who knows exactly what he wants and how to get it. Of course he won't reveal how to doddering old pedants like you and me, who are only good for sitting by the warm fire and discussing religion. The young are so self-interested, don't you find? And cruel.

'Did I ever tell you,' he continued, 'the maxim of the ancestor of some of our greatest emperors, Temujin, the Khan of Khans, who, it is said, conquered the whole world with his armies? He was a soldier, Ma Na Si, like you, and – yes – like our Major Lin. Do you know what he said?' The hooded eyes closed as the Mandarin quoted in a dreamy voice: 'There is no greater pleasure than to overthrow an enemy by guile, to slay him, to enslave his children and burn his crops, and to take his wives and daughters to your bed.'

'That sentiment is monstrous, and barbaric. It's evil,' said the doctor.

'Yes, it is. It contradicts nearly all of your Ten Commandments. But it does have a ring of honesty about it, does it not, Ma Na Si? A soldier's creed? In fact, it is as absolute and implacable in its way as the strictures of right and wrong that you yourself obey in your own religion. Only the values are reversed. How I would like to witness a conversation between my Temujin and your Jesus Christ. That would be a diverting exchange, would it not?'

'Da Ren, I cannot have you joking about such matters. There is a limit.'

'But I am not joking, Daifu. You and I, we represent two opposites. You the idealist, I the pragmatist. Or so it seems. But are we so far apart? Will it be that one day you, my friend, will play the pragmatist? And will I play the idealist? Who knows? Who knows what Fate has in store for us in these changing and troubled times? What will be your test? And what will be mine? Will we each be true to what we believe? Or shall we find ourselves in the relative position of young Ma Na Si here, securing tactical advantages in the field?

'But listen, what is that thumping noise which is drowning the speech of the engineer? And what is that screeching whistle? Is this finally the sound of civilisation that we have been waiting for? Is this the progress you have been promising us, Daifu? You will excuse me if I observe that civilisation in this instance seems to be taking on rather violent, physical dimensions.'

All eyes were on the railway track and the rapidly approaching cloud of smoke. The air pounded with the sound of steam and the rattle of cars over rails. A groan of astonishment welled from the crowd, which undulated like a black speckled serpent as each person tried to stand on tiptoe to get a better view. Even those on the platform – the majority of whom had certainly seen a train before – rose as if hypnotised by the thundering mass of polished black and red metal hurtling towards them. The smokestack and the boiler were now clearly visible. The whistle howled like wolves in a forest; the siren screeched like a gale on a snow-face. Grey smoke belched from the stack, and blue steam billowed on either side like waves parted by a schooner in full race. Herr Fischer, who had abandoned his speech – he had ruefully realised half-way through that nobody had been listening to him anyway – made out the grinning whiskered features of Engineer Bowers who was gleefully tugging at the cord. His Chinese stokers, leaning from the cab, were grinning in their excitement. Herr Fischer realised that Bowers planned to bring his engine into the depot at full steam, for maximum spectacle, confident that the brakes would bring the whole juggernaut to a stop before they hit the buffers. And now, like the Flying Dutchman driven to harbour by a storm, the train had reached the gates of the camp.

'Bravo, Fischer! Bravo!' he heard the doctor shout beside him.

'Magnificent,' he heard Delamere cry.

He snatched a quick glance at his Chinese guests. The Mandarin was seated impassively, as was the military officer. The chamberlain, however, was cowering back in his chair evidently afraid. The crowd, too, was showing signs of nervousness; there was some jostling to and fro, but the line of railway coolies kept them away from the track and out of harm's way. Everything would be all right, he told himself.

He heard the jarring scream of the brakes, and saw that Bowers had calculated it perfectly. With a rattle and groan of metal the engine shuddered in its tracks. He could see fireworks of sparks cascade from the rigid wheels. The engine still seemed to be hurtling forward at great speed but Fischer knew that it would be at rest in a hundred yards. He felt disposed to cheer.

Then he saw a man standing in the tracks.

The crowd spotted him at the same moment. There was an eerie exhalation, something between a shout and a collective gasp. Bowers saw him too; he did everything he could, throwing the reversing lever and opening the throttle. Spouts of steam jetted from either side of the engine, but the train could not decrease its speed more rapidly than it was doing already. Those nearest the tracks were trying to edge backwards while the ones at the back were pressing forward to see what was happening. With horror Herr Fischer saw that in the ensuing mêlée some were being trampled underfoot. Their screams mingled sickeningly with the general cry of alarm from all sides. Helen Frances recognised the man as soon as she saw him and a chill ran down her spine. Her father spluttered, 'Him again!' and the blood ran out of Tom's face.

It was the Boxer priest, standing calmly in the tracks as doom thundered down on him. He raised his hand, a magus warding off an evil spirit, then he was enveloped in steam, and the metal monster was screeching over where he had stood.

The engine came to a halt a few feet from the buffers. There was one last rush of steam, and after that a quiet descended on the railway camp. The dying hiss of the cooling engine and the whimpers and cries of those who had been trampled only intensified the silence.

Herr Fischer was as shocked as everyone else. He even felt responsible for the accident, but in spite of this, or even because of it, he felt that the only way to restore order was to continue with the ceremony. Ignoring the fact that Dr Airton, the nuns and Tom had already rushed from the rostrum to see if they could help the injured and the priest, he bowed in front of the Mandarin. 'Your Excellency, please,' he said, gesturing him to stand and follow him to the rostrum. There he pointed at a lever, which he directed the Mandarin to pull. He and Charlie had designed this carefully. When the catch was released a bottle of champagne swung from a pole and exploded with a hiss on the hot boiler of the engine. At the same moment, cords tying down a net on the roof were loosed and a shower of dried petals scattered into the air blowing over the train and the crowd.

'On behalf of the Peking–Mukden Railway Company, I formally declare the Tientsin–Shishan branch line open,' said Herr Fischer.

It was then that the schnapps arrived. It was also the signal for the small band, which Charlie had spent months training, to launch into a disjointed but cheerful version of 'Garryowen'.

It took some while and exertion on the part of Major Lin's troops to restore order. The monstrous machine had frightened the crowd; they were shocked by the apparent death of the Boxer priest; and they had become even more alarmed when no trace of his body could be found under the wheels of the train. Was Boxer magic stronger than western magic after all? Were the stories true that followers of the Harmonious Fists could not be injured by the ocean devils' weapons or machines? For many this was the first time that they had come across any evidence of the Boxer movement at first hand. They had all heard about it and knew that it had flourished in other towns. But today the sheer evil nature of the foreign machine – its infernal noise and hellish emanations, the panic it had unleashed at its approach – and the bravery and successful defiance by a Boxer cult leader, despite these fearsome aspects, had caused many to think seriously again about what in the past they had only considered to be the fanatical speeches of rabble-rousers and quacks. What had really angered them was Fischer's callous scattering of flowers, and the band that had tactlessly played its triumphal western tunes. It was as if the foreigners were deliberately mocking their superstitions, and jeering at the death of the priest. Some remembered the arrogant speech of the foreign engineer – not many had bothered to listen at the time, but now his words were recalled and embroidered. Had he not boasted that he was conjuring new forces that would erase their old traditions? That monstrous machines like this fire-cart would in future reduce the load of the honest working men, the carters and hauliers, whose livelihoods depended on transporting the goods that would now be carried by this machine of metal and fire? Had he not gone further and said that the new western science – magic by another name – would change the way of life of the people, breaking the order of the old society and replacing it with new ideas? Was this not an attempt to challenge the eternal cosmic order and shake the Dragon Throne? It did not take long for the crowd's mood to turn ugly, and for the first stones to be thrown at the train, breaking the windows in some of the carriages.

Major Lin had to send a company of men to rescue the doctor and his wife, the two nuns, Tom and Helen Frances, who were still below offering medical assistance to those who had been trampled. They were surrounded by a mob of angry young men who first screamed abuse, then pelted them with mud and finally with harder projectiles, one of which hit Sister Elena on the temple giving her temporary concussion. It was enough for Major Lin's soldiers to fire a volley in the air to cause the men to scatter, and the doctor and his party calmly continued with their work, guarded by the soldiers. Fortunately few were seriously injured. They treated the patients quickly and efficiently, and it was not long before they could return to the safety and warmth of the ceremonial platform.

Bowers and his crew, and the two passengers who had travelled with them to Shishan, also had to be escorted to the platform. Bowers, a tall, bearded man of a puritan bent, was anguished with remorse that he had run a man over, and baffled when he was told that the body had disappeared. 'I saw him,' he said. 'I saw him tumble under the wheels. Saw it with my own eyes. There's no devil could survive the onrush of a train. If there's no body there then some other person's moved it. There's no other way to explain it.'

Manners had recognised one of the passengers from the train. 'Taro-san,' he called across the tent. 'You old dog. You accepted my invitation.'

He crossed over and embraced a tall, well-proportioned Japanese. The man was both elegant and relaxed in his western clothes. He wore a trim tweed suit and patent leather boots. He had a black military greatcoat hung casually over his shoulders. He sported a narrow moustache and his eyebrows were set in a humorous frown. 'My dear friend Manners,' he said, in perfect English, 'when I received your telegram telling me about the hunting here, how could I resist?'

'Come, let me introduce you,' said Manners.

The Mandarin had seated himself by a small table on which were piled a plate of corned-beef sandwiches. These he was sampling with his schnapps. If he was at all perturbed by the ugly behaviour of the crowd he did not show it, and in fact was exhibiting the same levity and bonhomie that had characterised his behaviour since his arrival.

He looked up at the two men with a smile. Taro clicked his heels and bowed deeply. 'Da Ren, may I present Colonel Taro Hideyoshi, who is attached to the Japanese Legation in Peking,' said Manners.

'Ah, yes,' said the Mandarin, nibbling a sandwich. 'I have heard of you, Colonel. Ma Na Si Xiansheng has spoken of you, and so has the commander of my garrison, Major Lin Fubo.'

'The major and I had the honour of meeting during the late war, Da Ren.' Taro's Chinese, like Manners's, was fluent. 'Lieutenant Lin, as he was then, and I were opponents, but we rapidly developed a friendship of soldiers.'

'Is that what it was? Not the relationship between a warder and his captive? Major Lin seems very grateful to you. You must have been kind to him. In your culture and mine we respect the obligations of friendship. We also consider it shameful to be defeated in battle, and we tend to despise those who have allowed themselves to become prisoners. There might have been a contradiction here. I am so glad that you and Major Lin, with your friendship of soldiers, were able to resolve it.'

Colonel Taro smiled. 'Ma Na Si Xiansheng in his letters has often spoken to me of the sagacity of the Mandarin. I am very honoured to make his acquaintance.'

'I am certain that Major Lin is looking forward to renewing your acquaintance, Colonel. I assume from the warm way he speaks of you that it was an intimate friendship?'

'Your Excellency is very kind. Indeed it was a very warm friendship,' said Taro. 'May I ask, where is Major Lin?'

'He is outside shooting the peasants who became scared when your steam train arrived. No doubt he will return shortly.' The Mandarin picked up another sandwich. 'Colonel, you are welcome in Shishan. Ma Na Si has spoken to me of your plans to hunt here. Indeed, he has discussed these with Major Lin, who has reported them to me. I am more than interested that the three of you will be successful in your sport and that you will bag the quarry you seek. You understand that in my position I cannot join you in this hunt, although I look forward – I very much look forward – to seeing the trophies.'

'I am encouraged by your Excellency's support. I can inform you that I, too, have made my own minister aware of my intentions to hunt here, and informed him of what quarry I seek. He wishes me every good fortune – indeed, he did me the honour of giving me some useful suggestions, and has indicated to me which trophies he would particularly like to see. Of course, he, like you, Da Ren, is prevented by his duties from joining us personally.'

'It is gratifying that we all have such an early understanding, Colonel. Let me know through Major Lin how I can be of assistance to you during your stay. I am certain that he will look after your comforts. Of course, being such an intimate friend, he is in a position to know exactly what your requirements are. This is he now, Colonel, flush from his military victories. I will not delay your joyful reconciliation any further.'

Major Lin had entered behind the doctor and the party that had been treating the injured. He did not see Colonel Taro at first. He was somewhat distractedly pulling off his gloves and his padded greatcoat and was warming his hands by the stove. He was startled when a smiling Taro tapped him lightly on the shoulder, and it was with a petulant frown that he turned to see who had disturbed him. He froze in mid-movement.

'Taro-sama.' The word came out as a gasp. The Mandarin and Manners, watching from the other side of the tent, saw the colour drain from the young officer's face, and a look almost of terror distort his pallid features.

'My old, old friend,' said Taro, taking Lin by the arms and embracing him. Trembling, Major Lin shrugged himself free of the other man's grasp. His twisted lip quivered, his features contorted with conflicting emotions. It was only after a noticeable effort that he was able to smooth them back into their habitual expression of coldness. He clicked his heels, bowed sharply from the waist. 'Colonel Taro, you are welcome to Shishan,' he said.

'How touching,' said the Mandarin. 'I had not appreciated that the friendship of soldiers could be so passionate.'

'Colonel Taro said that it was an intimate friendship,' said Manners, smiling.

'I suspect that Major Lin would like to forget quite how intimate it was,' murmured the Mandarin. His voice lost its ironical tone, and he looked up at the Englishman with a hard eye. He spoke very quietly: 'Ma Na Si, you and I both know what happened when Lin was that man's prisoner, and how he bought his life or at least his release from hard labour with his own dishonour. I am not one to cast blame. I benefit from the military knowledge, which Lin learned while he was Taro's – friend. And it was in the past. We all have pasts, Ma Na Si, do we not?

'But now we have an interesting situation. The past has returned to haunt our brave young officer. I am relying on you to guide these negotiations to a successful conclusion. The relationship between these two men is – how shall I say it? – nicely weighted. I am gambling, Ma Na Si, that in the delicate balance between obligation and shame – and Major Lin, as you know, feels both – the weights will come down slightly on the side of shame. In the balance between love and hatred, the scales will fractionally favour hatred – for then Major Lin will drive the hardest bargain for me. But the scales must tip only gently, or otherwise there will be no deal.

'Do you understand me? Of course you do. That's why I am speaking so frankly. I am revealing nothing that you had not calculated already. For you sit on the balance of the scales, Englishman. I would remind you that you will not profit if the scales fall too heavily in either direction.'

'There is an expression, Da Ren, that an Englishman's word is his bond.'

'Your word is worth nothing. You are an opportunist. My friend, I only trust your self-interest. And your hunger.'

'And my respects go to you too, Da Ren.'

'Ha! Ma Na Si, we understand each other. That is why I like you. I will give you one word of advice, however. Be hungry – but do not be greedy.'

'Meaning?'

'Fan Yimei, the girl in the brothel, she belongs to Major Lin. Content yourself with your theft of the red-headed English girl from her young fool. Dally with the other whores in the Palace of Heavenly Pleasure. Leave Fan Yimei to the Major.'

'I see,' said Manners. 'I won't ask how you know these things. It is true that Fan Yimei is comely and I had . . . noticed her. I am surprised, though, that such a great one as the Da Ren takes interest in the ownership of a whore, or the disposition of a barbarian's heart.'

'You do not have a heart, Ma Na Si. You are also impertinent – but I do have an interest in this girl. At least, I have placed her under my protection. Her father once – never mind. I cannot move her from that house but she can be my gift within it. It is one way of protecting her. She also serves my policy, and for the moment she is given to Major Lin. He has a passion for her. It is a difficult time for him. I do not want him made more upset than he is already.'

'And once our deal is concluded? When it no longer matters whether Major Lin is upset?'

'Oh, you are arrogant, Englishman. But I agree. When the deal is sealed we will talk. Expect to pay a high price for her. I will think of some suitable exchange. No, no further talk now. It is nearly time for me to leave, and for courtesy's sake I must exchange banalities first with your comical colleague, the engineer, and his half-foreign interpreter.'

Dr Airton, who on his return had intended to have a long talk with the Mandarin, had been surprised and slightly chagrined to see him in such close conversation with Manners. It was impressive how the relative newcomer had managed to ingratiate himself so quickly with the important people in Shishan. He also seemed to be on intimate terms with Major Lin, which was remarkable, knowing that cold young officer's hatred of foreigners. He had just seen the major embraced, of all things, by the natty Japanese visitor who had arrived on the train. Lin's face had been a picture! What had impelled the man to do such a thing? The Japs really were unfathomable. Knowing Lin, the doctor had expected violence. However, it was now ten minutes afterwards. No explosion had taken place, and the two were still talking amicably in a corner. It was a mystery, but not one the doctor cared to ponder on overmuch. What he really wanted was a cup of tea.

'Dr Airton?' A loud American voice was addressing him. It was the second passenger, a soberly dressed, elderly but fit-looking man wearing a Homburg hat and a travelling cape. 'May I introduce myself? My name is Burton Fielding and I am with the American Board of Commissioners for Foreign Missions based in Tientsin. You kindly sent us a letter.'

'My dear fellow, of course, so I did. About poor Millward. Well, well, to be truthful I never really expected a reply. It seemed a trifle impertinent on my part.'

'Not at all, sir. My board took your letter very seriously. We are all deeply concerned, especially about the tragic and ghastly loss of his son, which as I understand it unbalanced Mr Millward.'

'Well, he was pretty unbalanced already. One tries to be charitable but . . .'

'Say no more, sir. You expressed yourself most eloquently in your letter. I will be here for three days, until the train leaves again, and I hope that in that time I may achieve an understanding with Mr Millward that will save further embarrassments for you and the rest of the community.'

'What can I say? Welcome to Shishan. I'm sorry that your arrival was marred by such a gruesome accident on the track.'

'Sir, these are unpredictable times. If it's not Boxers then it's something else.' Fielding's sudden deep-throated laugh was infectious. 'But who said missionary work was going to be easy? Doctor, you've heard of the School of Life and Hard Knocks? That's where I've graduated. I take things as they come. Give me a yoke of common sense in front and the whip of the Lord's will behind. Reckon that's enough to get me across most rivers and obstacles. My philosophy is to be pragmatic, trust in Jesus, take life and people as you find them, and don't, for heaven's sake, start worrying your head about things you can't control.'

Something in the lilt of Fielding's voice was excitingly familiar; the expansive imagery and the slow American drawl suddenly reminded Airton of his magazines. 'Mr Fielding, may I ask, where in the United States do you hail from?'

'I come from a town called Laredo, sir, which is in Webb County, Southern Texas. Mexican border way, near the Rio Grande.'

'The Rio Grande?' said the doctor, his eyes shining. 'That's cowboy country.'

'Yes, sir, it surely is. Father was a preacher, missionary to the Pueblo Indians till a *bandido* got him in a canyon and filled him with lead. I came back from college in Albuquerque to attend the funeral. I guess it was standing by my pa's grave, with the dry mountains around me, and cactus shimmering in the desert haze and silence hanging in that dome of sky so you just knew that God was all around you, I guess it was then and there I decided I would be a missionary like my pa, only I came further afield than he ever did and here I am.'

'Nellie,' said Airton to his wife, who had quietly come up beside him, 'would you believe me if I told you that this gentleman is from the Wild West – the Rio Grande? And tonight he will be staying with us!'

'That would be too much of an imposition, ma'am,' said Fielding. 'I intended to put up with the Millwards tonight.'

'No, sir,' said Nellie. 'I don't know who you are and why you've come here but I can tell you one thing for sure, that under no circumstances will I allow you to stay with the Millwards. They won't have you and, once you've seen their place, nor would you want to rest there. Besides, if you really do come from the Wild West, then you have a tryst with my husband that is likely to go on into the wee hours. The poor man may look like an elderly and respectable father of the Kirk, but the truth is that he is more juvenile than my little son, and only dreams of robbing trains and being a cowboy. His library is awash with comics and shockers – a sad example to his flock and a shame and embarrassment to his family. So you see, sir, whoever you are, you are a godsend. I am relying on you as the real thing to cure him of his delusions.'

Fielding's laugh boomed round the tent. 'Put like that, ma'am, I guess I don't have a choice. Doctor, didn't think I was coming all the way up here to save *your* soul! Don't know what fiction you've been reading either, but I reckon dealing with the Millwards will be easy in comparison to converting a man away from a belief in Buffalo Bill. Ma'am, my name's Burton Fielding. I don't know if I'll be equal to the task but I'll sure be honoured to accept your hospitality.'

Abruptly the Mandarin got up from his chair. He waved his hand languidly at Herr Fischer, and moved towards the entrance. Jin Lao hurried to drape his fur cape over his shoulder and raise the felt flap for his superior to pass. It was the signal for all the other Chinese to leave. The palanquin was waiting below. Major Lin's guard were ringed round it, but after the scenes earlier the crowd had dispersed, and the railway coolies had retired muttering to their quarters. Rubbish drifted over the mud of the empty yard, where in melancholy splendour the engine and carriages slumped inertly on the rails. The violence and energy had seeped out of them. It was a wonder how such lifeless mounds of metal could have earlier aroused such elemental terrors. The Mandarin climbed into his palanquin and moved away, the guards falling into line. No drums played or horns blew. Soon they were gone.

The Europeans were also putting on their coats.

'Magnificent ceremony, Fischer. Marvellous show,' said Frank Delamere, as he left with Tom Cabot and his daughter.

'Do you really think so?' asked Fischer earnestly.

'Oh, yes,' said Delamere. 'Made history as you said.'

'I'm sorry, Jin Lao, you can't have the foreign boy this afternoon. He's occupied. For once with a paying customer.'

Mother Liu enjoyed the fleeting pout of displeasure that crinkled the old man's face. She had to look closely to catch it. By the time he had put down his cup of tea his features had regained their usual opacity.

'I was beginning to tire of him anyway,' he said airily. 'He whines.'

'That's because he's miserable,' said Mother Liu. 'The creature's realised Ren Ren doesn't love him any more.'

They both laughed.

'He should have gathered that long ago,' Jin Lao said. 'However, I had hoped that he might have some affection for me. I always treated him kindly. I was very upset when—'

'When he tried to slit his wrists, and we had to tie him belly down on the bed for a week? It didn't seem to indispose you at the time. In and out you flew like a swift making its nest in the palace eaves. I've never known you so skittish. Like a frisky goat.'

'Well, it was tantalising.' He smiled. 'The poor dear boy. His pillow wet with tears. It made me sympathetic.'

'It made you lecherous.'

'Oh, what a sharp-tongued she-devil you are.'

Mother Liu smiled complacently and poured more tea.

'So come, tell me,' said Jin Lao, 'who's this paying customer? Or is it a secret? It must be someone with enormous wealth, or you wouldn't have risked it. I hope his discretion is as deep as his purse. Isn't it rather dangerous to put so exotic a ware on the open market? Remember the pains we went to to obliterate any evidence that the boy exists.'

'We don't have secrets, Jin Lao, you and I. You know how much I'm obligated to you and the Mandarin. You're so kind as to remind me of it every month. How much have you collected from me today? Three hundred taels?'

'Considerably less than I usually ask,' murmured Jin Lao.

'But I'm doing considerably more for you, aren't I? First it was Lin and his monopoly of my best girl and best pavilion. Free of charge. Then it was open house for the foreigner, Ma Na Si. He's important to the Mandarin, you say. Let him have his pick of the chickens. All right, he's a bit of a charmer, he's popular with the girls and he pays generously too, unlike some – but many of my customers don't like the idea of a barbarian having first lick in the stable. It was all right in the old days when we could fob off that disgusting De Falang with a slut like Shen Ping, may she rot in hell. But this Ma Na Si is discerning.

'My son doesn't like it, Jin Lao. He's not a happy boy. And after that incident at the railway depot last week I doubt there are many other citizens of Shishan who'd be willing to entertain a barbarian in their home. Haven't you heard? They're all evil magicians trying to overthrow the Empire. Or so Ren Ren tells me.'

'What a trying time you must be having.'

'And now Ma Na Si's bringing in that foreign whore – using my house for his own secret love nest! I don't even get quit-rent.'

'What foreign whore?'

'You know. The red-headed woman who looks like a fox spirit.'

'De Falang's daughter? Well, well.'

'I thought you knew about it. He told me the Mandarin had sanctioned it. They take over one of the pavilions in the afternoons, fucking and smoking opium. All very furtive. She comes in a closed sedan wrapped in a cloak like you do. I'm the only one who's allowed to know about it. And that's the way I've kept it. Heaven help me if Ren Ren found out. But what am I running here, I ask myself? A bordello for barbarians?'

'There do seem to be a lot of them about,' murmured Jin Lao sympathetically. 'De Falang? Is he back too? I'd hate to imagine him meeting his daughter here. That would be a comic scene from the opera.'

'Spare me. No, he's only been here once or twice with his merchant friends, and always in the evening. I offered him Chen Meina but he wasn't interested.'

'Pining after little Shen Ping, no doubt. Have you broken the tragic news to him?'

'Of course not. He thinks she went back to her village.'

'He always was a credulous animal.'

'Jin Lao, are you pretending or did you really not know about the foreigner's love nest?'

'No, Mama, I did not know about it. It was cheeky of Ma Na Si if he used the Mandarin's name to persuade you. You were right to accommodate him, however. We value this man at the *yamen*. But how interesting about the girl. So De Falang's stuck-up daughter is a whore? And an opium smoker? Well, well. I see possibilities.'

'And so do I, Jin Lao.' The two smiled at each other knowingly.

'Tell me,' asked Jin Lao, as if he had been struck by an inconsequential thought, 'how does Ma Na Si get on with Major Lin? Does their unlikely friendship continue?'

'I can hardly credit it. They eat together. Talk into the night. Sometimes they look at maps and pore over lists and documents. The only person they allow in the room with them is Fan Yimei, but she never tells me anything. Can't think why Major Lin lets Ma

Na Si near her. Anyone can tell the barbarian's got the hots for her. Actually, I've half a mind to give the little bitch to him. Get my own back on all three of them in one go. You wouldn't stop me, would you, Chamberlain dear? I know there's no love lost between you and the major. Wouldn't you like to see him cuckolded? Shame that he'd probably murder Ma Na Si when he found out and, of course, Ren Ren would have to punish little Miss Virtue afterwards – well, a visit for her to the garden hut's long overdue. I'd flay the flesh off that one's back myself.'

'You're in a bilious mood today. Did something at lunch disagree with you? What you propose is diverting, but it's not very businesslike. You are forgetting, I think, that the Mandarin wants both Major Lin and Ma Na Si alive and co-operating.'

'What are they up to, Jin Lao? All these meetings? What are they plotting? I've been racking my brains about it.'

The old man smiled knowingly. 'Matters of state, my dear Mama. It is not intended that you should know.'

'Of course, matters of state are only for you wise ones at the *yamen*. So tell me, where does the Japanese man fit in?'

This time she knew she had taken Jin Lao by surprise. She knew it because his mouth opened and closed, his eyes flicked rapidly from side to side and he tugged at his chin.

'The Japanese man? What Japanese man? You mean the one who came on the train?' he asked, recovering quickly. 'The Englishman has brought him to the brothel, I suppose. What of it? I don't see why you are making a mystery of that. Why shouldn't he bring his hunting friend for a night of pleasure?'

'No reason at all, if that's what it was, but he brought him to see Major Lin. And now the Japanese man comes by himself to see Major Lin, and on these occasions even Fan Yimei is sent out of the pavilion. Major Lin and the Japanese man meet alone.'

He stared at her. She laughed triumphantly. 'Come, admit it, Jin Lao,' she crowed. 'You don't know what's going on, do you? This time you're not in the Mandarin's confidence at all, are you? In fact, I would guess that you haven't been for some time. Does he trust Major Lin now and not you?'

'We are both of us servants of the *yamen*,' he said, in a small voice, his brow furrowing. 'The Mandarin tells me only what I need to know and no more. I have always served him faithfully.'

'You're so modest,' said Mother Liu.

He frowned, ignoring her sarcasm. He sipped slowly at his cup of tea. 'Yes, the Major did seem to recognise the Japanese when he first arrived,' he said. 'I thought that it was strange at the time. But what possible relationship could there be between Major Lin and the Japanese? We know Lin was once a prisoner. I'm missing something,' he said. 'Something else is going on, which I don't see.'

'More than matters of state, perhaps,' said Mother Liu, grinning broadly. 'I told you the foreign boy has a paying customer. Who do you think it is?'

'Of course,' said Jin Lao. His eyes shone palely. A gentle smile radiated his pale features. He looked more than ever the ancient scholar. 'Of course. And Lin arranged it?'

'Major Lin did – and he paid. First money I've ever taken from him,' said Mother Liu.

'Was it, indeed? Well, well, an officer of China procuring on behalf of the Japanese Imperial Army. Makes you wonder about their relationship in the past, doesn't it? My dear Mama, how pleased I am that I have a friend such as you. I never come away from your sitting room disappointed.'

'I'm sure you don't, if every time you take away three hundred taels.' She laughed.

'Now, now, what's a small amount of money between friends? Forget about all that. My mind is fixed on pleasure:

> "The bee steals wild nectar
> And savours its first taste;
> The golden oriole pecks at the peach
> Melting the soft pulp in its mouth . . ."

'Come, you have deprived me of my foreign boy, what other diversion have you planned for me this afternoon?'

'You can watch the Japanese stepping tigers with the foreign boy,' she said, 'but that might make you jealous. How about something more exotic? What if I take you to see the lovemaking between a foreign devil and a fox spirit? Does that appeal?'

'They're here this afternoon?'

'They are. And after you have laughed at their antics, you can go to the hot tub I have prepared for you, and there a handsome young flautist from Yang-chow will be waiting for you, with instructions to satisfy your every desire.'

'It's no longer any fun, is it?'

They had made love and were lying spooned against each other on the red sheets under the garish hangings embroidered with menageries of mythical beasts. Henry gently removed his hands from Helen Frances's breasts, rested his head on his elbow, and contemplated her quietly. 'Why do you say that?' he asked, after a long pause filled only by the tick of the grandfather clock in the corner of the room.

She did not reply. A tear welled from her eye and dropped on to the brocade pillow. Carefully Henry removed a strand of hair from her sticky forehead.

'Hold me,' she said, in a small voice. She turned and burrowed her head against his chest.

'I know you never loved me,' she said after another long silence. 'No, don't say anything, darling. I knew from the beginning it was just a – a game for you. You've been loved by so many beautiful women. I was just a—'

'Don't,' he said.

'I didn't love you either at first. I was flattered and curious and excited . . . And it was wonderful. In the cave, and after. That night when you climbed through the window, and the doctor . . .'

'. . . walked up and down on the lawn outside smoking his pipe and gazing at the moon.'

'Yes. And never saw your horse though it was tethered right in front of him. That was so funny.'

Neither of them laughed.

She tightened her grip on his back. 'Christmas was such hell,' she said, her voice breaking.

He kissed the top of her head. 'I know,' he said. 'I felt for you.'

'Tom's so much in love with me.'

'You don't love him,' he said.

'No, but I'm fond of him. And my father thinks of him as the son he never had. The two of them were so happy. Wearing those silly hats, trying to light the Christmas pudding.'

He stroked her hair.

'I'm not sure if I can pretend any more,' she said.

'What has changed?'

'Tom, I think. He's more serious. Maybe it's his work. Maybe it's all this talk of Boxers. Sometimes I can't help thinking he suspects something's going on between you and me. He's grown solemn. He used to be boisterous and playful. Now he's stiffer. No, that's not the word. He's become more thoughtful and responsible.' She laughed bitterly. 'He's even taken up smoking a pipe. He was furious with you, by the way, after that ghastly ceremony at the railway when you were being so beastly to Herr Fischer.'

'Tom's an Englishman. He likes fair play.'

'But he's no longer the big, good-hearted idiot he used to be. It was easy in the beginning, when he first came back from Tsitsihar. He'd pick me up in his arms, and swing me round the courtyard, always inanely happy to be with me, showering silly presents on me. Calling me "old girl" and "HF" and "chum". And I would despise him. He'd kiss me and I'd smell your sweat on me from the afternoon. He'd hug me and I'd think of your touch on my skin. I thought he deserved to be cheated for being so trusting. So I didn't care. In fact it was – thrilling.'

He kissed her cheek. 'But now you're feeling a belated attack of conscience?' he murmured.

She closed her eyes, and there were tears in them when she replied: 'I don't have a conscience any more. I'm only alive when I'm with you. I'm only myself when I'm with you. I'd live any lie with anyone if you loved me . . . but you don't.'

Abruptly she rolled away from Henry and swung her legs off the bed. 'Where's the pipe?' she whispered. 'I want another pipe.' She pulled aside the gauze curtain and stepped naked into the pool of pale sunlight on the carpet. 'Where is it?' she cried petulantly, pulling a drawer from a desk, kicking aside a stool. She dropped to her knees, defeated. 'I want a pipe,' she moaned.

There was a scratching outside the door, a shuffle and a whisper. Helen Frances hurled a cushion in the direction of the sound, and there was scurry of startled feet. 'That horrible old woman,' she screamed. 'Peeping Toms. I hate this place.' Her shoulders slumped. Her head fell forward and silent tears ran down her cheeks

Henry knelt behind her, his cheek against hers, wrapping her in his arms. In his protective embrace, they swayed from side to side.

Then he got up, went to a cupboard and pulled out the long

flute-like tube with the metal bulb at one end. From a little lacquer box he scraped out some black paste, which he rolled between his fingers kneading it into a ball. He dropped the ball into a small cup on the side of the pipe opposite the metal bulb. From the table he picked up a candle, and with the pipe and the lit candle went back to Helen Frances and knelt beside her.

She had curled into a foetal position on the cushions, her head on a wooden rest. She reached for the pipe and put her mouth round the end. Her eyes met Henry's.

'This is the last time I'm giving you this,' he said. 'I would never forgive myself if you got into the habit.'

She giggled mirthlessly. 'Haven't I picked up enough bad habits from you already?'

Slowly he moved the candle flame back and forth beneath the bulb. As the metal heated, the opium ball in the cup began to melt, emitting a sweet-smelling blue smoke. 'Let out your breath,' he said. 'Right. Suck in. Now.'

She pulled the smoke into her lungs, coughed, lay back and closed her eyes. Henry repeated the process, sucked a bowl of smoke into his own lungs, then, after a moment of languor, replaced the pipe and opium in the cupboard. Then he picked up Helen Frances and carried her to the bed. They lay together side by side, lazy with the drug. Her head rested in the crook of his arm. Idly his hand stroked her shoulder, moving over the curve of her arm to brush her breast. Her own fingers traced over his belly. She nuzzled against him, luxuriating in the warmth that filled her body. 'Henry?' she murmured.

'Yes?'

'When you're here alone in this place, when I'm not with you, with all these ladies available, do you . . . do you ever . . . ?'

He kissed her mouth. 'Sssh,' he whispered. 'Don't.'

'I wouldn't mind if you had,' she said. 'If I was a man I'm sure that I would . . . I was looking at one of them as I arrived today. She was very beautiful. She was standing in the door of the pavilion opposite, across the path. Such a pale face, and gorgeous eyes, deep grey lustrous eyes . . . She was slender, graceful, with lovely hair, but she was sad, sad. Everything about her was sad. Who is she?'

'That was probably Fan Yimei,' said Henry.

'I liked her,' she murmured. 'Our eyes met, you know, for a

fraction of a second. She looked so ... understanding. Funny. She was the first Chinese I've ever seen who I felt could be my friend. Isn't that odd? And I've never even talked to her. Have you ever ... ? With her?'

'No,' said Henry.

'Perhaps you ought to,' she said. She moved her mouth along his shoulder, kissed his ear, his neck, his chin. Her hand touched him below. He began to respond. She pulled herself forward on his chest, and looked him sadly in the face. 'This'll be the last time, Henry.'

'Why?' he breathed, feeling the caress of her hand. 'I thought you enjoyed this.'

'I live for this,' she said.

'Then why?'

'Because you won't be mine and I can't live two lives.'

'Oh, dearest,' he sighed, 'it's not that I want ... I do, I really do ...'

'Love me?' she whispered. She was sitting across his belly. 'You don't have to say that, darling. I understand.' She guided his hands to her breasts, and sighed herself as he touched her nipple.

'I have a job to do here,' he whispered. 'Darling, it's a role I have to play. I'm not the person you ... Oh, God, if only I could ...' He groaned as she lowered herself on to him, riding him.

'It doesn't matter. I understand,' she breathed. 'It doesn't matter. I'll be all right. I'll be all right. I promise. I understand ...' She panted the words, rocking to the movement below her.

'You don't understand.' He arched up and clasped her back, keeping himself tight inside her, maintaining the rhythm. His mouth found hers and they sucked each other hungrily. 'You can't. You can't marry that oaf,' he whispered urgently, as his tongue withdrew, but she only heard him groan, as she was beginning to groan, and whimper as the passion and the heat grew greater, and the sweat ran between their two bodies, which now had a movement and life of their own, oscillating violently towards a moment of final release ...

Jin Lao snapped the spyhole shut. 'Exotic, as you say, dear Mama. A most curious display, but very untalented. And the woman is extraordinarily ugly.'

'Every woman is ugly to you, Jin Lao. The question is, will she be ugly to others?'

'For those libertines, I suppose, who have become satiated with every other possible variety, the prospect of bedding a fox fairy may have some appeal.'

'Might it appeal to the Mandarin, Jin Lao?'

'It might,' he said, 'but how will you accomplish her procurement? You are dreaming, dear friend.'

'You saw she took the drug. That can be a hook.'

'Yes, but she is protected by a father and a lover and a doltish fiancé who, like some farmer happy to receive soiled goods from the town stews, is foolish enough to want her even when Ma Na Si is finished with her. How do you propose to deal with them?'

'Maybe I won't have to, Jin Lao. You were there when the fire-cart came, and you saw the Boxer priest magically vanish. My son tells me that the Harmonious Fists will one day soon be powerful in Shishan. And what will a foreigner's protection be worth then? What will even the Mandarin's protection be worth then?'

Jin Lao looked at her long and hard.

'Mother Liu, who knows what the future will bring? It is safer not to speculate. All I can say is that if any eventuality arises like the one you described, the procurement of a foreign she-devil will be the least of our concerns. I prefer my prognostications to be limited to what is tangible, and in this context I think you mentioned something about a bath?'

Arm in arm the two friends made their way back along the garden path. Mother Liu wrapped her shawl closer round her body. There was a chill in the air that portended a fall of snow.

Chapter Nine

Little Brother can imitate the Striking Crane;
Master Zhang says
practice will make us worthy of the gods.

The children were clearly up to something.

It was puzzling how tractable Jenny and George had become at bedtime, especially on nights when the Airtons had guests, and even on ordinary nights they scurried off to their rooms immediately after their supper without a protest.

When Nellie came to announce that it was time for lights out, there were no pleas for 'just a few more minutes', or 'Can I finish the chapter?'. Books immediately snapped shut and were placed unprotesting on the side table. In one fluid movement the children slid out of bed and on to their knees for their goodnight prayers. Then as briskly they wriggled back into bed again, sheets up to their noses, big eyes looking up innocently, awaiting the good-night kiss, and there was not a murmur from them when the candle was snuffed. It was all very mysterious.

Nellie might have discovered the secret if she had thought of lifting up the heavy linen tablecloth during her own dinner. There she would have found them, their arms folded round their knees, their eyes shining in the shadow, ever watchful of the forest of legs that might at any time stretch and kick and discover them. For several weeks now the truants in their hideaway had been listening to the real bedtime story unfolding in the adults' dinner conversation, something much more exciting than they could ever find in any adventure books by Henty or Captain Marryat.

For it was at dinnertime that their parents talked about the Boxers.

They had given up trying to warn their parents of what Ah Lee and Ah Sun whispered to them in the kitchen: tales about the ever-growing and invincible army that had been spreading its magic and menace over the countryside. The children themselves had seen the Boxer priest tumble under the wheels of the train, and vanish like a magician without receiving any hurt. His white pallid face and sightless eyes haunted them in their dreams. And now that the big American man, Mr Fielding, had come to stay, they were convinced that finally they would get some real answers. Not only was this minister, for an adult, extraordinarily impressive (he had been a cowboy in the Wild West), but in his role as Commissioner of Foreign Missions he had travelled all over China, and more than that, as he told their father on the first night, he had actually met the Boxers face to face!

And now he was describing them!

'Down south the Boxers are part of the local scenery,' Mr Fielding was saying. He had just lit his second cigar. 'You'll find them lounging in knots by the side of the road in any village in Shantung or Chih-li. Usually there'll be some martial arts demonstration going on in the background: some bravo stripped to the waist twirling a great sword round his head while the crowd admires him, or maybe it'll be a demonstration of strength, smashing bricks with bare hands – it's amazing what they can do. Normally, they don't pay much attention to you as you pass, maybe give you a hostile jeer or a catcall, but they'll laugh if you answer back in kind. They're simple peasants beneath, for all their colourful exterior.'

'Colourful?' interjected their father. 'You mean their uniforms?'

'Well, you could call them uniforms. More like the sort of fancy-dress costume you'll find in the wardrobe of an actors' travelling troupe – yellow tunics and red bandannas, sky-blue sashes round their waists, and blood-red characters painted on their chests. Some have raided the village arsenals and clomp around in ancient armour, brandishing great big snickersnees.'

'You make them sound comical.'

'They're not comical, Doctor. Might as well call Cochise comical because he wore a buckskin loincloth and a top hat with a feather in it. I spent some time with the Apache when I was a young preacher. Worked in a reservation – one of those squalid hellholes where we attempted to break the spirit of a proud and savage people, introducing them to civilisation through starvation rations and the bottle. I gave them scripture classes, God help me, and I remember the patient hatred in their eyes, while flies crawled over their faces and their pride. They were a broken people and it makes me sick to think of them. But, Doctor, if you had seen a Chiricahua Apache on his horse with a rifle in his hand, as I did once after Geronimo led the break-out from San Carlos in the seventies, then you would have seen a man. Proud as an eagle, free as the wind, for all he was wearing what you or I would call rags, and his possessions amounted to his weapons and a few knucklebones or beads. Scary as a mountain lion, as ruthless a killer as ever trod God's earth, the odds were ever against him, yet he held his head high. Doctor, I hate to tell you this but that man had something in common with the Boxers I see in this country today.'

'You mean they're dangerous savages?'

'If you provoke them, they could be very dangerous, but that's not what I was referring to. What I saw in their eyes was pride, Doctor, pride. You and I have lived in China many years, you longer than me. We've become used to the downtrodden nature of the Chinese peasantry. Come, don't deny it. Does the farmer look you in the eye when you give him surgery? Does the muleteer keep to his path when you come by on your horse? No, sir, the one greets you mumbling with his eyes averted, the other is anxious to step out of your way. There's a sycophancy ingrained into every Chinaman from birth. It's a society of superiors and inferiors, where you either bully or grovel, and the peasant's the lowest of the low – but when a Boxer brave beards me on the highway, I'm looking at a man. He's not a savage like the Apache, but he stares me in the eye with the same menace and, by God, I treat him with caution and respect and go on my way as fast as I possibly can.'

'Are we missionaries really in danger from the Boxers, do you believe, Fielding?'

The children heard the American sigh as he thought over this question. They heard the clink of glass as he poured himself more port.

'Danger? Physical danger? I don't think so. Not yet awhile. It's the poor converts who are being threatened. They'll turn on their own kind before they turn on us. There are corroborated stories of murders of Christian villagers in Shantung and Chih-li. There's certainly incendiarism going on in outflung parishes. Burning of Christians' houses, torching of churches, that sort of thing. These are terrible times and those farm-boys in their mad state are capable of devilish cruelty. I daresay the Boxer bands have their share of criminals and bandits who egg them on. Convert communities all over north China are naturally pretty fearful . . .

'What scares me, though, is how the Government and people in power might try to manipulate these disturbances for their own ends. So far – largely – the mandarins have come out on the side of law and order. Perpetrators of violence against Christians are still being punished. Yet the Boxers are a sword that can cut in two directions. I hear that the anti-foreign factions at Court – Prince Tuan and his like – have been quietly supportive. Whatever else, the Boxers are growing in numbers. I feel that there's some sort of tacit encouragement going on. That at least one faction sees an opportunity to scare us, squeeze a few concessions out of us, get even a bit for some of their diplomatic humiliations over the past few years.'

'The Government would not break their treaties,' said Dr Airton. 'They know just what sort of retribution that would bring down on their own heads from the powers. But I'm alarmed by what you say about the converts. There is tension between convert and local community at the best of times. Ordinary land disputes sometimes flare into religious quarrels. And there are other resentments.'

'I am afraid that our good work has inadvertently created a tinderbox. Is Shishan's Christian community large, Doctor?'

'Not large, no. There are three or four Christian villages in the vicinity. Sadly I can make no claim to having converted them. I'm afraid that they owe allegiance to the Church of Rome rather than the Reformed Church. My two Italian nuns take on such pastoral work as there is, which is difficult without a priest, but they do make visits there from time to time.'

'I've noticed that your arrangements here are commendably charitable, Airton.'

'It is a special circumstance, Fielding. One day a new priest will be appointed by Rome to replace the late Father Adolphus, and then I will lose two excellent nurses – but if what you are saying is correct, it seems to me that we missionaries of all persuasions should be showing some solidarity now to counter the Boxer superstition. But I wonder, I wonder. Can we really take them so seriously?'

'I advise you to take them very seriously indeed. Don't misunder-stand me, sir, I will not be intimidated by the Boxers or any man. I haven't put out any call to the American missions to evacuate, and I won't do so. I don't see the need. In fact, in this time of trial I think it behoves us to stay. It's our duty. We need to be calm. If we keep our heads and trust in the Lord, then we'll all be safe enough.'

He paused. The children heard the thump of his cigar being stubbed out in the ashtray above their heads.

'In the meanwhile, what we do *not* need at this time are mad dogs like Septimus Millward embarrassing our good name and confirming every prejudice against us.'

'Ah,' said Airton. 'You've met him, then?'

'Yes, I went to his dwelling, if such you can call it, this afternoon. The squalors of an Arapaho reservation are more refined. Doctor, I nearly despaired when I saw the skeletal state of his family. I asked him why they were not eating, and do you know what he said? The Lord has commanded them all to fast until the prodigal has returned.'

'Yes, he believes his murdered son is alive.'

'Apparently he's thriving. Mr Millward is a regular receiver of celestial visions, as you know. The latest bulletin has the boy Hiram luxuriating in abomination and vice among the stews of Babylon, which he says are located in front of Baal's temple.'

'Mad, quite mad.'

'I'll say, especially when he told me that this stew of Babylon is located above a dumpling shop in the market square of this very town. He saw his son's painted face gaze out at him from a window while the minions of Satan were beating him below.'

'You know, he was once beaten in the market square. He was trying to prevent a beheading. Actually, it was the execution of his son's murderers, whom he maintained were falsely accused. As it happens there is a brothel above a dumpling shop and it is right opposite the Confucian temple.'

'Then, sir, there's method in his madness – but, Doctor, Doctor, he is clearly deranged. What disturbs me is that this personal tragedy of his seems, if anything, to have intensified his missionary zeal. His compound, filthy as it is, is full of orphan children and infants, playing in the mud among the dogs and chickens. There must be a hundred of them. And when I was there I saw his wife return with two new infants in her arms. Apparently she'd just discovered them abandoned outside the Buddhist monastery where she had gone for alms. Imagine. Somehow they all survive there. God knows how they sustain themselves. There are adults too. Cripples and beggarly types, whom he tells me he has baptised. He says he is teaching them to speak with tongues. Yes, tongues. And he is planning a new evangelical campaign to bring the Word of God to the Palace of Babylon itself. I fear he means the Mandarin's *yamen*. All this motley crew will march there in a procession and after that, when the evil-doers have been cast down, the Lord will consider returning him his son. Don't laugh, Jesus has personally commanded him to do all this in a vision.'

'He seems to have been very open with you.'

'He was affability itself. He saw me as the commander of his order to whom a report was due. I suppose it's true. He does technically report to the American Board of Commissioners for Foreign Missions. It leaves me in a quandary. I cannot criticise his saving of orphans or his conversion of beggars but his approach is very dangerous. His compound is unhygienic. If any of those orphans were to take ill and die . . .'

'The old accusations would surface that we Christians rear orphans to steal their body parts for our rituals . . .'

'Exactly. And this march he is planning . . . Can you imagine anything more provocative at this time?'

'Can you order him to return to America?'

'Not really. This is only a fact-finding visit. A removal would have to be a decision of the whole board, perhaps of the bishop himself. And enforcement is . . . well, difficult. Good Lord, it would probably have to involve the civil authorities. But I have to do something, for his own sake.'

'And the sake of his children,' said the doctor quietly.

'Well, let us pray nothing untoward happens for the next couple of months. It will take that long for our bureaucracy to get in motion. At least Shishan is linked to the railway now, so you and I can communicate with more ease. I hate to burden you with a matter that should not be your concern, but I would be obliged if you were to keep me informed. And I promise that I will return to deal with the poor man in one way or another as soon as I can.'

'My dear fellow,' the children heard their father exclaim, 'I am as anxious as you are that the troubles of this sad family are resolved.'

'The tragedy is that Septimus Millward once showed such promise. I've seen the reports from Oberlin. He was an inspiration in his class, you know. His knowledge of the scriptures was exceptional, and he showed a greatness of heart that commanded respect and devotion. There was not a person who knew him who did not love him. There was much rejoicing when he and his family decided to come to China. A David was going to do battle with the heathen. He embraced the most difficult postings in the hardest conditions, and the letters he wrote back were always joyful, enthusiastic, full of compassion . . . It was after he came to Shishan . . . Something possessed him here. Demons. Fancies . . .'

'Come, come, Fielding, I thought we had dealt with possession by demons when we were talking about the Boxers. Next thing you'll tell me is that poor Millward has taken up the martial arts.'

'Give him time.' The American's laugh boomed and his falling hand shook the crockery on the table. 'Give him time.'

As the two children scurried back to their room, George whispered to Jenny, 'Did you hear that? Mr Fielding thinks that Mr Millward is possessed! Like the Boxers!'

'He's a Christian. He can't be.'

'No, but he can be by Christian spirits. By angels, like – like St Michael. Ah Lee said that if we're to fight the Boxers we've got to match their magic with ours. Maybe Mr Millward is our secret weapon! Only nobody realises it.'

Shortly after the departure of Mr Fielding, Helen Frances returned to stay with them. She had surprised everyone by suddenly taking up the old invitation to work in the hospital. This delighted the children at first, but it did not take them long to realise that Helen Frances had changed in an undefinable way.

She was still kind and good-natured, and smiled at them dreamily when she saw them – but she did not romp and play with them as she used to. There was something distant about her. In the evenings, after work, she would sit for hours at a time, with an unread magazine dangling from her hands, gazing into space. She no longer rode horses, or took any exercise. Tom and her father would sometimes visit, but she did not look excited to see them and her smiles, when she talked to them, seemed forced. Mr Manners never came to see her, and that perhaps disappointed the children most of all.

What was very strange was that her physical appearance had altered. The children remembered her as a ruddy, healthy girl, full of energy and spirit. Now, her cheeks were pale, and there were blue shadows under her eyes. In some ways she appeared more beautiful than ever – her hair burned a brighter red against the whiteness of her skin, her green eyes were somehow even more lustrous than before, though they shone with a sad, pale fire, unlike the infectious brilliance the children remembered. There was a languor about her, however. It was as if she was drained of energy.

'It can't all be tiredness,' said George one day, after she had gently declined to play the hoop with them in the yard. 'Mummy and Sister Elena never look tired after working in the hospital.'

'She's still new,' said Jenny. 'Maybe she's not used to it yet. And it is gloomy, working with those awful opium addicts. I wonder why she chose them anyway. She spends hours there.'

'Don't know. They give me the spooks, those addicts, wandering round with their shining eyes and their ribs showing, bumping into things or sitting on their beds like ghosts. Sister Elena said Helen Frances specially volunteered for the opium ward. She told Daddy she didn't want to work anywhere else.'

'Do you know what I think?' asked Jenny. 'I think she's suffering from a broken heart and that's why she wants to be with miserable people all day.'

'Oh, no,' groaned George. 'Not more boring love-affair talk about Mr Manners. Look, Jen, I promised to stop going on about the fox fairy. Why don't you put a brace on all that love rot? She's marrying Tom.'

'She's getting so pale she does look a bit like a fox fairy now,' said his sister reflectively. 'Anyway, I think they were in love. We saw their legs and feet touching under the table last autumn, didn't we? Didn't we?'

'Shut up, Jen. You really are boring. She's marrying Tom.'

And there the exchange ended, with Jenny sticking out her tongue at George and George chasing Jenny across the yard and pulling her hair. Two nights later, however, they heard a conversation that turned their childish banter into something altogether more serious.

It was the occasion when Tom and Helen Frances's father had come round for dinner. It was their last evening in Shishan before setting off on another expedition to Tsitsihar. The children had looked forward to this dinner for a week. Nowadays their parents never mentioned the Boxers at table and sitting under it every night had become dull. Once they had fallen asleep and woken up with a start to find all the lamps turned down and everyone already abed. The flit through the dark house had been scary. Tonight, however, Mr Delamere was coming and he always had interesting stories to tell.

They were nearly caught on their way to the dining room. Helen Frances was standing alone in the hall, looking at herself in the mirror. She was so absorbed in her own reflection that she did not notice the scuffle as the children backtracked along the corridor. There they stood in the shadows, wondering. They could hear the voices from the sitting room and were curious as to why Helen Frances was not with the others. They watched as she closed her eyes and silently leaned her forehead against the mirror. There was the saddest expression on her face. Then she straightened her shoulders and moved wearily towards the sitting room. At the door she paused, setting her face into a smile before going through the door. They heard the boom of her father's voice greeting her, and her voice trilling in reply. The subsequent general murmur hid the patter of children's feet as they rushed into the dining room and under the tablecloth, just in time. It was only a moment after they settled that Ah Lee came in and began to lay out the soup plates.

It was a cheery meal for a change. Mr Delamere was on good form, boasting about the fortune he and Tom would make when they sold the soap to their new customer, Mr Ding, in Inner Mongolia. They were going there with eight carts and ten armed guards.

'Of course there're no secrets with you fellows,' Mr Delamere added confidentially, 'but actually we've had to be pretty close about this trip. My partner Lu suspects that one of the other merchants is in league with Iron Man Wang. I'm not meant to say who, Airton, but let's say it's a respectable general trader we both know.' He dropped his voice to a whisper. 'Jin Shangui,' he hissed. 'He lets Wang know when the shipments are taking place so the bandits can ambush us.'

'My dear Delamere, if it's a secret, you shouldn't be telling me,' said the doctor. 'Anyway, I don't for a moment believe you. I've known Jin for years.'

'To be truthful I was a little surprised too,' said Frank, 'but Lu's pretty sure of it. Course, we all remain chummy on the surface –

but we don't tell Jin what we're doing any more, or we spin him a yarn sometimes to put him off the track. Quite the secret agents nowadays, aren't we, Tom?'

Tom did not reply. He and Helen Frances had hardly said a word all meal.

'I don't understand all this talk of secrets and merchants,' said their mother, from the head of the table, 'but I've heard of Iron Man Wang. Mr Delamere, I hope you and young Tom are going to be careful on this great adventure of yours. Bandits are menace enough, but with all these rumours of Boxers threatening harm to God-fearing people as well, I for one get worried.'

'You don't have to worry about Boxers,' laughed Mr Delamere. 'They won't come this far north. At least, they haven't done so yet. And we've faced Iron Man Wang's boys before, haven't we, Tom? Or, rather, you did, you brave fellow. Mind you, it'll be interesting on the way back from Tsitsihar when we're loaded up with all the silver we're getting for the alkali. Helen Frances, my dear, you didn't know that your fiancé and your papa are going to be rich, did you? I expect the board of directors of Babbit and Brenner will vote their hardworking sons of the soil a substantial commission when they hear of the profit we'll be making for them this time. Have you ever seen a wagon loaded with silver, Doctor? It's a beautiful sight. That's why we're taking the armed guards. Not for the outward journey, but for the return.'

'I think you ought to be more discreet, Papa,' said Helen Frances, breaking her silence for the first time.

'Nonsense, girl,' said Mr Delamere, helping himself to crème caramel proffered on a tray by Ah Lee. 'It's all in the family here. Who could be eavesdropping at the Airtons?' The children saw his heavy torso turn in his daughter's direction. 'You're a bit pale, chicken,' he said to her. 'Have you been unwell? Or are you sad to see your old father go off on a trip again?'

'She won't be pining for you, Delamere. It's young Cabot she'll be missing,' said Airton jovially.

'Yes, now you mention it, we haven't had a word out of Tom all evening either. What a gloomy pair they are. Glad my old skin's too thick for Cupid's darts. They look miserable the both of them. Parting is such sweet sorrow, eh?'

'I was wondering if it would be impertinent to ask,' the doctor cleared his throat, 'if a date had been fixed for the wedding?'

'Yes, Tom,' the children's mother said. 'It's a pleasure having dear Helen Frances staying and we do value her help in the infirmary, but we wonder from time to time what your ultimate plans are. I daresay she's been missing you immensely. She's lately been very quiet, and I agree with you, Mr Delamere, she has looked a little off-colour.'

The children noticed that Tom was punching his fist softly into his palm under the table, and one of his feet was gently tapping the floor. They had the impression of enormous energy being tightly controlled. Suddenly the large hands vanished from their view and there was a rattle of the table above them.

'Mrs Airton, Dr Airton, may I trespass on your hospitality?'

'By all means, Tom,' said the doctor, in the sudden hush this outburst had caused.

'I wondered if I might have a few moments alone with my fiancée. We can – we can join you in the drawing room a little later.'

'Why, of course,' he said, after a pause. Then, 'How stupid of me. Of course you must have some moments alone together. Whatever was I thinking?'

'Probably of the port and cigars we're going to miss by retiring from the table early,' muttered Mr Delamere.

'Mr Delamere,' said Nellie, 'you may have your glass of port, and your cigar, with coffee besides – but in the drawing room. Come. I think these two young persons have much to say to each other.' And chairs scraped, two pinstriped pairs of legs and a bustled dress disappeared, Mr Delamere's grumbling diminished out of earshot, and in a moment only Tom's flannels and Helen Frances's striped skirt remained, the bodies above them unmoving. The children gazed at each other wide-eyed in the unnatural silence as the engaged couple confronted each other across the table above their heads.

'Off to Tsitsihar again tomorrow,' said Tom, after a pause. 'Won't see me for a while. Five to six weeks at best.'

He seemed to wait for a reply, but none care.

'Mr Lu's confident enough that Mr Ding will purchase all the alkali. It'll be Babbit and Brenner's big breakthrough. Everything your father's worked for.'

'I'm glad for him,' murmured Helen Frances. 'And for you.' The children had to strain to hear her voice.

Tom waited, as if he expected her to say more. 'Well, I'm glad too,' he said, after a while. 'Yes, it's very – gratifying.' He paused. 'The journey . . .' he continued. 'Look, don't worry about us. We'll be all right.'

'Father shouldn't be telling everybody about the silver.'

'No, he shouldn't.' The children noticed that Tom's foot was tapping the carpet again. His hands were twisting the side of his chair.

'He's become so boastful. Stupid. Juvenile.' Helen Frances spat the words. The children started at the shrill vehemence. 'I'm sick of him. Sick of him. Drinking. Boasting. Drooling sentimentally over his little girl. I'm *not* his little girl. Has he even thought of the danger he's putting you in? Is this deal so important that he has to risk your lives on the road? He's monstrous, and you're a fool for going along with him.'

'Come on, HF,' sighed Tom, 'we're taking all precautions. We've gone that way before. This is an ordinary business trip.'

'Not with Boxers about, and the bandits knowing your movements. But you're as bad as he is, aren't you? What a pair you are. Jolly adventurers. Everything a joke, or a game of cricket. How I despise you.'

Tom had gone rigid again at her outburst. But Helen Frances's hands had also tightened under the table: Jenny could see her knuckles pale in the gloom, and her legs and body shaking under her dress. Like Tom earlier she seemed to be forcing back some strong emotion she could hardly control.

'HF, what's the matter?' asked Tom quietly. 'You've been acting oddly for weeks – months, actually.'

'Not you too?' said Helen Frances scornfully. 'Are you going to nag me like Nellie? "Och, Helen Frances, aren't we a wee bit pale again today? Och, Helen Frances, aren't you going to finish your chicken soup?" If people would only leave me alone. Leave – me – alone.'

'Your father and I are concerned about you,' said Tom, lamely.

'My father and you? It's always my father and you, isn't it? What an inseparable pair you've become. Is that why we're engaged? Am I part of the deal? So we can all be a jolly threesome doing great things for Babbit and Brenner?' She laughed. It was an ugly sound. 'The two of you don't need me, Tom. I'm no part of your nice little boys' club. The two of you should be happy enough now I've left you to come and work here. You can both drink and joke to your heart's content, can't you? Has my father introduced you to one of his fillies yet? You do know about his goings-on before we arrived?'

Tom breathed out heavily. 'Well, old girl, if I hadn't seen you touch nothing but water all evening, I'd have said you'd had one too many. I really don't know what you're talking about.'

'Pure, honest Tom. You really are too good to be true, aren't you?'

Tom pushed back his chair. The children could hear the click of his feet as he paced back and forth. Helen Frances seemed to quieten. Her hands settled on her lap. After a few moments Tom sat down again. 'I've never asked you what happened between you and Manners,' he said, his voice softer but somehow firmer than before, 'while we were away in Tsitsihar, and afterwards. I've never questioned you or him. Mrs Airton once told me something about a rainstorm . . . You must understand something about me, HF, that I'm a simple fellow. I'm not imaginative, or clever. I take things at face value. And I'll trust people until I know I shouldn't. Maybe that's foolish. To think the best of people. Maybe it's cowardice. Running away from facts. But sometimes you hope – you just hope – that if you let things be, they'll turn out for the best.

'No, don't say anything. It's my turn to speak now. You've had your go at me. I don't think you hate me, although for the last few weeks, whenever you've spoken to me, your words have been . . . well, not what a fellow wants to hear from the girl he's in love with. I don't think I gave you any cause to be angry. If I did, it was unintentional and I'm sorry.

'But I don't think, actually, you are angry with me or your father. I think you're in a bate with yourself. The few occasions at school that I blew my rag, as often as not I was only taking out on the other fellow some rage at my own mistakes. I don't know how a woman's mind works. But I think it's probably the same. Let me say this once and for all. I don't care what happened between you and Manners. If it's over, HF. If it's over. As long as it's over I don't want to know. It's past. Forgotten.'

'Forgotten?'

'I love you, HF,' said Tom simply. 'I mean it. Forgotten. Unless he hurt you.' His voice hardened. 'If I find out that he hurt you, then I'll kill him.'

George gasped, Jenny quickly put a hand over his mouth, but neither of the adults heard. Tom was punching his palm again under the table. They saw his chest expand as he took a deep breath. 'If it's not over, on the other hand . . . If it's not over . . .' His voice stumbled. He sighed, took another breath. 'Then you must tell me, old girl, and I'll get out of your way.'

The children dared not move. Helen Frances reached in her purse and withdrew a handkerchief. It was damp when she replaced it. Presumably she was weeping. Her voice, however, when she spoke was calm and flat. She sounded tired. 'It's over. He didn't hurt me. You don't have to kill him. Does that satisfy you?'

Tom slumped in his chair, letting out something between a groan and a sob. There was a long pause. The children could hear the grandfather clock ticking in the hall. There was a laugh from the sitting room.

'And us?' he said, after a while.

'I don't know,' said Helen Frances.

'Our engagement?'

'I don't know,' she said, clenching her fists.

Tom thumped his own fist down on the table. The plates and glasses rattled. A wine glass fell and the children saw the tablecloth stain red and drips pool on the parquet.

'Sometimes I think I will kill him anyway. The bounder. The cad. The . . .' The explosion was over as soon as it had begun. His voice faded. Helen Frances said nothing.

Another explosion. Tom was on his feet again. George and Jenny heard him banging back and forth, back and forth.

'God, HF. Why? Why?'

She said nothing.

The children heard the steps move round the end of the table to Helen Frances's side. Suddenly her body was dragged upward, off her chair. Craning their heads they could see Tom's great arms in a bear's embrace around her but she hung limply, unresponsively. He seemed to be shaking her. 'I love you. I love you,' he groaned, but her head was turned away. After a while he replaced her gently in her chair. The sound of the pacing continued.

'I'm away for six weeks, two months.' The words came out

woodenly. 'When I'm back I'll ask you if you still want to marry me. My feelings for you won't have changed. I'm yours, HF. You're life for me. Nothing less. I loved you from the moment I saw you, at your aunt's house. You came in and the gas-light burned brighter. That's the best I can describe it. You radiated me. I never dreamed . . . On the boat that night when you . . . I felt, how can a chap deserve such happiness? I suppose I should be thankful. I'll always have that memory.'

The pacing stopped.

'But didn't we have such fun together? Don't you remember how we used to laugh? Our eyes would only have to meet and we'd read each other's thoughts . . . I blame myself. I shouldn't have left you alone all day. I shouldn't have got so intoxicated like your father with that bloody soap yard. I should have been with you, so you wouldn't have had to go riding with him . . . with that . . .'

'Don't, Tom. It wasn't your fault.' Helen Frances's voice hardly exceeded a whisper.

Tom began to say something, but stopped himself. Then the children heard him sigh.

'If the answer's no when I get back, I won't make it difficult for you. Excuse me if I don't stay around in Shishan. I couldn't bear that. Babbit and Brenner will give me some other outpost somewhere. I don't care if they don't. I'm sure life will go on. As I said, I'll have my memories. And if a chap chooses to nurse a broken heart, well that's his own affair, isn't it?

'But think hard, old girl. Think hard while I'm away. It doesn't matter if you throw away my life, but don't throw away yours.'

His voice choked. 'Excuse me. I can't bear to face anybody else this evening. Pass on my thanks to Mrs Airton. Make some excuse . . . Oh, God, HF, your hair in the light of that candle . . . How I love you . . . God go with you, my dearest. Think of me sometimes.'

The door to the corridor opened and softly closed. The children listened to Tom's footsteps fade. Helen Frances had not moved. She continued to sit rigidly in her chair, then her body slumped and began to heave with silent sobs. A hum seemed to emanate from deep inside her, which developed into a shrill wail of misery. She rocked from side to side as the keen from inside her grew louder. Jenny could not bear it. She left her hiding-place under the tablecloth and hugged the weeping woman. Tears were running down her own face. The keening stopped. Helen Frances put her arms round her and the two wept silently in each other's arms. Like a mole, George put his own head into the light. In a moment he, too, had been swept into the embrace. The three rocked silently together, and it was this tableau that Frank Delamere saw, a cigar in his mouth, when he peeped in from the sitting room.

'I say,' he called to the Airtons behind him, 'here's a subject worthy of Burne-Jones. Mariana crying her eyes out at the moated grange with a couple of cherubs as comforters. No sign of Sir Lancelot. No doubt he's so overcome with sorrow at a separation too grievous to be borne that he's sloped off already. Ain't it touching? Well, well. Cheer up, old girl. We're only going to Tsitsihar. Back before you know it. Don't worry, the wedding bells will ring soon enough. Airton, how come your children are up so late? Getting a little liberal, aren't you? It was six o'clock to the nursery with a loaf of bread in my day.'

Two miles away, in the Palace of Heavenly Pleasure, Fan Yimei was coming to a decision. Major Lin was away with his troops. She was alone in the pavilion.

Across the courtyard she could see lights in the windows of the pavilion that mirrored hers. Earlier the Englishman Ma Na Si had been having dinner there, followed by a bout of drinking with his Japanese friend. Originally Major Lin was to have joined them (no doubt for another interminable discussion about gun-running) but there had been disorder in one of the outlying villages – a group of hooligans, maybe one of the bands of Boxers that everyone was talking about, had been inciting disturbances against local Christians, and a barn had been burned – so the Mandarin had ordered Major Lin to go there to restore order. He had grumbled, but obeyed. He had said that he would be away for at least two days.

She had observed that the Japanese man who reminded her of a snake had already left Ma Na Si's pavilion a short while earlier, following Mother Liu to the main building. She knew where he was going, and she felt a deep pang of sympathy for the white catamite who waited for him. Colonel Taro had repelled her from the moment she met him. For all his courtesies and good looks she sensed violence lurking behind the velvet charm. His eyes never smiled: lizard-like, they would flick from person to person, coldly, appraisingly. He had a terrible effect on Major Lin. The more relaxed and ingratiating the Japanese became, the stiffer and more curt was her lover's response to him. He took propriety to the extremes of discourtesy, as if he loathed this man he had to do business with. Yet in pauses of conversation, when Taro's attention was elsewhere, she would observe Lin looking at the Japanese, with a wistfulness in his eyes that was almost spaniel-like. It was the gaze of a worshipper or a lover.

Lin always drank more than usual before and after the Japanese colonel's visits. And invariably at night when he and she were alone after his drinking, the rod would come out and he would demand to be beaten. He had also become brutal with her, slapping her, forcing her to her knees in front of him. If he took her it was in the dog position. Sometimes she would wake in the night and hear him crying. She had always suspected that her lover was hiding some shame. She had assumed that it dated back to the war. Now she no longer doubted what it was. As a slave herself she had come to recognise the symptoms.

Her suspicions of Taro's proclivities had been confirmed a few days before, when Mother Liu, angry and preoccupied, had summoned her to the main buildings. Mother Liu's creature, Su Liping, had led her up flights of stairs she had not known existed and down an undecorated wooden corridor flanked by cells. In one of the rooms Mother Liu was waiting. She lifted a blanket from a figure huddled on the bed. It was like revisiting a bad dream. For a moment she had the delusion that the bloody, bruised flesh was that of Shen Ping returned from the grave. Then horror gave way to curiosity and surprise. This was no girl and no Chinese but a thin, pinched foreign boy. Mother Liu gripped her by the throat. 'You won't breathe a word, do you hear? Or you're a dead woman. I want you to clean this brat up. Fix him up and get him well, like you did last year with that bitch Shen Ping. I don't want this one dead on me. Not yet. There's still money to be made from him. Do you understand? I've picked you because you have a healing touch, and you're intelligent enough to know when to keep your mouth shut. You'd better not disappoint me. Do you hear?'

Numbly she had set about her task. It was obvious that the boy had been beaten, but not in the indiscriminate manner of Ren Ren. The cuts were clustered on the buttocks and upper thighs (a dim part of her mind registered that there were scars on Major Lin's body in the same area). The real torment had been the cigarette burns on the boy's nipples and genitals. The boy was conscious and in whimpering pain, and screamed when she placed the ointment on his wounds. The pale eyes in his puffed red face followed her movements with fear. When she tried to talk to him he shook his head violently from side to side. 'No words,' he whimpered. 'No words. Ren Ren will . . . Ren Ren will . . .' and his narrow face had screwed up with terror.

It had taken time, but by the third day her gentleness had won him over, and he began haltingly to answer her questions, in surprisingly fluent Chinese. She asked him if it had been Ren Ren who had beaten him. 'No,' he told her, his eyes widening. 'I haven't done anything wrong. Really I haven't done anything wrong. Please don't tell him I've done anything wrong.' He forced a smile. 'He sometimes comes to me when I'm good.' Then tears began to stream down his face. 'I did try. I did try. The old men like me. He never punishes me for the old men. He used to reward me – sometimes if I did really well he stayed the whole night with me afterwards. And this time I tried so hard. When this one explained about the pain, I did listen. He said that there could be no love without punishment. So I let him . . . I let him . . .'

'Ren Ren?' asked Fan Yimei, confused.

'No!' the boy cried. 'Ren Ren loves me. It was the other man. It was the devil man Mother Liu said I had to specially please. The Japanese,' he whispered.

Then Fan Yimei knew. And her horror of Colonel Taro increased. She told herself that many men become violent when drunk. That was not abnormal. Many men gave way to violent passions when their senses were befuddled by liquor – her own Major Lin was typical. But Colonel Taro was different. He was like Ren Ren, a sadist who enjoyed inflicting pain, only unlike Ren Ren, who had the appetites of a brute, this Taro practised cruelty with refinement and patience: the more he drank the more deliberate and passionless he became. 'He says that love is an art,' the foreign boy had whimpered as she bandaged the wounds on his back and thighs. 'He says that love is an art.'

And with her understanding came sympathy for Major Lin. If

Colonel Taro had been his captor during the war, then everything was explained. The poor, proud man . . .

She knew that she should be alarmed about her own situation. She did not know why Mother Liu had let her into the secret of the hidden room and the extraordinary presence of a foreigner in the brothel. Perhaps it was as the old tyrant had said: she remembered her nursing of Shen Ping. More likely, in Mother Liu's mind, Fan Yimei was dispensable, or would be when Lin was finished with her. Well, what was different? She knew already that the hut at the bottom of the garden awaited her one day. Mother Liu had nothing to fear. The secret was safe. Where did she have to run? Who did she have to tell? But she did feel sorry for the boy who was imprisoned here.

Then that afternoon her sympathy for his predicament had turned to alarm for his safety. She had been aware that Ren Ren and his hangers-on were having a carousing and gambling session in one of the dining rooms of the main building. She had not been prepared for their eruption into her courtyard in the early part of the afternoon, or for the noisy demonstration that followed. They were wearing yellow scarves wrapped round their heads and one carried a silk banner with a picture of a black stick and the word 'Retribution' painted on it in bloody characters. Another man pounded on a drum while Ren Ren, stripped to the waist and holding a sword, shouted and leaped into the air, apparently possessed or drunk, in a travesty of martial arts. She had been ordered to stay in her room out of sight because she was told that a *yin* force would contaminate the magic they were conjuring: female pollution would deter the gods from descending into the bodies of the martial artists. Or so Monkey, one of Ren Ren's more odious henchman, had barked at her as he bolted her into her room, but it had not prevented her peeking through the cracks in the door to see what was going on, or listening to the shouts as Ren Ren and three of the others danced themselves into a frenzy. She did not believe that any god would wish to inhabit Ren Ren's body, so she presumed that he was play-acting or showing off – but she knew him well enough to realise that whatever game he was playing it boded badly for somebody. 'Save the Ch'ing! Annihilate the foreigners!' they were shouting, and 'Death to the foreign devils.' One of them had run up to the locked pavilion opposite and yelled in a high-pitched voice, 'This is where one of them brings his fox-spirit whore. Kill! Kill! Kill!' and the others had laughed as he pissed against the doorpost. The performance had lasted all afternoon, and only finished when Ren Ren had collapsed on the ground exhausted. The group had then drifted off in twos and threes in the direction of the outer gate. 'To the altar in the Black Hills,' one shouted, 'where the heavenly army descends.' Another began to sing and they all took up the crude doggerel:

> 'No rain comes from Heaven
> The earth is parched and dry
> And all because the churches
> Have bottled up the sky.
>
> 'The gods are very angry
> The spirits seek revenge.
> En masse they come from heaven
> To teach the Way to men.'

Waving their swords and spears they left, even Ren Ren, leaning on a friend's arm. The sound of the drum and the angry voices faded. Fan Yimei sat on the edge of her bed, exceedingly disturbed.

She had never paid much attention to the other girls' gossip about the Boxers. Her father had taught her not to believe in magical spells and she did not credit the stories about gods descending to the earth. Nor could she become excited about an army that would spring from the soil to purge society of evil-doers and restore the wrongs that the dynasty was suffering at the hands of the foreigners. It would have to be an exceptional army, she thought bitterly, to consider righting the wrongs of poor creatures like herself suffering inside the walls of the Palace of Heavenly Pleasure. Not if it was an army made up of men.

And what had the problems of the dynasty to do with her anyway? She was as much cut off from the world outside as a Buddhist nun in a convent. She smiled at the conceit. Yet the life of the flower girl had its own equivalent of monastic rules, its own perversion of celibacy, and rituals of oppression that had been hallowed and condoned for centuries. It was part of the same social order that the Boxers were saying they wanted to save and preserve. So, what should she expect from the Boxers if not more oppression? The Palace of Heavenly Pleasure, in its way, was as much a symbol of tradition and established order as the temple, or the *yamen*, or even the dynasty itself. There had always been flower girls. And always men to exploit them. And here was Ren Ren himself rushing off to join the Boxers. What more needed to be said?

Such animosity towards foreigners was new. She remembered the kindly doctor who looked like a mouse and had tried to save her father's life. What sort of threat could he be to the dynasty? Or blundering, foolish De Falang, who probably even now did not know what had happened to his Shen Ping, believing Mother Liu's lies that she had been sent away to the country. What harm could he be to anyone? The missionary's son? He was a victim like her. And that left Ma Na Si.

Ma Na Si. As always when she thought of him, she was startled by the vivid impression of a smile and laughing blue eyes, which immediately came to her mind as if he was physically present in the room. Yes, she admitted to herself, perhaps there was something dangerous about Ma Na Si. Despite herself she had become curious about this courteous and confident foreigner who had so effortlessly exerted a mastery over Major Lin, and even persuaded Mother Liu to offer him the privileges of the other pavilion for his foreign mistress. Not since that first terrible evening – the evening of her friend's murder – had he addressed anything but polite compliments to her. As was only proper – she was Major Lin's concubine – he ignored her, or pretended to. Yet there was something there. Sometimes she would look up from her *chin* and see his blue eyes observing her, and if their eyes met a slow smile would break over his tanned features, and once – she could hardly believe it – he had winked at her. On that occasion she blushed and looked down at her hands, and when she looked up again his head had been bent in close confabulation with Major Lin. She wondered if she had imagined it: he hardly looked at her for the rest of the evening. Nor did he ever direct such a personal gesture at her again. Yet ever since then she had felt that there was an unspoken complicity between them and, deeper than that, she had read in his clear gaze an interrogation, as if he had been trying to seek the true character behind the flower girl's mask. And sometimes, when he smiled in her direction, she caught herself hoping that he had seen something, and she would give way to the idle fancy that the appraising look of this barbarian was one of respect.

She had been startled by her own reaction when Ma Na Si had taken the pavilion opposite and the visits of the foreign woman began. Many were the gloomy winter afternoons that she waited by her window for the black-cloaked form of the woman to hurry from the gatehouse and disappear inside the pavilion. Ma Na Si in his white shirt would open the door and pull the figure inside. She never did manage to see the woman properly, though once a strand of brilliant red hair slipped from beneath the hood, and fluttered in the breeze; she had watched transfixed as a long freckled hand moved nervously from under the cloak to smooth it away. But it was not the foreign woman who fascinated her. What she was waiting for, and dreading at the same time, was the glimpse of Ma Na Si's own face when he greeted his paramour, and each time the radiant smile of welcome had pierced her heart. At first she could not understand her feelings. She could never admit to herself that she was jealous, yet when she first saw Ma Na Si's arms embrace the black cloak, her lips tightened, her chest constricted, her eyes misted and a vein in her temple throbbed. She never allowed herself such a self-indulgence of emotion again. She watched sadly and calmly, as she watched everything that went on in the Palace of Heavenly Pleasure sadly and calmly. After all, this was only one more slice to a spirit that had learned to endure the Death of a Thousand Cuts.

And then the woman's visits ceased. There had been no assignation for a month now. Ma Na Si still came to the pavilion, but always by himself, and on these occasions Fan Yimei sensed a weariness in his step, as if sorrow was weighing on his shoulders. He would remain alone in his room for hours, allowing the afternoon to fade and the dusk to settle before calling for the lamps. At first Mother Liu had brought girls to him, Su Liping and Chen Meina, but they never stayed with him long and once he angrily turned Su Liping away. Ren Ren had been called, and there was an ugly scene, with much shouting and fist-shaking on the part of Ren Ren. Money had resolved whatever the altercation was about. Ma Na Si had thrown a pouch of gold at Ren Ren's feet, and watched sardonically as the young man scrabbled for the coins.

Most evenings he would dine with the Japanese colonel; sometimes Major Lin would join them. On these occasions Major Lin would return drunk in the early hours. Fan Yimei suspected that when Ma Na Si was by himself he also drank heavily. Once, when he was leaving after one of his solitary vigils, she saw him swaying on the steps, then he righted himself and walked quietly away. Fan Yimei sat among her own shadows, wishing for an impossibility – but eventually she put aside the thought. She had learned many years ago that hope was her greatest enemy was hope.

Tonight it was not hope that impelled her across the courtyard but fear. She had thought about the implications of what she had seen in the courtyard this afternoon. Ren Ren might have been play-acting at being a Boxer, but there was more behind this than his usual operatic vanity. The slogans he and his friends had been chanting were none of their own invention. The threats made against the foreigners were therefore real. Her first thought was for the boy. She knew enough to realise that his life hung by a thread of secrecy; she did not doubt that Ren Ren and Mother Liu between them had already thought of a way to dispose of him should there be any danger of him being discovered. Even she had heard about the execution of the peasants who were supposed to have murdered him. The boy was therefore already as good as dead. Now that Ren Ren was espousing the cause of the Boxers, here was a ready-made foreign victim in his power. His only hope was escape back to his own kind. She thought of Ma Na Si. She had no plan, but if anyone could help him . . . Anyway, Ma Na Si needed to be warned himself . . . She had an opportunity this evening . . . No one would see her . . .

She was already half-way across the courtyard before she saw how hopeless and unrealistic was the task she had set herself. The boy's main tormentor was the Japanese, and he was Ma Na Si's friend. And why should the Englishman help her, anyway? Or even believe her?

What could she offer him to persuade him?

The blood drained from her cheeks as she realised the answer. And then she was standing still on the pavilion steps, questioning herself. Had she not known that all along? Was it really the boy she had come to save? Her knees quivered and she tottered on her lotus feet as a wave of shame and despair engulfed her. She leaned against the pillar, and tears welled in her eyes.

Panting, she turned to leave. At that moment the door opened and Manners appeared. He was dressed in his shirt and braces and he had a bottle of wine in his hand. His eyes were bloodshot and puffed. He was swaying. 'I'm sorry, Ma Na Si Xiansheng, I'm sorry.' Her voice was a whisper. 'I did not mean to disturb you . . . I'm leaving straight away. Sorry. Sorry.'

Manners peered at her. Then, leaning on the railing of the verandah, he stared into the shadows of the courtyard. Nothing moved. He turned back to her. 'No,' he said. 'Please don't leave.'

'I mustn't. I can't,' breathed Fan Yimei.

'For a few moments. Sit with me. Talk with me. I could . . . I could do with company tonight,' said Manners.

'I can . . . I can call Mother Liu,' said Fan Yimei. 'Perhaps Chen Meina . . .'

'No,' said Manners. 'You misunderstand me . . . Please.'

'Major Lin . . .' she started.

'I know,' he answered. 'I know . . . But please. For a short while. Keep me company tonight.'

Fan Yimei remained very still, her head bowed. Manners moved a heavy hand up and wiped a flick of hair from his forehead. He shrugged, made as if to say something, then reached forward and gently lifted her chin, looking deeply into her eyes as he did so. 'You're crying,' he said. 'Please don't cry. Here.' He reached into his pocket and dabbed her cheek with his handkerchief. 'You're remarkably beautiful,' he said softly. 'I've never thought you belonged here. I've watched you. You listen and understand. You're educated. What was the tragedy that brought someone like you to this hellhole? . . . This country,' he sighed, 'so many tragedies . . .' He stepped back and contemplated her. 'I wouldn't hurt you,' he said. 'Not for the world.'

The two stood facing each other, one with her head bowed, supporting herself against the pillar, the other larger figure swaying in the doorway. Eventually she nodded. 'There is a boy,' she said, in a small voice. 'I will ask for your help.'

'Yes,' he said, after a pause. 'Whatever.' He turned heavily and went into the room.

Fan Yimei followed and the door closed.

The courtyard was silent. A bough swung in the light breeze. A dog barked in the alley outside.

A figure moved from the shadow of the trees, a slight figure on tottering feet. It was Su Liping. Cautiously she crept forward, up the steps and on to the balcony ringing the pavilion. Silently she slid along the wall. Hardly daring to breathe, she moved the small panel that disguised Mother Liu's peep-hole. Trembling, she put her eye to the aperture, and watched for a long while.

Next afternoon George and Jenny with Ah Lee as their escort went for a walk down the country path that ringed the bottom of their hill. It was a bright spring afternoon. The trees were sheathed in a furze of green buds. The winter nakedness of the millet fields was beginning to be covered in a blanket of shoots. Plum blossom was already visible among the orchards. From a distance they could hear a cuckoo, the first after the long winter. It had been their mother's idea to get the children into the fresh air, to gather wild flowers for the vase on the dining-room table.

George was talking excitedly about the Mandarin's annual tiger hunt, which was to take place during the following month in the Black Hills. As usual, invitations had arrived for the foreigners. Last year their father had gone and they had been lucky. A tiger had been found. At bedtime he told them frightening stories of how the huge beast at bay had disembowelled one of the hunting dogs with its paws, and knocked over one of the spearmen, horse and man, how it had broken out of the ring of hunters and charged towards the hillock where the doctor had been waiting with the Mandarin, and how the Mandarin had drawn his bow and slain the tiger with three arrows fired in quick succession, all in the time it took for the doctor to take a frightened breath and fiddle with the safety-catch of his gun. George could never forget the size of the dead animal strung on a pole and carried by four men when the triumphant procession had returned to Shishan.

They were bitterly disappointed that they were not considered old enough to go with their father and Helen Frances, and it was only a small comfort that their mother had agreed to stay behind and keep them company. This year they would have been particularly excited to see Mr Manners and his Japanese military friend among the hunters. They were convinced that Mr Manners would perform extraordinary feats of heroism.

George had found a curved stick, which he had tucked into his shoulder like a rifle. A hunter stalking his prey, he had crept on ahead of Jenny and Ah Lee, who were occupied in gathering violets from the bank on the side of the road. The road curved there and a large willow tree hung down from the bank obscuring the path ahead. George manoeuvred carefully through the drooping branches; in his imagination he was creeping through dense jungle, listening for the growl of the tiger. With a cry he leaped through the willow branches and exploded into the road on the other side, his rifle cocked and ready to fire. 'Bang! Bang!' he cried.

He found himself face to face with a Chinese boy his own age. The boy, stripped to the waist and nut brown as any peasant, contemplated him silently with his arms folded. George was aware of big white eyes in the dark face, looking at him curiously at first then narrowing superciliously when he saw the stick George was aiming at his face.

The next thing George knew was that the boy had vaulted into the air, at the same time emitting a high-pitched cry like that of a seagull or a crane. For a second he seemed to hang in the air, one leg and arm stretched forward, the other leg curved behind him. Then George felt the stick rip from his hands, as the boy's foot snapped it in two. One end of the stick flicked up and tore his cheek and temple while a glancing blow on his shoulder rolled him into the mud. When he looked up from where he had fallen the boy was standing as he had first seen him, his arms folded, contemplating him. Behind him lounged several tall young men, some holding spears and swords, most with yellow scarves wrapped round their heads. One of the men rested a hand on the boy's shoulder. The boy looked up at the man with a proud smile. George began to cry.

Ah Lee and Jenny appeared round the bend in the road, their arms full of flowers.

Ah Lee screamed something and ran forward dropping his flowers. The man who had congratulated the boy blocked his path. As Ah Lee tried to edge to one side the man in the headscarf moved to counter him. The other men and the boy began to laugh.

Gently the man pushed Ah Lee's chest so he tottered backwards. Ah Lee cursed and swung a blow at the man's head. Effortlessly the man ducked, his leg snaked out and Ah Lee fell on his behind in the mud. 'You turtle's egg,' he hissed, and launched himself at the man, who caught his head in a shoulder lock and began to twist.

The other Boxers were shouting, '*Sha! Sha! Sha!*' which George knew was the word for 'Kill'.

Jenny stood frozen in the middle of the road clutching her flowers.

Suddenly the Boxers fell silent. With a start George recognised the Boxer priest in the middle of them. It was as if he had appeared from nowhere. He was wearing the same strange clothes decorated with pomegranates that George had noticed the last time he had seen him during those unforgettable seconds when the man had stood in front of the oncoming train. Sightlessly, expressionlessly, the priest made a gesture with his hand. Then, turning his back, he moved off down the road that led to the Black Hills. The man who was strangling Ah Lee spat, and dropped his victim to the ground. He kicked the groaning body, then turned after the priest, who was already far down the road. The others followed, including the boy, and in a few moments the road was empty, except for George who was now crawling towards a wheezing Ah Lee, sitting in the dust, clutching his neck and shaking his head, and Jenny standing where she was frozen, her bluebells and violets pressed against her open mouth, her eyes round with horror and fear.

Chapter Ten

*The gods have descended. It is true. I saw it – with my
own eyes.*

D r Airton sat alone by the campfire hugging his mug of tea.
The embers crackled into flame, the tall trees loomed, the
shadows edged closer, and a drum thudded softly in the forest. He
assumed that it was the beaters celebrating the success of the hunt
– but the noise welled and subsided and was sometimes quenched
altogether when the wind gusted. He would not have been able to
swear from which direction the sound was coming or from how far
away, or even whether he was imagining it, and this made him feel
dislocated and unsure. The presence outside the ring of firelight of
the few guards left behind by the Mandarin gave no reassurance; if
anything their hovering added to the indefinable sense of menace.

The doctor usually enjoyed camping. He loved the starry nights
and the scent of woodsmoke. He felt awed and humbled by vast
spaces. He loved the wet dawns and the heart-stopping mystery
when the first rays of sunshine blew away the night mists and
blazing Nature was revealed in all her glory. Nellie had once asked
him what it was in his western shockers that so appealed to him, and
he had answered, in all seriousness, 'The great outdoors, my dear.
These are stories about men who live in Paradise.' And he believed
it. Whatever squalid gunfight or robbery was the ostensible subject
of the penny dreadful, it was the shining backdrop of the prairie
that compelled his imagination. His thoughts used to soar over the
cacti as he scanned the printed page. The stockman laying his head
on his saddle at the end of a hard day's riding, the thin column of
smoke rising from the chuck wagon to a sky of scudding clouds,
thunder murmuring over the faraway hills, and cattle lowing by
the deep-flowing river – this was mankind living at peace in the
canvas of Creation as it had been before the Fall, or such had been
the message he had laboured to pass to his bemused congregation
of Catholic nuns and Chinese invalids in a recent sermon. He had

quoted from the psalms: 'The heavens declare the glory of God: and the firmament sheweth his handiwork.' For him cowboys lived in nothing less than an Eden fashioned by the God of the sunrise and the sunset, and sleeping under canvas brought him close to it.

Only tonight it was a darker deity who presided over this camp in the Black Hills.

He shivered and pulled the blanket closer round his shoulders. 'Pull yourself together, man,' he muttered. 'You're becoming as agitated as an old woman who's misplaced her teeth.'

He closed his eyes and held his breath in an attempt to quieten his thumping heart, but the mocking image of the Mandarin flashed behind his retina – and the anger and disappointment, which had been growing for a fortnight, welled in his bosom.

It had taken three whole days, and even then an audience had been denied. Three whole days, during which George had tossed on his sickbed, and Jenny had huddled in her nursery chair, not speaking, not responding even to her mother.

He could hardly bear to recall that first scene of horror and pandemonium – Sister Caterina bursting into his office shouting at him in a gush of Italian so that it took him several moments to understand what had happened, then the pounding run through the courtyards and corridors to the infirmary, where Nellie and Helen Frances were struggling with the children shaking uncontrollably in their arms. Nellie had been dabbing at the blood that was running down his son's head. And he had seen immediately the blank terror in his daughter's eyes and her unnaturally pale complexion. For a long second he froze, his mind unable to cope with the implications. His own blood roared in his ears, blocking any sounds. Nellie was calling out to him but he could not make out what she was saying.

The scene seemed to take on a nightmarish aspect of farce, as if a Punch and Judy show were being staged in slow motion in a morgue. In the foreground his son's lifeblood pumped silently over his wife's dress. Behind this central tableau, Ah Sun was beating her husband with a dust tray, screaming curses at him for failing to protect the children; Ah Lee, half swooning on the bed, held his strained and swollen neck in one hand, trying ineffectually to ward off the blows with the other. On the other side of the room, Sister Elena, who might have been expected to help, was relieving her consternation by yelling and gesticulating at the major domo, Zhang Erhao, who stood hangdog by the window, clearly failing to comprehend any of the nun's contradictory instructions. Outside the window the moon faces of the opium addicts stared in blankly.

After an age, his physician's instincts took over and started him into mechanical activity. He could not remember now what he had said or how he had restored order. It had taken only a short examination to apprehend that mercifully there was no serious physical hurt inflicted. George was bruised and had a nasty gash on his temple, Jenny – thank Providence – was untouched, and Ah Lee, while in pain, had no injury that would not soon be mended. There was no denying, however, the terror and shock to which the children had been subjected. It had therefore been in a state of barely controlled rage that he had struggled into his formal clothes and walked the interminable two miles to the *yamen* – only to find that the big wooden gates were closed and his path barred by two well-armed *yamen* runners.

'Do you not know who I am?' he had shouted in their impassive faces. 'I am the foreign *daifu*, the Mandarin's friend. I demand to be let in.'

The two guards had grinned at each other and folded their arms.

He had pushed past them and banged on the gate with the end of his cane, only to be seized and thrown roughly to the ground. The smiles on the *yamen* runners' faces had changed to scowls and one had drawn his sword.

The small door in the gate creaked open and the chamberlain, Jin Lao, stood smiling above him. 'Honourable Daifu, why are you lying on the ground? Your clothes are covered in dust.'

'Jin Lao! Jin Lao! I never thought I'd be so glad to see you.' Airton panted to his feet. 'You must take me to the Mandarin. A terrible thing has happened. I must see him right away.'

'A terrible thing? I am grieved to hear it. Has another of the mad American's children run away, perhaps?'

'No, man, it's my own children.'

'Your own children have run away? This is indeed upsetting.'

'You are a peacock, sir. I demand that you take me to your master. My children were attacked by Boxers. Do you understand? Boxers. I know where the band is heading. If we hurry we can stop them.'

'How intensely dramatic! Children attacked by Boxers, well I never – martial artists, did you say? That seems a trifle strange. The morning exercisers who practise *t'ai chi* and *qi gong* in this town are not in the habit of attacking children, certainly not foreign ones. Did your children provoke them in any way?'

'Jin Lao, you are either being deliberately obtuse or you are mocking me. You know very well whom I mean by the Boxers. Now, will you or will you not take me to the Mandarin?'

'Let me first enquire: your children are badly injured? Maimed? Or was this attack of a sexual nature?'

'I cannot believe what I am hearing. No, Jin Lao, it was not a sexual attack. And thankfully – providentially – neither are my children seriously injured, though my son, George, is very bruised and frightened.'

'Bruised? I am sorry to hear it,' said Jin Lao. 'Can you describe the man who gave your son these bruises?'

'Well, the one who did it was a boy, actually. About George's own age. Or so I gather. I wasn't there. My servant told me the boy had Boxer skills. There was a band of them. Now, please, Jin Lao, we have wasted enough time. I need to talk to the Mandarin.'

'I deeply regret, Daifu, but I cannot take you to him.'

'Why not, man? I told you. There are Boxers out there getting away.'

'The Mandarin is resting,' said Jin Lao, 'and I cannot disturb him with a story substantiated only on the hearsay of a servant about a brawl between two little boys. You have admitted there were no serious injuries. The odd bruise is hardly a matter for the *yamen* court.'

'Oh, you snake of a man,' whistled the doctor. 'Is it cumshaw you're wanting? I should have known. Here, take this money and let me in.'

Jin Lao's parchment face did not alter its expression. 'Put your money away, Daifu. I understand that you are overwrought. Otherwise you would not think to bribe an official of the *yamen*.'

'But the Mandarin—'

'Is resting. When he wakes I will report what you have told me, and if he wishes to pursue the case I have no doubt that he will summon you. I suggest that for now you return to your home.'

'I am not going until I see the Mandarin. No one has ever prevented me from entering here before.'

'Before, Daifu, you came at the da ren's invitation, and the da ren's pleasure. May I remind you that I, too, am an official of the *yamen*. I have taken your petition. I will inform the da ren, and he may or may not respond to you, but if he does it will be at his own convenience. There is nothing more that you can do here today. I suggest that you go home.'

And Jin Lao barked an order. The two *yamen* runners resumed their aggressive stance in front of the gates. Jin Lao, with a curt bow towards the doctor, stooped through the door, which closed behind him. One of the runners raised his eyebrows ironically at the doctor as it slammed.

'Snigger as much as you like. I'm not going,' muttered Airton, shaking the sand off his hat. 'You'll see. There'll be hell to pay when the Mandarin finds out.'

So he had waited. And waited. The evening sun glinted on the rooftops of Shishan. A cuckoo called from the wood on the hill. The gates remained closed. Towards dusk an old woman appeared carrying a teapot in a basket. She poured and the elder of the two runners, a waggish man with a well-worn face and stumpy teeth, offered the doctor his bowl. Airton refused huffily. The man shrugged, reached within the folds of his robe and extracted an earthenware bottle. He unstopped it, lifted it to his nose and mimed delight at the smell, then smiling broadly, he offered the liquor to the doctor. Airton turned away, his ears burning. He waited for the laughter to come, but it didn't. The *yamen* runner took a sip from the bottle himself, offered it to his companion, then replaced it in his robe. The vigil continued. A chill wind blew. The *yamen* runners busied themselves with lighting then raising the lanterns above the gate. Airton pulled his jacket tighter round his body. The friendly guard blew on his hands, then pointed at the moon, which had risen palely in the sky; then he mimed a yawn and a head lying on a pillow. He peered at the doctor quizzically. Airton looked despairingly at the closed door. The *yamen* runner shook his head sadly. After a moment Airton nodded once, twice, then turned and made his way slowly down the hill.

Three weeks later, hunched by the fire in the clearing, he lived again the shame of that walk back to his house. Everyone he passed seemed to mock him. A group of women giggled; he hurried on by. Another threw a bucket of slops across the street behind him and he quickened his pace. He threaded his way through the busy high street with his head bowed. He seemed to hear catcalls of jeering laughter from every alleyway.

He preferred not to recall the desolate return to the hospital, Nellie's recriminations, the nuns' tears, and the pathetic sight of his children in their cots – George's battered face and, worse, the rigid, wide-eyed silence of his daughter. He felt a strangling impotence: her terrified stare was an accusation of him both as father and physician. He had sat by her throughout the night, watched her into fitful sleep, held her tightly when she burned and screamed in her nightmares, and only with the dawn had he relaxed. That was when she awoke and recognised him and began to sob in his arms. 'Promise me, Papa, you'll never let the Boxers come again. Promise me. Promise me,' she had begged him, and he had promised again and again before he allowed herself to fall into a normal sleep.

The light of morning and a reviving cup of tea had put him in a calmer mood, and he was able to reflect that perhaps he had not been snubbed by the Mandarin, after all. More likely the vengeful Jin Lao had never passed on his message. He determined to write, therefore, directly to the Mandarin. He doubted whether even Jin Lao would dare to obstruct a letter. The Mandarin would certainly call for him when he heard what had happened. Zhang Erhao was duly packed off to the *yamen* with an envelope under the doctor's most impressive seal. He also sent messages to Herr Fischer and Henry Manners at the railway camp asking if they had experienced any incidents involving Boxers. Herr Fischer himself arrived at the hospital in the afternoon, all concern. The Honourable Manners was absent as usual, he reported, probably enjoying himself in the town, but speaking for himself he had seen or heard of nothing untoward and neither had Charlie. Was Airton sure that it had been Boxers and not some other band of armed vagrants? Again they interrogated Ah Lee, who against Airton's instructions had already left the sick ward and was back at work in the kitchen – but the cook, while giving a histrionic account of what had developed in his telling to be an epic battle, was not able to provide a convincing proof that it had really been the 'Harmonious Fists'. The doctor and Herr Fischer decided that certainty must await the Mandarin's own investigations. In the meanwhile they should take precautions to protect their properties. They agreed to remain in daily contact. Fischer rode back to his camp and the doctor settled down to wait for the Mandarin's summons, resuming as best he could his duties in the surgery – but no summons came.

Nor did it the next day, or the day after. Instead, on the morning of the third day after the accident, one of Major Lin's officers had arrived, with four armed and mounted soldiers, a sedan chair, and orders that the doctor was required to attend the *yamen* court forthwith. He protested that he had not completed his morning surgery. Nor was he dressed for an official audience with the Mandarin. The young lieutenant had politely, but firmly, made it clear that this was no invitation to take tea. The criminal court was in session and the doctor had been requested to give evidence. He would be obliged if the doctor would enter the sedan chair that had been provided for him. He might observe for himself that a suitable escort had been prepared for his safety.

'Is this in answer to my letter?' The doctor had pushed aside the curtains of the sedan to ask. 'Is this to do with the attack on my children?'

The officer riding beside him had not even turned his head.

When they reached the *yamen*, the soldiers, dismounted but still holding their rifles, formed two in front, two behind him, like a court-martial detail. The lieutenant, his sword drawn and sloped against his shoulder, led them through the gate.

'Here, am I under arrest?' the doctor called. 'Why the guard?'

Instead of going straight through the main courtyard to the Mandarin's apartments, the lieutenant led them through a small door leading to a bricked-in corridor lined with benches, which opened into a smaller courtyard, to which the doctor had never been before. Soldiers with spears guarded a gate beyond. The courtyard itself was full of men and women squatting on the ground or leaning against the walls. They came from all classes – the doctor recognised the brown silk gowns of merchants and the blue cotton pyjamas of peasants. They had the blank expressions of people waiting all night at a railway station for a train long overdue. Dull eyes surveyed him incuriously. Then he noticed that in one corner a man was crouching on his heels weighted down by a *cangue*. In another, three iron cages hung from a pole. With horror, the doctor identified ragged arms and legs inside and bodies contorted into positions where they could neither stand nor lie nor sit. In the shadow of the left-hand wall his eyes made out manacle rings and chains. The lieutenant halted his detail. 'We wait here,' he said.

'What is this place?' The doctor had to make an effort to keep his voice firm. 'Have you brought me to a prison?'

'As I told you, this is the *yamen* court. Be patient, Doctor. Your case will soon be heard.'

'My case?' said the doctor – but the lieutenant had sauntered over to the gate, in front of which sat a dark-spectacled official with a pen and parchment. Anxiously the doctor watched the two conversing. He felt a tugging at his trouser leg and looked down to see the exophthalmic eyes, open mouth and twisted shape of a beggar. One of the soldiers hit out with his rifle butt and the man crawled away. High-pitched laughter erupted from his right. A young, well-built, shaggy man manacled by his hands and feet to a pole was winking facetiously at him. Airton turned away.

'I demand to know what is happening,' he said quietly, when the lieutenant returned. 'Does Liu Da Ren know that I have been brought here like this? Like a common criminal?'

But the lieutenant ignored his question, merely beckoning him to follow him. 'Your case is ready to be heard now,' he said. 'Come.'

'What case? Am I on trial? On what charge? This is madness. I am a foreigner, sir. I am not subject to Chinese courts.'

'Come, Doctor, you are wasting time,' said the lieutenant.

The gates opened into a candle-lit hall. It took a moment for Airton to adjust to the gloom. At the end of the hall was a raised table covered by a red cloth. Behind the table sat the Mandarin, in splendid blue robes. A servant with the official yellow umbrella stood behind him. Next to him sat a younger man, also in blue robes, also under an umbrella, and he, too, wore the green button and peacock feather hat. While the Mandarin sat impassively and stiffly, no hint of expression on his wide face, the young man next to him lounged in his chair, covering his mouth with his fan to hide a yawn, his moist brown eyes lazily surveying the room. He looked very much at ease.

The doctor was confused. His mind ran rapidly over everything he knew about Chinese protocol. There was nobody of equal rank to the Mandarin in Shishan, that was for certain. Then who was this handsome fellow whose manner signified equal if not higher status than the Mandarin?

Beneath the table sat the scribes and court officials. With no surprise he recognised Jin Lao, who was studying a scroll.

There were three figures knowtowing on the ground in front of the magistrate's table, two adults and a small boy. The man on the left had his hands bound behind him. An armed *yamen* runner stood two paces away. There was something familiar about the man bound on the ground, the long thin neck and the stick-like limbs. With a start of anger and fear Airton recognised Ah Lee.

The lieutenant stepped forward, clasped hands above his head, knelt and bowed. 'May the court behold the foreign doctor, Ai Dun,' he shouted.

'The court beholds him,' said the Mandarin gruffly. 'The officer may retire.'

Jin Lao raised his reedy voice. 'It is customary for the accused to kowtow.'

'The foreign doctor may be excused a kowtow,' said the Mandarin. 'And you will not refer to him as the accused, Chamberlain. As you know he cannot be tried by this court. Foreigners are protected by treaty and the extra-territoriality laws, none of which have been repealed.' He turned to the man beside him. 'As far as I know that is still the case, Prince, is it not?'

The young man smiled. 'I am very much afraid that it is. What a shame. I would have enjoyed the sight of a hairy barbarian attempting to bow in a civilised manner.'

'You may proceed, Chamberlain,' said the Mandarin.

Jin Lao began to read, in the stilted, falsetto voice that convention demanded of an indictment. The phrases were literary and opaque, and the doctor had to struggle to follow the sense, his mind lulled by the lilting rhythm and shrill crescendos of the delivery. He might have been listening to a virtuoso performer at the opera (he had always thought that Chinese formal proceedings modelled themselves on the opera), but Jin Lao was no theatrical king with flags and a beard and a painted face. The barbs and thrusts of his language were a spear pointing directly at the doctor, wielded by someone whom he now realised he could never again dismiss as a functionary but must treat as his deadly enemy. Airton felt the man's eyes on him, gloating, triumphant, reptilian. Long nails unrolled elegantly out of the chamberlain's robe in the direction of the cowering Ah Lee, pointing the power of the court in accusation like a magician's wand – but the snake eyes still flickered on the doctor, drawing him also into his spell. Airton could feel the perspiration growing on his hot forehead; at the same time he felt a chill of fear. Jin Lao was talking about his children. In a *yamen* court. This was deeply unreal. He felt that he had stumbled into a dream, or a nightmare.

Behind the flowery language the charges were simple. There had been a children's quarrel. The foreign *daifu*'s son and daughter had one day set upon and attacked some smaller village children in a spirit of hooliganism, which was only to be expected from barbarian brats untrained yet in the ways of their own country, let alone those of a civilised society. An older boy in the village, grieved to see his brothers and sisters so abused, had bravely come to their rescue and in so doing had inflicted some well-deserved chastisement on the foreign bullies, including, regrettably, a few bruises and cuts on the body of the doctor's son. This was a minor matter, of no formal interest to the *yamen*; a certain rough justice had been turned on the perpetrators of an act of juvenile delinquency; there the matter should have ended. It was then, however, that this foreign *daifu* – a barbarian who had been uniquely honoured and revered in Shishan, recognised for his apparent good works and privileged by the favour of no less a person than the Da Ren Liu Daguang himself – showed his true colours, his pride and his arrogance. Incensed that anyone would dare to reprimand his children, he had boldly marched to the *yamen* itself and demanded that the weight of Chinese justice be turned on innocent children's heads, merely to satisfy his revenge for a perceived slight – against himself and the Christians whom he represented.

At the mention of the word Christians the doctor was startled to see the young man next to the Mandarin, who had been yawning through the earlier parts of Jin Lao's speech, suddenly frown and nod enthusiastically. The Mandarin himself remained impassive, waving Jin Lao with a slight movement of his fan to go on.

He himself had been forced, Jin Lao continued, to interview the foreign *daifu* on that unpleasant occasion outside the *yamen* gates – and unedifying it had been. The doctor had been so enraged and irrational with anger that at one point he had rolled in the dust, and the violence of his language had shocked the guards. He had concocted a story that his children had been attacked by criminal gangs of martial artists. His intention had obviously been to deceive the *yamen* into punishing an innocent village – presumably one that had spurned his missionary activities. Here, again, the young man on the bench nodded vigorously. This was not only to be revenge for a personal slight but another attack by the Christians on their enemies. Jin Lao had told the raging man to go home, which eventually he did, but little did anyone know what vengeance he still harboured in his heart.

Frustrated by his inability to use the law for his own advantage, the foreign *daifu* had taken the matter into his own hands, and ordered his servant, a Christian in his pay ('See him – this insect grovelling before us today'), to go to the village in the night and to find the boy who had hurt his son. He had been ordered to inflict wounds on the boy that only a doctor skilled in the art of healing, and therefore knowing, too, the ways in which a body can be most effectively injured, could imagine. The servant had been so obedient of the wicked instructions of his master that it was feared that the young hero of the village would never walk again. 'So do the Christians behave!' Jin Lao had cried. 'See their handiwork!'

He pointed his finger. A guard – Airton recognised the friendly *yamen* runner who had offered him a drink at the gatehouse – gently lifted up the middle of the three kneeling figures, the boy, whom he now saw was wrapped in a cloak. Supporting him, the guard let the cloak fall to the floor, and the boy was presented stark naked to the court. Only there was hardly any whole flesh to see among the welter of bruises and lacerations that covered the tottering body. The doctor noted the misshapen angle that indicated one leg was broken and needed to be set, the drop of the shoulder suggesting dislocation. Then he winced and turned his head away, a tear in his eye. 'Animals,' he wanted to cry.

'See their handiwork!' Jin Lao crooned on. 'Does the Christian doctor avert his gaze? Does the foreign healer not wish to examine his patient?'

The Mandarin's rough voice rasped through the mood that Jin Lao had created. 'The court has seen this evidence. Get this boy out of here and find him a doctor. This is the *yamen*, not a grotesque stand at the fair. Chamberlain, make your case – and quickly.'

Jin Lao bowed. 'My Lord Prince Yi, Liu Da Ren, I will present one witness more and then I am done.'

He pointed to the third kneeling figure, who rose jauntily to his feet when pushed by the guard. Airton saw a young, well-built man with a sour face and traces of smallpox scars on his cheeks. His expression was half a sneer and half a smile.

'And who is this?' said the Mandarin.

'A patriot and a model citizen,' said Jin Lao. 'He is the restaurant owner, Master Liu Ren Ren. It was our good fortune that he happened to be in the village on the night in which this misdeed was done. Unfortunately he was too late to prevent the beating of the boy, but he was able to recognise and apprehend the villain and identify him as the servant of the Christian doctor. The city owes him our thanks. None of the villagers would have reported this matter,' he added darkly. 'They would be afraid of the Christians. We have Master Liu to thank for bringing this evil matter to justice.'

'And what were you doing in the village that night?' asked the Mandarin.

'I was visiting my auntie,' said Ren Ren. 'She lives there.'

'He is filial as well as public-spirited,' said Jin Lao.

'Is he?' said the Mandarin.

'The case seems cut and dried to me,' said the Prince. 'This is typical of the sort of outrage that the Christians have been getting up to in other parts of the empire. I was right to come here. I think that you should get on and punish them.'

'Them?'

'All right, the Christian servant, then. These pernicious extra-territoriality laws . . . You can reprimand the master and punish the man.'

'We judge them guilty, then, Prince, without giving them a chance to refute the charges?'

The young nobleman raised his eyebrows and smiled affectionately at the Mandarin. 'My dear Daguang. How punctilious you are! What is the point of questioning them? They are Christians. Christians lie. Their guilt is adequately proven already by your chamberlain, who has done a most worthy job. You are to be congratulated. Get on, get on, my dear fellow. Deliver an exemplary verdict, and then we will go to lunch.'

'Prince, I hear you,' said the Mandarin. 'But if we flout the extra-territoriality laws and it gets to the notice of the Legations . . .'

'Oh, I wouldn't worry about that,' smiled Prince Yi. 'As I told you, there are to be some changes. Great changes. These are very exciting times.'

'Da Ren, I will speak.' Airton's throat was dry with tension and he had to repeat himself to be heard. Prince Yi dropped his fan in surprise.

'Good heavens, the barbarian really can speak the language. How amusing.'

The Mandarin sighed. 'Daifu,' he acknowledged, and nodded for Airton to continue.

'Mandarin. Da Ren. I beg you to open your minds and hear the truth. What has been described is a – a travesty. I do not know who was the monster who savaged that poor boy, but it couldn't have been Ah Lee. He's been in my hospital for the last two days. He's been injured himself. This is a malicious attack on my family, my servants, my faith, using innocent victims as tools. You know me, Da Ren. You know why I came to see you. It was to warn you of the Boxers—'

'So do the self-serving accusations from the lying Christians begin again,' Jin Lao started, in his high falsetto.

'Silence, both of you,' growled the Mandarin. 'Daifu,' he addressed Airton directly, his eyes narrowed. 'You are not being judged by this court.' He glanced coldly at Prince Yi, then back at the doctor. 'In fact, you shouldn't be here at all. Not under the present statutes. Nor am I convinced that you ordered this crime. Chamberlain, you have given us supposition on that point not proof.' He paused. 'The case of the doctor's servant is another matter, however, and for him punishment is due.'

Airton found himself shouting, 'How can you believe these lies? It is obvious that Ah Lee is innocent. He wouldn't harm a fly.'

The Mandarin spoke quietly. 'Daifu, please. I do not wish to show you indignity by expelling you. I can do nothing else but punish your servant because he himself has confessed.'

'*Confessed?*'

The Mandarin's face had returned to its impassive expression. 'Yes, he signed a confession, acknowledging his own guilt. Here it is. He does not implicate any accomplice or directly say that he was under orders. It is an atrociously written document – but interestingly he does abrogate any rights he may have as a Christian to be tried in any other court of law. Surprising that a cook should know so much about the law. However, it makes things easier for me. It will prevent you protesting to your consulate, Daifu. I think that in consideration I will lessen his punishment from the usual hundred strokes for assault to fifty strokes.' He picked up a pen and scribbled his name on the charge. 'Fifty strokes it is, to be administered forthwith, plus a week in the stocks. Officers, let it be done. Tremble and obey.'

'Well, well, what a soft heart you have,' Airton heard the Prince say as he and the Mandarin got up to leave together. 'You really need not worry about the reaction of these Christians, you know. Wait till you hear what I have to tell you over lunch. We must hurry. I continue my journey north this afternoon.'

'Excuse me, Prince. I have a word to say to the doctor.'

He paused only a moment by Airton to say gruffly, 'In China we do things in our Chinese way, Daifu. I ask you to try to understand. It is important. You will still join me on the hunt, I hope.'

'The hunt?' But his head was swirling with shock.

He was conscious of another presence by his side. Jin Lao's rheumy eyes in the perfect parchment face gazed at him benevolently. 'Daifu.' He bowed, and his thin lips curled into a beatific smile. 'I hope that you are satisfied that I did as I promised and investigated this crime.' Airton did not answer, and Jin Lao moved on, followed by his young witness, who sauntered past the doctor, insolently looking him up and down as he passed. Airton heard a laugh and the word 'Rat-eater' flung back as he disappeared through the gate.

After a moment he moved forward to where Ah Lee was still crouched on the ground guarded by the *yamen* runners.

'My friend, my friend, what have they done to you?' whispered Airton, when he saw the bruises on his cook's face. 'Are you hurt?'

Tears welled in a black eye as Ah Lee shook his head.

'Then why, why did you confess to such an impossible thing?'

'They came in the night. They held a knife to Ah Sun's throat. They said they would kill her and cut me, and I was frightened,' he muttered. 'They also said that they would take the missies, Helen and Jenny, and – and—' His head fell and his body shook with sobs. 'And I knew I would go to hell and eternal damnation fire if I lied, but if they hurt Missie Jenny and Missie Helen . . .'

'You won't go to hell and damnation fire, my dear friend.'

The friendly *yamen* runner cleared his throat. 'Daifu, it's time. Don't follow us. You don't want to witness this punishment. It's not for a Xiansheng like you to see – but don't worry too much either. He's a tough, stringy chicken, this one. He'll be all right. I'll see he gets back to you in one piece.'

Sitting by the campfire in the Black Hills three weeks later, the wind gusting the sparks, Airton could not forget the pleading face of his cook as they led him away. Nor Ah Sun's cries and laments when the twisted, beaten body was returned on a handcart from the *yamen* a week later. Nor the weak but still eager smile which was all Ah Lee could manage from his sick bed, to which this time he really would be confined for several days.

Shivering, Airton reached for the kettle and recharged his mug. He knew that he should retire to his tent; rest was what he needed, peace, contemplation – but the memory of his experience in the *yamen* still haunted him. Not to mention the new shocks he had received today – shocks that his mind half refused to face or believe. And then there was that wider sense of unease, the chilling darkness, and the drumbeats from the forest – a growing conviction, which he was reluctant even to admit in his rational consciousness, that something lurked out there tonight, which was primordial and evil.

It had been a day of violence. The camp had been woken before dawn with the rumble of drums and the screeching wail of horns and trumpets. The doctor had emerged from his tent to witness the exotically uniformed beaters disappearing into the mist between the trees. The Mandarin, Liu Daguang, resplendent in his red armour, a bow and a quiver of arrows on his back and a long, pennanted spear in his mailed hand, had clattered into their clearing from his separate camp, rearing his horse, laughing boisterously, a war god in his prime, chivvying, encouraging. The sleek hunters, Henry Manners and Colonel Taro, in their leather leggings and tweed capes, appeared with their horses, Lao Zhao and another muleteer standing behind as gun-bearers. There was the rattle of harness and the Mandarin's charger was steaming and pounding the ground in front of him.

'Daifu, you are not ready. Come. The omens are propitious. Nay, better, my old wounds throb, signifying we will kill today. Hurry.'

'Da Ren, when can we talk?'

'Talk?' The Mandarin let off one of his high-pitched giggles. 'Today's not a day for talking, Daifu. Today's a day for killing.'

The doctor had hoped that he could stay behind in the camp with Helen Frances, and avoid the hunt. Both he and Nellie had advised her not to come to the Black Hills. She was not the healthy girl she had been – although the doctor could not account for her change into the languid, morose creature she had lately become; he had frankly been too preoccupied with his children and Ah Lee and the Boxers to worry about his assistant; he suspected that her state had something to do with affairs of the heart and her protracted engagement to Tom, and that sort of thing he was happy to leave to Nellie. But shortly before their departure from the mission, focusing suddenly on the black rings under her reddish eyes, the unhealthy pallor of her skin, he had wondered whether there might not be some physical ailment underneath it all. 'If I didn't know better I'd have said you looked like one of the opium addicts,' he had joked with her, as he had examined her tongue. She had responded with a strange smile. 'Well, maybe the fresh air will do you good,' he had told her, 'though I'll not allow you any great exertions. Nor do I suspect that a decent young girl like you will want to get too close to such a dangerous thing as the hunt itself.'

'I want to see the hunt,' she had said.

'Maybe you and I will wait in the camp until they bring back the trophy, and then we can join in the celebrations,' said the doctor. And she seemed to have assented. At least, she had said nothing more. The ride to the Black Hills had been dreary. The doctor had expected that Helen Frances would have looked forward to an excursion with her old friend Henry Manners – it had been some time since they had ridden together – yet he was surprised that the two largely ignored each other, Manners riding ahead with the Japanese colonel, whom the doctor did not like. Since the Mandarin also kept to himself, absorbed in paperwork inside his sedan chair, and Helen Frances remained taciturn and silent, even though she rode beside him, the doctor felt isolated and chagrined, and increasingly frustrated that he had no chance to talk to the Mandarin, which had been his primary purpose for coming on this expedition in the first place.

And now, as the Mandarin in his armour cantered round the fire, Major Lin and his soldiers wheeling behind him, Manners and Taro mounting their horses, the doctor was shocked to see Helen Frances in full riding habit also climbing on to her horse, assisted by Lao Zhao. There was no help for it. Although he hardly felt prepared, he quickly called for his own horse. In a few moments, led by the yelling Mandarin at a fast canter, the party was thundering after the beaters into the trees, the doctor holding on to his hat in the rear.

And the hunt had been as beastly and bloody as he had expected it to be. The beaters had done their job well, and soon Manners's and Taro's guns and the Mandarin's arrows were taking their toll of fleeing deer, hares and wild pig. Ever ahead they heard the baying of the dogs, tracking the main quarry, whether bear or tiger the doctor did not know. From all directions came the sound of the beaters' drums and the harsh calls of their trumpets, driving whatever animals remained in the ring to the chosen killing ground. It was all the doctor could do to stay on his horse. He felt no inclination, as Manners and his friend were doing, to attempt to fire from the saddle at such a breakneck speed. In fact, he felt no inclination to fire at all. He wanted this to end.

It ended in a clearing with a bear at bay. They approached to a gurgling waterfall of sounds from the hounds, murmurs and barks and whines mixed in diabolical frenzy. The beaters had ringed the glade and were pounding thunder on their drums. Polemen were dancing out of the black giant's reach. Fangs open and lathered, yellow eyes mad as a demon's, swaying on her back paws, roaring in her rage, the bear waved and swatted at the dogs leaping at her neck. Some of her victims lay crumpled, whining and broken on the ground. The Mandarin trotted his horse to a stop. The others gathered in a half circle around him. He raised his right arm high. One of Lin's men blew loudly on his trumpet. The drums ceased beating. It was a signal. The polemen ran back. Huntsmen making strange whistles ran among the hounds, some of them trailing meat, and slowly the murmur died. After a few more jumps and tumbles, most of the hounds followed the lures and withdrew. The bear swayed where she stood, puzzled by the sudden silence. She roared once, twice, then dropped on her front paws, growling, the yellow eyes glaring suspiciously at the group of horsemen.

'Ma Na Si Xiansheng,' said the Mandarin lightly. 'Whose is

she to be? And with which weapon? The gun, the spear or the bow?'

'I am certainly no equal to the da ren with the bow,' said Manners, with a smile.

'And an ancient bannerman trained only in the old ways of war knows little of the new-fangled sports rifle,' said the Mandarin.

'It seems we must compromise on the spear, then,' said Manners.

'It is the traditional weapon,' said the Mandarin.

'On foot or on horseback?' asked Manners.

'On foot is best,' said the Mandarin. 'I will go first and you will follow me to back me up. Your friend?' He looked towards Taro, who bowed an acknowledgement of the invitation, before deliberately, insolently turning to Major Lin. Taro's eyes danced with humour as he passed on the unspoken challenge. Major Lin flushed, but maintained his stern expression, looking straight ahead.

'No, I thank you, Da Ren-sama,' said the Japanese. 'On consideration, I will be proud to observe the triumph of Your Excellency and Mr Manners.'

'Doctor?' said Manners, dismounted, uncloaked, his hands raised high as a huntsman pulled a studded leather jerkin over his head and sheathed his arms in huge metalled gloves. 'No pikemanship for you today?'

'Certainly not, Manners, and if you want my view I think that you are behaving like a damned fool.'

'I was always that, Airton. Only today I feel safe enough. It's not always one has a doctor immediately on hand in case of accident – and, for that matter, a nurse.' He smiled up at Helen Frances, who looked down coldly at him. 'Will my lady give me her favour to take into battle?' he asked. Helen Frances turned her head away, biting her lip. 'Obviously not,' he said.

'Ma Na Si,' the Mandarin was shouting, 'it is time to kill our bear.'

Airton watched in disbelief as the two men sauntered into the glade, their spears sloped casually over their shoulders. The bear saw the movement and rose blearily on to her hind legs, the gigantic shoulders swelling as she stretched her forepaws wide and ready to receive them, her head with its fangs shaking slowly from side to side. The Mandarin and the Englishman walked deliberately towards her.

Suddenly the Mandarin was running forward with the spear pointed. A great paw swished, the Mandarin rolled, thrusting as he did so, and the bear roared as the serrated edge of the spear sliced into her breast. The Mandarin was on his feet again, nimbly running backwards, eyes on the bear, spear at the ready. The assembled beaters shouted applause. 'Ma Na Si!' the doctor could hear the Mandarin roar over the noise. It was Manners's turn. But now the bear had dropped on to her forepaws, growling, angry, in pain. As he moved a step forward, the whole mound of meat and fur and lethal claw charged. 'Butt on the ground,' the Mandarin shouted. 'Quickly.' Manners dropped to one knee, jamming the end of the spear into the grass, the point facing the charging beast.

'That won't hold her,' the doctor heard himself moan, and he felt Helen Frances's hand on his arm. In agony he watched the bear close.

The Mandarin was running towards Manners's position and with graceful fluidity knelt beside him. A second spear faced the charging bear. Airton could not bear to watch. He heard a gasp from the men around him, a sigh from Helen Frances, and opened his eyes.

The two men were straining under the weight of the bear. She was impaled on the two poles, which bent and swayed above them as her enormous bulk twisted and writhed in her agony. Teeth and curved claws slashed down at her tormentors. Blood and froth drenched them. She was making a determined mewing sound as she herself strained for the kill. Manners and the Mandarin had to duck and sway to keep their unprotected heads out of reach. The beaters had become silent as they watched the desperate struggle of men and beast.

There was a crack like a whiplash. The Mandarin's spear shaft snapped. The bear's paw swung and a back-hander smashed into the da ren's shoulder hurling him to the ground. The bulk of the bear sank lower on to Manners's straining spear. The doctor could see his body arc with the effort of pushing up this impossible weight. He knew that soon the spear in the bear's body would tear through the remaining muscle and flesh and the animal would plunge down on to the man and that that must be the end of him. Airton could see the Mandarin crawling groggily away, calling something he could not make out. Then he was aware of loud hoofbeats and Major Lin was riding into the glade, followed by Taro. He saw Lin hurl something towards the Mandarin, who in one movement had caught his bow and quiver and had fitted an arrow to the string. Turning elegantly, he loosed his shaft almost point-blank into the she-bear's breast. At the same moment there was a crash of a gun and the bear's head exploded into blood and pulp. Taro swerved his horse and fired again. The bear slumped on the spear. The struggle ceased.

Then he heard more hoofbeats. 'Helen Frances! Don't,' he cried. 'It's still dangerous . . .' But she was galloping towards Manners, and he was following, and next thing he knew she was off her horse and Manners had stumbled to his feet and she had buried her head against his bloodstained chest.

'What did I tell you about having a nurse on hand?' said Manners smiling. Then exhaustion hit him and he stumbled to his knees, his head flopped on to her shoulder. An arm seemed to curl naturally round her back and her behind as he fell. Helen Frances, shaking, pressed her body against his. The doctor had dismounted and was hurrying forward, but the sight of the tight embrace – the extraordinary familiarity of it – embarrassed him and he held back. 'Helen Frances? What are you doing?' Helen Frances's head slowly raised and Airton saw tears in her eyes behind her dislodged hair. She gazed at him blankly, shuddered, and then, with a start, she recognised him. The blood of the bear streaked her cheeks. 'I'm sorry, Doctor,' she whispered. 'I thought . . . I thought . . .'

'Never mind, girl. I understand,' he said – although his mind was pounding with a sudden and unwelcome realisation. '*They are lovers!*' a voice was shouting in his temple. 'Come on, girl, we must get that jerkin up and over his head. Careful now.'

They lowered the body to the trampled grass. Airton's mind was rushing, but his hands went through the professional motions as he checked Manners's pulse and heartbeat and probed gently for internal injuries. *Lovers!* the suspicion screamed in his mind. My God, what will Nellie say? We abetted it. Oh, Lord! Poor Tom! Helen Frances, the professional nurse again, was calmly staunching the blood from a cut to Manners's upper arm. He groaned, but remained unconscious. The doctor's racing mind was distracted by a sound from the other side of the great carcass, which still loomed above them, now much admired by the gathering beaters. It was the Mandarin's booming voice. He thought of calling over to him to ask if he needed treatment as well, but instead he found himself listening.

'Colonel Taro.' A trick of the wind brought the Mandarin's voice to him clearly, although he was hidden by the bulk of the bear; nor did the chatter of the beaters obscure the sound. 'I am obliged to you for your kind attention to saving my life. However, I think you will find that this is my shaft already embedded in the creature's heart.'

It was perhaps the coldness in Taro's reply that made Airton concentrate and listen. 'Da Ren-sama,' the Japanese hissed, 'if I had known exactly the foolishness that you and the Englishman intended I would have intervened earlier. You two may kill yourselves at another time, but I remind you that we still have business to conduct, which affects your country and the empire of Japan. I cannot let you or Manners sacrifice our imperial interests in fruitless heroics with a wild animal.'

Had he heard correctly? Imperial interests? What had Manners – or indeed the Mandarin – to do with Japanese Imperial interests?

'I am disappointed,' the Mandarin replied. 'I had heard so much about your code of honour – your *bushido* – and had expected a samurai like yourself to appreciate the chivalrous traditions of the hunt.'

'Da Ren-sama, please do not play with me. You of all people know that war is not a sport, and neither is the business of taking power. I have come to these mountains not to hunt but because the agreement that Manners and Lin are broking has reached a satisfactory conclusion where you and I can agree.'

'Perhaps we can agree. I need to hear the details.'

'You will hear the details tonight – from Manners who, thank Providence and the accuracy of my rifle, is still a living man.'

'It may be that I will meet you tonight. However, I have another meeting, which has a bearing on this matter.'

'Another meeting? Here? ... I see ... So-o ... You're still negotiating with those bandits for Russian guns? I should have guessed. That's why we're in the Black Hills, is it? And you talk to me of honour, Da Ren-sama?'

'Colonel, for there to be a bargain there must always be another bid with which to compare it. All life is negotiation and compromise of one kind or another. I think that you are experienced enough to know that – even though you are still very young.'

'I have no wish to be old, Da Ren-sama, as you are lucky still to be. But I will bargain . . . for a while longer.' The doctor heard the sound of fading hoofs. Taro had ridden off.

Airton shook himself back to his task in hand. 'Put his shirt on him again, Helen Frances. Don't want him catching a chill.' But guns? Imperial Japanese interests? Negotiations with bandits? These were the words that repeated themselves like exploding mines inside his brain. With horror Airton looked down at the man he was treating, and experienced a tremor of repulsion. Manners was stirring out of his swoon but his eyes were still closed, his head cushioned in Helen Frances's lap, and there was a trace of a smile on his handsome brown face. Who was this man? What was he up to? It sounded like treason. Certainly it must be villainy. But if that were true . . . ? And if it was true that Helen Frances had become involved with such a man . . . ? A criminal? A gun-runner? For the moment the reaction of an angry Nellie when she heard about it was uppermost in his mind. Then he realised something else. The Mandarin was in on this too! The man he had trusted since he arrived in Shishan. His friend. His benefactor. The man whose wise advice he had looked forward to receiving this very day about the Boxers, his children, Ah Lee's unjust punishment, the disturbing overtones in that courtier's remarks about the Christians – important matters of life and death that affected the whole community in the doctor's charge. Yet he had just heard this paladin discuss gun-running with an agent from a foreign power! And proposing a meeting with bandits! Bandits who in the past the Mandarin had sent expeditions against. Or had he? Had anything not been a lie? Whom could he now trust?

'Daifu,' he heard the laugh of the Mandarin above him, 'I see that you have already bound the wounds of the conquering hero, and provided him with a beautiful handmaiden to tend him back to health. You must not tell the big soap salesman too much about Ma Na Si's deeds today or he will be jealous. Yet what a glorious victory we achieved together, this Englishman and I! Did you see our struggle? Did you see it? A bear is better than a tiger! We will feast tonight on her paws!'

'I saw you knocked down by the bear, Da Ren. Shall I examine you?'

'No, I thank you. I am enjoying the pain of the blow that the she-bear gave me – albeit it is a great bruise and throbs. Why? Because it reminds me of the noble creature we slew. I carry the wound in the she-bear's honour. Do you still wish to speak to me, Daifu, now that the killing is over? I have time as we ride back to camp.'

'Thank you, Da Ren,' the doctor found himself muttering. 'It is not perhaps convenient just now.'

The Mandarin looked at him curiously. 'Not convenient? Yet this morning you were so importunate?'

'Da Ren, there was nothing of importance . . .'

The Mandarin wheeled his horse. 'You have nothing to ask me about the proceedings of our courts? Nothing about Christians or Boxers? Or the changing winds that seem to be blowing over this country? Or the reason why I was so lately honoured by a visitor from the Imperial Court – whom you met? Which reminds me of a neglect in courtesy on my part. I never asked you about the health of your children. Are they recovered?'

'Yes, thank you, Da Ren, my children are well again.'

'I cannot guarantee that I will have time again on this excursion for another talk, Daifu. You know how I enjoy our conversations. Will you not ride with me now? Ma Na Si seems to be in perfectly adequate hands.'

Airton found himself gripped suddenly by a cold anger, and the words flew out: 'How do you dare to ask after my children's health after what you did to us in that court? And what about our conversations, Da Ren? What do they mean to you? Have you ever told me a word of truth? I don't know you, Da Ren. Not any more, and more's the pity, because I believed there was a noble soul somewhere inside you.'

The Mandarin clicked his teeth, steadying his horse. 'Well, well, the poison of the she-bear seems to have affected you more than she has Ma Na Si or me, Daifu. But, then, there are mysteries in the hunt that arouse strong and curious passions. You are perhaps right. This is not the day for a talk. There will be other days – when you know me better again, and if, dare I say it? you come to know yourself.

'I have much to do tonight and I must leave you, but there is one thing I will say about our conversations – which I have always enjoyed. I know, you see, that you are trying to convert me. You view our dialogue as a civilised debate between a ruthless and pragmatic pagan, and yourself, a man of ideals. You consider yourself fortunate in that you have a faith and try to run your life on an absolute code of what is right and wrong as laid down in your Bible. You are like some of our more serious-minded Confucianists – the academicians not the practical men. I, on the other hand, am an administrator and do what I have to do to suit the circumstances at any given time. Yet are you sure, Daifu, that the conversion process is not a two-edged weapon? Are you not a little influenced yourself by, shall I say, my relative approach? Will you never compromise your ideals to circumstances, Daifu? Ever? For greater gain?

'You may be surprised, but I am as interested in your soul as you are in mine. Is there not a story in your Book about Satan taking your Jesus to a high place to tempt him with the riches of the world? I like that story very much. Oh, I do hope that one day we can resume our debate. Perhaps we can arrange a little test like the trip to the high place and make a wager on the outcome.'

'Are you mocking me?'

'Know this, Daifu. There may come a time soon when all of us will have to be practical, if we are to honour our responsibilities and protect our families. Remember my words. I never speak lightly – and I am your friend.'

'It is not good enough for you to say that, Da Ren. You treated my servant monstrously. An innocent man.'

'You are a surgeon. There are times when a healthy limb needs to be chopped off to preserve the whole. I respect your Christian dream. Your perfect world. Unfortunately I think you will find such perfection only in Heaven. Life is a sea of sorrow, Daifu, a sea of sorrow – but never forget that I am your friend.'

The Mandarin smacked his whip on his horse's rump and galloped off, followed by his retainers and Lin's men.

The rest of the day had passed in a blur. The doctor had accompanied Manners and Helen Frances back to the camp. Nobody spoke. Helen Frances was as morose as ever and Manners preoccupied. The doctor had almost convinced himself that his suspicions were imagined. Anyone observing the two might have thought that the girl and the young man actively disliked each other. Helen Frances excused herself from the Mandarin's invitation to sit at the top table at the feast in the great tent, and rather perversely – rudely, the doctor thought – sat with Lao Zhao and the muleteers. Manners and Taro, meanwhile, caroused loudly with the Mandarin, who was boisterously toasting all and sundry and loudly singing his own praises and that of Manners for their feats of the afternoon. The doctor did his best to be sociable in the circumstances, and drank more than he wanted to. After dinner, Helen Frances excused herself to her tent pleading a headache. Airton went to the campfire in their own clearing to light a cigar, expecting the others to join him. All of his new forebodings were realised when Manners and Taro remained behind with the Mandarin and Lin in the Mandarin's tent. So they were discussing something together, after all, something that required a secret meeting, which went on for nearly three hours. What on earth was he to do? He thought of writing to Sir Claude MacDonald, then felt foolish. What was his proof? And was it his business?

'Still up, Airton?' Manners appeared behind him, startling him. 'Sorry to have left you to yourself. Railway matters to discuss with the Mandarin.'

'Quite so,' said Airton. 'Will you have a cigar with me?'

'Thanks, but I won't. Been a bit of a hard day one way or another. I'm off to my tent. Taro might, though. He never sleeps, do you, old boy?'

But Taro was not with them. They saw his figure standing by the tree-line; he was smoking and apparently contemplating something in the forest. Airton strained his eyes. There was movement in the gloom – red lanterns, the shadows of horses, a muffled shout, a jingle of harness, the sounds and shapes subsiding like wraiths into the haze.

'Well, well, look at that,' said Manners. 'Mandarin himself, if I'm not mistaken. And Lin's troop. What dark deeds are they planning in the woods tonight? Some pagan ritual, perhaps. A sacrifice to allay the spirit of the she-bear we killed? How spookish these woods are, don't you think? Don't stay up too late, Doctor. You don't want to be taken by fox spirits in the night!'

'I'll be all right,' said Airton. 'Don't worry about me.'

Taro came briefly to the campfire to finish his cigar. They exchanged uncomfortable courtesies. Airton never knew what to say to the Japanese. Taro excused himself politely. The doctor was left alone in the night, with his thoughts and the cold, inside and outside – and shortly after, in the distance, he heard the drums begin to beat.

*   *   *

'Do you consider yourself to be a superstitious man?' the Mandarin asked Major Lin. The horses were threading their way through the pines, the lantern of the guide bobbing ahead between the branches.

'I am a soldier,' muttered Lin.

'Quite so. Please remember that tonight – whatever you see or hear. Are you confident of your troop?'

'They, too, are soldiers, Da Ren. I picked the bravest as you ordered.'

'A man may be brave in the daylight but undone by the dark. Fear – like reality – can be manipulated. You will need to be vigilant, Major. Remember at all times that we will be dealing with men no different from ourselves.'

'Surely there is nothing to fear from common bandits, Da Ren? And we have met Iron Man Wang before.'

'Be vigilant, Major. That is all I ask.'

They rode on. The wind sighed in the pines. The night mists blurred the outlines of the tree-trunks through which they were winding in single file. After a while they became conscious of dim lights flanking the trees on either side of them, torches held by unseen escorts keeping pace with them, watching them, steering them forward. The leather of their harness creaked, and a horse snuffled loudly, but no one spoke. Some distance off a horn blew. Eerily, from all around them, drums began to thump.

The trees faded away and they broke into a black clearing, lit in the centre by a bonfire. Three men waited, silhouetted against the flames. The man in the middle was not tall, but his wide shoulders and bull neck indicated massive strength. He was leaning on a double-headed axe. The reflection of the firelight flickered over his flat impassive features and reddened the straggling ends of his thick beard. A fur cap drooped over his forehead shadowing his eyes, but the poise of his body indicated suspicion, tension and watchfulness.

The Mandarin and Lin halted, and the eight troopers quietly wheeled into a protective half-circle, rifles held at an angle by their sides. As they did so, the lines of torches that had accompanied them on their march ringed forward, still behind the line of trees, and soon there was a circle of dim lights weaving around the glade. The unseen drums rose to a crescendo, then ceased. The Mandarin dismounted and, accompanied by Lin, strode briskly towards the men waiting by the fire.

'Master Wang, what a theatrical greeting you have arranged for me.'

Iron Man Wang grunted. He passed his axe to the taller of his two companions, and pointed to a table and bench laid out on the grass. 'We eat first. Drink,' he said. 'Talk when the others come.'

He led the way forward and swung himself heavily on to a stool. Without waiting for the Mandarin to be seated he reached for an earthenware bottle and cup and poured himself a draught of white liquor, which he drained noisily. Then he pushed the bottle and cup towards the Mandarin, who had seated himself delicately on the bench opposite. Major Lin and Iron Man Wang's two companions watched carefully from the sides. The Mandarin sipped the liquor. 'Good,' he said. 'A Shantung wine. I am honoured.'

'Got it from one of the merchant trains you let me have last year. Ten big pitchers.'

'I remember poor Jin Shangui telling me about his loss. The wine he eventually served at his nephew's wedding feast was inferior.'

Iron Man Wang cleared his throat and spat. Wiping his mouth with the back of his hand, he pointed at some covered dishes on the table. 'Meat,' he said. 'Eat.'

'Later, perhaps. And who else have you invited to this – feast?'

'Old man Tang.'

'I thought that this time you would be working independently of the Black Sticks. I'm not sure that I approve.'

Iron Man Wang's dark eyes flickered peevishly. 'Yes? Well, maybe none of us have any choice any more. Tang'll tell you.'

'I will be interested to hear.'

'Drink,' said Iron Man Wang. 'He'll be here soon.'

The hidden drums began to thud again, slowly at first, at heartbeat rate; then they mounted to the same crescendo as before, and stopped as suddenly. From the other end of the clearing the Mandarin made out figures approaching on foot. One was a thin, bent figure draped in a heavy fur cloak. The other was being led by a small boy. The fire flickered over a bald head and coloured robes. There was something familiar about the man's shape and the cut of his costume, but in the darkness the Mandarin could not be sure. As the figures moved towards them slowly, another circle of unseen torch-bearers moved around the glade, adding to the glow of fire ringing the wood behind the trees; the lights shifted and changed position like glow-worms in the dark; it was as if the outside of the glade was being invested by pale spirits. Just the other side of the fire the man in the cloak made a sign for the boy and the priest to stop; they remained in the shadows as he pulled his own way painfully to the table. There he slumped gratefully beside the Mandarin on the bench.

'I really am getting too old for this,' said the tin merchant, Tang Dexin, releasing his hood to reveal his white pigtail, 'but this is a momentous day. Da Ren, I am honoured to see you with us. You make an old man happy. Please give me a moment to catch my breath.'

'It is equally an honour to be received by the Grand Master of the Black Stick Society. An unexpected one, however,' said the Mandarin. 'I had looked forward tonight only to the company of Master Wang, and the opportunity to discuss some private business.'

'I know about your business,' said Tang. 'It is of no matter now.'

'Is it not?'

'I would advise you not to pursue it. Iron Man and I do not think that this is the time to be treating with barbarians, especially the filthy Russians who already occupy much of our sacred territory in the north. And if the presence of that Japanese soldier on your hunting trip means what I think it does, and you are considering a counter to the Russian proposal, I would advise you to reconsider that too. Chinese do not need foreign guns. If you will forgive an old man the impertinence of offering a respectfully meant admonition, I believe that the da ren has been too indulgent to the foreigners in our city. We do not need them. Or their toys.'

'Really? You and Master Wang have suddenly become very patriotic and altruistic. Master Wang? Iron Man? Is this right? Are you are no longer interested in helping me in my transaction?'

The bandit shrugged. 'Tang'll explain,' he said sullenly.

'I think he'd better,' said the Mandarin.

'I hear that you were recently visited by a prince from the Imperial Court,' said Tang.

'That is no secret. The Prince Yi was conducting a tour of inspection. Not unusual at this time of year.'

'I understand. However, on this occasion I believe that the Prince also imparted news about some recent deliberations in Peking relating to the Christian laws?'

'I will have to dismiss another of my house servants. I do recall a private conversation on such a subject with the Prince over luncheon. As I imagine that your eavesdroppers are efficient I presume you know all the details.'

'Not all the details, Da Ren. Enough to know that there are factions in Court who believe that the empire is in danger, and that it is time for loyal Chinese – all loyal Chinese – to join forces to save the Ch'ing from their enemies and the dark forces that threaten our country.'

'There are many factions at Court and many contrary views.'

'What is important is that this time the Old Buddha herself appears to support the more patriotic elements gathered round Prince Tuan. The star of your old master, Li Hung-chang, the collaborationist, is fading – fast, it seems. You are aware that forces are building in this country that call for the expulsion of the barbarians, their religion and everything evil they have brought here.'

'I am aware that groups of rabble-rousers have been arrested in various parts of the empire for hooliganism and insurrection.'

The old man sighed, and pulled his fur coat closer round his shoulders. 'I do hope that tonight we can come to a mutual understanding.' His mouth cracked into a smile and a gold tooth glinted in the firelight. 'The Black Sticks are desirous of your continuing friendship, you know. I am sure that I speak also on behalf of Iron Man Wang – and the other great forces that are with us and still building.'

'In my experience interests are more reliable than friendships. You might begin by telling me what common interests the Black Sticks and Iron Man's bandits have with the Harmonious Fists. You are, I presume, alluding to the Boxers? The *bonze* in the shadows is the mountebank priest who demonstrated his conjuring tricks at the railway camp, is he not? Why do you not bring him into our circle? Or are you his mouth tonight? I recall that he is both blind and mute.'

'You will hear his eloquence before the night is over, and if you are fortunate you will also see his vision. We are entering a time of wonders, Da Ren . . . wonders.'

'As I told you, I respect only interests. And I fail to see the benefit to either of your organisations of joining a peasant rebellion.'

'If the Court supports us we cannot be in rebellion. Do you think that the Black Sticks are merely a criminal gang, Da Ren? I doubt that there are more loyal or devoted servants of the Emperor and the dynasty than Iron Man Wang and myself. And yet we have lived in exile, underground or on the wrong side of the law, watching evil thieves and barbarians stealing our heritage, watching our beloved Emperor succumb to the bullying of foreigners, seeing the poisonous magic of the Christians spread like a cancer over our land. Iron Man may live in a forest, among the animals, but his are the ancient virtues . . .'

'Plundering merchants' caravans?'

Iron Man Wang grunted irritably. Tang Dexin smiled.

'A tax on those who deserve it: is that not how you once described it? Iron Man has done very well – to our mutual profit in the past, and perhaps for a while longer to come. The silver shipment from Tsitsihar, for example, will be a useful addition . . .'

'The English soap merchants will be accompanying Lu Jincai. Is that really a good idea?'

'Is the da ren so concerned about the safety of the barbarians?'

'An attack on a foreigner always creates complications, and paperwork.'

'Perhaps not for much longer.'

'"Exterminate the foreigners. Save the Ch'ing." Do I take it that the Black Stick Society is now formally adopting the motto of the Boxers? I thought that you were more practical.'

'Da Ren, we have known each other for many years. Will you tell me honestly that you do not appreciate what is happening in our country? Do you really not see the Harmonious Fists for what they are? And what forces they have unleashed? It is not an army of men alone who will drive out the foreigners. But when the gods themselves in their thousands come to support us . . .'

'My dear friend, Tang Dexin—'

'Da Ren, Da Ren, I did not believe it at first. Why would I? Like you I seek truth from facts. But my eyes were opened by the remarkable things I have seen. Look around you. Listen. Do you not feel it? Listen with your senses and not your mind. Listen with your heart.'

The Mandarin had thought it was the wind intensifying but he now realised that the sighing in the air of which he had become half consciously aware was in fact singing, a faraway chant, male and female voices fading in from different directions and dying again, with a hint of mournful flute behind. The lights swirled behind the trees. Drums thumped at irregular intervals.

'So now you are presenting me with conjuring tricks. What are you going to produce next? Ghosts? Maybe you are getting old, Tang Lao. You are hardly showing respect for my intelligence. Or do you mean only to intimidate my guards?'

But Tang Dexin had turned on his stool and was peering behind him. Iron Man Wang had already risen to his feet and was groping for his axe, as if for comfort. His eyes stared. A muscle was quivering in his cheek.

The blind priest, led by the boy, had moved into the firelight. He was motionless but his arms were outstretched and his sightless eyes were fixed at a point above the trees. The singing sound grew louder.

A white phosphorescence appeared to be growing at the top of some of the pines, drifting upwards in filaments of yellow and green smoke.

'Fireworks, Tang Lao? Very pretty.'

But the old man ignored him and continued to stare. Imperceptibly his hand moved to his mouth and he began unconsciously to suck his thumb.

Some of the phosphorescence was now drifting downwards through the higher branches of the trees, like strands of diaphanous material weaving and twirling to the pulsating of the drums and the sighing of the faraway song. It was fanciful, but the Mandarin believed that he could make out vague white shapes in the smoke, the glint of silver on white arms, the trail of a dress gliding behind the pine branches. The music – lute sounds now mixed with the flute – grew louder.

Carefully the Mandarin turned to observe the effects on his men. Major Lin was standing behind him, motionless, his mouth twisted open, eyes narrowed, one hand on his pistol holster. The soldiers sat rigidly on their horses, staring, frightened. Iron Man Wang and his men seemed similarly amazed, and Tang Dexin was making low moaning sounds. He seemed entranced.

There were unquestionably figures moving, or rather gliding, at the tops of the trees. The Mandarin recognised several *apsaras*, the elegant sky maidens of Buddhist manuscripts and monastery paintings, who appeared to be floating in the shimmering haze. The smoke changed hue from yellow to red and in the new pink glow the Mandarin thought he saw a procession of gorgeously dressed ladies in white veils and silks moving slowly among the higher branches. The invisible female singers touched beautiful, haunting heights – despite himself, the Mandarin felt a wistfulness and a languor, almost desire burning in his loins – then the song and the vision of the ladies began to fade as suddenly as they had appeared, to be replaced by loud, insistent drumbeats and discordant braying of trumpets, the music of the palace giving way to the call of the camp of war. Larger, stranger shapes were forming in the higher branches.

He had lost track of time. Something pulled his attention away from the treetops to the glade itself – and he started with shock. The glade had filled with men.

There were hundreds of them. They were standing in ranks and companies like an army drawn up on a battlefield. Each troop had its uniform and colour. Red turbans and red tunics bearing spears and pikes. Yellow turbans and yellow jackets wielding heavy swords. One group appeared to be dressed in tiger skins, carrying banners. There was a small company of girls, diminutive in their uniform red pyjamas, but their eyes shone defiantly and they, too, were armed with swords and others held up large red lanterns. The Mandarin had spent a lifetime reviewing troops. He saw at a glance that here was a disciplined array. Nor did he disparage the extreme youth of most of the men – at least half seemed under sixteen or seventeen – or their clear peasant origin: burnt, wide-eyed, rustic faces gazed at the sights above them in the trees with the foolish, open wonder of children. But, then, the hardier, older men scattered among them were staring too, and the few here and there who had the effete look of the city wastrel – elements of Iron Man's gang and the Black Sticks? he wondered. The realisation, however, that hit his professional eye and sent a chill to his belly was that if these were the Harmonious Fists they were not the rabble he had imagined. Raw and inexperienced they must be, but no different from the young recruits like himself who had lined up in village squares to join the Hunan Braves forty years before, and they had grown to become one of the most formidable armies the empire had ever seen. Yet what diabolical force had had the power to gather such numbers in such a time – in secret, without any organisation of which he was aware – in his own district without him knowing? It was unnatural.

The smoke in the treetops had shifted and now dank grey swathes of smoke seemed to be stretching a platform into the air. The ghostly white shapes he had seen before he dropped his eyes were becoming more substantial. With a chill, he recognised what they were. There, on a horse, in the air, wild beard and topknot clearly visible above the armour, his fierce brows beetled in a resolute grimace recognisable from a thousand statues in a thousand temples and wielding his enormous spear, was the war god, Guandi, shining and shimmering in the night, a stone statue come to frightening life. There was a loud cry as several hundred men drew in their breath in fear or gasped in wonder. The inarticulate human sound rose for a moment above the thunder of drums and trumpets. The Mandarin was shocked to hear his own cry among it, and small it sounded.

The Boxer priest stood in the same outstretched position as before, although now his lips were moving in what might have been silent incantation or prayer. The firelight shifted the shadows on his pallid features, but the sightless white eyeballs remained fixed on the sky. He showed no awareness of the growing ranks and companies forming behind him, yet the Mandarin had the feeling that he was orchestrating the gathering as much as he was somehow conjuring the phantasms in the trees . . . but, of course, he told himself with an effort, that was what he was meant to believe. He must resist the entrancement. He forced himself to concentrate: there are walkways in the treetops, actors, he told himself, fireworks and wires, yes, wires for the *apsaras* to swing themselves – this is opera, this is circus, this is illusion. These are men . . .

Another long-drawn gasp of surprise welled over the drumbeats. All around the circle of treetops other figures were forming out of the phosphorescence into recognisable shapes, marching sturdily forward to stand with their weapons on the cloud. The Mandarin recognised Guandi's companions from the War of the Three Kingdoms, Liu Bei, Zhang Fei, Zhuge Liang, and their arch enemy Cao Cao, the latter's white beard waving in the breeze. And there was the Shang warrior, Zhao Yun, and one-legged Sun Bin of the Warring States. There was another gasp as the crowd recognised the protagonists of *The Journey to the West*: the magical monkey god, Sun Wu-kong, his boon companions Sandy and Piggy. The greatest roar of all was reserved for the appearance of the Jade Emperor himself, flanked by his enormous guards. The glistening figures hung in the dark night above the tree-line, indistinct because of the distance from the ground, but clearly identifiable from their folklore incarnations – and they were moving, even conversing, gazing benevolently at their worshippers below.

The unseen drums were beating at a furious rate. The Boxer priest slowly folded his arms. His heavy head fell forward and the white holes of his eyes seemed to stare directly at the group by the table. The Mandarin realised that he was walking deliberately towards them, towards him. With an effort he composed his features to look back into the sightless eyes. The blind man stood above him and, though it was impossible, he seemed to be contemplating him, studying him, reading his mind. The Mandarin felt a trickle of sweat on his forehead.

Then the priest was standing above Tang Dexin, who cowered into his fur, averting his eyes. The priest paused for a long moment, then walked to where Iron Man Wang stood rigidly with his axe clutched in two hands. Stretching out his hand the priest touched the haft, and gently lifted the weapon out of the bandit's grasp, swinging it lightly as if it was a weightless object. He reached out his other arm, took Iron Man Wang's hand, and led the bandit towards the fire. Iron Man Wang offered no resistance. In fact, he looked like a man in a trance, a schoolboy stumbling after a strict master resigned to whatever punishment he deserved.

The priest released Iron Man's hand but kept the axe. He moved slowly towards the centre of the clearing where the firelight flickered over the front ranks of the Boxers. Eager faces watched the priest's progress, although many others could not take their eyes away from the visions floating above their heads. Iron Man followed a pace behind. The priest raised his head in the direction of the first manifestation which had appeared, the war god Guandi. Then, with both hands, he raised the axe above his head as if he was making an offering. His body curved gracefully into a bow and he sank slowly to his knees, then rose and fell as effortlessly to perform the nine times kowtow due an emperor or a god. Iron Man stumbled to his knees and did the same in more clumsy fashion. He was still kneeling when the priest returned to him with the axe, which again he raised above his head, then placed in Iron Man's hands. He stood back with his arms folded, waiting.

Iron Man looked nervously to his sides, and up at the figure of Guandi, whose cloak was now swirling in the breeze and who was raising his own great axe above his head. Hesitantly Iron Man raised his axe into the same position. Slowly at first, but growing more confident with every turn, he swung it around his head in great arcs. He hurled the axe into the air with one hand and caught it effortlessly with the other. Then he was thrusting forward and lunging back, the haft twisting and turning round his body like a baton. Imperceptibly Iron Man had begun to dance. His body was shaking as if from an internal force, while his feet leaped and kicked with an elegance that seemed incongruous in such a bulk. The two blades of the axe spun on the axis of the haft, flashing red reflections from the firelight round the glade. As the speed and the violence of his movements increased, Iron Man made whooping shouts on his thrusts. The Mandarin was amazed at how fast he was moving. This was martial arts of an advanced skill.

The priest had turned to the war god again with his arms upraised. There was a great murmur from the ranks of the Boxers. The figure of Guandi and his horse seemed to be growing and fading at the same time; green smoke swirled around his huge frame. Then he was gone. Where there had stood a horse and a god, now there was an empty black space. At that moment, Iron Man stopped dead, caught in mid-movement, one leg on the ground, the other bent, axe above his head; he stood like a temple statue. The Mandarin stared. It was still Iron Man. There were the shaggy brows, the rough beard, the flat cheeks, but the expression had altered imperceptibly, and what he saw was the fierce and unmistakable scowl of Guandi.

'Did you see that? Did you see that?' Tang Dexin was whimpering.

There were roars from the Boxers: 'Guandi! Guandi!' There was an excited movement among the ranks as all strained to see what transformation had occurred before their eyes.

Slowly Iron Man straightened his legs, brought the axe to his shoulder, and turned to face the ranks. He seemed to stand taller and to move with a grace that was not his own. He raised the axe above his head and crashed it to the ground so that one of the heads was fully buried in the grass. 'Exterminate the foreigners and save the Ch'ing!' he roared, and the whole crowd followed the chant.

He and the Boxer priest moved together among the ranks and companies, examining the excited recruits. They peered closely into men's faces and when they seemed satisfied they would pull out a candidate from among them. Most of the young men so picked stepped forward eagerly, and kowtowed energetically behind the priest and Iron Man as their weapons were proffered to whatever god had been chosen for them. Soon the whole glade was filled with figures twirling and dancing to the frantic beat of the drums and whatever internal madnesses had been unleashed inside them. And one by one the figures on the cloud faded and disappeared and there on the ground would be another rigid possessed statue where a moment before there had been a wild martial artist in a trance; a statue that, after a moment, would move and walk among the Boxers with the characteristics of the god into whom he had been transformed.

Tang Dexin was rocking his narrow shoulders back and forth in his furs, giggling uncontrollably now. 'I told you, Da Ren. I told you, Da Ren. You wanted guns for your precious soldiers, I give you a militia led by the gods!'

'Major Lin!' the Mandarin called. 'Major Lin!'

'Here, Da Ren.' It took him a moment to come to attention, and it was a dazed reply. Like the others he had been hypnotised by the spectacle.

'If you are indeed a soldier, get your troops together now and form around us. And remember what I told you, we are dealing with men.'

'But, Da Ren, you saw—'

'I saw men, Major. Nothing more. Now quietly gather your troops. We are leaving this place. In good order, I hope.'

'Da Ren!' Lin bowed curtly, and ran back to his troopers, who were huddled around their horses' heads muttering and pointing.

The Mandarin turned, and his heart stopped when he saw Major Lin gesticulating with one of the sergeants who was waving his carbine with a wild face and angry eyes. He held his breath when Lin pushed his pistol into the man's forehead, and exhaled with relief after what seemed to be an age, during which the man shuddered, came to his senses and saluted his officer. Good. Lin knew his soldiers. The two of them should be enough to get the rest back into order. It should not take long. He had feared that he might already have lost them to the Boxers. He turned to the gibbering Tang Dexin. 'So Iron Man is to lead a patriotic militia financed by the Black Sticks?'

'The god Guandi will lead the militia, Da Ren. You saw him descend.'

'And when am I to be favoured by the arrival of this divine assistance in Shishan?'

'When it is time, Da Ren. The gods will choose the propitious moment to rid the country of the barbarians. Already they have graced the Imperial Court with wisdom. It will not be long now. But you must prepare for the day.' Tang leaned forward and grabbed the Mandarin's sleeve. 'You are still the Tao Tai, Da Ren. Yours is the authority. But we will be there for you. I knew that you would support us when you saw.'

'Exterminate the foreigners! Save the Ch'ing!' was the cry from all around them. The Mandarin saw that the Boxer priest and Iron Man, and the others selected to be leaders in the bizarre ceremony, were moving back towards them with purposeful strides.

'They've become invincible, you see, Da Ren.' Tang Dexin was giggling. 'Can't kill a god. Not with one of those foreign toys. You see, there's no need to buy guns any more. Shall I show you? I think I should show you.' He reached inside his fur and pulled out a small pistol. 'Why don't you take a shot at Iron Man Wang now? See what it will do. Don't worry, it won't hurt him. That's the point. Oh, don't you want to try? Then let me.'

'Sit down, Tang Lao, if you wish to live.'

But Tang Dexin, a wild smile on his face, had risen cheerfully to his feet and was stumbling towards the approaching group, the pistol outstretched. 'Iron Man, my lord Guandi, we must still demonstrate your invulnerability to the da ren. I would be so honoured.'

It happened very quickly. The Boxer priest stopped and seemed to sniff the air; then he pointed his finger at Tang Dexin, who cowered backwards. As he did so, as if by involuntary action, the gun fired, twice. The Mandarin saw that it was still pointed directly at Iron Man Wang, and at almost point-blank range, but the bandit did not flinch, and continued to stride forward in his new godly gait. But as he did so, he lifted his axe to his shoulders, and swung with both arms. Tang Dexin's head bounced off his body, and the fur cloak subsided slowly to the ground. There was a shout of triumph from the Boxers.

'Guandi! Guandi.'

The little boy who tended the Boxer priest ran forward, and picked up the white pigtailed head before it had fully rolled. He gave it to the priest who held it high. Iron Man Wang leaned on his axe. The Boxers shouted their slogans, rattling their spears, waving their banners. Some of the other newly made gods inspected the head dispassionately. One of them, a sour-faced, pockmarked youth, who was familiar to the Mandarin although he could not place where he had seen him, took the head, his own face twisting into an evil smile – it seemed of triumph – then he dropped the head on his foot and kicked it high over the crowd of Boxers, where it was caught with shouts and hurled from hand to hand.

'Exterminate the foreigners! Save the Ch'ing.' The chant had become an insistent chorus, as loud as the drums.

'Da Ren!' He somehow heard the voice shouting into his ear. 'Your horse! Quickly!'

Automatically he felt for the bridle and swung himself into the saddle, his eyes not leaving the knot of men. The blind priest's sightless eyes bored into him. The young, sour-faced Boxer captain grinned. Iron Man leaned balefully on his axe. 'Tao Tai, you may leave,' he said, 'but you will be ready for me when it is time to kill the foreigners.'

The Mandarin swung his horse and followed Major Lin and the troop at a gallop out of the glade. Suddenly and inconsequentially, he remembered where he had last seen that sour-faced young man. He had been the witness in the trial of the doctor's cook.

Finally the doctor went to his tent. The drums were still beating far away in the forest. He lay fully clothed on his camp-bed, and dozed fretfully, but his mind was churning and deep sleep would not come. In a half-dream he rehearsed over and over again a conversation with

Nellie, somehow set in Ah Lee's kitchen, with the cook and Ah Sun in the background plucking chickens and scattering feathers; he was trying hard to explain to her why Henry Manners was to become their new son-in-law and marry Jenny once the doctor had bought a battleship and a field gun, and meanwhile Helen Frances must be kept on her pills ... but Nellie was being typically obdurate, showing not the slightest sympathy for his difficult position ...

He started awake. There was the sound of hoofs and the panting of horses outside the tent. He recognised the Mandarin's voice and Manners's reply. Blearily he raised his pocket watch to the night lantern and peered at the dial. It was four o'clock in the morning. What were they doing at this time of the night? As quietly as he could he crept to the tent flap and peered outside. The Mandarin was on his horse, a blanket draped over his shoulders, and Manners, wearing nothing more than long johns (he must have been roused from his bed), was standing beside him. They had obviously just concluded whatever conversation they had been having. Manners stretched out his hand. The Mandarin, seeming preoccupied, considered for a while, then reached out with his own and briefly returned the Englishman's handshake. Then immediately he turned his horse away and moved out of the clearing at a slow walk.

The doctor expected Manners to return to his own tent, but instead he walked to where Colonel Taro had pitched his. He paused a long moment there. The doctor waited for him to wake the Japanese and tell him whatever news he had heard, but Manners seemed to reconsider, yawned, stretched – then slowly made his way towards his own tent. To do so he had to pass Helen Frances's. Again he stopped. The doctor, watching, felt a flutter of fear in his stomach. Manners stood by the tent door irresolutely. He turned to go. Then sharply he called out Helen Frances's name – once only – and waited. There was a long, long silence, and Airton at last began to breathe again; she had not heard him in her deep sleep. Then he saw the door flap move and a haggard, tear-streaked face framed in red hair appear, shining wraithlike in the starlight. Two white arms snaked out, drawing Manners into their embrace, and the two disappeared into the darkness of the tent.

The doctor slumped on his washing stool and put his head into his hands.

* * *

'I thought you'd died,' she said, after their lovemaking, feeling his head in the familiar position on her breast. 'I thought that the bear had killed you.'

'Can you forgive me,' he said, nuzzling her, 'for trying to show off to you?'

'You weren't doing it for me. I saw the glint in your eyes when you were talking to the Mandarin. You'll always be selfish and follow your own way. And I'll love you anyway. See what you've made me. Do you care?'

Henry sighed, and rolled away so that he was lying on his back.

'Don't stop,' she said softly. 'It's been so long since you touched me.'

He slipped his hands under her arms in a tight embrace. 'You have to believe in me,' he said urgently, his eyes staring into hers. 'It's not as it seems . . .'

'Yes, I know. You've said that before. If only I really knew . . . But I don't care, Henry, what your secrets are. It doesn't matter. Really. I'll be leaving soon anyway. I can't hide things here much longer. I think that Nellie woman suspects already.'

'Nobody suspects us,' Henry murmured, kissing her. 'Trust me.'

'Trust you?' She pushed him away, then leaned over him, a strange smile on her face. 'Trust you?' She laughed shortly – a hard, bitter laugh. She shook her head. 'It's Tom I feel sorry for. That's obviously over, isn't it? Anyway, I don't deserve him. I thought I'd make for Shanghai. I'm told people can disappear there – among the opium dens.'

'Oh, God, Helen Frances, you're not telling me you still . . . ?'

'You think I just gave up up when I left? Oh, no, Henry. Why do you think I work in the hospital? In the opium ward? Don't worry. I enjoy my . . . habit. It's about the only thing I have left that reminds me of you.'

'What have I done to you?' whispered Henry.

'Used me,' she said, kissing him. 'But I told you, it doesn't matter. That's you. And me, for that matter. I'm to blame as much as you are. More so.' She smiled down at Henry, who was breathing heavily, his mouth twisting as though unsure what to do or say. She used one hand gently to straighten his hair, the other to stroke his chest. 'You could take me away with you,' she said, in a small voice. 'I'd settle for the half-decent thing not the whole.'

'I – I can't leave now,' he muttered. He gazed at her wildly. 'I can't.'

She laughed and flopped on to her back, stretching her arms.

'Of course you can't,' she said. 'Railways,' she added. 'So important. The doctor thinks they'll bring the Chinese to Jesus. Is that what you're doing as well? Bringing Chinese to Jesus?'

'Helen Frances, dearest, I promise you . . . I'll think of something . . . Please don't . . .'

But she put a finger first to his lips, then she covered his mouth with her own, and then she lowered herself on to him and told him to love her again.

Far away in Tsitsihar, in the last cold darkness before morning, Frank Delamere, Lu Jincai and Tom Cabot were checking the loading of the silver chests on to their wagons while Mr Ding fussed beside them offering well-meant but largely unhelpful suggestions.

At about the same time in the Black Hills, dawn trailed pink clouds over the clearings where the huntsmen were rousing, in a camp where only one man, Colonel Taro, still slept peacefully that night.

An equally florid sky irradiated the larger sleepless clearing where chastened companies of Boxers were seated round their fires, eating gruel and peering at the innocuous-looking trees from which, a few hours previously, they had witnessed the descent of the gods. Iron Man Wang, looking little like a god this morning, was seated with his new captains under a rough wooden shelter examining a map and growling orders through a leg of mutton he held in his large hairy hand. Behind him the Boxer priest slept on a mat, attended by his boy, his sightless eyes open to the sky.

It was already raining four miles to the east, where Ren Ren, now a Boxer captain, was riding proudly through the forest, bearing orders in his satchel from Iron Man Wang to the Black Sticks elders, bringing them the news of the change of leadership in their society, and calling on them to attend their new grand master. Ren Ren did not mind getting wet. He was thinking how he would surprise his mother with the news of his new status. He liked to surprise.

And it was also raining in Shishan, where Fan Yimei was looking out of her window towards the main house in which the foreign boy was imprisoned. Now that she was alone – with both Lin and Ma Na

Si away – she had had leisure to kneel at her small shrine and pray for a plan to rescue him. Saving Hiram had become the only meaningful purpose in her useless life. She thanked the Merciful Lady Guanyin for giving her this opportunity to redeem her sins and failures. She had failed with Shen Ping, but Providence had given her another chance. She knew that Ma Na Si would help her now that she had given herself to him. He had promised, and he was a man who could be trusted. Now all she needed was a plan.

And outside the city walls, in the mission, two children whimpered and tossed through their nightmares while their mother slept in a chair between their cots. In the hospital, Ah Sun was spooning congee into her injured husband's mouth to his great embarrassment. In another, more dilapidated mission in the west of the city, the Millward family were on their knees in prayer.

Black clouds rolled over north-east China, presaging a storm.

And hundreds of miles to the south, grey mists hung over the capital city, swirling round the green and black roofs of the Legations where Sir Claude MacDonald and the other ministers slept.

The great sprawl of the Forbidden City still slumbered in the dark of the morning, although the lanterns on the watchtowers were paling as light penetrated through the heavy cloud. Lamps burned bright, however, in the Dowager Empress's state rooms, where the old lady, cowled in a cloak to keep away the cold, was reading a document presented to her by Prince Tuan and some of the other senior courtiers. Her chief eunuch and adviser, Li Lien-ying, stooped attentively by her side.

'So let it be,' she said, lowering her spectacles and reaching for the brush and the vermilion ink. ' "Exterminate the foreigners and save the Ch'ing." '

PART TWO

Chapter Eleven

*We march for our Emperor; we will drive the foreign devils
from Tientsin into the sea.*

D r Airton was fussing, as he always did when one of the nuns
was about to make an expedition to an outlying village.
Some years previously when Sisters Elena and Caterina had first
announced their intention to carry on Father Adolphus's pastoral
work, he had conjured up all sorts of dangers and had offered to
accompany them on their visits. Nellie had had to remind him of
how inappropriate this would be. 'You don't want to make our dear
Roman colleagues think that you're scheming to steal their flock and
turn them into Presbyterians,' she had told him, before rounding on
him for being foolish. 'Besides, Elena and Caterina were wandering
alone around the Chinese countryside for months before you arrived
in Shishan. Whatever makes you think they need your protection?
They're doughty Italian peasants, my dear, and they'd probably end
up looking after you.'

And, indeed, he had to admit that the nuns had never come to
harm, even though some of the Catholic villages were days' journey
away, nestled on the slopes of bandit-infested mountains. Father
Adolphus had been an indefatigable traveller within the parish he
had created. Not only was his saintliness revered, but the old priest
had also possessed Jesuitical skills of organisation and diplomacy.
And he had won the respect of even the non-Christians who lived
side by side with his converts in these remote hamlets. The doctor
had heard many stories of how the white-bearded old man on
his donkey had averted this dispute over a well, or practised the
wisdom of Solomon over that family quarrel, or mediated on a
generations-old land feud to the satisfaction of all parties.

Father Adolphus had established small churches in some ten
or more different villages, claiming between them as many as a
thousand converted souls. He had chosen as his pastors worthy
men who were liked in their communities, but it was rarely they

who managed to keep the hotheads at bay after Father Adolphus's death, or stem the resentments that naturally arose each year when the Christians refused to pay the traditional dues to the local temple. If harmony was maintained, it was due to the memory and example of the good old man. The doctor therefore recognised the importance of the nuns visiting regularly. Not only were they the link with the wider Christian community outside: they also provided continuity with the saintly Adolphus, and this had a settling effect on Christian and non-Christian alike. So, whatever his fears for their personal safety, he knew that he could hardly forbid them to go.

He realised, too, that the recent incidents in some villages where non-Christians had apparently burned Christian property could not be ignored. These incidents, Boxer-inspired or not, were serious enough for the local militia under Major Lin to be called to investigate – although no malefactor, as far as he knew, had yet been punished. In these troubled times it was even more important for the nuns to keep in communication with their parishioners.

'But it's still my right to fuss,' he said to a laughing Sister Elena, who was loading a pack mule by lantern-light in the dark hour before dawn. She had exchanged her nun's coif for a simple peasant scarf, and her plump figure was even more shapeless than usual under the heavy padded jacket and trousers. It was the nuns' custom, when journeying beyond the confines of Shishan, to dress in the sensible travelling clothes of the Chinese.

'Now, I repeat, have you packed enough food for the journey?' asked Dr Airton.

'And I repeat yes. Yes. Yes. Yes. Yes. *Mamma mia!* You are like my grandmother. *Carissimo Dottore*, you will see. On my return, I am as fat as this mule with eatings. You will have to give me medicines for swollen tummy.'

'Very well,' grunted the doctor. 'I suppose you know what you're doing. You've been to this village before?'

'Many times. Many times,' said Sister Elena, straining to tighten a rope. 'Listen. I am going to be among friends. You need have no fears. They love me in Bashu. And Caterina, when she goes to Bashu, they love her too. They say welcome, welcome, and give us foods, and strong wines too. You have nothing to worry.'

'I daresay. I daresay – but I don't know why you refuse to take a groom with you.'

'For why do I want a *mafu*? I am a sister of the poor. Not a lady in fine clothes, fa-la-la. Oh, Doctor,' she grasped Airton's hands, 'do not worry so. The Lord Jesus will protect me, and the good Father Adolphus who is always watching from Heaven.'

For once she was being serious. The doctor looked down at the crabapple cheeks and the warm brown eyes intent on his own, and noticed the care marks on her rough skin, the crow's feet and the lines that crossed her forehead. Sister Elena looked older than her twenty-eight years. 'Doctor,' she said, 'it is for you that I worry. Caterina and I, we notice you are changed since you come down from the Black Hills. For why, Doctor? For why are you so alarmed? It cannot just be these fantastical Boxers. Is it . . . Miss Delamere?'

Airton tried to pull away his hands. 'Why do you say that?'

'It is the way that you are looking at her. When you think that nobody is noticing. Your eyes – they have pain,' she said simply.

'What nonsense.'

'No, Doctor, we see it, Caterina and I. And you are right to worry about Miss Delamere . . . Miss Delamere is not well. Listen to a simple peasant girl. Her soul, it is troubled, and maybe there is more.'

'What do you mean?'

'Women they see things, and you, *Dottore*, I think you also see, although maybe you prefer not to see. But she is a fine lady, Doctor, full of love and life.' Her hands tightened her grip. 'You will help her, Dr Airton, through this dark time? Sister Caterina, she tells me, say nothing. But I think that you know something is wrong, very wrong, and you will do what is right.'

'I don't know what you – what you are talking about,' muttered Airton, his whiskers quivering slightly.

Sister Elena's shrewd eyes held his for a moment longer. Then she smiled, and in a quick movement leaned forward and pecked the doctor on the cheek. 'Thank you, Doctor. *Grazie*. You are a good man.' And she released his hands. 'Oh, you make me late,' she complained, glancing at the pink clouds appearing above the roofs, 'and I have to ride far today if I am to reach Bashu by sunset. Goodbye, Doctor, I will see you in four days, maybe five. Lao Zhang, please open the gate. I am ready.'

Airton cleared his throat. 'Goodbye, my dear.' His cheeks had reddened and there was a moistness in his eye. 'Look after yourself,' he called. And he watched her clatter out of the compound.

He did not move from where he was standing. His major domo, Zhang Erhao, closed the gates and looked at him curiously as he passed. Airton pulled his pipe from his pocket but made no effort to fill it, just twisted the stem in his fingers, gazing at the ground.

He knew what he had to do, but he had always held off taking any action. Sister Elena was right: he *had* been behaving out of character ever since his terrible experience in the Black Hills. For the first time in his life he had not shared with Nellie what he had discovered. Nor could he bring himself to tell her his suspicions about Helen Frances's condition – no, they were more than suspicions. He was a doctor and saw the signs: it was a fact, and if he could see it, others would soon notice as well. Obviously the nuns had sensed something already. He must face it. The girl was pregnant. With Manners's child. *With Manners's child.* At the thought his mind clouded with confusion. Her father and Tom would be returning any day. What was he to do?

Then there were his darker suspicions. There was something else about her, which could not be explained by morning sickness. Her pallor, listlessness, the black shadows under her eyes. For months he had denied the obvious conclusion. A well-brought-up girl like Helen Frances? How could it be possible? Yet now he saw her in a new light, as Henry Manners's paramour, and what could not be possible where that man was concerned? Yet he had done nothing, despite the Hippocratic Oath, despite his role as guardian. He realised, to his shame, that he had been hoping that the lovers between them would create their own solution, by eloping, by marrying, by going away; by doing anything so that the responsibility would not be his. How he despised himself. What a hypocrite he felt when he stood in the chapel and preached a sermon on the Good Shepherd looking after his flock. For the first time in his life he was living a lie. And what would the Mandarin say if he knew? He would laugh.

And now weeks had passed. The lovers had not solved his problem for him. In fact they had hardly seen each other during that time. It was true that Henry Manners had called at the mission a day or so after their return from the Black Hills. They had all sipped tea in the stilted fashion of the English abroad, Nellie making small-talk, he abetting convention in a jocular manner that made his skin crawl. Helen Frances had come when she was asked and listened silently to the conversation, contributing the monosyllabic utterances that they had now come to expect from her. He had seen how Manners had tried to catch her eye, or manipulate the situation so that he could be alone with her. The doctor, feeling like a pander, had manufactured an excuse to take Nellie with him to the kitchen and leave the lovers alone – but when they returned, the two were sitting like statues: Helen Frances immobile in her high-backed chair, Manners resting his chin on his forearm gazing into the fire. A week after Manners had left, he had suggested to her that they visit the railway camp – the ride would do her good, he said – but she had muttered something about being busy in the wards. It was as if she wanted to retire into the darkness of her own soul. Even Nellie was finding the atmosphere strained, although he believed – he certainly prayed – that she did not realise the cause.

Yet something had to be done. She was ill. She was pregnant. God forbid, she might even be planning to take her own life.

And where was his compassion? Was he so concerned about moral appearances in their little foreign community that he would not lift a hand to help a lost soul?

'Oh, you hypocrite. Oh, you Pharisee,' he murmured, and clasped his face in his hands. The pipe fell to the ground.

After a while he drew out his pocket-handkerchief and wiped his eyes. Then he blew his nose. He squared his shoulders and made his way deliberately through the corridors and walkways until he came to the dispensary behind the opium ward. He tried the door. It was locked. He always kept a spare set of keys in his jacket. It took him some time to find the right one. He pushed open the door and saw Helen Frances sitting on the floor by the window. She had removed her apron and unbuttoned the top of her dress. She was breathing heavily and he saw the shadow of her breasts moving rhythmically under her chemise. One white freckled arm was out of the sleeve and lay limply at her side; it looked as if it were detached from her body. Her hair was untidy and fell in haphazard locks over her face, which was smiling seductively. Her lustrous kitten eyes catching the early-morning light gleamed a welcome that reminded him of the merry girl who had first come to Shishan such a short and such a long time ago.

'Oh, Dr Airton,' she cried cheerfully. 'How clever of you. You've discovered my little secret.'

Airton bent over, picked up the syringe and looked at the empty container of morphine. 'Oh, the brute,' he sighed, 'the brute. What has he done to you, my poor, poor girl?'

An hour before that same dawn Fan Yimei was lying next to Manners in his pavilion. Gently, so as not to waken him, she lifted the heavy hand that had flopped on to her shoulder and laid it softly back on the mat of hair that covered his chest. She eased herself through the curtains and reached for her gown, which had fallen on to the carpet.

'Do you have to go so soon?' said Manners, through the yawn of someone who had just woken from a deep sleep.

'You know what will happen to me if they find me here.'

'Nothing will happen to you. I will prevent it.'

'That is not in your power.'

'You are very beautiful, you know,' said Manners. 'Prize porcelain.'

'I am pleased that I satisfy you.'

'You've also become a mite cold to me of late. Also like porcelain.'

She did not reply, concentrating on tying the sash around her waist. When she was ready, she secured one side of the curtains and sat delicately on the bed. Manners reached for her hand but she pulled it away. 'You owe me payment, Ma Na Si Xiansheng.'

'That again?' said Manners. 'You refuse all the money and presents I offer you.'

'I believed we had a bargain, Ma Na Si Xiansheng.'

'Xiansheng. Xiansheng. Can't you be less formal? We're lovers, for God's sake.'

'No, Ma Na Si Xiansheng, I am your whore.'

'I've never thought of you as that,' said Manners quietly.

'Then you are wrong, and you . . . insult me.'

'Oh, for God's sake. Listen, what you ask of me is impossible. This boy – if he exists, and I find it hard to believe – is locked in the most secure part of this establishment.'

'I told you. I can lead you to where he is.'

'Past Ren Ren and all his guards?'

'You are resourceful. You will find a way.'

'My dear girl. Look, the best thing to do – as I've told you a hundred times – is to report the matter to the authorities.'

'Then you condemn him to instant death. He will have disappeared before the first *yamen* runner arrives at the gate.'

Manners laid his head back on the pillow. 'And what happens to you if I do rescue him?'

'It does not matter what happens to me.'

'It does not matter what happens to you,' Manners repeated. 'Come on, old girl.' He reached for her waist. Fan Yimei turned, her fragmentary self-control lost. Red spots of anger burned her cheeks. Her eyes screeched silent despair. Her long fingernails scratched a pink line on his chest. She pummelled his arms, his face. Then she turned away from him, panting, and straightened her back, although she still quivered with impotent rage. Her features settled into a white mask; a tear ploughed its furrow through the powder on her face. 'I am already dead.' It was hardly a whisper.

'All right,' said Manners.

'Ma Na Si Xiansheng, I do not understand.' She turned and regarded him suspiciously.

'I said, 'All right.' I'll do it. On one condition.'

'What – condition?' There was scorn in her voice.

'That I take you out with the boy.'

'That is impossible.'

'That's my condition.'

'No,' she said. 'No. That is not . . . necessary.'

'I am taking you out with the boy. Otherwise, the bargain's off.'

'No, only the boy.'

'I'm not negotiating with you, darling.'

'We already have a bargain. I have – provided my service. Many times.'

'I'm changing the terms.'

'I belong to Major Lin.'

Manners kissed her lips. 'Not any more.'

'And your mistress? The red-haired girl? Whom you – love? What about her?'

Manners kissed her again and wiped the wetness from her cheeks. 'What about her?' he whispered

'How will you do it?' she asked.

'I haven't the foggiest idea,' he said in English. Then, in Chinese: 'We'll make a diversion,' he said.

'Yes,' she said, thoughtfully. 'A diversion. Good. What is your plan?'

'Trust me,' he said.

After a moment she nodded. 'When?' she asked.

'Soon,' he said. 'Today. Tomorrow. Be ready.'

Fan Yimei looked hard into his eyes. Her expression softened. With a faltering finger she touched his lips. Then she pulled away from him, dropped to her knees, and bowed, her topknot sliding along the carpet. '*Duoxie! Duoxie!* Thank you, Xiansheng.'

'No more Xianshengs, all right?' Manners pulled her gently to her feet, kissing her forehead.

'Yes, Xiansheng,' she said. 'I must – I must go now.'

Manners released her. 'Wait for my call,' he said, and after she was gone, 'A diversion? God help me! Give me gun-running any day.'

'Do you think that they are plotting something?' asked Mother Liu lazily. She had finished her breakfast and had said her prayers at her shrine. The girl Su Liping had delivered her report and she had just called Ren Ren into her boudoir to discuss the affairs of the day. As was her custom she had prepared a pipe or two of opium and was now absorbed in heating a pellet over a candle.

Ren Ren, dressed in his usual clothes (the Harmonious Fists uniform had only been used for night-time raids on Christian villages), was sprawled on the bed, nursing a headache. He had drunk heavily the night before after a meeting with the Black Sticks council.

'Why do you say that?' he grunted. 'He's an animal, like all the other barbarians. She's a whore. They fuck. What's sinister about that?'

'You always were crude, my dearest,' said his mother, resting her head on the wooden pillow and putting the pipe to her lips. She sucked the smoke into her lungs, and sighed contentedly. 'The point is that it's not just fucking they get up to. Little Su says they spend a lot of their time talking.'

'Maybe he's one of those flowers who can't get his stalk up.'

'He's almost as well endowed as you are,' said Mother Liu, 'and active with it.'

'Yes? Well, perhaps he's aroused by her reciting poetry to him. You always said that she was an artistic little bitch.'

'No, I don't think that Ma Na Si is interested in poetry. It puzzles me. What do you imagine they discuss so intensely?'

'If you're so interested I'll take her down to the shed and beat it out of her.'

'There'll be time for that, my darling one, but not yet.'

'I don't know why you don't tell Lin that the barbarian is taking liberties with his whore. I'll kill the Englishman myself if he's too lily-livered to do it on his own account. As well as dealing with the girl.'

'My poor Ren Ren. Denied his pleasures for so long. You must learn to be patient, and think of business first.'

'I don't see what business you can get out of letting two of our clients have their way with our chickens scot-free, and one a barbarian at that. We might as well open our doors, stick incense sticks up our bums and offer our own fragrant holes to anyone who wants to suck on them.'

'What a charming turn of phrase you have. I hadn't realised that you took so after your useless father. I'm sure that you didn't inherit such vulgarity from me. Anyway, since you ask, you have a lot still to learn about the basic politics of business – even if you are all high and mighty now with your Boxers and Black Sticks.'

'Be careful, Mother. There are some things that even you must not joke about.'

'Who's joking? I'm very proud of you. I think that your new exalted position will be very good for business – when the time comes.'

'Well, that time's coming very soon, Mother. Very, very soon. We won't be pandering to foreigners much longer, that's for sure. They'll be dead, every one of them.'

'Even your dear little catamite next door?

'I'm tired of that whining brat. I've a mind to get rid of him anyway.'

'Well, be careful how you do it. I won't be upset. He's more than repaid our investment. What we received from the Japanese alone . . . But the constant subterfuge is tiresome, and our guests become wearied after a while with even the most exotic fruits. Take Jin Lao. He won't touch the boy now, and once upon a time he thought he was "peach blossom after rain". He's past his usefulness, dear.'

'There's another thing I don't understand. You and Jin Lao. Why do you spend so much time closeted with that ancient fairy? If he wasn't as bent as a fish-hook I'd be thinking he was jigging your old bones. What a thought! His crinkled old frog poking about in your dried-up cinnabar grotto! Giggles in the graveyard, eh, Mother dear? What a horrible prospect.'

And he snorted with laughter, shaking the bed. Mother Liu looked at him coldly. With dignity, she reached for another opium pellet to heat over the flame.

'Just look at your face, Ma. Never could take a joke, could you? All right, all right. I apologise. You and Jin. It's a business relationship, I know.'

And he flopped over in a renewed burst of laughter.

'As it happens, it is a business relationship,' Mother Liu said coldly, 'and a very profitable one. Which reminds me. When the time comes, there's one of the foreigners I need you to spare. For business reasons . . .'

'Oh, yes? And who would that be?'

'The fox-spirit girl. The red-headed one. Old De Falang's daughter.'

'The ugly bitch? The one who whored with the Englishman? She's stale goods. Why do you want her?'

'I have a special client who's interested. That's why.'

'Go on. Tell.'

'You'll know in good time. Don't worry. You won't be displeased. It may even help you in your new career.'

'I can take her to the shed first?'

'Of course you can. She must be trained properly.'

'All right, then. I'll get her for you. What do you want me to do with Ma Na Si and the Fan bitch in the meanwhile?'

Mother Liu was already smoking her second pipe. 'Something in my bones tells me they're up to something. There's something more than just lust. Why would an intelligent girl like Fan Yimei risk so much? We'll tighten the watch on them. And it might be useful to have some of your boys around for a while. Just in case. Indulge the worries of an old woman who's learned a little about survival in this sea of sorrow. Can you do that for me, my dear, dear Ren Ren?'

'Of course,' shrugged Ren Ren, and yawned.

* * *

'You should have come to me earlier,' said Nellie.

Helen Frances looked sullenly at the floor. The grandfather clock ticked loudly from the dining room. From the kitchens came a dim wail – Ah Lee singing Chinese opera as he cooked their lunch.

Airton was standing by the mantelpiece puffing at his pipe.

'Nellie,' he began, but froze under his wife's glare.

'I imagine you thought I would be unsympathetic,' Nellie continued. 'I suspect that you have always been a little afraid of me, Helen Frances. I know you don't like me.'

Helen Frances raised her head and looked the older woman in the eye. 'I don't need your sympathy,' she said. 'I told you. I would have left earlier. Only – only I didn't have the money. If you pay me my salary for April and May, I can go by the next train.'

'And where would you go?'

'Does it matter?'

'I think it would matter to your father – and Tom.'

'Mrs Airton, I know what you think of me. Let us not prolong this unpleasant interview. I have asked your husband for my salary. Do me that charity at least. Let me leave on the train that arrives from Tientsin tomorrow.'

'Your father and Tom are expected any day.'

'That is why I want to leave Shishan tomorrow.'

'You want to run away?'

Helen Frances's eyes blazed. 'Yes, Mrs Airton, if you please, I would like to run away.'

Nellie glanced at her husband. Airton nervously cleared his throat. 'My dear, you know we cannot allow that. Your condition—'

'My condition, Doctor, is one for which I alone am responsible. There is nobody else to blame. And I do not ask for your help.'

'And what would you have us tell your father?' asked Nellie calmly.

'Tell him the truth,' said Helen Frances, shrilly. 'The sooner he knows what a disgrace I have been to him the sooner he will forget he had a daughter. And as for Tom, it would be a kindness.'

'I do not think that you appreciate how much you are loved,' said Nellie.

'Mrs Airton, do I need to remind you? I am a fallen woman. Isn't that what you think of me? I have fornicated, Mrs Airton. And, Mrs Airton, I have enjoyed fornicating. And I am an opium

337

eater. Doesn't your precious Bible tell you to cast out sinners such as I?'

'My Bible tells me not to cast the first stone,' said Nellie.

'Oh, don't give me cant, Mrs Airton. I know how much you despise me. And don't tell me you plan to save my soul. I'm not one of those pathetic Rice Christians in your infirmary whom you think you can bring to Jesus with a plaster and a bowl of hot noodles. If you really want to help me, give me my salary so I can purchase a train ticket out of here. My damnation's my own affair and nobody else's.'

'And Mr Manners? He proposes to go with you and look after you?'

'No. He has nothing to do with my decision.'

'The man who ruined you has nothing to do with your decision?'

'Nobody ruined me, Mrs Airton. I am responsible for my own actions. Henry has been . . . chivalrous throughout. You will not understand that, but what I feel in my heart for Henry is gratitude and respect, above all, gratitude.'

'For giving you an illegitimate baby?'

'I knew that you would not understand. Henry's is a free spirit. He freed mine.'

Airton coughed. 'This is all getting way above my head. As far as I'm concerned, the man is a cad, a liar, a seducer – and worse besides. He must also be some sort of Svengali if he has this hold on you still, after he's mistreated you so abominably. Well, the opium may account for that.

'I am merely a doctor and for me the question is a practical one. How to get you better again, off this habit. It won't do you any good gallivanting round a strange land with little or no money and therefore no means to satisfy your addiction. The consequences, moral and physical, are too terrible to contemplate. And then there's the question of the baby's health. You intend this child to live, I suppose? For that we must ensure the health of its mother. You, my dear. And I can't look after you if you're attempting to run away from whatever furies are lurking in that silly head of yours on a railway train.

'So, I'm not going to allow you to go to Tientsin tomorrow, and that's that. And before you start telling me how responsible you are for your own actions – we've had enough of that modern twaddle, thank you very much – let me remind you that you are under twenty-one and therefore subject to the authority of your father. And since we are your appointed guardians in his absence, that means you will have to do what we tell you to do. And, my first instruction to you, young lady, is to take yourself down the hall to your room, go to bed and rest. Your treatment starts tonight. You've worked in the ward and you know how tough it's going to be. But I'm here, and so is Nellie – who loves you, too, though you're too much of a dolt to see that – and we're going to see you through, and save your bonny bairn who, if I am not wrong, is the only innocent party in this tragic affair.'

'He's right, you know, my dear. We do care deeply for you, and we will look after you,' added Nellie.

'I will not be made an object of your charity or hypocrisy,' said Helen Frances. Two red spots burned on her sallow cheeks.

'Call it what you like, but I don't see that you have a choice. It's for your own good and the good of the child.'

'My bastard,' said Helen Frances.

'Your baby,' insisted Nellie.

Helen Frances opened her mouth to retort, but her face squeezed involuntarily, crumpling like a dried-out persimmon, and her shoulders began to shake. Sobbing, she threw herself at Nellie's feet and clutched the hem of her dress. Her words came out in great gulps between her tears. 'I beg you . . . I beg you . . . please . . . Be merciful . . . please . . . Let me go . . . I can't . . . I can't face it . . . My father . . . To-om . . . How can I . . .'

Nellie knelt down beside her, hugging her tightly, pressing her cheek fiercely against the hot, tear-streaked face, as if seeking by will-power alone to transfer her calm to the shaking girl. Helen Frances's body jerked and shuddered in the death agony of her independence like a newly caught marlin drowning in air. Her sighs were like the whisper of a dying breeze heard through rigging at sea. At last the convulsions subsided. Nellie rested Helen Frances's head against her broad bosom and began to stroke her hair. 'There, there. There, there. It'll all be fine. It'll all be fine.' Helen Frances, overcome, stared with round, bewildered eyes, a stunned fish netted in Nellie's strong arms.

Nellie lifted her gently to a kneeling position. She grasped both hands tightly and looked commandingly into her face, forcing her to return the gaze. 'Now, listen to me, girl. You must be strong. Stronger than you've ever been before. Yes, you will have to face your father, and your fiancé in due course, and it will be terrible for you, and for them. But that's for another day. Now I'm going to take you to your room. Edward will give you – what you need. And then I want you to sleep.'

Helen Frances nodded submissively.

'Good. That's my girl.'

If the virtues of charity and forgiveness were having an airing at the Airtons' mission, the trumpets of a more martial Christianity were sounding in the Millwards' establishment. Septimus had prayed and fasted, and was now in the figurative process of girding his loins to fight the good fight.

He had been thrown into temporary confusion after the visit of the commissioner of American missions, who had ordered him to desist from evangelical activities until the board had given judgement on his 'case'. At first he had meekly succumbed to higher authority. It had taken him weeks to understand the terrible temptation by which the Devil had sought to snare him. It had come to him in a vision, shortly after he had collapsed from malnutrition; providentially that angel of mercy, his wife Laetitia, had obtained dispensation from the saints to allow him to break his fast and have a bowl of gruel. It had been in the fitful sleep following his meal, his wife and children gathered around his bed in prayer, that the Angel Gabriel had revealed to him in a dream the truth about the creature who had called himself Mr Burton Fielding. He knew that there was a real Mr Fielding; he had seen his name on correspondence and on the lists of board members printed at the bottom of pamphlets published by the Commission. That had not been the Burton Fielding who had visited Shishan, however. Septimus had been deceived by a Principality of Darkness, a demon sent by Lucifer in Mr Fielding's form, to steer him from the true path of righteousness. It had been that simple, and he had been beguiled.

Now he had made atonement. He had continued his fast. He had beaten his flesh with rods – or, rather, he had allowed Laetitia to administer the chastisement, reprimanding her on occasion for her weakness when she did not deliver the blows hard enough. A fortnight later he had been granted another vision, the memory of which even now made him tremble with humility. God the Father had been present, but it was the Son Himself who had raised him to his feet, and bathed the wounds on his back – he knew then that he had been forgiven. The Saviour had afterwards arrayed him in silver armour, with cloak and greaves and a shining helmet, and in his hands He had placed a burning sword. St Michael had mounted him on a horse called Steadfastness, and a host of angels had been delegated to follow him into battle. On waking he knew what he had to do.

The problem was that he was so weak from his fasting that he could hardly stand, and it had taken all Laetitia's care to restore him to something resembling his old strength. Even yet he was not fully recovered. He was subject to blackouts, and a curious array of spots would float before his eyes; cleaning his glasses did not help. Nevertheless he knew that he was ready. If the body was weak, his spirit was strong. The Lord of Hosts was with him.

And today was the day. He had roused his family early. Together they had prayed, and sung several hymns. Then they had gathered in the yard, all except one daughter, Mildred, who would remain to look after the orphans and babes. They carried nothing in their hands except rush torches fashioned into the shape of the Cross – since Hiram had left they had dispensed with the band. The Lord would provide them with all the other weapons they needed. In solemn and silent file, Septimus led them out of the gate and over the drains.

Before them lay the House of Babylon in which the Lord had revealed that his prodigal, Hiram, lay in bondage. Today Septimus would do battle with the forces of darkness; he would bring down the Temple of Abominations; he would free the good people of Shishan from their enslavement to the powers of evil. He might even save his son, Hiram, in the process but that was not so important.

The doctor had administered a measured dose of morphine and had left Nellie to put Helen Frances to bed. He had resumed his position by the mantelpiece, smoking his pipe. Nellie had sat with Helen Frances until she was satisfied that the girl was asleep. Now Nellie, too, had returned to the sitting room. She slumped into her armchair, lay back and closed her eyes. 'Oh, Edward,' she murmured, 'what are we to do?'

Airton was surprised and confused to see that she was crying. Clumsily he knelt beside her and took her hand.

'I'll be all right in a moment,' she said, wiping her eyes. 'It's just that . . . oh, when I think of that poor, poor girl, it makes me want to . . .'

'Manners is a monster,' said Airton.

'Oh, we're all to blame. To think that this affair must have started under our own roof, when we were meant to be protecting her. I should have seen what was going on.'

'You weren't to know,' said her husband.

'I'll never forgive myself,' said Nellie. 'And I shouldn't forgive you either, you silly man, for not letting me know earlier what you suspected.'

'I didn't want to upset you,' said Airton lamely.

'That poor, poor girl. Can you imagine what she must have been through? She probably believes she hasn't a friend in the world. Thank you,' she said, taking the cup of tea, which her husband had poured for her. 'It's not that I can condone what she has done. She's right in a way, you know, when she says it is her own responsibility. Even if she was led on by that unspeakable man. She has sinned, Edward, and brought hurt on herself and others.'

'We mustn't be too hard on her . . .'

'Why ever not? She has been a vain, silly, headstrong girl, who has given way to lust and evil temptations. This will break the heart of her father, not to mention that noble fellow who has been foolish enough to want to marry her.'

'I suppose there's no question of that going ahead now.'

'Helen Frances told me just now that her greatest shame and fear is that Tom will still want to marry her. She says that's the main reason why she wanted to leave. He's such a gentleman with all those stupid notions of self-sacrifice and doing the right thing. And he truly loves her. You can see it in his mooning expression every time he looks at her. He's just the good-natured type of fool who would be prepared to bring up another man's bastard.'

'It would be wonderful if her child could be born in wed-lock.'

'The man who should be forced to marry her – at pistol point, if I had my way – is the Honourable Henry Manners. Let the two of them reap the fruits of their crime together. What did she say about looking after her own damnation? Let them both be damned together.'

Airton sighed. 'You say these things, Nellie, but you don't mean them.'

'I'm sorry, Edward. I'm tired, and I'm angry. With her. With myself. With you. What a ghastly, ghastly tragedy it is.'

They sipped their tea.

'We'll have to break the news to Frank and Tom as soon as they return,' said the doctor, in the hesitant tone of somebody who would like to be contradicted.

'Can we hide it from them?'

'I suppose not,' said Airton.

'Can you cure her of her addiction?'

'Yes. With time.'

'And the bairn? Will the mother's addiction harm it?'

'It need not be so. If Providence is on our side I hope that we can avert the worst effects. It's still early in the pregnancy.'

'Let's trust to Providence, then. And pray for some degree of forgiveness and understanding from her father and Tom.'

'Amen to that,' said Airton, putting down his cup. 'Whatever is that noise?' He moved to the window and peered through the shutters. At that moment Ah Lee burst through the doorway, followed shortly after by Jenny and George, who had tumbled out of their schoolroom and into the yard at the first sound of the disturbance. Ah Lee was pointing inarticulately. It was George who cried out first: 'Father, come quickly. It's Uncle Frank. They're back, and I think that Tom is wounded. He's covered in blood, and he's lying on the cart not moving. Maybe he's been killed.'

'Whatever is it?' muttered an irritable Mother Liu, woken from her afternoon siesta by the tapping on her door. 'Come in, then,' she barked angrily. 'Oh, it's you. What do you want?'

'I'm sorry, Mother, I'm so sorry,' squealed Su Liping, nervousness mixed with excitement on her coquettish face. 'I hope I've not disturbed you.'

'Of course you've disturbed me. What is it? It must be something important or you wouldn't have dared. Out with it.'

'It's foreigners, Mother. They're in the square outside and they're making a demonstration against our house.'

'Are you mad? What foreigners?'

'The funny ones, Mother. The missionaries dressed in Chinese clothes, with all the children. They're trying to break into the noodle shop downstairs.'

'The noodle shop? Our noodle shop? All right. I'm coming. Help me with my slippers. Where's Ren Ren?'

'I don't know, Mother. I think he went out. He made me go with one of his friends before lunch, that horrible Monkey, and before we were finished he came in and told Monkey to get dressed, saying something about having to go to some village. They left immediately and I didn't even get a tip although I did the Wild Duck Flying Backwards position for him, and the Butterflies Fluttering.' She pouted.

'Never mind all that. Did he say how long he would be away?'

'No, Mother, but I think it could be a long time. He was dressed in travelling clothes and he wore leggings for riding a horse.'

'And what about his other men? Here, pull, girl, a girdle doesn't tie itself on. Where are his other men? The ones I told him to keep watch on this house.'

'I think they've all gone. They seemed to be in an awful hurry.'

'You mean there's *no one* left here? No men left here at all?'

'Well, there's the porter, and the cooks, and Chen Meina is with the fat draper from Shuangqian Street, and Xiao Gen is with the two old twins who come to her once a week to do the Cat and Mouse Sharing a Hole, and—'

Mother Liu, her face purple with anger, slapped the girl hard on the cheek. Su Liping screeched and burst into tears. 'Mother, why did you hit me?' she wailed. 'What have I done wrong?'

'Shut up and let me think,' snarled Mother Liu. 'I am surrounded by idiots. The biggest is apparently my own son. Leave that,' she snapped, pulling her girdle away from Su Liping's fumbling fingers.

Half dressed she hobbled to the door, Su Liping tottering after her. Their lotus feet made progress difficult, but Mother Liu's anger drove her forward and along the corridor at a trotting pace. She paused by one of the doors and put her eye to the spyhole. Inside the foreign boy was sitting on the bed, one leg manacled by a chain to the post. His face was alert, one hand to his ear. She became aware of a dull murmuring sound coming from outside the building. Mother

Liu grunted, and moved on. At the end of the corridor a window looked out on to the square. It was high on the wall, so Mother Liu had to enlist Su Liping's help to get on to a bench, which allowed her the elevation to raise the paper-covered window on its hinges and peer outside. There was an immediate welling up of the roar of the crowd, and she could identify shouts, laughter and jeers.

Su Liping had climbed up beside her and pointed. 'There they are, Mother, right below us. Do you see them?'

A large mob of layabouts had surrounded the Millward family, mocking them as they formed a half-circle on their knees in prayer. Mother Liu saw that each of the foreigners was holding up a cross apparently made of straw. The father, a tall, skeletal figure, with an unkempt yellow pigtail and beard, was muttering some sort of incantation in a reedy voice. There was a woman beside him looking up at him with a worried expression. Some of the children, ranging in all sizes from gangly youth to small toddler, had their eyes tightly closed, others were gazing round at the crowd in sheer terror. Strangely, half of them, including the parents, seemed to be wearing pebble spectacles, which glinted in the afternoon sunlight.

'They look harmless to me,' said Mother Liu.

'They were shouting at our house earlier. It is difficult to understand their funny Chinese, but the man was saying something about a lost son. Living here.' Su Liping looked at her mistress innocently.

'Was he indeed?' answered Mother Liu. 'You know that's nonsense?'

'Oh, yes, Mother.'

'Well, I'm not going to waste my afternoon looking at a bunch of mad foreigners praying, if that's all they are doing. Help me down.'

'Oh, look, Mother!' screeched Su Liping.

Mother Liu glanced again, then froze. The tall skeletal man had reached into the folds of his robe and pulled out a large green bottle. He carefully poured what appeared to be some sort of brown liquid on to his cross. Then he passed the bottle to his wife who did the same. Reaching into his belt, the man extracted two metallic objects which he beat together in his hands. With horror, Mother Liu saw the first spark. Within moments the man's cross had ignited into a flame.

'Get me down from here,' she screamed, pulling at a startled Su Liping's sleeve. 'Get me down.'

In a moment she was hobbling at breakneck speed back along the corridor to where the curtain covered the secret doorway that led to the stairs.

'Buckets!' she yelled, as she reached the next floor. 'Buckets! Water! Quickly!' Doors opened and puzzled girls and a few startled clients emerged. One girl, stark naked, appeared like a nymph in a temple frieze flanked between two venerable but equally exposed old men, who were trying to cover their flaccid immodesties with their long white beards. A fat man dressed and made-up ludicrously in the costume of a female lead in Peking Opera was clinging to Chen Meina. 'Don't just stand there!' screamed Mother Liu. 'Find some buckets and water. They're threatening to burn the building down.'

It was not a sensible thing to say. There was, of course, immediate panic. The next thing she knew was that she was being pummelled and pushed along in a scrum of bare flesh and bedclothes down the narrow, circular wooden staircase that led to the ground floor, landing in a tumble at the bottom and bumping her head on a vase. Dazed, she heard the patter as bare feet ran into the courtyard, the screams and shouts fading outside.

With an effort she pulled herself to her feet. Su Liping appeared with two of the cooks, straining under the weight of a tub full of soap-sudded water. 'Where shall we take this, Mother?' asked Su Liping nervously.

'Follow me,' she muttered, somehow overcoming the sense of dislocation and dizziness caused by her fall. She led them into the room Ren Ren used as his office. Taking down one of the crude pornographic paintings that he had hung around the walls, she touched a hidden spring, and the panel moved aside. A few steps led them into a cellar, where sacks of flour and pots of rice wine were stacked in disorderly heaps on the flagstone floor. It was the storeroom of the noodle shop. 'This way,' she called, pointing to another set of steps, which led up to a ragged leather curtain covering another doorway. The cooks and Su Liping strained behind her with the tub. The noise from behind the curtain was deafening. Mother Liu in her frenzy ripped it from its rails.

They stared in disbelief.

It might have been a scene from the opera, *Monkey in the Peach Orchard*, where the child acrobats playing Sun Wukong's anthropoid followers wreaked havoc in heaven. The little noodle shop was a tumble of struggling bodies, upturned tables and benches. The Millward children, like eels avoiding capture, were here, there and everywhere, dodging the leaps of the townsfolk who were trying to secure them, jumping over the heaps of struggling bodies that had fallen in the attempt. In the centre of the shop the tall figure of Septimus was wrestling with three burly porters, one of whom was hanging on his back with his arms around his neck, trying to pull him down. Laetitia was pinioned on the ground, flailing with a ladle in one hand, tugging with the other at the pigtail of the young, bare-chested man who sat astride her. Mother Liu was relieved to see that the firebombing with the crosses had apparently been only partially successful. Smoking rush torches lay everywhere on the ground, obviously having failed to catch light. A few flames licked up one wall of the shop, however, where a torch had fortuitously ignited a spilt barrel of gaoliang wine. Two of the waitress-cum-sing-song girls who serviced the rougher clientele below stairs were bravely but ineffectually flapping at the small blaze with a tablecloth, at the same time kicking off the attentions of two of the smaller Millward children who were trying to bite their ankles. With more concern Mother Liu noticed that the struggle with Septimus was moving ever closer to the bank of open charcoal stoves, which were used to cook the noodles. If they were overturned there would be a disaster. There would be no controlling the conflagration then.

But with superhuman effort the panting cooks had brought the big tub up the stairs. They now excelled themselves by lifting the heavy wooden barrel with its dripping soap-suds to shoulder height, and with a shout hurled it forcefully, if unscientifically, upwards into the air above the struggling mass. Then they bolted, with a scared look behind them at Mother Liu, back the way they had come. Discretion was clearly the better part of valour when the prospect of incineration was concerned, even if this involved the possibility of incurring the wrath of Mother Liu.

Their missile, however, achieved its effect spectacularly. The tub seemed for a frozen instant to hang in mid-air. In the next, there was an explosion of water and suds, which descended like a cloud over the combatants, drenching one and all; it also incidentally extinguished with a hiss the little blue lick of fire climbing up the wall. Then, most decisively of all, the tub itself descended, directly on to the head of Septimus Millward. Mother Liu caught an instant of recognition in the magnified blue eyes behind the spectacles, as the doomed missionary felt the weight of the instrument of retribution falling on him from on high. It poleaxed him, then shattered into its component hoops, its fragments clattering down to cover his prone body.

There was a despairing cry of 'Septimus!' from Laetitia, and a wail from the children, and that was effectively the end of resistance. It did not take long for the children to be secured, one by one, and to be held squirming in the arms of their captors. Mother Liu herself collared a tiny bespectacled girl, who was trying to hide behind the stove; she pulled her out by the ear, pinched her neck viciously, and thrust her towards a burly muleteer, who picked her up and held her kicking under his arm.

When Jin Lao and the *yamen* runners arrived, Mrs Millward and her children were corralled within a square of tables; Laetitia cradled the still unconscious body of Septimus on her lap, trying vainly to stop the flow of blood from the cut in his crown.

The townsfolk, who had been chattering and celebrating their victory, fell silent and moved aside to allow the venerable official and his guards to pass.

'Well, well, Mother Liu, how you have been inconvenienced.' Jin Lao smiled.

'I hope that you will take these incendiaries and punish them with the full weight of the law. Look what damage they have done to our shop.'

'Yes, indeed. Ren Ren won't be pleased, will he? That women and children could be so violent! What is the world coming to?'

He was interrupted by an impassioned outburst from Laetitia who, seeing the presence of authority, began to plead in her broken Chinese.

'Can anybody tell me what this barbarous woman is saying?' said Jin Lao. 'If she is attempting to speak in a civilised tongue it is none that I can understand.'

A babble of voices greeted him from the onlookers, each with their own interpretation of what the mad foreigners had been saying.

'I see that I am in a roomful of scholars,' he said. 'You,' he pointed at a big, bearded man, who wore the leather apron of a tanner. 'Do you understand what this woman is saying?'

'She says her son's here, sir. Kidnapped upstairs in the brothel.'

'Does she?' said Jin Lao. 'I recall we executed some felons for murdering one of her children last year. Has she lost another?'

'Same one, sir,' said the man. 'Says he wasn't murdered after all. Kidnapped and brought to the brothel, sir. Of course it's stuff and nonsense. They're all mad, as anyone can see – but that's what she's saying.'

'I see. Well, if that's the motive for the vandalism then I suppose that the matter should be investigated. Are you keeping a foreign boy in your establishment, Mother Liu?'

'Of course not, Jin Lao, sir,' said Mother Liu sweetly.

'I would be surprised if you were,' said Jin Lao, 'especially a dead one, or a ghost. That would be very untidy,' he said pointedly. 'I will have to come and inspect your house, of course.'

Mother Liu's eyes flashed angrily. 'Surely that will not be necessary? You can't believe such malicious invention.'

'Whether I believe it or not, the law must take its course,' said Jin Lao. 'I will come to inspect your house tomorrow afternoon. Does that give you enough time . . . to prepare?' He smiled again.

This time Mother Liu also smiled. 'Plenty of time, Jin Lao. I am sure that you will find everything perfectly in order – by then.'

'I would expect nothing less,' said Jin Lao.

The Millward family, their hands bound, were shuffled out by the guards. Two of the townsfolk were deputed to carry the groaning Septimus on a stretcher. His head had been bandaged and a quick inspection by a local physician had confirmed that his wound was not serious. Jin Lao gave orders that they should be taken back to their compound, which would be guarded until such time as the Mandarin had decided what action needed to be taken.

Mother Liu, with a patience that she did not feel, eventually persuaded the curious crowd to leave the teashop with promises of free meals when the establishment was reopened. She satisfied herself that the damage was not extensive. Another hour was spent appeasing the angry customers in the brothel. The venerable twins were particularly irate. Standing in the courtyard in their birthday suits had not done anything for their dignity, and one had stubbed his toe in the stampede down the stairs. A promise of another game of Cat and Mouse Sharing a Hole, this time on the house and with a rather chagrined Su Liping, who was more attractive in every way than the sturdy Xiao Gen, finally placated them. It was nearly dark before she had finished – and she still had to deal with the foreign boy. She found herself cursing Ren Ren as she plodded slowly up the stairs to her private floor. Where was he when she needed him? And when had she ever needed him as much as today?

Her head throbbed. She wondered if she was getting too old for this sort of life. What she needed was a cup of tea, and maybe a pipe. Well, there would be time for that. She could handle the boy. It would not be the first time that the well at the bottom of the garden had been used for such a purpose. Somehow she would manage by herself. She had in the past. She only needed some excuse to lull his suspicions. A client waiting in one of the pavilions? A promise of freedom, perhaps? She would loosen the bricks on the side of the well; a hard push. Nobody would notice.

At the top of the stairs she had to pause to catch her breath. She hobbled slowly down the corridor, pausing again by Hiram's door. Wearily, she reached for the cover of the spyhole, and started when this slight pressure pushed the door wide open. Her heart thumping, she surveyed the empty room, and the broken chain.

The boy was gone.

'Are you all right, Hiram?' asked Henry. Now that dusk had fallen and he was satisfied that there would be no pursuit, he had slowed his mare to a walking pace and they were threading their way through the lanes that wound towards the river and the railway camp. He was steadying Hiram on the pommel of his saddle. Perched behind him on the cruppers of the horse, her arms clinging around his waist and with a long cloak draped over her shoulders, was Fan Yimei.

'I'm fine, sir, I guess,' Hiram replied. The boy was subdued but otherwise – on the surface at least – appeared none the worse for his ordeal.

'Stout fellow. I'll make you a promise. Word of a British army officer, and you know how dependable that is. You'll never have to go back to that place. Do you hear me? That's a promise. My promise, which means it's as solid as a tablet set in stone. Never, ever, ever. And neither will you.' He nodded over his shoulder at Fan Yimei.

'I do not understand the words you say when you speak in your own language,' she answered, 'but after what you did today I am for ever in your debt. I am your slave.'

'Nobody's anybody's slave, Fan Yimei. We had a bargain, remember? And, besides, slavery's not allowed where I come from. Abolished by Act of Parliament in 1833!'

He sensed that a more serious response was needed and pulled the horse to a stop. He felt for her cold hands and cupped them in his own. 'Listen. You no less than Hiram have been living in a nightmare, but now it's over. It may take time for you to realise that, but you're free. You'll never have to go back, not to Major Lin, or Ren Ren, or Mother Liu. And you don't owe anyone anything either. Certainly not me. Anyway, what did I do?' He laughed, kicking the horse on again. 'I said I wanted a diversion and I got one, out of the blue, but it was all thanks to this boy's father here. Never dreamed it would be so easy. I don't think anyone even noticed us. All those naked people in the yard so intent on preserving their dignity! The porter was so distracted by all that flesh on view that we just walked past him. He wouldn't have recognised us anyway under our cloaks. Probably thought we were honest burghers of the town creeping out before our wives found out . . . I haven't had so much fun for years! And I didn't even have to break any heads! Mind you,' he said ruefully, 'I would have liked to give Ren Ren a thrashing. That would have been a duty to society.'

'Please do not joke, Ma Na Si Xiansheng. I still fear Ren Ren. Even now when I am out of his power. And Major Lin, he too will be angry. You say you can make me disappear, but it is for you I fear when they come to seek their revenge.'

'Nobody will even suspect me. When I next go back to the Palace of Heavenly Pleasure, Major Lin can have my shoulder to cry on. I'll be all sympathy for his loss, his bosom friend as ever before. Anyway, he's still got business to do with me on the Mandarin's orders. He can't touch me – even if he did suspect.

'And don't worry for yourself. You'll be perfectly safe at the railway camp until the train comes to take you to Tientsin. Once you're there, I'll set you up with some people I know, and you can begin a new life as a respectable matron. Well, not too respectable, I hope. You're too pretty for that fate!'

'It is a dream, Ma Na Si Xiansheng. Like this ride. I had forgotten what the stars looked like in the open sky, and the smell of the countryside.'

'You're smelling night soil at the moment, my darling. It stinks.'

'No, it is fragrant. You cannot appreciate how beautiful are all sights and sounds and smells to one who has been released from a prison. This morning I was dead, a lump of earth, nothing in a void of nothing. Now it is as if the goddess Nu Wa has come again to breathe life into dead clay, creating stars and sun and moon again as she did at the beginning of the world. And for this new life I have you to thank, Ma Na Si Xiansheng. Even if I wake up tomorrow, and I find myself back in my prison, I have you to thank for ever for giving me this dream.'

'It's not a dream, my dear. And you're not going back there. Not ever again.'

'Mr Manners?'

'Yes, Hiram.'

'Will I have to go back to my parents?'

'I wouldn't recommend it in the short term. I imagine, after your father's escapade today, he'll be something of a marked man with the authorities. You'd be better to stay with me for a while at the railway camp until the heat dies down. I can get a message to him, though.'

'I don't ever want to see my parents again,' said Hiram, in a small voice.

'I suppose that being free means you don't have to,' said Henry, after they had ridden some time in silence. 'Look,' he said, pointing to some lights that winked on a hill to their right. 'That's the Airtons' place. The mission and hospital. I'll take you there one day if you like. Airton's got children. They're a bit younger than you, but they've horses and animals, and books. You've a whole life to catch up on, young man.'

'Is that where the doctor with the whiskers lives, Ma Na Si Xiansheng?'

'Of course, you knew him, didn't you? You told me that he was once kind to you.'

Fan Yimei looked up at the lights. She did not reply. She was thinking that there was another person who also lived up there among those lights. Ma Na Si had told her that the red-haired girl worked in the hospital. She thought that she might have been jealous – if she had only believed in her heart that she really was free.

Airton looked exhausted and there was a spot of blood on his cuff. Gratefully he accepted the cup of tea from his wife. Frank Delamere was sitting uncomfortably on the sofa, still in his travelling clothes; his usually florid complexion was white with dust, which had also greyed his black moustaches. The little porcelain cup in his big hands looked singularly out of place, as was his rough presence altogether in the neat sitting room. His round eyes blinked in anticipation of the worst.

'Well, he'll live,' said the doctor. 'You did a good job bandaging him up. He didn't lose as much blood as might have been expected. And he's got a tough constitution. Luckily the bullets didn't cut any arteries although his left arm is shattered and one of his legs broken. I was more worried about the wound in his groin. What did it by the way? It was a nasty, ragged cut.'

'Some sort of pike,' muttered Frank.

'Well, again, he was lucky – but only by half an inch or so, or he wouldn't have survived the journey.'

'That boy's a damned hero,' said Frank. 'A damned hero.'

'He's not over it yet. There was some infection, but I believe I've cauterised it in time. He'll be fevered for a couple of days – I'm afraid he's raving a bit now. But he's a strong lad. He'll get through.'

'Thank God for that.' Frank's eyes had moistened. 'I really thought . . .'

'It was a close call,' said Airton. He noticed the shaking teacup in Frank's paw. 'Here, man, what are you doing with that? Nellie, give him some whisky.'

'Do you know? I wouldn't mind . . .' said Frank.

'Give him the bottle, and pour a tot for me while you're about it. Now, Delamere, are you in a fit state yourself? Can you tell us what happened, man?'

'We were ambushed,' said Frank. 'By Boxers.'

'Boxers? Are you sure of that? They weren't just bandits? Like before?'

'Boxers. Bandits. What's the difference?' said Frank. 'There were hundreds of them, lining the trees where the northern road skirts the forest under the Black Hills. They knew we were coming. I'm damned sure of that. Lu's gone into town already, determined this time to find out who the informer really is.'

'So Lu's all right? I was wondering when I didn't see him with you.'

'He got a sword slash on the shins. Nothing serious. Not like Tom. Or Lao Pang, one of the muleteers. He was killed, poor fellow, in the first volley.'

'I saw from Tom's wound that they had guns. A rifle bullet at that, not a musket ball. That's new, surely?'

'They had a few guns. Luckily they didn't know how to fire them effectively or we'd all be dead. The whole thing was very rum. A lot of them were wearing uniforms. Yellow tunics and orange headgear. That's why I called them Boxers.'

'You'd better start at the beginning. Pour yourself another glass.'

'Nothing much to tell. Trip went well. Old Ding did his stuff for us in Tsitsihar. Bought all we brought and more, and paid us over the odds when we got the processes going for him. Good little cove, that Ding. So, of course, we travelled carefully, off the road when we could. Can't be too careful when you've got a strongbox full of silver pieces on your wagon. It all seemed to be going well. There were a couple of weeks when we didn't see anybody – just endless miles of salt flats and plain. Very dreary, though Tom got in a bit of hunting. He's a hero, that boy, a damned hero.'

'So you said. Go on.'

'Lu insisted we go at a slow pace, off the road. He wasn't taking any chances – but we knew we'd have to go by the Black Forest at some point. There's no other way into Shishan. Lu wanted us to take an even longer way round, half-way to Mukden and back again so we could come in through the southern pass, but it wasn't really on. Supplies were running low, and with six mounted muleteers we thought we had the firepower to withstand any surprise attack from Iron Man Wang and his thugs. We were wrong.

'We did take precautions. Tom and Lao Zhao scouted ahead when we reached the narrow pass through the forest. Saw nothing suspicious, not a sight, not a sound. They must have been hiding deep in the trees. That was rum, too. You don't expect such organisation from bandits.

'We rode in just before noon, when the sun was at its highest and there was at least some visibility. Couldn't go too fast because of the wagons but we made the quickest pace we could. We got through the worst bit, and I thought we were scot-free. Then, suddenly, all hell broke loose. Never seen anything like it. Smoke from the bushes, bangs of muskets and cracks of rifle-fire. Bullets hissing over our heads like geese and arrows whistling like pigeons. That's when Lao Pang got it, right in the neck. Gurgled for a bit then rolled off his mule. Lots of blood. Pretty nasty shock.

'And then they were all around us. Boys mostly, or so it seemed. Young fellows dressed in carnival costumes – but they were dangerous enough: white rolling eyes in brown faces, thrusting with their spears and pikes and swords. We were firing back by that time with our repeaters, and they were being bowled over like coconuts, but on they came with horrible yells, slashing and thrusting. "This won't do," I shout to Tom, who's clubbing and firing at the devils around him like some latter-day Lancelot in a mêlée. "Let's ride for it," I say. "What about the silver?" says he. "Damn that," says I. "There are too many of them." So we set our spurs into our horses and gallop through the throng, Lao Zhao and the other muleteers following behind. We ride into the mass of them as if we're the Charge of the Light Brigade taking the guns. And then, would you believe it? we're through, and there's quiet all around us except for some chirping birds among the trees, and butterflies fluttering over the wild flowers.

'"Where's Lu Jincai?" asks Tom, looking very worried. And sure enough Lu's not there. I remember with a pang of guilt that Lu had been driving the wagon with the silver. "They must have got him," I say. "I'm going back for him," says Tom. Before I know what's happening he's snatched my repeater from my hand, rammed in a new clip of cartridges. He's already reloaded his own, and with a rifle in each hand he's off and away, galloping back the way we've come. Lao Zhao follows him, as irrepressible as Tom. But that's the effect Tom has on people, born leader. God bear witness, I'm proud that he's to be my son-in-law.

'I got the full story later from Lu, who by this time has been surrounded and overwhelmed on the wagon, struggling under a mass of filthy peasants all reaching to untie the box of silver, which Lu is holding on to for dear life. He told me that if they were going to snatch it it would be over his dead body, and he meant it too. But it doesn't come to that, because Tom and Lao

Zhao are suddenly riding out of nowhere, guns blazing in either hand, and the Boxers are rolling off the wagon like shot rabbits. Tom's caught them unawares, you see. They think the battle's over and they've got the loot in hand. So they've relaxed and some have put down their weapons.

'Tom leaps off his horse on to the cart and takes the reins. Lu's got the presence of mind to snatch up a repeater and start blazing away, and Lao Zhao grabs the lead horse by the bit and belabours it about the head with his gun-butt till it starts galloping and the other mules in the yoke follow the lead.

'And somehow the Boxers are all so stunned that they let the heavy wagon build up speed and get away. Some bravos come up thrusting with their pikes and get crushed under the wheels, and the marksmen with the rifles are still blazing away from the bushes. That's when Tom is wounded, although you wouldn't know it. He keeps his hands firmly on the reins until they're out of danger. I told you he's a hero.

'By this time I and the other muleteers have got our wits together again and we too are riding back to the rescue, and that's when I saw them, bowling through the pine trees. What's that picture from the South African war? It's been in all the illustrated papers lately. Saving the guns at the Modder river. Well, I'll tell you, if there'd been an artist who could have pictured Tom and Lao Zhao and Lu on that careering wagon, saving my silver with all the banshees from hell behind them, well, that's a picture which would have sold . . . You *bet* it would.'

Frank, beaming with pride, sentimental tears pouring down his cheeks and turning the caked dust to mud, drained his glass and poured more whisky.

'How did you get away?' breathed Nellie, amazed and a little thrilled to be listening to such a story in her living room.

'Well, it wasn't difficult after that. There was a bit of a chase but the advantage was on our side by then, you see. We were out of the ambush, and it was us doing the volleying, with better rifles and a damned sight better marksmanship. Don't know how many we killed. After a while they found it all a bit too hot for them and they sort of faded away. It was only then that we realised what had happened to poor old Tom. Do you know? He kept firing right to the end, with one useless arm. It was only when he knew we were safe that he allowed himself to pass out. What a fellow!'

'So you patched him up as best you could and brought him here?' said Airton.

'That's right. That was the most hellish part of the whole affair,' said Frank, in a more sober tone. 'We couldn't travel fast, you see, not with Tom in that condition, but every moment delayed we feared more for his life. After two days he had dropped into almost permanent unconsciousness and . . . well, I thought he was done for. It took another day to get to you.'

'I think that you and Lu Jincai and the others did a magnificent job,' said the doctor quietly.

Tears were welling in Frank's eyes again. 'You see, it was going off to save our silver that got Tom almost killed. If he'd . . . if he'd been . . . for that! How could I forgive myself?'

'Tom was wounded saving the life of one of his comrades,' said the doctor. 'The silver doesn't come into it. As the Evangelist says, "Greater love hath no man than this, that a man lay down his life for his friends." You have nothing to be ashamed of, old fellow, and you are right, Tom has behaved like a hero.'

'You're very tired, Mr Delamere,' said Nellie. 'Stay with us here tonight.'

'Tomorrow we'll go to the Mandarin and report this outrage,' said Airton, 'but Nellie's right, first you need some rest. And perhaps a bath.' He chuckled.

'I suppose I am a sight,' said Frank. 'Look, you're very kind, but first I think I ought to see Helen Frances. I suppose she's down in the infirmary with Tom? She must be very upset.'

Nellie and the doctor exchanged glances. Nellie nodded almost imperceptibly at her husband.

'Delamere,' said Airton gently. 'She isn't at the infirmary. In fact, she doesn't know anything about this yet. She's here, in one of the bedrooms, asleep. I'm afraid she's not very well.'

'Not well?' repeated Frank, stupidly. 'Why, what's wrong with her?' He half rose from the sofa. 'If she's ill I must go to her.'

'Sit down a moment longer. I'm afraid that I have some rather bad news for you,' said Airton. 'You see, since you were gone, we discovered that Helen Frances has . . .' He coughed nervously. 'That Helen Frances has . . .'

'Contracted an influenza,' said Nellie quickly.

Airton looked at his wife in amazement.

'She's caught a cold?' asked Frank, with some bewilderment. 'Is that all?'

'Well, it's more serious than a cold,' said Airton, conscious that his cheeks were burning. 'It's a new strain of influenza, quite contagious, and – she's been very ill,' he finished lamely.

'She's all right, isn't she?' asked Frank, now very bemused. '"Flu's not usually life-threatening, is it? It's not pneumonia or anything like that? She's not in danger, is she?'

'Oh, no,' said Airton, 'It's just a 'flu. But she really has been very ill, and well, for the moment . . .'

'You're not telling me I can't go in and see my own daughter?'

'We don't think that she should be upset now, Mr Delamere,' said Nellie soothingly. 'She really is quite weak, and I think that the doctor fears that if she were to hear about the terrible things that have happened to you, it would excite her. Isn't that right, Edward? Why don't you have your bath, Mr Delamere, and a good night's sleep? In the morning when we're all quite recovered, and your daughter is feeling stronger, we can acquaint her with the news that you're home again . . . and also tell her about Tom.'

'Very well,' said Frank, a little grumpily. 'Tomorrow, then. But she is all right? Recovering and all that?'

'Oh, yes,' said Nellie. 'It's just that the doctor feels she should not be disturbed tonight.'

After Ah Lee had been called, and Frank had been led off to his bath, Nellie lay back in the armchair and sighed. 'What on earth got into you, dear?' asked Airton, dumbfounded. 'Why the lie?'

'Oh, don't you see, Edward?' she answered. 'With Tom hanging between life and death, how can we tell him the truth? Frank Delamere, bless his heart, is the most temperamental and indiscreet man we know. Goodness knows how he'll react. And what if he told Tom? Letting Frank share a secret is like making a public announcement. I will not have the life of that fine young man on my conscience when we can delay a week and tell him when he is strong enough to withstand the shock. If he hears now he'll lose the will to live. Surely you comprehend that?'

'Well, how are we to maintain the secret?'

'You keep Helen Frances in bed and treat her for influenza, and any other plausible illness you can conjure out of your medical books. Don't worry about her not looking ill enough once the withdrawal symptoms for the opium habit begin. And together, tomorrow morning, before she sees her father, we will tell her what is at stake. Believe me, she will co-operate. She doesn't have any choice.'

Airton nodded compliantly and meekly sipped his whisky. 'Nellie,' he said, after a long pause, 'there's someone else I'm even more concerned about.'

'Who?'

'After Frank's story today we cannot deny the danger of the Boxers. And Sister Elena's out among the Christian villages.'

'I know,' said Nellie. 'It's been on my mind too. But there's nothing we can do about it tonight.'

'I'll send Zhang Erhao after her first thing in the morning.'

'Until then we can only pray that she's all right. Oh, Edward, what a day! What's suddenly happening around us? Our little world is falling to pieces.'

Evening was falling when Sister Elena reached the outskirts of Bashu. Pastor John and his two daughters, Mary and Martha, had been waiting for her on the hill and they were as relieved to hear the sound of her horse's hoofs as she was to see them.

The two girls were as merry as she remembered them. Mary was fourteen, and in village terms a beauty. The high cheekbones and snub nose were those of a northern peasant, but the peach pink of her skin, the mischievous eyes, which curved upwards like phoenix tails, and the oval red lips, cheeks dimpling with smiles were those of a coy princess from opera. Her shining plait, tied with a blue ribbon, swung behind her as she walked, or rather danced, along the path, reminding Elena of a colt or a deer, frisky with the joy of springtime. She could not imagine a less likely bride of Christ, but it was Mary's ambition to be a nun, and Elena and Caterina had promised, with her father's approval, to take her to the convent in Tientsin when she was sixteen. Twelve-year-old Martha was the opposite of her sister, a small, serious child, whose wide eyes, when fixed contemplatively on Elena's, had a knowledge and a sadness within them that made Elena want to clutch her to her bosom and squeeze her tenderly. Elena loved both the girls, whom she had known since their infancy.

Laughing, they were singing the verses of the hymn, which Caterina had taught them two months before:

> '*Yesu ai wo, wo zhidao*
> *Shengjing shuoguo wo hen hao . . .*'

> 'Jesus loves me, this I know
> 'Cos the Bible tells me so.'

Usually Sister Elena would have walked along beside them, singing with them, but this evening she was not in the mood – and it was not just the tiredness from her journey. Walking beside Pastor John, she noticed that he also was more than usually subdued. Despite the girls, it had been a sombre walk the last mile into the hamlet.

Mother Wang greeted her warmly, but Sister Elena noticed a look of concern behind her smiles. After a quick supper of corn broth and chicken, they retired early. Sister Elena lay awake for some time listening to the others breathing on the *kang*, rehearsing in her mind the strange events of the day.

It was not that the roads had been deserted. Any number of reasons might explain that. Nor was she particularly surprised by the tension she had discovered among the Christians of Bashu. It was natural to be worried about the rumours, of Boxers and burnings of property. That was one of the reasons why she had made the journey.

What had alarmed her was the meeting that she had had at her midday halt with the company of militia led by Major Lin. They had been watering their horses at the well when she arrived. She had greeted them in her usual hearty manner, but had received silent stares from cold faces in return.

The major had strolled up to her as she was eating her meal alone in the shade of a sheep byre. 'You speak our language?' he had asked sardonically. The scar and the twist of his features gave him a menacing air.

'I speak a little,' she had answered.

'Will you tell me where you are going?'

'I am going to Bashu,' she had replied.

'The Christian village,' he said scornfully, and spat, the sputum narrowly missing her boots. 'Your Christians are causing much trouble these days.'

'I have heard that much trouble has come upon them.'

'It makes no difference,' he said. 'The peace is being disturbed. Why are you going to Bashu?'

'They are my people,' she said simply.

'They are not your people. You are a foreigner. They have only been affected by your foreign ideas. They refuse to pay taxes.'

'They do not pay temple dues, but they obey the law.'

'Foreign laws.' And Major Lin spat again. 'Do you realise that it is dangerous to travel the roads alone? Things can happen to a woman.'

'I am confident that soldiers like yourself can protect honest citizens going about their business.'

'My men and I are returning to Shishan. We have been keeping the peace among your Christian villagers for these last weeks. Now we are returning home. You may ride with us – for your protection.'

'I am going to Bashu.'

'I strongly advise you against it.'

'It is my duty.'

'I, too, have done my duty. I have warned you of the dangers you face.'

'What dangers are there for me in Bashu, Major?'

He looked at her coldly, then turned on his heel.

'What dangers are there for me in Bashu, Major?' she called after him.

He turned to face her again. 'You have been warned,' he said. 'It is not my responsibility what happens to you.'

He barked an order and his men began to mount up. His sergeant brought him his own grey pony and he swung himself into the saddle at the head of his troop. Soon they were clattering in a cloud of dust down the road.

Now she lay on the *kang*, hearing again the major's hostile words. '*You have been warned,*' he had said to her. Warned against what?

It seemed that she had only just fallen asleep when she was woken by the sound of cocks crowing, and the shuffle of her fellow sleepers as they roused themselves for the day. They were the natural sounds of the morning.

'*You have been warned.*' She heard the words again in her mind. '*It is not my responsibility what happens to you.*'

Chapter Twelve

*This city is so big – but we stride through the streets
like the heroes of old.*

H elen Frances was sitting on her made-up bed fully clothed,
a defiant, surly expression on her face. She had opened the
shutters and bright morning sunshine suffused the room. Nellie,
who had remained with her back to the door, noticed that Helen
Frances had packed all her clothes into three portmanteaux, which
were lined up in front of the emptied sideboard. The room was
light and airy; the Scottish scenes framed on the white walls gave
the place a cheeriness that none of the three people contemplating
each other felt.

'Why are you out of bed?' asked Airton quietly, pulling up a
wooden chair so he was facing her.

'I've changed my mind,' said Helen Frances. 'I want you to give
me my money and then I'm leaving – after you've given me the
morphine you promised me last night. I'm taking the train away
from here.'

'Did I promise you morphine last night?' asked the doctor,
ignoring her last remark. Helen Frances's eyes widened, then her
face pinched as she frowned. Nellie was reminded of a snarling fox.
'You did. You know you promised me, Doctor.' It was a harsh, shrill
sound; to Nellie, it was the voice of a stranger. 'I need it. It's been
twelve hours. Last night. You promised you'd come again in the
morning.'

'I have come again in the morning, my dear,' said Airton.

Helen Frances's suspicious eyes flickered from the doctor to Nellie
to the sideboard. 'Well, where is it? The tray? You brought it on a
tray last night. Where is it?'

Airton looked at her impassively. She had been sitting in a
composed position but now she began to shake and her pressed
knuckles were as white as the counterpane she clutched in her
trembling fingers. 'Please, Doctor, don't torment me. Give me my

dose. Just one phial.' Her eyes gleamed with sudden hope. 'Or my pipe. Give me back my pipe with the paste. The one you took from my drawer. That's mine. Mine, Doctor. Please give it back to me. You can't take away what's mine. Mrs Airton,' the imploring eyes turned towards the figure by the door, 'please ask your husband to give me some morphine. Or my pipe. Please.'

'I think you should be getting back into your bed,' said Nellie.

'Listen, I saw my father this morning, as you wanted me to.' Helen Frances's words were tumbling out one after each other, and a bead of sweat was running down her forehead. 'I let him come in and I lay there, and pretended I had flu. I lied to him as you told me to. I did my part. Now you've got to do yours and give me the morphine you promised me. And then I'll go. And you won't have to see me again. *That's what we agreed,*' she screamed suddenly. 'That's what we agreed.'

Airton tried to reach for her hands but she wrenched them away, and rolled over the bed so she was standing on the other side, breathing heavily, her fists clenched. 'I'll tell my father the truth,' she hissed. 'That you're keeping me here against my will. That you started me on the drug. I'll tell him – I'll tell him—'

With a rush she pushed Nellie aside and reached for the door handle. Nellie put her arms around her body pinioning her. Airton grabbed her kicking legs. Sister Caterina, who had been waiting outside the door, came in, and briskly assisted Nellie. With surprising ease the three carried the fighting, scratching, biting girl and laid her on the bed. As the women held her down, Dr Airton, breathing heavily after the exertion, reached in his pocket for some cut lengths of rope and, with some difficulty, caught her flailing arms, one after the other, and tied her hands to the bed rail. Later, pulling off her boots, he did the same for her kicking feet. Helen Frances lay spreadeagled on her back. All of them, including Helen Frances herself, were exhausted after the struggle, and for a while the only sounds in the room were sobs and panting.

There was a tear running down Caterina's apple cheeks, but Dr Airton's and Nellie's faces were grim set. Helen Frances, her white face peering through a tangle of fox-coloured hair, gazing up at her captors with wide, amazed eyes, resembled a hurt animal.

The doctor's voice was stony: 'No, my dear, you won't be getting any more morphine from me. That's not what I promised you last night. I promised to make you well, and that's what I'm going to do.'

Nellie saw the horror dawn on the girl's face and felt her own cheeks twitch as she struggled to keep her composure. She had to look away, but she heard the small voice rising piteously from the bed: 'But that's not fair. It's not fair. You don't keep the opium away from your Chinese patients. Not totally. I've seen you, and you've explained to me. You give them reducing dosages. I need the drug too, Doctor. You know I do. You can't . . . you can't . . . deprive me.' Helen Frances's head began to shake. 'You can't do this to me,' she cried.

'Listen, Helen Frances. You must be brave. You won't be on your own. Either I, or Mrs Airton or Sister Caterina will be with you all the time. It's true I give the Chinese addicts reducing dosages but most of them have been opium-smokers for many years. If I tried to break them of their habit abruptly they would probably not survive – but you're young, you're strong, with a habit of only a few months' duration, and I think I can cure you completely of your craving. Anyway, I'm going to risk it, for your sake, for the sake of your father and Tom and, most importantly of all, because you're carrying a baby inside you. And I think, deep down, you want me to help you. To save you from yourself. To save your baby.

'You can scream and struggle and yell as much as you like, but that won't change anything. I'm sorry, but for the next few days you will remain strapped to the bed. In a while Sister Caterina will help you remove those day clothes and make you comfortable in a nightdress. There'll be water for you, and food if you want it. I'm going to make you take some soup whether you want it or not.'

Helen Frances's eyes, like two glittering stones, remained fixed on Dr Airton as he spoke. Her expression was one of shock and dismay.

'Listen,' said Airton, 'I think you should know while you're still rational and can understand me what will happen to you when your body is deprived of this drug. Please pay attention. There is no disguising the hideousness of what you are about to undergo, but knowing may help you.'

As he said this he glanced up at Nellie as if to seek support. Gently she rested a hand on his shoulder. When Dr Airton spoke again, it was matter-of-factly, but he could not completely hide his emotion. 'In a short while, after only a few hours, the first effects will be visible. You will find yourself yawning uncontrollably, you will weep, you will perspire. You will have a runny nose. Finally you will sleep. It will be a restless, fitful kind of sleep and you will have terrible nightmares. And when you wake you will wish that the nightmares were real because they will be more pleasant than the waking reality. Your whole body will be aching. You won't be able to lie still. Your pupils will contract. You will have severe leg pains. And then you will begin to vomit. Uncontrollably. And I'm afraid that you will also experience severe diarrhoea. You'll be in a state half waking, half unconscious, wanting oblivion but unable to slumber. If you're aware of yourself at that time you will be disgusted with yourself. I'm sorry – but it doesn't get better. You'll experience fever, high blood pressure, you'll be delirious – but don't worry, I'll be there, carefully monitoring you and seeing you come to no harm. It will seem to be a nightmare without end. Some patients attempt to kill themselves. That's why I'm tying you to the bed – but believe me, my dear girl, it will come to an end. In two or three days you will reach the peak of your suffering, and then slowly, slowly, you will return to normal again, I promise you this, by everything I know. And one day – pray God – you will wake, and you will be yourself again, and you will have lost that craving. It may take as little as ten days. It may take longer. But that day will come.'

He sighed, avoiding Helen Frances's eyes, which bored into his with hatred. 'There, Helen Frances, I've told you the worst. I've spared you nothing. I've told you because when you are experiencing this hell and torment, there will be a small part of you that will understand what is happening and why. Cling to that part of yourself, because it will bring you through. Now I'm going to leave you while the ladies undress you. I'll be back soon.'

Hurriedly he left the room.

To Helen Frances, lying helplessly on her back, the concerned faces of Nellie and Sister Caterina hanging above her own, the fingers gently unbuttoning her clothes, the cool hands stroking her perspiring brow were like the embrace of demons dragging her soul towards hell. For a while she lay rigid under their ministrations, then she spat in Nellie's face; her eyes blazed, her lips stretched back over her gums, revealing her gnashing teeth and, in her impotence and despair, she howled, as a she-fox caught in a trap moans at the uncaring sky.

As soon as he had received the intelligence from Zhang Erhao, the foreign doctor's chief servant, that one of the witch women, the nuns, had left alone for a remote village that morning, Ren Ren had gathered his men together, rousing some from their dalliance with the girls and others from half-finished meals.

He was still smarting with irritation after his interview with his mother that morning. He did not like to be mocked but there was always irony in his mother's tone, even though she was too clever to put it directly into words that he could challenge, which suggested that she thought he was a fool. He, a full Blood Brother of the Black Stick Society and now a captain of a company in the Harmonious Fists, trusted by Iron Man Wang himself and all the other leaders! Well, he would prove to her that he was not a fool. She had asked him a favour. She had asked him to bring a foreign woman to the brothel. He would show her how quickly he could achieve that task. It wouldn't be the fox-spirit bitch but who would appreciate the difference? One bit of white meat was like another, equally rancid as far as he was concerned. If his mother wanted to show off to the old Mandarin and Jin Lao – that was what he assumed this was all about – then she could do so with the nun.

He had already determined to get rid of the whining boy. A day or two with the witch woman in the hut – which he would enjoy – and she could take over the boy's quarters. Who would know? He didn't care if the other foreigners missed her. The day was coming soon enough when they would all be getting their reckoning. And by leading a raid on a Christian village he would be earning high marks with Iron Man Wang and the Harmonious Fists. So who was a fool then?

With Monkey and the others he galloped on their stolen horses out of the town to the ruined temple hidden among the woods close to the river. This was where his company of Boxers, a hundred strong, were training in the martial arts. He knew that there were similar encampments in hidden spots all around Shishan. One day soon they would all receive the orders to descend in a body into town and then blood would flow. For the moment strict secrecy was being kept. Ren Ren approved of this. He had been a runner in the Black Sticks long enough to know the need to keep knowledge in small, unconnected cells. That way power could be concentrated for those to whom the cells reported. The grand master was now Iron Man Wang and it was he who controlled the whole web, like a fat spider chewing a juicy fly. One day that spider would be Ren Ren – one day! But for the moment it paid him to be loyal. For now he enjoyed being a Boxer, with power and magic at his command. Sometimes he even convinced himself that he believed it all.

It took the usual hours of delay and confusion to get his company ready for action, so it was already late afternoon when they set out on the road to Bashu. There was a nervous moment when, ahead of them, they saw Major Lin and his militia. There was no time for them to hide, but it did not matter. He presumed that Major Lin had his orders not to interfere with them. He and his troop rode past the column, eyes ahead, as if the host of Boxers had not been there. In one way Ren Ren liked that. He could fantasise that they were a host of invisible phantoms heading into the night to wreak their righteous revenge. On the other hand, he would also have liked it if Major Lin had returned the salute that he had proudly given him as he passed – one soldier recognising another – but Major Lin had ignored him. Arrogant turtle's egg! Well, he would get his comeuppance one day. Ren Ren would make sure of that.

The night march was tiring, and cold; the three hours during which they rested before dawn were uncomfortable and Ren Ren found it difficult to sleep. He was bad-tempered and morose during the first stages of the march the next morning and cuffed Monkey when he started on one of his interminable jokes. He cheered up when the morning mist lifted and they found themselves at the top of the hill looking down on Bashu.

He gathered his lieutenants and passed on his orders. Half of the company was to circle the village, staying among the trees, but ready to catch anyone who tried to break out of the trap. Once they were deployed the rest were to follow him into the hamlet. He allowed two hours for his men to get into position, and whiled away the time playing dice with Monkey and his friends. Meanwhile, he ordered one of the Boxers up a tree to report what was happening in the village. Just before noon the boy called down that a crowd was gathering in the square and shortly afterwards he announced that there seemed to be some sort of meeting taking place between the elders. Yes, there was a woman among them who might be a foreigner.

'Good,' said Ren Ren, gathering his winnings. 'They're all in one place. That'll make it very easy for us. Let's get going.'

Sister Elena felt frustrated and inadequate. The meeting had lasted an hour already. Headman Yang, a black-browed bully of a man whom she had never liked, and the other representatives of the village had been hostile from the beginning. It grieved her. She had thought she knew these people so well. There was Lao Dai, the muleteer-cum-innkeeper in whose house she had frequently stayed. Next to him was Wang Haotian, Pastor John's uncle, who had often invited her to apple-picking picnics with his nieces in his orchard on the hill. At the end of the table sat amiable, foolish Zheng Fujia, Little Butterfly's father, who had fussed outside the bedroom all night when she had gone to deliver his grandson. Even these men, as familiar to her as family, whom yesterday she would have counted as friends, looked coldly across the table with flickering hatred in their eyes.

She wished that the sun, burning down on the open table in the square, was not so oppressive. It gave her a headache. In Italy they would have been sitting under vine leaves, but here there was no shade. She had to concentrate hard to follow the rough dialect, especially when the meeting degenerated into an open exchange of abuse between Headman Yang and his cousin, the loud-mouthed Miller Zhang, who had forced his way into the debate, despite Pastor John's urgings to him to stay away, flanked by his two villainous-looking sons. Miller Zhang was a Christian, but everyone knew that he had only taken the vows to give him an edge in the land battles he was always having with his cousin.

She wished that Father Adolphus had been there. He would have found the wise words to bring the two sides to harmony. Or even Dr Airton, whose twinkling sense of humour might have alleviated the tension. She felt alone and depressed. Above all, inadequate.

Pastor John had tried hard to limit the agenda to the most pressing of the many grievances in the hope that some compromise might be found on the main issues, but the meeting had started with a long, bickering exchange of veiled insult and mutual recrimination, most of which passed over Elena's head. Pastor John had remained largely silent at this stage. He wanted some of the anger to exhaust itself before he came in with what he hoped would be a conciliatory message that would lead to a positive resolution.

His opportunity had come after the Buddhist priest had spoken. The *bonze* had made some measured remarks about the temple tax, explaining how the Christians' refusal to pay had reduced the temple's ability in turn to contribute to many of the village projects, such as the new drainage scheme and the New Year Festival celebrations. He had not grudged the Christians' right not to pay, as many villagers did. He merely noted that it raised problems for the temple finances.

Pastor John judged that this was a propitious moment to make his own speech. Adjusting his spectacles, and with a final glance at his notes, he addressed the elders courteously. It was, as he intended, a calm, reasoned speech, which at first seemed to strike a chord among his listeners. He had called upon their common ancestry, their pride in the village, their years working together through good harvests and bad, the fact that there should be no divisions among relations and friends. Could there not be mutual respect, he said, between those who happened to believe in one God and those who believed in many? Unfortunately of late, friction had grown up between Christians and non-Christians, but the reasons for the friction often had little to do with religion itself. If the issue was a tax one – the payment of dues to the temple, for example (and he thanked the Buddhist priest for his wise words) – let them discuss other ways in which the Christians could contribute to the good of the village. If there was still an issue between Headman Yang and Miller Zhang, let the wise heads of the village get together to find a resolution, as Father Adolphus had done in the past—

He had not been allowed to finish. The mention of the land dispute was a signal for the two cousins on either side of the table to abuse each other again, each accusatory remark of one matched by a more deliberate insult from the other. At one point it looked as if they would come to blows. Pastor John banged on the table, and attempted to restore order by calling on both sides to honour the memory of Father Adolphus.

This was a mistake. Headman Yang turned away from his cousin to face Pastor John. He scowled at him, then turned his sneering face full on Sister Elena, and deliberately spat on the table in front of her. 'That is what I think of your Father Adolphus,' he said. 'He was nothing more than an evil magician who used his arts to deceive honest people and bring advantage to you Devil-worshipping Christians. Now you are trying to bring his succubus, his witch, to do the same.'

The Christians on Elena's side of the table rose in angry protest. Miller Zhang reached for the knife in his belt, but Pastor John banged the table, crying, 'Order! Order!'

In the stillness that followed, Pastor John attempted to remonstrate: 'How can you be so insulting, Headman? And so ungrateful for all the good things our friends have done for us over the years? I beg you, please apologise to our Elder Sister for your thoughtless remark. We in the village may have our differences, but Elder Sister is guiltless of anything but kindness to us.'

Headman Yang threw back his head and laughed. 'Guiltless? Tell that to my cow, which this morning came down with a sickness – right after *her* arrival in our village. Or your mule, Lao Dai, the one that died when the other foreign witch came here two months ago. Guiltless? Our mothers live in fear for their children's lives. What happens if the witch goes after one of them?'

'My grandson had a fever this morning,' said Zheng Fujia nervously. 'His little head was burning when my daughter brought him back from the river – after she met this one,' he said, pointing at Elena, 'by the washing pool.'

Elena, her mouth open in shock, tried to formulate words to protest. Simultaneously she became aware of a noise all around her. She had been so concentrating on the debate at the table that she had hardly been aware of the crowd of bystanders, Christians and non-Christians, in their separate groups, who had been watching the proceedings. Now the air was filled with angry shouts. An old woman thrust a bony finger at her and screeched, 'My little granddaughter cries for vengeance. You poisoned her, gave her medicines, and two weeks later she died!' and another man was shouting something about a plague of ringworm in his sheep.

'It's not true. It's not true,' she whispered, turning in a pathetic desire to justify herself to Pastor John. 'That child had a brain disease. I only gave her some medicines to stop the pain. I never pretended I could save her. How can they be saying such things?'

But Pastor John was on his feet, his usually placid features quivering with rage, his shoulders and fists shaking. 'How dare you?' he was shouting, in a remarkably loud and carrying voice. 'How dare you mouth this evil, superstitious rubbish at us? You accuse us of devil worship when your temples are full of plaster idols! Why do you think we become Christians, if not to get away from the foolish, wicked ignorance in which you are all mired? Don't you realise that the Lord Jesus offers us a way out of our slavery into a better world?'

Headman Yang was also on his feet, his face radiated by a triumphant grin. 'Hear him!' he shouted, in an even louder voice. 'He admits, did you hear? He admits he wants to trample on our traditions. You heard him mock our gods. He wants to make a better world, he says, and calls us slaves! What's that but an attack on the Emperor himself? Villagers, are we to allow this treason in our midst? Treason and black magic, threatening our very homes!'

'I'll give you treason, you bag of goat's piss,' screamed Miller Zhang, and leaped across the table to strike the headman. The two embraced in a biting, hair-pulling, knee-jerking, scratching struggle. On all sides Elena saw other Christians and non-Christians standing off against each other, pushing, shouting, some exchanging blows. The old men on the benches looked at each other in confusion. Pastor John seemed stunned. Elena felt she had to do something, and suddenly found herself propelling herself forward so that she was standing on the table. More in frustration at her impotence to stop this terrible brawl than because of any conceived plan, she threw back her head and issued a long, high-pitched, ululating shriek. It pierced the noise around her like a whistle at a football match, bringing both game and grandstand to a halting silence. Faces turned to stare at the foreign woman with her raised arms and her thrown-back head, who stood transfigured above them. 'Stop! Stop! Stop! For the love of the Blessed Virgin, stop,' she was still screaming, but the words were strange to her audience because in her confusion she had used Italian. After a moment she, too, paused, aware of the growing stillness around her. She blushed, a little embarrassed, turning towards Pastor John as if asking him what she should do next.

Then a voice from the non-Christian side of the village shouted, 'She's made a spell. In her devil's language. Witch! *Wupo!* WITCH!'

And the chant was taken up: '*Wupo! Wupo! Wupo! Wupo! Wupo!*'

It seemed as convenient a moment as any, and Ren Ren gave the order for Monkey to fire his musket into the air above the commotion. The echo of the explosion reverberated round the square, hushing the startled villagers, who gazed in confusion at the armed, uniformed figures who had positioned themselves silently round the perimeter and at strategic positions blocking all exits. None of them had seen Boxers before but they knew immediately from the yellow turbans, the orange sashes and their studied martial-arts stances who they were.

Ren Ren, followed by Monkey and his other lieutenants, strolled into the silence, past the tableau of frozen, frightened figures, into the centre of the square. 'Friends,' he said. He spoke conversationally but his drawl sounded brittle in the tension. 'Friends. It seems that we've arrived at a perfect time. Have you caught a witch? That's very clever of you. It's a foreign one, I see. A fat, ugly bitch, isn't she?'

Sister Elena, still on the table, felt her knees shaking, but she knew she had to control her fear. 'I am Sister Elena, from the Christian mission in Shishan. I don't know who you are, but there will be trouble if you harm anyone here.'

Ren Ren smiled. 'Who's the headman?' he asked quietly.

Headman Yang tumbled forward and prostrated himself at the young man's feet. 'Master, we meant no harm,' he mumbled into the dust.

'If you've been identifying witches that's no harm done at all,' said Ren Ren. 'In fact, it's highly commendable. Helpful, even. But I am confused. We've been hearing terrible stories, haven't we, Monkey? That this whole village has been overrun by Christians. It makes me wonder why a good headman, who's presumably loyal to the empire of the Ch'ing, allows his village to be overrun by Christians and traitors to the Emperor. Are you a Christian yourself?'

Through the convulsion of terrified sobs and protestations at his feet that followed, Ren Ren established that, no, Headman Yang was not a Christian. On the contrary, he hated and feared Christians. They had been casting their spells on innocent villagers, and stealing their land. He himself had suffered, he and his whole family, from their magic, only there were so many of them, so many of them – forgive him, Master – there was little he could do . . .

'You can get off your feet and stop snivelling,' said Ren Ren. 'That'd be a start. Then I suppose you'd better point out to me which ones are the Christians, and I'll show you how to deal with the turtle eggs.' He turned to give orders to his men, but was stopped short by the tall figure of Pastor John, who with great dignity had risen to his feet and blocked his way. Ren Ren looked up at the calm, weathered face and grizzled grey hair. 'Who are you?' he asked.

'With respect I would like to ask you the same question,' said Pastor John, 'and by what authority you come to intimidate our community. I am a schoolteacher and my name is Wang. I also have the honour and privilege to be the pastor of the Catholic church in this village. We are not witches, sir, and we are loyal subjects of the Emperor. I would like to see your commission, please. With respect, you and your . . . soldiers do not on the face of it appear to represent any regular forces of the Ch'ing empire.'

For a moment Ren Ren and his lieutenants looked at Pastor John with amazement. Then Monkey began to giggle. 'Shall I show him our commission, Ren Ren?' he asked, pulling a great sabre from his belt.

'Not yet,' said Ren Ren, smiling. 'The man's made a point. We've been lacking in courtesy, it seems. We ought to have introduced ourselves. With respect, Mr Christian Schoolteacher,' he addressed Pastor John sarcastically, 'I'll be showing you my authority in a moment. Don't go away.'

In three fast strides he had reached the table. Sister Elena stepped back as he climbed upon it but Ren Ren grabbed her wrist. 'Stay,' he whispered. 'There's a good little bitch.' He released her and turned to survey the crowd. All eyes were focused anxiously upon him. Smiling broadly, he held up a hand as if to acknowledge applause. His teeth flashed like a showman's at a fair. 'There's a gentleman over there who's just asked me who we are.' He pitched his voice loud. 'He wants to know by what authority we come here. But I think most of you good people know who we are, and who's sent us to Bashu. Are there any of you still guessing?'

His question met a predictable silence. 'Xiao Tan,' he called to one of the Boxer guards. 'Come over here and show them what you can do.'

The young man he had appointed ran forward to the centre of the square, pulling off his tunic as he did so. He bowed to Ren Ren, then began to move his body in an elegant demonstration of *kung fu*, kicking, jumping, punching. Swirling faster and faster, he leaped his own height off the ground, his legs scissoring as he did so. He landed smoothly on one leg while his fists were still moving in a pink blur. His sharp intakes of breath mixed rhythmically with the hiss and swish of his limbs in an almost musical sound that matched the beauty of his movements. Suddenly he froze, balancing at an impossible angle. Those close to him could see that his eyeballs had rolled upwards under his eyelids. He appeared to be possessed or in a trance. When he moved again it was with an odd, inhuman gait, sloping or galloping across the ground. He paused, standing on one leg. He cocked his ear in one hand, as if he was listening to a faraway sound; his mouth and nostrils twitched as he sniffed the air, his eyes blinked and rolled; his movements were alert, simian. There was a gasp from the crowd, for the character standing live in front of them had been familiar to most of them since childhood.

'You recognise him?' Ren Ren called. 'Of course you do. That's Sun Wukong, the Monkey God himself, and he's taken the boy's form. Monkey's just one of the gods we can call down from Heaven to help us. Look at him. Look carefully. Watch how he moves. See for yourselves what it's like to be possessed by one of the gods! That's the power we have. Can you imagine? It gives us invulnerability and supernatural strength in our martial arts. It makes us Boxers of Heaven. Heavenly Boxers. That's who we are. We are the Tiger Company of the Shishan Chapter of the Battalions of Righteous Harmony. We're a loyal militia, sworn to serve the Emperor, and we have Heaven behind us.'

Ren Ren pretended disappointment when there were no cheers. 'You should believe it, you know,' he said. 'The gods *are* coming down to earth to make an invincible army here below. We are their vanguard. But you should be asking yourselves why they are coming, good people of Bashu. Why you are being so honoured. Because our country's in danger, that's why. The Middle Kingdom and the throne of our Emperor are being threatened by the magic of foreigners – by the sorcery of Christians.

'You've got Christians here among you, haven't you? People like yourselves, aren't they? Except for their funny rituals, perhaps, and their special attitude towards paying bills, you might think they're harmless on the whole. They even talk nice, don't they? About brotherly love, and coming to Heaven through Jesus. Don't be deceived. That's what's so diabolical and dangerous about them. They look like us, but if you look inside their hearts you'll find stinking malevolence and corruption. In every one of their black hearts plots are fermenting. Oh, yes, their faces may give you sweet smiles, but inside there's only one thing they want: to destroy you, and your families, and your village, and bring down the empire itself.'

He watched with satisfaction the effect of his words, as people in the crowd began to distance themselves from their neighbours.

'We have to be constantly on our guard,' he continued. 'The gods are with us but our enemy's magic is also strong. Sometimes the evil is so strong that even the gods find it difficult to prevail against it. Sometimes the rank evil of the Christian is so foul that it can pollute the purity of the vessel holding the god within us. Our gods can withstand the bullets of our enemies, but not always can they withstand the black magic of the Christian wizards. That is why we have come to exterminate the witches and demons who call themselves Christians wherever we find them.

'And that's why we're here in Bashu. We wanted to see what sort of danger you were in – and what do we find? You've already identified a witch.' He grasped Sister Elena's hand and pulled her to his side. 'This one here, I take it? Well, she's ugly enough, that's for sure. And she smells rancid, and she looks foul, but is she really an evil witch? Shall we prove it one way or another? How about a little demonstration, good people of Bashu, to see just what danger you are really in?'

He paused for dramatic effect. 'My lord Sun Wukong,' he called. 'May it please you to honour us with your presence on this stage.'

As the simian creature loped towards the table, Ren Ren made a quick movement, catching and twisting Sister Elena's two hands behind her back. As the possessed Boxer jumped on to the board, balancing on one leg, cocking his head in a perfect imitation of the Sun Wukong they all knew from the opera, Ren Ren pulled out a knife. Sister Elena was so surprised that, despite the pain, she did not cry out, but Pastor John, watching from below, gave an angry shout. He was immediately grabbed by two of Ren Ren's men, and prevented from coming to her aid, his mouth gagged. 'Now let us see whose magic is the stronger,' shouted Ren Ren, and he slit the front of the nun's jacket and vest open from collar to waist, cutting the string of her pajama trousers at the same time so that they fell to her knees. Elena's sex and belly were fully exposed to view; a little crucifix dangled between her heavy breasts. There was a gasp from the crowd, no doubt partly caused by shock at this sudden nudity in someone they had been used to venerate, but there was even more surprise at the dramatic effect on the Monkey God. He emitted a high-pitched screech, and growling and muttering, seemed to shrink from his heroic posture, collapsing to the boards of the table where he shook and shuddered, his back arching as if in pain. With a final groan the body slumped into a swoon, feet drumming the table, and lay still. This was but momentary, however, for at the next instant the young Boxer, looking tired but with no hint now of possession, was sitting up scratching his head, clearly wondering how he had got there and startled by the sight of a naked foreign lady beside him.

'Surprised?' asked Ren Ren, rhetorically. 'You shouldn't be. That's what happens when one piece of magic overcomes another. And in this case the pollutant effect of the witch was so foul that it drove the Monkey God back to heaven. He couldn't bear the sight of her disgusting parts, you see. The lewdness of a witch and whore, who fucks with Christian devils . . .' Ren Ren ran his hand under Sister Elena's loins, then theatrically smelt his fingers. 'Ugh! What a pong! The stench of corruption and evil.

'But don't be disheartened, good people. We've other magic just as powerful. I only wanted to show you how dangerous a foe we face, and how evil these Christians among you really are. We've proved she's a devil. How many others are there down there like her?'

No longer interested in Sister Elena, he pushed her off the table. She fell winded to the ground where, in her shame, she clutched what remained of her clothing and curled, foetus-like, sobbing. None of the Christians dared approach her. Their scared eyes were fixed on Ren Ren.

'Never mind the witch. She's a spent force now we're here. She'll be despatched, of course, as soon as I get her back to the Harmonious Fists headquarters. What concerns me more is what we're to do with all the other Devil-worshipping Christians you have here. Your own people.

'They won't get away, if that's what anybody was thinking. We have this square sealed tight, and my men are already scouring the houses for anyone hiding there. It won't take us long to sort out who's who. You all know who they are anyway, don't you? And, if I'm not mistaken, we'll probably all be able to smell who they are before long. If they're not shitting in their pants already they soon will be.'

He stalked round the table.

'Can you smell their fear of us? I can. And their malevolence? I can. Let's take this pastor, this schoolteacher, the one who wants to see my credentials. You there. Headman. Why don't you advise me? What shall we do with him? He's already confessed to being head of the Christians here. And you told me that the Christians have been making magical attacks on your family. If he's their leader, he's got to be some sort of wizard too, hasn't he?'

Ren Ren cocked his ear comically, in part parody of the now departed Monkey God. 'Speak up,' he said. 'Can't hear you. Whisper whisper. Moan moan. You're more bashful than a bride on her wedding night. Come on, what shall we do with him?'

'Kill him!' a loud female voice called from the crowd.

'Fact. It's always the women who are the most bloodthirsty,' said Ren Ren. 'Well? Is that what you want too? You're the headman here. Is that what we should do? Kill him? Shall we?'

One or two more voices repeated the call. Soon there was a hesitant chorus of scared villagers demanding Pastor John's death. Headman Yang, his eyes wide with fear, eventually nodded. 'Yes. Kill him,' he said. 'Please. Kill him for us.'

'Bring him up here then, 'Ren Ren ordered, and the bound and gagged Pastor John was pushed up on to the table. 'And you come up too,' he added. Headman Yang nervously climbed up beside him.

'Now, how are you going to do it?' asked Ren Ren. 'Knife? Axe? Pitchfork? I know you peasants can be very imaginative . . . Oh, you wanted me to do it for you, did you? No, no, no. That's your responsibility, Headman. Your village, after all.'

Ren Ren played with him for some time, then lost patience. He pulled out his own knife and thrust it into Yang's hand. 'That's his heart,' he said. 'Just shove it in. Pretend you're killing a sheep.'

Yang, his mouth twitching, turned to the gagged Pastor John. 'Forgive me,' he muttered. 'Old Wang, I'm sorry. He's forcing me . . .'

Pastor John's eyes flashed their contempt.

'Just get on with it,' said Ren Ren.

Yang squeezed his eyes shut and, with both hands clutching the knife's handle, stabbed downward into Pastor John's chest, groaning as he did so. Ren Ren, his face leaning close to that of Pastor John's, smiled when he saw the old man's eyes widen with pain, and heard the choking behind the gag. 'Satisfied with my authority now, are you?' he whispered. 'No more questions about my commission?' and he spat on the body as it dropped to the ground in its death agony.

The crowd watched Pastor John's execution in silence, but there were three piercing screams. Two young girls and an old woman ran forward, reaching vainly through the cordon of Boxers for the body of their father and husband. Idly, Ren Ren noticed that one of the girls, the pink-faced one, was very pretty. She might do as a gift for his mother, he thought. The old lady was always looking for new stock. She seemed the right age too. Later, he thought. He would think about that later.

'Now who's next?' he asked the panting and bloody Headman Yang, who was staring at the stained knife he was holding in his hand. 'Let's be a bit more methodical about this next time, shall we?'

It took little encouragement for the villagers to identify and denounce the Christians, and it was quite an easy task for the Boxers to herd then into the small hall on the side of the square, which Pastor John had used as his church. There was no resistance. They had all been cowed by the presence of the Boxers, Ren Ren's intimidating theatricals, Sister Elena's humiliation and the murder of Pastor John. Even Miller Zhang and his two sons gave up their knives without a struggle and meekly followed the others into the church, awaiting their fate.

It was not long coming. The Zhang family was the first to be called to face the tribunal that Ren Ren had set up in the square. The same elders who had debated with the Christians earlier in the morning were now seated again at the table as judges of their fellow villagers. Ren Ren paced behind smugly, an impresario admiring his own production.

Miller Zhang and his sons stumbled blinking into the sunlight and had to pass through a cordon of villagers to get to the table. Many had gone back home to get their pitch-forks and hoes, and such was the hatred of this family in the village that a few blows were struck even before they reached the tribunal.

The trial was perfunctory. Headman Yang had recovered his composure. In fact, he was looking pleased with himself, having convinced himself that in stabbing Pastor John he had committed a noble, even heroic act. The land issue was not mentioned. Miller Zhang was too proud to disclaim his family's Christianity. In fact, he had flaunted it so much in the past that he could hardly deny it now. He also knew that Yang would never allow him to recant. He had decided while waiting in the dark church that he would die bravely. Whether he ultimately did or not was difficult to determine. On Yang's signal he and his sons were surrounded by villagers with hoes and hacked to pieces.

There was a longer debate over the next victim, a cobbler, whose harmlessness – unlike the Zhangs – had never aroused any animosity in the village. He knelt and wept, confessed freely to his error and promised to give up his Christianity. Ren Ren in the end had to intervene, pointing out the obvious truth that all Christians were liars so his retraction could hardly be genuine. The cobbler died under the hoes.

The next trial was shorter. Ren Ren congratulated the tribunal. 'You're getting into the rhythm,' he said. 'That's good.'

Sister Elena was still lying, ignored and traumatised, on the ground. She was aware of what was going on, but it seemed distant and unreal, as if she was watching a play. Part of her knew that that she was displaying cowardice. It was her duty to do something to protect these people, friends of hers, who were being murdered before her eyes – but at the same time she felt powerless, unable to move. Calling on the saints for strength was no use – something had died in her when she saw her beloved Pastor John fall to his death. She could not reach that quiet part of herself, full of love and warmth, which had always given her strength when she was troubled. She felt abandoned and defiled. She wore her nakedness like an accusation, clutching the rags around her body as if she was trying to hide a crime. And every few moments she would hear the ugly, triumphant yells, and the hideous thud of the hoes that were extinguishing her parishioners' lives. She closed her eyes on her own darkness of the soul, and wept self-pitying tears.

She felt rather than saw the kindly presence kneeling beside her. She opened her eyes and focused on the wrinkled face of the village *bonze*, who was smiling at her out of the sunshine as he offered her his own saffron cloak. 'I do not understand your religion,' he said, 'but I have never thought it was evil. Come, wrap yourself up. There are people who need you now, whom you can help before their long journey.'

She did meekly as she was told, tying the neck fastening of the long cloak with fumbling fingers. The priest gave her his own girdle, which, tightened, closed the cloak and ensured her modesty. She followed the bent figure across the square. A Boxer guard stood threateningly in front of them. The *bonze* waved him gently aside. 'I am taking her to the hall where the others are,' he told him. 'I will be responsible for her.'

The guards at the door of the church were there to prevent people coming out not going in. 'I must leave you here,' said the *bonze*. 'You have been hurt and confused, but you will know what to do when you get inside. And I will be lighting incense this evening and praying for a happy reincarnation for you and Mr Wang. You know, he was always my friend. We will perhaps meet again, beyond this sea of sorrow.'

Sister Elena nodded, and in her Buddhist cloak entered the church. It took some moments for her to adjust to the darkness, and for a moment she felt panicked by the wall of wailing that assailed her ears. She did not feel strong enough to cope. She was more conscious of her inadequacy than ever before. Then she began to distinguish figures in the dim light. She saw Mother Wang sitting on the bare stone floor, her eyes running with tears, her mouth opened and her face frozen in a mask of abandoned lament. Mary had buried her head in her lap, and her body was shaking with sobs. Little Martha was kneeling beside her, a desperate expression on her thin face, wanting to console her mother but not knowing how. Elena looked down the nave and saw other women she knew slumped in similar attitudes of grief and fear. There were a few men left in the church – mainly the elders, the young had been taken first – waiting their turn to be summoned. Some were kneeling on the ground in prayer. Others were slouched against the wall, gazing at their feet in blank despair. She heard another triumphant yell from the crowd outside and shortly afterwards two Boxers came in and, after looking round, selected one of the praying figures to drag away. A chorus of screams greeted his departure, fading again into the anonymous wail when the heavy doors banged shut again.

She felt a little hand grasp hers and saw Martha's quizzical face looking up at her. 'Oh, Auntie, what kept you away? We so missed you here.'

Elena reached for her and hugged her, tears welling in her own eyes as she buried her face in the child's shoulder. For a while the two rocked together, sobbing silently.

'They came to the house,' said Martha, 'and forced us to go with them to the square, and we saw Father . . . we saw *Baba* . . .'

'I know, I know,' whispered Elena, rocking her. 'Don't think of it. Not now.'

'But they lied to us. They told us we were going to go away. That we were to leave the village, and we were to get our valuables and belongings. And then they just stole them and there was nothing we could do.'

'I know,' said Elena. 'Don't think of it, little one.'

'But don't you see? Don't you see? What that awful man said about us Christians being witches. It's got nothing to do with it. They're just robbers, Auntie. They're killing us only because they want to steal from us . . .'

Elena reached for the hot little face and kissed it. 'Hush, my darling,' she said. She felt another arm around her waist, and the lithe body of Mary was in her arms. She looked up, and saw other figures around her, expectant faces looking at her. The wailing had subsided a little as, one by one, the Christians in the church noticed that Sister Elena had returned.

Lao Yi, a farmer who had been one of the first in Bashu to befriend and be converted by Father Adolphus, was contemplating her with his honest features. 'Elder Sister, is there anything that can be done to save us?'

'Oh, Lao Yi, I don't think so,' said Elena, feeling her heart break a little.

'I didn't think so,' he said. 'I was never very clever, you know, and I couldn't learn the scriptures. Father Adolphus was often angry with me for getting the stories wrong, but you can tell me, can't you? There is a purpose to this? The Lord does have a purpose?'

'Oh, yes, Lao Yi, the Lord always has a purpose,' said Elena, trying to hold back her tears. 'Even if we cannot understand what it is.'

Lao Yi nodded. 'I thought so,' he said. 'Then everything's fine, isn't it? Elder Sister, I'm glad you're with us at the end. Look,' he paused shyly. 'I know you're not a father, or even a lay pastor like John, but I thought, maybe, you can lead us in a few prayers, or hymns. Some of us are quite frightened, you see, and there's nothing like a hymn or a prayer, is there, to cheer you up?'

When the Boxers next came in they were surprised to see a woman in Buddhist robes standing at the altar, with the Christians kneeling in a half-circle around her. In a strong voice, she was reciting a prayer, the Magnificat, the others murmuring the words along with her. When the Boxers tapped Lao Yi on the shoulder, he stood up promptly, genuflected to the altar, and then, straightening his shoulders, walked resolutely in front of them to the door. This time there were no screams or wails. The prayer continued to the end. Before the door closed, Lao Yi heard the first lines of a hymn, and as he stepped into the sunlight he began to sing in his rough, tuneless voice:

> 'Yesu ai wo, wo zhidao
> Shengjing shuoguo wo hen hao . . .'

> 'Jesus loves me this I know
> 'Cos the Bible tells me so.'

Five more times the Boxers came in, and then all the men were gone. The women continued to sing, although many had tears running down their faces.

They were singing when the doors banged open and Ren Ren, flanked by his lieutenants, with Headman Yang and several villagers holding bloody hoes and pitchforks, strode into the church. Heads turned in fear, but Elena, her eyes fixed on Ren Ren, forced herself to continue, louder, defiantly, with the words of the psalm, and although there was faltering, the murmuring accompaniment continued. It happened to be the twenty-third Psalm, which Dr Airton had translated and for which Sister Caterina, who was talented in that way, had composed a catchy tune. As she sang the words she felt strength and a purpose she had thought she'd lost: 'Yea though I walk through the valley of the shadow of death, I will fear no evil: For thou art with me; thy rod and thy staff they comfort me, Thou preparest a table before me in the presence of mine enemies . . .'

She held Ren Ren's stare across the hall until he looked away. He laughed nervously. Then, winking at his companions, he began to clap his hands in ironic, slow applause, shouting, '*Hao!* Good!' in parody of an audience expressing appreciation for fine singing at a performance of Chinese opera. Grinning, the others followed his lead. The singing wavered under the handclaps, and died, and the scared faces gazed as if hypnotised at the blood, which was dripping from the hoes.

Sister Elena was not to be deterred. She closed her eyes to steel herself and in a loud voice that somehow did not sound like her own she began to chant the Lord's Prayer: 'Our Father who art in heaven Hallowed be thy name Thy kingdom come . . .'

Ren Ren knew how to make his voice carry further.

'The way these witches flaunt their incantations! They never give up, do they? It's as if they're asking to be burned. Well, isn't that convenient? Because that's exactly what we've come here to do.'

The meaning of his words did not sink in for a moment. Then one of the women screamed, and Elena's prayer was drowned in a low moan that grew to a wail of terror.

Ren Ren, who knew he had command now, raised his hand. 'Ladies, ladies,' he said. 'Please. We're not going to burn all of you – well, not till we've had a bit of fun first. Don't want to be wasteful, do we? Some of you we might not burn at all – if you're good to us, that is.'

As he was speaking the other men were circling the women, who cowered as they passed. The reason why they had come here was clear to all now, and some of those with young daughters were attempting vainly to shield them from view. They were therefore the more easily spotted. With a leer one of the villagers with a hoe reached out, grabbed a girl of sixteen and pulled her from the clasping hands of her mother, who fell on her face, crying. Within minutes, ten or eleven girls were huddled where they had been thrown near the door. Still the men prowled.

One of the older girls – Sister Elena recognised her as the wife of the farmer, Zhang Aifan, who had been among the first men to be taken out and killed – threw herself forward and flung her arms around Ren Ren's legs. 'Take me,' she squealed. 'Take me. I'm not really a Christian. I don't want to die.'

'No, you're ugly,' said Ren Ren, and kicked her back into the circle. 'Where's that one I saw earlier, the pink thing? Ah, there you are.'

With a shock Sister Elena realised that he was looking at Mary, who had pressed herself up against her mother. With a pang in her heart, she saw that the young girl's eyes were wide with terror. She realised she had to do something. She knew that it would be useless but she could not stand by and let Pastor John's daughter be taken and dishonoured – but Martha moved first. A small erect figure, eyes blazing, she stood with her fists raised in front of Ren Ren. 'You're not taking my sister!' she said, in a high, clear voice. 'She's going to be a nun.'

Several of the men laughed, but Ren Ren was contemplating her, smiling, appraising her. 'What a brave one,' he said. 'I've a good mind to have you as well. You'll grow into a nice chicken in a couple of years. She'll be good for the virgin trade, don't you think, Monkey? Take her for me, will you?'

As Monkey reached to grab her, Martha bit his hand. He roared with pain, plucked his knife from his belt and slit her throat from ear to ear. 'Sorry, Ren Ren,' he said, wiping her blood from his tunic, 'but that hurt.'

'*No!*' Sister Elena screamed. She was running down the nave and saw Monkey reach for his knife, and Martha's quizzical eyes, calm, frowning a little as she fell. She realised that she was too late, but her anger propelled her forward. Ren Ren had taken Mary from her mother and was dangling her by her waist, her legs kicking. He and Monkey saw the nun coming at them at the same time. Elena threw herself at Monkey, her nails scratching for his face. Instinctively he stabbed upwards with his knife, before her weight and the force of her rush knocked him off his feet. As he rolled away from her, his knife remained buried in her upper chest.

She lay on her back, bewildered, numbness spreading over her breast and into her arms and legs. She heard the gurgling sound of her own breathing, and from afar the peevish voice of that man, that horrible man: 'What's the matter with you, Monkey? That's two of my chickens you've killed. You're a fucking turtle's egg.

That's what you are. Did you know that?' Language, she thought idly, what terrible language; Father Adolphus would not approve. Above her she saw Mary's face, hanging strangely in the air above her. She saw the shocked expression on the girl's face, and tried to form words to comfort her; she felt her lips move but she thought that she might only have achieved a smile. Then she felt a crashing blow on her stomach, and her head seemed to explode. Everything went dark.

Ren Ren had dropped Mary, who whimpered in a huddle in the middle of a big pool of blood on the floor. He was standing with his hands on his hips looking at two villagers, who were proudly pulling a pitchfork out of the dead nun's belly and a hoe from the remains of her skull. One of them was giggling stupidly, the other whooping triumphantly.

'Fucking peasants,' he said, shaking his head. Then he gave orders for the girls who had been chosen for the men's pleasure to be taken outside, for the doors to be barred, and for the building to be set alight. As the first flames began to lick up the side of the church, and the sound of women's screams reached a crescendo inside, he wondered how they would transport back to Shishan the goods that his men had started to bring out of the Christians' houses.

All was quiet at the Airtons' mission. A sliver of moon revealed itself for a moment as the clouds parted, and a pale light illuminated the room at the end of the corridor where a girl lay bound to a bed. The room stank. By the head of the bed was a bucket half full of vomit. Soon Sister Caterina would take it out and change it but she was occupied for now with bundling the diarrhoea-stained sheets she had just removed from the bed into a basket. Helen Frances was naked. All her nightdresses were soiled, and there was a stain on her white thigh where she had not yet been sponged. In a chair the doctor dozed, exhaustion making him oblivious of the animal grunts and snarls that, for the last five hours, his patient had been emitting through clenched teeth as she rolled and strained against the ropes. The moonlight revealed her staring eyes, which, fixed unblinkingly open, seemed focused on nothing, unless they were gazing inwards into whatever delirious dreams were shaking and tormenting the body on the bed. Only occasionally consciousness would appear to return to them, but then they would clench shut as the unbearable pain in legs and arms would arch the body upwards. When Caterina saw this she would stop what she was doing, and hold Helen Frances's head, steering it to the bucket, for the vomiting inevitably followed these attacks. It was a sort of routine, which the doctor, the nun and, when she could spare the time, Nellie had become used to over the last day and night. And somewhere, hovering between dream and wakefulness, the mind that was Helen Frances's, struggled to understand what was happening to her and to overcome the hatred she felt for her tormentors, and even more for herself.

Two days later Frank Delamere was sitting in a restaurant with his merchant friends, Lu Jincai and Jin Shangui. Ever since he had heard about the mysterious disappearance of old Tang Dexin, and the rumours that he had been a black society member and an associate of Iron Man Wang, Lu had dropped his suspicions of Jin, and some of their old intimacy had been restored. The food, as usual, was delicious but Frank found his two friends tense. They had been plying him with questions about his and the doctor's interview with the Mandarin, which had taken place that morning.

'Well, it was all a bit strange,' said Frank, helping himself to another cup of hot rice wine. 'Certainly the doctor thought so, and he's attended many more of these audiences than I have. Normally, apparently, the doctor's used to seeing the Mandarin alone in his private rooms, but this time we were taken to the main audience hall, which was an intimidating place. And there were a lot of unsavoury characters hanging about whom the doctor hadn't seen before. Quite unlike the sleek-looking officials you're used to seeing in the *yamen*. It was all very odd.'

Jin and Lu exchanged glances. 'Can you tell us who they were?' asked Lu quietly.

'Haven't a clue. Rough-looking fellows, one or two in sheepskins, lounging against the wall as if they owned the place. One of them, would you believe it? was picking his teeth with his knife. And the guards just ignored him!'

'Didn't the Mandarin say anything?' asked Jin. 'He is usually punctilious about the formalities.'

'No, that was the odd thing. The Mandarin didn't say much at all. Just sat there on his dais with a blank expression on his face, looking as if he wished he were somewhere else, as if the whole thing were a frightful bore.'

'Then who conducted the audience?'

'That sinister-looking chamberlain of his. He did most of the talking. Unsavoury fellow. Not quite right in the head, to my mind. Had a bee in his bonnet about Christians. Kept ranting and raving about Christians disturbing the peace, and planning all sorts of villainous activities.'

Again Jin and Lu exchanged glances.

'Naturally they were still a bit flustered about old Millward's exhibition the other day. That's not surprising. It was bizarre enough behaviour by any standard – even for that bedlam of eccentrics. Of course we told them that Millward's a maniac, that we had nothing to do with him, that his own society is about to have him strait-jacketed – but he didn't seem to take the point. Way he talked to Airton, it might have been that the doctor had planned the whole thing, given Millward orders. Doctor took it very calmly, repeated our position patiently, but I could see he was a mite upset. Especially that the Mandarin didn't intervene. Well, who wouldn't be?' He drained his cup and poured another.

'Did you tell them about the attack on our wagon train?' asked Lu. 'The wounding of Mr Cabot?'

'Well, eventually – when we could get a word in edgeways after the chamberlain's ranting about the Christians. I've no complaints about that side of things, actually. They said all the right things. You know, great regrets, great embarrassment that a guest in their country should be attacked and injured. Promises to hunt the villains down. Asked a few questions about where and when it happened, and how many of them there were. Asked us to pass on congratulations to young Tom for his bravery – that was the Mandarin, one of the few times he spoke – and hope he gets well soon. Usual stuff. A bit perfunctory, I suppose, and I didn't like the ruffians grinning on the side – but they've promised to look into it, and consider some form of compensation, depending what they find out. Couldn't really ask for more.'

'Did you tell them about your suspicions about the Boxers? The strange uniforms?' asked Lu.

'That was another funny thing. They didn't seem very interested.

Pooh-poohed the idea, saying everyone had heard these rumours before and that they were a bit below the dignity of such an eminent court as the *yamen* to consider. The doctor pressed them, stressing that our attackers were wearing yellow turbans and had some pretty good discipline – but the chamberlain told him, rather rudely, I thought, that he was being credulous, and hadn't we considered that Iron Man Wang or whichever bandit was directing this might not have dressed his own men in such costumes simply because of the rumours, knowing that would make everyone more scared of him? I suppose that's possible, if you think about it,' Frank finished glumly, reaching for the rice wine again. 'Clever in its way. The villains round the walls certainly seemed to think so. Laughed as if the chamberlain had made some joke, though I didn't see the humour.'

'Are you not drinking a little excessively, De Falang Xiansheng?' asked Jin, as Frank hailed the waiter for another pot of rice wine.

'I suppose I am,' said Frank. 'But do you know? I need to get a little drunk after the last few days, holed up in that mission. Airton's a good fellow, but he portions out his precious whisky as if it's the communion cup or something. And what with concern for poor old Tom – who's mending fine by the way – and my daughter down with some sort of illness that nobody's prepared to tell me much about, well, it hasn't been easy.'

'I am sorry to hear about your daughter,' said Lu, again after a glance at Jin. 'What is ailing her?'

'Well they say it's the flu, but what's rum is they're so secretive. Maybe it's some woman's thing they're shy to talk about. She was uncommunicative the only time I was allowed to see her – don't know what's got into her these last few months – and Nellie's as protective as a mother hen, and the doctor goes in at odd hours with a tray of syringes. You know, old friends, I'm a bit at my wit's end with worry about her.' Frank's face had reddened and his eyes had misted sentimentally. 'She looks awful.'

'Have they talked to you about the other Englishman, Ma Na Si Xiansheng?' asked Lu carefully.

Frank looked up in surprise. 'No. What's he got to do with it?' he asked, somewhat belligerently.

'It may be nothing, De Falang, but since the madman's attack on the Palace of Heavenly Pleasure the other day there have been many rumours spreading round the town. Lao Jin and I were there last night, and some of the girls were talking freely. They were telling us some strange stories about Ma Na Si and a – foreign woman who used to visit him regularly in his pavilion there.'

Frank's face achieved the unusual feat of turning from red to white to red again. 'I don't know what you're implying, my friend,' he said, in a low growl.

'Please, De Falang, this is painful for me, and Jin and I discussed the matter long before we decided to talk to you. I only do so because there may be lives at stake.'

'Go on,' said Frank, coldly, as he poured himself a cup from the new pot, drained it and poured another.

'De Falang Xiansheng,' said Jin quietly, 'did you perhaps hear that, during the raid by the Christians on the Palace of Heavenly Pleasure, one of the girls escaped?'

'No, I did not hear any such thing,' said Frank, 'and I'll thank you for sticking to the point.'

Jin continued, undeterred, 'The girl was Fan Yimei. You may remember her. She was a close friend of your once-companion, Shen Ping.'

'I may remember her. What about her?'

'Fan Yimei had a particular position in that establishment. She was the permanent mistress of Major Lin Fubo, who heads the Mandarin's militia. Major Lin, who returned from the country yesterday, is extremely angry at the loss of Fan Yimei, I am told, and will want vengeance on whoever is responsible.'

'Good for him,' said Frank. 'I still don't know what you're getting at.'

'There are other rumours, De Falang.' Lu took up the story. 'It is said that Fan Yimei was not the only one who escaped during the disturbance. It is being whispered that the Lius were keeping a foreign boy, perhaps the son of the preacher Millward, in an upstairs room as a catamite, and that during the commotion he also disappeared.'

'What bloody nonsense!' exploded Frank. 'Everyone knows that the boy was killed by bandits and his murderers were executed. And what's this got to do with my daughter?'

'If it is true, De Falang, your daughter may be in danger, for it is widely believed that it was the Englishman, Ma Na Si, who effected the escape of both Fan Yimei and the boy.'

'There you go again. You can bloody well come out straight with it. What has been going on between Ma Na Si and my Helen Frances?'

'If it is true that Mother Liu and her son were keeping this boy, they will be doing everything in their power to destroy the evidence, and eliminate anyone who can accuse them. For otherwise they will be found guilty of kidnapping – and worse besides. They will certainly suspect Ma Na Si – and anyone who is close to him. And that will almost certainly include your daughter, who has visited Ma Na Si – I am sorry, my old friend, but that cannot be denied. Jin and I made very thorough enquiries. I fear that she may even be pregnant by him. Alas, your story about her illness would seem only to confirm that.'

Jin and Lu looked at Frank tenderly. His features were broken in anguish and he could not bring himself to speak.

'Ren Ren came back to Shishan also this morning. Now he knows. I cannot emphasise enough how dangerous that young man is to you. He will stop at nothing, believe me.'

'Why should I possibly fear a little brothel boy like Ren Ren?' whispered Frank.

'Because he is more than that now. I hear that he is powerful in the Black Stick Society. There are also rumours that he leads a Boxer band. In ordinary times going to the authorities may have been a solution, but the situation is changing for the worse, as you yourself saw when you went to the Mandarin this morning. Is it not strange that the Mandarin did not speak? And that there were unfamiliar people in the *yamen*? I fear that we are facing very troubled times.'

'We tell you this to warn you, De Falang,' said Jin. 'There is still time for you to take your daughter and Mr Cabot and leave Shishan. Perhaps you should also warn the other foreigners. We are your friends and we strongly advise you to do so. I believe that the Boxers are a real threat, whatever people say, and they will shortly be coming to Shishan. If that is the case, the Mandarin's writ will no longer apply. Any foreigner – and any friend of a foreigner – will be in deadly danger. Besides, Ren Ren now has a motive to get rid of you and your family. If the Boxers come to Shishan he and his like will be all-powerful.'

'I'm not afraid of him,' growled Frank.

Lu looked at Jin, who nodded. 'You should be, dear friend,' he said. 'He has already murdered one person you love.'

'What do you mean?'

'It grieves my heart to tell you, and I had hoped to spare you, but it is almost certain that he murdered your companion, Shen Ping. I hoped that you would never know.'

Frank stared.

'She did not return to the countryside as I told you. She was beaten and tortured by Ren Ren for daring to fall in love with you, and then she hanged herself when Mother Liu persuaded you that she had been unfaithful to you. Ren Ren might have put that noose around her neck with his own hand. Perhaps he did. I am sorry, my friend.'

Frank tried to say something, but words did not come. Tears were rolling down his cheeks. He dabbed uselessly at his face with a napkin, sniffed, stood up, sat down again, then groaned – a terrible, despairing sound – and lurched towards the door.

Lu and Jin tried to pull him back, but he shook them off. 'I'm sorry, gentlemen,' he muttered through his sobs. 'I am a little indisposed.'

Lu and Jin returned to the table and the remains of the meal. They looked at each other, but neither had anything to say.

After a long pause, Lu Jincai said, 'De Falang has forgotten to take his hat.'

'Poor De Falang,' said Jin.

'Poor us,' said Lu Jincai, after another long silence.

When Frank left the restaurant he had no clear idea of what he would do or where he would go. He reeled back at the noise and bustle, and the intoxicating smell of the busy main street. A muleteer driving a heavily loaded wagon yelled at him to stand aside, and Frank lurched backwards, stepping into a puddle of horse urine and unidentifiable animal droppings, which covered his shining black pumps – he was still in morning dress, following the call on the *yamen* – with a dirty yellow slime. He felt the hot sun beating down on his uncovered head, and had to squint in the dazzling white light to make any sense of the movement around him. He had not realised quite how much he had drunk or how disoriented he had become. Passers-by stared sourly, or smiled curiously, at the red-faced foreigner swaying in the street.

Frank was hardly aware of where he was; nor did he care. In his mind was one image: the laughing face framed in silk pillows of a girl whom he had hardly thought about during the last few months, but whose merry eyes now twinkled ironically at him in their two narrow slits above the familiar flat cheekbones, and whose wide mouth with its wicked white teeth was half open in what he knew must be a gentle rebuke.

The memory of her pierced his heart, and his blood throbbed violently, almost choking him with grief and remorse. Other images came to his mind, as vivid as if he was watching the scenes unrolling in front of him on a flickering cinematograph: his interview with Mother Liu, the hard-faced smile as she twisted her pearls and broke his heart with her unspeakable and relentless description of Shen Ping's treachery; wicked words that he now knew had been lies, which only someone as foolish and gullible as he could have believed; the smirk of her son as he passed out of the door in despair; the long night he had spent at his desk, whisky bottle, paper and inkstand before him, penning the cruel letter of rejection, which he realised now must have helped to seal his dear girl's fate. Lu Jincai's recent words seared in his memory like accusations of the Furies: '*daring to fall in love with you . . . hanged herself when Mother Liu persuaded you that she had been unfaithful to you*'.

Frank blundered aimlessly down the main street, oblivious of the people who had to step quickly out of his way. Another image haunted him and possessed him, the same face of his dear Shen Ping, but now drained of blood and colour, dangling on a cord in a dark room, her glazed eyes reproaching him for his blindness.

Without consciously deciding to do so Frank reeled off the high street into an empty alley. The stink of the open drains, coupled with the effects of his drinking, caused him to retch, and he vomited into the gutter. On his knees, his hands in the filth, he began to sob, his heavy body shaking with helpless sorrow.

Then he recalled the other words of Lu in the restaurant: '*She was beaten and tortured by Ren Ren . . . Ren Ren might have put that noose around her neck with his own hand.*' And, while feeling no less guilty for his own betrayal, he became angry. His head was clearer now that he had vomited, and he understood the full horror and significance of those words. *Beaten and tortured.* Tortured? His Shen Ping tortured? Beaten? Now the image in his mind was of a sneering, pockmarked, rat-like face, staring back at him sardonically, unrepentantly, chewing on a melon seed and spitting it out at his feet.

'Ren Ren,' he hissed, on hands and knees by the gutter. He saw Ren Ren's hateful reflection in the murky water, not his own. 'I'm going to kill you,' he addressed the smirking image, almost fondly, 'after I've torn you limb from limb.'

Clumsily, he pushed and heaved himself to his feet, staggering until he had retained his balance. 'I'm going to tear you,' he roared, down the empty alley, 'limb from bloody limb.'

He was still disoriented and did not really know where he was, but a determination to pound down the doors of the Palace of Heavenly Pleasure and wring his enemy by the neck propelled him forward – in the opposite direction to that which he had come. He burst out of the alley into another half-empty side-street, absorbed in his own thoughts. Part of his mind was reminding him that it was not only Ren Ren he had to deal with: there was also Manners and his disgraceful treatment of his daughter. 'One at a time. One at a time,' he muttered in his anger, the vicious image of the brothel boy still uppermost in his sights.

He was dimly aware of a small group of people blocking the far end of the road where a nondescript *pailou* marked a crossroads. They were dressed in the blue tunics of artisans and they appeared to be watching a performance of some kind, although Frank could not see what it was. All he saw was an obstacle on his way to the Palace of Heavenly Pleasure that he had to push past.

He shoved and elbowed his way through the ring of townsmen, who were startled enough to give way to him. He found himself confronting an athletic young man giving a demonstration of martial arts. Something about his dress – the yellow turban, the tiger-skin tunic, the red belt – was vaguely familiar, but Frank did not want to think about that now. He only wanted to get on and complete his business with Ren Ren. On the other hand, as soon as the red-faced foreigner stumbled into his circle, the young man stopped what he was doing, put his hands on his hips and blocked Frank's path.

Frank tried impatiently to sidestep him to his right. The man moved lightly across to block him. Frank tried to get past on his left, and the man blocked his way again.

He heard laughter and a few jeers from the artisans, but the young man was staring at him steadily.

Frank lifted what he thought was his cane to strike the fellow aside. Then he realised that he hadn't brought it. There was more laughter as his hand flapped inanely up and down. The young man kept his eyes on Frank's face.

'I've had enough of this,' Frank growled. 'Get out of my way.'

The man remained where he was.

This time Frank swung a clumsy punch at the man's head. The man ducked aside, easily avoiding the blow, while Frank found himself staggering, off balance. There were more cat-calls from the onlookers.

With a roar of rage Frank threw himself forward, stretching out his arms to seize the man and throw him out of his way. As he hurtled forward, the man neatly stepped back, reached inside the folds of his tunic and pulled out a tasselled hatchet, which, in a graceful movement, he threw up into the air, caught, and with a downward strike, buried in Frank's chest.

This time there was silence from the bystanders. Frank looked down at the expanse of his white dress shirt and appeared to be studying the blood, which was seeping over it. Possibly he had noticed that it was of a similar colour to the crimson tassel on the hatchet. With some difficulty he brought up his hand to feel the weapon that was so incongruously attached to him. The tassel slipped through his limp fingers as more blood gushed out of his mouth, and he toppled on to his front.

For a moment the group stood still, a fascinated tableau around the body. Then, one by one, they slipped out of the circle and ran away. The Boxer paused a while, perhaps determining whether he should lift the heavy body and retrieve his axe. Leaving Frank untouched, however, he picked up his satchel, and ran with light steps under the *pailou,* and disappeared down one of the bisecting streets.

Frank's bloodshot eyes stared angrily down the road. After a while flies began to buzz around the sticky congealing substance that had stained his moustache and chin and was now filtering into the sand.

Chapter Thirteen

The foreigners cower behind their walls,
but we are unafraid.

Herr Fischer was sitting at his map table, rehearsing in his head what he might better have said during his infuriating encounter with Manners that morning. His thoughts about that 'damned Honourable' were as black as the contents of the big mug of coffee, which he was stirring with his spoon.

He had hardly slept the night before. He had fretted through the day over the non-arrival of the train from Tientsin. At two in the morning he had given up his vigil, and staggered to his tent. He had taken off his boots and changed into his red striped nightgown and cap, but hardly had his snores begun to flutter his whiskers or flicker the candle on the side table than he was being shaken awake again by the whistle of the locomotive and the hiss of steam as it settled into the sidings. He checked his watch: fifteen hours and twenty-two minutes late.

He had found the engineer Bowers incoherent with exhaustion. His explanation of the delay had consisted of a confused mutter about obstacles on the line and crowds of angry peasants throwing stones. There had been no use in interrogating the dour, bearded fellow in this state so Fischer had sent him straight to his quarters where he was still sleeping. He had been impressed, however, by the professionalism of the man. Despite his tiredness, Bowers had spent another twenty minutes shunting the engine and guard's van round the loop, repositioning them at opposite ends of the train, so that when it left the next day on its return to Tientsin the engine would be proudly pulling from the front in a manner that would make the punctilious Herr Fischer proud.

There had been few passengers on the train. The Chinese on board had gathered their bundles and disappeared into the night. The American missionary, Burton Fielding, the only passenger in first-class, had also been uncommunicative, and had left quickly for the Airtons' in the mule cart that had been waiting for him all the previous day.

Fischer and Charlie had inspected the engine and carriages in the lantern-light, locking the doors of the carriages, securing the brake in the van, uncoupling the engine before banking the fire in the firebox. The pale orange of pre-dawn was already illuminating the sky before they had finished their various duties.

It was while he was making his way back to his quarters for a shave and a wash that he saw Manners coming out of his tent, followed by a European boy with a tousled head and a Chinese woman dressed in an elegant blue gown. Herr Fischer was not a stupid man, and he prided himself on his keen powers of observation and analysis, the indispensable attributes of a senior engineer. And he was also objective enough, he believed, to look facts squarely in the face. A single glance was enough to assess the situation, and closer examination of the detail merely reinforced his hypothesis. The conclusive evidence was provided by the paint on the woman's face and her fully combed headdress, tinkling with ornaments. Her profession could not have been clearer if she had held up a sign with her portrait on it. And there were even traces of eye makeup on the boy, who was wearing embroidered silk pyjamas! He had wondered for a moment how a foreign boy of this persuasion could have got to Shishan. Then he dimly recalled that Charlie had once told him of the people-smuggling business that went on in Shanghai and in the south of China. Was there any wickedness, however improbable or ingenious, of which Manners was not capable? Herr Fischer composed his features into what he hoped was the magisterial expression of a Cato or Cicero. His shoulders stiffened as he prepared his stern and sad rebuke – but before he had a chance to speak, Manners, far from showing any guilt or remorse or discomfort at being found out, merely raised his hat.

'Morning, Fischer,' he had greeted him brazenly. 'Good day for a ride, don't you think? I see the train's come in. That's good. I've some passengers for you.'

The tower of dignified oration that Fischer had been constructing tumbled, and what emerged was a disconnected rockslide of recrimination and complaint. How dare Mr Manners take that impudent tone? Had he no shame? Did Mr Manners not care about his family name? He demanded an explanation of this latest outrage. He knew that the Englishman was debauched, but never before had he dared to bring his fancy women to the railway camp. Not to mention this painted boy, this – Ganymede! It was clear that the three of them had spent the night together in the tent in contravention of morality, civilised behaviour, and the rules of the railway company. Even Manners could not deny this. Herr Fischer had discovered him *in flagrante delicto* . . .

'You do have a prurient imagination,' the man had replied, with a hateful coolness. 'If you were to observe a little more closely you would notice that there are two camp beds on the ground outside the tent. Hiram spent the night in one, and I in the other. Very peacefully, I might add. I think that you owe our guests an apology, old boy.'

And then he had insolently proceeded to introduce the creatures – as formally as if they had all been at a cocktail reception – as his friends, Miss Fan Yimei, who was preparing for a journey to Tientsin, and Master Hiram (he did not give a surname), her companion.

'I had intended to explain it all to you at a more appropriate time,' he had continued, unabashed by the scowl of disapproval on Herr Fischer's face. 'I am certain that when you understand the circumstances you will appreciate that discretion is involved, and you will be as eager as I am to help.'

'Discretion, Mr Manners?' In his anger Herr Fischer had attempted a heavy irony. 'For your paramours? You are asking me to provide a private compartment on the train for their disportings perhaps? With curtains and a double bunk?'

'I am not discussing ticketing arrangements. In fact, I don't think it's the time or place to be talking about this at all. You appear a little tired, Herr Fischer, and I promised my friends that I would take them riding. I'll call on you later in the day, when you are calmer.'

At which point Herr Fischer had lost his temper completely. 'Yes, I will talk to you later in the day, Mr Honourable Manners,' he had shouted. 'You have gone far enough. It is not only these disreputable people whom you have brought to our railway. You have from the moment you have arrived my authority flouted, and treated the corporation which employs you with contempt. And, what is more, you have done no work. You are—' His mind whirled to think of a suitable word to describe his disdain. 'You are a passenger here, Mr Manners. I am writing to the board once and for all. You are discharged, Mr Manners. I discharge you, do you hear me? Now and here!'

'Then you'll have no objection if I take my friends for a ride?' The man had smiled at him. And sauntered past him in the direction of the stables, his two companions glancing with nervous curiosity at him as they sidled past.

Well, he *would* sack Manners, Fischer decided, as he stirred his coffee. He did not care what authority was protecting him. He would take the matter to the highest levels. Even if the consequence was his own resignation. It was intolerable! The man was his subordinate yet he had no idea what he got up to during his long absences in town. He was certain that whatever Manners was discussing with the Mandarin was of no benefit to the railway. He was dubious that such a relationship even existed; he rather suspected that Manners wasted his whole time in that infamous bordello where he had once had the temerity to take Charlie, poor fellow.

Why the railway board had sent Manners to Shishan in the first place was beyond his understanding. He suspected that there was something Oriental behind it all, favours being exchanged or some other typical intrigue. Whatever the reason, it was damnable that he, Fischer, had been used, however passively, in these machinations. He, *Gott sei Dank*, was a simple engineer, with a set task, a budget and a timetable to complete. He would do his duty as a professional – and no more. 'From now on, no more,' he said to himself. 'I am no *Junker* Honourable – but I know my duty, and I have my honour too.'

He took a big sip of coffee and scalded his tongue. This did nothing for his temper, so when Charlie burst into the tent, he shouted at him uncharacteristically to get out, and if he had to come in again, to knock first like a civilised human being.

Charlie ignored him. His face showed none of its usual irony or humour. The staring eyes and twitching lips revealed a man who was badly scared. His voice was calm, however: he was obviously calling on all his reserves of strength and self-control. 'You are needed now, Herr Fischer. The workers – we have a strike on our hands, and I cannot control it.'

This brought Herr Fischer immediately to his feet, all thoughts of Manners forgotten in the emergency. 'What are they doing now?' he asked briskly.

'Some are stoning the train. Others are pulling up the rails that lead to the bridge.'

'Better in that direction than the line to the tunnel and Tientsin. Who is leading them?'

'The foreman, Zhang Haobin.'

'Lao Zhang? But he's not a troublemaker.'

He started for the door. Then, reconsidering, he returned to his desk, pulled a revolver from a drawer and stuffed it into his belt. He gathered a hunting rifle and some cartridges from the rack by the wall. 'Do you use these?' he grunted at Charlie. The Chinese shook his head, his expression of distaste. 'Then carry them to Mr Bowers's tent. Wake him if he is sleeping and tell him to join me immediately. I wait for you here. Be quick now.'

Charlie ran on his errand. Herr Fischer looked carefully round the tent. He swept up some papers and knelt by the Chubb, turned the combination to open the big metal safe. He stuffed the papers inside, then pulled out a wad of American dollar bills, which he put into his pocket. As an afterthought he reached for the black book in which he meticulously kept the accounts and, with some tearing of the lining, squeezed it into the inside pocket of his jacket. He locked the safe, grabbed another rifle and cartridge case from the rack, and walked, with a deliberate step, to the door.

It was the silence that struck him as ominous. There were none of the ordinary sounds of the camp. From his commanding position he could look down on to the track and the bridge. A crowd of coolies and earth-carriers were milling about, without any particular purpose that he could identify. Then he observed that the majority of them were watching some of his railway workers under the direction of Zhang Haobin heaving with iron bars at the rails and the sleepers. There was the clear tinkle of metal against metal, which carried over the still morning air, but otherwise no sound – not even a shout. Certainly not the roar of a mob of angry workers, calling out their grievances and demands. The funnel and steam dome of the engine were visible behind the tents to his right, and from that direction he also heard a clattering of stones on metal – but, again, no human voices raised in anger.

Puzzled, he occupied himself by loading his revolver and his rifle. After a few minutes Charlie returned with Bowers, looking incongruously formal in his blue, brass-buttoned jacket, and high peaked cap. The rifle slung over his shoulder, his upright bearing, the black beard and solemn face reminded Herr Fischer of a police constable. He wished that he had one or two real policemen at his command.

'Good man, Bowers. You slept well?'

'Adequately, sir,' answered the sombre fellow.

'Then you are ready to join me for a little conversation with these hooligans here?'

'I'll be happy enough if we can prevent them from damaging my engine.'

'Excellent,' said Herr Fischer. 'We take a stroll together, *ja*? Come on, Charlie, lead the way.'

The three moved slowly down the hill, Charlie glancing nervously from side to side.

'There is nobody who is with us?' Fischer asked Charlie quietly.

'Not this time. They're all in on it, or intimidated into it.'

'I see. And who is doing the intimidation?'

'Can't tell. In the past when we had trouble I was able to speak to them. At least hear what they had to say. This time they stoned me when I got near.'

They had reached the outskirts of the crowd, which parted to let the armed men through. As he looked at the faces lining their path Herr Fischer detected few signs of outright hostility. There were sneers and frowns and whispers; some of the younger workers, muscled torsos stripped proudly to the waist, tensed and squared their shoulders threateningly, but these were the minority. Most of the weatherbeaten faces looked at them blankly, some sullenly but more with open curiosity. There were several smiles, and the occasional nod of recognition. Fischer found himself nodding back to one or two of the veterans, who beamed at him.

Most curious, he thought. It was patently a strike, and that was worrying, especially if the whole workforce was involved – but he did not feel particularly threatened personally. There was an atmosphere of excitement, but none of the bitterness in the air that he normally associated with strikes. He was conscious, however, of the disparity of numbers should the situation deteriorate.

'Mr Bowers's men – the engineers and stewards who came with the train last night – where are they?' he asked Charlie.

'They're huddled in their tent. Wouldn't come out even when Mr Bowers threatened them.'

'Bowers? This is true?'

'Aye,' was the short answer.

'Then, gentlemen, it appears that we are on our own.' He spoke cheerfully, but he was conscious of a fluttering in his belly, and silently ran through the prayers he knew, wondering which would be most appropriate in these circumstances.

The last of the faces moved aside to let them pass, and they found themselves confronting the foreman, a grey-queued, stubble-headed man with lined, honest features and a habitually melancholy frown. As the three stepped up the bank to the rails, the workers bent on destruction froze with their crowbars in mid-air, and gazed questioningly at Zhang Haobin.

'All right, lads,' the foreman said sadly. 'Rest for a spell.' He faced Herr Fischer, waiting patiently for the German to address him.

'Mr Zhang,' started Herr Fischer politely. 'We are interrupting your work.' Charlie translated.

'It's no matter,' muttered Zhang.

'May I ask, what are your reasons for destroying our fine railway? You, among others, have worked on it with hardship and pride for many years.'

Zhang hung his head gloomily, but when he looked up it was directly into Herr Fischer's eyes. He muttered the first sentence sullenly, then gathered confidence and projected his voice so that the workers around him could also hear.

'He says that it is true they worked hard, but that was before they knew they had been deceived and that it was a mistake to build this line for foreigners and traitors,' translated Charlie. He spoke coldly. Anger had driven away his nervousness, and there was a red spot on each cheek. 'He says that he and his men have no quarrel with you, Mr Fischer, who have been fair with them. Nor with Mr Bowers. But they are under instructions from the new powers – as he calls them, I do not know to whom he refers – that foreign magic must be destroyed. So he is attacking the railway line.'

'Tell him that I find his arguments interesting, but that I am not aware of a new government in China or a change of policy in the railway board. Tell him also that I am surprised that he speaks of the railway in such a superstitious manner.'

Zhang listened carefully to Charlie's translation, and calmly gave his reply. Whatever it was angered Charlie who snapped something back at him. The workers near Zhang began to murmur, but Zhang raised his arms in the air to quieten them. When he spoke again, his words were hard and deliberate, and what he said seemed to infuriate Charlie even more – but Herr Fischer touched his arm gently. 'Just interpret for me, Charlie. There's a good fellow.'

'This insolent man spoke disrespectfully of the railway board and accused His Excellency the Minister Li Hung-chang of being a traitor to the Dragon Throne. I told him that if there are any traitors they are turtle's eggs like himself and those who are sabotaging the reconstruction of our country.'

'That was brave of you, Charlie, but in the present circumstances I suggest we make our remarks more moderate. What else did he say?'

'He says that he is working under the orders of the *Yamen* itself. I know that is a lie. He and his men have been listening to the ignorant peasants who seek to throw back our new civilisation and destroy all that is good in our country.'

'Nevertheless, Charlie, please keep that opinion to yourself and maintain a strictly interpretative role. Tell Mr Zhang that I hear him, but that as the director of this railway section I need to see any new orders in writing. And tell him that if such orders have been delivered to the Mandarin, we should wait until they are produced before we embark on any action we may later regret. Tell him that no great damage has been done yet, no harm done, I repeat, and that I respectfully request that he gives orders to his men to desist from their present work until the situation is clarified. That is reasonable, do you not think, *ja*?'

Rather grudgingly, Charlie translated, although his tone still appeared hostile to Herr Fischer's ears. Zhang Haobin, however, nodded at each of Herr Fischer's points, then turned to consult some of the other workers around him. A lively debate ensued.

'What are they saying?'

'It's all treason,' sneered Charlie. 'They're talking about the Boxers – the Harmonious Fists. It appears there was some sort of visitation in their camp last night. Apparently it is the gods telling them to do this,' he said sarcastically. He listened as Zhang, having reached some sort of consensus of opinion with his men, spoke again. 'As I thought,' he said. 'Sheer superstition. They claim that they have orders from a higher authority even than the temporal powers. Gods came down to talk to them, would you believe, and who can disobey the orders of the gods? Even so he claims that the *yamen* is in full agreement with these heavenly instructions. One of these acrobats-turned-gods apparently produced a memorial with the Mandarin's seal on it. It is comical, is it not?'

'So are we to wait until this memorial is produced?'

'No, the orders of the gods are good enough for them. I will ask them which god is greater than our Emperor on the Dragon Throne, who is in daily communication with the Jade Emperor in Heaven. And remind them that to disobey him is treason.'

'No, Charlie,' said Fischer, but he could not prevent him. There was an even louder growl from the crowd and this time even Zhang did not try to pacify them. He barked something back that caused Charlie to laugh. 'He says the Jade Emperor himself was one of the gods who came down to the coolies' camp last night and that he heard him with his own ears.' Charlie snarled three words that Herr Fischer recognised: 'Liar!' 'Traitor!' and 'Turtle's egg!'

Fischer watched with horror as a dogspike arced out of the crowd, descending it seemed to him in slow motion and hitting Charlie on the head. He fumbled with his gun but his arms were pinioned from behind. He heard a shot. Obviously Bowers had been quicker off the mark but he, too, was pinioned. Fischer caught a brief glimpse of blood dripping down to the black beard as he hung between the arms of two burly navvies. Then he saw the crowbars rising and falling, rising and falling. He thought he was imagining things. He distinctly saw Charlie's smiling face rising up above the knot of people who were trying to murder him. Then it continued to rise, higher into the air, and Fischer realised that they had decapitated him and stuck his head on one of the crowbars.

Now he heard the full roar of a crowd. The silence had broken.

He could not take his eyes away from the head of Charlie, which, moving on the end of the pole, seemed as animate as if it had been alive. His young companion seemed to have recovered from his bad temper and his lips were moving in what could have been one of his ironic remarks about the superstition and follies of his fellow countrymen. Then Fischer realised that it was not the tongue moving, but light glinting on the blood that was dribbling from the gaping mouth. He heard an insistent voice in his ear, and saw the foreman, Zhang Haobin, speaking to him urgently, but he could not understand the words. Zhang nodded in melancholy frustration. He closed his eyes as if trying to remember something, then he said in broken English: 'You. Master. Belong camp,' and then, patting the stubbled pate of his head to help him remember the right word, 'Friend,' he finished, pointing at Fischer's chest, then his own.

Fischer's first reaction was one of anger. How dare this foreman call himself a friend? He had just murdered, or allowed his men to murder, in front of his very eyes the best companion he had ever had. A growling sound came from his throat, and his vole's face snarled, and he struggled in his captors' arms, wanting to tear with his nails and scratch . . . Then he remembered Bowers and their helpless position. And he realised that the anxious face in front of him murmuring, 'Friend,' seemed genuinely to want to help them.

'Do what you will,' he muttered, no longer struggling against those who constrained him, shaken and overcome by an overpowering wave of grief for Charlie. He was hardly aware of the rough but not unkindly hands steering him and Bowers back through the crowd, and up the hill again, towards the office tent from which they had started.

It was the familiarity of his tables and charts that brought him back to reality, and recalled him to his sense of duty. His conscience told him that he was an engineer and that he must do something practical. A decision to bathe and bind the wound on Bowers's temple was an easy one to make and implement. Coming up with a plan for what to do after that, however, he realised with some alarm, was beyond his experience, and he understood just how much he had come to rely on Charlie for all matters relating to the Chinese. Without Charlie he could not even speak to anyone. He was worse than deaf or dumb. A prisoner in his own tent, Herr Fischer suddenly comprehended that the only person who might be able to help him was Henry Manners.

The ride had not been the success Henry had hoped. The sights and sensations were not enough to bring the boy out of his shell. Hiram had sat on his pony oblivious of the countryside through which they were passing. Fan Yimei had tried hard to help by describing an excursion with her father as a child, in which he had told her the names of all the flowers and shrubs and what sort of brush-strokes he would use to paint them, and how father and daughter had later run along the path imitating the various birds that skimmed then as now over the ripening fields. Hiram had merely nodded; the thin line of his mouth stayed clenched and the blank eyes in the white face reflected nothing but the nightmares that continued to haunt him. After a while Fan Yimei herself retreated into melancholy introspection. The picnic by the riverbank passed in silence.

On the ride back Henry had tried to excite them with the prospects of their new life in Tientsin. He would give them a letter to pass to his friend, George Detring, manager of the Astor House Hotel, who would install them in one of his best suites and look after them until Manners himself had finished what he had to do in Shishan. Then he would rejoin them and find them a house of their own in the city. That would not be long. His business with Major Lin was nearly concluded. Detring, in the meanwhile, could assist Hiram to find a place in the prestigious Tientsin grammar school. As friends of Manners they would be treated with honour and respect. Fan Yimei, he joked, could even promenade with the English ladies in Victoria Park, and they would look at her over their fans, imagining that she must be some exotic princess of the blood, exiled to Tientsin after a mysterious court intrigue.

His humour had fallen flat.

Neither did Henry's remarks cheer Fan Yimei. Talk of English ladies had only reminded her of Helen Frances. She had no illusions of what life would be like as the mistress of a foreigner, despised by both races. She knew that, one day, he would tire of her. She wondered if he had already done so. For the two nights in the strange tent she had lain awake waiting for him to come to her, longing for the protection of his arms even though she knew he did not love her as he loved the red-haired girl. She had not understood why he had remained outside on a servant's bed next to Hiram. She had told herself that it was because Ma Na Si was concerned for the boy and did not wish to leave him alone with his devils. That would be characteristic of his nobility and generosity. She did not feel that he owed anything to her. He had repaid his part of the bargain, and more besides. Rather, she owed him a life, however he wished to tax her for it. Nothing was worse than the hell from which he had rescued her. If she continued to live, it would be on whatever terms he demanded. Even if he did what he threatened, and made her free.

In the meanwhile she could help to look after the boy. As a fellow victim of Ren Ren she was at least qualified to do that. She believed that she could reach him: she had done so once before when she had tended his wounds after his beating by the Japanese. She understood the anguish he was undergoing now, and the causes. She remembered her own nights as a girl in the Palace of Heavenly Pleasure, after the rapes and the beatings and those other humiliations she could hardly bear to recall. She felt again the incomprehension of the child who has been abandoned, that sense of guilt and self-loathing, for no child believes that the evil which happens to it is undeserved. She lived again that greatest shame of all, the closely guarded secret known only to the tortured and the damned and that no time can efface or burying obscure. She knew the love of the tortured for the torturer – the punisher – even as he inflicts his pain. That terrible intimacy, longed for as much as feared. She knew Hiram's shame, because she herself had shared it: they had both been lovers of Ren Ren. Deep, deep inside them, they shared that shame.

They rode in silence through the chattering summer countryside each locked in their own thoughts. Preoccupied as they were they did not notice the quiet of the railway camp, and only when no *mafu*s turned out to meet them at the stables did Henry grasp that something was very wrong.

'Hiram,' he said, 'I want you to stay here and look after Fan Yimei. If I'm not back in ten minutes, or if you sense anything out of order at all, I want you to get back on your ponies and ride, as hard as you can, away from here. Make for the doctor's house – you remember the way we came – but stay hidden. Ride off the road where possible. Will you do that for me?'

The two of them were gazing at him in astonishment. Henry grasped Hiram's hands, and looked urgently into his eyes. 'You're the man here, and you've a lady to protect. I don't know what's going on but I have to find out what's happened to Herr Fischer and the others. I'll probably be back before you know it – but if I don't come in ten minutes, will you do as I asked?'

For the first time since his rescue there was a spark of animation in Hiram's eyes. 'Yes, sir,' he said hesitantly.

'Good man.' He embraced him, then kissed Fan Yimei on the fore-head. 'You're to stay with Hiram, whatever happens,' he ordered. 'Do you understand?' She nodded, her eyes contemplating him steadily.

'And take this,' he said to Hiram, pulling his revolver from its holster. 'This is the safety-catch. You click it, so. Only use it if you have to – but remember my promise. Neither of you is ever, ever going back to that house.'

He ran to the tent-lines. He peered cautiously round the corner of the first tent, then stepped lightly over the guy ropes and disappeared from their view.

Bowers was phlegmatically boiling the kettle on the tent stove. There was a bandage round his head, but he seemed none the worse for that. Herr Fischer was pacing up and down, mutter-ing in German. They had spent an hour and smoked six pipes between them discussing what they should do or, rather, Herr Fischer had come up with one inconceivable plan after another, and Bowers had watched him, occasionally shaking his head. When Fischer had exploded his last plan, and laid another curse on the head of the absent Manners, Bowers had suggested a cup of tea.

'If you'll excuse me, sir, for hesitating a view,' he said, when he had poured two strong cups, 'in situations like these it's Providence we'd best rely on. We've not been served badly so far. We have our lives, and there's not much even a bunch of coolies can do to break up a good engine manufactured in a York yard. So far so good, say I, barring of course the sad loss of your friend. While the three gentlemen standing outside the door have our guns I think it would be foolhardy to try anything too adventurous, so I say, let's wait and see what happens.'

'But what can we do?' Fischer waved his hands. 'We are prisoners of murderers and crazy men who believe in demons.'

'Yes, sir, it's not pleasant – but you did mention Mr Manners, sir, as being a resourceful fellow. And if there is a government in Shishan still I doubt that they'll take too kindly to the smashing up of state property. I dare say it'll all turn out right in the end, sir, if we give it time.'

'But where is Manners?' Herr Fischer squeaked in frustration. 'I tell you, he is picnicking. That is what he is doing. Picnicking with whores. He may be hours.'

He was startled to see the enigmatic Mr Bowers chuckle. 'Excuse me, Mr Bowers, I see nothing humorous either in our situation or in what I said.'

'No, sir, forgive me.' Bowers coughed, his face still red with mirth. 'I was only thinking how the Lord will sometimes pick the strangest instruments to work his wondrous ways.'

And it was rather in the fashion of a winged saviour or a *deus ex machina* at the end of a melodrama that, a few moments afterwards, Henry Manners appeared. The two engineers gaped as the tent flaps shook and a figure wearing a coolie's hat and a railway worker's straw raincoat straightened to reveal itself as the English *Junker*. Under his arm were three Remington rifles, one of which he threw casually to Mr Bowers and another to Fischer.

'Gentlemen,' he said. 'Excuse my attire. English serge is a little conspicuous today. I suggest you follow my example.' He reached behind him through the tent flap and pulled in a bundle of clothes. 'The three guards at the door are . . . resting, shall I say?, and won't miss their garments, but we don't want to be here when they wake. Coast seems clear otherwise, and I have some saddled horses at the stable.'

'But my railway camp, Mr Manners? Are you suggesting I abandon it?'

'Yes, Herr Fischer, considering that it has been overrun by your workers and is already being redecorated with the heads of some of your colleagues.'

'Heads? My Charlie was brutally murdered but—'

'It seems others have shared his fate. I recognised your stoker, Bowers. The grin on the end of his pole is nearly as cheerful as Charlie's. It's getting bloody out there, gentlemen. Very bloody.'

The black-bearded engineer bowed his head, but his face was steady when he looked up again. 'There's no chance of us getting to the engine, sir?' he asked. 'If we could only drive that away . . .'

'Sorry, Bowers, it's an ant's nest out there. Come on, Captain Fischer, your ship is sinking fast. It's time for you to abandon the poop deck. Sensible rats should be scampering. Now. Before it's too late.'

But it was already too late, as they found out before they left the tent.

Hiram saw all that happened. When he and Fan Yimei had noticed the dust on the hill and heard the thunder of galloping horses approaching, Fan Yimei had wanted to return to the camp to warn Henry. He had tried to prevent her but she had beaten the rump of her mare with her stick and lurched off in the direction of the tent lines. Hiram, grasping for her reins, fell off his own horse, which bolted. So he had been lying on the ground, invisible behind a rock, when the stream of uniformed cavalry had poured out of the trees, rapidly overtaking Fan Yimei, whose bridle was quickly caught and her pell-mell canter halted. The officer commanding the troop, an elegant man with a cruel, hawk-like face, had trotted his white stallion up to her, and the two of them had gazed at each other for some time, he impassively, she with a look of defiance mixed with resignation, her eyes wild. In a quick movement the man had lashed at her with his cane, leaving a thin red mark on her white cheek. Then he had snapped an order, and two soldiers moved to take their positions on either side of her. Guarded thus, she could do nothing but follow the column as it continued its ride to the camp.

Hiram watched the dust settle as the horses disappeared among the tents. He had learned as a child, playing with the Shishan street urchins, how to move silently and inconspicuously. With great care he followed in the same route that Mr Manners had taken earlier, keeping within the shadows of the tents and crawling on his belly across the open spaces. He found himself a hiding-place among a pile of tin cans that had originally contained diesel oil and were now left abandoned. From here he had a good view of the administration tent. Here the soldiers had halted in a fan, their carbines levelled at the entrance. Behind them milled several hundred railway workers, peering to see what was going on. The hawk-faced officer had dismounted and was talking to a grizzled railwayman, who seemed to be in authority. He was pointing in turn at the entrance to the tent and to three naked coolies sitting sheepishly on the ground rubbing sore heads. Hiram was relieved to see Fan Yimei still sitting on her pony with her two guards, one of whom was holding an umbrella over her head against the strong sunshine.

He watched as the officer strolled towards the entrance of the tent, and called loudly, 'Ma Na Si.'

A conversation followed, which he could not make out. The officer returned to his line of horsemen and gave an order. One of the soldiers fired his carbine into the air. The sharp crack echoed round the still camp, followed by a murmur from the assembled railway workers. The officer waited for about a minute, then barked another order. The soldier fired his carbine towards the top of the tent. The bullet nicked the metal tent pole and there was a clanging sound as it ricocheted.

The tent flap opened and three men in Chinese peasant clothes stepped out. One was Mr Manners, the other Mr Fischer and the third was a tall, bearded man he had never seen before. They were holding rifles and, for a moment, Hiram thought that they were about to use them. He pulled the revolver from his belt and slipped off the safety-catch.

Then Mr Manners laughed and threw his rifle on the ground. The others did the same. Quickly six soldiers ran forward and pinioned their arms.

The officer turned towards the crowd and raised his voice in what sounded like a proclamation. Hiram could make out the words 'safe conduct' and 'protection'.

Mr Manners was smiling nonchalantly at his captors. Then he looked in the direction of Fan Yimei and started. Her face expressed alarm and she called something Hiram could not hear. Mr Manners tried to struggle out of the grasp of the two men holding him.

The hawk-faced officer looked slowly from one to the other. His lips curled in a lopsided sneer. He walked towards Mr Manners, his sabre furrowing the sand behind him, took a rifle from one of the soldiers, rammed the butt into his belly, and again, down on his head as he fell. Deliberately he kicked Mr Manners in the side, in the face, and brought the gun butt with full force down on the back of his head.

Hiram felt hot tears stinging his eyes. He pointed the revolver at the officer's back, but the barrel shook, wavered, and inclined to the ground. He stifled a sob of anger and shame, but he could not take away his eyes.

The officer handed over the task of beating Mr Manners to his men. The two soldiers picked him up and he hung in their arms while a stocky sergeant punched him. His face was a mask of blood and bruises. They continued long after he was unconscious. The crowd watched in silence, and the only sounds were the thump of the blows and whimpers from Fan Yimei, who was being held back by her captors. The officer watched sardonically.

After an eternity the officer gave the order to stop. There was no visible life in the body. They left it lying in bloody contortion where it had fallen on the sand.

The two other foreigners had watched in scared silence. The officer now moved towards them and bowed. He gave orders that they should be released from the grip of the soldiers. Two horses were brought for them, and a small company was despatched to ride off with them in the direction of Shishan.

The officer spent some time more in conversation with the railway foreman. Orders were given for the crowd to disperse, and soldiers were sent in the direction of the makeshift station. After an hour the troopers who were left prepared to saddle up. As an afterthought the body of Henry Manners was thrown over one of the troopers' saddles where it hung limp and lifeless. The cold-faced officer rode out of the camp with his men behind him. He paid no attention to Fan Yimei, still escorted by her two guards at the back of the column. She had long ceased crying and her face was now as cold and expressionless as his.

When he judged that the coast was clear Hiram moved silently from his hiding-place, leaving the way he had come. Without a horse he had no need to travel by the road, and within minutes he was skirting a course through the millet fields in the direction of the town.

Nellie had coped magnificently, thought Airton. She never ceased to amaze him and, not for the first time, he thanked Providence for bestowing on him such an indispensable helpmate. A lesser woman – he was no expert on the sex and much of his knowledge was drawn from his collection of romantic novels – would have pleaded the vapours and withdrawn to her boudoir. Not that there was a boudoir to go to in such a relatively small house, but she might have panicked, as he nearly did, when Zhang Erhao burst in on them with the dreadful news. Shortly afterwards Frank Delamere's body had been brought, wrapped in sacking and tied to a handcart, to the mission gates.

Airton and Sister Caterina had been in the middle of a complicated operation to remove the swollen appendix of a farmer, so it had fallen to Nellie to face down the curious crowd that had followed the corpse from the town. With Ah Lee's and Zhang Erhao's help she had separated the handcart from the people peering and touching the bloodstained sacking and pull it into the courtyard, after which she had single-handedly drawn the heavy bars to lock the gates. She had first, however, had the presence of mind to notice Frank's two merchant friends, Lu Jincai and Jin Shangui, standing irresolutely on the edge of the crowd. They had organised the passage of the body from the town but now they were both in a state of nervous exhaustion. She had pulled them into the compound, sat them down in the hospital waiting room and ordered Ah Sun quickly to prepare them some tea. Leaving Frank – what could she do for him? – she saw that the greater need was to comfort his two friends, so she had sat between them, holding their hands, until the doctor had finished with his patient. In any other circumstances the two Confucian gentlemen would have run a mile before allowing themselves to be touched in such an intimate fashion by a foreign woman, but so great was their shock and relief to be away from the mob that they were unprotesting, and with their free hands dutifully sipped their tea.

That all seemed a long time ago now, and much had happened since, but he vividly recalled the curious scene, and the disbelief, and shock, when Lu Jincai, recovering his presence of mind and a little of his dignity, pulled from inside his robe a package wrapped in grey silk, which he untied to reveal an axe with a red tassel and told them that this was the weapon that had killed Mr Delamere. Thinking back, the doctor realised that that was also the moment when he knew that their lives and their circumstances in Shishan would never be the same.

He had repressed the chill that coursed down his neck and spine and asked the question to which he already knew the answer: 'That's a Boxer weapon?'

'Yes, Daifu,' said Lu Jincai quietly.

'So they are in Shishan?'

Lu Jincai nodded. Jin Shangui was cleaning his spectacles with a silk handkerchief he had pulled from his sleeve.

'Well, what's the Mandarin doing about it?' he asked, a little over-belligerently.

There was no reply. The two merchants looked down at the floor.

'I see,' said Airton. Then reason revolted in him, and he spoke angrily: 'No, I don't see,' he said. 'We're talking of murder here, bloody murder, of a foreigner. The Mandarin has no truck with Boxers. What's he going to do about it?'

The merchants remained silent. Jin Shangui shrugged. Airton felt his wife's hand on his knee. 'Calmly, Edward,' she whispered. 'These good men are not to blame.'

Lu Jincai had a sad smile on his handsome face. 'Shangui and I have feared this for some time,' he said. 'Who knows why the world should go through cycles of madness, but Fate metes them out to each generation. Now we must all be prepared to face . . . difficulties. Great difficulties. This is only the beginning, Daifu. We must be thankful that the suffering of our dear friend, De Falang, was not great. Truly, he would have known little pain. Perhaps a little surprise, before the end.' His smile broadened affectionately. 'In truth, he was a little intoxicated at the time. I believe that the gods were merciful to him as they are to great, simple men whom they love. Who knows? We who face perhaps a more terrible future may one day envy him that quick and easy end. I am speaking to you what is in my heart, Daifu.'

Airton cleared his throat. His cheeks were hot and he felt a sentimental tear forming in his eye as he thought of Frank, dying alone in the sand.

'Your words are hard,' he said, 'but I think that poor Delamere was lucky in his friends.'

'We may have to answer for that one day,' said Lu quietly. 'These are not understanding times.'

'But you are Chinese,' said Airton. 'Surely the Boxers are only directing their cruelties against foreigners?'

'This is China, Daifu. We reserve our greater cruelties for other Chinese. It is our way. It has always been our way.'

'Then you were brave to come here,' said Airton, when he had collected his emotions.

'De Falang was our friend,' said Jin Shangui simply. He had finished cleaning his spectacles, but they seemed to mist up again as soon as he settled them on his face.

They had saddled the children's ponies for the two merchants to ride back to Shishan. Lu Jincai thanked the doctor for his consideration and promised to return them when he could. As they left, by a back way to avoid the small crowd that was still hanging about the front gate, Lu Jincai had warned the doctor not to trust anyone, even his servants. 'It is the times,' he said. 'There will be pressures on every man.' There had been something final in their farewells.

Airton and Nellie had returned with some trepidation to the first courtyard where Frank's body still waited on the cart. Flies were buzzing over the bloodstained sacking, although Ah Lee was trying vainly to wave them away. It took a few moments for Airton to determine what he had to do.

He had blocked his mind to the thought of how they would break the news to Helen Frances in her sick condition, and to Tom who was recovering from his wounds. First they would have to find somewhere to lay out the body and presumably tidy up the damage of the wounds and prepare Frank for burial. Well, Caterina could help with that. They had had enough experience together of preparing corpses during the plague. He was concerned about the nun, however. It was days since they had had any news of Sister Elena, and now with this murder, it would be a wonder if Caterina did not anticipate the worst for her colleague, whose continued disappearance was beginning to be worrisome. Well, that was another problem with which he would have to deal in due course. He found himself comforted suddenly by the fact that Burton Fielding had arrived in the early hours of the morning. He was in the house with the children, resting after his hard journey. At least there was a man he could rely on, a practical man of action, inured to hardships in the Wild West. They would discuss together this evening how they would approach the Mandarin for help. They might perhaps seek the protection of some of his soldiers to guard the mission or at least to secure his aid in evacuating the women and children to Tientsin, should that be necessary . . . But all that would come later. First he had to deal with Frank Delamere. Poor, poor drunken Frank, who had finally had a drop too much. He was angry with himself that he could even think of such a joke but, to his shame, he was beginning to feel a little lightheaded. Frank's murder had undermined his certainty about their comfortable existence. The horror of it, coupled with Lu Jincai's ominous forebodings about Boxers and the Mandarin's diminishing control of his city, had unnerved him, had confirmed his own fears after his unsatisfactory experience in the Mandarin's court that morning, not to mention his nagging worry about Sister Elena, and the fact that Tom lay in one ward wounded by gunshots and Helen Frances lay in another fighting the effects of opium addiction. All these formed a tableau that had all the characteristics of a bad dream.

He had not had time even to unwrap the sacking covering Frank's body before he heard a loud banging at the mission gate. Leaving Caterina he had run down the corridors of the hospital in the evening's waning light to find that Nellie and Burton Fielding were there before him. Ah Lee and Zhang Erhao were standing by the bars obviously scared to open them. 'Open in the name of the *yamen*,' he heard from outside, followed by another thunderous pounding on the doors.

'What do you think?' he asked Fielding.

'If the man's saying open in the name of the *yamen* I think you'd better do just that,' was the laconic reply.

'You're right,' said the doctor, feeling a sudden spurt of hope. 'It might be a message from the Mandarin. About the murder. Maybe they're starting an investigation after all.'

'If you don't open up you won't find out,' said Fielding.

'Do you think it might be the Mandarin himself?' said the doctor, gesturing to his servants to pull back the bars.

But it was not the Mandarin. It was Septimus Millward, and his family, and another unruly crowd pelting the American missionaries with mud.

A *yamen* runner, whom he did not recognise, was proffering a document for him to sign. 'You are the *daifu* Ai Dun? We are handing over these incendiaries and criminals for your safe-keeping pending their trial. His Excellency the Mandarin has decided that all ocean barbarians are to be housed together until the emergency in the city is over.'

'Emergency? What emergency?' spluttered the doctor – but the man did not answer, only proffering the piece of paper, brush and ink for the doctor to sign his name.

'Better do as he says,' said Fielding, observing the Millwards warding off the missiles of mud and vegetables, 'or before long they'll be so filthy you won't have enough bath-water to clean them all – and I guess they're coming in anyway, whether we like it or not. Strange,' he added, 'I was going up to town to see them myself tomorrow. Reckon the mountain's come to Muhammed instead.'

Again it was Nellie who took the situation in hand. As soon as the gates were safely closed, the Millwards, ignoring their deliverers, dropped to their knees in the courtyard. Septimus, the extremely soiled bandage round his head resembling a Bacchanalian wreath because of all the cabbage and spinach leaves hanging from it, raised his arms heavenwards and loudly thanked the Almighty for preserving His chosen ones, adding for good measure a few invocations for the Lord of Hosts to smite the ungodly and the depraved.

Nellie was having no truck with this. 'Now, come on, you,' she cried sternly, pulling a surprised Septimus by his beard. 'Up you get, and your unholy brood with you. It's baths and beds for the lot of you, if you are to be my house guests. You can do all the praying you like, but only after I've put a hot meal inside you first. Do you hear? My goodness, the state of those poor wee bairns. It's enough to break your heart.'

And perhaps the strangest event on that unsettling afternoon was that the Millwards meekly followed her.

The doctor and Burton Fielding had remained alone in the court-yard. Neither spoke for a while, then Fielding reached into his pocket for his case of cheroots. 'Enjoy this one out, Doctor. We'll have to make the rest of them last.'

'What do you mean, Fielding?'

'I mean the situation's becoming pretty clear-cut. Seems we're expected to hole up in Fort Laramie with the women and children while the redskins rampage on the warpath outside. Trouble is, I don't see any US cavalry coming to rescue us. And don't repeat that last remark to the ladies, will you?'

'I simply cannot believe that the Mandarin would—'

'You may be correct. You know the man and I don't . . . But I don't think we can be certain that the Mandarin's in a position to help us, even if he wants to. My advice to you, Doctor, in a situation like this, is to be self-reliant, cut your losses. I say first light tomorrow we load our loved ones on to our wagons and high tail it to the railway camp, before that engine I came in on this morning steams back to Tientsin. When it does leave we want to be on it.'

'You're not serious? My dear Fielding, that sounds like the counsel of panic. And how can we just leave? I have sick here who need to be tended. It's unthinkable.'

'You know your duty, Doctor. I know mine. If it was my kith and kin I know what I would do. Thank goodness my responsibility lies only with that misguided family who've just arrived here. I was coming here to take them out anyway. The board's decided they're a menace to themselves and the community at large so I'll be leaving, with the Millwards, even if I have to tie them up to make them go. I'd intended to stay longer but there it is. Guess it's up to your own conscience what you decide to do.'

'Fielding, Fielding . . .' Airton did not know what to say. He felt that he was drowning in the rush of events and decisions. 'Even the Millwards have their dependants. What about all the orphans in their mission?'

'If anyone's looking after them it's not the Millwards, is it? Mandarin's seen to that by sending them over here. Look, Doctor, it comes to the point where you can only do what you can do. In desperate situations you must make hard decisions. If you can't save everybody you save whom you can.'

'I suppose I'm not convinced yet how desperate our position has become. I could ask Nellie if she and the children . . . But, then, there's also Helen Frances and Tom. Helen Frances is really in no state to travel. And Nellie wouldn't leave her. She'd refuse flat. I know her. So would Tom. And then there are all my Chinese patients . . .'

'Hard decisions, Doctor. Hard decisions,' murmured Fielding, puffing on his cheroot.

Within two hours there was another banging on the mission gates, causing yet more alarm in the hospital. This time Lin's troopers were bringing in Herr Fischer and Mr Bowers 'for their protection'. Nellie, Fielding and the doctor had taken the two frightened men up to the house and listened in silence to their terrible story, too numbed now by the earlier events of the day to show any undue reaction or surprise. Herr Fischer had broken down in tears when he had tried to describe the death of Charlie. The news that Henry Manners had also apparently been beaten to death by Major Lin only elicited a sad shake of the head from the doctor, while Nellie took his hand and squeezed it with the gentlest pressure. After the two men had told their tale, drunk their glass, and finished the bowl of soup Nellie had produced for them, there was little more conversation. They were all exhausted and decisions of any kind could be left until the morning. For now it was enough to know that they were trapped in Shishan.

There is a natural safety valve in civilised society that makes people cling to the idea and the forms of normality even in the most impossible circumstances. Two days after the death of Frank, the unlooked-for arrival of the Millwards and the railway engineers, Nellie was managing her extended household as if she were conducting a house party. As the doctor sat at the writing desk in his study preparing his memorial to the *yamen* he could hear the sounds of children playing in the corridors, and from the kitchens came the clatter of pans and the usual shrill arguments between Ah Lee and Ah Sun. The comforting smell of stew wafted into his study.

As proud as he was of Nellie, he also felt a great paternal pride in his two children. who had not shown any rancour at having to give over their playroom to the Millward family. Here, for the first time ever perhaps, the Americans were not living in squalor. They had adapted quickly to Nellie's punctilious regime of aired mattresses and blankets, stowed clothes and regular inspections, Nellie holding a big feather duster and Laetitia following meekly behind in her magisterial wake. It had been touching to see the Millward children, on the first morning after their arrival, looking at George and Jenny's toys stacked on the shelves, half with wonder and longing, half with fear as their eyes turned to their father reading his Bible in the corner.

George and Jenny had rapidly sized up the situation. There was a moment's uncomfortable silence after the doctor had introduced them. Then George, with a whoop, had lifted the smallest Millward child on to the rocking horse where she sat blinking behind her spectacles. After a few furious rocks she was gurgling with delight. Jenny had handed out dolls to the girls and George had unpacked his box of toy soldiers for the boys. Laetitia had continued to look nervously at her husband, but Septimus remained immersed in his reading. That the children did not know what to do with the dolls and the soldiers made no difference to George and Jenny. Their patience and good nature had been endless, and now there were signs of a growing friendship between some of the older children. Hence the noise in the corridor. Nellie and Airton had been prepared for some eruption or protest from Millward, but the man seemed to have withdrawn into his own world. He spent the day turning the pages of his Bible, eating his meals in his room. Nellie felt she had achieved a small victory when, on the afternoon of the second day, Laetitia had offered hesitantly to help her with the housekeeping.

Altogether things had gone better than expected, thought Airton. The general situation remained uncertain, but at least there was order, and even a degree of cheerfulness, in their little world.

Things had seemed black on the morning after the 'Day of Catastrophe' as Fischer had described it, in his curiously pompous English. Airton had risen early and hurried through his rounds in the hospital. He had been relieved to see that the appendix patient was in good condition and he was pleased by Tom's fast recovery. Tom was already itching to be allowed out of bed and frantic with curiosity about the noise and commotion he had heard the day before. The doctor had taken the decision there and then to tell him the truth about everything that had happened. He was bound to find out sooner or later. He had even told Tom about Helen Frances, keeping none of the facts from him. Tom had taken it like a man. When he heard that Frank had been murdered he bowed his head. Otherwise he showed no sign of emotion. He listened with a stony face as the doctor described Helen Frances's affair with Manners, her pregnancy and her drug addiction. It did not seem to surprise him. He merely nodded at each unpleasant detail. There had been no way to sugar the pill so the doctor's own telling had been precise, even cold, and Tom had seemed to respond in the same vein. He only asked two questions after the doctor had finished.

'And how is HF? Will she recover?'

The doctor had told him that it was too early to say. She was still undergoing treatment for withdrawal. She had suffered, but she was strong, and he saw no reason why she should not conquer her addiction, given time and care. She was still weak and he would not allow her to be disturbed. The baby was growing healthily inside her.

'I'm pleased to hear it,' Tom said shortly. 'She's lucky to be in the care of a good doctor.' Then came his second question, in a voice so calm it had almost scared Airton: 'And the father? Manners? He is dead, you say?'

'He was beaten to death, Tom.'

'You know that for a fact?'

'That's what Herr Fischer told us. He and Bowers saw it happen.'

'Thank you, Doctor. I would like to rest now. I'll join you in the house in a while.'

'Tom, I don't think you should move from the ward until you have . . .'

But something in the young man's expression caused the doctor quietly to withdraw. And, of course, Nellie had been angry when he told her that Tom was now in possession of all the facts. She had accused him of being a man with no common sense or sensibility, and he had surprised himself by rounding on her: 'Hold your tongue, woman. Do you not yet understand the situation we are in? Tom, like all of us, must come to terms with this emergency, and he won't do so if we continue to mollycoddle him.' And he had ordered her to get on with her house chores while the men held a council. He had felt a glow of satisfaction when she had surrendered to him with 'Well, you know best.' He could not remember when he had stood up to his wife in this way before. It was therefore with an unfamiliar sense of authority and resolve that he stepped into the dining room, where Fischer, Fielding and Bowers were finishing their breakfast, and, in as objective terms as he could, laid out the situation as he saw it.

'Gentlemen,' he told them, 'you all know what happened yesterday, and we are naturally alarmed, but there is even more that we don't know. Obviously there is something seriously amiss in the city of Shishan. Delamere's death proves that the Boxers are here and powerful enough for the Mandarin to want to gather all of us together for our protection. Yes, protection. That's what the officials who brought you here told us. As you pointed out to me last night, Fielding, I know the Mandarin and I have no reason to believe that he is not the friend to us that he has always been. I believe him when he says he wants to protect us. I also believe that the sensible course is not to do anything rash, like trying to escape from here, as some of us may have been thinking.'

At this point he looked at Fielding, who smiled and waved his pipe for him to continue.

'How can we escape anyway? The railway line's closed to us and we don't have the wherewithal to set up a mule train. No, escape is impractical and not even desirable. We've all been in China for a long time and we've all had experience of these flare-ups. They blow over when authority reasserts control. In the meantime it's important for us to keep our heads.'

'Excuse me, Doctor,' Fielding interrupted, his features still humorous, 'in the circumstances that's a rather loaded phrase. It's keeping our heads that's of most concern to us all. Are we really just going to sit here and take what comes?'

'No, Fielding, I'm not proposing that we do nothing. I intend to write a letter to the Mandarin, a memorial as it were, expressing not only our dismay at the events that have taken place but also our willingness to support him in this crisis, assuring him that he need expect nothing but co-operation from us. Believe me, gentlemen, the Mandarin, and only the Mandarin, has our interests at heart and he will be in a position to help us. This I firmly believe, as I believe that Providence will not forsake those who put their trust in her.'

'You're going to write a letter?' Fielding smiled. 'That's it?'

'Well, Fielding, have you a better suggestion?'

'It's not my mission,' said Fielding. 'All I can say is, if I see a chance of getting out of here I'll take it, Mandarin or no Mandarin.'

They were startled to hear a sound from the door. Tom, leaning on a crutch, his arm in a sling, made his way painfully to a chair and sighed as he slumped into it. 'Excuse me, gentlemen,' he said, 'I heard most of what's just been said. I believe the doctor told us, Mr Fielding, that there is no way out of here at the moment. In the circumstances I agree with what he proposes.'

'That we rely on a letter, and Providence?'

'You're an ordained minister, Mr Fielding, you know more about Providence than I do – but the doctor was talking about finding ways to persuade the civil authorities to come in on our side. And, yes, perhaps a few prayers might help in getting them to do so – but I have some other suggestions, Doctor, with your permission.'

'Yes, Tom?' said the doctor uncertainly.

'A letter to the Mandarin is a wise move, as you suggest, and I agree with you that, at the end of the day, order will probably be restored. But it does no harm to prepare for the worst – and it may be that it will take some time for the Mandarin to settle his problems with the Boxers. He has Major Lin and trained troops who are loyal to him . . .'

'The men who murdered Henry Manners,' said Fielding.

'Yes,' said Tom, 'but Manners was a man who made his own enemies. I don't know what personal quarrel may have existed between him and Major Lin. I know they had dealings, probably of a dubious kind. Some of us know what a man like Manners was capable of.'

'Even so, Tom.'

'All I'm saying is that there are no grounds to believe that Major Lin, whatever his shortcomings or personal enmities, will not remain loyal to the Mandarin – but even that in the short-term may not be enough for us. We must conceive of the possibility that the Boxers may attack us before civil order is restored.'

'Go on,' said Fielding.

'Well, I believe that if we're well prepared we should be able to hold them off. We've a good position on a hill. We have hunting rifles and ammunition. And plenty of stores. There's even a well in the garden for water.'

'Yes, but . . . this is a mission, Tom. A hospital.'

'It's a building, sir, and a building can be protected. It's brick, with a corrugated-iron roof so it's difficult to set afire. We can put bars over the windows and strengthen the doors. We can make firing-holes. Look, sir, I'm not saying anything like this will happen, but it does no harm to be prepared.'

'So it's to be Fort Laramie, after all!' laughed Fielding. 'What did I tell you?'

'I think the idea is preposterous,' said Airton. 'How can we turn our hospital into a fort? It's far too large.'

'We may have to abandon the hospital,' said Tom quietly. 'We can defend this house, however.'

'No, a thousand times no,' said Airton. 'I will never abandon my patients. And what will the women think, and the children, if they saw us preparing for a – for a war?'

'They'll think that you were a good shepherd defending his flock in the best way he can,' said Nellie, who, unnoticed, had also come into the room. 'And a brave man, my dear, as I've always known.'

'I'm for it,' said Bowers, breaking his silence for the first time. Herr Fischer, still in the depths of remorse for Charlie, nodded also.

'It may only be a precaution, sir,' said Tom. 'I also believe that the Mandarin will come to our aid long before we need to pick up a gun. You still need to write that letter, sir.'

'Guess it'll give us something to do to while away the time,' said Fielding. 'I haven't barricaded a cabin since the last Apache uprising in 'eighty-six.'

'Then you'll be able to instruct us on what to do, sir,' said Tom. 'Doctor, will you not consider the idea?'

And, of course, the doctor had agreed – and now he did not regret the decision. The preparations, as Fielding had said, had provided occupation and done much for morale. He could not believe that there was any need for them but he was used already to the bars on the windows that strengthened the shutters. It made little difference to their lives. In summer they had to keep the shutters closed anyway. In the meanwhile he had worked hard on his letter to the Mandarin, consulting his dictionaries to produce the most exact words, and racking his memory of the classics to turn out the perfect phrase.

He was content that the hospital functioned nearly as normal. Sister Caterina had insisted on staying on in her room there so that she could be close to the patients. Elena's disappearance still troubled her but he had to admit that she was coping marvellously, bustling through the wards with her usual cheeriness. If she felt any alarm for her friend she did not show it in public, although she spent most of her free time now in the chapel, praying.

Of course, the patients had become aware of the tensions. Some had made excuses and discharged themselves before they should have done so, and there were no new patients or outpatients – but that was only to be expected. He had been disappointed when his major-domo, Zhang Erhao, had failed to turn up for duty, but again he did not blame the man. He would certainly not be one to cast the first stone. On the other hand the good spirits of the patients who had stayed – many were Christian converts – had cheered them all. He had never seen Ah Lee or Ah Sun cope with their heavy duties with more enthusiasm. 'We are Christians and marching in the same army of Jesus,' Ah Lee had told him proudly, and he had clapped him on the back. The doctor was moved as much as he was amused. One of the droller episodes in the civil-defence preparations had been when Tom attempted to teach Ah Lee how to use a gun. After a while they had mutually decided that in Ah Lee's hands a kitchen chopper would be more effective.

It had taken the small community remarkably little time to adjust to their new conditions and to treat the firing-holes, the bales of grain packed against the doors and the barricades at every opening of the building as normal fixtures of the household.

There was a moment of sadness during the second afternoon when the doctor had conducted a simple burial service for Frank Delamere in the small plot in the garden where the Airtons had laid their own still-born child shortly after their arrival in Shishan. A rough wooden cross now stood next to Teddie's carved stone. Everyone had attended, except the one person who mattered: Frank's daughter, Helen Frances, did not know yet that that her father was dead. She was still in too precarious a state to be told. The children threw a wreath of wild flowers on to the grave with her name on it, and at one point in the service the doctor saw Nellie looking up at Helen Frances's boarded window with tears running down her cheeks – but there was no help for it. These were terrible times.

They had done their best in the circumstances. That was his only comfort. Airton was sure that Frank would have liked something grander than this furtive gathering round a grave in the hot Manchurian sun. Frank would have considered his brief address pedestrian, and probably pompous to boot. He conceded that Tom's remarks had been much more moving because of their simplicity. Frank was an old rogue, Tom had said, and he would have been a difficult father-in-law, but no man had been more generous and Tom loved him, as his daughter did. Tom would miss him, as a friend. That was all, but it was enough to cause wet eyes all round. Well, Frank and Airton had had their differences but underneath his disapproval he had had a genuine liking for the man too and he would also miss him. His eyes misted. Perhaps when this emergency was over, and Helen Frances was herself again, they might think of a more suitable memorial. A service in the cathedral in Tientsin, perhaps, with choirs and Ave Marias and a sung Nunc Dimittis or whatever else the papists preferred. That would be for happier days. Happier times.

Now all he could do was work on his own memorial for the Mandarin and soon he had lost himself in the task. When it was finished to his satisfaction he folded the closely written sheets and carefully placed them in a red envelope. The only problem he faced now was how to get it to the *yamen*, but that could be resolved tomorrow. One of the patients could take it, perhaps, for a bribe. In the meanwhile he was looking forward to this evening's entertainment. As in old times, Nellie and Herr Fischer had promised a concert with piano and violin, after dinner.

Nellie had given a competent rendition of one of Chopin's nocturnes, and afterwards Herr Fischer had surprised them with an impassioned playing of Brahms' Concerto for Violin. There had been tears in his eyes as he moved his bow over the 'Allegro non troppo', Nellie struggling slightly to follow the score. All could feel the intensity of his feelings as he mourned his Charlie. The doctor had tears in his own eyes by the time it came to the 'Adagio', and he noticed that Bowers was sitting upright on the sofa, the cup of tea in his hands untouched. It had been something of a relief when the heart-rending music was over, and Nellie and Fischer started on a rousing medley from *Carmen* to finish the evening. It was half-way through 'The Smugglers' Dance' that they heard the drums. So lost were they in the music that, for a moment, it seemed to be an unlooked-for accompaniment to the gypsy strains, but Nellie and Fischer froze, and then they all froze as the alien noise from outside seemed to thunder inside the very room.

Fielding was first to the window, peering through the firing-hole they had bored through the shutters, followed as quickly as his crutches could take him by Tom. Fielding silently relinquished his place to Tom.

'What is it, Fielding? What did you see?' asked Airton urgently.

'It's all black out there, Doctor. Maybe some movement. I don't know.'

'Quickly, Doctor, the door,' shouted Tom. 'It's your nun, Caterina. She's running to the house.'

Nellie, Airton and Bowers ran into the hall, and for long moments struggled with the bars and bolts. Outside they could hear the thumping of fists on the wood and Caterina's frightened calls. When the door was open the white-cowled figure fell weeping into Nellie's arms. Hurriedly Bowers and Airton locked the door again. In the few moments that it had been open the doctor had seen running figures on the lawn, and his blood chilled. 'Did you see, Bowers?' he whispered. 'The costumes. The turbans.'

'Aye,' said Bowers.

'Good Lord, Tom was right. They're here.'

'Aye,' said Bowers. 'Did you also notice the flames, sir? I imagine they've fired the hospital.'

'Oh, my God. Oh, my God.' Airton leaned against the wall. He saw two small figures at the end of the corridor, peering at him anxiously. 'Get back to your bedroom. At once,' he shouted angrily – more angrily than he had intended – and Jenny and George disappeared like scuttling rabbits.

'Oh, my God, my God,' he said.

'Aye,' said Bowers. 'Excuse me while I take my rifle, sir. I'll be covering the main bedroom,' he added.

In the living room Tom already had his rifle ready and was peering through the firing-hole. Fielding was nowhere to be seen. He had presumably taken his post in the dining room next door. Herr Fischer was administering a glass of brandy to Caterina, who was shaking in one of the armchairs. The drums thumped insistently outside.

'Edward, I'm taking the children to the playroom with the Millwards,' said Nellie. 'Perhaps you can bring Caterina along when she's had time to recover.' As she passed him she whispered, 'Don't question her now. She's in a terrible state of shock. They burst in on her at the hospital and, Edward, they're killing the patients. There was nothing she could do.' She slipped away.

Airton clenched his fists. This could surely not be happening – but there was Caterina, her peasant face contorted into an ugly mask of fear, and Tom was pushing his rifle through the firing-hole, cocking the bolt. 'Tom, what are you doing?' he cried.

'They're massing on the lawn, Doctor. It's difficult to see, but some are holding torches. There must be a hundred at least. Can't see any guns. Most are carrying swords and spears. I'm going to fire a warning shot.'

'My God, Tom, do you think that's wise?'

Tom ignored him. 'Fielding,' he shouted. 'I'm going to fire once. Into the air. Can you do the same?'

'Sure thing,' came the answering call.

'Bowers,' Tom yelled, 'hold your fire.'

'Aye,' came the distant answer.

The drum noise was suddenly extinguished by the two explosions and suddenly there was a smell of smoke in the air. The echoes died away and the pulsing sound of the drums resumed.

'What do you see, Fielding?' Tom called.

'They're staying, Tom. No, hold on . . . My God, some of them are beginning to dance.'

Airton felt an unreal sense of calm. This really was happening. Everything he had read about was true. 'It's martial arts, Tom,' he said. 'They're drawing down the powers of the gods into their own bodies. They think it makes them invulnerable to bullets.'

'Do they now?' said Tom. 'Fielding,' he shouted, 'Bowers, we're going to let them dance a bit more, then we'll show them what being invulnerable to bullets means.'

'You mean to fire on them, Tom? To kill them?'

'Yes, Doctor.' Tom turned to face him. 'They've set fire to the hospital and killed the patients. They'll do the same to us. What do you want to do? Negotiate with them?'

'No, Tom,' said Airton, making his decision. 'I believe that we have another rifle somewhere. Perhaps you can tell me where I would be most useful.'

'Thank you, sir,' said Tom. 'I was wrong to doubt you.' He clapped him on the back 'You'd better defend the kitchen door. See how the servants are getting on, while you're about it. Don't want the cook panicking and letting the enemy in. When you hear me firing you fire too. Aim low.'

Airton was ashamed that he had forgotten the servants till now. Quickly he ran the length of the corridor. He found Ah Sun crouching under the big kitchen table and Ah Lee standing by the boarded-up door his chopper at the ready. A delighted expression filled the cook's face when he saw that the doctor was holding a rifle. 'Oh, Master,' he said, 'so you have joined the army of Jesus too! We will die together and go straight to Paradise.'

'I hope we won't be doing that just yet,' said Airton, fitting a magazine to his rifle, and taking his position by the door.

It was the longest five minutes he had ever waited. Through the narrow firing-hole he saw the Boxers anticking on his lawn. He was surprised to find that he felt no hatred for them. If anything, they reminded him of the puppet displays of mythological heroes in the market, and the image of the fairground remained. He remembered the country shows of his youth. A part of him told him that when the time came it would be as easy to shoot at these mannikins as it had been to shoot coconuts off a stall. Another part of him saw the irony: here was a so-called man of God ready to inflict death on his fellow man – but then, almost to his own shame, another more pleasurable fantasy engaged him. How appropriate this was for a lover of western penny dreadfuls. He, Airton, the great romantic, had finally found his place behind the covered wagons of his imagination ready to defend his family against the redskins. The persistent thumping of the drums might have been Indian tom-toms.

Over the noise he heard a faint shout. It must be Tom giving the order to get ready. He squeezed his eyes to the sights, concentrating on a large figure in a tiger-skin costume brandishing an axe. His finger started its gentle pressure on the trigger. 'Dear Lord, forgive me,' the silent words formed.

He heard running feet, and Caterina's screaming voice. 'Hold fire, Doctor,' she cried. 'Mr Cabot has told me to tell you to hold fire.'

He pulled back, startled. 'But why, Caterina?'

'It's Major Lin. He has come with his troopers.'

Merciful God, he thought, the US cavalry after all, and the next thing he heard was the welcome sound of horses on the lawn.

'The Mandarin has promised you protection, and that will be given to you,' said Major Lin coldly. He was sitting astride his horse by the front door of the house. Behind him his troopers were fanned out keeping an eye on the Boxer braves who were now assembled in loose formations, watching in sinister silence. Airton, Fielding and Tom were standing on the porch holding tightly to their rifles. Out of the corner of his eye, Airton could make out Bowers's weapon protruding from his firing-hole. The whole scene was lit up garishly by the blaze of the hospital at the bottom of the hill. 'On what surety do we have that?' he asked.

'My surety,' said Lin. 'There is no other.'

'How can we believe you when your men allow these Boxers to remain armed after they have burned my hospital and killed my patients?'

'How we deal with the Boxers is a Chinese matter. It is unfortunate about your hospital. No doubt one day you will be compensated for the loss of your property. Is compensation not what you foreigners usually demand?' Lin's tone was mocking. 'As for the patients inside, I understand that they were Chinese. So that is also a Chinese matter and none of your concern.'

'I had a responsibility for them,' expostulated Airton. 'Those men butchered them.'

'You are wasting my time, Doctor. I am offering protection only to foreigners – under the terms of the extra-territoriality treaty.' Again there was sarcasm in his tone. 'Do you wish to hear my terms?'

'Terms?' said Airton. 'Go on.'

'First, you will hand to me all the weapons you are holding in this house. My men will search the house to make sure that none are concealed. We do not want any accidents to occur to yourselves or others. You will not need weapons because my men will be protecting you.'

'Go on.'

'Second, the protection I offer applies only to the foreigners in the house. Any Chinese you are concealing here must leave. At once.'

'Well, that's unacceptable. Is there any more?'

'You will undertake to obey the law that has been imposed in this emergency, and therefore will stay in this building – which is being protected – until further notice.'

'That's all?'

'That's all. My men will bring you provisions on a weekly basis. You may use the well in the garden once a day under supervision of my soldiers.'

'And if we do not accept your terms?'

'Then you will be treated like malefactors and any infringement of our emergency laws will be punished.'

'I see,' said Airton. 'Well, your terms are not acceptable – and as you have noticed, we have guns and you have guns so it seems as if there is to be a stand-off. At least I can undertake that any attempts you make to enforce your so-called emergency laws will be costly to you. Thank you, Major Lin, but we prefer to protect ourselves.'

Lin raised his arm in a signal to his men. After a moment Airton and the others saw the Boxers by the gate step aside. 'Oh, my God,' whispered Tom, 'he's brought his old cannons from the walls.'

They watched in shocked silence as the string of mules drawing the heavy field guns were whipped and pulled up the slope.

'I think that my guns are bigger than yours, Doctor,' said Major Lin. 'Do you wish me to give you a demonstration?'

'Checkmate,' muttered Fielding.

'No, Fielding,' hissed the doctor. 'He wants us to hand over Ah Lee and Ah Sun. We can't do that.'

'We can't fight artillery.'

'We'll have to. I will not . . . I will not . . . I cannot hand over my servants to be slaughtered. Let me talk to him. Major Lin,' he reverted to Chinese, 'we agree to all your conditions except one. We will not hand over our Chinese servants to you.'

Major Lin made a pretence of yawning. 'Then I withdraw my offer of protection,' he said. 'Good evening.' He drew up his reins.

'Listen, Major Lin. Please, I beg you. I have a memorial here, yes, here, you see.' With fumbling fingers he pulled from his jacket pocket the letter for the Mandarin. 'Please. Please give this to the Mandarin and let us – let us for the moment leave this matter of the Chinese in our house until he has made a considered decision. All the other terms we agree to. Even the weapons, but please consider. In the name of humanity.'

Major Lin examined the envelope uninterestedly, then slid it into his saddlebag. 'I already have my orders from the Mandarin,' he said.

'I'll tell you what I'll do. I'll pay you for them. A ransom. Yes, a ransom. I have money. Here.' Airton fumbled for his pocketbook. With his other hand he grasped at Lin's bridle in a desperate attempt to keep him from going. Suddenly he heard a familiar voice behind him. 'Master, please let us pass.' Ah Lee and Ah Sun were standing on the porch, bundles of possessions under their arms.

'Ah Lee.' He had tried to put anger into his voice, but it cracked. 'Get back into the house. That's an order. Ah Sun. Tell him.'

Ah Lee was smiling, although tears were running down his cheeks as they were also shining on Ah Sun's wrinkled features. 'Master velly stubborn,' he said, in his pidgin English. 'Think he velly good to poor Ah Lee and Ah Sun. But Master also velly mean man.' He shook his head comically. 'Velly low wages. Scottishman, always mean. Ah Lee belong better job, better master. Maybe find cook job in Heaven hiyah? Makee bacon flied egg for

Jesus. He velly good master. Ah Lee Ah Sun velly, velly happy belong Jesus.'

Ah Lee put down his bundle and embraced Airton. 'Lemember ol' fliend sometime?' he said simply. 'Better this way,' he added in Chinese. 'Look after Missy Nellie and Master George and Miss Jenny,' he continued, in pidgin. 'You have velly good children. Ah Sun and I, we think they like own glandchildren. Goodbye, dear Master.'

Ah Sun, sobbing, clasped Airton's hands. She was too moved to speak, as was the doctor, who stood indecisively as the two servants left him and made their way slowly towards the gate. 'No,' he roared, attempting to run after them but Fielding held him and Major Lin moved his horse to block his way.

One of the Boxers stepped forward as the two old servants approached. With shock Airton recognised the features of his major-domo, Zhang Erhao, although he was now wearing a turban and full Boxer regalia. He made an elaborate bow to Ah Lee, as if welcoming him to their throng. Ah Lee spat in his face. The Boxer ranks closed round them and Airton could see them no more.

Lin's soldiers searched the house efficiently and gathered their weapons – there was only a minor disturbance when Nellie barred the door to Helen Frances's room and had to be pushed aside. Shortly afterwards the troop left, leaving sentries at the doors. The Boxers also dispersed, although the drumbeats thumped on into the night. The foreigners gathered in the Airtons' sitting room, sinking into the armchairs and sofas as if they wanted to hide from themselves. No one had anything to say. After a while Septimus Millward came into the room, followed by his wife and children. He surveyed the others quietly. 'Gentlemen,' he said. 'We're in the hands of the Lord. Don't you think that it's time for a prayer?' In his fine baritone he began to sing: 'Praise to the Lord, the Almighty, the King of Creation . . .'

One by one the others joined in. They took some comfort in the hymns and prayers, which Septimus intoned till the early hours of the morning. Standing over them like a stern Old Testament prophet raising his staff against the forces of chaos, Septimus seemed to have come into his own. It was a reflection of their appalling predicament that, for the first time in anyone's experience, he did not appear crazed to the other foreigners in this dwindling community.

Outside, the heads of Ah Lee and Ah Sun, mounted on poles by the gateposts, appeared attentive, as if they were straining to listen to the impromptu service in the house. But, in fact, it was only a trick of the air currents being sucked into the fire that still raged in the wreck of the hospital below.

Chapter Fourteen

Many of our men appeared to die, but Master Zhang says
it is not so for bullets cannot hurt us. Why then has Little
Brother not returned?

Christian Mission and Hospital
Shishan, Manchuria, China

Sunday 16 June 1900

My dear James,

It is now four days since the burning of our hospital by the
Boxers, and our forced incarceration in our quarters. I have
not written earlier because the terrible slaughter of the patients
and the servants in my care weighed heavily on me. Yet we have
cause for hope.

Every day we see signs that Providence has not abandoned us.
Two days ago our enemies were surrounding our house, beating
on their drums and taunting us, day and night, with their shouts
and chants, performing their hideous dances and rituals on our
lawn. They gestured obscenely at us with their weapons, knowing
our defencelessness, calling on their gods to bring violence on
our heads, and accusing us of diabolical crimes while threatening
bloodcurdling retribution. You can imagine the terror of our
children who trembled between their sheets while the nightmarish
screams tore the night outside. What comfort could we give them,
brave little creatures that they are? Only Major Lin's pickets
stood between us and murder, and weak reeds we considered
those undisciplined soldiers to be. Yet somehow the crisis passed.
Septimus Millward believes that in addition to the pickets from
Lin's cavalry there were also angels with burning swords standing
at our door, protecting us. Well, figuratively I suppose there might
have been. The Lord saw to it that we came to no harm.

Then yesterday we woke to a strange silence. For the first
time in days we could hear the delightful sound of birdsong.

For a moment I imagined myself back in our dear little cottage in Dumfries, lying in my old cot listening to the chattering of a summer morning, with sunshine outside and the prospect ahead of a day's fishing on the burn. Lifting the shutters we saw that the Boxers had indeed gone. The only movement was that of the soldiers yawning as they sat round their breakfast fires.

No explanation was given – the soldiers are under instructions not to speak to us – but in my heart I felt a surge of confidence and thanks. I am convinced that my letter to the Mandarin has now reached him and that he has given the instructions that caused our persecutors to be removed. I do not understand the present politics of Shishan but I assume that the Mandarin is dealing with his problems one at a time, cutting his coat to circumstance. When he has restored peace and order in the city then he will come for us. For the moment he is protecting us as best he can.

My strong good helpmate, Nellie, sends you her love, as do the children, who are now living through their own adventure as exciting as the ones you send them in your book parcels at Christmas. Pray that this one will also have the sort of happy ending that one looks for in such tales! Tell dearest Edmund and Mary, when you visit them at their school, that their parents miss them as ever, and assure them that we are ALL RIGHT!

Tuesday 18 June 1900

The Boxers have not returned. We have been blessed by a third night of calm.

Major Lin has been true to his word at least, as far as provisions of food are concerned. Today we received sacks of rice and vegetables, and three large sides of fresh pork. This will make a welcome change from the monotony of canned bully beef on which we have been subsisting. Fortunately our own larder was only recently stocked, and we have tins of preserved food which, if sparingly used, will last us for more than a month. Nellie is a strict quartermaster, and our meals are of necessity Spartan affairs – but each day she manages to surprise us with some treasure out of her trove. Last night we enjoyed a plum pudding from Fortnum's, a gift at Christmas from the Gillespies.

Herr Fischer poured a drop of brandy over the steaming dessert, and the children made great play of blowing out the lamps so we could enjoy the delicious blue flames when Nellie brought the burning dish ceremoniously to the table.

You can see from this that we remain in good heart. We keep ourselves busy. There is nothing like work to drive away disconsolate thoughts. Nellie has been ingenious in inventing household chores. She has recruited Mr Bowers to be her helper in the kitchen where he supervises the stores. He has labelled and numbered every can of beans! And every measure of cooking oil is marked in his ledger! Sister Caterina, Mrs Millward and two of her daughters are our washerwomen. We have clean sheets every day, not to mention a fresh set of clothing. The house sometimes smells like a laundry! Meanwhile Herr Fischer, with Mr Fielding as his lieutenant, has been placed in charge of polishing and dusting. Fischer approaches the work with Germanic efficiency, holding his feather duster under his arm like a field marshal's baton. There is not a speck of dust left in the house and the surface of the piano gleams like a mirror. So do the floorboards! Even Tom, who still has difficulty walking, keeps himself occupied polishing the silver. I imagine that no ship-of-the-line could be in such glistening condition as our humble dwelling. There cannot be many other places of enforced confinement in the world that could qualify for entry in the *Woman's World* magazine as an Ideal Home!

Septimus Millward and I are the only ones who are excused from these chores. Ever since the extraordinary service he conducted on the night of the Boxers' arrival Mr Millward has been our pastor. You may find this strange, considering what I have told you about him in the past. Neither has he changed. He is still the deranged fanatic believing in his visions. He is uncompromising, and his sermons – of the old hell-fire and fury type, which ordinarily the likes of you and I would go lengths to avoid – do not even border on the lunatic: they go well beyond! Yet there is no questioning the absolute certainty of his faith, and there is something in our present circumstances that makes such certainty comforting. I find it difficult to explain. Anyway, we tolerate him and, as Dr Fielding said, what else are we to do with him? His preparations for his evening service at least keep him locked in his bedroom out of harm's way, and also away from his children who, in Nellie's view, have suffered under his tyranny for far too long.

I am still occupied, of course, with my medical duties, which as you can imagine in our enlarged community keep me as busy as if I were a general practitioner. Besides my two chief patients, Helen Frances and Tom, I have to deal with any number of small ailments from burns to headaches, and one of the gentlemen (I will not mention which) has a nasty case of piles! It is fortunate that my medical bag was with me in the house when we became besieged and that there was a whole box of stores that I had not sent down to the hospital, including – of paramount importance – a supply of morphine. Not that I need so much as I did. Up to now there has been no need to restart Helen Frances on the drug. The poor creature is now almost cured of her addiction. She has suffered terribly and there were days when I despaired of her recovery and of being able to save her child. You remember when you once visited me in the hospital in Edinburgh? I showed you patients fighting addiction, so you know the bestial state to which they succumb at the peak of their withdrawal. There are still weals on the girl's wrists and ankles from her struggles when I had to tie her to the bed. It is no fault of hers. She has been the victim of a terrible invasion of her body and mind. The perpetrator was Mr Manners, who seduced her, then introduced her to opium. A terrible crime, yet I should not speak ill of the dead. He is now beyond worldly punishment. And his end was a cruel one.

Thank goodness that Helen Frances is young and strong. I am glad to say she is now recovered to the point that she is eating normally and putting on weight. There is even something of a return of her former beauty – though I doubt whether the sadness that now lines her face will ever entirely leave her. Strangely, it gives her an ethereal look, a sort of haunted languor, which is not unattractive and reminds me of a Pre-Raphaelite painting. *Mariana at the Moated Grange*, perhaps. The parallel is not inappropriate.

At least she is beginning to take an interest in life again. Coward as I am, I gave Nellie the awful task of telling her everything that has happened while she has been 'out of this world'. The murder of her father. The death of her lover. Boxers and so on. We had the morphine ready to hand in case the anguish overwhelmed her – but there was no need for it. She took the news with surprising calm and resolve, only asking to be led to the window and for the shutters to be opened wide enough for her to see the grave of her father. Then she cried awhile. The strength of the girl, especially after what she has been through, is truly amazing. That night Sister Caterina remained in the room with her but she slept soundly. She tossed and turned, and once or twice she cried out, but altogether she passed a peaceful night, much like any other.

I do not know why I am writing to you at such length about this. I suppose it is because I cannot unburden my worries to anyone here. As far as our little community is concerned I must be the strong, all-knowing physician and the head of the household, brimming with confidence and authority. I never thought of myself as being a leader yet such is the role I have to play now – but I am concerned, James. Not so much about the Boxers – I believe the danger from that quarter is receding. I am very worried about Helen Frances and Tom. I do not know what to do about them.

You see, Helen Frances won't see him. Her calm when Nellie told her about Henry Manners's death was rather frightening. Unnatural, even. She hardly seemed interested to hear about it. Yet she gets into a hysterical state when I suggest that Tom should visit her. She shakes her head on the pillow. She closes her eyes and clenches her teeth. It is not as if Tom has been showing much desire to see her either. He asks about her politely, but perfunctorily, and appears relieved when I change the subject or leave him to get on with his polishing of the silver. These poor children, each of them so wounded by the cruelties of life. I have been a physician long enough to know that, ultimately, healing of the body can only take place when the mind is also made whole; it does not require a mountebank in Vienna to state that obvious fact. Yet what can I do if they refuse to confront each other?

This is where the physician reaches the boundaries of his healing powers. And I have no answer. Yet I suspect I will have to do something to make a reconciliation even if it is not their desire. Helen Frances cannot remain bedridden much longer and she will have to find a role in this household, at least while the emergency persists. What will happen to our our fragile sense of morale if two of our number will not talk to each other?

My dear James, I had intended this letter to be reassuring and I fear that instead I have been burdening you with my doubts and fears. This is wrong of me and the circumstances do not even merit it for, as I told you before, I am convinced that the worst is over, and that even now the Mandarin is working for our release. Of course I was disappointed that there was no letter or message from the Mandarin when Major Lin brought the food supplies today. Indeed, Major Lin was his usual cold self and remarkably uncommunicative about anything. He brought the supplies, then he left. But I am not disheartened. Not at all. Adversity teaches patience.

Oh, she had tried. How she had tried.

She could remember little of what had happened to her in the days, weeks, months, eternities that she had been incarcerated in this little room. She had an image of herself lying on the bed, a wild trussed animal, struggling, slavering, snarling, straining against the ropes. It was as if she had been separated from her own body and could see herself from above. She saw her own bared teeth and rolling eyes, her own back arching and her legs kicking violently against their bonds. She saw the doctor in his baggy black coat with his little leather bag sitting on a chair by the bed; his eyes were closed but his hands covered his ears and tears ran down his cheeks. She saw her own mouth twisting out hideous words and her eyes burning with hate. And this other floating part of her had felt a sudden rush of sympathy for the poor man, who was only trying to help her. And she had determined that she would help him, and fight this thing on the bed with him.

And one day she had woken and known that she was herself again, and when the doctor had come in with his tray and his bottles and the syringe, she had weakly brushed it away, and fallen asleep again, and this time there had been no dreams.

That had been a blessed week. There had been noises outside her little room, drums and shouts, but they had seemed far away and nothing to do with her. She was only aware of her own body, the blood flowing in her arms and legs, the thump of her heart, the rhythm of her breathing, the warmth in her womb where she knew that another life was growing. Sleep, food, sleep, and a feeling of returning strength. No thoughts, but for the returning sensations in her body, and this other life, which she could not yet feel but which was nevertheless there inside her. And sleep without dreams.

Then Nellie had come in and told her about the deaths of her father and Henry. And with the news of their deaths her own life had begun again. She had not understood the full import at first, not until Nellie had helped her from the bed to the window, and lifted the shutters and shown her the wooden cross in the fenced garden off the lawn where her father lay. And she had wept, silently, and Nellie had probably thought that these were the tears of a dutiful daughter, but really she was crying for herself, because now she could no longer hide from what she had done and what she had become, nor escape the self-hatred for the damage she had caused. Her father and Henry were dead. Seeping up from deep within her, like water bubbling from a poisoned well, came the knowledge, and the guilt, that somehow she herself was to blame.

She had lain on the bed afterwards, looking at the familiar cracked ceiling, and the broken plaster seemed an emblem of her own ruined life.

Where was that confident girl from the convent, stepping out into a world of promise, so full of excitement, enthusiasm and *joie de vivre*? The intelligent girl, top of her class, 'Helen Frances, you're a modern young lady now ready for a modern century – but don't let that famous curiosity of yours get the better of you,' and giggles from the admiring school hall as she had stepped up to collect her prizes.

That curiosity – no, that hunger for every sensation life had to offer – had betrayed her, as surely as she herself had betrayed every person who had loved her, or been kind to her. Her father, her simple father, who had wanted the best for her and who had gazed at her in wonder when she had first come to Shishan, a sentimental tear in his eye, and called her his princess. Had he known? Had he sought his own death, blundering into that alley where they had found him, because she had broken his heart? The doctor and Nellie, whose hospitality she had so flagrantly abused. Could she ever make amends? And Tom. How cruelly she had treated Tom.

Tom. Kind, gentle Tom.

Stupid, boorish Tom.

She had never really loved him. He had been a toy, a convenient pastime, when her whole world had been opening up, and passions were waking inside her, which she had lavished on the most convenient male receptacle to hand. She had experimented with his love, indulging it as she was indulging herself with all the other sensations of Asia. Tom, malleable Tom, who had only been another spice in an Oriental banquet of exotic dishes arrayed for her pleasure. Oh, she had pretended to believe it was real at the time. She had fooled herself as much as anyone else. And Tom had been lovable in his way, and her affection for him was certainly no less than that she had felt for the collie she had brought up as a puppy at her aunt's house – but her tears for that collie had not lasted longer than the week following its death under a cart. And her affection for Tom had not survived the first moment when she had seen Henry galloping his horse to Sir Claude MacDonald's party. From then on Tom had been only a pleasant habit, an adornment, a nosegay, while she herself was pretending to be brilliant in Shishan's parochial society.

How could she have been so wicked?

But was it wickedness to hunger and yearn for the touch of another man whose very presence fired and transformed her into a selfless vessel of passion? The last thing she had felt when she was with Henry was that she was sinning, especially not in the act of love when their limbs had been wound and wet together, and her very soul had felt as one with his. It had only ever been natural and right, as nothing else had ever been right in her life. No, it had felt like a sin when she had broken away from him, because a part of her still cared for what the world and society said or thought.

She knew what the world thought of Henry. She saw it in the averted eye, she heard it in the unsaid words, whenever Dr Airton or Nellie mentioned her baby. To them he was a ruthless adventurer, a seducer, a bounder. But what did they know? Henry had not seduced her. Hers had been the hunger, she the huntress, and Henry, like helpless Actaeon, had fallen to her hounds. And when they were together, when their bodies were wound round each other, hers had been the primal desire. And she was proud that she had woken desire in him. Had he loved her? She hoped that he had, in a small way. But what right had she to claim him? To tie him down to some domestic parlour where she knitted and he came home for tea? It would have been like trying to tame the wind. He was a free spirit, a creature of the wild, a stag, a stallion. She knew his faults, his unfaithfulness, and loved him for it the more. He was her unfulfilled self. His was the freedom that she as a woman could never have. She knew that he was in Shishan for some important mission, whatever it was, and that she could only ever be a part of his life. She had left him because she did not want to trap him any further. The world would think that it was he who had hurt her but that had never been the case. She had hurt only herself. And now he was dead.

And she was left, mourning the brilliant, tropical storm that had illuminated her universe and now had faded from the sky, leaving only dark clouds behind it, hanging over a flat, dull sea. A sea in which she could not even drown herself, for she had to go on living.

For his baby still lived – she owed the doctor for that. And she had her duty.

Dull, boorish Tom. She shuddered now when she thought of him, but she would marry him if he still wanted her. The doctor had woken her back to life, and she owed life a debt. She had drunk its cup to the full, but now she had to taste its lees. And she was willing to do so as reparation for the damage she had caused.

Dawn, Friday 21 June

I write in haste. The Boxers have returned. Fielding and Tom were right and I was wrong. Lin's pickets have deserted us. We do not know what it portends, but fear the worst.

I am hiding my letters to you, with some valuables, under one of the floorboards in the dining room. If you should ever read these words think kindly of your brother and his family. I entrust Edmund and Mary to your good care. Bring them up as Christians.

There is so much to say but the drums are throbbing outside.

May the Lord protect us all.

Edward Oh, but it is sad that it should end this way. Jenny and George are so young.

We have survived a terrible day. This morning I was tempted to utter the words of despair: *eli, eli, lama sabachthani?* But God has not forsaken us. We are together, we are safe. Providence continues to watch over us and the wings of His mercy enfold us and keep us from harm.

The Boxers must have returned in the early hours before dawn. They were silent at first and they might have crept up upon the house unnoticed, had it not been for the presence of mind of Mr Bowers, who happened to be up early, as is his habit as a railwayman. He was reading his Bible in the sitting room when he heard a noise. Going to the window he saw shapes sliding through the shadows towards the house. He recalled that in the storeroom there was a box of Chinese firecrackers, which I had once confiscated from George and Jenny. Quickly he retrieved these, and also a toy popgun from the children's room. He thrust the barrel of this through one of the firing-holes. In the dim light no doubt it resembled a real rifle. He then moved quickly from firing-hole to firing-hole, lighting and hurling out the firecrackers one by one. The household was therefore woken by what sounded exactly like gunfire. This was his intention, of course. It had the right effect on the Boxers, too, for they scurried away in fright. The sight was no doubt comical – the turbaned and pantalooned figures scampering into the gloom like startled children caught playing in the costume wardrobe – but none of us was in the mood for mirth. Nor did we feel any elation at our victory. We were appalled that the Boxers were back. We also knew that firecrackers would not keep them away for long. Shortly after the foiled attack, the drums began to beat, as well as the horrible taunts and chants, the memories of which had filled our nightmares since the last time we were besieged.

Oh, it is a horrible sound, James. An endless repetition of their slogan 'Destroy the foreigners and save the Ch'ing' followed by screams of '*Sha*! *Sha*! *Sha*!' which means, 'Kill! Kill! Kill!' with verses of unrepeatable lewdness and insult, describing our supposed crimes. I imagine that the cries of devils in Hell cannot be more fearsome, or revolting.

What was incomprehensible, and certainly most alarming,

was that Lin's soldiers, our guardians such as they were, were nowhere to be seen. Their makeshift tents were gone, as were their cooking pots and their other litter. It was suddenly clear to us that we were to be abandoned to the Boxers.

You may imagine our feelings of betrayal.

We gathered in the sitting room, in our dressing-gowns, or with trousers hurriedly pulled up under our nightshirts, as forlorn a group of ragamuffins as you could conceive. The children were extremely frightened, and it was as much as Nellie and Sister Caterina could do to stop their crying. One of the Millward boys was wailing like a siren, as hideous a noise as the yells coming from outside – but I am being uncharitable. I hope I am never to see such frightened white faces again as long as I live. Hurriedly, we men held a council of war. Bowers and Tom were calm, but Fischer was in a bad way, and Fielding was not helpful, criticising me for accepting Major Lin's terms so easily and surrendering all our weapons. As if we had had any choice at the time.

I will pass over the acrimonious exchanges. Eventually we determined on a plan, hopeless in my view, but anything was better than nothing in those terrible circumstances. When the Boxers attacked, Bowers and Fielding, as the most able-bodied men, would defend the doors as long as they could with choppers, spades and any makeshift weapons they could come by. This would buy time for Fischer, Millward and myself, with Tom, on his crutches, to break out of the small window at the back of the house. Somehow we would find a way down the steep hill slope taking the women and children with us. Bowers and Fielding would join us when they could get away. No one proffered any suggestions about what we would do after that. The truth is that we had no idea – but there was something repulsive about the idea of waiting passively for the Boxers to break in, and a quick death seemed preferable to the thought of being burned alive. We believed that this would be our most likely fate if we stayed. And who knows? Some, if not all, of us might get away.

Septimus Millward would have none of our plan. 'The Lord has placed me here and here I will stay,' he intoned, in his ringing voice, and I am afraid that we all gazed at him, speechless with astonishment. Burton Fielding rounded on him, telling him that the Lord usually helps those who help themselves, and Tom tried to reason with him, asking him to consider the safety of his wife and children. 'This is as good a place as any for us to await our passage to Heaven,' was his answer. 'Who am I to question His Grand Design?' He was not to be moved.

I found myself burning with anger against this obdurate man. I think I called him a silly old fool. There was no way that some of us could seek a way to safety leaving this man's family to burn with their tyrant of a father. It was unthinkable and, anyway, I was worried about Helen Frances, who was in no condition yet to walk far. Since the other men would be needed to defend our retreat, the only one of us with the strength to carry her was Septimus Millward.

Our arguments raged back and forth. Millward ignored us, falling on his knees in that ostentatious way of his with his head raised in prayer. It was now nearly nine o'clock. For some hours it had been light and Mr Bowers, who had positioned himself next to the window, giving us occasional reports of the gathering Boxer strength, now called to us that there were ominous signs of activity on the lawn. No fewer than twenty Boxer Braves were dancing their ritual of possession, which we knew usually preceded an attack.

In exasperation I rounded on the company: 'What do we do?' I asked. 'Do we fight? Do we run? Do we stay?' The silence that followed told me it was I who had to make a decision, and quickly. 'Millward,' I cried, 'we will follow our plan. I cannot force you to join us but I plead with you to allow Mrs Millward and the children to come with us to safety.' Laetitia stood up. She was ashen-faced. 'The children and I remain with Septimus,' she whispered. I looked down at the plaintive expressions of her little ones, and heard my own voice, as if coming from afar: 'Then we will leave without you,' I said. I think that I added, 'May God protect you.' James, that was undoubtedly the most terrible moment I had ever experienced in my life.

Without a further word, Bowers and Fielding left us to gather their weapons. Nellie, giving me an unfathomable look, hurried off with Sister Caterina to prepare Helen Frances for the journey. I stood by the window, looking out at the Boxers, feeling helpless.

I do not know what would have happened if the Miracle had
not intervened. Truly, it was a desperate plan to which we had
committed ourselves. But as I watched the Boxers on the lawn,
leaping in more and more frenzied dance, I heard a trumpet
blow, long and hard and discordant, from behind their ranks.
The drums ceased beating. The chanting stopped. In the strange
silence, the dancers froze, then hesitatingly, questioningly,
looked behind them, as if embarrassed by being caught in a
faux-pas at a country ball. A loud voice shouted a command,
and a moment later the twenty figures were loping back to their
fellows. And then, strangest of all, the whole host turned, and in
silence disappeared. It had taken only a few moments, but where
there had been a horde of devils screaming for our blood, now
there was no one.

About half an hour later Major Lin and his cavalry trotted
through our gates. We watched him get off his horse and walk
purposefully to our door on which he banged with his gloved
hand. I went out to on the porch to meet him, but before I had
a chance to say a word, I was astonished to see him bowing to
me with a curt snap to the waist. He was apologising! He told
me that the scoundrels in his troop who had been left to guard
us had been bribed to vacate their positions. After the Boxers
had done their worst to us, they would have been found tied
up and gagged as if they had been overpowered by the Boxers.
Fortunately one of their number had ridden to Lin and reported
on the others. Lin had come as soon as he could, and the Boxers
had retreated when they saw the dust of his approaching horses.
He said he was ashamed that such indiscipline had occured
in his troop. The perpetrators would be punished. He would
personally see to it that it never happened again. A guard of his
more reliable soldiers would replace the men who had showed
such dereliction of duty.

So we are safe again, my dear brother – although we are
prisoners as before – and my confidence in the Mandarin
is restored. It is clear that the civil authority as represented
by Major Lin, who reports to the Mandarin, after all, is in
command in Shishan and feared by the Boxers. This bodes well.

I feel very strongly, however, that it is not only a temporal
power we have to thank for our deliverance. When I returned

to the sitting room after seeing Major Lin, Millward was still on his knees. He did not say anything, but there was a look in his expression that seemed to signify 'I told you so'. And was he not right to trust in the mercy of our only Saviour, for surely it was He and He alone who today saved us from harm? Among us, it was only Septimus Millward – that obdurate man – who held fast to his faith, and who was it who was vindicated?

My head is dropping. These are great mysteries. For now I can only express humble thanks that today the Lord chose to preserve the lives of my beloved Nellie, George and Jenny.

I commend you to Him, my dear brother,

Tuesday 25 June 1900

Little of note has happened since I last wrote to you, but since the attack last week a strain has descended on our beleaguered household, and there is a noticeable lack of the good humour that characterised the first days of our incarceration.

Major Lin's men are efficient at preventing the Boxers coming close to the house, but for all that they are a menacing presence beyond the fence. Their drums pound eternally, day and night. Our voices are hoarse and our throats sore from making ourselves heard above the din; for much of the day we communicate among ourselves in gestures like Cistercian monks under a vow of silence. Our nerves are taut, and all of us find it difficult to sleep, so we are tired and irritable, and less forgiving of each other's idiosyncrasies.

Every day there is a demonstration of some kind. The soldiers allow this, presumably to give our besiegers a chance to let off steam. It is the usual display of martial arts and invective. We watch because there is little else to do. It has elements of a fairground show, and would be innocuous if it were not for the hideous and murderous intent behind their antics and sword-waving. Did our Romanised ancestors behind their city walls watch the war dances of the wild Saxon invaders with a similar mixture of scorn and fear? This morning for a change there was a spectacle of female Boxers, they call them the Red Lanterns. These fierce-eyed damsels in red pyjamas appear to be the priestesses of the cult – but don't imagine, dear brother, that there is anything feminine about these young harridans, and there is certainly nothing sacred: they have been trained to do the same dances with sword and spear as the men, and the shrieks and abuse that come out of their pretty mouths are even more loathsome and unnatural for being delivered in soprano.

The strain is terrible on our little ones. White-faced, they huddle together with big, staring eyes. George and Jenny try their best, the darlings, but the toys that only a week ago provided such delight now lie unused on the floor. George sits for hours with one of his books of adventures, but I see that his mind is elsewhere; the pages do not turn. The Millward children have reverted to the old ways, and kneel for hours with their mother while Septimus chants his prayers, albeit almost inaudible under the drums. I do not know from where that man gathers his strength. Or perhaps I do. For all his madness, there is something admirable in his single-minded devotion. He is perhaps the only one of us who remains unbowed under our persecution. He has become an unconscious influence on us all. Yesterday I was surprised to see Sister Caterina kneeling among his family as he led them in prayer.

Burton Fielding, however, cannot conceal his loathing for Septimus and he will leave the room to avoid being in his company. It is as if Millward challenges his authority. But Fielding has been behaving strangely since the attack. It is tragic to see the decline in a man whom I once so respected and whose advice I so valued. There is nothing left of his laconic humour, and conversation with him is now a catalogue of bitter complaint. He blames me particularly for our predicament, saying that if only we had listened to him we would all have escaped when there was a chance to do so. He is hardly less damning of the others. In fact, he seems to despise us all. He keeps morosely to himself, glaring at us with an intensity that might be hatred. So we tend to ignore him. I hesitate to impute cowardice to a man who, if we are to believe him, once outfaced the savage Apache, but he appears to have given way to despair.

Thankfully, the rest of us remain relatively confident of our eventual delivery. Bowers, in his quiet way, exudes calm, Fischer has a blind faith in ultimate rescue by the railway board, and there is no questioning Tom's bravery and cool-headedness in a desperate situation. Tom, however, worries me. Against my better judgement and without my knowledge, three days ago he went to Helen Frances's room. I do not know what they said to each other, but there was certainly not the reconciliation for which I had fervently prayed. The poor fellow acts and behaves as if nothing has happened, but there is a grim set to his face, and a cold deliberation in his manner, which speaks to me of a broken heart. There is no trace in this icy stranger of the affable, easy-going young man who charmed us all when he came to Shishan last year. On the contrary, there is something ruthless and impenetrable about him that is almost frightening. Even Jenny, who loved him and was always presuming on his good nature, now avoids him. The saddest thing is that he does not notice or care. And Helen Frances? Well, as far as her health is concerned, her recovery is little short of remarkable – as a physician I could not be more pleased with her – yet she will hardly speak, even to Nellie. She lies on her bed, staring at a crack in the ceiling. Who knows what is going on in her mind? While, outside, and in our heads, the drums keep beating, beating, beating.

I wish that I could re-institute the busy activity that kept us so optimistic and high-spirited in the early period of the siege, but I am afraid that our spring-cleaning days are over. I did not tell you when I last wrote to you because I did not then know but there was a serious consequence of the Boxer attack on our house last week. Some time during the commotion the Boxers blocked our well. We are now totally reliant on our guards who twice a day take the long walk to the stream at the bottom of the hill. The water is brackish, and four buckets a day are hardly enough to quench our thirst, especially when most of it spills on the climb up the hill. We are rationed to a pot of tea in the morning and evening, and we have a cup each of the 'natural' liquid at lunchtime. If I tell you that the heat for the past few days has reached the mid-eighties you may imagine our privation. There is no question of washing our clothes or ourselves. I have no doubt that the consequent itching discomfort is as contributory to the strain as the irritation of the drums.

In this heat and hardship my thoughts often return to our

beloved Scotland, and I dream of the breeze in the heather.
When this is over I have determined that we might take a little
furlough. I would enjoy a long walk with you, my brother,
among the hills and glens. And to be reunited with dear Edmund
and Mary, to whom I send my fondest love and that of their
mother and brother and sister. Visit them for me now and again
at their school, James, if you have the time.

Oh, these drums. These drums. How I long for a moment –
just a moment – of quiet!

She had waited in her small room for Tom to come. She had waited
looking blankly at the broken plaster and her ruined life. She lay on
her bed like a sacrificial victim of her dashed hopes.

And after many days he did come. He let himself in quietly and
leaned his bulk against the door.

'So,' he said, after a long while.

'I'll marry you, Tom, if you still want me,' looking up at the ceiling
and the cracks.

A hard laugh, brutal, such as she had never heard before.

'That's not really on now, HF, is it? Can't quite see myself raising
a bastard's bastard.'

Helen Frances watched an ant crawling out of one of the cracks.

'Anyway,' continued Tom, into the silence, 'it's all a bit academic.
You do realise our situation, I suppose? If we're not hauled out to
be executed we'll probably be burned alive in here. Me, you and your
unborn baby. Sorry, dear.'

The ant disappeared down the side of the wall out of her vision.

'Not really the time for marriage bells, is there? Anyway, they
wouldn't be heard above the drums.' Tom laughed again.

'Have you been drinking?' Helen Frances asked quietly.

'Drinking? I'll say I have. Not that the others seem to have
noticed. To them I'm still good, honest, cool-headed Tom, the
amiable cuckold. I'm their big white hope, even if I am a cripple.
But, then, you probably haven't noticed that I've been hobbling on
crutches, have you? You've been lying in bed recovering from your
drug addiction. Doctor said I wasn't to see you because you weren't
fully recovered yet – but I'm not quite the fool I look. Or maybe I
am. Don't care, really. Not any more.'

'Poor Tom.' She turned her head for the first time to look at him.

'Is that sympathy, my dear? How jolly, jolly decent of you. Knew your heart was in the right place, even if you were fucking all and sundry behind my back.'

'Only Henry,' she said, turning her head away.

'Only Henry?' Tom laughed. 'Oh, well, that's a relief. Only Henry. Then you have my deep condolences. So sorry the little shit was beaten to death. I am, you know,' he added. 'I'd have liked to do it myself.'

'Why have you come here?' she asked softly.

'Well, my dear,' Tom said, with false joviality, swaying slightly, 'that's a very good question. Do you know, I was sitting in the dining room having a little tipple, all by myself when – you know what sentimental creatures we men are – I suddenly started thinking about my dear, lost love. And I thought, Well, she's not that far away, is she? And what with old Henry gone, maybe she's lonely. So here I am.'

Helen Frances looked at him coldly but said nothing.

'And I started wondering, you see,' continued Tom. 'What was it old Henry had that I didn't?'

Tom opened his mouth and was about to deliver another barb, but instead he shook his head. Leaving the support of the door he lurched into the room, and slumped into a chair. Helen Frances started, then sat up in bed with the sheet pulled to her chin. There was a lost expression in Tom's eyes, and his mouth hung slackly.

'Why, HF, why?' It was almost a whimper, and his eyes were filling with self-pitying tears.

'I loved him,' she answered.

'Didn't you think that I loved you? That I wanted you?'

'I know you did,' she said.

'We were engaged, for God's sake. And you gave yourself to him. You let him—'

'Let him what, Tom? It wasn't like that, you know.'

She watched the big man sobbing as he rocked on the small wooden chair. She had no feeling for him. She might have been watching an actor in a play, but she remembered the duty to which she had reconciled herself. This was the man whom she would marry if he wanted her. Because of Henry's child.

'It's all right, Tom,' she said. 'It's all right.'

'We're all going to die here, HF,' moaned Tom, through his sobs,

'We're all going to be killed by the Boxers, and I'll die . . . I'll die without ever having known a woman.'

She had been moving forward on the bed to try to give him some comfort, but at these words she froze. 'Is that why you came here?' she asked. 'You thought I'd sleep with you?'

'No,' groaned Tom. 'But you gave yourself to Manners. You whored to Manners.'

'Is that what you really think of me, Tom? That I'm a whore?'

Tom was not sobbing now, but his chest was heaving and he wiped his nose. In the manner of drunks his mood had suddenly changed and there was a sly look on his face, like that of a child wheedling for apples. 'Would you?'

'Sleep with you? Is that what you want?'

Tom hung his head, but the sly look had not left his face. 'I didn't mean what I said,' he mumbled. 'It's the drink. I still love you, HF.'

Helen Frances looked at him coldly. She pushed back the sheet and contemplated him. He looked back at her with an expression half misery, half bravado.

'You don't have to,' he muttered.

She untied the bow of her nightdress and, still looking at him coldly, pulled it over her head, baring herself to his gaze. Neither of them moved.

'Are you going to sit there?' she asked, after a while. 'Or are you going to whine some more?'

Tom slowly and clumsily raised his big frame to his feet, and stood swaying in front of her. 'HF?' he said hesitantly, leaning towards her, one hand stretching gingerly forward. She flinched back, unable to help it, when she felt his cold fingers on her breast.

'So that's it,' said Tom. His arm dropped. 'You bitch,' he hissed, and slapped her face, knocking her backwards. 'If I ever touch you again,' he said, 'it'll be to wring your bloody neck. Whore.' He staggered out of the room, slamming the door.

She lay on the bed, her cheek stinging. More ants were crawling from the crack in the ceiling. She watched them. Drums were beating outside. She reached for her nightdress but she did not put it on. She rolled it into a ball and hugged it, her knees up to her chest in the foetal position. She buried her face in her pillow, but she could not cry.

Saturday 29 June 1900

The most extraordinary thing has happened!

It was late in the evening. Most of us had already gone to bed and Herr Fischer was preparing in that fussy way of his to take the first watch – laying out on the dining-room table his timepiece, his Bible, his handkerchief, his pipe, his pouch, his flask of brandy, his little framed portrait of his mother (it is tiring to watch the man!). I was trimming the lamps and checking the shutters before turning in myself.

I happened to be winding the grandfather clock – it is strange how one clings to one's old habits from a time when there was a degree of normality in our existence – when I was startled to hear a quiet rapping on one of the shutters. I might not have heard it at all, had there not been at that moment a cessation of the awful beating of the drums – we have been favoured recently with blissful periods of quiet; even the Boxers tire occasionally, it seems. At first I took the noise to be the knocking of a branch. There is a tree close to one of the dining-room windows and it was windy outside (the mounting heat and the high pressure has caused the evenings to be stormy of late although, alas, there is no rain) – but the rapping was too persistent and too regular to be explained by natural causes. Carefully I lifted the shutter an inch and, with my lantern, peered outside. I saw a white face wearing a Boxer turban, and my spirits sank. I imagined that the house was under attack again. Then I noticed the urgency in the eyes, a pointed, distinctly unChinese nose, and I heard a voice, in English, whispering, 'Let me in. Let me in.' And then: 'It's Hiram.'

You can imagine my shock. The only Hiram I knew had been murdered months before, and I had even attended the execution of his murderers! For a mad second I was wondering if here before me was a ghost! But I looked more closely, and it was undoubtedly Hiram Millward. There was the narrow, pinched face and the same suspicious, foxy look I remembered. This was no ghost. 'Quickly,' he was whispering. 'Let me in before they see me.'

Calling for Fischer, I opened the shutters – I had the presence of mind to extinguish the lantern first – and the two of us hauled the boy into the room. We led him into the sitting room and in the lamplight we gazed in astonishment at this slight figure dressed from head to toe in Boxer regalia. 'My dear boy, you're alive,' I said. I must have sounded foolish, but I really was lost for words.

He was clearly in a state of exhaustion. His legs were swaying, he could hardly keep his eyes from closing, and he was shivering. 'Quickly,' I ordered Fischer. 'Bring his father, while I administer brandy.' I propelled Hiram to a sofa where he sat down without protest. He gagged on the fiery liquid at first, but managed to get down a couple of sips.

The next thing I knew Septimus Millward was standing in the doorway; his eyes were blazing and his beard seemed to be on fire in the lamplight. He cast a huge shadow into the room. Hiram on the sofa looked up and saw the stern figure gazing down on him, and seemed to shrink into the cushions. His white face became, if anything, more pallid with fear. For a tense moment father and son gazed at each other. Septimus's look was implacable. I feared an explosion. Then in two large strides he was by his son's side and he lifted him up, and hugged him in a huge embrace, burying his head in Hiram's bony shoulder, his great breast heaving with emotion. When he raised his face again tears were running down his cheeks and into his beard. Then I was amazed to hear him chuckle as he caught my eye. 'I don't know if you've got a fatted calf on hand, Doctor,' he said, in the mildest tones I have ever heard from him, 'because it sure would be appropriate. For this my son was dead, and is alive again; he was lost, and is found. Excuse us now. Hiram needs his mother.'

So there it is, James. The prodigal returned. Father and son went off together to their room, and we have left the family since to their reunion. No doubt in the morning we will discover more. We are nigh speechless with amazement, and none of us can guess at the meaning of this extraordinary reappearance of one whom we all believed dead. For now there is a bubbling sense of joy in my heart, which is why I am sitting up into the night and writing to you at length. The Lord knows, we need something to cheer our present dire existence, and what could be more joyful than this mysterious resurrection? Truly I wish that we did have a fatted calf to kill. It is a long time since we were able to 'eat, and be merry'.

I have one nagging doubt, however. Three men were executed for that boy's murder. The Mandarin authorised it and presided over it. Was it an error? Was it itself a judicial murder? Who, really, is this man on whom our lives depend?

Sunday 30 June 1900

Our joy in Hiram's return is rather muted by the news he has brought. It appears that our circumstances are even more dire than we imagined. Ours is not an isolated case. The whole of north China is aflame with rebellion. What is worse, the Imperial Court has publicly espoused the Boxer cause. There is no doubt of that. Hiram showed us a copy of a memorial, which he had torn down from a wall. There, in black and white print under an Imperial seal, is the instruction for loyal subjects to go out and slaughter all foreigners.

The rumours spreading through the town are alarming. Boxer and Imperial armies – there seems little distinction between them – have launched great attacks against the foreigners in Tientsin and Peking. The diplomatic missions are under siege. Some say that they have already fallen and that the British minister's head has been sent to the Empress Dowager on a platter. The foreign community in Tientsin continues to hold out, but a relieving army from Taku has been defeated, and several of our naval ships have been sunk under the guns of the Taku forts. Trophies, and even body parts taken from the foreign slain, are passing from town to town. Hiram, attending a Boxer celebration in the market square, saw held up for public view a bloodstained scarlet tunic, a necklace of ears, and other unmentionable parts of the human anatomy.

From what we could gather from the boy, the situation in Shishan is precarious. The Mandarin apparently runs only a paper court in the *yamen*. The real power in the city belongs to Iron Man Wang. Do you remember me telling you about this semi-mythical bandit king who held sway in the forests of the Black Hills? Well, he is no myth. He is a bloodthirsty monster of a man who has taken control not only of the Boxers but also of all the criminal syndicates in the town, and he metes out life and death from his headquarters in a dumpling shop off the public square. He keeps the Mandarin in position only to provide himself with a legal sanction for his murders. Each ransacking of a merchant's house is done under a warrant from the *yamen*.

Nobody is safe from his depredations, since it is easy to taint anybody with the stigma of being a 'Christian sympathiser'. I fear very much for our good friends, Mr Lu and Mr Jin.

The fact that the Mandarin endorses these crimes – even under duress – appals me, but in doing so he apparently retains some freedom of action. Major Lin's militia still take their orders from him, even though Iron Man Wang's henchmen have replaced many of his palace retainers, and bandits now have the run of the *yamen*. Perhaps we should be grateful that the civil administration continues to exist. It seems that the Mandarin retains some bargaining power, and can ameliorate some of the worst excesses. The Mandarin represents Imperial authority after all, and I presume that Iron Man Wang, for all his local power, recognises that ultimately he must retain the good graces of the Court, in whose name it is now apparent that all these atrocious deeds are being performed. This is small comfort to us, because it begs the question, if the Mandarin is committed to obeying the orders from Peking, and Peking demands the destruction of foreigners, how long can he continue to protect us?

Hiram is convinced, from what he has seen and heard, that there is actually no desire to protect us. Our predicament is well known and much talked about in the town. The current rumours, and the popular belief, are that we are being preserved for a show trial after which we will be executed, every one of us. Apparently a date has already been decided and a memorial is being prepared.

I confess that, for the first time, I am beginning to accept that my confidence in the Mandarin has been misplaced. I do not need a gloating Burton Fielding to tell me that I have probably been mistaken all along in putting my trust in such weak clay. I will pass over my feelings in that respect because they are too turbulent. It is a black, black day, brother, and we will require all our fortitude if we are to survive a future that has suddenly become so uncertain.

Monday 1 July 1900

The boy Hiram is remarkable.

He sat modestly on my sofa after luncheon, fully recovered

after a long night's sleep. Septimus was beside him, nodding sagely or beaming indulgently, like an impresario showing off his prodigy. The more horrific the experience his son described the more complacent the father appeared to be. I suppose that strange, literal man is taking the parable to heart. What matter the sin of the prodigal if he has repented and his father has granted forgiveness? What import the suffering so long as the sheep has returned to the fold? There is no denying Septimus's happiness at his boy's return, but his equanimity appeared inhuman to some of us – because what Hiram had to tell us would have wrung tears from a stone; certainly it took all my self-control to keep my composure – and Nellie left the room. Hiram spoke quietly and matter-of-factly about experiences that would have broken the spirit of stronger men but that he, despite his youth, has come to terms with, and put behind him.

Do you realise, James, that while we were continuing our comfortable and smug existence in Shishan, that boy, in the centre of the city in which we lived, was suffering the tortures of the damned? He was lured by ruffians into a house of shame, and imprisoned in an upstairs room. There, day by day, and month by month, he was subjected to such unspeakable indignities and cruelties that I hope you cannot imagine them. He lifted his shirt and showed us the marks of cigarette burns on his back as well as the scars left by what I gather was a routine beating with rods. Who knows the marks of Sodom that scar his poor soul? For he was made the plaything of brutes. I gather that for most of the period he was chained to a bed. Oh, it is loathsome even to contemplate.

Yet he does not dwell on the cruelties. He speaks of the kindnesses he encountered in that hell. There was a girl – a prostitute – who looked after him as best she could, tending his wounds and passing on to him by her example the courage and the will to endure. It was this Magdalene who persuaded Henry Manners – yes, that rascal who ruined poor Helen Frances – to rescue him. It is strange to listen to Manners being spoken of in terms of praise and hero-worship, but the boy considers him his saviour, and will hear no ill word spoken against him. Neither will he accept that Manners is dead, although he apparently witnessed his beating by Lin. It was in fact to discover the

whereabouts of Manners that he donned the disguise of the
Boxers and returned to the heart of danger in Shishan.

I am speechless with amazement when I consider the bravery
of this poor, persecuted creature who, rescued from perils,
returned willingly to face even greater perils for the sake of
his friend. He lived among the Boxers, ate with them, took
part in their rituals. He frequented the teahouse in which Iron
Man Wang holds court, and even spoke to his chief persecutor
in the brothel, a man called Ren Ren, who is now high in the
Boxer Council. How he managed to remain undiscovered I
do not know. He merely shrugged when I asked him and told
me that during his incarceration he had learned how to act a
part. Apparently he was able to conceal his western features
by wrapping his turban round his face like a Tuareg and he
tried only to go out among the Boxers after dark, staying in the
shadows cast by the torchlight. That he got away with such a
slight disguise is remarkable. His boldness was breathtaking, but
when questioned he is shy and self-deprecating. Such courage
in a boy of fifteen! He says that his daring paid off. He heard
stories of a prisoner being held in the dungeons of the *yamen*,
a foreign devil who had committed crimes so terrible that he
was being kept for special punishment in a remote, solitary
cell. There was a great mystery surrounding this prisoner:
it was rumoured that the Mandarin himself was conducting
the interrogation, presiding personally over the torture. The
gossip was that the secrets this man held affected the safety of
the empire. Hiram decided that he must penetrate the *yamen*
to investigate the rumour, and did so, taking advantage of a
demonstration by a troop of Boxers who had gone there to
pledge their loyalty to the Ch'ing.

Somehow he found his way into the dungeons, even to the
locked door of this secret cell. Through the bars he saw a figure
suspended in a hanging cage. It was naked, and the arm hanging
out of the cage was bloody and bruised, but on one of the fingers
was a thin band of gold not unlike the signet ring Manners used
to wear. Hiram called to him by name, and there was a response.
The hanging hand made urgent gestures, as if signalling Hiram
to go away. The prisoner spoke, in hoarse, broken Chinese. It
was difficult to make out the hissing words but Hiram thought

he heard: 'Go. Go. Go to the doctor. It's not what it seems. I'll come presently. Go.' At that moment Hiram was startled by the footsteps of approaching guards and he hurried away – but he had convinced himself that he had found Manners, and Manners was giving him instructions to wait for him at the mission. In his own mind, his task was accomplished.

Yet he did not immediately come to the mission. He still owed a debt of loyalty, he believed, to his friend, the courtesan, whom Manners had also helped to escape from the Palace of Heavenly Pleasure. She had been captured by Lin's troop at the railway camp and presumably taken back to the brothel where before she had been kept as Lin's own paramour. Hiram feared very much for her because he believed that she would be punished for her desertion. And here is the most astounding thing. He made his way deliberately into the very establishment where he had been held in bondage for so long. The consequences of recognition would have been unthinkable, yet he found the courage to return there, and this for the sake of a friend. He took a terrible risk but he found the girl. She had been savagely beaten by Major Lin, but Hiram thought that this was a lighter treatment than she might have suffered from the brothel-owner, this man Ren Ren who is known to have tortured girls to the point of death. Such horrors and this boy speaks about them so casually! The girl had persuaded him that she was safe under the continued protection of Major Lin, who, after her chastisement, had apparently restored her to her former position as his mistress. Hiram passed on to her a revolver, however, which Manners had given him and which he had secreted under the folds of his clothing all this time. I am afraid to say that at this point in Hiram's narration Burton Fielding stormed out of the room in disgust. 'The use we could have made of a revolver!' he snarled. 'And this boy gives it to a whore!' We were all rather embarrassed, but Hiram continued his tale as if nothing had happened. There was little more to tell. Shortly after this he had left Shishan and made his way through the countryside to our mission. Even so, he had to wait two days among the besieging Boxers before he judged that it was safe enough to approach our house.

What a story, James! I have rarely heard such a tale of

hardship, cruelty and courage. Of course, we had not the heart
to express to Hiram our doubt that the prisoner whom he had
seen was really Manners. His meeting was inconclusive to say
the least and the so-called message smacked more to me of the
delirious uttering one might expect from a poor soul suffering
the pain of prolonged torture. And why, if it was Manners, did
he speak in Chinese? Yet there is no harm in allowing the boy to
believe in Manners's survival if it gives him comfort – as long as
Helen Frances does not come to believe in it; that might reopen
wounds better left closed.

Oh, James, what terrible times we are living through, and how
dark all of a sudden the future seems. The saddest thing for me is
that the one man in whom I put my trust seems to have betrayed
us utterly. The Mandarin may have protected us up to now, but
it seems that it is only to keep us for a worse fate to come.

That I should have been so intimate with him, counting him
among my friends, and yet all along to be deceived about his
real nature! I condoned evil and called it pragmatism. I mistook
venality for compromise, and opportunism for wisdom. I realise
now that I was winking at murder – worse than murder, for it
was committed under the veil of the law.

Hiram's story alone convinces me how utterly mistaken I
have been. For whatever reason (money? blackmail?), it is now
certain that the Mandarin connived with criminals, and executed
innocent people in order that the terrible crimes being done to
Hiram would not be found out. Who, except mad Millward,
would continue to believe in the boy's continued existence after
a *yamen* trial had condemned his murderers? Yet again Septimus
has been proved right when wiser heads have been befuddled.

There is a lesson here, James, a lesson. Septimus reposed
his trust in the Lord, and he believed what his heart, or his
Voices told him, when everyone else, including myself, was
blinded by what they thought was their reason. Whatever is
to come – and, frankly, with Tientsin and Peking under siege,
and even the Imperial Court against us, what hope remains
for us? – we would be better to take a leaf out of Millward's
book and trust to that Higher Power, giving ourselves
humbly into His Hands, counting not the little tribulations
of this world, but seeking to prepare our souls for that

Homecoming which the Grace of our Lord Jesus Christ has promised us.

Again, my admiration goes out to that young boy, for perhaps the bravest act in a catalogue of bravery was his decision ultimately to come and join us, even though he knew that we are doomed by imperial decree, and that if he came here he, too, would share in our fate. He may talk of Manners, but fundamentally I believe he wishes to be with his family, and to be reunited in their love before the end comes. I know the comfort that I myself feel in having Nellie and the children close to me. If there was any hope of saving them I would lay down my life to preserve them – but having no hope of that now, just knowing that we will live and die together is mercy enough. In fact it is more than mercy. It is a sort of joy. For what can prevail against love?

It is late. I must sleep. We must be strong to face tomorrow, and the next day, and the next, and however many remain for us.

Have sympathy for us. The drums outside have begun to beat again.

And more days had passed, and she had decided to get up. She saw Tom in the pantry, and she smiled at him, but he only muttered and moved away. Nellie and the doctor were kind to her, and Herr Fischer held both her hands and told her how pleased he was that she had recovered from her illness. But everyone in the house had been distracted – she gathered that they had had news that their execution was now certain. She spent some time knitting with Jenny: the little girl seemed to take some comfort from her company, and when she was with Jenny she did not have to think. She was sad, however, that such a sweet little girl would have to die soon.

For herself she was relieved. There were no more choices now. It was as if her wretched life had been given a reprieve. She longed for the nothingness, the extinction.

Thursday 4 July 1900

Well, now I know what it must feel like to live in a condemned man's cell and, this may surprise you, it is not as intolerable as one might expect. Strangely, the thought of imminent dissolution hardly bears down on the spirit at all. For Christians such as we, what is death anyway but a release from care and the crossing over of a bourn to a happier world? What is tiresome is the waiting. We would be much happier if we knew with more certainty when it is to be.

It may surprise you, but during the last few days we have returned to some degree of cheerfulness in our little household. We hardly pay attention any more to the howling and screaming and the drums outside. I had thought that Hiram's ominous news would have unmanned us all, but it is rather the contrary. Now we know that the worst is likely to happen we have ceased worrying about it.

Each of us seems to be adapting in our own ways. The Millward family act as if they are on holiday, so delighted are they with Hiram's return. Nellie told me the other day that she actually heard Septimus telling a joke. It was not a particularly funny joke so I won't repeat it, but his behaviour of late has been what I can only describe as waggish, if you can imagine a stern Old Testament prophet being such a thing. He is even taking part in some of the children's games. George has set up his clockwork railway set in the playroom and Septimus is, would you believe it?, the solemn stationmaster, with a scarf around his neck and Bowers's cap on his head. From time to time he blows a whistle. It is very droll.

Bowers and Fischer have become the firmest of friends. They have established a routine of Bible-reading in the morning and chess in the afternoon. To our delight Fischer has taken to playing his fiddle again in the evenings, and he and Nellie now regularly perform a little concert for us. It is difficult to hear against the noise of the Boxers outside, but we strain to listen.

Sister Caterina has taken the contemplative route, praying for many hours of the day in front of the icon of the Virgin Mary in her room. She tells me that she feels very close to poor Sister Elena for whom we must presume the worst, and is happy because she knows that the two of them will soon be reunited.

Tom and Helen Frances? I feel very sad for them. They have not been able to resolve their differences. I suppose that it does not matter so much now, but I would have liked it if they had come together again. As you know, I am a hopeless sentimentalist. Nevertheless, there appears to be no rancour between them. Helen Frances is up and about and, if not fully restored to her old self, at least her health is restored, as is much of her former beauty, though she looks older and somewhat sadder. She and Jenny have become inseparable, sewing together and chatting about I know not what. Poor Jenny, I see that she would have grown up to be a lovely lass if she had had the chance. Tom has taken one of the children's jigsaw puzzles and seems happy enough just being by himself. He, too, looks older and sadder but occasionally, when he is concentrating, he unconsciously whistles a merry tune; I may be an incompetent physician, but I am satisfied that if a man can whistle, there is little really to worry about him, body or soul!

And Nellie and I? We spend much of our time sitting together, occasionally talking about Scotland and our many happy memories, but usually we are content to be silent together, like the auld man and wife in the story, nodding by the fire. One day Nellie noticed that we were holding each other by the hand, and she blushed, remarking that this was a fine time to be beginning a second honeymoon!

The one Malvolio in our happy circle is, I am sad to say, Dr Fielding, who cannot reconcile himself to our fate. Thankfully he no longer rails and criticises as he did, but it is sad to watch him pacing restlessly up and down the room, lifting the shutters to watch the Boxers outside. We tend to ignore him, as we do the Boxers. It is better that way.

Dear James, do not be sad for us. We are quite content.

I had intended to write a long formal letter to you as the executor of my will, asking you to look after this, and take care of that – but material things that once had such overwhelming importance, especially to us money-minded Scots, hardly seem to matter much now. I know you will do what is right with my little estate, and that you will see that my dear Mary and Edmund are well looked after. Truly I could leave them in no better hands. Dear James, you have always been friend as much as brother to me, and I know that you will be a faithful father to my children.

I hope this is not my last letter to you, but it may be. It is only a matter of time. In any case, there is little more to say. We are leaving this world of trouble and cruelty, confident that we will travel together to whatever Paradise those who have always trusted to our Saviour are heirs to. We are terrible sinners, with the most miserable failings, but somehow I know that the Lord will treat us mercifully. And I have no doubt, my dear James, that sooner or later you and I will also be reunited there, and we will walk the heather once more. (Can there be Heaven without heather?)

Goodbye for now, James. Scotland for ever!

Sunday, 7 July 1900

Dear James,

It is as we expected. Lin came today. He brought with him a memorial from the Mandarin. He has finally answered my letter. It is not the reply I hoped for when I wrote to him. It is a formal proclamation acknowledging my 'appeal for mercy', but then it goes on to tell us that the foreigners 'have been justly condemned for their iniquities' and that we must await the 'sentence of the Emperor'. So much for a trial. It seems to have already taken place in our absence.

Perhaps it is better this way. I am glad that Nellie and the children will be spared the indignity of kneeling in a *yamen* court. I asked Lin when our execution is to take place, but he was his usual cold self. We will 'be informed', he told us. I imagine that it will not be long now.

Perhaps there is some humanity in the man. He brought with him a cartload of luscious water-melons, a gift for the condemned. You can imagine how welcome a treat this was for people who have been parched on small quantities of brackish water for the last few weeks.

We carried them into the kitchen, and made a great pile on the table. The children could hardly wait to fall on them. With rather doubtful humour Bowers brought down the chopper slicing the delicious fruit. 'Chop-chop! Chop-chop!' he said.

Oh, James, but you would have laughed to see . . .

Chapter Fifteen

Every day we attack the walls without success.
The ocean devils' magic is hard to overcome.

'You would have laughed to see . . .' Airton smiled as he sat at his desk, wondering how to describe the look on Bowers's so solemn face when he had realised the inappropriateness of his chopping remark, and his hangdog sheepishness afterwards. He wanted to describe it in a humorous way. After all, this might be the last letter he would ever write to his brother, and he wanted to communicate to James the good cheer that had blessed this household despite, or perhaps because of, their appalling predicament. Never before in his life, he realised, had he felt at such peace with himself. Never before had he felt such pleasure in the simplest things, or appreciated how truly wonderful it was to be alive. It was almost intoxicating. Even the ugly metal paperweight on his desk seemed to have a beauty of form. He felt suffused with love, for his family, for his fellow prisoners, even for the inanimate objects in the house. The motes of dust swirling in the rays of sunlight coming through the shutters made him think of flying angels. Of course he dreaded what was to come. He hated the fact that his children would suffer pain. He knew that all his fortitude would be required – but, strangely, even though his rational self reminded him of all these things and he knew that the time allotted to them was only a matter of days, the joy and intensity of living for the moment were enough to put all evil thoughts aside. It was like the holidays of his youth, romping on the beach in a golden for-ever, with no thought of the hospital ward or the study to which he would inevitably have to return. He wondered whether they had been granted a taste of the Heaven that was to come. A perpetual present bathed in the glow of love.

Absentmindedly he reached into his pocket for his tobacco pouch, but instead of the familiar soft leather he felt his fingers touching something hard. Surprised, he pulled out a small canvas package. Using his paper-knife, he cut the string tying it. Inside was a folded piece of paper and a ring, a gold signet ring. With a shock he recognised the emblem, a griffin half rampant, and a Latin motto *auxilium ab alto*. The last time he had seen this was on Henry Manners's finger.

The folded piece of paper lay on his blotting-pad. He had a reluctance to touch it. He felt resentment, revulsion. Until this – thing had arrived, everything had been so clear-cut. The path ahead was laid out. The slow fugue of martyrdom, in all its quiet beauty, was playing to its fall. All they had to do was accept what Fate had ordained for them. Therein lay peace. But now there had come a jarring note of discord. He knew instinctively that whatever this message contained it would bring complication to their existence. The mere idea – and he could hardly doubt it now – that Manners was still alive alarmed him. The uncharitable thought came to him: Oh, why could he not have remained safely dead? All that Manners had ever brought to them in the past was trouble. The very fact that it had been Major Lin who had delivered the package denoted intrigue. The package could have come from no other quarter. Lin was their only link with the outside world. Yes, he remembered now how Lin had uncharacteristically stumbled over his spurs and clutched the doctor's lapels to prevent himself falling. He must have slipped it into his pocket then. Airton resented the familiar emotions that were rising unbidden into his breast and that he thought he had conquered for good: those of fear – and, worse, of hope.

With trembling fingers he unfolded the paper and read the bold, incisive script. It was short, but very much to the point.

All are condemned. I can save you, your family and Helen Frances but nobody else. Say nothing to anybody but be prepared to move quickly. The window of your room after midnight. Lin will be the messenger.

Dr Airton dropped the paper. Then he laid his head on the desk and groaned.

'My dear Ma Na Si,' said the Mandarin, 'for a man being tortured to the point of death, your cries are extremely feeble. Please give some consideration for my reputation. We have an audience skulking somewhere outside, and I would hate that Iron Man Wang should have so poor an opinion of my abilities.'

'My apologies,' answered Manners, and let out an animal roar of pain. 'Is that better? When do I actually expire?'

'You are impatient, like all foreign devils. You should know that the art of torture in this country is much refined over many years, and we are expert at keeping people alive for excruciating lengths of time. I would ask you, please, to put more concentration into the task. The split bamboo that has been carefully inserted into your rectum should now be tearing at some of your lower organs. A very loud scream would be much appreciated, then I might allow you to faint for a while.'

Henry howled.

'Thank you. That will do. You may now consider yourself unconscious.'

'Thank goodness for that,' said Henry. 'I never was very good at amateur dramatics.' He looked down ruefully at his bloody legs where the manacles had chafed his skin to a nearly raw condition. 'Not that I have been acting overmuch lately.'

'No, the cage must have been very uncomfortable. Of course, it is designed for smaller criminals so you will have felt even more cramped than the usual occupants. That is one of the penalties you must pay for being a large, and very hairy, barbarian. Perhaps you will write a book one day describing our heathenish and diabolical practices.'

'I'll leave that to the missionaries,' said Henry. 'If any survive. Do you really have to execute so many?'

'The imperial edicts are very clear on that point. I am, as you know, a loyal civil servant. And, anyway, for the moment I am not exactly the master of my own establishment. Iron Man Wang has a bloodthirsty appetite, which I am afraid that I will have to indulge.'

'You know that the powers will come back with an army? Very foolish of the Empress to attack the Legations. China can't win on this one.'

'I am sure that you are right, and no doubt they will utterly destroy this very weak dynasty – but we are, thankfully, a long way from Peking. And chaos provides opportunities for the unscrupulous – especially if they have guns. Who knows? Your powers may even be grateful for a loyal local ally who has cleaned his city of bandits and Boxers responsible for the most wicked of atrocities.'

'You're an evil man, Da Ren,' said Henry.

'That is what my dear friend, the *daifu*, keeps telling me. But you should not be one to complain, Ma Na Si. Under our arrangement, I will have the guns but you will have my gold. Think of the rewards your government will bestow on you for providing so amply to their coffers. That is, if your government should ever receive the gold. In a disordered land so many things can go astray. What was I saying about chaos breeding opportunities for the unscrupulous?'

'I'll bear that in mind. We have to get out of here first, though. While I'm still unconscious I wouldn't mind if you could tell me the arrangements. You will still hold to your bargain about the doctor and Helen Frances?'

'If my conditions are met.'

'I am painfully aware of your conditions.'

'You should be grateful for my generosity. It is foolish in my position to spare anyone but yourself. You are necessary to me. The others are not. But I confess that I have a soft spot in my heart for the *daifu*, and his agreement to my proposal concerning your own paramour would be an interesting development of a philosophical debate that has afforded me much pleasure over the years. Of course, I will have to spare his wife and children too. So high-minded is he that he may not agree to come on his own if they are not included in our arrangement.'

Henry coughed a bloody gobbet of spittle on to the stone floor. 'Your bastard of a major might have damaged my lungs as well as breaking my ribs. You're an evil, lecherous bastard too, by the way. And I'm a bastard for letting you have your way.'

'You don't really have a choice, if you want to keep the girl. My advice all along to you has been to let her go and find another, but there is no accounting for western sentimentality. I resent your use of the word "lecherous", however. You are the lecherous one. If you are hurting from your beating by Lin you have only yourself to blame. Did I not warn you to avoid that courtesan of his?' The Mandarin stretched, and yawned. 'Am I lecherous?' he asked distractedly. 'No, but I am curious. Did I tell you that I once saw your woman from my palanquin? Her hair was of a most intriguing colour.' He smiled. 'Like fox fur. Come, come, these are bathhouse conversations. I am allowing myself to be distracted from my torture of you. A long drawn-out scream would be welcome if you can manage it. Please try to imagine that you are a man waking from unconsciousness to an agony of pain.'

'You haven't answered my question: how will I be getting out of here?'

'Did I not say? How remiss of me. In a coffin, my dear Ma Na Si, in a coffin. How else?'

'And when I have collected the doctor and the others, where are we to be taken?'

'Initially to the Palace of Heavenly Pleasure. Can you think of anywhere more appropriate?'

Dust puffed up from white summer roads as the pony-trap clattered down the hill. The harness jingled and the frame creaked under their weight. All around them the bushes were exploding with flower and bloom, and the oak trees swayed above their heads. Of course birds were singing and the sunshine made a warm glow of their faces. In the far distance they could see Ashdown Forest rising in blankets of gorse, and mountainous white clouds erupted into the sky, ships and castles and prancing stallions. Helen Frances was sitting on her father's knee. His tweed coat was rough on her bare arms, but she hugged him, half scared, half excited, totally content, and the sun beat down, and the cool breeze of their passing brushed her skin, and her father rattled the reins whooping out his jovial laugh, and the pony-trap gathered speed, while farmers, hoes on their shoulders, paused to watch their hurtling passage, and waved. The air was scented with all the perfume of all the flowers in the world. She looked up with adoration into Frank's deep-set brown eyes, which twinkled with merriment under the heavy black eyebrows. 'Hold tight, my little darling,' he roared. 'We're coming to the ford.' She hugged him tighter, hardly daring to look, and then there were fountains of water bursting around them, and the thunder of the weir, and they were through, and Frank was laughing, laughing, and she was screaming and laughing and crying, and the trap was bouncing along the dirt-track road, the seat was squeaking as it lifted them up and down, up and down, a rhythmic cradle rocking to and fro, to and fro, and she reached up and stroked her father's florid cheeks and bushy black moustache . . .

And the movement continued up and down, up and down, and she was laughing and screaming and crying, and inside her she felt a heat she could hardly contain, volcanoes of fire in her belly, suffusing her breasts, her arms, her thighs, her cheeks, and her head was shaking from side to side, and when she opened her eyes again she saw Henry above her, his features contorted as he thrust and thrust, burning, burning, and she squeezed with her thighs, her calves and her heels pressed into his behind so that he would go further, and further, and further inside her, and her fumbling hands pulled his wet hair down on her neck and breast, sweat mingling, flesh tingling, stomachs slapping and sucking. And Henry groaned, and molten lava surged from her loins to her womb and throughout her body, and the movement became a shudder, and then Henry lay beside her and she saw the beauty of his form, the perfect white limbs, the hollow of his belly, and she moved over him and drank the moisture in the matted hairs of his chest, and his stomach, and touched his red stalk and watched it rise again, and her mouth closed over the delicious soft flesh, kissing, caressing, sucking . . .

Sucking the smooth wood of the opium pipe, waiting for the sickly sweet smoke to enter her lungs and take away care. Anticipating the ensuing languor, the peace, the absence of all thought or desire. Such a little puff of smoke: that was all she needed. Just one pipe. She could even see the poppy paste heating over the candle. Surely it would be ready soon. She sucked the pipe, tasting the tar. Surely it would be ready soon . . . but the paste bubbled over the candle, and she sucked the pipe. And the smoke did not come . . .

She woke in despair. For a moment she did not know where she was. In a panic she looked for the familiar curtains of her home in Sussex and listened for the rustle of thrushes on the sill. But all she saw were the shutters that could not keep out the bright sunlight of north China; nor could they block out the stifling heat of a north China summer, or muffle the calling of the Boxers outside. And above the dripping, sweat-soaked sheets on which she lay hung the hated white ceiling, where a spider was swinging patiently on a strand from a crack in the plaster.

She hated her dreams. What right had her father to come back to life again and make her relive the happy times of her childhood? What right had Henry to make love to her, reigniting those still fires in her loins? Henry and her father were dead, and that was fine, because she, too, would be dead soon, and then there would be an end of it.

Every day she hoped that this would be *the* day. Sometimes in her imagination she had a chance to kiss the blade before it was wielded to strike off her head. She even imagined kissing the executioner's hand, like a grateful penitent genuflecting to the cardinal's ring. And she hoped that there would be no Heaven after, just nothing, an eternal nothing, oblivion that neither sleep nor the opium pipe nor the syringe could bestow.

And now she would have to get up for another day. She had slept very late. It must be afternoon. Mechanically she put on her skirt and blouse. She was tidying her hair when there was a knocking on her door. It was the doctor, and he looked extremely flustered. 'I'd like you to sit down,' he said. 'I have some rather startling news.'

She sat down on the edge of the bed as commanded. The doctor was fumbling in his pockets. 'My pipe,' he said. 'Would you mind? It's a disgusting habit, I know, and this is your room, but it does help calm my nerves.'

She watched him as he fussily lit his pipe and puffed away. 'It can't be worse news than we already know,' she said, after a while.

'No, my dear, no. It's the opposite. It's good news.'

'You don't look very happy about it,' she said.

'Oh, I am. I am. It's just – I don't know the best way to tell you. And bits of it may come as a shock.'

She waited, a little bored.

'It's – you see – it seems that there may be a chance of a rescue.'

'I don't want to be rescued,' she said.

'There you go again,' he said. 'You don't mean that. Well, I've received a letter – very secret, you mustn't tell the others, not immediately – but it seems that some of us have been chosen to be spared.'

'Some of us?'

'Yes, unfortunately only some were named, but there it is. Some is better than none. Well, you were one of the lucky ones. With my wife and Jenny and George, thank goodness. And, of course, Tom. Yes, Tom is one of the lucky ones. Yes, definitely Tom was one of the names mentioned. In the letter.'

'The letter from whom, Doctor? Can I see it?'

'No, I've burned it. Better that way. Can't let this slip out just yet, get into the wrong hands. In fact,' he lowered his voice, 'I haven't told anyone else except you.'

'You're being very mysterious, Doctor. Why only me?'

'I want your help, Helen Frances. With Nellie. She's very head-strong, as you know, and – well, she may refuse to go if she knows that I'm not escaping with her.'

'You're not one of the lucky ones, then?'

'No. No, alas, not. No, nobody would want a silly old man like me along. Strictly women and children. That's as it should be. Right and proper.'

'But it's not just women and children, is it? What about Laetitia Millward and her children? You didn't mention they were on the list, did you? And why is it that Tom is? Look, I don't want to go. Doctor, you must take my place. I mean it.'

She was startled to see Airton's agonised look.

'Oh, Helen Frances. Don't you think I want to live? But I can't. I can't go with you. My place is here, with my – with my flock, for want of a better word. I can't leave them. Don't you see that?'

Helen Frances suddenly realised the truth. 'Your name *was* on the list, wasn't it? And you're trying to save me instead of yourself.'

'You're a silly girl,' the doctor snapped, but his cheeks had flushed a deep red. 'Who do you think I am? God? To choose who will live and who will die? You think that I'm capable of such – blasphemy?'

Helen Frances reached out for his hand. 'No, Doctor, I think you're a very kind, brave and generous man. But I'm not worth saving. And you have a wife and children to protect.'

Airton pulled his hand away. 'Listen to me, lassie. I did not substitute your name. You were specifically chosen. And you are going, if not for your own sake, for the sake of your unborn babe. And Tom. And I need you to go, because otherwise Nellie might not. She'll go to look after you.'

'She'll go to look after her own children. Doctor, you're not telling me everything. The Mandarin wouldn't want to save me. He doesn't even know who I am. Why? Why me?'

Airton's trembling fingers fiddled with his pipe. 'It wasn't the Mandarin who sent the letter,' he brought himself to say, after a while. 'It was Manners. He's alive.'

Everything suddenly shone with a still clarity, as if a phosphorescent lamp had illuminated the room. She noticed the thread on the sleeve where the doctor had lost one of his buttons. She saw the stitching in the rug where it had been frayed away, and the blue enamel wash-basin and jug on the stand, and the dust on the mirror, and the little framed watercolour of the Hebridean islands on the whitewashed wall. It was as if time had stopped, and she and the doctor had become figures in a photograph, frozen in an eternal moment. Then, with a crash, the noise of drums returned, and she felt the blood rushing to her head, and the still room began to turn, and the worried look on the doctor's face was almost comical as he reached out to steady her. 'I'm all right,' she heard herself say, from a far distance, and then she was floating above a tropical sea where, in the black starlit night, a lightning storm began to rage.

'How is she, Edward?' Nellie asked. She had been waiting in their bedroom.

'Oh, shocked. What do you expect? But she'll be fine.'

'You told her the story, then? That she must come to persuade me?'

'Aye.'

He sat on the bed beside her and reached for her hand. The two of them sat in silence.

'You're determined, then?' Nellie asked, after a while. 'To abandon your good wife and wee bairns? Nobody will think the worse of you, you know, if you come with us.'

'I have my duty, woman. You know that.'

'Self-important and selfish to the last.'

'Oh, how can you say that?' He turned to her with sorrowful eyes. 'We discussed it and agreed. Helen Frances needs Tom to protect her from Manners, and I'm needed here. We went over it again and again.'

'I'm teasing you, you silly man.' She reached out for him, and he nestled his head on her expansive breast, which soon began to shake, as unbidden tears streamed down her strong features. 'Oh, but how I wish, Edward, how I wish.'

'I know. I know,' he whispered, moving her head to rest in turn on his chest. He kissed her auburn hair with its streaks of grey.

They held on to each other for some time. Then Nellie roused herself and dabbed her cheeks with a handkerchief, which she kept up her sleeve. 'Look at me,' she said. 'I'm becoming as silly and sentimental as you are. And I'll have to retidy my hair.'

'You're fine as you are,' said Airton.

'No, I'm not, I'm old,' said Nellie. 'What a pair we are. How have we lasted so long together?'

'Habit?' suggested the doctor, and Nellie laughed, but then her brows furrowed, and she turned to her husband with an intent expression.

'You know I'm only going because of the children? You know I'd stay with you, Edward, if it weren't for the bairns?'

'If I'd let you stay,' said Airton.

'You couldn't stop me, you dolt. I'd stay with you, I'd stay with you . . .'

'Till a' the seas gang dry?'

'Oh, aye, Edward. Sing that for me. Sing "The Rose".'

And rising above the noise of the drums outside, Edward Airton's voice rang, a surprisingly strong baritone:

> *'Till a' the seas gang dry, my dear,*
> *And the rocks melt wi' the sun:*
> *And I will love thee still, my dear,*
> *While the sands o' life shall run.'*

It was already night when the *yamen* gates opened and, under Major Lin's supervision, the coffin was carried out to the cart. The usual *yamen* Runners had long been replaced by two of Iron Man's bandits, who demanded to know what it contained.

Henry, cramped inside, chilled when he heard Major Lin's languid reply. 'Open it and find out for yourselves.'

He heard the rasp as the coffin lid was prised open, then felt cool air and saw lamplight through the straw and offal that covered him.

'It stinks,' said one of the guards. 'What is it?'

'A traitor,' said Lin. 'They all stink, don't they?'

'*Ta made*, he doesn't even look human. Not much left of him. What did you do to him?'

'Interrogated him,' said Lin.

'You were thorough about it,' said the guard. 'That's all I can say. Where are you taking him?'

'To his family. For burial.'

'They'll love you for that. You'd better get on with it, then. Exterminate the foreigners.'

'And save the Ch'ing,' finished Lin.

Henry heard the lid replaced, and tightened the handkerchief round his face, which even so could not keep out the rotten, fetid smell. In a moment he was being jostled as the cart moved down the hill. He felt blood dripping on to his forehead, and it took every measure of self-control not to retch.

There was another inspection at the city gates, and only after they had left the city walls behind them did Lin order the small convoy to stop. As soon as the coffin lid was open, Henry clambered out, desperately pushing aside the sheep entrails and the pork hanks that were wrapped in the remains of his clothes. He knelt in the mud, swallowing big gulps of clean air. His naked body covered from head to foot with blood and muck was black in the moonlight.

Major Lin surveyed him with contempt. 'Ma Na Si, now you actually look like the animal you are. There's a stream by the side of the road where you can wash. Take these clothes. Be quick. And don't try to run. My fingers are just itching for an opportunity to shoot you down.'

'And Fan Yimei, she is also well?' Henry called, over his shoulder.

'Don't tempt me, Ma Na Si. Please don't tempt me,' said Lin.

The chamberlain was smoking a pipe of opium with Mother Liu. He was tired, after a strenuous hour with a peasant boy who still stank of the farm. He had not enjoyed it. Perhaps he was getting old. Perhaps it was the times. Mother Liu was really dredging the wine pot, these days, for her regular customers. All her talented chickens, boys and girls, were now fully occupied with entertaining Iron Man Wang's brutes, poor things. He could hear them, even from Mother Liu's secluded room, roaring in the tea-house, and roistering in the dining rooms below them. Animals. He forced himself to listen to what his old friend was saying. These tedious negotiations – but it was important to see this one through.

'Yes, there will be six of them. Two children,' he repeated, for at least the tenth time that evening. 'You'll easily be able to hide them on your secret floor.'

'But the danger, Jin Lao . . .'

'That's exactly why you will be paid so very high a fee. And you will have the gratitude of the Mandarin on top of it. That's invaluable.'

'Nothing's invaluable, these days. And think of the compromise to Ren Ren. He's a high official now, a Boxer captain. What will happen to him if Iron Man Wang finds out?'

'Nobody will find out.'

'I'll do it for twice what you're offering.'

'That's absurd. You could establish five more brothels with the money I'm already giving you.'

'Three-quarters then.'

'Half.'

'All right. But the girl stays after, and maybe the two children, if I like them.'

'I can't promise that. This is the Mandarin's affair.'

'How long will he remain a mandarin if I tell Iron Man that he's hiding six foreign devils in the attic?'

'How long do you expect to enjoy your ill-gotten earnings if you do so? Who do you think it is who's protecting you? How long will you last with Iron Man Wang as your patron? Don't threaten me, old friend. You know I have your interests at heart.'

'Your own, you mean. I have just as much dirt on you as you have on me.'

'Mother Liu, why do you have to be so unpleasant on such a delightful evening?

> "Idly I watch the cassia flowers fall
> Still is the night, empty the hill in spring
> Up comes the moon, startling mountain birds,
> Once in a while in the spring brook they sing."'

'Jin Lao. Do control yourself. This isn't the time for poetry. Look, I can persuade Ren Ren. The money's enough – but he'll want something more for his pains. Give him the girl. What's she to anyone after the Mandarin is finished with her? Be practical, Jin Lao. Think of a poor old woman and her difficulties with her unruly child.'

'Give me another pipe and let's be done with this haggling.'

'Then you agree?'

'I didn't say that. I'll consider your request.'

'That's not good enough.'

'All right, then. I'll consider your request kindly.'

'Oh, Jin Lao, you are, as always, the fountain of generosity. How do I, a poor old woman, deserve such a friendship? Now, what was that delightful poem you were reciting to me?'

> *'Abide with me; fast falls the eventide;*
> *The darkness deepens; Lord with me abide.*
> *When other helpers fail and comforts flee,*
> *Help of the helpless, O abide with me.'*

The doctor watched Nellie sitting at the piano, the light from the gas lamp lighting her hair, and her beautiful neck rising from her necklace of pearls. The sad music of the hymn crumbled his self-control and he felt hot tears running down his cheeks. Across the room he saw Helen Frances, one hand in Jenny's, the other holding her hymnal. She noticed his distress and smiled at him. He nodded gratefully. Gradually he pulled himself together. He knew that he must show strength – but his heart was breaking. Perhaps his son, George, sensed that something was troubling his father. His little hand reached upwards, and Airton held it tightly, his eyes misting again.

Oh, let it be soon, he was thinking, let midnight come. I can't bear this much longer. At least let this hymn end soon, but verse followed verse, each plonking note from the piano like a dart piercing his soul.

> *'I fear no foe, with Thee at hand to bless;*
> *Ills have no weight, and tears no bitterness.*
> *Where is death's sting? Where, grave, thy victory?*
> *I triumph still, if Thou abide with me.'*

Septimus Millward stood erect, one arm raised to his breast, his beard lifted, singing with vigour. His wife Laetitia's shrill voice accompanied him. His children were arrayed, in order of size downwards, in two neat rows on either side of their parents, Hiram standing proudly next to his father. Look at them, thought the doctor. They will die as a family, together, and happily. He felt a surge of envy, wondering how he would be able to go on once Nellie and his own children had left him. He had a moment of terror as he imagined himself kneeling alone in the sand under the executioner's sword. Would he blubber? Would he disgrace his family, his name, his God, and die like the coward he knew himself in his darkest moments to be? Then he saw Burton Fielding standing away from the others, head turning from side to side, with distracted eyes. There but for the grace of God, he thought bitterly. No, he would be strong. He would not be like Fielding. This was the right choice, the right thing to do, the only thing to do. The Tempter had offered him a chance to escape his duty, and he had spurned the temptation. He was doing what was right. Oh, but it was hard.

The dirge-like hymn rolled to its last stanza. Airton tightened his hold on his hymnbook, and his baritone rose above the others, stronger if it was possible even than Millward's rich, confident tones:

> *'Hold Thou Thy cross before my closing eyes;*
> *Shine through the gloom and point me to the skies.*
> *Heaven's morning breaks, and earth's vain shadows flee;*
> *In life, in death, O Lord, abide with me.'*

They took the children into their own bedroom for this last night. George and Jenny slept fretfully under the sheet, the noise of the drums disturbing their dreams. Dr Airton and Nellie had long ago said whatever they had to say to each other. There were no more words. They sat side by side, holding hands and looking at their children. A small leather suitcase lay on the floor, packed with clothes.

Just after midnight the doctor thought that he heard a sound, but opening the shutter he saw nothing but the bare lawn. They waited. The hall clock struck one.

'Do you think it was a hoax, Nellie?' he whispered. 'Or that something's happened to him?'

She squeezed his hand. They waited. The hall clock struck two.

'Oh, I can't bear this any longer,' muttered Airton. 'I want to scream.'

'Be brave, Edward. Be brave,' said Nellie.

'You don't know how much I love you,' he said.

'I do,' she said. 'I do.'

They both started at the brisk tap on the window. Each froze. Neither wished to admit that the moment had come. There was another loud rap. It was Nellie who roused herself and briskly opened the shutters. She stood back, her hands to her mouth. A figure dressed in black climbed quickly into the room. They watched him stride purposefully to the door, open it a fraction and look out. He seemed satisfied by the silence in the corridor, and turned towards the Airtons, stepping into the lamplight as he did so. Nellie gasped, and Airton started. 'My God, man, what's happened to your face?' whispered the doctor.

'Not a pretty sight, I suppose. I've been enjoying *yamen* hospitality for the last few weeks,' said Manners. 'Have you a mirror? Yes, I see what you mean. Very ugly. But never mind all that. Where's Helen Frances?'

'In her room,' said Nellie.

'Well, get her. As quietly as you can. We haven't much time.'

Nellie slipped out.

'So, Doctor, I trust you are well.'

'As well as could be expected,' said Airton.

'I'm pleased to hear it,' said Henry.

'I'm not coming with you,' said Airton.

'Are you not?' asked Henry.

'No, my place is here, with the others. They need me.'

'You know what's going to happen to those who stay behind?'

'I have a good idea, yes.'

'Then you're either very noble, very brave or very stupid. In any case it doesn't matter. You're coming.'

'You can't force me.'

'No, I can't – but if you don't come neither do any of the others.'

'You can't mean that, man. You'll take the women and children with you. A barbarian would do no less.'

'No, Doctor, it doesn't work that way. All come, or none do.'

'I've given my place to Tom Cabot.'

'I'm afraid it's not yours to give. Seriously, Doctor, if you don't come with me, I'm leaving without any of you. You'd better make up your mind quickly.'

'You'll leave without Helen Frances?'

'Try me.'

'But what does it matter to you whether I come or not?'

'It doesn't. But it does to the Mandarin. They're his terms. He's the arbiter of life and death, not me.'

'This is madness. I don't believe you.'

He would have argued more, but at that moment Helen Frances burst into the room, a Gladstone bag in her hand, her hair dishevelled. She stopped short at the sight of Henry, and for a moment the two of them stared at each other awkwardly. Then with a cry she threw herself into his arms. 'Oh, my darling, they told me you were dead, you were dead. Oh, thank God, thank God, thank God . . .' and she covered his bruised face with wild kisses of joy.

The children were sitting up in bed with their mouths open, and Airton stood by helplessly, not knowing what to do or say. That was the point when Nellie returned to the room, one hand supporting Tom who was leaning on his crutches. He looked at the lovers once, then turned his head away. Airton's face went white with alarm.

Henry had been facing the door and, in the interval of her kisses, he too had seen Helen Frances's fiancé enter the room. Gently he disengaged her. She turned her head to follow his look. 'Oh, God,' she said, and stepped aside, but she did not leave go of Henry's arm. 'Airton,' Manners breathed, 'trust you to make a pig's ear of it all. I can't take him, you know.

'Hello, Tom,' he said, in conversational tones.

'Manners,' Tom muttered, not raising his head.

'We both look rather worse for wear, if you don't mind my saying so. Boxers in your case?'

'Yes,' said Tom. 'On the road back to Shishan. You?'

'Lin's beating, with the odd thrashing by the Mandarin's prison warders after. Not really a gentle experience.'

'Well. You survived, didn't you?'

'Yes, I did,' said Henry

'I could've wished you hadn't. There was a time when I was glad you were dead.'

'I understand,' said Henry.

'I would have liked to kill you myself. For a long time – oh, well before the Boxers came – I dreamed of little else.'

'I put the horns on you. It's understandable.'

'No, that's not my point,' said Tom, looking up with an anxious expression on his face. 'You were – you were always the better man, you see.'

'Bollocks, Tom.'

'You were. That's why the other night when HF . . .'

'Oh, Tom, don't say it,' pleaded Helen Frances.

'No, it's true,' said Tom. 'HF, I never deserved you. I'm grateful for – for the time we had together, what you gave me . . . And now I'm glad Henry's alive again for you.'

'I can't take you with us, Tom,' said Henry gently.

'I never intended to come. Sorry, Dr Airton, I led you on a bit, I'm afraid, when you asked me this afternoon. I saw the opportunity to see Henry, and HF, for just one last time, to say what I had to say. Settle my account, so to speak. Apologise once and for all for being such an ass.'

'Oh, Tom,' said Helen Frances. 'I'm so, so sorry.'

'No, don't be sorry. I'm not sorry. I think I can face this particular wicket rather well, in fact. Maybe cheer up some of the others on the way. It won't be nice for the Millward children, or Caterina. And Fischer and that Fielding are in a bit of a funk. Team needs stiffening up. The old folks when they hear about it may yet find it in their hearts to be proud of me. One last match well played and so on. I have a letter for them, by the way. Maybe one of you could take it for me.'

'You're a brave man, Tom,' said Henry. 'I'm proud to know you.' The two men shook hands. 'Tom, I'm afraid we have to go,' said Henry.

'HF, the other night . . .'

'Nothing happened, Tom. Nothing.' She reached up to peck him on the cheek, then impulsively hugged him. It was Tom who finally pulled away.

'Godspeed, HF.'

'Godspeed, Tom.'

She touched his cheek. The big man hung on his crutches, his head bowed. She turned briskly away and picked up her portmanteau. Nellie had got the children out of bed. They were wearing their day clothes, and were now holding their mother's hands, their eyes big with wonder at this dramatic turn of events.

'Now, Doctor, are you coming?' said Henry. 'I haven't the time to argue. You know what it means if you say no.'

'I – I can't,' said Airton.

'Then I can take none of you. That's the deal I made with the Mandarin.'

'Mr Manners, what is this?' asked Nellie. 'Edward, what is he saying?'

The door burst open, and Burton Fielding stood in the room, a knife in his hand. 'I've seen you rats,' he shouted, 'skulking down the corridors. I've heard you cowards, planning your breakaway. But don't think anyone is going anywhere without me.'

'Who the hell are you?' asked Manners. 'This is like a vaudeville show.'

'You want to know who I am?' he yelled at Manners. 'Whoever *you* are. I'm the superintendent of the American Board of Commissioners for Foreign Missions in China, and the senior minister here, not that any of you skunks show any respect for authority. Especially that cowardly cur Airton over there, who I see is the first to try to make a bunk of it, abandoning his duties. Well, if anybody's leaving, I am,' he finished, 'and I'll slice anybody who tries to stop me.'

They stared at him – as much in pity as amazement. Fielding's eyes were blazing, and he was waving his knife like a madman. He might have caused some hurt had not the large figure of Septimus Millward suddenly appeared behind him, and held him fast, twisting the knife out of his hand so it dropped to the floor.

'Gentlemen, ladies, I was woken by the commotion. Dr Airton, is this misguided man bothering you?' he asked politely, gagging the struggling Burton Fielding with his large hand.

'We were just leaving, actually,' said Henry. 'Or I hope we were. Doctor?'

'How can I?' snapped Airton angrily. 'I can't be party to any bargain with the Mandarin.'

'Then your sensibilities do you credit, but you'll be condemning your wife and children, and Helen Frances, to death. That's your choice,' said Henry, 'and I'm asking for the last time. Major Lin will be wondering what's going on and will be coming for me any minute.'

'Nellie, what do I do?'

'Edward, I can't make this decision for you.'

'Oh, my God,' cried Airton, covering his face with his hands. 'Help me.'

They all watched him in his agony. Only Septimus in his long Chinese gown appeared calm. He broke the tense silence. 'Excuse me, Doctor, it's none of my business, but do I understand that this man is offering you the choice between life and death for your family? And are you standing in the way of it? Are you not thereby putting yourself just a little in danger of succumbing to the mortal sin of pride?'

Airton slumped to the floor, breathing heavily. 'I want nothing else,' he said weakly, 'than to escape with my family, but how can I? How can I?'

'Through the window?' was Septimus's helpful suggestion. 'That's how I'd do it.'

'Come on, you silly man. Up you get,' said Nellie. 'Tell us what to do, Mr Manners. Shall we follow you?'

One after another, they climbed through the window, and jumped down on to the grass, Henry supporting them from below. Septimus, who had locked the struggling, gagged Burton Fielding in the wardrobe as a temporary measure, handed down the ladies' two portmanteaux, and the doctor's medical bag, which he had noticed in a corner of the room. Henry gestured towards the shadows of the trees, where the cart was waiting. Luckily clouds were covering the moon so there was a good chance that they would not be spied by the Boxers, whose fires they could see burning down the hill. Henry hurried them along, carrying the ladies' bags. Nellie steadied the stumbling George and Jenny, and Helen Frances carried Airton's medical bag. The doctor, unencumbered, took one last agonised look behind him. Burned in his memory for ever were the faces in the window, not only of Septimus and Tom, but also of Herr Fischer, Caterina and Mr Bowers who had also presumably been wakened by the disturbance caused by Mr Fielding, and who had arrived in time to watch their pastor leave them. Their faces were sombre, wistful and, to the doctor, reproachful. None of them waved goodbye.

Those faces were all that the stunned doctor saw as they made their escape that night. He seemed hardly aware of what was happening, and had to be steered by Henry through the thick undergrowth. Lin and his soldiers were waiting for them by the cart, gesturing angrily to them to hurry. The Boxers might surprise them at any moment and the troopers had their carbines at the ready. Lin looked with displeasure at the portmanteaux, but threw them in all the same before bolting the tailgate. Slowly they moved off through the trees, the troopers leading their horses.

Only when they had reached the open road did Lin relax and

order the soldiers to mount. Then they made a fast pace under the stars, bumping along the dirt track.

They stopped by a small farmhouse where there was a stack of hay in the courtyard. Lin ordered them to lie flat on the rough boards, and the soldiers proceeded to pile the hay on top of them. The doctor thought, I am being buried for my sins, but the reproachful faces continued to gaze at him when he closed his eyes.

They reached the city gates where there was an inspection of the cart. They heard rough voices demanding to know what Major Lin was doing arriving in the city in the dead of night. They heard him explaining that he was bringing hay for his stables, and what business was it of theirs at what hour he came or went? Perhaps they would like to take it up with the Mandarin, whose orders he was following. The gates creaked open, and they rattled on.

Before they reached the square they turned into a side-street. At last they stopped, and they heard Lin commanding them to get out of the cart. They pushed their way through the suffocating hay, scratching their faces as they did so. They were in a dark alley. Two stone lions guarded a wooden door. They were given black woollen cloaks, with hoods to cover their faces, then Lin rapped on the door. A hard-faced woman was waiting for them, her face caked in white powder and makeup. 'Major Lin, how pleased I am to see you again,' she simpered. 'And Ma Na Si Xiansheng. It's been such a long time.' She raised her lantern and identified Helen Frances. 'It's not the first time that you've graced our establishment, is it, Xiaojie?' She reached bony, ringed fingers forwards and gently pinched Helen Frances's cheek. 'And still as pretty as ever, I see.' Helen Frances flinched away. 'Well, do come in. Do come in,' said the woman, hobbling on her lotus feet along the lantern-lined path. 'You must all be very tired and hungry after your arduous journey. What sweet little children you have,' she cooed. 'It's the famous Ai Dun Yisheng, isn't it, unless I am much mistaken? Welcome, Daifu, welcome. All friends of the Mandarin are welcome here, you know. We are so honoured to have this chance to entertain you in our humble home.'

They moved through the courtyards. Helen Frances shuddered slightly when she saw the familiar pavilion, and Henry put a protective arm around her shoulder. The children gazed in awe. They had never seen such a palatial mansion.

'Now, you must be very quiet as we go up the stairs', said the woman. 'The house is sleeping, but you never know who may be about. We are entertaining so many people, these days. So many guests – none of them, of course, as welcome as yourselves.'

They climbed the dark stairs, the woman puffing ahead of them. The odour of stale perfume pervaded the building, and they heard odd creaking noises coming from inside some of the rooms off the second landing, and once a loud brutal laugh, followed by a shrill squeal. George whimpered with fear. She turned, revealing a cruel smile as the lamp illuminated her face. 'There's nothing to be afraid of, little one. That's only guests amusing themselves. I'd offer you a peep, but I'm sure your mother wouldn't like that,' and she chuckled to herself as she led them along the landing.

Up to a bare wall, or that was what it seemed like, but the woman lifted a scroll, and behind it turned a catch, and a door swung open to reveal another flight of steps. 'Not far to go now,' she said. 'One at a time, please. Be very quiet. Isn't it exciting, little ones? A secret door! Oh, what sweet little creatures you are,' and she stroked Jenny's hair. Nellie pulled her daughter away. Mother Liu laughed.

They reached a bare wooden gallery. 'That's my room,' she said. 'Please don't hesitate to knock on my door at any time for any service whatsoever. And this is your room, Daifu.' She opened a door to a room blazing with candles. It was dominated by a large red-covered four-poster bed, while on the floor were two futons which had presumably been prepared for the children to sleep on. Nellie's eyes, however, were drawn to the paintings on the walls, which revealed lovers in various indecent positions. 'Ah, you've noticed my art collection.' Mother Liu smiled maliciously. 'They're by the finest artists, you know. I do so hope that you will be comfortable here, and enjoy your time with us.'

Still smiling, she closed the door behind her. They could hear her voice cooing along the corridor. 'And for the lovers. Oh, I have a wonderful room prepared for you, Ma Na Si, and for your lady friend . . .'

Nellie dropped her portmanteau on to the sumptuous carpet. 'Well, my dear, it seems that Henry and our Helen Frances are to spend a night of sin together,' she said brightly.

Airton had slumped on the bed, his head in his hands. With an effort, he brought his attention back to what his wife was saying. 'Yes,' he muttered. 'Yes, I suppose they are.'

'Not much that we can do about it,' said Nellie. 'Anyway, it wouldn't be for the first time. Let's assume they're already married in the sight of God.'

'Aye,' said Airton, weakly. 'That would be generous.'

'Come on, you.' Nellie turned her attention to the children. 'Jenny, will you stop gawping at those pictures. You're far too young to understand them. Come on, into your beds now. And you, young man. We'll all need our sleep for the days ahead of us.'

When she was satisfied that the children were comfortably tucked up, she sat down beside her husband, who was sitting on the bed, gazing listlessly at the floor. 'Edward,' she murmured, 'is this place what I think it is?'

Airton groaned.

'What would your brother James say, or my aged parents for that matter, if they knew we were spending a night together in a brothel? Can you imagine their long, solemn faces?' She smiled. And then she began to laugh, a deep-throated, hearty laugh, which rocked the bed on which they were sitting.

The laughter disturbed Airton from his introspection. 'Have you gone mad, woman?' he rounded on her. 'Do you realise where we are? Oh, what have I done? What have I done? Did you see their faces, Nellie, when we left them? And all to bring you to this Babylonian sink of iniquity. What have I done?'

Nellie kissed him. 'You've saved my life and that of our children, that's what you've done. You've been a good husband and father. And you were very brave. You've nothing to reproach yourself for, Edward, nothing. And I love you the more.'

But Airton dropped his head into his hands, the reproachful faces of Sister Caterina, Herr Fischer and Frederick Bowers accusing him of his desertion. He felt foul, corrupted, damned, to the extremities of his soul.

'You can sit there feeling sorry for yourself if you like, my dear,' said Nellie, after a while, 'but I'm tired and want to go to bed.'

One by one she blew out the candles until the room was perfectly dark. Airton was left alone in the blackness contemplating the faces of all the people he had betrayed.

* * *

As soon as the cackling Mother Liu had closed the door on them, Henry and Helen Frances had fallen into each other's arms, scrabbling with their hands to tear away each other's clothes, devouring each other with their lips, teeth, tongues, grunting in their haste to press naked skin against naked skin, flesh against flesh.

'Oh, my darling, your bruises. How I've . . . how I've . . .'

'Oh, my love, my love. The thought of you . . .'

Each incoherent sentence was stopped by a hungry kiss.

Panting they wrenched away from each other. Henry hopped on one foot as he pulled off his boots. Helen Frances had already ripped the shirt from his back, and he her blouse. She fell back on the bed as she unclasped her skirt, wriggling out of it and throwing it aside. Henry had already kicked away his trousers. She lifted her arms, moaning with impatience as he pulled her chemise over her head. She lay back on the pillow, raising her lower body so that he could enter her. Blood tingling, eyes burning, hands trembling, she reached out for him.

But Henry stood frozen, staring at her.

Perplexed, she raised herself on her elbows.

'Darling? What is it?'

'Your stomach,' he whispered.

She sank back on the pillows.

'My God, I didn't know,' he said.

She groaned. A tear formed in her eye. 'I couldn't bring myself to tell you,' she whispered. 'I knew . . . I knew in the Black Hills. That's why I said I wanted to leave Shishan. But surely it's different now? It doesn't matter now?' Her eyes pleaded. 'It's different, isn't it?' She was weeping.

'Yes, it's different,' said Henry, his eyes widening. 'Oh, God,' he said. 'Oh, God, what have I done? What have I done?'

Her eyes implored him. 'Love me.' It was hardly a whisper.

'Oh, my darling,' he cried, taking her into his arms, covering her face with kisses.

'Oh, God, if I'd known . . . I'd known.' Softly his palm cupped the light protuberance of her belly, where the life was growing inside. 'Oh, darling, forgive me. Forgive me,' he murmured. Her mouth met his. Gently he settled his body over hers. She gasped, and squeezed his back when he entered her.

Downstairs in one of the dining halls of the Palace of Heavenly

Pleasure, Iron Man Wang's men were firing their rifles at the ceiling in a drunken debauch. The noise, like faraway firecrackers, hardly reached them. Their bodies moved to a rhythm of their own creation. The old four-poster squeaked, and for a while it seemed that in this private world of touch, heat and smell into which they had retreated, nothing could harm them. Not this night. Not while their arms were there to enfold each other; nor afterwards, when her head lay on his shoulder, and he breathed the scent of her hair, tangled in his own. For this one night they were protected, if only by each other from all the devils that stalked outside.

Chapter Sixteen

*The Imperial troops are brutal. They do not understand the
deep magic.
Master Zhang says be patient. Victory will come.*

M ajor Lin's troops arrived at the mission shortly after ten. This
time he did not bring melons.

Herr Fischer opened the door. He was in his nightshirt and was
holding a teapot.

'It's time,' said Lin shortly.

Herr Fischer blinked when he saw the grim-faced soldiers standing
menacingly behind their officer, and the two covered travelling carts
waiting by the gate. He understood. '*Ja*. I will inform the others,'
he said.

Troopers with fixed bayonets followed him into the hall.

It was all quite orderly. The Millwards were ready first. The
children followed Laetitia in file like a school crocodile towards
the gate. Septimus strode solemnly behind, a prayer book clutched
to his chest. His other hand kept a firm grasp on Burton Fielding's
elbow, steering the cowed minister forward. After a half-hour in a
cupboard and the rest of the night in enforced prayer with Septimus,
the superintendent of the American Board of Commissioners for
Foreign Missions in China had become a much humbler man, if
slightly dazed by the experience. Caterina came out next, wearing
her Ursuline robe and wimple and holding a rosary. Frederick Bowers
had put on full railwayman's uniform. He and a frock-coated Fischer
helped Tom down the steps.

They were thankful for the protection of the covered carts as they
ran the gauntlet through the Boxer lines. There were the expected
jeers and shouts, and some missiles were thrown at them. Sister
Caterina was sitting closest to the tailboard of her cart, and could
see the grimacing, angry, hate-filled faces, jostling for a view of
their condemned enemies. She noticed one man because, unlike the
others, he was smiling. With a start she recognised Zhang Erhao,

who had once shared the daily chores of the hospital with her as Dr Airton's major-domo. Their eyes met and he spat, a yellow gobbet of phlegm, which stuck to her robe. The cart jolted on.

It was a relief to reach the open countryside.

It was a glorious day. Great clouds rolled in a deep blue sky. The leaves on the elms were rustling in a slight breeze. Magpies and choughs flew among the branches. In another circumstance, on just such a day, they might have been going on an outing, in just such a cart, with Jenny and George. Sister Caterina suddenly thought of Elena, and began to weep.

'Come on, old girl.' She felt a large hand on her shoulder and saw Tom's red, smiling face beside her. 'Here, give me your hand.'

Faintly, from the cart in front of them, where the Millwards were, they could hear the sound of a hymn. They could make out some of the words. Septimus's strong voice carried over the clatter of the wheels, the shrill voices of his children accompanying him.

> 'We shall reach the summer land,
>   Some sweet day, by and by;
> We shall press the golden strand,
>   Some sweet day, by and by . . .'

'Look, I don't know that one,' said Tom, 'but we can do better than the Yanks, can't we? Come on, Bowers. let's give them an English hymn. Come on, Caterina, you've got a lovely voice. Drown me out because I sound like a foghorn . . . All right, I'll start.' And taking a deep breath he began to sing:

> 'There is a green hill far away
> Without a city wall . . .'

Come on, chaps. Join in.'

Bowers chuckled. 'Did you say foghorn, Mr Cabot? Sounds more like a croaking frog to me. Let's show you how we sing in the Dales. With a pint or two inside us, perhaps. It's a beautiful morning and there'll be time enough for religion before the long day's done. Now, this is an old song my mother taught me. You foreigners may find the words a little strange at first, but just follow along,' and clearing his voice he began to sing 'On Ilkley Moor Bar t' At'.

Tom joined in enthusiastically:

'"*Where hast thou been since I saw thee, I saw thee
On Ilkley Moor bar t'at . . .*'

Herr Fischer found he could not help laughing. 'You English. Oh, you English,' he said. 'You never behave appropriately,' but he began to follow:

'"*I've been a courting Mary Jane,
I've been a courting Mary Jane . . .*"'

His harsh, guttural bass hardly added to the harmony, but he had a smile on his face as he sang.

'That's good, Mr Fischer. That's good. We'll make an Englishman of you yet,' said Bowers. 'Now, Sister, will you join us for the third verse?'

'"*Then thou will catch thy death of cold, death of cold
On Ilkley Moor bar t'at . . .*"'

Weakly, at first, she too joined in, but her voice strengthened and soon they were all bellowing out the nonsensical refrains, and laughing between the verses. And after 'Ilkley Moor', Bowers led them through 'Do Ye Ken John Peel?'. Then Tom sang the 'Eton Boating Song', and Herr Fischer remembered a drinking song from his days at Heidelberg, and Sister Caterina sang 'Funiculi Funicula'. And then, by common volition, they began all over again with a resounding repetition of 'Ilkley Moor.'

Major Lin rode behind them on his grey mare, a stern expression on his face. He wondered whether these prisoners really knew the fate so imminently in store for them. That they could roister in such a way! Had they no fear? A Chinese would have comported himself to his death with dignity. Yes, even scum like Iron Man Wang and his bandits, or the scabbiest peasant. How he loathed these foreigners. Even now they appeared to be mocking him. He hated them almost as much as he hated the Boxers. Undisciplined rabble. He longed for an ordered society, a restoration of the old virtues, a respect for the majesty and terror of the law. Well, he would impose order with the Mandarin's guns. But these foreigners – why did they not show fear?

The little convoy moved on through the lanes, and the singing rose from the carts of the condemned to the blue dome of sky above; from one cart came 'Praise My Soul, the King of Heaven', from the other 'Ilkley Moor Bar t' At.'

When they were in sight of the city walls, Major Lin stopped the convoy. They would walk the last quarter-mile to the city square.

They were stripped of their fine clothes. Chinese criminals walked bare-chested to their execution. Even the women were stripped to their skirts, although they were allowed to hold up the fronts of their dresses in some preservation of modesty. It did not seem the time to worry about such things, and neither Caterina nor Laetitia showed any objection. It was somehow beneath their dignity to do so. There were too many of them for them all to be given *cangues*, so only four, Septimus Millward, Herr Fischer, Burton Fielding and Frederick Bowers were loaded with the heavy wooden collars. Tom was spared this because of his disability. A stretcher had been prepared for him, but he indicated angrily that he would walk on crutches, and Major Lin let him have his way. Nor did Lin insist that they be shackled. It would merely have burdened the march. The irons were thrown back into one of the carts.

Yamen officials were waiting for them. Chamberlain Jin was in his palanquin. He had the responsibility of leading them to the square. Bannermen stood with their pennants flapping. Others held long sticks, their task if necessary to beat their way through the crowds. A drummer had a big tom-tom tied to his chest, and two musicians were adjusting their long horns; their role was to walk near the front of the procession to give warning to passers-by to stand aside.

There was the usual Chinese chaos as everyone found their places in the line of march. Major Lin sat on his horse irritated by the delays. Finally Chamberlain Jin waved an elegant hand out of his palanquin, and Major Lin barked the order to begin.

The heavy drum began to thump. The horns began to blare.

At a desperately slow pace – that of the children and Tom on his crutches – the procession began to move.

The gate tower loomed above them. Soldiers and ruffians were leaning over the crenellations to catch a glimpse of them. Then they were swallowed by the dark cavern of its inside, the spikes of the portcullis hanging threateningly over their heads as they passed within. And out the other side, where a blaze of sunlight hit their eyes, blinding them for a moment before they noticed the thick crowds lining the road. Even the balconies of the houses were filled with people. So many of Shishan's citizens had come out to watch the foreigners die. But this was not the usual Chinese crowd. It was silent. It was as if they could not believe what they were seeing. Burton Fielding stumbled under the weight of his *cangue*, his head bowed to the road in front of him. The others somehow carried themselves upright. Septimus Millward strode proudly in front, eyes looking neither left nor right, although occasionally he cast a fond glance at Hiram, who was walking by his side. The women had forgotten their modesty and were holding hands with the smaller children, one on either side. Tom strained on his crutches at the rear, Frederick Bowers held a steadying hand on his shoulder. The black-bearded railwayman gazed at the crowd on either side with equanimity.

'Colourful-looking lot, aren't they, Mr Cabot?' he said. 'Sad to be born a heathen, don't you think? You know, I never had much time for China's famous five thousand years of civilisation. Hasn't seemed to have brought them very far, to my way of thinking.'

'They're certainly not behaving in a very civilised way today,' Tom muttered, between panting breaths. 'You know, I think it's time for another song.'

'"Ilkley Moor" wouldn't be very appropriate now, sir.'

'No, something more rousing,' said Tom. 'Something to show them what we're made of.' He gathered his breath, and called over the procession to Septimus, 'Millward! Do you know "Onward Christian Soldiers"?'

'I certainly do,' called back Septimus. He lifted his lion-maned head and began to sing. His family, dutifully trained, joined in, and so, one by one, did the others. Even Fielding mouthed the words. The Christian clarion call to arms evoked by the thin voices rose above the drums and the horns, and there was a murmur in the crowd. Major Lin turned sideways on his horse, looked behind him and frowned, but he could do nothing about it. The chamberlain leaned his head out of his carriage. His long-nailed fingers hanging on the side of the palanquin began unconsciously to tap the rhythm of the tune. He smiled, thinking of the spectacle to come. A voice in the crowd shouted out, 'Exterminate the foreigners! Save the Ch'ing!' but it was only one voice. The bulk of the crowd remained silent, watching, wondering.

The small band of pilgrims marched singing to their martyrdom.

They had slept late into the morning. The children were still sleeping when Nellie and Airton rose. He looked at his watch. It was well after noon.

'Let them sleep on, Edward, they're exhausted, poor little things,' said Nellie.

They did their toilet. There was a wooden pail full of water and a ladle in one corner of the room, next to an ample chamber pot. When they were dressed, they sat on the bed. There seemed little else to do. 'I'm a mite hungry,' said Nellie. 'Do you think we could ask that awful woman to make us some food?' but there was no need, for outside the door in the otherwise empty corridor the doctor found a tray on a stool. There was a pot of tea in a warmer, cups and little wooden receptacles containing cold sweetmeats and some *mantou*. 'Room service?' said Nellie.

'Aye,' said the doctor glumly, and poured some tea.

'No sign of the lovers?' asked Nellie.

'No,' said the doctor.

'Well. I suppose all we can do is wait for something to happen, then,' said Nellie. 'Somebody must have something planned for us.'

'Aye,' said the doctor, his mind elsewhere.

Someone knocked on the door. It was Henry. He had a grim expression on his face. 'Doctor, I think you had better come and see this,' he said. 'But, Mrs Airton, you might like to stay in your room.'

'Whatever it is,' said Nellie, 'I'm coming with my husband.'

'So be it,' said Henry. 'But it won't be pleasant.'

They followed him into the gallery. They could hear the murmuring, roaring sound of a crowd. Helen Frances was standing on a bench that allowed her a view out of the high window. Her face was ashen, and she wore the same grim expression as Henry.

'I'll help you up,' she said to Nellie, reaching out a hand. The four stood on the bench and looked below. They could see the curling roofs of the temple directly opposite them, and the grey tiles of the city stretching to the distance in all directions. They also had a very good view of the square, which was filled with excited people. The centre of the square was empty, a bare ring of sand, in the middle of which stood a large man, stripped to the waist and leaning on a sword. He was exchanging pleasantries with the crowd. 'Oh, my God,' cried Airton. 'It's to be an execution. Oh, Manners, it's not . . . it's not . . . Is it?' Henry did not reply. As they watched there was a movement in the crowd and they saw the Mandarin, accompanied by a bear-like man in shaggy furs, with whom he was conversing, laughing at something his companion was saying, and following them were a raggle-taggle parade of officials and others who looked like thugs. This official party made their way casually to chairs that had been arranged for them at one side of the square. 'Iron Man Wang,' said Henry, 'and his ruffians. Well, I wouldn't have expected anything else.'

Nothing seemed to happen for a while. The Mandarin and his companions were smoking their long pipes. The hairy man next to him was drinking from a gourd. The crowd became restless. A group dressed in Boxer uniform took up the by now familiar chant, 'Exterminate the foreigners! Save the Ch'ing,' but like the sporadic bursts of song which erupt in a football crowd and die down again, the chant sputtered out. Egged on by the throng, the man with the sword began to twirl it round his head, performing some sort of martial-arts dance. There were cheers. Then he, too, stopped, and gradually the crowd became silent, waiting.

As they also waited, frozen, on their bench in the gallery.

Then they heard the slow beating of a drum, and braying horns. The crowd stirred, and craned their heads expectantly. Another sound rose faintly above the drums. Singing! 'Oh, Edward,' breathed Nellie, 'it's "Jerusalem, the Golden". I can't bear it.'

They watched. A troop of bannermen marched into the square and took their places along the edges of the crowd. Major Lin followed them. He was dismounted now, and was walking beside the thin, white-haired figure of Chamberlain Jin, who bowed to the Mandarin, before taking a position, slightly in front of the others at the far end of the square. More bannermen entered. And then they saw Septimus Millward, his arm round his son's shoulders. One by one, they recognised the others, Tom hobbling on his crutches at the rear. The hymn came to an end. Septimus, ignoring the crowd, stood tall in the sand, stretching out his arms – he could not raise them very high because of the *cangue*. Then he opened his prayer book. The others knelt in a ring around him and began to pray.

The white-haired official had unrolled a scroll. He read the charges in a high, incantatory voice, ending with the resounding, 'Tremble and obey.' The Mandarin, who had put down his pipe, nodded, and after a moment, gestured with his hand. The big man with the sword bowed deeply. There was an intake of breath from the crowd.

Two men, the executioners' assistants, ran over the sand towards the condemned foreigners. Arbitrarily they selected Burton Fielding, who was nearest. He began to struggle and cry out as they unlocked his heavy *cangue*. The crowd murmured with satisfaction. Septimus Millward paused from reading his prayer book, and said something loudly to his whimpering compatriot. Whatever it was it seemed to have an effect, for Fielding suddenly relaxed, and he was unresisting as they dragged him to the centre of the square. Septimus went back to his reading. None of the others raised their heads to look, concentrating on their prayers – but the doctor and the others in the gallery saw. They were powerless to look away. Fielding was forced into a kneeling position, his hands were pulled behind his back, and with one blow his head was knocked off his body.

Henry put an arm round Helen Frances, who leaned on his chest, crying quietly. Dr Airton and Nellie stared stone-faced, petrified in their shock and disbelief.

Herr Fischer was the next to be chosen. Unlike Fielding he did not struggle when they came to remove his *cangue*. He bowed curtly to Septimus, and then to Bowers, shrugged off the pulling hands of the executioners and walked stiffly of his own accord to where the man with the now bloodstained blade stood. He sank to his knees, crossed himself, then pushed his own hands abruptly behind his back. This time there was silence from the crowd when the neat grey-haired head rolled in the sand.

Tom was ready when they came back for the next victim. In the interval of Fischer's beheading he had taken the opportunity to shake hands with Bowers, and kissed Sister Caterina gently on the forehead. Before the two assistants even reached him he was pushing his own way with his crutches towards the executioner. There was a murmur from the crowd: it might have been admiration for his courage. There was a hush when he flamboyantly threw aside his crutches, and dropped to his knees. In the silence, even as far away as the gallery, they could hear him whistling.

'"Jolly Boating Weather",' said Henry quietly. 'Out of tune, but that's Tom. Brave man. Brave man.'

'Oh, Henry, I can't look,' said Helen Frances.

'Don't,' he said.

The sword blade fell.

For variety, they chose a woman next. Sister Caterina seemed nervous, glancing from side to side at the crowd, covering her breasts with her hands – but she walked steadily enough. She appeared confused when she reached the executioner, staring with fascination at the stained blade and the pools of blood in the sand. The executioner was gentle with her and told her to kneel. She did so, crossing herself. One assistant pulled back her arms, the other pulled her hair forward, leaving her neck clear – but the blade was getting blunt now and it took two strokes to cut off her head.

'Oh, Caterina,' whispered Nellie, and now she, too, began to weep, softly like Helen Frances. Airton stared rigidly, his hands clutching the window-sill. He had cut himself on the sharp edge and was bleeding, but did not notice.

There was a long pause as a stone was brought in to sharpen the blade. The executioner rubbed his sweating body with a towel, and drank greedily from a pot of wine, which was brought out to him from the dumpling shop. There was a buzz of excited conversation among the crowd. The now smaller group round Millward continued to pray. The heads of Fielding, Fischer, Tom and Caterina lay in the sand where they had fallen. Flies were already buzzing round them.

Eventually they came for Bowers. He marched to his execution like a guardsman, and it was quickly over. His head rested next to Fischer's. They might have been conversing together in a macabre sort of way. Now only the Millwards were left.

Laetitia had wrapped her arms round her two smallest children, Lettie and Hannah. They would not leave their mother and the assistants allowed them to come with her to the centre of the square. Before they knelt down together, Laetitia gently removed the girls' pebble spectacles, and then her own. The executioner swiped off the children's heads and after that their mother's. It was neatly done.

Hiram was next. He kissed his father's cheek, then walked towards the executioner, head held high. Not for long. His elder sister, Mildred, followed. She, like Sister Caterina before her, seemed shy about exposing her budding breasts. She whimpered a little when she saw her mother's and her brother's heads lying in the sand, but she was dispatched quickly, and her own head soon joined theirs.

That left four more Millward children and their father.

The executioner was visibly tiring now. Perhaps it had been the wine he had drunk in the interval between the beheadings. So he allowed his assistants to dispatch the children while he took a rest, taking the opportunity to drink more wine as he did so. The crowd, which had remained rather mute through the last decapitations, did not seem to care. Isaiah, Miriam, Thomas and Martha, who had stopped praying once their mother had been taken away, were clutching their father's legs in their terror. The assistants patiently unclasped their little hands, and pulled them struggling after them. They did not decapitate them. They slit their throats with butchers' knives. It was quicker that way.

Neither Nellie nor Helen Frances observed this last performance. After Laetitia's death they had witnessed enough, and now they were sitting on the bench, Helen Frances shaking in Nellie's arms, Nellie staring wide-eyed at the wall. Only the doctor and Henry remained at their observation post, the doctor rigidly locked in a position from which he had hardly moved during the last hour. Henry would occasionally glance towards him. He was concerned about him.

Only Septimus remained alive. Once his children had been removed from his protection, such as it was, he had closed his prayer book and stonily watched their dispatch. Now he turned towards the Mandarin, pointing his finger, the Old Testament prophet, no doubt summoning the wrath of the Lord to fall upon the Mandarin's head and on those who had sponsored this dreadful crime. Airton could not make out the words, but they seemed to have little effect. The hairy man next to the Mandarin, who Henry said was Iron Man Wang, laughed uproariously and toasted Septimus with his bottle. The Mandarin, from what the doctor could see, merely looked bored. He gestured with his hand to the executioner to hurry.

Septimus turned on his heels and walked towards the executioner, easily pushing the two assistants out of the way as he did so. He stood for a moment looking directly into the executioner's eyes. The man gazed back impudently for a moment, then turned away his head. Septimus reached out his hand and patted him gently on the shoulder. Then he knelt down of his own volition, allowing the rather cowed assistants to take off his *cangue*. He dropped his head in a final prayer. Only then did he allow one of the assistants to pull back his arms. The other reached gingerly for his blond pigtail, baring the neck. The executioner hesitated, then struck, but Septimus's obstinate head appeared to remain firmly fixed to his body. It took four more heavy blows before the flesh, muscle and gristle parted, and Septimus's head rolled in a leisurely fashion to join his family.

It was over.

Or nearly so. The doctor remained rooted to his spot, ignoring Henry's hand on his shoulder. He saw the Mandarin get off his chair and walk towards the slain, observing the bodies dispassionately, like a hardened general inspecting the aftermath of a battle. Then he raised his head and seemed to gaze directly at the window where the doctor stood. The Mandarin's expression was impenetrable, but he seemed to be trying to communicate something to the doctor, if only to let him know that he knew he was there, and that he had witnessed this. He turned abruptly on his heels and walked away.

'Come down, Doctor,' Henry was saying. 'There's nothing more to see.'

After a moment the doctor turned, noticing his bloody palms as he did so. He shook his head, then turned towards Henry, grasping his sleeve. 'I'm a Judas,' he whispered. 'I should have been there with them.' His staring eyes bored into those of the younger man. 'I should have been there.'

'Come down, Doctor,' said Henry softly. 'Let me give you a hand.'

They heard a cooing voice floating down the corridor and saw Mother Liu hobbling towards them. 'Oh, there you all are,' she simpered. 'How lovely. Enjoying the sunshine and our pretty view. I do hope you are all comfortable and have eaten well. I have very good news for you. Yes. The Mandarin, the Mandarin himself, is coming to see you tomorrow.'

Chapter Seventeen

When it rained some of us wanted to return to our farms –
but the troop commander executed those who tried to leave.

The first reaction was of denial and shock. Later Helen Frances became hysterical, shaking in Henry's arms as he tried to restrain her. She wanted to run, anywhere, to escape this claustrophobic painted room, the stifling hangings, and the memories of what she had witnessed during the afternoon. 'Did you see it?' she screamed. 'His head! His head! Tom's head!' and 'I'm wicked. Wicked. I want to die! I want to die!' He had to wrest his razor away from her, and pull her back when she began to bang her head against the gilded mirror, and he had to pinion her hands so she would not scratch her face or tear his with her nails. He held her while she twitched on the bed, her eyes staring wildly, saliva and tears mingling on her cheeks, and he kissed her wet brow, and whispered to her, 'We have to live on. We owe them that. We have to live. Don't you see that, darling? Don't you see?'

But she did not respond, either to his words or his caresses. Her violent convulsions ceased when her body became exhausted, but her mind remained locked in her waking nightmare. She lay rigidly in his arms, her blank eyes fixed on the horror of heads and disconnected trunks and pools of blood in the sand. In desperation he slapped her face, to wake her, to bring her back to him, and she focused for a wild moment, clutching his arm, whispering confidentially, 'Laetitia was a good mother. She took off the babies' spectacles first so they wouldn't see.' She giggled – a mad, chilling sound like a jackal's yelp. 'But they cut off the babies' heads all the same. Snip. Snip. Snip. Like trimming the roses! One, two, three . . .' Her words became incoherent moans, as she rocked uncontrollably from side to side.

Henry walked deliberately to one of the cabinets, pulling open the drawers until he found what he was looking for. He took out a long pipe, a candle, and a packet containing black paste. He rolled the paste into a ball, placing it into the receptacle on the pipe. He took it to the girl lying on the bed. She smelt the pungent odour, which calmed her. She sucked the first pipe greedily. Henry rolled another ball, and she smoked again. 'Thank you, thank you, my darling,' she murmured, before she slept.

Henry sat for a long while, holding his head in his hands.

Later she woke and reached for him, and they made love. 'Stay with me, stay with me,' she murmured, when he had climaxed. 'Don't leave me again,' and he remained inside her, holding her, moving with her, travelling with her through the long, dark night.

In the morning she emerged from a languorous dream. She tried to retain it for as long as she could until the images jumbled and disappeared. Lazily, she stretched out her hand for Henry but it flailed over an empty bed-sheet. 'Darling?' she said, opening her eyes.

Henry, fully dressed, was sitting on the end of the bed looking at the floor. 'How are you feeling?' he asked curtly.

Images from yesterday flooded into her mind, chilling the warm glow and physical contentment that had permeated her limbs when she woke. She had a vivid impression of Tom kneeling in the sand, whistling defiantly. Tears came to her eyes, yet to her surprise she found that she could contemplate the memory without anguish now. It was as if she was recalling a sorrowful pageant, one that had affected her deeply but that had passed, leaving behind not pain or confusion, only a crushing sense of loss.

'I feel sad,' she answered, 'but I remember what you told me, that we must go on living.'

'That's right,' said Henry. There was a tight, almost bitter note in his voice. 'God help us, we must go on living, however we can, whatever it takes.'

Helen Frances sat up in bed, the sheets falling off her. 'Henry?'

She saw purple-shadowed, bloodshot eyes in an unshaven face, eyes that she felt were assessing her, clinically examining the long strands of auburn hair falling over her pink breasts, her freckled arms, her round, slightly protuberant belly. She began to feel nervous, and self-conscious. 'Henry, what is it?' she said.

'God, but you're beautiful,' he replied. 'I don't know if I can go through with this.'

'For God's sake, Henry, what's the matter? Go through with

what?' Unconsciously she had pulled back the sheet to cover herself from his penetrating stare.

'I might as well say it straight,' said Henry. 'I had to bargain for your lives. The Mandarin demanded a price. And he'll probably be calling for his payment today.'

Helen Frances tried to overcome her mounting concern. 'Is this something to do with your secret business here?'

'Partly,' said Henry. 'I'm alive because he needs me. I think he would genuinely like to save the doctor too. He considers Airton to be a philosophical sparring partner. A friend. Not that that would have been reason enough in itself for the Mandarin to let him live. His devious Oriental mind is incapable of altruism. To save you, and the Airtons, I had to bargain.' He paused. 'Actually, my dear, you were the bargain,' he added bitterly.

She suddenly felt a cold calm. It was as if something that she had half realised had become clear. Or as if something she had been secretly dreading had come about. Ludicrously, she remembered an infraction of the rules she had once committed at her school. She and another girl had crept into the kitchens one night and stolen a pie. For two days nothing had been said. Then, on the afternoon of the third day, she had been called to the headmistress's study, her crime discovered, and her first feeling had been one of relief that the suspense was over. The two days that she had spent with Henry since her rescue had been a time out of time. She had even convinced herself that he really loved her. Until the executions of yesterday afternoon she had been happy, unbelievably happy – yet she had known all along that this was undeserved after all the hurt she had caused and the mistakes she had made, and that it could not last. It was even fitting that now it should be Henry, her false idol, who should be the instrument of whatever punishment life had in store for her.

'What would you have me do, Henry,' she said, 'as part of your bargain?'

'It was the only thing he would agree to. I tried everything. I begged. But there was only one condition he would accept.'

'So what is this condition? I can guess, but I'd like you to say it. My lover,' she added quietly.

Henry sighed. 'He said he once saw you from his palanquin. He was attracted by your red hair.'

Helen Frances had been expecting it, but it was still a shock. She felt a chill coursing through her blood, and her temples throbbed. 'Oh, Lord, Henry, what have you done?' she murmured.

'I've saved your life, and the Airtons' lives. In the only way I could.'

'By selling me into the Mandarin's harem? Is that what you've agreed? Am I to spend the rest of my life as an Oriental concubine?'

'No,' said Henry. 'You're to spend an hour alone with him. That's all. Mother Liu told us he will come here later today.'

'Only an hour,' she repeated. 'That's all.'

'I thought, with opium . . .'

'Maybe I wouldn't notice what was happening to me. That's delicate of you, Henry. It would be . . . what? Just another bad dream?'

'Something like that,' muttered Henry.

'I don't suppose I have a choice?'

'Not if you and the Airtons are to live.'

'I see.' She gave a brittle laugh. 'Then I suppose it will be my saintly duty. Do you think the nuns in my convent school will be proud of my martyrdom? Not that I have any virtue to sacrifice. You've already seen to that, haven't you, Henry? What price virtue and honour in my case? You've made a very easy bargain, I think, in the circumstances. I congratulate you.'

'There's no fate worse than death, Helen Frances. None. Life's what matters, not bloody middle class sensibility. Do you think that I wouldn't have tried any other way if it had been possible? Oh, God, Helen Frances,' barked Henry, 'what else was I to do? It was the only way to save your life. You'd have been in the square, decapitated along with the others if I hadn't agreed. You'd be dead. So would Airton, Nellie, Jenny, George. This way you live.'

'Oh, yes, we must go on living. That's your great philosophy, isn't it?'

'Listen, the Mandarin may not even do anything to you. He's an old man who's making a philosophical point with the doctor. That's all this is about. They argue about pragmatism. He thinks the doctor's agreed to prostitute you to save our lives. The Mandarin's point is proved. Everybody's venal. That's that. And we stay alive.'

'What are you saying now, Henry? The doctor's party to this too?'

'Of course he isn't. He doesn't know anything about it. The Mandarin only thinks he does. What does it matter? You live, my darling, and that's all I care about. You live. You live.' He shook his head, clenching his fists. 'I couldn't lose you. You're – you're life to me now. I'd do anything, say anything, lie, cheat, kill, partner with the Devil to save you. This is the only way I know how. Oh, God.' His head sank into his hands.

'You know, Henry,' said Helen Frances coldly, 'that's the closest I've ever heard you come to a protestation of love. Ironic, really, since you're in the process of whoring me to a savage. I feel sorry for you.'

Henry stood up, his head bowed. He paced the room, but after a few steps he turned to face her. The agony that had been showing in his face during their conversation had been replaced by a cold, supercilious calm, his mouth had settled into its usual sardonic smile, and when he spoke it was with his habitual drawl. 'You've every reason to hate me for what I'm about to put you through, old girl, but as long as you're brave enough to go through with it, I'll be content. You may never want to see me again afterwards. I'll be content. Life without you will be painful but I'll get by. Or maybe I won't. It don't matter a toss, one way or the other. I'm only worth the next gamble I play. That's the life I've chosen. Whether I win or lose, it's all the same. But it does matter to me what happens to you. You've done what no other woman ever has. Got under my skin. It's remarkable, really. I thought I was immune. Anyway, I'm going to make damned sure that you survive this.

'If I thought the Mandarin was going to hurt you, I'd kill him, but he won't hurt you. He's a pathetic old man who'll give you an unpleasant half-hour. He may paw you. He may even try to get inside you. Well, there are worse things that can happen to a girl. What if he does fuck you? Your virtue doesn't lie between your legs. It lies in your soul, Helen Frances, in that big heart of yours. It's the courage with which you face life and all its unpleasantness. It's your radiance and humour. It's the free spirit that sparks life into everyone around you. It's everything I love about you. That's not something the Mandarin can touch. He won't even get near you, not the real you.

'Take opium, if you must, to get through it. The pipe's on the table there. If you're as strong as I think you are a few smokes won't make you an addict again, but don't overdo it. I feel guilty enough for having started you on the damned drug in the first place. Prepare yourself however you like – but go through with it. You'll be saving the only life that is precious to me.

'Excuse me. I'm going into the gallery outside – for a cheroot.'

He left, banging the door behind him.

Helen Frances dressed slowly. She finished her toilet, and sat on the stool next to the low table. The pipe lay in its own reflection on the polished mahogany. She picked it up and put it to her lips, tasting the lingering fragrance from her smoke of the night before. She closed her eyes. Her hand moved to the package of poppy paste, and her fingers distractedly picked out a pinch of the black, treacle-like substance, going through the familiar motions of rolling it into a pellet. It took a conscious effort to stop herself. She opened her eyes. For a long while, she sat, the pipe in one hand, the poppy paste in the other, staring into her own thoughts. She sighed. A tear rolled down her cheek. She replaced the pipe on the table, and put the pellet back into the package. Wearily she rose to her feet and, after stowing the pipe and paraphernalia back in the cabinet, she went out and joined Henry in the gallery. Neither spoke. Henry smoked. She put her arm round his waist, nestling her head against his side. After a while, he put his arm round her shoulder.

There seemed nothing else to do but wait.

At that moment the Mandarin was also contemplating an opium pipe. He rarely indulged in opium smoking outside his own quarters, but after a half-hour interview with Iron Man Wang he needed something to calm his temper. He waited patiently while Fan Yimei prepared the pipe for him, observing her lissome form with satisfaction as she knelt on the carpet kneading the paste.

He was sitting – or, rather, reclining – on a *chaise-longue* in Major Lin's comfortably furnished pavilion within the Palace of Heavenly Pleasure. Occasionally he would use this facility for those meetings that, in formal terms, never took place. He had never allowed Iron Man to call on him officially at the *yamen*. And he, the Mandarin, could hardly make house calls on a dumpling shop. This pavilion served as a useful, and deniable, alternative.

Iron Man had been as crude as ever, arrogant, threatening. His pig eyes had peered insolently into the Mandarin's face, close enough for the Mandarin to smell the garlic on his breath. 'You cheated me, Brother Liu,' he had hissed. 'You didn't give me all the Christians, did you?'

'All we could find,' the Mandarin had replied lightly, although he had felt the skin of his temples contract with anger. 'Were fifteen heads not enough to satisfy your appetite?'

'My men tell me that there are others. A doctor. His woman. Children. Why were they not executed in the square? Where are they?'

'Major Lin?' The Mandarin had turned to his lieutenant. 'Why were the *Daifu* and his family not brought to the execution ground with the others?'

'They were not present, Da Ren, when we called on the mission,' said Major Lin. 'My orders were to bring to execution only those who were there.'

'Surely you don't mean that someone allowed the doctor and his family to escape?' exclaimed the Mandarin, in a tone of incredulity. 'With all the troops and hundreds of Boxers guarding the house? These Christians must indeed possess magical powers if they can achieve a disappearing feat like that! That they managed to evade the vigilance of all your men, Iron Man, and the gods who are helping you! Astounding!'

Iron Man had merely grunted. He held out his beaker for Fan Yimei to pour more wine.

'Games, Brother Liu? Do you really want to play games with me?'

'That's not a threat, is it, Iron Man?'

Iron Man Wang gave him a long, black-browed stare.

'What about the other foreign devil, the one who you were interrogating?'

'Ma Na Si? He died.'

'So I heard. Did he tell you where the guns were concealed before he died?'

'Alas, no. He was a tight-lipped one, even under torture. I must have lost my touch.'

'Are you playing games again, brother?' Iron Man smiled.

He rose to his feet, agilely for such a bulky man. His great axe suddenly appeared in his hands. With efficient force he slammed it down on one of the lacquer stools, slicing cushion and wood into two neat halves, the tray with the tea on it shattering to the floor.

'Thought I smelt a rat under there,' he said, in the silence that followed.

'Major Lin,' said the Mandarin, 'you will escort our guest to the gate, or into the brothel, or wherever else he wishes to go. Then you will order that sergeant of yours to go with his men and scour both town and countryside until they find these missing Christians. Our friend desires their heads for his collection and we do not wish to disappoint him. Will that be all, Iron Man? Are you satisfied?'

'For now,' said the bandit. 'Don't think that I'm not carefully watching you, my brother.'

'As I am watching you,' replied the Mandarin. 'With deepest respect, of course.'

And, thankfully, that had brought the interview to an end. Iron Man Wang and Major Lin had left. Now he took the opium pipe from Fan Yimei, but he held her off from lighting it, taking her chin in his plump hand and examining her features. 'You are very beautiful,' he said, after a while. 'Unlike your father, who was an ugly fellow. But you have the same intelligent eyes.'

Fan Yimei froze, but she felt her cheeks burning. A vivid memory of her father, smiling down at her as he wrote in his study, flashed before her eyes. 'You . . . knew my father?' she stumbled.

'Very well,' said the Mandarin, smiling gently at her confusion. 'We had a friendship that spanned many years. Dear Jinghua. I see him now as clearly as on the day I first met him, in General Tseng Kuo-fan's camp, forty years ago.'

Fan Yimei found herself clutching a corner of the carpet to prevent herself shaking.

'He didn't talk to you about me?' the Mandarin continued. 'I'm not surprised. He was always a little perverse, my friend Jinghua. Other men might have boasted about a relationship with a high government official. Not your father. Or perhaps he did not wish to be reminded of those early years of military service. They were terrible times.'

He spoke in a low voice, meditatively, as if he were reciting a history of a different age. 'He never spoke to you about the great rebellion, did he? Or of his career as a professional soldier. Well, it was never a distinguished one. He was always more of a poet than a warrior, and he never felt comfortable with all the blood we shed. He believed . . . Never mind. As I said, they were terrible times. But

armies need their poets, men who can inspire courage through fine
words, or make us dream of our homes when we are campaigning
far away. I know that you have a reputation as a musician. It is one
of your talents. You probably inherited that gift from Jinghua. There
were many evenings, crouched round the campfire, in the rain, after
a defeat, when your father's lute cheered our hearts, and made us
laugh away our fear. I did not see him for years, and it was a long
time after I came to Shishan that I discovered he was living here. We
met, once or twice. A proud man, your father. Never one to crawl
and beg favours from the powerful, as I had become – but there was
one evening, oh, it must have been a year before the plague, when he
and I drank wine together. The years dropped away and we became
Hunan Braves again. It was a good evening.'

He smiled, remembering. 'Yes, it was a very good evening. And on
that night he asked me a favour, laughing, because he never thought
that it would be one he would have to call in. You were there,
although you don't remember, a studious little girl in the next-door
room, practising endless scales on your *chin*. He was proud of you.
I think you know that. You were to him like the son he never had.
We listened to you for a while – you played very well, even then –
and he asked me, when we were both drunk, happily, sentimentally
drunk, he asked me – there were tears rolling down his cheeks and
mine, even as we chuckled at the great improbability of your father
asking me a favour – he asked: "If anything ever happens to me,
will you look after her?"'

Fan Yimei heard his words as if from far away. In her mind
was the face of her father, smiling, intoxicated, loving, droll. The
Mandarin was wrong. She did remember that evening. It was a
rare occasion for her father to drink wine, and he had been sick
afterwards for two days. She had admonished him in her childish
way for associating with bad company – but she had never known
the identity of the man with whom he had been drinking or that it
was the Mandarin.

'Of course I agreed,' the Mandarin continued. 'We drank on it, in
the old Hunan way. I did not see him after that. The plague came. I
was busy. Yes, I did hear that your father had died, but so many died
then. Forgive me. We were living from day to day. I looked for you
when I could. First I heard that you, too, had perished. One more
nameless victim in a nameless grave. I made offerings for you and

your father in the temple. And life went on. We grow accustomed to sadness, and loss . . .'

He paused. His brows furrowed, as if he was remembering something painful. Fan Yimei stared at him, her mouth half open, her mind whirling. The Mandarin sighed. Then, in the same flat voice with which he had begun his monody, he continued: 'It was years later, when one of your uncles was up before me in the *yamen* court. Actually it wasn't the court, but the persuasion room next to it where truth is always to be found. He was an evil man, this corrupt banker uncle of yours, who had stolen from his own family, including your father, as well as from all those others who put their trust in him. And he told me that he had sent you here, that he had sold his own brother's daughter, my friend's daughter, into a brothel. It probably won't bring you any comfort to hear that his end was a cruel one. That at least was in my power to arrange. But a deserved death in itself could not right the wrong that had been done to you . . . Yes, I will have that pipe now.'

Fan Yimei lit the candle, and the Mandarin sucked in the heavy smoke. 'Thank you.' He closed his eyes, and lay silent. She sat, head bowed, at his feet – two still figures in a room. 'Should I have bought you out?' He spoke after a while. 'Easily enough done, even at the extortionate prices charged by Mother Liu. But what would have become of you? You would have been unmarriageable. I could have kept you in my chambers, made you one of my concubines, in name if not in fact, but my wives would have guaranteed that your life became a misery. You would have found yourself in as much of a hell as the one in which you were living here. Perhaps a worse one. I considered sending you to a temple. But for someone like you to live the half-life of a nun? I thought and I thought, and I could see no future for you other than as some listless chattel, an unwanted cuckoo in someone else's nest. So I settled you on Major Lin. It seemed practical. He is not a bad man, though he has his problems. Pragmatically – I try to be pragmatic, life is a balance of this and that – I thought that the two of you might be good for each other. At least your status as kept mistress offers you some protection. And I believe that Lin is fond of you in his way. Forgive me. It was not a perfect solution.'

Fan Yimei said nothing. There was nothing to say.

The Mandarin pulled himself up so that he was leaning on one elbow. 'Yet you did manage to surprise me,' he said. 'You possess many of my friend's virtues: courage, compassion, patience . . . Yes, I have been watching you over the years, I see the father in the daughter. You also have Jinghua's talent for doing the unexpected. It was you who persuaded Ma Na Si to rescue that wretched American boy, was it not? You inconvenienced me at the time. There might have been repercussions – there would certainly have been if the situation in this country had not so dramatically changed. Yet I was delighted and proud that you had performed such a noble act. I was also glad that Ma Na Si had taken you under his wing. I wish that you had escaped with him. There is no place for you in our society, but there might be in his. The complication is that he loves another, or thinks he does.'

'You speak of him as if he were still alive,' Fan Yimei said quietly.

'He is very much alive,' said the Mandarin. 'You are shortly to meet him. That is one of the reasons why I have revealed so much to you today. I know that there is little for which you have to thank me, but I was your honoured father's friend, and it is for his sake that I am asking you this favour now.'

'I do not understand, Da Ren.'

The Mandarin was no longer reclining but sitting forward on the couch, looking closely into Fan Yimei's confused eyes.

'Listen, then. An intelligent person like yourself, who has survived so many years in an establishment such as this, will be versed in politics. Believe me, the politics of the state are different only by degree from the politics of the boudoir. Your Mother Liu in her little world is no less an empress than the Old Buddha in Peking. All life is a struggle for power; power is the currency of survival. We temper it with compromise and we balance competing strengths. We stave off open conflict because in conflict there is always danger. But there will inevitably come a time when compromise is exhausted. That is the situation in which I find myself now.

'During the last few weeks, I have been forced into an accommodation with that disgusting bandit whom you saw here earlier. The reason is simple. He presently holds more power, in men, in weapons, than I do. You will also have gathered from my last exchange with Iron Man Wang that our relationship, such as it is, is coming to a crisis. I am being forced into a position where I will have to retreat in order that I may return with enough force to regain my dominance of this city. Never mind how I plan to accomplish this. All you need to know is that both Ma Na Si and Major Lin are essential to my plans. I cannot afford that there should exist any more bad blood between them.

'We will shortly be leaving Shishan. You will accompany us. I will not leave you to the vengeance of that abominable woman and her son. After some persuasion on my part, Major Lin has agreed to take you with him. Mother Liu will be in no position to prevent this – but if this is to work, I need you to be loyal to Major Lin.'

'I am his bondmaid,' murmured Fan Yimei. 'His slave.'

'You have run away from him once, with another man. And that same man will be with us on our journey.'

'There will be no impropriety,' said Fan Yimei.

'It is not propriety that concerns me. It is whether you are strong enough to control your emotions. Ma Na Si will be accompanied by your rival, the red-headed girl. He will, no doubt, be making passionate love to her. I need you to be strong enough not to show any jealousy. In fact, I want the opposite. I want you to be her friend.'

'You mentioned survival, Da Ren,' Fan Yimei said softly. 'In our world – my world – we have an expression for women in my position. We call ourselves "sisters in sorrow". If I have survived so long, it is because I have learned never to hope. You have no need to fear that I will shame you, or Major Lin, in any way.'

The Mandarin touched her cheek gently with his hand, and stroked her delicate eyebrow with his finger. 'There will come a time when it will be appropriate for you to hope,' he said finally. 'I have learned that there is one area where no power holds sway, and that is over the human heart. I ask for an interlude, that is all. Act your part for a while longer. Then I will make you free to win Ma Na Si away from his fox woman, if you can.'

'You are good to me, Da Ren.'

'Oh, no, I may be many things, but goodness is something to which I would never dare to aspire.'

Major Lin strode into the room. 'I have done what you have ordered, Da Ren. My troopers are now riding uselessly round the countryside.'

'Thank you. We must humour these bandits for a while longer. I, meanwhile, have been well entertained by this lovely girl of yours. You are extremely fortunate, Major. She has been telling me how much she admires you. She firmly rejected the advances of an ugly old man.'

Major Lin bowed curtly, a sour expression on his face. 'You remind me as ever of the gratitude I owe you, Da Ren.'

'You deserve it, and more. Now, did you tell that wicked woman that Fan Yimei was to move to the private quarters with the foreigners? She understands our need to have someone we can implicitly trust to report on their activities.'

'I told her, Da Ren, but she said she wanted more money.'

'She always wants money, Major. That is why we can rely on her.' He yawned. 'I really shouldn't have taken that opium. It makes me lethargic. I suppose I must complete my business with the foreigners now. Is the woman ready to take us?'

'She and her son.'

'The Boxer captain? What an honour. It is remarkable how easily the most unlikely people can be bought. I find it amusing that our foreign devils are being protected by the Harmonious Fists. Fan Yimei, thank you for your hospitality. You will no doubt wish to pack some things before we move you to other quarters.'

They were still standing in the gallery when the Mandarin, Major Lin, Fan Yimei and Ren Ren reached the top of the stairs. The Mandarin was draped in a dark cloak and hood presumably to prevent recognition should there be a chance encounter with any of Iron Man's followers on the lower floors, but both Henry and Helen Frances knew him immediately by his confident, rolling stride. He paused when he saw them, acknowledging their presence with a slight incline of his cowled head. Mother Liu was waiting for him at the door of her room. She bowed unctuously, requesting that he enter and refresh himself with a cup of tea. He nodded curtly, and went inside, followed by the others. The door closed and the gallery was still again.

Helen Frances could feel Henry's hand closing over hers, willing her to be strong. Now that the moment had come, however, she did not feel particularly scared, although she was aware that she was breathing faster, and there was an empty feeling in her stomach, and – this shocked her – a tingling sensation, of anticipation, in her loins. She realised that she had not only accepted what would happen to her but, in a perverse way, was excited by the prospect. She had a sudden memory of the Mandarin as he had been on the day of the bear hunt, resplendent in his armour, hot and bloody and triumphant after his kill, virile and strong, a man of power. She had never really thought of him as a man before. He had been an alien presence, with hooded, cruel eyes, and flat Mongoloid features, a storybook villain, like Aladdin's wicked uncle in the pantomime, and he was old, with a curled, grey queue, and, like all Chinese, he smelt of musty pork – but now she wondered what it would be like to be enclosed in his arms. Oh, she had come a long way from her convent school. That wicked curiosity of hers, which had always been her undoing. Guiltily she clutched at Henry, burying her head in his chest, pressing herself against him.

'It'll be all right,' he said uselessly, a slight choke in his voice that she had not heard before.

'I love you,' she pleaded. 'I love you,' as if by saying the words she could extinguish the betrayal she contemplated in her mind.

Mother Liu, followed by Fan Yimei, was making her way slowly down the corridor towards them.

Henry translated for Helen Frances. They had prepared a hot bath for her. She should go with them now. They would bathe her and dress her. Before long the Mandarin would come to her room.

She felt his arm tighten round her waist, steadying her. Mother Liu simpered up at her, an arch expression in her cunning eyes. 'What's she saying?' Helen Frances whispered.

'She's congratulating you on your good fortune,' said Henry. 'Apparently the Mandarin has a reputation as a mighty lover.'

'Lucky me,' said Helen Frances.

'You asked,' he said quietly.

Mother Liu gestured and the slim figure of Fan Yimei, who had been waiting a few paces behind her, moved elegantly to Helen Frances's side. There was something familiar about this graceful girl in the blue and red silk gown – the stillness of her carriage, the serenity of her features. Helen Frances remembered the mysterious, sad-eyed creature whom she had glimpsed in the pavilion opposite them in those happier days when a more innocent version of herself had come trysting here with Henry.

'This is Fan Yimei,' Henry was translating. 'She'll help you with your bath.'

'You know her, don't you?' said Helen Frances. There was something in the way he was looking at her – and how the girl kept her eyes fixed on the wooden floor.

'Oh, Helen Frances, let's just get it over with,' said Henry, letting her go.

She kissed his cheek. Fan Yimei was waiting quietly. Helen Frances, head erect and shoulders back, followed her down the hall.

Henry watched her go. Mother Liu observed him sardonically. 'Proud, superior Ma Na Si. Noble, virtuous Ma Na Si, who conspired against me and stole the foreign boy away. You and that bitch Fan Yimei thought you could change fate. Did you see the boy die in the square yesterday? Did you change fate after all? And now I see you pimping that woman of yours, as if you were Mother Liu herself selling another chicken. Are you changing Fate still, Ma Na Si? Or are you yourself not just a little like Mother Liu – that poor old woman – doing what she has to do to survive?'

'I can do without your philosophy,' growled Henry.

Mother Liu laughed. 'I'm no philosopher, Ma Na Si. All I do is sell clouds and rain. As you are doing. I hope that you have secured a fair price from the da ren for his hour with your chicken. Are you sure that you will get your reward? You'd be surprised how many of my customers think they can dip their jade spoon into the bowl and leave without paying. Don't take it to heart, Ma Na Si. Just a friendly tip from someone in the same trade. This is such an uncertain world.'

She threw this last sally over her shoulder as she hobbled back along the corridor to her room, her shoulder shaking with laughter.

Helen Frances lay drowsily on a mat while Fan Yimei rubbed sweet-smelling oil on her back and limbs. Her body was still tingling from the bath. She had been embarrassed at first to strip in front of Fan Yimei, and even more so when the Chinese girl had taken off her own robe and joined her in the wooden tub. Her white, freckled body seemed coarse when compared to Fan Yimei's smooth, olive skin, and she did not know where to look or put her hands – but

Fan Yimei had been sensitive to her discomfort. Her sad eyes had contemplated the English woman calmly, gesturing to her to lie back and relax. She had waited patiently as the heat of the water had had its soothing effect, easing Helen Frances's tension and suffusing her body with a warm, languorous glow. Fan Yimei allowed her to soak, and dream. Then, gently, she had taken her hands, indicating that she should stand. Like a nurse bathing a child, she had ladled hot water over her skin and gently soaped her from head to toe. Helen Frances was by now lost in the sensual experience and did as she was told, luxuriating as more hot water was poured over her and she was soaped again. This time Fan Yimei scraped off the suds with a wooden spatula, and Helen Frances felt a painful yet pleasurable tingle where the wood grazed her skin. Taking her hand Fan Yimei helped her out of the tub. She experienced a shock as Fan Yimei upended a bucket of cold water over her head, but afterwards she realised that she had never in her life felt so fresh or clean. Fan Yimei gave her a towel and gestured her to a stool. With another towel Fan Yimei dried her hair, leaving it as a turban on her head; then she took her hand and led her through a side door into the adjoining bedroom. Here, lying on a mat, she was oiled and massaged, the slight girl at one point walking on her back, expertly stretching the vertebrae with her tiny, lotus feet; Helen Frances felt the stumps in their wet bandages gently pressuring beneath her skin like a child's knuckles pushing through a sponge. She had been disgusted by the idea of bound feet in the past, but now she only wondered how Fan Yimei could keep her balance on such thin points. She accepted the strangeness, because in a deep part of her she had already surrendered to these new, pleasurable sensations. She knew that this was an elaborate ritual to ready her for the Mandarin's pleasure, that Beauty was being prepared for the Beast, but she no longer cared. She felt Fan Yimei's soft hands spreading the oil on her shoulders, and heard herself sigh with content.

Fan Yimei helped her into a loose robe of thin green silk, and combed her hair so that it hung in a fiery red cascade down her back. Helen Frances watched in the little mirror as the Chinese girl applied white powder and rouge to her cheeks, vermilion to her lips, blue shade to her eyelids. She could hardly contain her surprise and wonder as the features of the convent girl transformed into those of a courtesan before her eyes. She had never imagined that she could be so beautiful. She stared at the stranger she had become. Gently Fan Yimei opened the front of her robe and she felt a tickling sensation as the girl applied rouge to her nipples. From a drawer Fan Yimei brought out a necklace of amber beads and hung it so that it fell into the cleft of her breasts. Helen Frances fingered them and felt the cool stone. The strange painted image in the mirror that was her and not her smiled, then started. In the grave reflection of Fan Yimei behind her she saw tears welling in the corners of the girl's soft eyes. Helen Frances turned on her stool and looked up at her. Hesitantly she grasped her hand. 'I'll be all right,' she said in English, then in her faltering Chinese: '*Wo – hen hao.*'

'*Shi, nin hen hao, hen mei. Nanguai* Ma Na Si *zhemma ai nin.*' Fan Yimei spoke softly, but Helen Frances could not understand her. Did *mei* mean beautiful? And was Ma Na Si Manners? And surely *ai* was love?

'I don't understand,' she whispered.

'*Shi, nin bu dong.*' Fan Yimei leaned forward. Impulsively she kissed Helen Frances on the forehead. '*Zheige xinku shijie – ni ye kelian. Lai!*' she added. 'Come!' Helen Frances understood the last instruction, and she would have understood anyway, for Fan Yimei was pointing at the bed. It was time.

'What the devil did he mean, he's glad I've kept to my bargain?' the doctor exploded, when the Mandarin had left his room. 'What choice did I have? Does he expect my gratitude for not murdering my family? What bargain is this, Manners? Is there something you haven't told us?'

Manners sat uncomfortably on the chair, looking at the carpet. Nellie held the children on the bed and kept her silence. The doctor, dishevelled and unshaven, was pacing the little room. He had not slept since the massacre of the previous afternoon. To his family's concern he had lain frozen on the floor in a rigid attitude of prayer, refusing food or drink or any comfort that Nellie and the children had tried to give him. He had only roused himself when the Mandarin, with Henry, had entered his room; but he had not responded to the hearty greeting and he had avoided the bear-like embrace and turned away his head when the Mandarin had spoken to him. 'You can tell this man – this monster – that I don't converse with murderers,' he had said shrilly to Henry in

English. Henry had not translated, but the Mandarin had appeared to understand.

'Yes, he is sad for the fate of his fellows,' the Mandarin had nodded, 'and, of course, for now he blames me. There will be time in the future for us to talk when he has considered these things. The fact that he has agreed to my bargain – which affords me double satisfaction by the way: first, for the transient pleasure it is about to afford me, second, for the longer-lasting virtue that it has preserved my friend from a terrible death – makes me think that, at bottom, he is a practical man. Like you and I, Ma Na Si. Yes, he will come round to me in time, and we will be friends again.

'For now I have merely come to thank my dear friend for conceding so gracefully on the philosophical challenge with which I have presented to him. He has in this instance gracefully accepted defeat, like a chess master acknowledging a superior gambit. I am rewarded by the preservation of his own life – which I had unjustly feared he might have thrown away on a point of useless principle – and, of course, for the preservation of the fox-headed lady. That was a more difficult play, perhaps, and one on which I thought I might lose the game – but your good sense prevailed, Daifu. Thank you. That is more important to me than my physical reward.'

'You'll kindly tell this man that I don't understand a word he's talking about and that he's not welcome here, whether he thinks he's saved our lives or not,' said the doctor angrily, again in English.

'I think he has saved our lives, Edward,' said Nellie quietly. 'Monster that he is, we are still in his power. Might it not be wiser to show him some respect?'

'Not after the horrors of yesterday, woman. I will no longer compromise with evil. Manners, I say again, he is not welcome here.'

The Mandarin had been watching this exchange shrewdly. 'There is no need for you to translate, Ma Na Si. It seems that on this occasion it is the woman who is showing more sense than the man. But that is not strange. Women, for all their frailty, understand necessity better than us men. I see that the doctor is still blessed, or cursed, by his complicated ideals. That is good. There is meat for more debate in the future. For now, I will thank him for honouring the most sensible bargain he has made. Stay here with him, Ma Na Si. You know where I will be. Of course, my thanks go very much to you as well. You have been exquisitely accommodating, as a go-between.'

He had left, and the room seemed smaller in his absence, though the tension remained.

Henry lifted his head and looked the doctor in the eyes. 'I don't know what he means by a bargain,' he lied, 'beyond the choice you rightly made of leaving the mission to save your family. And Helen Frances,' he added bitterly.

The Mandarin strode down the corridor. He was feeling in the best of spirits. He would have liked to stretch out his arms and chuckle aloud, but he saw Mother Liu and Ren Ren waiting at the end of the corridor. For their benefit he glared superciliously, preserving a dignity he did not feel.

'She is ready and waiting, Da Ren,' Mother Liu cooed. 'A pretty, pretty creature, to be sure. Oh, Da Ren, it is, of course, right that you should be the first to enjoy her exotic charms, yet I can't help but think, afterwards, what a grace she would be to our establishment. So interesting for our regular customers. If she could be properly trained. Chamberlain Jin and I have spoken many times . . .'

'I am aware of your discussions with Chamberlain Jin,' said the Mandarin shortly.

'Then could you only consider? After all, what is one foreigner more or less? And when you have finished with her . . . ? I would pay a high price,' she said coaxingly.

'Out of the money I have already given you?'

'You know what a dangerous position we are in, agreeing to keep these foreigners. Ren Ren and me you can trust – with our lives – to keep silent. Loyalty for us is not a matter of money. But if anybody else were to hear of this . . .'

'I will give you my answer tomorrow. In principle I agree. You charge a high price for your silence, woman.'

'Oh, Da Ren, your generosity is a legend.'

'No, it is your greed that is legendary, Mother Liu. Now, shall we stay chatting in this draughty corridor? Or may I enter? And by the way, if I hear the merest movement of that peep-hole of yours while I am inside then it'll be I who will inform Iron Man Wang that it is you who are harbouring foreigners upstairs. Two can play at blackmail, my dear Mother Liu.'

'Oh, Da Ren, as if I would even dream of spying on you . . .'

Chuckling at her discomfort the Mandarin pushed open the door and went inside. The curtains on the bed were drawn. Standing on the carpet in a submissive attitude was Fan Yimei. He smiled with pleasure to see her. He was struck again by her beauty. She reminded him of Jinghua when he was a young man. He could even recognise in her downcast eyes the look of unstated disapproval that he had known so well in his old friend. 'How is your rival, my dear?' he asked.

'She is ready for you, Da Ren.' She made a delicate gesture at the curtained bed.

'And are you pleased that I am taking her away from your lover? Do you think that Ma Na Si will want her in the same way after I have used her?'

'I think Ma Na Si loves her, Da Ren, as she does him.' She looked him fully in the face. 'It is not my place to be pleased or not but – I do not think my father would approve of what you are doing.'

'Ha!' laughed the Mandarin. 'You are like him. Too good for this world and yourself! But not afraid to say so, it seems. Well, well. It appears that my friend the *daifu* has allies even in the bedchamber.'

'I do not understand you, Da Ren. I had not meant to be insolent. Please forgive me.'

He cupped her chin in his hand and looked at her kindly. 'If you were not the daughter of my friend,' he said regretfully, 'and if I were a younger man . . . Come,' he said, 'away with you. Off you go. My assignation is with the fox lady, and what will happen between the two of us is a matter only for her and me, but Yimei . . .' She paused by the door. 'I have never forgotten your father. Believe me, he would be proud of you today. Now go.'

She left.

The Mandarin sighed, and stretched. Through the thin pink curtains he could see red sheets moulded over the shape of a woman's body. He could make out a head on a pillow resting in a flame of auburn hair. He listened and could hear the whispering sound of her breath. He wondered what she would be feeling, knowing that he was there, waiting for the curtain to be pulled aside. Was she afraid? Was she excited? He felt the familiar stirrings in his loins.

He waited until the sensation subsided. He prided himself on his self-control. The pleasure of sex lay in the anticipation. The longer the delay, the greater the eventual reward. He began to hum. It was one of the songs of the Hunan Braves, one that Jinghua used to play, in very different surroundings. He had not thought of the tune for years. He stopped, sensing a movement in the sheets behind the curtains. Let her wait a little longer, he decided. He took up the air again.

Slowly he pulled off his boots and then his robe, hanging it carefully on the frame in the corner. Underneath he was wearing white cotton pyjamas. He thought of removing these, then thought better of it. He would take this very slowly.

Carefully he pulled back the curtains at the end of the bed. She was holding the sheets to her chin. The first thing he noticed was her pointed nose, so unlike the flatter Chinese noses. He wondered how foreigners kissed. Her face was covered in makeup. Fan Yimei must have painted her like that. She looked different from when he had seen her on past occasions, from his palanquin, at the railway ceremony, during the hunt in the hills. The paint gave her a sophistication he had not associated with her. She looked older, more experienced, not unattractive, but he had been expecting a young, frightened girl. She was watching him with her strange green eyes. Yes, there was anxiety there, but not exactly fear. Did he imagine it or was there pleading in her expression? Was this foreign girl like any other girl? Alone with a man, wanting to be approved? How brave she is, he thought. How did Ma Na Si persuade her? he wondered.

He closed the curtains behind him, moving to the side of the bed to sit by her. Her green eyes followed his movements. She flinched as he reached under the bedclothes but relaxed when he only pulled out her hand, pressing it with his. He examined the long fingers and the strange mottled freckles on her arm. Like smallpox scars, he thought. Ugly, but interesting. He smiled at her, looking directly into her eyes. They were not green, really. A sort of hazel colour flecked with grey. He was glad they were not blue eyes, such as some foreigners had – milky pale things that looked like the eyes of the blind. There was light and fire in these eyes, he thought, though for now they contemplated him nervously. Carefully, he reached his hand behind her head and ran his fingers through the thick, red hair – the fox fairy's hair that had attracted him. He had expected it to be tough and fibrous, and was surprised by its softness, the way the strands slid through his fingers like silk. He smiled at her again, and this time he was rewarded by a slow quiver of her lips as she tried to respond. Brave girl, he thought, brave girl. Worthy of Ma Na Si.

Gently he laid her arm back on the sheet. Her eyes widened with alarm as he stood over her. He carefully pulled away the sheets uncovering her all the way down to her feet. He untied the sash of her gown and lifted it over her shoulders, running the sleeves down her arms, so she lay naked to his gaze. She was a thin thing. He could make out all her ribs and there were blue veins visible on her chest. He was glad that the brown freckles and smears were restricted to her arms and legs and part of her shoulders. The rest of her skin was pale, white, wraithlike perhaps, but again, not unattractive. He admired the bluish hollows over her surprisingly round stomach and throat and thighs. She had quite full breasts too, larger than most Chinese girls. She was not as hairy as he had imagined; the fine filaments on her belly and thighs were like goose down, and the thick red bush that covered her groin . . . well, that was intriguing. He had wondered if the colour below would be the same as the flaming hues on her head, and now he knew. He felt the stirring again in his own loins. In fact, he realised, he was quite hard under his pyjamas. He wondered if she had noticed and what she thought. He looked at her face. Her eyes were closed and her mouth was partially open. He could see the tips of her teeth.

He sat down beside her. He ran his fingers through her hair, resting his hand behind her head. With his other hand he gently stroked her body, moving his palm over her shoulders, down her thin upper arm, over the swell of her breast. He held the small pink button of her nipple, rising out of its pale puckered areola, between his two fingers. He closed his mouth over it, kneading it with his lips and tongue, feeling it harden. As he pulled away he was struck by her odour. She had a sour, milky smell, different from the smell of women he was used to. Again, it was intriguing. Not unpleasant. Arousing, even – but how foreign she was. Her eyes were open now, watching him, lids half closed. He wondered if he was exciting her. There was a dreamy look in her eyes that might have been desire – but he could not read this woman as he could read one of his own kind. Was she enjoying this? He continued his exploration, moving his hand across her ribs, over her round, protuberant belly, down her thighs, then back again, smoothing his palm over the red, wiry hairs, feeling for the familiar mound, the cinnabar grotto. His fingertips touched soft flesh and, yes, there was moistness there. She was responding to him. He wondered what it would be like to kiss her. Would that pointed nose press into his cheek? How strange she was. If only she did not have such large, ugly feet, he thought, she might be considered beautiful.

Hesitantly Helen Frances lifted her own hand to touch the face of the man who was leaning over her. He felt a cold palm on his cheek. Her eyes, looking directly into his, stared with urgent enquiry. Her slightly frowning brow, the teeth in the half-open mouth, the quiver of the upper lip reminded him of an inquisitive little animal, a peering fox cub or a small beaver. For a moment he was nonplussed and sat rigidly on the bed, allowing the long, cool fingers to descend from his face to penetrate the folds of his pyjamas, tickling in turn his chest, his belly, moving downwards towards his own secret regions. The hand reached his waistband and could go no further. The solemn face below him looked questioningly at him, then stared in fascination as a hardness he could not control raised the cloth that covered his groin, and his growing excitement became visible to her. His own hand moved almost unconsciously to untie the silk cord. He wanted those cool fingers to go further, to touch his arousal, to enfold his jade flute . . . He slipped the knot, the cold fingers moved on, he felt them ruffle over his hairs . . . But no, with an effort of will he asserted his self-control. This was inappropriate. He stopped her there. The green eyes widened in surprise as he pulled out her hand. He held it pressed between his palms, and sighed, feeling after a moment his hardness subside. He smiled at her puzzlement.

'No, my little fox lady,' he whispered. 'I cannot allow it. For all I have said, I value my friendship with Ma Na Si. The debt between us is paid and you will tell him that I have not harmed you. I will not take his treasure although I see it is freely given. I in turn am in debt to him, and to you.'

She had not understood a word. He dredged his memory for the English words. 'Sank – you,' he said clumsily, after much thought. 'You – be-yoo-ti-fu'. No – berong – old – man.'

Slowly, understanding penetrated her face. Her features quivered, and crumpled, and her green eyes filled with tears. Her body began to tremble, and she shook with silent sobs. The Mandarin stood over her indulgently, gently pulling the sheets to cover her. He leaned down and kissed her forehead, smelling again for the last time that strange, milky odour. Then he closed the curtains quietly behind him.

As he put on his official gown, he began to hum the song of the Hunan Braves.

And he was humming as he stepped out of the door into the gallery where Mother Liu and her son, joined by Major Lin, were waiting. Ma Na Si was also there, standing sheepishly a little distance away. Ignoring the brothel-keepers, the Mandarin strode towards him, but Ma Na Si would not meet his eyes.

The Mandarin laughed. 'Abashed, my friend?' he said jovially. 'That's not like you. Perhaps my little game has been worth it to see this humbler side of you at last.' He moved closer, putting an arm around his shoulder and speaking in a low tone so only the Englishman could hear. 'Remember the saying, Ma Na Si,' he whispered. '"Intercourse between friends is like a glass of clear water handed between gentlemen." Neither you nor I have anything to reproach ourselves for. Your fox woman is as you left her. Be assured of that. You will not hate me after you have spoken to her. Listen,' he said, pressing his mouth closer to Henry's ear, 'we are all involved in a game now. My wager with the doctor was trivial, but it does no harm that Major Lin has seen you apparently humbled. It may go a little way to assuage the vengeance he feels towards you for stealing his concubine. We need him, you and I, for our plans. Continue to act the aggrieved lover, although it doesn't suit you, and there may be peace between you. But beware of him. He is your enemy. It is dangerous enough here as it is. So much so that I am thinking of bringing my plans forward so we can leave tonight. Make sure all of you are ready when we come for you . . . Now, for the benefit of the others, look angry. They must think that in this whispered exchange I have been gloating over my defilement of your beloved. Spit at me, if you like. It will suit the melodrama of the occasion.'

'You bastard, you led me on,' said Henry.

'Would you have been able to persuade her if I hadn't?' asked the Mandarin.

Henry bellowed and swung a wide punch at him, but the Mandarin easily caught the bunched fist in his hand, twisting Henry's arm viciously behind his back. Major Lin ran forward and made to grab him, but the Mandarin only laughed, letting him go. Henry's eyes glared with very real anger, but he controlled himself. He brushed past the sneering Major Lin and ran down the corridor to the bedroom from which the Mandarin had come.

The Mandarin smiled. 'I think we can safely leave him to take stock of his spoiled goods,' he said. 'Come, Major, we have work to do. Mother Liu, thank you for your hospitality. If you are ready, we will leave now.'

'May I stay for a while longer, Da Ren?' Major Lin requested. 'I have things to arrange with Fan Yimei.'

'Join me at the *yamen*,' said the Mandarin, draping the cloak over his head, 'as soon as you're done. There may be some changes to those plans I discussed with you.'

Major Lin, Ren Ren lounging beside him, watched until the Mandarin, led by Mother Liu, had disappeared down the secret stairs. When they were out of sight, Ren Ren tapped on the door of one of the rooms leading off the gallery. The door opened, and Ren Ren's sinister assistant, Monkey, stepped into the light. 'Now then, Major, you asked for us to come here,' said Ren Ren. 'What exactly was it that you wanted us to do for you?'

'Forgive me, forgive me,' Helen Frances was weeping in Henry's arms, 'I tried, but he didn't – he wouldn't . . . He just looked at me, examined me, like I was some sort of animal that disgusted him . . . and he left, without – without doing anything . . . And now they're all going to die because I didn't . . . Oh, God, Henry, forgive me . . .'

She felt his kisses on her cheeks, her eyes, her ears, the tight pull of his arms round her shoulders. 'Nobody's going to die,' he said. 'It was just a game. A bloody game. One of the Mandarin's bloody games.'

'I would have done it,' she moaned. 'I would have done. I wanted to do it. Don't you see? I betrayed you. Oh, God – but he just walked away.'

'Nonsense,' Henry said. 'Nonsense. You had to steel yourself, that's all. You did what you had to do. You were bloody brave.'

'Hold me,' she whispered. 'Just hold me. Don't leave me again.'

And probably, after a while, her anguish might have subsided in his familiar embrace – but at that moment, with a crash, the door burst open and, through the curtains, she made out the shapes of three men forcing entry into the room. Immediately Henry leaped to his feet to confront the intruders, and she watched in horror as one of the figures kick-boxed with his foot and Henry's head crashed back against the bedpost. She had been too startled even to scream for help, and it was too late now, for rough hands were pulling her from the bed. She felt a stunning blow to her head, and she dropped on her knees. A kick in her back sent her sprawling over the carpet. She felt herself retching. Dizzily she was aware that she was being turned over on her back. She gagged as a rough cloth was forced tightly into her mouth and for a while she could not breathe. Strong hands pinioned her shoulders and arms to the floor. Someone slapped her again, and she opened her eyes to see a pockmarked Chinese face grinning over her. She saw Henry, also gagged, struggling against ropes that tied him to the bedpost. His eyes were angry white fires, screaming in their impotence. A tall figure in a white uniform stepped into view, and for a moment she felt a surge of relief when she recognised the handsome, familiar features of Major Lin, but then she saw the wolfish sneer, and the reptilian eyes, which coldly surveyed her nakedness; she saw him unbuckle and drop his belt to the floor and his fingers fumble with the buttons of his trousers.

And she screamed, and kicked with her lower body, but only moans came through the gag, and another man caught her feet and wrenched her legs apart. Lights exploded as she was slapped, again and again. She felt a heavy, stifling weight on her belly and chest, the scratch of thick serge and the cut of brass buttons on her breasts. The sour smell of garlic filled her nostrils and a man's breath blew on her cheek; and when she could focus, she saw the hate-filled eyes of Major Lin inches from her face. She felt his exploring fingers, and with all her strength she tried to shake away her attacker, but the other men's hands held her legs and arms fast to the ground and she could not move. She gasped at the sudden fiery pain. Major Lin, like a demented animal, was thrusting inside her, tearing flesh, splitting tissue, pushing deeper through the resisting folds. He grunted over her as he pushed; his spittle dripped on her face, and an explosion of pain ripped through her lower body as he broke the last obstacle, and her blood became the lubricant for his burning thrusts into her womb. She felt the hard thing inside her, violating her, ravishing her, jarring the very breath out of her body as it intensified its thrusts. It was as if time had stopped and she was caught in a slow-motion nightmare defined by pain and shame.

Over the shoulder of her ravisher she saw the beams of the ceiling, the pockmarked Chinese who was holding her down, and Henry at the corner of her vision, his face purple with his efforts to break his bonds, his eyes bulging despair and hate and wordlessly shrieking messages to her that she could not understand. Yet they might have been inhabitants of another planet for all their relevance to her now. Whatever was happening to her was an internal drama. Every painful thrust diminished her, tearing away another shred of the little self-esteem that remained to her.

She had a clear vision of herself being whipped in the hall of her school; everyone she knew was pointing at her naked body, reviling her for her foulness and laughing at the dirt that covered her. Major Lin climaxed and she felt her deepest parts running with his polluting, defiling liquid. The thrusting stopped, and the weight became heavier on her chest as he relaxed. The hard rod that had scorched and torn the inside of her had transformed into a soft, revolting stuffing of meat, swilling in a disgusting gravy of sperm and blood. She felt a trickle of the cold emission seeping on to her thigh, and began to gag with shame and self-hatred. How could she ever be clean again?

Major Lin pushed himself to his feet and pulled on his trousers. He gave one last, sneering glance at the girl he had raped. She was lying where he had left her. Ren Ren and Monkey no longer bothered to hold her now. She still lay with her legs apart. Her thighs were smeared with blood and there was a slime of pink liquid trickling on to the wooden floor. Lin spat, and his phlegm landed on her stomach. She did not react. He turned to Manners, whose struggles had also subsided.

'The da ren ordered me not to harm you,' he said to the gagged man, 'but he said nothing about your whore. That's what you made her, isn't it, when you gave her to the Mandarin? So you can look upon what I did just now as merely another bit of business for her.

As you gave business to my whore a while back. I think we can consider ourselves even now, Ma Na Si.'

He turned to leave, then stopped as if he had suddenly remembered something. He reached in his pocket and withdrew a few copper coins. 'I am being remiss,' he said. 'I haven't paid you for her services.' He flung the coins on the floor by Henry's, feet.

He left without another word.

Leaving Helen Frances to Ren Ren and Monkey. With great ceremony they tossed one of the coins. Monkey guessed tails, so it fell to Ren Ren to pinion Helen Frances's shoulders while the other took his reward. Monkey pulled his pyjamas down and knelt between her legs sniffing humorously. He made great play of lapping like a dog, then his excitement getting the better of him, he hurled himself on the recumbent body. Both Ren Ren and Monkey turned when they heard the noises from the bedpost. Henry was violently, and again impotently, struggling against his bonds. He was trying to shout too, because muffled sounds were coming through his gag. Ren Ren and Monkey laughed, and went back to their play.

Again Helen Frances felt the pain, the invasion of her body and the defilement. This time, weakened and broken by her shame, she did not struggle to resist, but Henry saw the tears running down her cheeks. They flowed in haphazard runnels across the bruises and the smeared makeup. Monkey's thin haunches wriggled and it was over.

Ren Ren sneered. 'Don't think that I'm going in that polluted hole, not after you animals have used it. Turn her over,' he said.

Roughly Ren Ren and Monkey rolled her on to her front. Ren Ren pulled her into a crouching position so that her bottom faced him and he, too, removed his trousers, adjusting himself between her parted thighs – but this time when they moved her the gag had slipped from her mouth. In her dazed state it took her some moments to realise that her mouth was free, but the intense agony of the new indignity that was being inflicted on her, and even more the horror when she understood what it was, made her scream, a piercing shriek that echoed around the walls of the room and penetrated the whole corridor outside. She screamed and screamed again until Monkey had beaten her into silence and replaced the gag – but by then others on the floor had been alerted and they heard the drumming of feet outside.

The doctor was the first through the door, followed by Nellie, and Fan Yimei. Ren Ren reacted quickly, pulling himself away from his victim and bounding to his feet – but they saw clearly enough what he had been doing. Helen Frances still crouched in the position in which he had been abusing her. They saw her nakedness and the ruin of her painted face. They saw the blood, and the bruises, and the foulness that stained the floor. They saw the drooping manhoods of the two trouserless Chinese men, the blood and filth that smeared their thighs; they observed the truculence on their guilty faces.

'My God. My God,' whispered Airton, leaning in shock against the wall. Nellie was already by Helen Frances's side, folding the girl into her arms, staring defiantly at Ren Ren as she did so. Fan Yimei stood hesitantly by the door.

'I can't believe this depravity,' shouted Airton, rage overtaking him. He directed the main force of his anger at Henry, ignoring the fact that he was bound and gagged. 'What sort of monster are you?' he cried. 'Was this – was this your bargain? My God, man! You told the Mandarin I'd agreed to this?'

Ren Ren and Monkey exchanged amused glances.

'And you – you creatures! What have you done to her? It's – monstrous! Monstrous!'

Ren Ren laughed, and Monkey giggled. This was too much for the doctor, who flung himself at Ren Ren, pushing the younger man's chest. His strength was feeble, but the carpet slipped, and both Ren Ren and Airton fell to the ground in a flurry of flailing fists. And such was the way they fell that Ren Ren, who was the stronger man, had his arms pinioned by Airton's knees, and had to shake his head to avoid the blows raining down on his face. 'Monster! Monster! Monster!' Airton was shouting, as he struck.

Nellie screamed and there was an eruption of movement from the gagged, bound Henry. Both had seen the knife Monkey had pulled from his sleeve.

'Edward! Behind you!' shrieked Nellie, but it was too late. In two steps Monkey had reached the struggling pair and raised the knife high above his head, ready to strike between the doctor's defenceless shoulder-blades.

A loud, cracking explosion echoed round the small room, followed by another. Monkey staggered backwards, blood seeping from a spreading red patch on his white shirt. He turned, and there was an expression of amazement on his face before he pitched forward, dead, and the knife clattered on the floor.

Fan Yimei stood in the doorway. A haze of smoke was rising from Hiram's revolver, which she held out at arm's length in her two small hands. She was shaking and the barrel of the gun was pitching up and down but she still pointed it forward into the room.

With a heave Ren Ren knocked the doctor off him and jumped to his feet. His eyes were blazing with anger and venom, his fists were clenched – but he froze when he saw Fan Yimei.

The foreigners in the room watched hypnotised as the slim girl with the revolver stared steadily at the half-naked Chinese man, her eyes fixed on his in a battle of wills. Only Henry knew what torments Ren Ren had inflicted on the girls in his power, and the terrors of his unspeakable regime – but the others could sense the deadliness of this silent exchange. For a moment it looked as if the man would gain his accustomed ascendancy over his slave. Ren Ren's lip curled into the beginnings of a cruel smile, and slowly he raised his arm, palm up, in an unspoken command for Fan Yimei to hand over the revolver. For a moment the gun wavered, but only for a moment. Nellie, who was closest to Ren Ren, saw his expression suddenly change, his head shake in disbelief, his mouth open as if to plead, and the pupils of his widening eyes dilate with fear. Then the revolver cracked again and Nellie saw his throat explode in a messy scatter of blood and bone. He toppled backwards, his body tangling with the pink hangings of the bed. The legs kicked and horrible, gurgling sounds rasped the silence, sawing on their stretched nerves. It was a long time before the twitching ceased

Fan Yimei dropped the gun. Sinking to her knees, she began to weep.

A ghastly stillness settled over the room. The doctor crouched in a prayer position where he had fallen; Nellie, Madonna-like with the recumbent body of the naked Helen Frances in her arms; Henry slumped in his bonds like a wounded St Sebastian, gaped at the twisted corpses. Frozen in attitudes of open-eyed horror, they resembled carved devotees worshipping at some hideous parody of a baroque shrine.

A film of smoke hung over the obscene tableau. Their ears still reverberated with the echoes of the gunshots – but gradually, through the ringing silence, the more familiar household noises seeped up from the stairway – a girl's cry, men's raucous laughter, and the drunken singing of Iron Man Wang's retainers revelling in the delights of the Palace of Heavenly Pleasure below.

Chapter Eighteen

*The enemy officers ride horses. The sunlight gleams on
their heavy guns.
I wish Little Brother were here.*

A child's voice broke the silence. 'Mummy?'
Nellie turned in alarm. George and Jenny were hovering
nervously outside the door.

All her maternal instincts welled to protect them from the horrors
they had, no doubt, already glimpsed in the room, but with Helen
Frances in her arms there was nothing she could do. In her anguish
she screamed at her husband. 'Edward, get them away!'

Airton turned his head blankly, still lost in his stupor, but the sight
of his children galvanised him. 'Oh, my God!' he cried, and flung
himself towards them. He threw his arms around them, covered their
staring eyes with his hands and pushed them back into the corridor.
With a violent effort he kicked shut the door behind him, as if to
keep out the butchery that had occurred there. Panting, he pulled
them down the gallery towards their own room, only stopping when
he realised that his grip on their wrists was hurting them. George's
eyes were filling with tears. Airton knelt in front of them, covering
their pale, frightened faces with his kisses.

'I'm sorry,' he sobbed. 'I'm so, so sorry. Oh, God forgive me.
What have I done?'

'Oh, Papa, don't cry,' said Jenny, hugging him. 'It's not your fault.
Really it isn't.' Choking, he put his arms around them, squeezing
them fiercely to his breast.

As he was doing so, he heard a voice behind him. In consternation
he looked up to see the cruel, smiling face of Mother Liu. 'The
poor dears,' she was crooning, as she hobbled down the gallery
towards him. 'Whatever could be the matter? The naughty little
things.'

He could hardly breathe for fear. He stared at her, his mouth wide
open, his limbs shaking.

Her shrewd eyes narrowed. 'Is something wrong with you, Daifu? You're not looking very well.'

'No.' His voice came out as a croak and he had to repeat himself. 'Excuse me. I'm fine,' he said. 'We're all fine.'

'I'm pleased to hear it,' she said, examining him.

He continued to stare at her. He was blocking her path down the corridor. She looked suspiciously over his shoulder. In panic he also turned to give a frightened glance behind him. She noticed the guilty movement. 'Will you let me pass please, Daifu?' She spoke quietly but her tone was threatening. 'Please let me pass. I have some urgent business with my son.'

'He's not here,' he said quickly. 'No, he left – with his friend. Yes, he's gone,' he repeated.

'With his friend? What friend? I met Major Lin downstairs. Ren Ren was not with him. He must still be here.'

'I mean, his other friend,' the doctor said. He realised he was sweating. 'They left together. You won't find them here. Downstairs, perhaps. Yes, downstairs. Why don't you look downstairs?'

Mother Liu tried to edge past him. Airton sidestepped her, blocking her. 'No, please, Madam Liu. I don't think you should go any further.'

She did not answer. She shuffled to the left, he to the right. Panting, she tried to push him aside. He grabbed her arm to prevent her. She stared at him in surprise and anger. She attempted to pull away her arm but he held on. 'Get your dirty hands off me, you foreign ghost,' she hissed. 'Let me by.'

He held on. Her eyes were two black coals of hatred. She wheezed as she struggled with him, swaying on her lotus feet. 'No, Madam Liu, you are not going down that corridor,' he muttered. He also was panting with exertion.

She spat in his face but he only tightened his grip on her sleeve. '*Ta made!*' she swore. With her other hand she reached for the hairpin that secured the bun on her head. He saw what she was doing, and desperately grabbed for her other arm, missing his hold in his panic. The long shining needle glistened in her hand.

He sensed a flurry of movement. Jenny had jumped up behind the old woman and caught the arm with the pin, pulling it backwards with all her strength. George was clinging to her legs. With a curse, Mother Liu toppled over, the doctor falling with her. With surprising agility she rolled away from him, and began to crawl at a fast pace towards the staircase.

The doctor felt a chill run down his spine. With sudden clarity, he realised that if he allowed her to reach the stairwell and cry out to Iron Man Wang's men, he, his wife, his children, Helen Frances and Manners would be dead within the hour.

He had to stop her, whatever it took.

He scrambled to his feet. On the floor lay the fallen hairpin. He picked it up and ran after her, panicked by the knowledge of what he was about to do.

Nellie in her desperation shouted at Fan Yimei. The Chinese girl was still slumped against the wall, staring blankly at the revolver on the floor. 'Get up, get up, will you, girl?' Nellie cried. 'Oh, can somebody not do something to help? Untie that man there. Get up, get up, woman, and untie Mr Manners.' Fan Yimei's eyes slowly focused.

For a moment she stared uncomprehendingly. Finally, realising the meaning of the European woman's frantic gestures she nodded, although she was still dazed by the momentousness of what she had done earlier. With an effort she pulled herself to her feet, and hobbled unsteadily towards Henry. She flinched as she stepped over Monkey's leg. She turned away her head as she pulled at the bonds. That way she would not have to see the contorted corpse of Ren Ren on the bed. 'Cut the rope with the knife,' Nellie shouted, when she saw that Fan Yimei was making no progress with the knots. Fan Yimei followed the pointing finger, and gingerly reached for the knife lying by Monkey's dead, outstretched arm. She was sobbing and panting as she sawed at the thick strands.

Eventually she cut through, releasing the tension on the cords so that Henry himself could wriggle out of his bonds. He tore in a frenzy at the gag in his mouth, and stood swaying on the bloodstained carpet. His chest heaved as he gulped air into his lungs. Fan Yimei staggered away from him, terrified by his rolling eyes and savage expression. His fists were clenched and he stood like an enraged bull seeking somebody to charge or maim. His maddened eyes flashed around the room, but when he saw Helen Frances, there was an immediate transformation. A despairing cry, half bellow, half howl, erupted from his cracked lips. His features crumpled, he dropped on to his knees; it was as if his body had suddenly been drained of spirit. Weakly he crawled towards her, his eyes pleading, his hand stretched out, his face a mask of horror, trepidation, and remorse.

The effect on Helen Frances, who had been lying comatose in Nellie's arms, was dramatic. Her eyes widened in fear. Henry reached to touch her and she flinched away. Whimpering quietly, her body shaking and shuddering with revulsion, she pressed herself against Nellie's bosom, watching warily the movements of this imagined would-be attacker out of the corner of one half-exposed eye.

Henry froze. After a moment he shook his head, moved backwards in his confusion.

Now that he was retreating, Helen Frances seemed to calm. Curling into a ball, she moaned, as if taking comfort in a reversion to infancy. Nellie cooed endearments as she would to a child, smoothing the wet hair on her brow. Gradually Helen Frances relaxed.

Henry, bewildered, was aware that Nellie was looking angrily up at him. 'Are you really surprised, Mr Manners?' she said coldly. 'You're a man. Men raped her. Do you wonder she's scared of you? She probably blames you directly for what happened to her. I know I do.'

'I – I . . .' But he had no words to answer her.

'Well, what are you going to do about it?' Nellie persisted, her voice rising in her fury. 'Have your brains evaporated with your manhood? You do understand that we're in danger here? That horrible woman will be returning any moment. I wouldn't be surprised if the whole house heard the shots.'

'What – what would you like me to do, Mrs Airton?' Henry managed.

'Hide the bodies, man. What do you think? We can't leave them here for all to see. Oh, come on, Mr Manners, do gather some self control. I can't do the thinking for everybody. And besides,' she looked down at Helen Frances, 'it's this poor wee lass who needs me now. Is that a bathroom next door? If you'll kindly ask this Chinese girl to help me move her, I'll be obliged. She'll need to be cleaned of the filth those brutes have put on her. Then Edward will have to examine her for her hurts. I don't doubt he'll be giving her the morphine again, after all she's been through. I can't bear to think of it. Oh, Mr Manners, you have a lot to answer for.'

Fan Yimei understood immediately what had to be done. Gently, between them, she and Nellie lifted Helen Frances to a semi-standing position; they helped her move, one hesitant foot at a time, into the bathroom, closing the curtain behind them.

Henry surveyed the bloody scene. For a moment he stood there uncertainly, perhaps overwhelmed by the apparently impossible task of transforming this charnel house into a semblance of normality. He closed his eyes, as if gathering internal strength, then, with violent decision, he pulled the bloodstained rug from under Monkey's body, flattening it on the floor. Overcoming his revulsion, he rolled the body on to it again, wrapping the stiff sides of the carpet over him so it half covered him. He pulled and pushed the makeshift shroud under the bed. The carpet left a red smear behind it on the floorboards.

He contemplated Ren Ren's body tangled in the bed curtains. Picking up Monkey's knife, he climbed on to the bed itself, straddling the corpse, so that he could reach the rings and cut away the part of the curtain that had not been pulled out already by the weight of Ren Ren's fall. He had just finished, the released body had fallen backwards on to the bed, when he heard a timid knock on the door. Leaping off the bed, wielding the knife now as a weapon, he ran to the door, flattening himself against the wall beside it. There was another timid knock, and the door inched open. Henry relaxed when he saw Jenny's worried face peering into the room. She noticed his at the same instant, saw the knife in his hand, and whimpered with fear. Henry squatted in front of her, taking her hand. 'It's all right,' he said gently. 'I won't hurt you.'

Jenny burst into tears. 'Mr Manners, please come. Please come,' she squealed through her sobs. 'Papa needs you, please come.' Desperately she pulled at his hand.

Henry paused only to pick up the revolver. With this and the knife in his hand he followed Jenny into the gallery. His heart sank as he saw the scene at the end of the corridor close to the stairs. Two bodies were lying tangled together on the floor. George stood beside them wringing his hands. 'Oh, my God,' he muttered, running forward. 'What the hell . . . ?'

His immediate apprehension that he had two new corpses on his hands was removed when the two bodies jerked into violent movement. Coming closer he recognised the doctor and Mother

Liu. The former had the latter literally pinned to the ground. Henry saw what could only be a hairpin embedded in Mother Liu's right shoulder. Seeping blood was staining her embroidered silk jacket a darker black, but the wound had not incapacitated her. Her eyes were glaring with hatred and anger, and her body was arching and writhing in its attempts to shake Airton off. She could not give full vent to her fury, because the doctor's hand was thrust firmly into her mouth. The blood streaming from the hand indicated that she had bitten it to the bone.

'Manners, is that you? Will you get a gag or something, and help me with this she-devil?' panted the doctor.

Henry's answer was to press the muzzle of the revolver between the woman's blazing eyes. It had the desired effect. Mother Liu immediately ceased her struggles. With his other hand Henry reached into his pocket and pulled out a soiled handkerchief. 'This will have to do for now,' he told Airton. 'Can you extricate your hand from her mouth?'

'I – I think so,' said Airton. 'Jenny, will you rummage in my medical bag and bring me a roll of sticky bandage. Quick, girl.'

With the bandage and the handkerchief they achieved a suitable gag.

'Oh, Lord forgive me, I've stabbed her,' moaned Airton.

'Never mind that,' said Manners. 'She'd have done worse to you. You'd better bind that hand of yours if you don't want to leave a blood trail down the corridor.'

'Aye, you're right,' muttered Airton gloomily. 'Oh, Lord, Manners.' He exclaimed, as he wrapped the bandage round his hand. 'What are we to do with her? I have to bind her wound too. We can't take her to that room. We'll have a madwoman on our hands if she sees what's happened to her son.'

'If I tie her to the bed in my room, can you look after her there? I'll leave you my gun. And you can keep the children with you. When I've – tidied in the other room we'll think again.'

With the gun against her head, Mother Liu did not struggle as they pushed her along the corridor. It was while Henry was tying her to the bed that the doctor, standing behind him, noticed a lady's portmanteau on the floor, spilling over with female clothes and one of Helen Frances's boots. So absorbed had he been in his struggle with Mother Liu that he had temporarily forgotten what had happened to her. Now his earlier anger and disgust returned in full force, especially when he remembered Henry's role in her defilement, that it had resulted from a bargain between him and the Mandarin done, unbelievably, in the doctor's name, and that, however indirectly, he himself was implicated in this atrocity, and therefore shared the blame. Shaking with fury, he lifted the gun Henry had given to him. He was shocked by the violent impulse to strike down this monster of an Englishman. The gun trembled in his shaking hand.

It was at this moment that Henry turned. 'I think that's done it, Doctor. She won't . . .' He saw the wavering gun and the venom directed at him from Airton's eyes. 'Do we really have the time for this?' he asked calmly.

'You monster,' hissed the doctor. 'That you could treat your own woman in such an abominable . . .'

'What took place I did not plan or envisage.' Henry used the same quiet tone.

'You cynical, lying . . .' Airton stopped, aware that his children were gazing at him, open-mouthed. 'Oh, God,' he moaned, clenching his cheeks. 'Forgive me. Forgive me.'

'Doctor, there'll be time for recriminations later, when we're all out of here. If we get out of here. For now, don't you think we'd both better get on with the jobs we have to do?'

Airton sighed, raising his eyes to the ceiling. 'Aye,' he acknowledged weakly. 'We're all passengers in the same boat now. Though the Lord alone knows where He's sailing her.' Quietly Henry left the room.

An hour later all that they could think of doing had been done. Mercifully there had been no other visitor to this secret floor to disturb them.

Henry, later helped by Fan Yimei, had achieved miracles in turning the butcher's shop back into a garish bordello. He had secured both bodies out of sight under the bed. Fan Yimei had taken bucket and sponge from the bathroom, and painstakingly wiped away all traces of blood from the floor and the walls. She had done the same for the bloodstains in the corridor. Where Monkey had fallen, the sheer quantity of blood that had soaked into the floorboards was impossible to clean. Their solution had been to cover the irremovable stain with a carpet taken from one of the other rooms. The bloodstained curtain at the front of the bed had also initially proved a problem. It was too soiled and tattered to rehang, and in any case it had been appropriated as Ren Ren's shroud. With some artifice, Henry had arranged the remaining curtains round the front of the bedposts, so a quick glance would suggest that all the curtains were still there. After ascertaining that there were spare sheets and coverlets in the cupboard, the bloody originals had been stuffed under the bed with the bodies. The furniture was back in its original position, the erotic paintings on the wall had been straightened. When he and Fan Yimei had finished, there was no obvious sign that anything amiss had occurred.

Meanwhile the doctor had dressed Mother Liu's wound, and double-checked that the old woman was securely gagged and tied. He had left the children on guard outside the door while he went to his own room to treat Helen Frances. She had been brought there by Nellie and Fan Yimei some fifteen minutes earlier, after they had finished bathing her. They had dressed her in her original clothes, and led her like a sleepwalker down the gallery. Now she was lying in the Airtons' bed. He had treated the bruises on her face with iodine, and ascertained that she was no longer bleeding below. As far as he could tell, no harm had come to the baby inside her. There was nothing that he could do to succour her broken spirit, or drive away the nightmare that replayed itself in her mind. He had been pained by the way she had initially flinched away from him. Obviously in her confused state she identified even her physician as another would-be attacker. Well, he had acknowledged sadly, that was to be expected: in her present state, she would have reacted with revulsion to any man who came near her. That was the worst of the horror that the brute Manners had allowed to be inflicted on her. Her poor body had been cruelly ravaged. Those scars would heal. There was no healthy prognosis for her spiritual and mental wounds. Pregnant, only recently recovered from a drug addiction, surrounded by horrors and murders and fears for their safety, and then savagely betrayed and assaulted in this way – he doubted whether any woman could survive such a trial without becoming severely unhinged.

It was only after Nellie had hugged her and rocked her and soothed her, telling her over and over again, 'It's Dr Airton. You know Dr Airton, darling. He's here to help, to help,' that she had reluctantly allowed him to examine her. All through his ministrations she had watched him with suspicious, frightened eyes. What alarmed him most was the self-hatred, which she would occasionally display, slapping herself and hissing words that sounded like 'Dirty. Dirty. Dirty,' And 'Wicked. Wicked.' Nellie had told him that in the bath Helen Frances had frenziedly snatched the soap from Fan Yimei's hands, and rubbed and rubbed it on her lower parts shrieking, 'How can I make myself clean? When can I ever be clean?' Fearing for her sanity, he had reluctantly concluded that the best salve for her at the moment was oblivion and, as Nellie had earlier predicted to Henry, his answer was to inject her with one of the vials of morphine in his medical bag. What he would do when he ran out of the drug he did not know, but at least it had had the merciful effect of sending her to sleep.

And now she lay quietly with Nellie watching over her. Nellie was using this respite also to see to the needs of her own disturbed children. They were sitting at her feet, listening to her read from *The Rose and the Ring*, one of the books she had snatched off the shelf when she was hurriedly packing the suitcase before they left the mission. She hoped that the romance, a favourite of the children, would take their minds for a little while off the terrible things they had seen and heard in the afternoon. Sadly she noticed that they were barely concentrating: it would take more than the amusing adventures of Prince Bulbo and Princess Angelica to wipe away from their imaginations the scars of this all-too-real adventure – but she read on resolutely because she had no other remedy to hand.

Outside her door Henry Manners, Dr Airton and Fan Yimei were standing in the darkening gallery. Dusk was falling. Bats were gathering in the violet sky outside the window. Henry had called the two others together to formulate a plan. He spoke quietly so that his voice would not carry into the children's room. 'Well, we couldn't have contrived a more desperate situation,' he said matter-of-factly, 'but let's not despair. We still have a chance of getting out of here. The Mandarin told me before he left that he was thinking of bringing our departure forward to tonight. That's fortunate, if it's true, because I doubt we could get through another full day here without being discovered. Unfortunately, he didn't tell me what his plan is – but I expect he'll send Major Lin to us after midnight. Doctor, have you your pocket watch?'

'It's just after eight,' said Airton gruffly, peering at his timepiece in the gloom.

'So we have four or five hours before he comes.'

'If he comes,' muttered the doctor.

'Correct,' said Henry. 'If he comes. Fan Yimei, what are the chances of someone coming looking for Mother Liu or Ren Ren in the next few hours? When will they be missed?'

'I don't know about Ren Ren,' she answered. 'Mother Liu usually visits the customers in the dining room about this time and allocates the girls. But sometimes she has a headache and doesn't appear.'

'Good,' said Henry. 'Then she'll have a headache tonight. What happens when she doesn't appear?'

'Ren Ren allocates the girls, and supper is brought to her in her room.'

'And if Ren Ren is not there?'

'I don't know. Perhaps she passes instructions to the girl who brings up her supper tray.'

'Well, that seems clear enough. Since Mother Liu won't be inspecting any banqueting rooms tonight, we can assume the girl with the tray will be coming here in due course?'

'I think so, Ma Na Si. And soon, I believe. It is already dark.'

'Do you know which girl it will be?'

'It depends on who is available, Ma Na Si. Not entertaining customers, I mean. Usually it would be Su Liping, her favourite, but sometimes it is one of the new girls who are being broken in.'

'So a girl – maybe Su Liping – will come up soon with Mother Liu's supper. What about our supper? Presumably someone is detailed to bring food to us as well. Will more than one girl come?'

'I doubt it, Ma Na Si. Noone else knows you are here. I think that Mother Liu and Ren Ren themselves must have organised your food before now. They would not dare to let anyone else in on their secret. If any of the girls knew you were here the news would spread throughout the house within a day, and Iron Man Wang would know of it.'

'Good. That's one thing less to worry about,' said Henry. 'We only expect the one girl, then, with Mother Liu's supper. We can fool one girl, can't we, Airton?'

'Can we? I don't see how.'

'I also wonder, Ma Na Si,' said Fan Yimei. 'Whoever comes will expect to see Mother Liu in her room.'

'Not if you meet her at the top of the stairs and tell her Mother Liu doesn't want to be disturbed. She'll leave the food outside Mother Liu's door. You pass on the instructions to her for the evening. She goes down again. Normal routine's maintained.'

'That might work with one of the new girls, but not Su Liping. She would certainly suspect something if it was I who told her this.'

'Then it will have to be Mother Liu who tells her herself.'

'But how, Ma Na Si?'

'With my gun trained on her head she'll say anything I tell her to. Come on, Doctor, we'd better move the crone to her own room. Sounds as if we've little time.'

'Manners, are you mad?' The doctor could hardly restrain his loathing of the man, and after what had happened earlier, he certainly had no confidence in his leadership. 'This is a desperate scheme. What if Mother Liu blurts out that she's speaking under duress? What if this girl, whoever she is, isn't fooled? Even if it works, there's Mother Liu's son's disappearance to consider. What if Iron Man Wang sends one of his men up here looking for him?'

'Then we'll probably be discovered, Airton, and we'll all die a horrible death. Have you a better idea? We'll be discovered for certain if we don't try to do something.'

'We don't even know if the Mandarin really will send anyone for us tonight. Have you his guarantee on that?'

'Dr Airton, I can't guarantee you anything – except that I'm not going to give up while there's the remotest chance of us getting out of here alive. If Lin doesn't come for us, we'll have to determine a way to get out of here ourselves. But with Iron Man Wang's thugs roistering below we can hardly do that now. We can only take each threat as it comes. The first is to deal with this blasted supper tray. Will you help me get Mother Liu, or not?'

Airton reluctantly assented, and while Fan Yimei waited at the top of the stairs, they went together to Henry's room where Mother Liu lay trussed on the bed. The eyes above the gag blazed malevolence, but she was otherwise calm. The doctor untied her while Henry trained the revolver on her. 'Get up,' he ordered. She obeyed. 'Tie her hands behind her back,' Henry instructed. Airton did so. Taking her arm, he steered her towards the door. Henry followed behind. 'If you make one false move, I'll put a bullet in you,' he threatened. At Mother Liu's hobbling pace they moved into the corridor.

It was nearly night now, and the gallery was swathed in shadow. Fan Yimei had thoughtfully brought out a lantern from Mother Liu's room and was hanging it on a hook on the wall. The yellow light illuminated her face. Mother Liu recognised one of her own establishment. She started with anger at the betrayal, mumbling something incomprehensible but vitriolic through the gag, and Airton could feel the fury in her quivering arm and shaking body.

Rage made her obstinate and she fell forward on her knees, refusing to go further. 'Get up,' Henry shouted. She refused, struggling as the doctor tried to lift her. Fan Yimei saw what was happening and, having secured the lantern, ran back to help.

They froze when they heard the clumping on the stairs. They were too late.

In the dim lantern light they saw a slight, pretty girl appear out of the darkness, stumbling under a heavy tray weighed down with dishes and a covered teapot. They saw her eyes widen when she noticed the two foreign men flanking the feared figure of Mother Liu, and she too froze, her mouth opening in wonder and alarm.

Henry ran forward. The girl dropped the tray, and turned to run away, but he caught her arm, pulled her round and pressed the gun to her forehead. 'Don't make a sound,' he hissed.

'Jesus and Maria,' she whimpered in her fear, 'please don't hurt me.'

This time it was Henry's turn to show amazement. 'What did you say?' he whispered, lowering the gun.

'Please don't hurt me,' she mumbled, through sobs. 'I've done nothing wrong.'

'You said, "Jesus and Maria." You're a Christian. Fan Yimei, what's a Christian doing here?'

'I don't know her, Ma Na Si,' said Fan Yimei. 'There have been several new girls brought in recently by Ren Ren and his men.'

'What's your name, girl?' asked Henry gently.

She sensed that he was not about to hurt her. 'Phoenix, Xiansheng,' she said, sniffing back her tears, 'but my real name is Wang Mali. Or that's what I was called before I was – I was brought here.'

'Mali,' repeated Airton to himself. 'That could be the Chinese version of Mary. Where do you come from, child? What's the name of your village?'

'Bashu, Xiansheng,' said the girl. 'But I've been told that I must forget my past.'

'Oh, Lord, Manners, that's the village Elena was going to before she disappeared. There was a girl called Mary there. There were two sisters, Mary and Martha. Elena and Caterina often spoke about them. Answer me, child, whose daughter are you?'

The girl was startled by his vehement tone. 'Pastor Wang,' she said nervously, and then her voice broke, and she sobbed, 'But he's dead. He's dead.'

Airton persisted. 'And Sister Elena, child?' His voice was fierce with the desire to know her fate. 'Answer me. The foreign nun who used to visit you. What happened to her?'

'She's dead too, Xiansheng,' she wailed. 'They killed her after they killed Martha. In the church. They killed – they killed everybody, and they forced me to come here, and they made me – made me –'

Airton's shoulders slumped and he bowed his head. Although his reason had told him it was not likely, he had never received news of Elena's death so a small part of him had continued to hope that she had somehow survived. Now his worst fears were confirmed. It was as if another hammer blow had beaten down on his head on top of all the other shocks he had received today.

By now Mary was weeping uncontrollably. Fan Yimei relinquished her hold on Mother Liu, ran to her, and embraced her, pressing her cheek against hers. 'Give me some time with her,' she said, looking up at Henry. 'I think we can trust this one. Don't worry, I'll tell her what to do. Let me calm her before she returns downstairs.'

'All right, you can use Mother Liu's room,' said Henry. 'Give her some of that tea if it isn't all spilled. Airton, we'd better put that woman back in my room and truss her up again. Now she's had her supper delivered.'

Airton expostulated. 'I will not have it,' he cried. 'Didn't you hear the girl? Mary's one of us, man. A Christian, and an innocent victim of cruel men who took her captive and sold her into harlotry. I knew her father. She was poor Elena's friend. Now we've rescued her, we can't just send her back again to men who'll abuse her. We must protect her.'

'Rescue her? Protect her? Do you hear yourself? We can hardly protect ourselves,' said Henry acidly, 'and we certainly won't be able to protect her or anyone else if we're discovered, which will be the certain result if your precious Mary doesn't go downstairs and report that all is well. Listen, Doctor, four hours. That's what we need. When the time comes we'll try to take this girl with us. For now she's more useful to us back in the brothel.' Angrily, he walked back to Mother Liu. 'What are you laughing at, bitch?' Mother Liu had been watching the altercation between the two men with interest. Her eyebrows were raised sardonically above her cold, calculating eyes.

It was two hours later. Dr Airton was in his room with his family. On the bed, Helen Frances slept, lost in morphine dreams. Occasionally she would turn restlessly on the bed, shaking her head or beating her breast with her hand, and once she sat up, staring, wide-eyed, murmuring clearly but quite mystifyingly, the words, 'Soap. Tom, please, give me more soap. Why won't you give me more soap?' and a tear rolled down her cheek. The doctor had another vial of the drug ready to hand, but her head sank on to her pillow, and she drifted back into her dreams.

Henry sat in the next-door room, guarding Mother Liu. She, too, was sleeping, her rasping snores muffled only slightly by her gag, which he had loosened so she would not suffocate. Fan Yimei was with him. Although they had much to say to each other, neither wanted to say it, so they sat in uncomfortable silence. Once Henry broached the subject they had last discussed fruitlessly on their final ride together before they were captured at the railway yard. 'You know that you don't owe me anything?' he said.

'If you say so, Ma Na Si,' she had replied quietly.

'For helping the boy, I mean,' he had continued.

'I understand,' she had answered.

'A lot has happened since then,' he said. 'It would never have worked.'

'Yes, I understand,' she had replied.

He had relapsed into silence.

'You must not blame yourself for what happened today,' she said. 'It is honourable to try to save a life, especially if it involves sacrifice. Your lady, too, was brave.'

'You know, I never intended . . .' He started, but could not finish the painful sentence.

'You were not to know what would happen,' she said. 'The blame does not belong to you. And the lady, she will heal in time. And she may forgive you, if she is wise.'

'The doctor will never forgive me.'

'He has never suffered before,' she said. 'He was wise, but only in the wisdom of the daylight, where certainties glisten brightly in the sunshine. He was a healer, and believed he could cast his light into the darkest corners. But now he is challenged by another wisdom, that of the night, in which there is no light and where nothing is certain . . . It is hard for him.'

'It is you who are wise,' he said softly.

'I have learned what sorrow is,' she smiled, 'yet I continue to live. Is that wise?'

'That's nonsense,' he muttered. She did not answer. 'You know that the Mandarin may not send for us today?' he said.

'It is better to believe he will,' she said.

'Yes,' he said. 'It is his messenger who concerns me. After what Lin did today I cannot let him live.'

'Yet if you take Major Lin's life there will be no one to save yours.'

'Tricky, isn't it?' said Henry. 'I'm not sure I'll be able to control myself when I see him.'

'You will,' she said. 'For you, unlike the doctor, are wise in the wisdom of the night.'

'Am I?' he said.

'You have always shown yourself to be so. Ma Na Si, when are you going to ask me to go below?'

'Could I ask you that? Wouldn't it be dangerous? With Iron Man Wang and his men on the prowl?'

'Yet if I do not go, who will lead Major Lin here? The Mandarin will have asked Mother Liu to see to it. They went to the gate together and he would have told her his plans. I imagine that it was her intention to inform Ren Ren and that was why she was looking for him when she and the doctor had their struggle. Unless someone is there to meet Major Lin, and inform him of the latest situation, then I fear that our plans may go awry.'

'Cannot the girl, Mary, bring him?'

'No, Ma Na Si. She will be entertaining customers. I have told her to be ready to slip away after midnight when hopefully whoever she has been assigned will be sleeping, but we cannot rely on her any earlier. And Major Lin does not know her, or trust her, so it will be I who goes to the gate and waits.'

'You are not afraid of meeting one of Iron Man Wang's men on the way down?'

'I know how to handle such situations. Believe me.'

'You're a remarkable woman,' said Henry. 'You saved our lives today, and you're about to do so again.'

'I killed two men,' she said sadly. 'I will have to live with that shame.' She stood up abruptly. 'Excuse me, Ma Na Si, but if I am to do this I must leave now.'

He bowed his head. He had nothing to say.

She slid into the dark corridor. From the stairwell she heard a burst of singing and the shouts of men challenging each other in a drinking game. She pressed the inside of her robe to check that she had not lost the pouch which she had found in Mother Liu's room, then slowly lifted the flap that covered the entrance to the stairs. She stepped into the corridor on the second floor. She could hear cries and laughter from the bedrooms on either side, but was relieved to see that the corridor itself was deserted. She hurried along it, but just as she reached the stairs she heard a shrill, jeering voice behind her. 'Can I believe my eyes? What an honour! If it's not the precious Lady Fan Yimei!'

She turned, forcing a smile. Su Liping was standing in the doorway of one of the rooms. She was naked except for a skimpy *doudu* covering her breasts and abdomen. In her hand hung a pitcher of wine. From her red face and her slurred voice, Fan Yimei could see that she was drunk. This would normally have been against house rules, but Fan Yimei guessed that there was a different regime now that the brothel had been taken over by Iron Man and his followers.

'So her superior ladyship has deigned to visit her humble sisters,' continued Su Liping, enjoying her own wit.

'I have just been summoned to see Mother Liu,' said Fan Yimei quietly, 'and was on my way downstairs.'

'Oh, summoned, were you?' said Su Liping, in a parody of an

affected voice. 'How very grand. Summoned, is it?' She bowed in a mocking kowtow.

'Who are you talking to?' Fan Yimei heard a rough voice from inside the room, and the figure of a man loomed behind Su Liping. She staggered aside to let him pass. He was also naked, a squat, bearded monstrosity, with a barrel chest. Fan Yimei had never in her life seen so much hair on a human body. With a shock, she recognised him. He was the bandit who had wielded an axe in Major Lin's pavilion in the morning.

'I know you,' he said. 'You're that stuck-up bitch who was with the Mandarin. You're pretty, though,' he added, surveying her carefully.

'Oh, you can't touch her,' giggled Su Liping. 'She's off-limits. She belongs to Major Lin. His personal property,' she said, in the same affected voice she had used earlier.

'Is she now?' growled Iron Man. 'We'll see about that. Come here,' he ordered.

Fan Yimei hesitated, wondering if she could ignore him and flee down the steps that beckoned behind her.

'With deepest respects, Xiansheng,' she said, in an appeasing tone, 'what Su Liping says is correct. I am under exclusive contract to Major Lin.'

'Don't Xiansheng me,' snarled Iron Man. 'I'm no Xiansheng. And I don't give a bugger for any contracts. I told you to come here.'

Fan Yimei realised that she had little choice but to obey. With as much grace as she could muster, smiling her most ingratiating smile, she moved towards him. She was startled when her arms were gripped by his two hairy paws. 'Contracts,' he snorted, and pulled her robe off her shoulders. As she felt him grasp her breasts, she was relieved that the pouch still nestled above her waistband and had not fallen on the floor. 'Nice little melons,' he was saying. 'Bigger than yours,' he addressed a pouting Su Liping.

'So you're Major Lin's girl,' he said, examining her. 'He won't be around much longer, nor the precious Mandarin, though they don't know it yet. You're mine now, girl, for tonight or for however long it takes me to tire of you. Go on. Get into the bedroom.'

'Oh, Iron Man,' whined Su Liping. 'What about me?'

'You can bugger off,' he snapped. 'Or stay and watch. I don't care.'

Sullen-faced, Su Liping followed them into the room. She slumped onto a stool and tipped the wine pitcher to her throat.

'Don't hog that, you greedy slut,' Iron Man shouted. 'Give it to me.' He snatched the pitcher from Su Liping's trembling hands, and sat on the edge of the bed. 'You,' he pointed at Fan Yimei. 'Strip.' He took a long gulp from the pitcher.

Fan Yimei trembled in apparent uncertainty, averting her eyes bashfully and covering her breasts with her hands. Professionally, she had already sized up this unwelcome client. She had determined that coy modesty would be the right approach. For all his crudeness, she thought that what attracted Iron Man to her was her refinement. Clearly, he resented Major Lin, and by roughly taking his concubine he was asserting some sort of vengeance on the more privileged classes of society, and the pleasures that until now had been denied him. If she appeared too eager, he would not only be disappointed, he also might suspect a trick. She knew enough of this man's reputation not to underestimate him.

'Shy, are you?' laughed Iron Man. 'Why don't you take some fortification, then? You'll need it for what I'm about to do to you, my little lady. Here, catch.' Lightly he threw the heavy pitcher towards her. She caught it easily, but exaggerated the weight and pretended to stagger with the strain of holding such a heavy container.

'Quite the little willow, aren't we?' sneered Iron Man.

'Please, Xiansheng, I don't drink,' she said, in a beseeching tone.

'You'll do what I tell you,' he shouted.

Fan Yimei made a pretence of trying to lift the pitcher. 'It's so heavy,' she whimpered. 'Can I – can I pour it into a cup?'

Iron Man roared with laughter. 'Go on, then. Pour it into a cup. Give us the tea ceremony while you're about it.'

It had been much easier than she had imagined. She whispered a silent prayer to Guanyin for this stroke of luck. Carefully she placed the pitcher on the carpet behind the table so it was temporarily invisible to Iron Man Wang and Su Liping. She took a bowl from the chest, and leaned over the pitcher, tilting it to pour. As she did so she emptied into it the contents of the pouch. She stood up, lifting the bowl to her mouth, and sipped gingerly, making a sour expression as she felt the fiery liquid on her tongue. With her foot she kicked the now empty pouch out of sight under the table. Iron Man laughed to see the discomfort on her face. 'Come on, empty the bowl,' he urged. Fan Yimei did so, making sure she coughed afterwards, inducing the tears that ran down her cheeks. She felt a moment's gratitude to Mother Liu for all the artifices she had so painstakingly taught her over the years.

'Please. No more,' she whispered, reeling slightly. She hoped her cheeks were burning a bright red.

'All right, give me back the pitcher. You want to see how to drink? This is how you drink,' he said, and gurgled half a pitcher's worth down in an extended gulp. 'That's better,' he said, smacking his lips. 'Now do what I told you to do. Strip.'

She had had worse clients. Patiently she made the desired sounds as the animal grunted over her. Out of the corner of her eyes she had the satisfaction of seeing Su Liping bad-temperedly picking up the pitcher, and retiring with it to her stool, drinking distractedly, occasionally directing peevish glances at the girl who had superseded her in the Boxer leader's affections. Fan Yimei lay under Iron Man Wang, moaning with assumed pleasure, and coolly calculated how long it would take for the sleeping draught to work. She was not overly concerned. There was still more than an hour before Major Lin was likely to appear.

Iron Man Wang shuddered, and rolled on to his back. 'I've had better,' he yawned. 'Get me the wine.' Fan Yimei was pleased to see that Su Liping was already asleep, her head back and her mouth open, snoring softly. She carried the pitcher to Iron Man, remembering to pretend that she was straining under its weight, although the container was now three-quarters empty. 'The little bitch,' he murmured, lifting it to his mouth. 'She's a worse tippler than some of my men. Let me rest a bit and then I'll do the two of you together. Twin Phoenixes Dancing? Isn't that what you call it?' He sat back on the bed, yawning.

Knowing that it would soothe him – and therefore help him to sleep more quickly, Fan Yimei overcame her disgust, and leaned over his loins, almost suffocating in his thick hairs, but moving her mouth as she had been trained. He grunted with pleasure. 'Ye-es,' he breathed. 'I like that. Ye-es.' She stopped when she heard him snore. She waited, then lightly smacked his cheek. There was no response.

Pausing only to swill out her mouth with cold tea from the pot on the table, she dressed quickly. She noticed Iron Man's huge axe leaning against the wall. She glanced at the sleeping figure. It would be so easy, she thought. She had already killed two men that day, and this was the Mandarin's enemy, as well as being the most serious threat to their own safety. She could save Shishan. No, she decided, there would be others to take his place. The world was full of monsters such as this, and the death of one would only bring the elevation of another, Besides, it was not in her nature to do such a thing. She could hardly believe she had fired the shots that had killed Ren Ren and Monkey. A part of her told her that if anybody deserved to die it was animals like them – and she had only done it to save the others – but she was deeply revolted with herself, and almost paralysed with remorse, and it took every effort of her will to keep going. But she could not let down the others, the children, the poor ravaged English girl, and Ma Na Si, whom she loved but who loved another. She thought of the Buddhist lore she had learned at her father's side. She was bound on the Wheel of Rebirth. What terrible lives she must have lived in her past incarnations that she was fated to suffer so much in this one. Her whole life had been one long-drawn-out expiation, but she feared that, for all her efforts, she was only gathering on her soul more sins she would have to expiate in future lives. She leaned her head against the door. Merciful Guanyin, she prayed, give me the strength to continue. She sighed. Iron Man and Su Liping snored in their different octaves behind her. She lifted the latch and stepped into the corridor.

The house was quiet now. She reached the stairs without incident, descending to the lower floor where the banqueting rooms were. The revellers had departed, the lights were extinguished. She stepped hesitantly into the darkness, feeling her way through the gloom towards the last ladder of stairs that led to the ground floor. She felt for the wall to guide herself, and gasped when she touched a human face. '*Jiejie*, it's me, Mali.'

She heard the whisper through her shock. Her first unconscious reaction was one of anger at the fright Mary had caused her, but she calmed herself. 'Good girl,' she said encouragingly. 'Go quietly to Mother Liu's floor and wait for me there. I won't be long.'

After she had got out to the courtyard, she relaxed. She moved quickly down the path into the next courtyard. The willows were rustling in the slight breeze. She paused to look into Major Lin's pavilion, her home for the last two years. The windows were dark.

Major Lin was not there. She passed into the last courtyard, along the avenue of lanterns, over the ornamental bridge, until she could see the shape of the gatehouse. The night-watchman's light was shining faintly. Plucking up her courage, she tapped on his window. 'Lao Chen,' she called, in as firm a voice as she could muster. 'Lao Chen.'

'Who is it?' came a sleepy reply. A coarse, heavy-browed face peered out at her, and smiled when its owner recognised her. 'Fan Jiejie,' he greeted her. 'What are you doing here at this time of night?'

'I've come with a message from Mother Liu,' she said. 'You're to expect visitors. Secret ones. Some time after midnight.'

'Not another midnight call,' he said wearily. 'I suppose I'm to make myself scarce like the last time?'

She had not been expecting this, but she immediately saw the opportunity. 'That's right,' she said. 'You can go home early. I'm to stay here by the gate to let them in.'

'All these secret goings-on,' he muttered. 'This could be the lodge for a Brotherhood, the way things have been happening here lately. What's it all about, then? Let me see, only two – no, three nights ago, it was the same thing. But then it was Mother Liu herself who came down and relieved me.' His brows furrowed with suspicion. 'Here, why's she sent you and not come herself to tell me? Or sent her son?'

'I can't tell you that, Lao Chen. They're both closeted in the house discussing something with that bandit, Iron Man Wang. I don't know what it's about – but she asked me to show you this.' From her sash she untied a string of jade beads, which earlier she had removed from Mother Liu's room. She had expected that she would have to show some evidence to prove her story.

'All right, I recognise them. Iron Man Wang, is it? Well, it must be serious. Don't think I want to know what's going on, after all. Give me a moment to get my things. Can't imagine what my wife will say when I wake her up two nights in one week.'

He grumbled off, and she sat down to wait on his straw bed. The hours went by.

With sinking heart, she began to fear that Ma Na Si might have been wrong, and Major Lin was not coming after all. She could not imagine what they would do.

* * *

Henry was pacing the gallery when Airton stepped out of his room. 'It's half past two,' he said coldly.

'Is it?' replied Henry, in the same tone.

'I don't think your Major Lin is coming,' said the doctor.

Henry continued to pace.

'Well, what are we going to do? What's your plan?' Airton pushed him.

'We'll give it until three.' Henry sighed.

'Then what?'

'We'll leave on our own.'

'I see. So we just walk out of here. Children. Women. One of them extremely sick – that's thanks to you by the way. We walk out past Iron Man Wang and his men, and then what? Assuming we get there, do we overpower the guards at the city gates?'

'We go through the back-streets to the Millwards' compound. That should be deserted now. We hide there and somehow get a message to the *Yamen*. Maybe we send Fan Yimei. Sorry, Doctor, that's the best plan I can think of.'

'Brilliant,' said Airton.

'Would you rather we stayed here?'

'I'm aware that is not an option, again thanks to you and your bargain with the Mandarin. Or should I say my bargain with the Mandarin? Well, it's all gone very, very wrong, hasn't it?'

'The best-laid plans . . .' murmured Henry.

'Aye, "of mice and men". You disgust me, Manners, you and your cynical manipulation of our lives.'

'I'll remind you that we still have our lives,' said Henry softly. 'Don't give up now, Doctor.'

Airton turned abruptly and re-entered his room. 'Nellie, dear, you'd better pack,' he addressed his wife, loudly enough for Henry to hear. 'Mr Manners has a plan.'

Henry continued to pace.

She was intending to leave when she heard the thump on the gate. Nervously, she lifted the spyhole. She saw horses and gleaming leather in the lantern light. Her heart thumped with relief.

As anticipated, Major Lin was there with some of his men, but he was also accompanied by a white-haired old man. She recognised him immediately. All the girls feared him. They knew of his perverted tastes and were not fooled by the smiling eyes in his deceptively saint-like face. This was the Mandarin's chamberlain, whom she had seen many times in the brothel. He was also, she realised with a sinking feeling, a long-standing friend of Mother Liu. Immediately she began to revise in her mind the story she had to tell. There could be no hiding the fact that Mother Liu was a captive upstairs – but that might be explained, she thought, if she told them that the foreigners had become suspicious of her and had acted foolishly out of excessive caution. It would be fatal, she realised, if this man were to discover the extent of what had happened, especially that Ren Ren had been killed. Chamberlain Jin might refuse to obey whatever instructions the Mandarin had given him.

He and Major Lin were initially suspicious when they saw that it was she and not Mother Liu who greeted them at the gate. They interrogated her closely, but accepted her story. Chamberlain Lin was amused, in fact, by her version of Mother Liu's humiliation. 'Bound and gagged?' He laughed, maliciously. 'And tied to a bed? Oh, I look forward to seeing this.'

She led the chamberlain, Major Lin and two of his men down the pathway through the still courtyards. All of the men, even the soldiers, were wearing cotton shoes, but the wood creaked as they climbed the dark stairs. Major Lin was holding his sword, and the soldiers their bayonets. If any of Iron Man's men had the ill-fortune to encounter them on their progress through the house, they intended their dispatch to be quiet. Warily, they crept along the lighted passage on the third floor, but there was no sound from any of the rooms except a few rumbling snores.

Fan Yimei lifted the hanging that hid the last flight to Mother Liu's private quarters, and they filed upwards.

They found the foreign party apparently already marshalled to leave. Gathered in the gallery, Nellie and Mary were supporting a drooping Helen Frances, who appeared half asleep, the doctor was in the act of picking up his medical bag and a small portmanteau, and Henry was taking the lantern off the wall.

'Thank God. Thank God,' exclaimed the doctor, when he saw Fan Yimei, followed in quick succession by Chamberlain Jin, and a soldier. The others were still on the stairs. 'They've come after all. We're saved.'

Then Major Lin stepped into the lamplight.

The nodding Helen Frances lifted her head at that moment and saw him. He was smiling. A crooked, wolfish smile. Her eyes widened with terror, her body shook uncontrollably, and she made little moaning sounds. Frantically, she tried to twist out of Nellie and Mary's grasp, but she had no power over her legs. She slumped to her knees, body shuddering, back arching.

'Edward, do something,' cried Nellie. 'I can't control her. She's having a fit.'

Hurriedly Airton groped in his medical bag for a syringe. George and Jenny, frozen where they were standing, stared in amazement. Henry, his face ugly with rage, made a rush towards the major, controlling himself only at the last minute. His eyes blazing with hatred, his fists clenched, he stood stock still in front of his enemy, who contemplated him calmly, his lips still curled in the cruel, lopsided smile.

'What an interesting effect you have on these foreigners, Major Lin,' was the chamberlain's languid observation. 'I would have expected them to be pleased to see you in their circumstances. But it appears to be rather the contrary. What could you have done to make them dislike you so?'

Major Lin had noticed Mary. He pointed a gloved finger. 'Who's she?' he barked.

Dr Airton looked up worriedly from where he was kneeling beside Helen Frances. She was sobbing on the floor, supported by Nellie. It would take a little while for the morphine to have an effect. 'Major, this young girl is a friend,' he said carefully. 'She's a victim of kidnapping who is now under my protection. I intend that we take her with us.'

'That is impossible,' said Major Lin curtly. 'She is not covered by my orders.'

Dr Airton rose to his full height. 'I insist,' he said, in the firmest voice he could muster. The effect was rather muted by the frantic appeal in his eyes, and his quivering lips.

Major Lin ignored him. He turned to give an order to one of his soldiers.

'None of us will leave without her,' said Airton shrilly. 'I insist she comes, Major Lin.'

Major Lin turned his sardonic expression back on him. 'You are in no position to insist on anything,' he said scornfully.

'Oh, Major, why wrangle?' said Chamberlain Jin. 'What's one more or less? This is wasting valuable time, but before I go I must pay my respects to Mother Liu. Indeed, I have been looking forward to that ever since your young lady told me about her embarrassing predicament.'

Major Lin lifted his chin in a curt order to his concubine. 'Go on. Take him to her. Quickly.'

Henry and the doctor exchanged a worried glance. 'I would not advise that,' Henry tried. 'Mother Liu is resting and has left strict instructions not to be disturbed.'

Chamberlain Jin smiled as he moved past him. 'Oh, Ma Na Si Xiansheng, please. I know exactly the sort of rest you have prepared for Mother Liu. Please don't worry. I won't disturb her in any way. That would spoil an otherwise excellent joke.'

They watched as he followed Fan Yimei into the chamber, and were relieved when he stepped out again a moment later without their prisoner.

'I owe you my thanks, Ma Na Si. I had never expected to be so entertained during what I imagined would be a desperate getaway. Such an angry look she gave me! "The wounded tigress glares at the hunters who would take away her cubs." By the way, where is her cub? You haven't tied up Ren Ren as well, have you? What a pity. That would have been perfection. Never mind. I am rather relieved that he is not here. No doubt he is out burning villages and slaughtering peasants with his Boxer friends as he likes to do. Such an angry young man. Oh, how comical she looked in her rage! She was furious when I paid out the taels owed her for your accommodation and left them on the table. And she couldn't even haggle. Such fury in a woman's eyes!'

'Chamberlain,' snapped Major Lin, 'we must leave if we are to reach the railway before daylight.'

'Of course. Of course,' smiled Jin Lao. 'But are the foreigners ready? This young woman appears to be sleeping. They seem remarkably reluctant to make their escape.'

Major Lin gave an order, and the larger of his two soldiers lifted Helen Frances over his shoulder. Neither Airton nor his wife protested. In her unconscious state this seemed as good a way to move Helen Frances as any other. Nellie gathered her children to her, and the party, frightened but relieved finally to be leaving this terrible hiding-place with its horrific memories, followed the soldiers down the stairs, and onwards through the sleeping house.

Fortune for the moment was with them. They encountered no obstacles on their way.

Outside the gates, among the troopers' horses, the familiar hay cart awaited them.

They clattered through the quiet streets. At the city gates there was the usual altercation with the guards, but this time they appeared cowed by the presence of Chamberlain Jin, whom they saw uncomfortably, and unaccountably, mounted on one of Lin's horses.

The fugitives huddled under the hay, thinking of the similar journey they had experienced only days before. So many tragedies had befallen them since, and none knew what the future would hold. They had escaped the city, but uncertainty lay ahead. They had been freed from their cage in the Palace of Heavenly Pleasure, but the wider countryside they could sense around them was filled with unimaginable perils. What escape could there be when the whole country raged with rebellion? Where might they find protection when every hand was raised against the detested foreigner? They knew that they were making for the railway camp. That was what Major Lin had told them. That was enough to think about for now.

The convoy hurried through the night.

They arrived at the railway camp as a dull morning dawned over the misty fields.

Su Liping woke with a start. Blearily she focused on her surroundings. She had a headache and she was disoriented. She badly needed a piss. She saw Iron Man spreadeagled on his back. Idly she wondered why Fan Yimei was not there with him. The stealing bitch, she thought, good riddance, and winced as she felt a throb of pain in her head.

The piss-pot in the room was full. She lurched down the corridor to the closet, and squatted on the hole. Her head felt terrible and she was nauseous.

Why was Fan Yimei not there? No girl left a client. That was Mother Liu's cardinal rule.

And what had she been doing with Mother Liu so late at night?

Usually Fan Yimei never left Major Lin's pavilion. It was odd, she mused.

Then, with a shock, she remembered what that new girl, Phoenix, had told her. Mother Liu was ill and not to be disturbed. It was inconceivable that she would have asked for Fan Yimei when she was having one of her vapours. If she had wanted anyone, she would have come for Su Liping.

And that was not the only odd thing. Fan Yimei had made only minimal protest when Iron Man had made her go with him. Obviously Iron Man was a catch. That was why she had insisted that she herself be assigned to him – but Fan Yimei had Major Lin and, anyway, Iron Man was rough trade, not her type. And there was another thing – all that play with the wine pitcher. Oh, yes, it had been very flirtatious – she herself had been taught similar tricks – but why had Fan Yimei been pretending to be seductive in the first place? She had a sudden suspicion. Forgetting her headache, she ran back to the room, to the table where Fan Yimei had poured the wine. It did not take her long to find the pouch. She picked it up and smelt it. The bitch! No wonder she felt nauseous.

Not bothering to put on her robe she ran to the end of the corridor and pressed the panel behind the hanging. She ran up the stairs and knocked loudly on Mother Liu's door. There was no answer. She opened the door. The room was empty. She went down the corridor, searching one room after another until she found her. Gasping with fright, she saw the ropes, and the gag. Frantically she started to untie them.

'*Ta made*,' screamed Mother Liu. 'Why's it taken you so long? Didn't you miss me, you stupid bitch?'

'Phoenix told us you weren't well,' Su Liping whimpered, untying her legs. 'Mother Liu, I have something to tell you about Fan Yimei.'

'I know all about Fan Yimei,' screamed the old woman, pushing herself off the bed. 'Where's Ren Ren?'

'Your – your shoulder, it's bleeding,' gasped Su Liping.

'Fuck my shoulder! Where's Ren Ren?'

'Nobody's seen him,' whispered the girl, now very frightened. 'The last we knew he was with you.'

Mother Liu's eyes widened with alarm. 'The *daifu*,' she gasped.

'The *daifu* – why was he trying to stop me going down the corridor?'

'I – I don't know.' Su Liping was quivering with fear.

'Follow me,' muttered Mother Liu. She was already hobbling towards the door. She quickened her pace down the gallery, stopping in front of the room that had been prepared for the Mandarin to meet the foreign girl. She seemed to experience a moment of weakness. 'Open the door,' she breathed. 'Open it for me.'

Su Liping lifted the latch. Mother Liu peered inside. 'Get the lantern from the hall,' she ordered. Su Liping ran to do as she was told.

'The carpet,' whispered Mother Liu. 'That's not the right carpet. Lift it up.'

She gave a little moan when she saw the bloodstains. She dropped to her knees and crawled slowly towards the bed

'Mother Liu,' whined Su Liping, her knuckles pressed to her mouth, 'what's happened?'

Mother Liu turned a white face towards her. Never had Su Liping seen an expression so terrible. 'Get out,' she hissed. 'Get out. Wake Iron Man Wang and tell him to come here. But get out, get out.'

With a frightened glance behind her Su Liping ran back down the gallery. As she was reaching the bottom of the stairs, she heard the screams begin, piercing, howling, inhuman shrieks that followed her down the stairwell, reverberated along the corridors and resonated in every dark cranny of the building to the depths of the floors below.

The once busy railway encampment was all but deserted. Most of the labourers had returned home; the others had joined the ranks of the Boxers. Major Lin's troopers were mounted round the perimeter on guard, their carbines at half-ready position, their wary eyes watching the approach of Major Lin . . .

The little convoy passed through the empty tent lines, past the sheds, to where the locomotive rested on the track. The Mandarin was waiting for them there, standing in the doorway of one of the first-class carriages. Despite all their efforts, the Boxers had not been able to damage the train, although the metalwork on the engine was now tarnished and dented. Some rust could be seen on the wheels, and there was not a pane of glass left unbroken in any of the carriages. By the engine, a small party of soldiers were handing up faggots of wood and sacks of coal and were stacking them in the tender.

The Mandarin watched sardonically as the Europeans climbed out one by one from under the hay. He smiled at their dishevelled appearance, and the straw that stuck to their hair and their clothes. His eyes narrowed in concern, however, when he saw Henry and the doctor lift the unconscious body of Helen Frances from the cart, and he called, 'Daifu, what is the matter with her? Is she not well?'

Airton's eyes blazed with hatred. 'You know very well what is the matter with her, you blackguard,' he hissed.

The Mandarin looked quizzically at Henry. 'She was raped, Da Ren, and assaulted . . .' His eyes flickered towards Major Lin, who still sat on his horse, smiling coldly. With an equally stony expression, Henry continued, 'It was done by Ren Ren and one of his friends.'

The Mandarin's face darkened. 'Major, is this so?'

'I know nothing of any rape, Da Ren,' he answered coolly.

'The major is being exact when he says that he has no specific knowledge that these two men committed rape, Da Ren, because he had already left us when they did it.' said Henry, picking his words carefully. 'He may, however, be interested to hear that those men are now dead. Yes, we killed them, Major, shortly after you left us. I am pleased for you to know this, Major, because you should appreciate that I am not the sort of man to allow any villain who has inflicted such a cowardly and despicable assault on a woman under my protection to live, and that I will have my vengeance, however long it takes.'

The Mandarin's brow furrowed as he heard the implicit challenge and saw the venomous eye contact between the two men.

'Yet you say that the perpetrators of this crime have already been killed by you, Ma Na Si?' he asked. 'I will hear more of this, and learn how you managed to conceal your actions from the others in the house. You must have shown great resourcefulness not to be discovered. I confess that I am a little puzzled as to why you are addressing Major Lin so vehemently. Are you accusing him of negligence that he did not somehow prevent this crime?'

'I would never accuse Major Lin of negligence,' Henry said, with a cold smile. 'I have never known a man to be so deliberate in his actions.'

The Mandarin shook his head. 'It is terrible that such a thing happened. You say that the woman was under your protection, Ma Na Si, but actually she was under mine. If you are casting around for responsibility for negligence, I am afraid that you must place it on me. The doctor there appears certain where the fault lies. I do not know what amends I can presently make, but it would seem more important for the moment to get her – indeed, all of you – safely settled on the train. I have converted the inside of these carriages into what I hope will be comfortable for you on our journey. There are beds and sitting rooms. Please make yourselves at home. When you are settled, Ma Na Si, I would like a talk with you. As you know, we have detailed arrangements to discuss. I hope that the doctor also will find it in his heart at some point to visit me – that is, assuming he can get over his antipathy towards me.'

He made ready to enter his carriage, but turned for one last word.

'I understand that the train will be ready for departure in a short while. The engine must be watered, or warmed. I do not understand these things. Let us hope that we may leave without any further mishap. You are the only railwayman here, Ma Na Si, all the others having unfortunately lost their lives during the recent turbulence. I hope you may give some instruction to the soldiers whom I have detailed to drive the train when we are ready to leave.'

The Mandarin had been true to his word. Despite the broken glass in the windows, the carriages had been sumptuously refurnished. In the carriage allotted to them, next to the Mandarin's, the original seats had been removed, to be replaced by comfortable armchairs and sofas, taken from Herr Fischer's quarters, and there were two Chinese four-poster beds, one at each end of the carriage. The floor had been laid with blue Tientsin carpets, and a pot of tea, with some sweetmeats, was waiting for them on a low mahogany table.

The children ran delightedly up and down these spacious new quarters, squealing with delight at their sudden freedom. Airton and Nellie settled Helen Frances in one of the beds. Fan Yimei and Mary busied themselves with the tea. Henry found himself ignored.

'I'm going to see the Mandarin,' he said, rather lamely.

'Yes, go to your friend,' snapped Airton. 'You'll be more welcome there than here.'

'Edward,' he heard Nellie sigh as he was leaving, 'can you not be kinder to the man? Do you think that he's not suffering too?'

Smiling ruefully, Henry crossed the gap between the carriages, and knocked on the door of the Mandarin's compartment. Inside, he saw an even more sumptuously furnished interior. There were blackwood cabinets, tables and chairs, and scrolls hanging on the walls. On one large table the Mandarin had been practising his calligraphy, but now he and Chamberlain Jin were sitting together on high-backed wooden chairs, porcelain cups in their hands. At the far end of the compartment Henry saw three women reclining on an elegantly curtained bed, playing cards. He assumed they were the Mandarin's wives.

The Mandarin stood up to greet him. 'Welcome, my friend, I am more relieved than I can possibly say that you all escaped safely. I can only repeat how sorry I was to hear of your young lady's mistreatment. I would like you to believe that it was never my intention that any harm should befall her. I have yet to hear how you punished the perpetrators, but I applaud that you did so, taking justice into your hands. In killing Ren Ren, you have rid the world of one of its more despicable inhabitants.

'But for now, sit down, drink tea. We have other important things to discuss. First I would like to show you that I have brought what is necessary to honour my side of the bargain.'

By the wall were two large lacquer boxes. He untied the yellow tassels that tied their lids. 'Examine both,' he invited. 'You will find inside them the payment your Japanese colonel requires.'

Henry opened the nearest box. The inside shone with stacked golden ingots. He nodded slowly, brushing his hand over the smooth metal. The other box contained silver: ingots and Mexican silver dollars. He ran his hand through the coins, which tinkled as they fell.

From behind him he heard a feline hiss. He turned to see Jin Lao leaning over his shoulder, the eyes in the parchment face almost glazed over with wonder and greed.

'You see, even my chamberlain has never seen such treasure,' said the Mandarin. 'You may weigh it, if you like, but I assure you that the required amount is there. It comprises the larger part of a fortune that has taken me many years to amass. It is yours to give to your own government or to the Japanese colonel or to keep for yourself – that is not my concern – as soon as you reveal to me where the guns are hidden.'

'Thank you,' said Henry, closing the boxes. 'I do not need to weigh it. I accept your word.'

'I am honoured by your trust,' said the Mandarin. 'It is now for you to tell us where we are to travel to in order to collect the guns.'

'Before I do so I would like you first to tell me what you intend to do with us after I have completed my part of the bargain.'

'You will be free to go, Ma Na Si,' said the Mandarin. 'What else?'

'There is the matter of how and, as importantly, where we are to go. The last I heard, the Legations in Peking were besieged, and an army setting out from Tientsin under Admiral Seymour had been annihilated, leaving that city also besieged. For all I know both Peking and Tientsin have already fallen to the Boxers. That does not leave us with many options.'

'You are right, Ma Na Si, when you say that Tientsin is under siege, as are the Legations. However, they still manage to hold out. You are right also that the admiral's army of marines and volunteers was initially repulsed, but it was not destroyed, and the last I heard they were still holding their ground in open country some twenty miles north of the city. They are not being allowed to retreat to Tientsin, but on the other hand our own armies have not been strong enough to overwhelm them.

'Meanwhile a new, much stronger foreign army has landed at Taku, taking our forts there by storm.'

'Has it indeed?' Henry whistled.

'Yes, Ma Na Si, it has. The successful assault from the sea occurred two or three weeks ago. It is expected that this army will in due course march up the Peiho river to relieve, first, Tientsin, and later this stranded admiral's forces. Indeed, they may already have done so. My news is more than a week old. No doubt, they will attempt to advance on Peking when they have gathered sufficient strength.'

'This is good news for me but bad for you.'

'On the contrary, Ma Na Si, I consider this excellent news. I say this as a patriot, believe me. Your forces will destroy the Boxers and overturn a decrepit dynasty. A newer, better China will be the result.'

'And you with your guns will hold a dominant position in north-east China?'

'You are speaking cynically, Ma Na Si, but you are right. I will be in a better position to serve my country, in its true interests.'

'So where does that leave us? When I give you the guns where do we go?'

'The chamberlain, Major Lin and I will disembark from the train with most of the men. We intend to remain a mobile force – as we speak, our troopers' horses are being herded into the freight wagons of this train. Of course, we will be strengthened by your heavy guns. I will loan you a small company of men and I will allow you to take the train on as far down the track as possible towards Tientsin. The troopers will help you to cross Boxer lines to your relieving forces. They will then return to me with the train. Is that not a reasonable plan?'

'It is a plan fraught with danger.'

'Yes, and uncertainty, but regrettably these are dangerous times. The doctor once taught me your English expression. "Nothing ventured . . ."'

'". . . nothing gained." All right, Da Ren, I am content with this plan.'

'Then you will tell us where the guns are?'

Henry smiled. 'The guns are hidden about one and a half days' journey from here, on the plain that lies on the other side of the Black Hills. There is a junction where the track forks, north to Mukden, south to Tientsin. The guns are located in a cave in a gully, about half a day's ride west of that junction. It is a place well known to both Colonel Taro and me from our hunting expeditions. I will be able to lead you there very easily.'

'You will lead us there, Ma Na Si? I had rather hoped that you might be confident enough to tell us the exact location.'

'The exact location is difficult to describe in words, Da Ren.' Henry smiled back. 'You might become lost looking for it on your own.'

The Mandarin laughed, and was about to make a rejoinder, when they heard a burst of gunfire outside. While the women at the far end of the compartment squealed in alarm, and Chamberlain Jin clutched the arms of his chair, the Mandarin and Henry ran to the window.

Up by the tent lines they spotted five or six of the troopers Major Lin had left on guard, galloping down the hill, firing their carbines as they rode. Against the tree line above them red and yellow banners were waving and hundreds of Boxers were streaming out of the woods. Mounted on a horse, signalling them on, was a squat, bearded man brandishing an enormous axe.

Henry, pressing his hands on the sill, pushed the front half of his body out of the window, looking to right and left along the length of the train. To his right, he saw troops jumping down from their compartments ready to face the threat. To his left the last horses were being pulled up the ramp of a freight wagon. Beyond them stood the engine. The wood and coal had already been loaded, but he saw that water from the tower was still being pumped into the back of the tender.

The Mandarin observed Henry's anguished expression. 'I take it that the train is not ready to depart?' he asked calmly. 'This will be a test, then, for Major Lin. It will be interesting to see how effective those laborious efforts of his in the past year to train his men in the methods of modern warfare have been.'

'I'd better go to the engine to see if I can speed things along,' said Henry.

'I wish you luck,' said the Mandarin. 'I need not remind you that our lives depend on your success.'

The Mandarin himself remained composedly by the window, observing Major Lin, who was lining his small force of riflemen into a firing formation, readying them for the onslaught of the Boxers that was about to envelop them.

Chapter Nineteen

*Killing. Such killing. I am alone. Master Zhang might tell me
why this happened, but he is dead.*

Henry jumped down on to the wooden platform and began to
run. As he passed the doctor's carriage he heard his name
called. Nellie was leaning out of the window. 'Mr Manners.'

'Mrs Airton, I have to see to the engine.' He halted impatiently.
'There'll be an attack soon. You must keep your heads down.'

'It's Helen Frances,' said Nellie. 'She has woken and is asking
for you.'

Conflicting emotions – anxiety, fear, hope – flickered briefly over
his expression. 'Is she – is she . . . ?'

'All right? Certainly not, Mr Manners, but she seems to have
come back to her senses. Well, some of them. She plainly desires
to see you. She's being coherent enough about that.'

Henry stood unresolved, but only for a second. Two soldiers
carrying an ammunition box jostled past him unceremoniously.
He shook his head. 'I – I can't, Mrs Airton. Not now. I must get
the engine started. Give her – give her my love,' he muttered, and
began to run again. 'Keep your heads well down,' he called, over
his shoulder.

'Give her your love?' Nellie repeated to herself, as she withdrew
her head back into the compartment. 'If only you had it in you
to give.'

As he passed the two freight wagons he could hear the neighing
of frightened horses and the drumming of their hoofs inside. The
soldiers who had been responsible for loading them were running
to join the rest of Major Lin's men. One figure had remained
behind, checking the bolts on the doors. Henry recognised the
shabby sheepskin and the filthy fur hat, even before the familiar
gnarled face turned towards him, and he saw the slit eyes and the

565

jagged grin of his old *mafu*. 'Lao Zhao!' he exclaimed delightedly, embracing him. 'I thought you'd joined the Boxers.'

Lao Zhao laughed. 'Those *wangbadans*, Xiansheng? Think I'd get a decent wage from any of those scum? Anyway, they stole my mules.'

'Follow me,' said Henry. 'I'll teach you to drive a train instead.'

They ran together past the tender. Quickly Henry pulled himself up the iron ladder to the footplates of the engine.

He sized up the situation at a glance. It was dire.

Two soldiers were standing on top of the piled coal manipulating the hose from the watertower into the hole at the back of the tender. They were having difficulty keeping the canvas funnel in place, and water was gushing everywhere. Being the boys they were, despite their uniforms, they were laughing about it and splashing each other – and this while the Boxers were rushing down the hill! At least the glass gauge at the front of the engine showed that the tank was over half full. He was more concerned about the boiler. A puzzled corporal was peering anxiously into the open firebox, out of which protruded logs of wood. There was a flame of sorts in there, and pale fumes of smoke were even coiling out of the stack, but this was no way to start an engine. With a sinking heart, Henry realised that it would take hours at this rate for the firebox to gain enough heat.

If he had had time, he might have commented caustically on Chinese priorities. Obviously great care and attention had been given to the decking out of the Mandarin's carriage to achieve a suitable state of luxury. Effort might have been better spent getting up steam, if the intention was to get out of there alive. He looked savagely at the pressure gauge. The needle on the dial had hardly moved.

There was no point in venting the rage he felt inside him. The soldiers on the tender and the footplate had realised his presence and were gazing at him hopefully, waiting instruction.

He leaned out of the cab to get a clear view of the action taking place beyond the platform. Boxers in incalculable numbers were pouring out of the tree line and down the hill. They would pass through the tent area and reach the tracks within minutes. He examined Lin's troop dispositions with a military eye.

At least the southern side of the railway yard, their rear in military terms, was relatively well protected. A high brick wall enclosed the loop of track that encircled a space about two hundred yards across. Here there were three sheds and a big pile of coal, and the tall watertower that abutted the western end of the platform. The brick walls made a strong perimeter and the iron gates at either end were firmly chained. The western gate would have to be opened for the train to leave, but Henry would think about that problem when he came to it. For now he was satisfied that the first attacks would not come from that quarter. Major Lin had made a similar calculation and left only a handful of men as lookouts there.

The danger came from the northern side. There was no wall separating the tent lines from the hill and it was here that the Boxers were massing. The only obstacles between them and the station platform were the three grey-brick buildings in which Fischer had kept his stores and offices. To get to the platform and the train the Boxers would have to rush through the fifteen-feet gaps between the buildings. It was facing these gaps that Lin had formed his companies of riflemen. He had them positioned in two lines, one standing, one kneeling. A wall of concentrated fire would meet any Boxers who attempted to come through. Henry saw that Major Lin was directing other men up ladders to the tiled roofs of the buildings, presumably to provide enfilading fire once the attack began. What puzzled him for a moment were the activities of a small company under the direction of a sergeant who appeared to be trailing lengths of wire from the buildings back to the platform. He guessed that the wires must lead to dynamite charges inside. Major Lin was already preparing for his retreat.

The numbers, of course, were overwhelmingly disparate, but he was satisfied. Lin had assembled his hundred men as sensibly in the circumstances as Henry himself would have done. 'They might hold. They just might hold,' he muttered. 'It'll all depend whether they can survive the first assault.'

'What did you say, Xiansheng?' Lao Zhao was looking at him blankly.

'Nothing,' said Henry. 'We're in good shape – but we have work to do.'

He began to give orders. He addressed the corporal: 'You there. I want you to go to Major Lin with a message. Tell him that he has to hold off the Boxers for two hours. Do you understand? Two hours.' The corporal saluted, and leaped off the train in his hurry to be away.

'Two hours, Xiansheng?' queried Lao Zhao. 'Does it take so long to start this animal? That's longer than it takes my old mare to warm herself up in the morning.'

'Two hours if we're lucky,' said Henry grimly. 'It may take longer. The engine's been lying here cold and untended for at least six weeks. We're about to wake a corpse, my friend. Let's hope we don't end up as cold as she is. Come on, we'd better do something about this firebox.'

Against their mother's orders – she was at the other end of the carriage talking to Helen Frances – the children were peering out of the window, and so it was that they saw the first attack.

Major Lin stood in a gap between his companies, pistol in one hand and sabre upraised in the other. The two lines of troopers aimed their carbines steadily at the empty space between the buildings. Motionless, they waited. The sun was high in a cloudless sky, and diamonds of reflected light flashed from their bayonets and cap badges. The leather of the soldiers' belts shone in a stark clarity of detail. A puff of breeze stirred a little dust devil on the open ground and magpies paused briefly on the roof of one of the buildings, ignoring the troopers lying flat on the tiles. Two hawks were circling high over their heads.

'*Sha-aa-aa-aa!*' It was a long-drawn out yell from a thousand voices, which rose to a sighing crescendo and, as suddenly, died. Still nobody could be seen.

A single voice shouted that now so familiar chant: 'Exterminate the foreigners and save the Ch'ing!' There was another loud scream of '*Sha-aa-aa! Ki-i-ll!*' And silence again.

The shimmering space between the buildings waited. The world waited. Major Lin turned a cold face to check that his troops were ready. Jenny heard a buzzing sound and started away as a hornet flew into their carriage. She saw the striped yellow and black body and the blur of its wings. She flapped her hand to wave it away, and when she looked out again, she thought for a moment that she was seeing hundreds of similarly striped yellow and black hornets pouring through the gaps of the buildings. A brigade of Boxers with orange and blue markings on their tunics, and yellow turbans, had filled the empty spaces, appearing as if from nowhere and moving fast, but these were no hornets. Their stings were swords and spears and axes. They were young men rushing on their enemy with their mouths open in a soundless yell, the whites of their eyes in their brown faces flashing hatred and a wild excitement, the sunlight glinting on their weapons and bare arms raised up to strike and kill. The dust swirled around their padding, cloth-shod feet as they hurled themselves forward.

Major Lin sliced his sword down to give the signal and, with a thunderous clap, the two lines of troopers disappeared in a cloud of spitting fire and smoke. They fired again and again, until their magazines were exhausted. The smoke began to clear when they were reloading, and through the haze the children could see the gaps between the buildings. Each alley was carpeted with dead and dying, and there were pools of blood in the sand.

'George! Jenny! Get away from that window!' They heard their mother cry out shrilly, and in a moment they were enveloped in her strong arms with their heads pressed down on the carpeted floor.

Outside there was another yell of '*Shaa-aa-aa!*' and another explosion of rifle fire. Jenny whimpered, but George peered through the gap in his mother's arms with wide-open eyes. He saw Helen Frances rocking on the bed on the other side of the carriage, her hands pressed to her ears. Fan Yimei and Mary were kneeling on the floor with their arms around each other. His father was standing by the table in the centre. He had cleared it of the bowls of compressed fruits and sweetmeats, teapots and cups, vases of flowers, and was carefully laying out his scalpels in their place.

There were more cries, followed by more firing, as the fanatical attacks continued. The huddled figures on the floor found themselves counting the minutes between the volleys. Each burst of firing was a relief because it meant that the lines were still holding, and when the minutes of silence stretched into longer and longer intervals their fear increased proportionately. The doctor finished laying out his instruments, his splints and his bandages, and cautiously moved to the window.

'Oh, Edward, be careful,' Nellie called. Then, 'Can you tell us what's happening?'

Her words were drowned in the crash of Lin's rifle fire.

'They're still in formation,' Airton said, in the silence after, 'but there are bodies lying right up to their feet. It's a slaughter,' he said, shaking his head. 'Oh, mercy, they're coming again.'

There was another thunderous roar of firing, but it was not followed by the familiar silence. They could hear shouts and barked orders, and a new sound, the horrific clatter of steel on steel. Dr Airton was pressing his knuckles on the sill, his eyes staring. His words were shrill and incoherent in his excitement. 'Oh, Lord, they've broken through . . . Yes, yes, the bayonets. Come on! Come on! . . . Oh, Lord, oh, Lord . . . There, man, there! Ah, got him . . . Oh, no, oh . . . Yes. Yes. They're holding. They're holding. Thank God. Thank God, the devils are running now, they're . . .' His words were lost in rifle fire, a volley followed by desultory shots. The women stared at him in fear and alarm. He wiped a hand across his forehead. 'That was close,' he breathed. 'Much too close. What discipline those soldiers have. They pushed them back with brute steel, Nellie. Brute steel. My God, I thought we . . .'

'*Shaa-aa – aaa!*' came another yell. The rifles fired, and fired again.

That was the last frontal assault for some time. They waited, hardly daring to breathe. After five minutes had passed they heard Major Lin barking orders. Shortly after, there was a knock on their carriage door. A sergeant stood respectfully outside with three wounded men. They were bleeding from cuts and slashes to the shoulders and head. Another, lying on a stretcher, was writhing with pain from a sword-thrust to his guts. They carried him into the carriage and laid him on the table. The doctor began his work, helped by Nellie who passed him his instruments and salves. He only looked up in surprise when he saw that Helen Frances was also standing in front of him. She was reaching for a roll of bandages and a bottle of disinfectant.

'What are you doing, girl?' he asked quietly. 'You should be resting.'

'You forget, Doctor, you trained me,' she answered, with only a small quiver in her voice. 'There are the other wounded men.'

'Thank you. Thank you, my dear,' he muttered, returning to the stomach wound.

They all started momentarily when the drums began to beat. It was the same monotonous, threatening rumble to which they had become accustomed during their weeks of incarceration in the mission. The children, who were sitting on the floor with Fan Yimei and Mary, shook a little as their well-remembered nightmare returned, but their parents and Helen Frances went back to their work after exchanging only worried glances.

The drumming muffled the firing that had begun again outside. The Boxers had thought better of their suicidal attacks and had sent snipers to climb the walls of the station-yard. A sharpshooters' duel began in which the advantage rested with the more experienced marksmanship of Lin's men, but a steady trickle of casualties arrived at the doctor's carriage. One soldier had an arrow through his arm. George and Jenny stared in fascination at the feathers and barb as the man sat placidly on a stool waiting his turn to be treated.

'What is Mr Manners doing?' whispered Nellie to the doctor, after they had put the final stitch in a patient's temple and were supporting him to the door of the carriage. 'It's been more than an hour since he went to the engine. Are we leaving here today or not?'

'The Lord only knows,' said the doctor. 'You know my view by now. I think we have only survived so far despite that man and his machinations.'

'Hush, Edward, Helen Frances will hear you,' warned Nellie. 'But why doesn't he start the train?'

At that moment Henry was lying on his back under the wheels with a rag and a spanner tightening the bolts on one of the connecting rods. He had already removed a crowbar that had been forced between the wheel and the rod in a clumsy attempt by a railway worker to damage the train. The connecting rod had been bent and he had spent some time hammering it back into shape. He had had to assign two soldiers to pound with sledgehammers the twisted metal back into true on a makeshift anvil formed by a smaller rod. He was now bolting the straightened rod back into position. The two soldiers had gone back to their lines. The repair was not pretty, but he thought it would function. Lao Zhao was leaning on the wheel smoking a pipe and watching him curiously. Henry recognised that expression on his friend's face from of old and knew that the muleteer had something to say to him, but he was not inclined to press him. He was too damned busy.

He had been busy ever since the battle started. He had watched Lin's men competently fight off the first attack, and after that he had given all his attention to the engine. Very quickly he had realised that the men appointed to drive the train were worse than useless, but at least the gauge glasses had shown him that they had filled the boiler with enough water to cover the firebox. The pathetic fire they had going would do nothing to start the engine but at least it would not crack the flues that contained the water around it. A blow-out would be unrepairable. Patiently, he had instructed them to remove all the logs and cut some kindling. He himself had rebedded the coal, and, with a paraffin rag and some gun cotton, had relit the fire, feeding in the kindling until he was happy there was an even flame. Then, carefully, he had added coal as necessary to secure the right heat. It would be at least half an hour before enough steam would be generated to give him the thirty pounds per square inch pressure required for him to start the blower. The draught created would then speed the burning process but it would still take another hour or more to get up enough steam for the locomotive to move.

Meanwhile there was enough to do. He had told the soldiers filling the tender to cease their efforts with the hose. They were spilling more water on to the coal than into the hole. The gauge showed him that the tank was three-quarters full, enough to be getting on with. With the train idle for six weeks, after having been attacked by a mob armed with stones, slabs and goodness knows what else, he thought it would probably be wise to inspect it thoroughly, especially the wheels on both engine and carriages. He had ordered the two soldiers and Lao Zhao back on to the platform, and had shown them what signs to look out for, and how to fill the oiling points on all the rod lugs and axles. He had also told them to check the bolt couplings between the carriages. Then he had sent them off with their tin cans. He had inspected the front of the engine, and that was when he had discovered the attempt at sabotage. It had been a heavy hour's work to get the connecting rod to rights again, pausing from time to time to climb back on to the footplate to check the firebox and the pressure gauges. He had turned on the blower, and when he had enough steam up, tested the injector. Now the boiler was merrily heating away, and he was satisfied – almost satisfied – that the damaged connecting rod would function.

He tightened the last bolt, and scrambled to his feet, wiping the grease off his hands with the rag. 'Come on, then. Out with it, Lao Zhao. What is on your mind?'

Lao Zhao spat, and puffed twice on his pipe. 'Xiansheng, would there happen to be any gold on this train?' he asked casually.

Henry started with surprise. 'There might be,' he answered cautiously. 'What of it?'

Lao Zhao made a big pretence of lighting his long pipe. 'I imagine that the gold would belong to the Mandarin?' he asked, his intelligent eyes contemplating Henry's face.

'So?'

'So, would it be appropriate for others to take an interest in this gold?'

Henry's expression was grim. 'Come on, Lao Zhao, what are you trying to tell me?'

'It is, of course, ill-bred for a man to eavesdrop on other people's conversations,' said Lao Zhao, 'but you did just now order me to crawl under the belly of this iron creature to feed oil into its many mouths, and I was underneath the carriage belonging to the Mandarin, just by the steps leading into it, when I saw Major Lin step down on to the platform.'

'He'd probably gone to report to the Mandarin on the state of the battle. So?'

'He was not alone, Xiansheng. An old man followed him out of the carriage and they talked on the platform above me, although they did not see me. This man is also a high official, I think.'

'Jin Lao,' said Henry.

'Yes, Xiansheng, I believe you are right. It was Chamberlain Jin. And this is what Major Lin was saying to him. They were speaking in low voices but my old ears still function and I could hear them quite well. The major said, "So you're telling me that he really does mean to give the barbarian the gold?" And the old man answered, "Yes, for the guns." And the major said, "But we need the guns and the gold." And the old man said, "You need the guns. I would be happy with the gold." And the major said, "The da ren is a fool. He's past his usefulness." And the old man said, "These are dangerous times and it is remarkable how easily accidents can happen on a perilous journey." And the major said, "You mean, we should make our move on the train?" And the old man said, "The soldiers are loyal only to you." And after that there was a lot of gunfire so I did not hear their final words. Anyway, Major Lin ran off very quickly to join his men, and the old man scurried back on board. I think he was a little frightened, Ma Na Si Xiansheng. But wasn't that an interesting conversation?'

'It was extremely interesting,' said Henry, abstractedly wiping his forehead with the rag.

Lao Zhao leaned back, cackling with pleasure. 'You've made your face all black with the grease, Ma Na Si Xiansheng!'

Henry smiled, his teeth flashing. 'I'm in your debt, Lao Zhao. I won't be ungrateful. Come on, we'd better stoke the fire.'

'Ah, yes, what a hungry beast it is,' said Lao Zhao, following him.

They had to step aside as a company of soldiers ran down the platform heading to the western perimeter where the Boxers were trying to climb over the wall.

Henry looked at the pressure gauge, which was reading only 82 pounds per square inch. Even with the blower on it would take another forty-five minutes to an hour for the pressure to reach the minimum 120 pounds with which he could attempt to move the train. And the Boxers now looked as if they were about to break into the perimeter. He leaned out of the cab to see down the line to the western wall near the gate where Lin's company was engaging the Boxers who had encroached over the wall. The soldiers had fired a volley and were now bayoneting the survivors. Sharpshooters were clearing the top of the wall. It had been efficient work, but he knew that there were not enough of Lin's men available to guard against all the possible points by which the Boxers might enter. He felt in his pocket for his revolver, which after Fan Yimei's execution of Ren Ren and Monkey had only four bullets left in the chambers.

'Lao Zhao,' he said, 'let me teach you what the railwayman does when there's nothing else to do but wait.' He pointed at the kettle on top of the firebox and the two enamel mugs. 'He makes himself a cup of tea.'

The Mandarin was standing by his desk, brush in hand, contemplating the two characters he had written in bold, almost savage strokes on the paper sheet. *wu wei*. Literally, it meant 'the negation of existence' but in this Taoist axiom there was a deeper connotation: that true wisdom can only be gained through the absence of conscious thought, that right actions can only be determined by a surrender to the events taking place around one, that the insignificant occurrences of one's own life are linked to a greater design, a harmony and pattern in which all plays its part, and which one can only understand if one does not seek to explain it; simply, that by non-doing, one achieves all. He smiled, listening to the firecrackers of shots outside the carriage, the shouts and screams, the running feet on the platform as one company or another was moved from one position of defence to another, and the crisis of battle took its course. Through the window he saw Major Lin waving his sword and shouting orders. He imagined Ma Na Si pulling levers and pumping fires at the front of the train – so much frantic activity all around him, yet here he stood, admiring the flower vase on his desk and the two characters of his own calligraphy, which spoke to him from the page. Inaction at the heart of action. The characters seemed appropriate in the circumstances.

He turned to look scornfully at Chamberlain Jin and his wives; their scared faces peered up at him from a gap between the settee and the table, which they had pulled around themselves as a barricade. For some time now the Boxer snipers had the range of the train, and occasional bullets would thud against the wooden walls of the carriage. Once an arrow had penetrated the window, hitting the fruit bowl on the table and knocking it to the floor.

'Chamberlain,' he said, 'it is noble of you to protect my women so assiduously from under the table.'

'The da ren – the da ren is pleased to mock an old man and his fear,' muttered Jin Lao hoarsely.

'Certainly not,' said the Mandarin. 'I witnessed an example of your bravery earlier when you left the safety of my carriage to accompany Major Lin outside. It must have been a very pressing matter that you should take such a risk with your life.'

'I – I merely wished to understand the situation better, Da Ren.'

'You were present when he described it to me.'

'Yes, Da Ren.' Jin Lao reached gingerly for a cup of cold tea to wet his dry throat. 'But there were one or two details I did not fully understand.'

'Really? I had not thought of you as a man who was interested in military matters.' The Mandarin was suddenly bored with the conversation. He moved to the window and peered outside. The firing had reached new crescendos, recalling the volleys of the earlier attacks. After a moment he turned again to the chamberlain. 'With your new-found interest in martial matters, you might be interested to know what is happening now. It appears that our Boxer friends have decided to clear our men off the roofs of the buildings. If they are successful I do not think that Major Lin's position on the open ground will be tenable much longer. Indeed, you might be lucky enough to see some fighting close at hand. I fear, however, that in the event of such a mêlée the numbers will be very much against us, and the train will probably be overrun, so your military education will be a short one. Unless, of course, Ma Na Si has found the means to start the engine at last. We are in an interesting predicament, are we not?'

But by then his words could not be heard above the wailing of his wives. He returned to his position by the window. He wondered if now was the time to put on his old armour and take up his heavy sword. He had no intention of being captured and subjected to the indignity of further interviews with Iron Man Wang. He looked out at the figures silhouetted on the roofs – turbaned men with swords and spears, trim, uniformed soldiers seeking to repel them with bayonets. It was the old world fighting the new, the battle cry of Imperial China raised against the new techniques and methods of the West, superstition against progress – and he had long ago thrown in his marker on the side of this progress. Now, standing at the window of the railway carriage, surveying the scene, he had the impression that nothing, in fact, had changed. He was watching Chinese fighting Chinese, much as he had done in his youth; the uniforms and costumes were irrelevant, as indeed were their weapons – Boxers, Taiping rebels, it was all the same, just another version of the perennial struggle for power that had rotted every dynasty in its time. If China was to change, then something more radical than bloodshed and wars was needed. Idly, he thought of his conversations with the foreign doctor, who preached a constitutional kingdom based on virtue. That really was a fine idea, and, who knows?, one day it might come about – but he doubted that he would see it in his lifetime, even if he should survive this battle. He knew that, topple this dynasty or that, Chinese would continue to fight Chinese. Rifles and bayonets would prove more efficient than spears, and heavy guns would give the edge over those who had only rifles. And there would be new Zheng Guofans with new equivalents of the Hunan Braves, and young men and boys, as he once had been, would continue to rally round flags, and their officers would urge them on with attractive-sounding creeds. Only later would they discover, if they became older and wiser, that it was the same creed, the naked struggle for power, garbed in different slogans, different uniforms, different banners.

He watched as one of Lin's sergeants, stabbed by a spear, pushed himself along the haft to bayonet the man who had killed him; both bodies toppled off the roof together in a hideous embrace of death. The soldiers behind him fired a volley, and for a moment the roof was cleared of Boxers, but more screaming, slashing figures came.

So they always would, thought the Mandarin. And no war would ever be ultimately decisive. That was the way it was. So it always had been. So it would continue. If he survived this, then he himself would buy Japanese guns, which would be the means for new wars, and the killing of more Chinese by other Chinese.

He sighed. What choice did he have?

Wu wei. Wu wei.

With mugs of tea in their hands, Henry and his team on the footplates watched the battle of the rooftops. It was certainly a desperate struggle, but Major Lin seemed equal to the task. Reluctantly, because he hated the man, Henry admitted to himself that Lin was a bloody good soldier. Two of the rooftops were now secure, with Lin's men lying flat against the ridge tiles firing into what he imagined must be the mass on the other side. On the third roof the bayonet struggle was still going on. Major Lin had kept his companies facing the gaps in the buildings, only taking out every fourth man to reinforce the soldiers on the roofs, and their rifle power was still strong enough to keep the occasional rushes and attacks through the alleys at bay. The attacks were less furious now, partly because it was difficult for the Boxers to step over the bodies of their comrades who had died in earlier attacks, and partly because by now they had a healthy respect for Lin's firepower. Henry wondered how long the ammunition would hold. Up to now there had been a steady relay of runners back and forth from the arsenal on the train, handing out spare magazines in the intervals between the volleys, but the supply could not be inexhaustible.

The battle on the third roof was not going Major Lin's way. An axe-wielding contingent of Boxers had pushed Lin's men back from the ridge, and it looked as if their snipers and archers would have a free hand to fire down below. Major Lin shouted an order, and the soldiers on the next building fired across. The confusion gave Lin's remaining men on the roof, with reinforcements scrambling quickly up the ladders, the opportunity to make a rush, and soon the third roof was as secure as the other two.

So they were holding on. But for how long?

He looked at the pressure gauge: 117 pounds per square inch. The boiler was heating nicely and there was a thick white smoke coming out of the stack. It would not be long now before they could get away. He had determined that he would start the engine when the pressure reached 135. The train might just crawl at 120 pounds per square inch steam pressure, but he thought that with the weight of the carriages – two loaded with horses – the engine would barely have the pull to move the wagons at walking speed, and the Boxers would be able to climb on with impunity. Ideally he should wait until the gauge reached 150 – that would be safer – but time was not on his side. A hundred and thirty five pounds per square inch was his compromise. It might just be adequate to get a head of speed. Maybe. The gauge read 119 now. It could be worse: at least it was heating quickly. At this rate . . . At this rate . . .

He calculated and made a decision. Turning to one of the soldiers he gave him his orders. 'Run to Major Lin. Tell him we're pulling out in thirty minutes. We leave in half an hour, do you understand? Tell him that and run back here again as fast as you can. And be careful.'

The soldier, a boy of eighteen with a blackened, girlish face, grinned and snapped a salute. 'Yessir!' he shouted in English. Henry wondered where he could possibly have learned to say that. He watched him anxiously as he ran across the open ground to where Lin was marshalling his men. The boy almost reached him – Lin had turned at his shout – when he stumbled, and fell forward on his face. Bullets were puffing up the dust. 'Damn,' said Henry. Lin was already shouting orders for a detachment to deal with this new burst of sniping from the walls. Henry turned to the other soldier on the footplate and registered the fear on his face. 'Dammit,' he said. 'I'll go and tell him myself.'

'No, Ma Na Si Xiansheng, I'll go,' said Lao Zhao. 'My belly's swirling with your tea and I need some exercise.'

'Dash it, be careful, then,' snapped Henry, angry because he knew it was wiser for the only person who could drive the train to try to stay out of harm's way. He did not relax until Lao Zhao, who had loped cautiously over the open ground like a hunter following a spoor, had returned, breathless but triumphant, to the footplate. Now he was happily pissing over the side.

'Major Lin says he will begin to evacuate in twenty minutes,' he said, over his shoulder.

'All right,' said Henry. 'We'd better be ready, then.'

He looked at the gauges. Water levels three-quarters full, that would do, 123 pounds per square inch steam pressure. Fine. He opened the firebox. Flames were dancing over the red bed of coals. He quickly shovelled in three spadefuls leaving the firebox door slightly open to enhance the draught over the fire. That would also do for now. What else did he have to think about? The gate. The gate, four hundred yards away, was still chained. It would be suicidal to open it now. The Boxers would rush through. Could he just steam through it? No, it was made of solid ironwork and tightly secured. The chains would have to be unfastened or he would be risking derailment. Damn. He would have to send Lao Zhao back again to Lin to instruct him to position some soldiers by the gate to open it when the train was ready to leave. They would probably have to fight off the Boxers as they did so. Damn.

He turned to survey the battle scene. Lin had not yet made his move. The soldiers were still standing in formation. He was puzzled for a second to see a puff of white smoke appear on the hillside just below the tree line. Then he heard a sharp crack, and a whining sound growing louder, passing overhead. With a boom, the coal stack in the southern yard exploded into red flame. He ducked as projectiles of scattered coal clattered against the side of the engine. He could hear a rising roar of cheers from the Boxers on the other side of the buildings. Guns! How could they have guns? Then he remembered the antiquated field guns Major Lin had kept on the city walls. He remembered the doctor telling him that they had been dragged to the mission. Iron Man Wang must have ordered them to be brought on here. There was another puff of smoke, but this time the explosion fell short among the tent lines. At least their marksmanship was not up to much, and the Boxers were in probably as much danger from stray shots as they were, but this completely altered the situation. A lucky hit on the train would strand them here. They would have to leave now, adequate steam pressure or no.

'Lao Zhao, you've got to go back again. Tell the Major we have to leave immediately. Tell him to get his men on the train. Hurry.'

Lao Zhao did not even pause to spit, but leaped off the engine and sprinted towards the soldiers.

'Dammit,' cried Henry. 'I didn't tell him about the gate.' Sod it, he thought. He would ram the gate, and hope for the best. 'You,' he shouted at the remaining soldier, 'be ready to shovel coal as if your life depended on it. Wait till I tell you—' 125 pounds per square inch. 'Come on. Come on,' he whispered, though clenched teeth.

He heard a volley of rifle fire. Encouraged by the arrival of their artillery pieces the Boxers had made another rush through the alleys. Henry peered anxiously through the drifting smoke. Yes, the retreat had begun. The soldiers on the roof were climbing down. They were joining the ranks of their comrades and kneeling to fire at the Boxers.

Henry ran through a last mental check-list of what he had to do. Couple the engine. Done. Release the handbrake of the tender. Done. Oh, God, he realised, with horror. He had forgotten the handbrake in the guard's car. That would also have to be released before they could move. There was no way round it. 'Listen,' he said to the soldier, 'look at this gauge here. When that needle points to 128, start shovelling in coal. Understand? Five full spadeloads. Don't close the box. Leave it as it is. Half open. Remember: when the dial reads 128 you shovel. Got it?'

He jumped on to the platform and began to run. The whole train shook as an explosion burst in the yard. He saw the orange black coils of smoke rising behind the carriages. They were getting the range. He glanced to his left and saw that Major Lin was attempting a fighting retreat – the men in square, firing, retreating a few steps at a time, and firing again. He passed the Mandarin's carriage and saw the sardonic face observing him from the window. He did not stop. He bounded up the guard's van steps and threw himself at the heavy red-painted wheel, turning until he felt that the pressure on the brakes was fully eased. He turned to leave, and his heart momentarily stopped. A Boxer was in the van.

It was a wiry, middle-aged man with a thin moustache. He wore a red tunic and carried a small axe and shield. The eyes in the wrinkled face were wary as he approached the foreign devil. Henry stepped backwards. The Boxer rushed at him, swiping with his axe. Henry managed to twist away. He kicked, and missed. The Boxer advanced again, and Henry retreated slowly. He could go no further because his back was against the brake wheel. His hands scrabbled against the wooden side of the van, and yes, there was the handspike on its rack. The axe came down again and clanged against the spike, which Henry had held up with his two hands, just in time. Henry kicked again and this time his foot contacted the man's groin. The Boxer moved back in surprise. Henry brought the handspike down on his head. Two more Boxers were pushing through the door from the guards' van balcony, and were staring at him, half startled, half afraid, their swords wavering hesitantly in their hands. Henry yelled and ran like a berserker towards them, slashing left and right with the handspike. He only stopped battering when he realised that he was beating air. Stepping over the bodies, he cautiously approached the door to the platform. He heard running feet and shots. Some of Lin's men had spotted the incursion and were dealing with it. Quickly opening the door, he leaped on to the platform and ran, ignoring the sound of steel on steel behind him.

As he ran, he noticed that Major Lin's fighting retreat had almost reached the platform. Bodies of Boxers lay in clumps over the ground that the troopers had so ably defended, yet more screaming battalions were massing in the gaps between the buildings. These were now in the hands of the enemy. He could see turbaned figures scrambling on to the vacated roofs. Soon they would be firing down at them. He heard Lin scream the command, 'Fire!' and a crash of shots went off just by his ear. He ran on. He was passing the doctor's carriage, and ahead could see Lao Zhao leaning from the engine cab waving him forward. As he looked, he heard the whine of a shell. The watertower exploded and the engine disappeared under a white wall of water and hissing steam. 'Bugger me!' he cried, stumbling to a halt. He was aware of Nellie Airton standing on the steps of her carriage looking down at him. There was an expression of alarm on her face. 'I beg your pardon, ma'am,' he muttered. 'Disgraceful language.'

'Never mind that,' said Nellie. 'What's happened to your arm?' It was only then that he noticed that his left forearm had been slashed by one of the Boxers' swords.

He looked up, confused, and saw over Nellie's shoulder Helen Frances's white, anxious face also looking down at him, her mouth open, her eyes shining with concern. 'Come on, you'd better get up here and have that bandaged,' said Nellie.

'I'm sorry,' he muttered, gazing at Helen Frances. 'I'm sorry. I haven't time.' And he ran on.

The engine and the footplates had been drenched, but thankfully the fire in the box was still burning and clouds of grey smoke were still issuing from the stack. The pressure gauge read 129 pounds per square inch. 'Right,' he shouted. 'Are we ready?' He pressed the pedal to eject any excess water in the pistons. With a whoosh, steam billowed out through the cylinder cocks on either side of the engine. He leaned out of the cab. Major Lin's men were now fighting on the platform, firing volley after volley to keep the Boxers at bay. The Boxers were now massed in a dense line in front of the buildings. They were ranked in impossible numbers. Banners waved over their heads. If they charged together no amount of bullets could keep them back. 'Come on, come on,' he breathed, pulling the cord to let out a long whistle, as if that signal could somehow miraculously hurry Lin's beleaguered soldiers on board. He remembered the wires leading to the buildings that he had seen earlier. Why didn't Lin blow the charges?

As he thought it, he observed the sergeant with the plunger. Major Lin, standing beside him, looked calmly at the massed Boxers as if they were parade-ground soldiers standing in line for his inspection. Almost dismissively, he waved his gloved hand. The sergeant leaned his whole weight on the plunger, and the three buildings disintegrated in flame. He could feel the shock of the explosion in the cab. The lines of Boxers were blown down like chaff before a scythe. Major Lin blew the whistle hanging from his neck and, in as orderly a manner as was possible in the circumstances, his men ran to the carriages assigned to them and clambered on board. Selected detachments mounted the ladders to the carriage roofs where they lay down ready to give a covering fire when the Boxers had recovered. It took three minutes to load them all. Major Lin waited until the last man was aboard, then unhurriedly climbed the steps. Leaning outwards he waved his sword at the engine.

Without further ado, Henry pulled back the reverser, and pushed the heavy throttle that regulated steam to the pistons. Agonisingly slowly the heavy wheels began to turn. Thump-thump, thump-thump. The engine was wheezing like a tired blacksmith. Henry heaved the regulator, careful not to let out too much steam in case the driving wheels slipped. One mile per hour, two miles per hour. 'Come on, come on.' But they were moving – moving towards a locked gate. A knot of Boxers, who had climbed over the wall, was standing there, waiting for them.

Meanwhile the Boxers by the houses had recovered from the blast. With a scream of *'Shaa-aa-aa!'* they charged. Lin's soldiers on the roof fired, as did those in the carriages out of the windows, but the firing had no effect on such numbers – and the train might as well have been motionless for all the speed it was going. 'Well, Lao Zhao, we tried,' muttered Henry, pulling his revolver out of his pocket. Lao Zhao grimly picked up the fireman's axe.

Had it not been for Iron Man Wang's artillery men's erratic marksmanship the train might well have been overrun then, but the next two rounds from these ancient guns could not have been been better directed if Major Lin had given the orders. The first exploded among the front ranks of the charging Boxers, disconcerting them and delaying momentarily the whole attack. The second burst on the gate, tearing one door off its hinges, smashing the chain and killing the waiting Boxers. Sedately, at three miles per hour, the engine steamed through the gap.

Fate, however, was not entirely on the side of Major Lin. The gunners on the hill reloaded quickly. Perhaps it was their annoyance after their earlier mistake, but this time they seemed to be taking more care with their aim. One shell exploded harmlessly between the coal heap and the ruined watertower. This was in line with their earlier haphazard marksmanship. The other shot, however, exploded under the coupling separating the last two carriages and the guards-van from the rest of the train. The connection was completely severed. The rest of the train, its load suddenly lightened, picked up speed and, ignoring the Boxers running along beside it, steamed off at a quickened pace down the valley. The three end carriages, with sixty of Lin's troopers on board, rolled to a gentle stop just outside the gate.

Major Lin, standing on the small balcony of what was now the last carriage, watched grimly through his binoculars as his soldiers – remarkably quickly, considering their tenacity in the earlier battle – were overwhelmed. The horde of Boxers surrounding the stationary cars resembled a speckled snake tightening its coils, or a dragon with red, yellow, green and black scales, slithering towards the coaches it intended to consume. At first Lin could hear scattered shots and he saw the white puffs of smoke as his men vainly tried to resist its encroachment – but soon the Boxer coils had enveloped the carriages. Their champions stood on the carriage roofs, which now fluttered triumphantly with Boxer flags. The writhing mass seemed to be sprouting limbs, like a giant upended caterpillar waving its legs. A closer look through the binoculars identified these as poles and spears, each one topped with the head of one of his brave men.

The train was steaming along the plain at a good twenty miles per hour. Rich farmland stretched on either side. A thin white stream of water flowed a slow course in the centre of the wide, otherwise dry riverbed. Looking down the long black barrel of the engine, appearing and disappearing through the grey smoke swirling from the stack and the white clouds issuing from the steam dome, they could see the bluish shape of the Black Hills lining the horizon ahead of them. They would reach the approaches within an hour and the tunnel about an hour and a half after that. Henry had passed a message back via Lao Zhao to Major Lin that he intended to stop the train at the entrance to the tunnel to re-water, taking advantage of the tower at the small construction workers' depot that he knew was located there. The engine was almost driving itself now, though Henry kept a careful hand on the regulator in case of unforeseen gradients. The three who remained of the original footplate party had settled into a simple routine.

The young soldier proudly relished his role as fireman, spading in the coal when Henry demanded, with ceremony and care. At first the boy had bitterly felt the loss of his friend – his girlish-looking companion who had died delivering the message to Major Lin – but he had now cheered up somewhat and was sitting on the tender, his rifle on his knees, singing a snatch of opera. Not for the first time Henry wondered at the hard-headed resilience of these northern Chinese peasants. Lao Zhao was with him on the footplate.

'Have you decided what you are going to do, Xiansheng?' Lao Zhao asked quietly, after his usual long-winded build-up to a serious question. He was idly whittling a wood splinter with his knife.

The wheels clattered below them.

'Not yet,' said Henry.

'Some people might have driven off this animal without waiting for Major Lin and his soldiers to get on board,' said Lao Zhao.

'Some people might have,' said Henry, 'if they could get a train going at a suitable speed to prevent Major Lin and his soldiers merely climbing aboard as soon as the wheels started turning, and if it didn't involve leaving them to the mercies of the Boxers.'

'Most of Lin's men were left behind,' said Lao Zhao. 'He has barely fifteen to twenty remaining who are not severely wounded.'

'It wasn't my doing that they were left behind,' said Henry. 'Poor devils.'

'No, it was Fate,' said Lao Zhao, 'but it was not inconvenient Fate. You have fewer soldiers to deal with now.'

'Now what could you possibly mean by that?' He could not disguise his grin.

'Ah,' smiled Lao Zhao, 'so you do have a plan! I would have been sorry if you had just allowed Major Lin and that Chamberlain Jin to kill you like a dog. I would have been sorry, too, if you allowed them to kill the Mandarin, for he is kind to poor muleteers such as me. And I would have been upset if the fox lady was killed, although perhaps Major Lin would have taken her for his concubine, as the old chamberlain will certainly make a catamite of that little boy, if he can get his hands on him . . . No.' He spat. 'I would not have enjoyed working for such people afterwards.'

'Afterwards? How do you know they wouldn't just kill you too?'

'They wouldn't kill me,' said Lao Zhao comfortably. 'Nobody has a quarrel with a poor muleteer like me. Somebody has to look after the horses, after all, whoever kills who. But I prefer working for you because you are foolish as all foreigners are and always pay me double the wages I am owed. And maybe you will also give me a little of that gold, which the Mandarin will exchange with you for your guns.'

'You paid very close attention to what Lin and Jin were saying, didn't you?'

'I told you, I have excellent hearing, Xiansheng. A hunter needs to have good hearing to track his prey.'

'Well, if I did happen to have a plan, would you help me?'

'Of course, Ma Na Si Xiansheng.' Lao Zhao laughed. 'Would you give me any gold if I didn't? Anyway, what can you do on your own with your bandaged arm in a sling? But please make your instructions simple. Remember, I am only an old muleteer, and I have no understanding of how this train of yours works beyond feeding its belly with great nosebags of coal.'

Quietly Henry explained what he had in mind. Lao Zhao closed his eyes in concentration, occasionally nodding, a wide grin cracking his lined face.

'The first thing you might do,' said Henry, thoughtfully, 'is to make your way back along the wagons – it's not difficult to climb along their sides. If Major Lin asks you what you are doing you can say you were looking for him because you need his instructions about watering the horses. What I need to know is where he has positioned his men. Are they all in the final compartment, as I think, or has he scattered them throughout the train? Do you think you could find that out for me?'

'I could do so very easily,' said Lao Zhao. He rose to his feet, opened the firebox a fraction and threw the whittled piece of wood into the flames. Then he climbed on to the tender, patting the young soldier playfully on the shoulder as he passed.

Helen Frances was sitting on the bed. She was weeping. The doctor was squatting on a stool in front of her, holding her hands in his and talking to her urgently.

There was a semblance of order in the Airtons' compartment now, after its sudden transformation during the height of battle into a surgical ward. The walking wounded had all been transferred to the last compartment with their comrades. Only two wounded soldiers remained, and they were lying on mattresses fashioned out of the sofa cushions, with red silk tablecloths as makeshift sheets. One was their first patient, the man who had received the sword thrust in the belly, and he was dying. Fan Yimei knelt beside him, holding his hand, occasionally wiping the sweat from his forehead and talking to him gently about his village, and his childhood. The other, whom the doctor had trepanned to remove a bullet from his skull, would also probably die, but mercifully he had been unconscious since the doctor had injected him with morphine. Nellie, exhausted by her exertions, was dozing in an armchair. The children were playing stones, paper, scissors with Mary. Their giggles from the other end of the compartment occasionally distracted the doctor from his chain of thought. Despite his tiredness – he could not calculate when he last slept – he knew he had to concentrate if this poor girl were to understand what he had to tell her.

At first, she hardly seemed to be paying any attention. Reaction had set in after Helen Frances's remarkable recovery from her sickbed, when she had taken up the heavy chores of field nursing like a professional. The doctor could hardly hold back his admiration for her. Now that there was nothing useful left for her to do, it was not surprising that her energy had drained away, and she had begun to tremble as she succumbed to the shock and horror of this most recent experience, on top of all the other ghastly events, and the struggle against her addiction. Nothing in the mission hospital had prepared her for the violent reality of bodies torn by battle – the smashed limbs, the sword slashes that revealed the insides of a man in anatomical detail, the surreal nightmare of having to remove an arrow from an arm, the amputated legs, the deaths of those they could not save. All this against the crash of battle outside, with the knowledge that, at any moment, their carriage might be overrun, in which case they themselves would face certain death, or worse. Well, the doctor thought, Helen Frances already knew what that worse could be, poor thing. Her recent actions had shown the wells of courage and strength that lay within her. He owed her his thanks, and much more than that. He owed her his protection, and that was why it was imperative that he should warn her now of the new danger she faced.

For there had been one other shock, not long after the train had left the butcher's yard of the railway camp behind. Major Lin had walked through their carriage on his way to report to the Mandarin. When he entered, the doctor had been involved with his trepanning, with Fan Yimei helping him, handing him his saw and his probes when he needed them, gazing as she did so in fascinated dread at the open brain in front of her. Nellie and Helen Frances had been bandaging the leg of another wounded soldier from which a bullet had been removed. Major Lin strode down the carriage, oblivious to the suffering of his men, his usual calm, sardonic expression on his face. He had paused when he came to Helen Frances, however, and his lip had curled into a cold grin. Helen Frances stiffened when he came near her, but with difficulty she had retained a calm expression, although the doctor noted that the colour drained from her cheeks. Major Lin smiled and touched her chin with his gloved hand. Her shoulders shook fractionally but she maintained eye contact, her grey-green irises widening and her mouth tightening.

Then Nellie had brushed away the gloved hand. 'How dare you?' she had cried. 'How dare you?'

Major Lin had laughed coldly, bowed, and unhurriedly gone on his way. Helen Frances closed her eyes. The doctor could see a tear glistening in her eyelashes, then she had flung back her shoulders, and rather fiercely returned to the bandaging of the wounded soldier's leg.

'Are you all right, Helen Frances?' Nellie had asked her – and she had nodded, but tears were running freely down her cheeks.

It had been at that moment that the awful truth had dawned on Airton, and he cursed himself for not having realised it earlier. He remembered her reaction in the brothel when Major Lin had stepped into the lamplight of the corridor on the night of their escape. The palpable fear she had displayed. He had had to sedate her. Of course. Major Lin had been one of her attackers. There could be no other explanation. And Manners had witnessed it – but he had not mentioned it. That could only mean one thing. Airton would not have credited it, had he not already known so much else about the man, and the depths of his perfidy. The treacherous, treacherous monster. It had not only been an arrangement with the Mandarin that had gone terribly wrong. Manners must have arranged the ensuing rape. He had made another bargain with Major Lin, to protect his own hide, or for some other cynical reason Airton could not yet comprehend, and had even gone to the lengths of having himself bound so that he would escape implication. For all their apparent animosity, Manners and Lin had been in league all along. For a moment his hand with the scalpel had shaken, as the enormity of it all hit him, and Fan Yimei had looked at him with curiosity and concern. His professional instincts had taken over, of course, and he had continued with the operation, but the unspeakable horror of his realisation remained. Poor girl. She probably didn't even yet know how she had been betrayed by the very man she thought she loved. He had to save her from herself, whatever it took.

So now, in the relative quiet, with Nellie asleep, he held her hands and told her what he knew of Manners. At first she would not listen. 'Henry,' she moaned. 'I want to see Henry.' And he told her that she was wrong to put her trust in such a man. She shook her head. 'No, he loves me,' she murmured. 'He loves me.'

'He loves nobody,' said the doctor. And he told her about the treason in which Manners was involved, the conversation with the Mandarin that he had overheard in the Black Hills. About the guns Manners was selling, on behalf of another power. He told her that a man who would betray his country would betray anyone and anything. The man was a criminal and a traitor.

'But he saved us. He saved us,' she moaned.

'He used us,' said the doctor, his voice rising. 'For his own advantage. He prostituted you.'

'I know,' she cried, 'I know, but nothing happened. It was a game. The Mandarin was honourable.' She shook her head in her confusion.

'A game?' hissed the doctor. 'He arranged your rape by Major Lin. Your rape, Helen Frances. Your rape.'

And she had shaken her head violently from side to side, whispering, 'No. No. No.'

But the doctor was relentless, relating all the circumstantial evidence, explaining Manners's foul motives, the extent of his deceit and treachery. She had to understand. She had to understand, he told himself through his tiredness. She had begun to whimper. He knew that the children had stopped their game and the others in the carriage must be staring at them. He felt the silence behind him, but he persisted, repeating the details of the brute's perfidy, explaining again and again the man's crimes. 'He does not love you,' he told her. 'He does not love you. He never loved you. Don't you see that, girl?'

And Helen Frances had screamed, through her tears, 'But he does. He does. He told me,' and he had to twist her wrist to calm her hysterics, and his own eyes blazed as he stared into her eyes, forcing her to accept the truth.

'But he lied, my dear. He lied!'

After a while she began to weep softly, and he put his arms around her and rocked her gently. 'I'm going to sedate you now,' he said quietly.

'Yes,' she whispered.

'And don't you worry. I'll be here to look after you. You need never see that man again,' he said. And she nodded, as she bared her arm, and let Dr Airton administer the syringe. 'Sleep now,' he said.

'What was all that commotion?' asked Nellie, yawning, as she woke from her sleep.

'Nothing, dear,' he answered. 'Get back to your rest. I was just giving Helen Frances a dose of morphine to calm her down. She had a little fit.'

'Is that wise?' asked Nellie. 'She was doing so well.'

'I think it's for the best,' said the doctor, slumping heavily into one of the armchairs. 'I think it's for the best.'

Henry's original intention had been to make his move at the depot by the tunnel where they halted – but Major Lin had been particularly vigilant, positioning his soldiers in a circle round the engine. The ostensible reason was that they were watching out for any of Iron Man Wang's bandits who might still be located in the Black Hills, but Henry noticed that the soldiers were facing inwards, with their weapons directed at him. Even so, if it had been only the soldiers who had got off the train, he might have risked starting the engine in the hope that it would have disappeared into the tunnel before they could try to clamber back aboard – but the Mandarin chose to get off too, as did Dr Airton and his children, to stretch their legs and take a breath of fresh air, although the atmosphere was dank among these gloomy precipices and peaks. So Henry and the young soldier had got on and replenished the water in the tender, while Lao Zhao had used the opportunity of the rest stop to feed and water the horses in the wagons.

The Mandarin had made a brief visit to the front of the train and congratulated Henry on their escape from the railway camp. 'You did well, Ma Na Si. I am indebted to you,' he said. 'I will miss your company when we have contracted our piece of business.' Henry would have liked to warn him of what Lao Zhao had overheard, but he had no opportunity because Jin Lao remained assiduously by the Mandarin's elbow.

He heard a brief altercation between the doctor and Major Lin, and was surprised when, a moment later, the doctor, protesting, was escorted by two soldiers to the engine and told to climb the footplates.

'Don't think this is any of my wishing,' muttered Airton irritably, in answer to Henry's raised eyebrow of enquiry. 'The prospect of any proximity with you fills me with disgust. But your friend Major Lin seems to think you need my help up here. God knows why. He doesn't seem to appreciate that I have wounded men of his under my care.'

Henry exchanged a glance with Lao Zhao, who spat over the side of the cab.

'Seems they're clearing any unwanted mules out of the stables,' he muttered significantly.

'Now what is that supposed to mean?' snapped the doctor.

'Nothing,' said Henry. 'If you're really interested in helping, I'll show you what you have to do.'

When everyone was aboard again, he ejected steam from the cylinder cocks, then set the reverser and pulled the regulator. The wheels turned. He pulled the cord as they entered the tunnel, letting out a long whistle, which was swallowed by the roar of the train as they rattled and thumped into the darkness.

Five minutes later they burst into light again – but it was a green gloom compared to the blazing sunlight of the Shishan valley, which they had left behind them. Here, in the midst of the Black Hills forests, dark firs formed an arch over their heads from the high banks on either side, and occasionally the space around them would narrow further as the track wound between high grey cliffs. Henry leaned out of the cab, peering at the track ahead through the unnatural twilight.

'Had we not better do something soon?' shouted Lao Zhao, over the clatter that the train was making over the sleepers. 'If I was planning something wicked, this is just the sort of evil spot I might choose. And so might they.'

'What is this man talking about?' asked the doctor.

Henry was peering ahead. The train clattered on. His mind was racing. He could make up any excuse to stop the train, but a suspicious Lin would surely have taken precautions as he had at the depot. He realised now that his plan depended on one forlorn hope.

Almost like a talisman, he clung to the memory of a conversation he had once had with Mr Bowers, who had complained to him that fallen trees were always a hazard on this stretch of line. Bowers had urged him to persuade Herr Fischer to send a team to cut away the forest on either side of the track. He had promised to pass on the message to Herr Fischer and, of course, he had not bothered, so nothing had been done about it. Six weeks had passed since anyone had used or inspected this piece of line.

'Doctor,' he drawled, 'you're a man of prayer. If you want to help, pray now for a fallen tree.'

'Now it's you who are talking nonsense,' said Airton. 'Or are you both mocking me?'

The train curled round the windy track. Ahead was an overhang that Henry thought looked promising, but not even a branch had fallen down the bank. Lao Zhao jumped down from the tender on to the plate. Neither Henry nor the doctor had noticed him leave, and he was now breathless on his return. 'I climbed back to look into the Mandarin's compartment. The three of them are in there. Lin, Jin and the Mandarin, and they appear to be arguing. It is as we thought,' he said matter-of-factly. 'You probably have little time.'

'I need a bloody tree,' snapped Henry.

'Are you two plotting something?' Airton asked angrily. 'You are, aren't you? You're plotting with Major Lin against the Mandarin. I know it.'

'Thank God,' sighed Henry. 'Hold on!' He pulled the handle to apply the air brakes, closing the regulator as he did so. The wheels locked hard, and there was a fearful jolt as the train skidded along the tracks – but after a moment it shuddered to a halt, the steel wheels screaming against the resisting rails, causing sparks to fountain almost as high as the cab. Lao Zhao turned the wheel of the tender brake. The wagons clattered and thumped behind them. The whole train concertinaed to a halt. The doctor and the soldier on the tender had fallen backwards, and it had taken all of Henry and Lao Zhao's strength to remain on their feet. He could only imagine the chaos in the compartments. He glanced forward round the cab. The cow-catcher in front had stopped feet away from the trunk of a small fir tree.

'Yes, Doctor, I'm afraid that we are plotting something,' said Henry, lifting Airton to his feet and twisting him round, 'and I'll thank you now to remain very silent. Oh, and by the way, that prickle you feel against your back is my revolver aiming at your liver. So please don't try to be heroic and do something you may later regret. It may not look it but I'm on the side of the angels.'

As he finished, a furious Major Lin climbed up the ladder. He was pointing his pistol at Henry's head. 'What is the meaning of this?' he was shouting.

'Look ahead of you, Major,' said Henry calmly, while keeping his own revolver, obscured under the sling in which he rested his wounded arm, firmly pressed against the doctor's back. 'Do you see that tree on the line? Don't you think you should order some of your men off the train to remove it? It's not a big tree so maybe four or five would be adequate to lift it.'

Lin leaned out of the cab to look. '*Ta made!*' he swore, and jumped down to give the necessary orders.

'Have you lost your senses?' hissed Airton. 'What are you trying to do?'

'To save our lives, if you'll believe it,' Henry replied, watching as a detachment of five men led by Major Lin ran forward past the cab. He glanced up at the young soldier on the tender who was leaning over the side enjoying the spectacle. Lao Zhao had disappeared.

'Major,' he called, 'I'm going to reverse the train a little to give your boys room to move.'

'Stay where you are,' shouted Lin.

But Henry had already released the tender brake, pulled the reverser and pushed the throttle, and the train slowly clanked backwards. It had gone about forty yards before a panting Major Lin caught up, pulling himself up the ladder. His face was twisted with anger. 'Halt this train immediately,' he shouted, pointing his gun.

'Whatever you say, Major,' said Henry. He pulled back the regulator stick and pushed the reverser, and the train came gently to a standstill.

Major Lin leaned backwards, still keeping his pistol trained on Henry, and looked down the track to where his men were straining with the tree.

'How are they doing, Major?' Henry asked politely. 'Do they need any help?'

Major Lin glared at him. The doctor felt his heart pounding as the moments ticked by.

'Get back here. Immediately,' shouted Lin to his men, when the tree had been pushed aside.

As he spoke, Henry rammed the throttle to its full stretch, pressing the lever as he did so to spread sand on the track and give the wheels extra traction. With a jolt the engine moved forward. Major Lin's pistol wavered as he swung backwards, unbalanced, struggling to keep his feet from sliding off the edge of the plate. Henry pushed the doctor aside. He pulled the hand that held the revolver out of the sling and fired. Major Lin's eyes registered his surprise. A choking sound came from his throat, and involuntarily he took his hand from the railing to clutch his wounded shoulder. For a moment he swayed on the edge of the footplate, looking in amazement at the red that stained his palm. Henry fired again, and missed, for as he did so Major Lin, his eyes wild with hatred, threw himself off, landing on his back on the bank, and there he lay, winded, as the carriages rattled past.

Henry turned towards the young soldier on the tender, who had scrambled to his feet. He was fumbling with his rifle. 'Don't even think it,' shouted Henry, but the boy was already raising his rifle, his scared eyes pleading. Henry fired, and the boy fell backwards on to the coals. His legs twitched and he was still. The unfired rifle clattered on to the footplate.

'Oh how could you?' wailed Airton, kneeling impotently on the footplate.

'Keep your head down,' shouted Henry, dropping to his own knees. Bullets clanged on the roof of the cab as they trundled past the men who had been moving the tree. Henry heard a thump and a scrambling sound. One of the men had grabbed the steps as the moving engine steamed past. He reached for the fireman's spade, and smashed it down on the head that emerged above the plate. The soldier fell backwards with a scream.

Panting, the bloody spade in his hand, he looked down at Airton who was sitting helplessly, shaking his head. 'What have you done?' he moaned. 'What do you think you can achieve by this? You know that the last compartment is full of soldiers.'

'Lao Zhao uncoupled it,' panted Henry. 'That's what he went off to do. The only enemy we have left on board is Jin Lao.'

'Jin Lao?' exclaimed the doctor. 'He's an old man.'

'A murderous old man. Look, Doctor, I'll explain everything later, but I must go back to the Mandarin's carriage now. I can't stop the train. We need to get a distance between Lin and his men. That means you'll have to drive it.'

'You must be mad. I don't know how to drive a train. Anyway, I won't,' said the doctor. 'I don't trust you. You're going to go and kill the Mandarin as you killed all these others.'

Henry ignored him. He was spading coal into the firebox. 'That should be enough,' he said. 'Look, it's simple. See this big lever? It's the regulator or throttle. It controls the speed of the train. The further you push it the faster you go. You have to use some strength but you'll manage. Don't go too fast with all these bends. That three-quarters mark is about as far as you'd want to push it in these conditions. That's the reverser. Another lever. It controls the direction of the connecting rods. It decides whether the engine goes forwards or backwards. You see? It's easy. Push, forwards. Pull, backwards. Anyone can do it. This is the lever for the air brake in case you have to use it. Stop the train if you see any more fallen trees on the line. That's it. Oh, yes, and this is the cord for the whistle. Pull it if you need me. Now you know as much about driving a train as I do.'

'I wasn't listening to a word you said,' said the doctor. 'I refuse to co-operate.'

'Please yourself,' said Henry, 'but I have to go.'

He picked up the fallen rifle and climbed on to the tender. He turned. Airton was still sitting disconsolately on the shaking footplate.

'Look, Doctor, trust me. Please trust me. I'm doing this for all of us.'

'You're a murderer,' shouted Airton, his face red with anger.

Henry sighed. Quickly he climbed down the back of the tender, and stood for a moment above the swaying coupling, choosing his moment to step across to the back of the wagon ahead, which held the horses. He climbed up the ladder, and at a swaying run, traversed the roof of the wagon, choosing his moment again to jump on to the roof of the next wagon, which also contained horses. He could hear them moving and snuffling below him. He ran on. When he reached the further end, he climbed down. The next carriage was the Mandarin's. He crossed over to the small balcony at the rear, pressing himself against the wall as he checked the magazine and released the safety-catch of the rifle. Taking a deep breath, he turned the door handle, and threw himself into the compartment.

In the second he did so, he realised that he was too late. The Mandarin was slumped against the far wall, a bloody wound in his chest. Chamberlain Lin stood over him, a revolver hanging from his thin elegant hand. He heard a sound on his left and saw the frightened faces of the Mandarin's wives huddled on the floor. It was a mistake to turn away his attention, even for that fraction of a second, for when he looked back the chamberlain's pistol was raised and pointing at him. They fired together.

The doctor stared in panic at the controls of the shaking monster, which was hurtling them forward. He peered nervously round the side of the cab, terrified that he would see another tree or piece of foliage lying on the track. At least the track was straighter here, the banks less precipitous. Oh, this would not do. Visions of what might be happening in the Mandarin's carriage behind him fought with fears of what would happen if the engine went out of control. Manners was a maniac. A ruthless killer, and, he, Airton, had not raised a finger to prevent him going back to do his worst. It had not even occurred to him to try. But what could he have done to stop him?

The huffing rhythm of the wheels suddenly altered to a metallic sound as the engine rattled over a small bridge that crossed a stream. The engine shook from side to side. He started in terror, and only relaxed a fraction when they had crossed the stream, and the wheels had reverted to their steady pant.

He had watched Manners driving the train earlier. He had seemed to be constantly adjusting several levers. One was that lever there, which he had called a reverser. Why was it called a reverser when the train was obviously meant to go forward? What was a reverser? Should he be pulling it, or pushing it? Or just leaving it alone? He felt utterly disoriented.

He could not do this. He wanted the engine to stop. Surely there was enough distance now between the train and Major Lin to make pursuit impossible? He didn't care. He just wanted the train to stop.

Could he stop it? Manners had mentioned a brake lever. But which one was it? That big red bar – that surely was the throttle, which controlled the speed. If he pulled it would the engine slow down? And should he be doing something with the reverser as he did so?

Oh, he could not cope. This farce could not go on. What was he, a doctor, doing, even contemplating trying to drive a steam train? Perhaps he should just leave everything as it was. Make his way back with the engine untended, rolling down the track with ghost controls. He might as well be a ghost for all the difference his uncertain presence on the plates was making to the situation. Since he had been left there, he had not touched a thing. And he must go back. He must, somehow, make his way back over the unsteady tender and the wobbling carriages as Manners had done with such ease. Of course, it might be too late now to prevent Manners doing whatever he intended to do to the Mandarin – but he owed a duty to his family. He must go back to rescue them from this maniac, this lunatic, this killer. But then he thought, What if there is another tree fallen on the line? If the train was derailed, all of them might be killed. There was no help for it. He had to stop the train.

He looked at the controls again, trying desperately to remember what Manners had done when he stopped the train earlier. Definitely he had pulled that throttle lever, and that other lever. Yes, he remembered, that was the one Manners had called the air brake. Why air brake when this thing was run by steam? Never mind that. He closed his eyes and prayed an incoherent prayer, the burden of which was, 'Please, God, forgive me for what I'm about to do in my ignorance. Only cast Your loving mantle over us, and save us. Save us.' Save me. Save me from the responsibility of driving this – thing.

Letting out his breath in a terrified shout, and using all his strength, he pulled on the throttle lever. What was that awful sound? He didn't care. Having started he must continue. He heaved at the brake lever, pulling it all the way, and was thrown forward by the sudden jolt. His head thumped against the dials, and then he was thrown back again against the tender. He looked up, dazed. Everything was steam and sparks, and screeching metal. The firebox door had banged open and he gazed almost hypnotised at the burning red coals, a vision of hell in front of him. The whole cab was shaking around him. He felt something heavy fall on top of him. It was the body of the boy soldier, which had been knocked forward when the tender banged against the back of the engine. The dead face bounced on the shuddering footplate. The blank eyes seemed to stare at him accusingly. The mouth flopped open as if to reprimand him. He shook with fear and repulsion. But thank God. Thank God. The engine was slowing. It was really slowing. Eventually it came to a stop, hissing and belching steam. And everything was still. Gloriously still. It took the doctor a moment to recover his senses. Muttering in disgust and horror, he wriggled and twisted himself away from the tangled corpse. Unsteadily he got to his feet. He was covered in blood and coal dust. He didn't care. He had to go back and confront Manners. He scrabbled for a weapon, any weapon, and saw the spade with which Manners had killed the soldier who had tried to climb up on the footplate. He picked it up. It clanged on the guardrail as he climbed down the ladder. It caught in the struts, so he had to pause to release it. He started running as soon as his feet connected with the bank. He only stopped when he reached the door of the Mandarin's compartment.

He heard the wailing noises before he reached the door. With a sinking feeling in his breast he recognised the sound. He had a sudden recollection of a trip he had made as a young medical student to the Outer Hebridean Isles. He and a friend had stumbled upon the funeral of a drowned fisherman. They had followed the villagers as they bore the bier along the clifftops to a windswept cemetery. And as the wind howled, the women had keened. He had never forgotten the shrill, eerie ululation. And he heard it again now from inside the Mandarin's compartment. His hand was shaking as he pulled the catch to open the door.

It took a moment for his eyes to adjust to the gloom. In the interval since Manners had left him and he had been alone on the footplate, the light had begun to fade and the sky above the cliffs had become streaked with red cirrus as the sun dropped slowly towards the tree line.

As he stood there uncertainly a dying ray from the sinking red globe illuminated the inside of the carriage with a pink glow – and he saw the bodies.

The Mandarin was propped against the carriage wall next to the door to the adjoining compartment. The grey, pigtailed head had sunk on to his chest, and his arms lay flaccidly by his sides; the fingers on the chubby hands were half curled, as if displaying for the curious his heavy jade rings. His three wives were kneeling beside him. They had been screeching and tearing at their clothes, but now they looked up in silent fear at the sudden apparition of the doctor, a black, bloody figure silhouetted like some demon against the pale mauve light behind the open door, brandishing a spade.

The old chamberlain was lying at the feet of his master. The pale dead eyes in the calm parchment face were skewed upwards, as if they were curious about the dark hole in the centre of his forehead. A silver revolver lay just out of reach of his long, tapering fingers.

Henry Manners had fallen against some boxes that were lined against the wall. One had been knocked over, and his body was partially covered by gold ingots, which glinted in the fading ray of sunshine.

'Oh, you thieving, bloody, murderous man,' moaned the doctor, falling to his knees. The spade slipped out of his hand. 'So it was all for gold. You killed these men for their gold.'

He was startled by a familiar voice, but it was speaking very weakly, in a breathy whisper: 'I see you have survived, my dear Daifu.'

Airton rushed to the Mandarin's side, and gently pulled aside the silk shirt, but a glance at the gaping chest wound and the froth bubbling out of the perforated lung told him that there was nothing medically he could do. The bullet had entered the Mandarin's chest about three inches above the nipple. There was evidence of rib fracture and he guessed that the right pulmonary vein and the right upper lobe of the lung were fatally damaged. It would be only a matter of time before the Mandarin would expire from blood loss. Rarely in his medical career had he felt such a sense of impotence. He looked around frantically to see if he could find any membranous material with which he could at least staunch the wound. On the table by the window was a piece of parchment. He carefully folded this and pressed the thick paper over the hole which was bubbling air and blood. He barely noticed the Chinese calligraphy on the manuscript: *'wu wei.'*

All this time the hooded eyes were contemplating him, and there was a hint of a smile on the pale face. 'No miracles for me, then, Daifu, like your Jesus can do?'

'Don't talk, old friend,' he whispered.

'I am glad that you can still call me friend,' said the Mandarin, forming the words with difficulty, punctuating them with deep breaths. 'I hope that you have enjoyed your train ride. I remember that you once told me of some bandits who attacked a train. I expect that you never thought that you yourself would one day . . .'

He stopped, weakened by the effort of speaking. He coughed and a thick film of dark, venous blood trickled down his chin. Airton clasped his hand. The Mandarin's eyes, which had closed in his pain, opened again slowly, and again the hanging mouth twisted into a smile.

'If you can find me a little water . . . I would be grateful,' he managed.

'Oh, Da Ren, of course,' murmured the doctor. 'Why didn't I think . . .' Of course. The blood loss would be creating a deep sense of thirst. Gesturing to one of the women to hold the staunch on the wound, he hunted the carriage for some liquid, settling for want of anything better for a pot of cold tea, which he poured into a cup, and pressed to the Mandarin's lips. He could only manage a little, but sighed gratefully.

'I would like you to know that I have always enjoyed my conversations with you,' he whispered. 'You did reveal many things to me. Yes,' he said, 'truly. You have a fine vision of what the world should be.'

'Oh, Da Ren,' muttered the doctor, tears running down his cheeks.

'But you were never very practical,' smiled the Mandarin, 'as I had to be.' He made a coughing sound, which might have been a laugh. More blood trickled out of his mouth. 'My poor Daifu. How difficult it has been for you. But perhaps I taught you a little of what it is to be practical. Before the end. No?'

He closed his eyes, and wheezed heavily. Airton wiped the beads of sweat from his brow and the blood from his face. He felt the Mandarin's hand clutching his tightly. The hooded eyes rolled open, stared fiercely into the doctor's face. After a moment the Mandarin relaxed. 'Not that it matters,' he breathed. 'We are all powerless pawns of an inexorable fate. Dying in this fashion is . . . ridiculous.' The large body shook uncontrollably. The froth bubbled in the lungs. Finally there was a long sigh.

Dr Airton closed the staring eyes. The women began to wail.

Ignoring them, he rose to his feet. It was only professional habit that caused him to examine the other two bodies. The Chamberlain was clearly dead, and he had no doubt from the contorted angle of Manners's body that he, too, was slain – presumably by the chamberlain after Manners had himself shot the Mandarin in cold blood. He must have returned the chamberlain's shot as he fell. A lucky and accurate hit, but Manners had always been lucky, and precise, as befitted an adventurer and schemer. Not any more, he thought, as he knelt beside him. There would be no more schemes now, thank God. He removed the ingots that covered him. That he should murder for this – this tinsel, this Mammon. He turned the body and saw the wound in the groin. Manners had bled prodigiously. Mechanically, he felt for the pulse – and started. He leaped to his feet, and stared down at the torn body – which was still living.

'My God!' He felt a chill run down his spine. What was he to do? The murderer was still alive.

Before Henry had stopped the train, Major Lin and Jin Lao had gone into the Airtons' compartment, and while the Chamberlain had trained the revolver on them, Major Lin had tied up Nellie, Fan Yimei, Mary and the children. This had been a precaution so that they would not be disturbed when they went back into the next-door carriage to give their final, fatal ultimatum to the Mandarin. Nellie, who was lying closest to the compartment, had heard a shot shortly after the train had got going again after the stop to remove the tree. A long while after that there had been more shots followed by a long, long silence. Nellie tried to explain all this to the doctor as he hurriedly untied them, but he was not listening. He did not want to listen. He knew in his own mind what had happened – the extent of Manners's villainy and the violent retribution Providence had brought down on him – and he was not prepared to entertain anything that contradicted his version of events.

Anyway, he had determined what he had to do to save his family. They would depart, taking the horses, which he had instructed Lao Zhao, who had appeared outside as he was leaving the Mandarin's compartment, to saddle. He had determined that they would leave this train of death. Better to face the forest. Better anything than to stay here. And they had to be speedy, for Lin and his men would certainly be following them down the rail track, and would arrive shortly . . .

Nellie had asked after Manners, and he had lied to her for the first time in his life: he told her that Manners was dead. He told her that their safety depended on him now, and he judged that it was vital that they leave. Immediately.

Something in his wild expression brooked no argument. Silently, one after another, they climbed down on to the track, and waited until Lao Zhao brought the horses. Helen Frances was dazed and sluggish, and it took all of Nellie's and Mary's attention to look after her. Only when she was mounted on her horse did her old instincts seem to come back to her, and without questioning why or where they were going, she sat firmly in the saddle waiting patiently for the instruction to move. When they were all mounted, the doctor remembered his medical bag, and climbed back into the carriage, where he saw Fan Yimei standing by the door leading to the Mandarin's compartment.

'Come on. You'd better get ready to leave,' he said brusquely.

'You are not taking Ma Na Si Xiansheng.' She spoke quietly. It was a statement, not a question.

'He's dead,' he said.

'You know that he is not dead, Daifu,' she said.

'Well, he's as good as dead,' snapped the doctor. 'He couldn't survive a hard ride. I'm sorry, but there's nothing I can do for him.'

Fan Yimei looked at him coldly.

'You don't think he would leave us behind if the circumstances were reversed?' cried the doctor.

Fan Yimei turned on her lotus foot and went into the Mandarin's compartment, closing the door behind her.

Airton stood for a moment, angered and bewildered. He was so tired that he could hardly think. He made a move to go after her, then thought better of it. She was Major Lin's concubine. For all he knew, Manners, Major Lin and she had been involved in their conspiracy together. The fact that Manners had fired a shot at Lin troubled him for a moment, but then he concluded that Manners had been attempting a double-cross. Thieves falling out over gold. It was the oldest story in the book.

He jumped on to the track, stumbled, picked himself up and ran to the horse that was waiting for him.

'Aren't you coming with us?' he said to Lao Zhao, who had been holding his reins.

'No, Daifu. I must look after the remaining horses.' Lao Zhao's tone was expressionless.

'God go with you, then,' said the doctor, and jerked his reins. Nellie called in some consternation. 'What about Fan Yimei?' and the doctor told her that she had decided to wait for Major Lin. It was not a lie. He believed it. 'Anyway, we can't delay, woman,' he snapped.

For a moment he was confused as to where he should lead them. The dank trees hung over them. Then he saw what looked like a path, which led up a gentle bank from the track. He kicked his horse and the others followed. Nellie kept a steady hand on Helen Frances's elbow. One by one, they disappeared into the forest gloom.

PART THREE

Chapter Twenty

I will creep out of camp when it is dark. I do not care if
they catch me.
I want to go home.

It was hardly a stream, not even a pool, just a puddle in a patch
of wet ground at the foot of a grassy slope – yet for Nellie, as
she crawled towards it, it might have been the waters of the Jordan
revealed to the Israelites after their wanderings in the wilderness.

She might have missed it entirely.

All afternoon she had staggered up and over the dry hills, using
what will-power she had left in her to put one weary foot in front
of another. She had no idea in which direction she was heading.
Every step was an effort. The raw knob of her hipbone, what
muscle remained in her matchstick legs, her swollen knees, burned
with pain. Her bare feet were blistered and bloody, but a voice
in her tired brain told her, 'Go on. Go on.' Something deep and
obstinate in her nature – perhaps it was the remnants of her pride
– had fought with the overwhelming desire to lie down, refusing
to accept that Providence, which had brought them so far, should
betray them so finally. Yet the bare, rolling hills had stretched to
the horizon in every direction, and each rise had revealed more of
the same: desert, surrounded by desert, and all the more terrible
because the hills were covered with grass. The green satin slopes,
shimmering and changing shade as the clouds shifted, mocked her
with promise: they were the colours of life, and the ground teemed
and rustled with grasshoppers and wildlife; there were marmots and
foxes in the hills, but there was no sign of the precious water that
sustained life. She had staggered on, clutching to herself the last rags
of hope, but after hours of fruitless searching, even that began to
slip away. The empty goatskin, which she was pulling behind her,
dragged like an anchor; her own brittle limbs became heavier to lift.
She heard that other voice in her head, also her own, treasonably
urging her to rest, to rest. At last she had fallen to her knees, sinking
into the deceptive comfort of the grass. The deceitful breeze had

wafted over her burning limbs, and she surrendered passively to its embrace. The Tempter would soon throw over her the blanket of sleep, and even though she knew that it would probably mean the end for them all, she could no longer resist.

And then the miracle had happened. A single ray of sunlight had broken through the great banks of cloud, and had shone like a torchbeam into the valley below. It shimmered only for a moment – the clouds rolled onward in their stately progress and the ray was withdrawn – but in that moment she saw them, the faint, reflected, sparkles of white, flashing like the diamonds on a girl's choker as she turned her head to laugh. Drawing on her last reserves of energy, she had begun slowly to crawl down the slope – she could no longer trust herself to stand. In her dazed state, she felt that the dry grass was parting before her of its own accord as grasshoppers and insects leaped away at her approach. The sun burned on her bare neck and her head throbbed. At last she felt moistness on her hands; the ground had become softer, muddier. She pulled herself onward, hardly daring to believe the evidence of her senses. Suddenly a face was looking up at her, that of a hideous old woman, with burning, red-rimmed eyes, gaunt cheeks, and yellow teeth that snarled out of desiccated gums. With horror she started away, then realised it must be her own reflection. She dropped her head into the brown pool; her cracked lips opened, and somehow the thick block of her tongue began to move again, and she drank.

She could not tell how long she had lain there, lapping in the life-sustaining liquid, feeling it flow through her body, restoring substance to her limbs, reviving her will to go on – but when, finally, she rolled over, lying on her back, gazing at the towering cumulus that floated in majestic unconcern in the blue sky above her, she knew that God in Heaven, for whatever reason, had spared them again, and they would live for another day.

She was summoning her reserves of strength for the long walk back to the dell where the others lay. Her heart ached, as she thought of her babes, their skeletal little arms and swollen bellies, their big, lustrous eyes in their prematurely aged faces, which somehow even now shone with confidence in her, and despite every new trial revealed a spirit that had not been entirely broken. She thought sadly of Edward and Helen Frances. Helen Frances moved like an automaton, these days: bravely she went through the motions, but her body was exhausted and her mind appeared to be elsewhere; the marionette's smile and the vacant eyes had something terrible about them, as if the soul inside was already on the point of departing. Nellie feared for her: the candle of life inside her seemed to be flickering towards its end. And Edward? Edward was physically fine – he had survived the hardships better than any of them – but he, too, had withdrawn into melancholy introspection. She no longer knew how to reach him through the barriers of his self-hatred and despair.

She wished that they could share the comfort which succoured her even on the worst of days. It was not just fancy, or wishful thinking, that there was a Guiding Hand leading them on. That they had survived through such terrible ordeals could not be mere chance. Every day they had evidence that Providence had not abandoned them. It had shown them roots when they were starving, revealed springs when they were parched, and so often surprised them with small kindnesses when every man's hand had been turned against them.

Only last week – or was it the week before? she had long ago lost track of time – they had been stoned out of one of the cave villages in the hills in which they had sought shelter. The village headman had called them devils, and he had been the first to pick up a rock to hurl at them. Yet on the outskirts of that same village, a little boy had run after them and given them food and a goatskin full of water – this very goatskin that lay beside her now. That had been a small miracle, one of many they had encountered on their odyssey. It had sustained them as they climbed the barren mountain that had ultimately led them to this region of desert grassland. They had replenished the skin several times since, once at a small waterfall, and again at a well by some deserted shepherds' huts, and they had rationed carefully the *mantou* and pickles the boy had given them. It was only during the last three days that they had been without any water or food at all.

And again Providence had favoured them, revealing this spring, which had revived her. Idly she tried to remember the words of the psalm, but all she could recall was the line 'Thy rod and Thy staff will comfort me.' They would need that rod and staff if they were to survive many more days in an environment that was so hostile. She sighed when she thought of all the hardships that they had already endured during their weeks of wandering. Was it August now? Or September? She did not know.

It seemed like months ago that they had left the train, so well equipped, mounted on such fine horses – but they had wandered in the forest for days, lost among the endless trees. Several times they found that they had retraced their own tracks. One night there had been a thunderstorm. It had not occurred to them to hobble the horses, and the animals had bolted in the night, taking away all of their provisions in the saddlebags. They had spent a day searching fruitlessly for them, and another, before accepting the inevitable. Nellie now remembered the ensuing days – weeks – of wandering in the dark forest as a nightmare without end. They had no food, and Edward had forbidden them to eat the few tempting berries they occasionally came across, in case they were poisonous. In those days he had shown a manic leadership, pressing them on relentlessly and unsparingly, his jaw fixed rigidly as he strode ahead. Nellie had not dared to ask him if he knew where he was going, so fierce was his expression as he paused time and again to look at the sun's position through the branches above him. After a day of trackless wandering, he had told them they would move at night so he could judge their position by the stars. The children found that even more difficult – the noises of the forest, rustling animals and shrieking birds, alarmed them – and Helen Frances, facing withdrawal pangs, for the morphine had gone with the horses, was occasionally hysterical, although Nellie had to admit that, in the circumstances, she was doing remarkably well even to walk at all. They might have died in the forest if on the third day they had not stumbled upon a woodman's cottage. The man had at first been kind, and given them food and shelter, but when they were leaving he demanded payment, and lifted his axe threateningly. Edward had been forced to give him most of the little cash he had had in his pocket. Then the man had been all smiles and had directed them towards another woodman's hut a day away. Here had been a father and his son who had unceremoniously robbed them of the little they had remaining, even taking Nellie's necklace with its silver cross, and her husband's signet ring – but at least they had given them food.

When they had arrived at the next human habitation, they were greeted with suspicion as paupers, or worse. In the two huts in a clearing lived a family who were engaged in slash-and-burn farming;

they had some pigs and a vegetable patch, but they were poor and had no intention of sharing what they had with mysterious foreigners. Reluctantly they allowed them to sleep in one of the animal pens belonging to the two brothers who lived in the second hut, but when they asked for food, the peasants shook their heads. It took them hours to get to sleep, unaccustomed as they were in those days to hunger pains, a condition that was now their constant reality. But Mary had woken them in the night. She had pointed to a cloth on the ground on which there were, unbelievably, a plate of hot green vegetables, a large bowl of rice, and half a breast of chicken. Edward had not been able to conceal his delight. 'How did you persuade them, Mary?' he had asked jovially, as he cut himself a slice of chicken.

The girl had looked sullenly at the ground. Then, after a long pause, she had shrugged her shoulders. 'I just asked the brothers for the food,' she muttered.

'The Lord be praised, there is Christian charity yet among us,' Edward had continued, smiling. 'You have hidden charms, young Mary, hidden charms, if you can melt the hearts of stony heathen like these.'

Nellie had realised even then what sort of payment the men must really have demanded from Mary for this charity, and she saw that Helen Frances too was looking miserably at her feet, avoiding any eye contact, but Nellie had remained silent, allowing Edward to enjoy his meal. What was the point in saying anything? Whatever Mary had done, she had done – and they had to eat.

A few days later, after more wandering and more hunger, they had received an even more than usually hostile reception from a woodcutter – he had threatened them with a fowling musket – and they had withdrawn to a glade close by to spend an uncomfortable night in the open. Mary had again woken them producing food, a dish of rabbit and cooked vegetables, but this time Edward had not been so obtuse. He had raged at Mary, calling her ungrateful, wicked, a whore, and dashed the plate out of her hands so it fell upended among the wet leaves on the ground. He had stamped his foot on it, breaking the plate, and ordered the shivering girl to fall down on her knees and repent her weakness. He had threatened her with God's wrath if she sinned again. Nellie and Helen Frances had waited in frozen silence, and George and Jenny had looked at their father with frightened, uncomprehending eyes. Only when Edward had exhausted himself, had Nellie calmly moved over to the weeping girl and put her arms around her. After a moment Helen Frances, avoiding the doctor's eyes, had knelt by the broken plate and begun carefully to retrieve the pieces of meat from among the leaves.

'You're not proposing to partake of these wages of sin?' Edward had cried, but the women ignored him, continuing with what they were doing.

'I think that you should apologise to Mary,' Nellie had muttered, after a while.

'For God's sake, woman, she's behaved like a whore. Have you not realised what she's just done?'

Nellie had contemplated him calmly. 'Mary's what she is, Edward,' she said. 'And she's feeding us, although she doesn't have to.'

Nellie often reflected back to that moment. It had marked for her the change in her husband's behaviour – his retreat into sullen melancholy, the awful passivity that had since overtaken him – and it had also marked for her the moment when she had quietly assumed leadership of their little group.

Nothing more had been said. Edward had sat on a tree-stump some distance off, while they silently ate what they could recover of the meal. Nellie had taken a portion to him, but he had shrugged her away. In the morning they had carried on with their journey.

So much had happened since – so many terrible things. There were many days during which even Mary was unable to produce food for them, and on the occasions when she could, nobody now said anything. They ate what she managed to provide, even Edward, although from that day on he had not spoken a word to her. One day she left them. They had long ago departed the confines of the Black Hills forests and were wandering through a plateau, pitted with deep gullies, in many of which were dwellings of the poor peasants who lived in those parts. They made their homes in caves dug out of the soft gully walls, surviving on the meagre crops they could gather from the terraces they had carved out of the steep slopes.

They soon learned to avoid these troglodyte villages, hiding where they could find shelter in the open countryside. They had not forgotten that they were foreigners and Christians in a country that had vowed to exterminate them. They saw no ostensible signs of Boxers, but in one village they came across a poster on a wall that contained xenophobic slogans and repeated the words of an unforgiving imperial decree. The villagers had looked at them with hostility, gathering in knots and pointing at them. They had left hurriedly, and some stones had been hurled in their direction. Afterwards they had kept their distance from human habitations. Without ever actually acknowledging it, they relied on Mary, who would slip away after they had all lain down to sleep. Usually there would be food of some kind waiting for them when they woke. Only one night she did not come back.

They had waited a day and a night tense with worry, hunger gnawing their bellies. On the second day they had made their way into the village. People stepped aside as they passed, and would not answer their questions. Finally they came upon an old woman, who pointed to one of the caves at the far end of the valley before hurrying away. There they had found Mary, cooking a meal at the hearth inside the cave. A grey-haired, wispily bearded peasant sat rigidly on a stool, ignoring them. Mary had burst into tears and told them that this man had agreed to keep her. She had had enough. She did not want to run any more. She was sorry. She asked for their forgiveness. Before they left, she had pressed on them several baskets of food.

The supply had lasted five days and after that they had no recourse but to beg for alms in the villages they came to, whatever the risks attached. Sometimes they found kindness and hospitality. Usually they were driven away with imprecations, and for one frightening night they were locked in a cell by the constable, but his wife had taken pity on Jenny and George and they were released in the morning.

Their emaciated bodies were covered with sores. Their feet were blistered in their rotting shoes. They were lice-ridden. Insect bites festered. It was a miracle that none of them had succumbed to illness more serious than diarrhoea, but at these high altitudes the heat was not oppressive in the daytime, and the nights were only cool. Nellie coaxed them on, rousing them in the morning when they did not wish to move, somehow finding the words to shame them into going on when they despaired.

Frankly she was amazed that Helen Frances had survived. There had been some very bad nights when she had screamed for her drugs, and the nights when she slept soundly were as bad: she would shout in her nightmares the names of Henry and Tom, or her hands would scrabble with the air as if she was fighting off an attacker. That she had a child growing in her belly was clearly visible now. Indeed, the swelling womb seemed to be sucking the life out of the rest of her body, like a hungry parasite demanding sustenance while its host starved. Nellie had become accustomed, when rationing out the portions of whatever meagre food they had been given, to loading Helen Frances's plate at the expense of her own; and sometimes her pity for her own suffering children meant that she took nothing for herself at all, splitting her whole portion between Helen Frances, Jenny and George. She was strong, she told herself, as she fought the pangs of hunger; she would survive, because her loved ones depended on her.

She felt a fierce, maternal love for Helen Frances. Sometimes, watching her thin frame waddling painfully along a stony path, realising that with the heavy weight in her belly every step she took was a matter of will, she felt through her sympathy a burning pride in her foster-daughter's courage. Breathing heavily, her face grimly set, Helen Frances never complained, though sometimes the strain became too much for her, and they all had to rest until she recovered the strength to go on again. On these occasions Edward would pace listlessly back and forth, or slump by himself on the side of the road. He was no longer the physician. Something had died in him. He would answer when spoken to, and once or twice Nellie observed him watching his two children with a tear in his eye, but for most of the time he remained wrapped in his own bitter thoughts. He avoided the others' company, never joining in their conversations round the evening fire. One day she noticed that his hair was nearly white, and his face had become worn like an old man's. Nellie could not think what was wrong with him – although it pained her to see him like this. Gradually – she was reluctant to admit it to herself even though she knew in her heart it was so – she had come to despise him. Sometimes she wondered if she had not come to despise all men, with their shallowness, their bravado, their violence, and their ultimate weakness.

Nellie would occasionally think of Helen Frances's irresponsible father, Frank. She doubted that the girl's deep reserves of will-power and her capacity for endurance were inherited from him. She wondered what sort of woman her mother had been – she knew that

Helen Frances had never known her, but Frank had always spoken of her as a goddess. Had Helen Frances inherited this extraordinary tenacity from her mother? Nellie knew that this was idle speculation. Wherever they came from, Helen Frances's qualities were her own. She also possessed something much more fundamental, something shared by every woman who had ever borne a child: the knowledge that another life was growing inside her. Nellie had seen her pregnancy as the cause of her weakness, the slow draining of her strength on top of the malnutrition that threatened them. Perhaps she should be thankful that Helen Frances was pregnant. For all that had happened to her, she was a woman and a prospective mother, with all the instincts and fierce determination of any mother to protect the life of her child. Far from weakening her, it gave her the will to live.

One thing surprised Nellie. Not once since they had left the train had Helen Frances ever mentioned Henry Manners, although she would sometimes talk of Tom with fondness and even humour. Nellie knew that Helen Frances was aware that he was dead: on their first night around the campfire Edward had described to them the terrible scene he had come across in the Mandarin's compartment. She herself had been surprised when the extent of Manners's villainy had been revealed, and she had expected that Helen Frances would react to defend him, or give some other evidence of denial, or at least of sorrow – but the girl had merely listened with her head bowed, and had never spoken of the matter again. Well, she thought, perhaps it was for the best. As far as the world would need to know, Helen Frances's child could be Tom's. Perhaps it would be kind even to invent a marriage. Sadly she acknowledged that there was no one alive who could gainsay this now. If Tom had not died a martyr's death he would have done the right thing. She was sure of that. Of the two men in Helen Frances's life, the scales of Providence had clearly fallen on the side of the most worthy, and Henry Manners, at the end of his miserable existence, had merely shown what a beast he was. It was sad – she had come to like him, even admire him, but his final treachery had been unforgivable. It was nevertheless remarkable that Helen Frances had put the memory of him so easily behind her . . .

What was she thinking? Nellie roused herself. Daydreaming by the pool, when the evening would soon be advancing and she had to return with water to her thirsty family! If she did not return quickly the social consequences of Helen Frances's pregnancy would be academic. As it was, she feared that the girl would not survive many more days. Even the miracle of finding this water might not be enough to save her.

Her tired body was reluctant to leave the cool spring, but she forced herself to sit up and fill the goatskin. Poor darlings, she thought. Jenny and George must be going mad with thirst. Well, she would reach them shortly. She had enough water in the skin to last them for today. And tomorrow she would bring them here. Perhaps George really would find a way to trap one of the marmots – the little white furry animals that inhabited these wastes and had first charmed, then later annoyed them as they stuck their whiskered heads over the ridges, always just too far out of reach to catch. A vision of hot meat stew suddenly overwhelmed her. She closed her eyes. Enough. She would go mad. She leaned down and picked up the goatskin, and took two steps, dragging it behind her. And froze.

The late-afternoon sun was throwing shadows over the grass, but the shadow she saw in front of her, in dark, precise clarity, was not projected by any natural phenomenon of hillside or cloud. Thinking that she was dreaming she turned, and was dazzled for a moment by the sun, but unmistakably, in front of the fiery ball, stood the silhouette of a man. He was of short, squat build and was sitting on a small pony. He was holding another horse on a rein. A shotgun hung over his shoulder, he had a fur hat at a rakish angle on his head, and he was wearing a tunic with wide skirts that came to the top of his boots. As her eyes adjusted to the glare, she saw that he was smiling at her.

Something in his kind expression put her immediately at ease.

For the children, the months they stayed with Orkhon Baatar remained in their memories as a golden period in their lives. Each morning, when the small hole at the top of the *ger*, the felt tent in which they all slept, began to pale with the dawn light, they would wake to see the comforting figure of Sarantuya, Orkhon Baatar's plump wife, feeding dried cakes of animal dung into the stove. Orkhon Baatar himself would have been up long beforehand, stepping quietly over the sleeping bodies to release his sheep from their pens and tend the horses. By the time the wooden door opened and his wrinkled, humorous face reappeared, greeting the waking family with a merry laugh and as often as not producing from behind his back a rabbit or a partridge he had just shot, the stove would be alight and the tea kettle on top of it beginning to boil. They would eat their breakfast, huddled in a ring round the stove. Orkhon Baatar would take his proud position on the one patterned carpet the family possessed and pass round the bowls full of curdled whey, which he would pour out from a copper jug. He knew how eager George and Jenny would be to get away, and he would tease them, inventing excuses as to why they should delay, feigning tiredness or a sore stomach, or discussing the weather with his wife in such interminable detail that the children would be fidgeting with irritation – but he always knew when their patience was getting exhausted, and then his eyes would twinkle, and his mouth would open in a smile revealing his jagged teeth, and he would ask, in his broken Chinese, if there was anyone here who would be willing to help him find his sheep today. That would be the signal for George and Jenny to leap to their feet, and rush out of the *ger* into the bright sunshine. (In their memories it never rained and every day was glorious.)

Soon they would have saddled and be sitting astride two of his short-legged ponies, following him at breakneck speed down the sloping valley to where his sheep were grazing on a hill. He would turn round occasionally to smile at them, his shotgun bouncing on his back. They always tried to overtake him, and he would deliberately slow down his horse, until they had nearly caught up with him, and when they were near he would howl like a wolf and, leaning forward in his saddle, gallop away to the bottom of the hill, wagging his finger at them when they caught up.

For the next hour as Orkhon Baatar checked his animals, the children would lie on the grass, inventing names for the shapes of the big clouds that rolled in the sky above them. Orkhon Baatar had taught George how to catch a grasshopper, and tie a piece of string round its leg so it would chirp in circles around him, but Jenny did not enjoy that game and she was happier making necklaces with flowers. When Orkhon Baatar returned he would squat in the grass beside them and, smiling, ask them what they wanted to do today. Sometimes they went down to the riverbank, where Orkhon Baatar would retrieve a dead mouse from the folds of his coat and tie it to a length of twine. This was the bait for the savage *taimen*, the huge salmon with teeth that protruded from its tongue and could grow in size to nearly five feet in length. While Jenny watched, Orkhon Baatar and George would wade into the river to seek a bush under which one of these monsters might be hiding. If ever they caught one it would give them a fight, which might last for half an hour, but when it was landed, Orkhon Baatar would always throw it back. It was unlucky to kill a fish, he told them. When people died their souls would go into the river and take the form of a fish. He would look solemnly at them as he said this, but then he would laugh so they never knew if he was being serious or not.

On other days they would just ride out as far as the fancy took them. A favourite destination was a rocky outcrop that rose mysteriously out of the grasslands about six miles away from Orkhon Baatar's camp. There was a cairn of stones on its slope, and always when they reached it Orkhon Baatar would dismount and lead them in a circle round the cairn three times before he was satisfied. Before they left they each had to search for a stone to place on it. Orkhon Baatar told them the first time they had come here that this was a holy mountain. He recounted to them the legend of the warrior who had fled with all that remained of his slain king's treasure after a terrible battle in which his master had been defeated. He had buried the treasure somewhere on these slopes and no one knew exactly where – for by the time he had finished his pursuers had overtaken him. There were too many to fight so he had galloped his horse to the top of the outcrop and, as his enemies surrounded him, he had spurred his animal over the cliff. He had been blown by the wind into the sky where he hid among the clouds, and was never seen again, so the secret of the king's treasure had always been preserved. George wanted to look for the gold, but Orkhon Baatar had told him that that would be a great sin. No Mongolian ever dug into the earth, he said, for the earth was alive and would feel the wound. He made them promise solemnly that they would never seek for the treasure, which would only bring evil upon them if they found it. After they had promised, he had winked at them and, laughing, led them to the summit of the rock from which the warrior had jumped. They had stood with the wind flapping their clothes, gazing in awe at the rolling grasslands, which stretched in every direction as far as the eye could see.

They would eat dried meat for lunch, which Orkhon Baatar kept in his woven saddlebag, and afterwards wind their way slowly home. The afternoon was a time for learning. Orkhon Baatar would teach them how to catch a running pony, galloping beside it and dropping round its neck a loop at the end of a long pole. He taught them how to herd the sheep in the evening back to their byres, and told them why they should gather the dung that the animals left behind. The sheep, he explained to them, provided every necessity of life. Their wool was used for clothing, and felt to make the *ger*; the milk provided them with sustenance in the form of yogurt or whey; the meat served for feasts. And the dried dung provided fuel for the fire. The most terrible thing, he said, was a cold winter, when sometimes a herdsman could not save his animals from perishing in the snow. Yet if the sheep died, it spelled famine for the family. If there was no dung for the fire how could they keep themselves warm? Let alone eat. No, the shepherd protected his animals – that was his duty, but it was also in his self-interest, because his sheep also protected him. One day he showed them how to cut the ringworm out of a sheep's stomach. They had been disgusted and nervous at first, but Orkhon Baatar told them that by doing this they were making the animals more comfortable and preserving them from harm. Every life was sacred, he said, and if they expected an animal to serve them, they in turn had a sacred duty to look after the animal. When it came to killing an animal a man should also show respect. To show them, he brought out a young sheep from the byre. It had a hurt foot and Sarantuya had asked him to prepare it for their supper: it had been a long time since they had tasted freshly killed lamb. They watched as Orkhon Baatar gently laid the sheep on its side. He pulled out his knife, cut a quick incision in its belly, reached his arm fully inside and squeezed its heart. With a mild bleat it died. He pulled out his arm and smiled. 'You see?' he said. 'She died painlessly, and none of her precious blood was spilled on the ground. Next time you will do it. I will teach you.' But George and Jenny had shaken their heads and run away. Of course, after a while, they did learn to do this, and many other things, which Orkhon Baatar taught them, before the golden days of summer passed into autumn, and they felt the first cold winds blowing through the steppes.

For Nellie and Helen Frances these were also days of calm and healing. They found comfort in the many domestic chores, whether it was cooking, or washing, or milking the ewes. They had rapidly become friends with the good-natured Sarantuya, who had welcomed them as sisters. Although at first they shared no common language – Sarantuya, unlike her husband, spoke no Chinese – they had quickly established a means of communication with her, using gestures of their hands and expressions of their faces, and sometimes they would draw pictures in the sand, laughing together as they tried to interpret each other's meaning. Over time, both women learned a few words and phrases of Mongolian, and could conduct rudimentary conversations with Sarantuya. They discovered that she was a thoughtful woman who, like her husband, had a practical wisdom as well as deep wells of earthy humour.

They also had their daily routine. They particularly enjoyed the walk after breakfast to the riverbank, where they filled the copper pitchers with water and once a week washed their clothes. These were always occasions for gossip and jokes. Sarantuya was nothing if not forthright and had no embarrassment about asking them the most personal questions, and they responded in kind. Sarantuya took a proprietorial pride in the advancement of Helen Frances's pregnancy. She would often rub her hand over the growing belly, sometimes putting her ear to it to see if she could detect any signs of movement. On the first occasion when she had felt the kick of the child within, she had given a great squeal of delight, clapping her hands, and hugging Helen Frances to her broad bosom. And for some time after she had rocked on her heels, clasping Helen Frances's hands in hers, and making clucking noises as tears of joy ran down her smiling cheeks. Within days she had decided that Helen Frances would bear a girl. She ran her hands over the womb, emphasising its round shape. Then she drew a figure of a woman in the sand with a more pointed belly, and followed it with a picture of a baby with an enormous penis and testicles. Then she crossed out both pictures, replacing them with a picture of a baby girl, and pointed at Helen Frances, smiling broadly. Nellie and Helen Frances gathered that a round belly denoted a girl, a pointed belly a boy, and now that this had been explained, the three giggled happily.

Once Nellie asked Sarantuya, again using a mixture of language and pictures, whether Orkhon Baatar and Sarantuya had children, and where they were. Sarantuya had smiled sadly, pointed at her own belly and indicated, with a swipe of her hand, that she was barren. Nellie and Helen Frances could not hide their concern, and embarrassment, but Sarantuya had taken their hands and made them understand that they should not be sad: this was something both she and her husband had accepted. Then she had pointed at the hill where, far away, Nellie's children and Orkhon Baatar were romping with the horses. 'Orkhon Baatar,' she said, thumping her heart. 'Jay-nee. Zhoorj. Like his own children. Orkhon Baatar's children. He very happy have Jay-nee, Zhoorj,' and she had smiled, with only a hint of a tear in her soft brown eyes. Nellie had a sudden glimpse of the tragedy that lay behind Orkhon Baatar and Sarantuya's simple life together, and she understood what might have been one of the reasons why they had been welcomed so warmly into this household. Impulsively she had embraced Sarantuya, and afterwards, if it was possible, she had felt even closer to her.

One subject that Sarantuya never asked about was Nellie's relationship with her husband. Indeed, they hardly ever spoke of Airton at all. Occasionally they would see him wandering, with bowed shoulders, over the hills. He kept to himself, joining them for their evening meal, where he sat, hunched and silent, waiting for Orkhon Baatar to pour out his bowl of *nermel*, the sour spirit made from distilled mare's milk in which he nightly sought oblivion. Some nights Orkhon Baatar would drink with him, matching him bowl for bowl, although neither spoke. There was an almost tender expression in Orkhon Baatar's eyes on these occasions as he observed the doctor succumbing quietly to his stupor. The liquor never seemed to affect Orkhon Baatar. On other nights, when he did not feel like drinking, he just left the pitcher for the doctor. Airton would sit with his back to the wicker frame of the *ger*, drinking steadily, while Orkhon Baatar entertained the others with rambling, humorous stories, or strummed his *er-hu*, or sang, full-chested, his rumbling, melancholy nomad songs.

Orkhon Baatar fascinated Helen Frances.

His had been the first face she had seen when she had woken from unconsciousness. She remembered the eyes, so warm, so understanding. They projected such peace, inspired such trust. She had thought at first that she had died, and that the face hanging over hers must be that of a devil or an angel. There was certainly something devilish about the features, the downturned mouth, the jagged teeth, the wispy moustache, the moonlike face cracked into wrinkles like a toad skin. It was illuminated by firelight, and shadows flickered over its yellow surface. She had never seen a face like it. It was alien, hardly human – but the eyes . . . The eyes were wise, as she imagined an angel's eyes might be; at least they were the eyes of a good man, and instinctively she had known that she was safe with him. She had felt his hand as he laid it on her forehead. It was warm, a bit leathery, but surprisingly gentle. The eyes above her closed, and the hanging firelit face became still, trance-like. She heard words in a language she could not understand, a deep, rumbling incantation, which must have come from the man's throat because his lips hardly appeared to move. After a while she had felt the hand on her forehead become hot, burning but not uncomfortable. She felt waves of peace and contentment flow through her body, and soon after she had slipped into a dreamless sleep. When she had woken again she had found herself in this *ger*, sleepy still and hungry, but there was a delicious languor in her every limb, and she had a strong sense of life within her, within her womb. She heard familiar voices, George's then Jenny's squealing excitedly, 'Come. Come. She's awake. She's awake.' And then Nellie was leaning over her, smiling, and over Nellie's shoulder she had seen the same strange man, standing bashfully by the door.

Nellie had told her the story of how she had ridden with Orkhon Baatar from the spring, as the evening light slanted over the hills. The little party, which she had left in the afternoon, were in their last extremities of hunger and thirst. Dr Airton had been kneeling listlessly by the embers of their fire, his arms around his sleeping children's shoulders. Nellie said that she had never seen such despair written on a man's face. He had hardly recognised her and did not seem to know what the goatskin was that she was offering him. It had taken Nellie several alarming moments to wake her children, but they recovered quickly enough after they had drunk the life-giving water. Nothing she could do would wake Helen Frances, though she squeezed water on her lips and shook her fragile shoulders. Finally she had realised, with horror, that Helen Frances had already slipped into the coma that preceded death. Her pulse had been so weak that Nellie could hardly feel it. All this time, Orkhon Baatar had remained on his horse, observing her.

She had screamed at her husband to do something, but the doctor had turned a blank face in her direction, and bowed his head. Desperately, she had turned her agonised face towards the

Mongolian who had brought her here. His sudden arrival had itself been a miracle. Could he perform another? He had stepped off his horse, and walked unhurriedly towards her. Kneeling beside Helen Frances's body, he had bent his head to her breast, listening for her heartbeat, then moved his nose close to her face, as if sniffing for breath. He had laid his hand on her belly, and looked up at Nellie as if for confirmation. 'Yes, yes, she's pregnant,' Nellie had screamed. 'But what of it? She's dying. Dying.' Orkhon Baatar had nodded. He muttered something, that sounded like the Chinese for 'Return.' Then, he had jumped into his saddle and, whipping his horse with his reins, galloped off into the dusk.

Nellie said that she had known at that moment what it was to be abandoned.

Orkhon Baatar had returned, however, not long afterwards. First he had reached into his saddlebag for a cloth bundle, which contained meat. This he gave to Nellie, gesturing to her that she should give it to the doctor and her children. Then he had efficiently relit their fire, and boiled water in a copper bowl. Taking from the folds of his coat what looked like strands of grass mixed with wild flowers, he crumbled them in his hands and dropped them into the bowl. Leaving time for whatever concoction he was making to infuse, he took the goatskin and knelt by Helen Frances, dripping a little water into her mouth. Then, to Nellie's surprise, he began to massage the prone body, all the time mumbling what sounded like prayers or incantations into her ear. He laid the bowl beside her head, lifted Helen Frances gently into a lolling position, raised the bowl to her nostrils and looked intently into her face as he did so to see if there was any sign of revival. After a moment he put it down again and renewed his massage and the incantations. When the mixture in the bowl had cooled, he soaked a cloth with it and dripped it carefully into Helen Frances's mouth. Then he massaged her again.

Nellie sat by the fire, watching him in utter despair – but she was too weak to protest that what he appeared to be doing was useless, hocus-pocus, or worse. After a while despite herself, she had sunk into slumber. She woke when Orkhon Baatar shook her shoulder. The sky was already pink with dawn. He was smiling. He took her hand, led her to where Helen Frances lay and gestured to her to feel the pulse. It was faint, but stronger than it had been the night before.

They had ridden through most of the morning, the doctor with the two children on one horse, Orkhon Baatar on the other, with Helen Frances drooped over his knees and Nellie holding on behind him. They had moved at a walk, threading between the folds of the hills. Just after noon they had arrived at Orkhon Baatar's *ger*. They had not realised how close they had been all these last days of wandering to the wide riverbed by which Orkhon Baatar was camped.

Orkhon Baatar had tended Helen Frances himself for two days, sitting patiently by her body, massaging her, feeding her with his herb teas, muttering his prayers. Presumably he slept, but the others never saw him do so. On the third day she had woken, and after a week she had been strong enough to walk.

Of course, her recovery had not been immediate. It took weeks before even a diet of yoghurt and heavy mutton broth could fill out her flesh into anything that resembled her former self. And as her body grew stronger, her nightmares returned, and with them her cravings, her hunger for the drug that she knew she could never find in these wilds. Nellie tried her best to comfort her, but felt powerless as she saw Helen Frances sinking day by day into deeper apathy and despair. Orkhon Baatar had watched her closely but he did nothing.

One evening, however, after a particularly bad bout of nightmare and restless sleep, he had woken her. He took her hand and gestured to her to follow him outside. A full moon floated high in a sky of bright stars, illuminating the ground over which they walked. He led her down the hill to the riverbank, and there he bade her sit down. From his belt he produced a pouch and gave her what appeared to be a dried mushroom, which he gestured to her to put into her mouth. She did so, noticing that he was doing the same. It tasted acrid but she forced it down her throat. They sat for a long while, listening to the sound of the rushing white water of the stream. As she sat there the noise appeared to become louder, and the hills around them to take on a stark clarity as if she was seeing them in daylight. Her head had never seemed so clear, and she felt a lightness in her body, a weightlessness. Suddenly she noticed an extraordinary sensation: she was floating above the ground. Amazingly, Orkhon Baatar also appeared to be floating. There was a merry expression in his eyes as he smiled affectionately across the short gap that separated them. Reaching across he grasped her hand, and the two rose into the air together – but that couldn't be because on the ground below them she could clearly see their own two bodies sitting facing each other. Was it some part of her consciousness that was floating above her own body, she wondered. Yet she could feel every sensation in the limbs of this incorporeal self, and the floating Orkhon Baatar also seemed real. She could feel the leathery grasp of his hand. He was laughing and pointing upwards at the stars, which seemed to be rushing closer towards them. They mounted higher and higher, and then, at a signal from Orkhon Baatar, plunged down again into the waters of the river, and she felt the strong current pulling her she knew not where . . .

She never mentioned that strange journey to the others. Indeed, when she woke in her bed next morning she wondered if it had been a dream – but it had not seemed like a dream and, unlike a dream, she could remember everything that had happened to her. Orkhon Baatar had travelled with her over continents, back in time and into her past. She had seen her childhood self, clattering delightfully along English country roads in the dogcart with her father. She had hovered above the liner where Tom and she were costumed in their fancy dress for the ship's ball. Resisting slightly, she had allowed Orkhon Baatar to pull her away from this pleasant memory, and he brought her to China, and here again she observed herself with Tom on a train, and then with Henry – with Henry in the Palace of Heavenly Pleasure. It was the day on which he had first given her opium and she had smoked it to impress him, although he had warned her not to do it. She wanted to fly down and snatch the pipe from her hands, but Orkhon Baatar had shaken his head. Later, she had seen herself in the dispensary of the mission injecting herself with morphine, and she had cried a little, but Orkhon Baatar had forced her to watch. She pleaded with him not to take her further, but he had shaken his head sadly, drawing her inexorably to Shishan and the execution ground, and then, despite her struggles – she knew what was coming next – to the room in the brothel where she watched herself being raped . . .

Mercifully that had been the end of that part of the journey. In a moment they had left the scene of horror. She found herself walking with Orkhon Baatar over the Mongolian grasslands. It was such a fine day that it was impossible to be dispirited. Great banks of white cloud towered above them and the country stretched for miles around. Orkhon Baatar began to talk to her as he walked beside her, his arms folded behind his back. He told her about the seasons, he told her where were the best pasturelands. She spotted a fox and they followed it to its lair. Inside were its three little cubs, their big eyes looking up at her endearingly. Orkhon Baatar pointed. A stag with great antlers was standing on the brow of a hill. Immediately they were by its side, running along beside it, whooping with exhilaration. He pointed at a floating speck in the sky. They flew with the eagles and the hawks. They sat by the banks of a wide, flowing river, which Orkhon Baatar said had the same name as his own. It was the sacred river to all Mongolians. By its banks the great Genghis had built his city. He invited her to swim in it. He took her clothes and she stepped into the water. She became conscious of another who was swimming beside her. She thought that Orkhon Baatar must have followed her in, but the face laughing at her side in the water was Henry's. His blue eyes were smiling and his teeth flashed in his sunburned face. He had splashed her and she had splashed him back, and then he had taken her in his arms and kissed her passionately, and she found herself responding, feeling only joy as he entered her, conscious of the life, which they had created together, forming in her womb.

They had sunk under the surface of the water after making love and followed the fishes as they darted through the reeds. Gradually the current took them onwards. After a while she realised that it was no longer Henry's hand she was holding. Somehow Orkhon Baatar had replaced him. His long hair drifted behind him, and his warm eyes reflected an enormous sympathy. She realised that he knew she felt an overwhelming sadness that Henry had gone. It seemed he could read all her thoughts. They floated to the surface and drifted under the glittering stars . . .

She understood, of course, that the mushroom had been a drug, and that these had been visions – but she was certain, despite that, that Orkhon Baatar had somehow been with her physically in her dream, travelling with her, protecting her from harm. She could not understand it but she knew it was so, and she believed that there had been a purpose to this vision, although she could not work out immediately what it was. Next day at breakfast when Orkhon Baatar had passed her the bowl of whey she had thanked him, putting a significant meaning into the platitudinous words, but he had only winked at her, and continued to serve. He had never spoken to her about it afterwards. He treated her with the same affectionate respect as he had before – but strangely, from that day forward, she began to feel well again. Nellie noticed it and commented. Also, her cravings disappeared, and her sleep was now rarely troubled by nightmares.

Much later, when she had a better understanding of the language, she asked Sarantuya if her husband was a shaman. Magic man was the word she used. Sarantuya laughed. 'To me my husband is always magical,' she answered coyly.

'But is he?' Helen Frances persisted. 'Is he a shaman? Can he do magic?'

Sarantuya only smiled, giving her a sly look out of the corner of her eyes. 'He is certainly wise,' she said, 'and a healer – as perhaps you know better than I. But I do not think that a simple shepherd can be a magic man.' And she had roared with laughter. That evening and for a few days afterwards, Sarantuya took a delight in calling her husband 'magic man' when she addressed him, but she was careful to preserve Helen Frances's face by keeping the reasons for the joke to themselves.

So the summer passed. The autumn made little difference to their lives. Orkhon Baatar had thick furs for them all, and a life in the open had made them inured to cold. They missed the hot sunny days of relaxation, but there were other pleasures. Orkhon Baatar excited the children with the prospect of going out to hunt wolves when the snows came and, to prepare them, each afternoon he coached them in firing his musket, grinning with delight when they hit their target, wagging his head and hooting when they missed. When he was satisfied that they could handle the gun, he rode off with them into the grasslands, and they took turns to fire at the marmots.

By the time the first snows came, dusting the hills in a thin coating of powder, Helen Frances's pregnancy was reaching an advanced stage. Sarantuya clucked over her and forbade her to accompany them to the river – not that they dawdled there long, these days. The weather was biting cold, especially if there was a strong wind. Helen Frances was quite content to lie in the *ger*.

She began to feel birth pangs on the day that George killed his first fox. He had bounded into the *ger* in the late afternoon, shouting that he had his own fox skin and Orkhon Baatar had promised to make a hat out of it for him. He was disappointed that no one else paid him any attention. His mother and Sarantuya were kneeling beside Helen Frances's mattress, exchanging worried glances, and Helen Frances herself was groaning in pain. It was too early for the waters to break: she was not due for another month, at least. This was certainly a cause for some alarm, although neither Nellie nor Sarantuya was panicking. They had prepared the kettle and were ready to fill the bowls with boiling water when the time came; clean cloths were laid out to hand, and with one Nellie was wiping the sweat from Helen Frances's straining brow.

Occasionally she would pass a withering glance at her husband, who was in his usual position by the wall of the *ger*, sullenly hugging his knees. She had asked for his help and he had refused, saying that Nellie and the Mongolian woman were quite capable of doing a simple piece of midwifery without his assistance, and what did she need him for, anyway, since she was clearly wearing the trousers now?

Orkhon Baatar and Jenny appeared a while later, having seen to the horses. Orkhon Baatar silently apprised himself of the situation, then he, too, sat by the wall next to the doctor, ready to help if he was needed. George and Jenny peered over their mother's shoulder until, irritated, she shooed them away. So they, too, sat down beside Orkhon Baatar, who winked at them, and held their hands.

He squeezed them tightly when the screams began.

'Heave, girl, heave,' shouted Nellie, encouragingly. 'My poor darling, my poor darling,' she whispered, in the pauses between the spasms. 'You'll be fine, you'll see,' but Helen Frances's eyes were rolling wildly in her agony, and her breath was coming in deep pants and no amount of wet towels on her forehead could soothe her pain.

The hours went by.

The screaming continued.

Nellie moved to where her husband was sitting. 'Edward,' she said quietly, 'it's not coming out. Will you help?'

Airton merely turned his head away. A tear was running down his cheek.

'You know you're being pathetic,' said Nellie. 'We need you now. Please help. I beg you.'

Airton kept his face turned to the wall.

Orkhon Baatar was looking up at her quizzically.

'Oh, explain to him, Jenny,' she said. 'I haven't the Chinese. Tell him the baby won't come out by itself. I think she needs a Caesarian. You know what that is? Good. Can he help? Does he know how to do one?'

Orkhon Baatar listened carefully to Jenny's translation. His eyes widened. He nodded questioningly at Airton. 'Is this not something the doctor should be able to do?' he asked.

'Look at him,' said Nellie flatly. She turned back to help Sarantuya, who was trying to hold down Helen Frances's shoulders as she vainly heaved again.

They had never seen Orkhon Baatar angry, but they saw it now. After Nellie had left him he had sat for a moment where he was, his face smouldering. Suddenly he leaped to his feet and stood above the doctor, bunching his fists. He reached for Airton's collar and jerked him to his feet. With his free hand he slapped the doctor hard on the cheek, and then, with the back of his hand, he slapped him again. Airton blinked at him, in amazement more than pain.

Orkhon Baatar pushed him back against the wall of the *ger*. In a quick motion he snapped his knife out of his belt. Airton's eyes widened in alarm. Orkhon Baatar pulled up the doctor's right arm and slapped the haft of the knife into his hand, closing his fingers on it. Then, his eyes blazing, he pointed at Helen Frances.

'I – I can't,' whispered the doctor. 'I haven't the confidence any more.'

Orkhon Baatar slapped him.

'Please don't make me do this,' he moaned.

Orkhon Baatar slapped him again. He pulled him by the back of the collar and propelled him forward, staggering, in the direction of the women, who were watching open-mouthed in astonishment.

'This – this is a hunting knife,' whispered Airton, staring at the weapon in his hand.

'You'll have to make do,' said Nellie. 'I'm sure it's sharp enough, but you'd better sterilise it in the fire.'

'What – what have I become?' It was a moan of anguish.

'I really don't know what you've become, Edward,' said Nellie, taking his arm. 'To me you're still my husband, and a doctor. Do try to behave like one. There's more than one life to save, and we need you now.'

Orkhon Baatar, still angry, would have stood over him to make sure he performed the operation, but Sarantuya gently pulled him back. In matters like this she had the authority, and she could see, from the way that the strange foreign man was examining his patient, that he knew what he was doing.

Without any other anaesthetic to hand Helen Frances had been made to drink a pitcher of *nermel*. At two in the morning, she was delivered safely of a baby girl.

When he had stitched up the wound, and satisfied himself that Helen Frances was as well as she could be – he could think of no better salve for the pain she had undergone than the baby, which she was holding to her breast – Nellie took his hand and led him out of the *ger*. Together they slumped against the felt wall. Nellie wrapped round them the thick goat-hair blanket she had brought out with her. She snuggled against him. For a while they said nothing, looking up at the bright stars.

Then Nellie kissed him. 'You did well there, Edward. I'm proud of you,' she said.

Airton did not reply. Nellie felt the motion of his shoulders.

'Is it weeping you are, you silly man?' she said, squeezing him. 'There's no reason for weeping now.'

'I'm – so – ashamed,' he said, through his tears.

Nellie nodded, and smiled. 'Well, you have been behaving a little oddly for a while, my dear,' she said. 'There's no denying that, but we've all been through terrible times, and you made up for it tonight.'

'I – can't forgive myself,' he said.

'Oh, we've all behaved badly at times,' she said. 'I know I've made mistakes. I'm not always as strong as I appear, you know.'

He did not reply. She shook his knee. 'We're together, Edward. We survived. All of us. We survived. And we're safe here, with these kind people. Don't you just know that there's a Providence out there among those beautiful stars that is continuing to take care of us? Be thankful. Don't be so glum.'

'It's Manners,' he said quietly.

'Manners?' she repeated, startled. 'What's he got to do with anything all of a sudden?'

'I believe that I misjudged him,' said the doctor hoarsely. 'I convinced myself that he was a murderer – that he'd killed the Mandarin because he wanted his gold.'

'So? That's what he did, didn't he, the beast?'

'I'm not sure now,' said the doctor, an agonised expression on his face. 'He told me when he left the engine cab that he was going to the Mandarin's compartment to save the Mandarin, to save us – and in my hatred of him I did not believe him.'

'Well, he was a liar. We know that.' She paused, looking at him with a puzzled expression on her face. 'Edward, why are you going on about Mr Manners?'

'But don't you see? You yourself told me. The shots you heard in the compartment were separated by a long interval. You said there was a single shot, followed much, much later by others. I don't believe it could have been Manners who fired that first shot. He was with me in the cab. He told me that Chamberlain Jin was an enemy. You see, I believe it was probably Chamberlain Jin who murdered the Mandarin, and therefore what Manners told me was the truth.'

Nellie was silent for a while. 'I see,' she said. 'You think that we've maligned a brave man?'

'I do,' whispered the doctor, staring into the valley. 'God help me for what I've done.'

'It's – unfortunate that we thought ill of him, Edward.' Nellie picked her words carefully. 'We'll – we'll tell Helen Frances in due course, naturally. Yes, that would be right and proper. In fact, it would be better if she could think well of her little girl's father. But I don't see for the life of me why you are torturing yourself about this. There's nothing you could have done to change what happened. Mr Manners is dead. He was killed.'

'He wasn't,' whispered the doctor, his eyes still staring. 'He was alive when I found him. Severely wounded, but alive.'

'He was what?' Now it was Nellie's turn to stare. 'You told me – you told all of us – that he was dead.'

'I lied to you,' said Airton flatly. 'Oh, God,' he choked, 'what have I done?' He banged his head with his hand. 'It was my hatred of him,' he said, as Nellie stared at him in horror. 'My anger. I wanted him dead. I wanted him to suffer for all the crimes I thought he had committed.'

'Edward,' Nellie whispered, 'are you telling me that you deliberately abandoned a wounded man on the train? You left him to be found alive by his enemies?'

'Yes,' he said weakly. 'I betrayed the Hippocratic oath. I left a man to die.'

'Oh, Edward,' she whispered. 'So that's what made you so withdrawn these months . . .' She sat with her back against the wall, gazing at the stars, but she no longer saw them.

'You see?' said her husband. 'I can never be forgiven for this, can I?'

'I don't know,' she whispered, her eyes staring. 'I don't know.'

His body began to shake with sobs. He made inarticulate cries as he wept. After a while she put her arm around him, and stroked his brow. He wept in her arms, while she stared rigidly into the darkness.

A shooting star flashed like a knife across the sky.

'Edward,' she said, turning to look at him. Her voice was as icy as the night. 'We must never – ever – breathe a word of this to Helen Frances.'

Over the next few days there was much fussing over Helen Frances and the infant. It was Nellie who had to take over the household chores because Sarantuya was besotted by the baby, rocking and cooing to her for hours. Helen Frances smiled contentedly from her mattress. She was still very weak. Nellie collected the water, prepared the food and cooked – but she had a helper in her husband. In fact, during those first few days Airton hardly left her side, except occasionally to examine Helen Frances and little Catherine, which was the name Helen Frances had chosen for her. When they were not busy, he and Nellie would go for long walks together in the snow. Sometimes George and Jenny accompanied them.

Orkhon Baatar and Sarantuya welcomed his new participation in the household with their usual warmth. It was as if his months of silence had never been. At first Airton reacted to the respect, if not reverence, they showed him with some confusion. Nobody would have recognised in this shy, humble man the smug, comfortable patriarch who had once presided over the mission at Shishan.

Of course, it had taken him time to adjust to the new circumstances, and to regain a degree of self-confidence. Orkhon Baatar had decided early on to take him in hand. While as a healer he might have shied away from such matters as midwifery, he had an unerring ability to detect a spiritual wound. For him it was as practical a matter as a case of ringworm in his sheep, requiring the same levels of patience and psychology as he would use in training a young colt.

The night after the birth, Orkhon Baatar had poured out the *nermel* as usual for the doctor, but Airton had tried to push away the bowl. Orkhon Baatar would not have it. He insisted that the doctor drink with him, and again he matched him bowl for bowl. Only this time it was Orkhon Baatar who became happily, deliriously drunk. He rocked to his feet, pulling his arms out of the sleeves of his coat, and sang one of his deep-throated songs. He forgot the words half-way through, and began to giggle. He pulled the doctor to his feet, embraced him and, still holding him, began to dance. Airton was embarrassed, but everyone laughed and clapped, and after a short time he got into the stamping rhythm. Orkhon Baatar picked up the pitcher and replenished the bowls. It did not take long for the doctor to become as drunk and merry as he. Before the evening finished, he had demonstrated a Highland reel and, tears flowing down his face, had serenaded Nellie with 'My Love Is Like A Red, Red Rose.' She had cuffed him gently, and called him a 'foolish, foolish man' before she kissed him. Orkhon Baatar, red-faced, swayed with his arms round Sarantuya's shoulders, sighing with pleasure.

One morning he insisted that the doctor accompany him and the children on their morning ride. He would not take no for an answer. He pushed the doctor's arms into the heavy sheepskin, and slapped the fur hat on top of his head, then dragged him, protesting, out of the *ger*. He heaved Airton into the saddle of the waiting pony and, when he was astride, cracked its rump with his own reins. Side by side, they galloped up the valley. Orkhon Baatar kept a watchful eye as Airton bounced on the bolting beast, sometimes reaching out a steadying hand, but he did not slow the pace. The children followed behind, as comfortable on these Mongolian ponies now as if they themselves had been bred in the grasslands.

There was heavy snow on the pastures. Orkhon Baatar slowed to a trot as they reached the top of the hill. He appeared to be looking for something, shading his eyes with his hand to ward off the sun's glare. The others peered in the same direction but all they could see was a uniform whiteness that stretched to the horizon, broken only by a rocky outcrop or two, and some clumps of trees on the leeside of a hill. Orkhon Baatar whooped and leaned forward in his saddle. His horse shot forward and, with no idea where he was going, the others followed.

At the bottom of a small hill, Orkhon Baatar jumped off his pony and, leaving it to graze on the tufts of grass that protruded from the snow, he gestured for the others also to dismount. He put his fingers to his lips to indicate silence, and proceeded cautiously to climb the hill. Airton followed nervously, panting with exertion. At the ridge, Orkhon Baatar flapped his hand signalling to them to keep their heads down. Very slowly he peered over the edge. He turned, his eyes shining, his jagged teeth revealed in a delighted smile. He put his finger again to his lips, then crooked it, indicating that the doctor should move up beside him. Not knowing what to expect, Airton lifted his head over the brow.

Below him, hardly twenty feet away, a large herd of reindeer was grazing against the background of the snow. It was the most beautiful sight he had seen in his life.

A fortnight after that the Russians came.

It was a darkening November evening, and Orkhon Baatar and the children had just finished feeding the sheep in the byre. It had been a dull, overcast day. There had been a heavy fall of snow the night before. They had not gone riding. The children had watched as Orkhon Baatar stretched the hide of the wolf, which George had shot two days before. It had been a glorious hunt and for two nights they had regaled the women with stories of their prowess.

Jenny saw them first, a straggling column of about twenty mounted soldiers who were making their way slowly down the riverbank. When they arrived at the *ger*, all of them, except Helen Frances and her baby, were waiting outside.

The young lieutenant in command revealed none of the surprise he undoubtedly felt to find a family of foreigners in a Mongol *ger*. He dismounted elegantly and saluted, then introduced himself as Lieutenant Panin, commanding a company of Don Cossacks. He spoke good English. There was only a trace of an accent.

Even Nellie, however, stepped backwards as he approached. The healthy, well-fed soldiers might have been aliens from another world.

Lieutenant Panin waited patiently, his eyebrows cocked, a kind smile on his round face. 'You are?' he asked politely.

'I'm sorry, I'm forgetting my manners,' she said, after a while. 'Your arrival is a bit of a surprise.'

The lieutenant nodded his head, a gleam of humour in his eyes. 'May I say likewise, madame?' he murmured engagingly. 'Your presence here, I mean.'

'We are the Airton family, from Shishan,' she said slowly. 'We are accompanied by another, Miss Helen Frances Delamere – Mrs Cabot, I mean. She's in the *ger*. She's just been delivered of a child. This is – this is Orkhon Baatar's *ger*.'

Lieutenant Panin bowed. 'Mrs Airton,' he acknowledged. 'If I may say so, you are a long way from Shishan.'

'We – we came here when the Boxers . . .' She could not finish.

'I understand,' said the lieutenant. 'Of course, it is well known what happened in Shishan. I had not realised that there had been any survivors of that atrocity.' He appeared to consider. 'Mrs Airton,' he said, 'if Mr Orkhon Baatar will allow us, I would like my men to camp here. We will not trespass on his hospitality. We are well provisioned. I would be honoured if you and your family will dine with me tonight. Perhaps I can acquaint you with what has been happening in the world, since your . . . since your . . .' He smiled. 'I congratulate you all on your miraculous escape. You must have a remarkable story to tell.'

'Lieutenant Panin,' Nellie called after him hesitantly, as he turned to give an order to his men, 'the Boxers? Are they . . . ?'

'Yes, madame,' said the lieutenant. 'They are defeated. An Allied army now occupies Peking.'

Sarantuya wept and hugged the baby, reluctant to hand her to her waiting mother. Helen Frances's eyes brimmed with tears and, indeed, there were tears on all their faces.

'I don't want to go,' cried George. 'I want to stay with Orkhon Baatar.'

He twisted his hand out of his father's grip and ran to where the Mongolian was standing. Orkhon Baatar picked him up and hugged him. 'Zhoorj. Zhoorj,' he said. 'You are a hunter and must be brave. If you do not go with your father and mother I will be worried for them. They need you to look after them.

You will return when you are older, and we will hunt wolves again.'

He lifted the boy on to his pony. 'This is yours now,' he said. 'It is my gift to you. When you ride him you will remember me, perhaps?'

It was true. Orkhon Baatar had refused to take the money, which Lieutenant Panin had offered him for the children's ponies, though he had reluctantly accepted a generous sum for the other horses, and for the old pony-cart in which Helen Frances would travel with her child.

The Airtons embraced their hosts for the last time. Helen Frances sobbed when she came to hug Orkhon Baatar goodbye. Her body shook in his arms. Airton had to lead her gently away. Nellie was the last to take farewell of Orkhon Baatar. She took his leathery hands in hers. 'The thanks we owe you are . . . I don't know how to begin . . .'

Orkhon Baatar hugged her gently. 'It is you who should be named Baatar, Nay-li. The Brave One,' he said. 'I will always remember you. And your husband is a good man,' he continued, 'worthy of respect. I regret that I was not able completely to heal the wound in his heart. With time . . .'

'Yes,' said Nellie, sniffing away a tear. 'Goodbye, dear Orkhon Baatar.'

'Goodbye, Nay-li Baatar.' He smiled.

Lieutenant Panin, who had been waiting patiently, judged that it was time. He gave the order to move, and the column began its slow progress south.

As they wound through the valleys, they saw, for a long time, a horseman keeping pace with them on the brow of the hills that sloped up from the riverbank they were following. Above them, great black clouds were rolling through the pale winter sky. On the horizon they could see approaching grey curtains of snow. The horseman reared his horse and appeared to wave his hat, then the cloud cover descended and he disappeared. Within moments, wet, silent snowflakes had begun to fall.

Chapter Twenty-one

Mother is dead. I have no home. The foreign soldiers hunt
and kill us.
Uncle says I must hide with Lao Tian and his bandits in
the forest.

The Legation was a ruin. After nearly two months of siege its
outlying buildings were burned-out shells. Only the residence
of Sir Claude and Lady MacDonald at the centre of the compound
retained anything of its former appearance. At least it still possessed
its walls and roof, though nobody looking at it now would have
guessed that this had once been the palace of Manchu nobility.

Its elegant veranda and filigreed windows were hidden under
sandbags. The now-deserted machine-gun emplacement above the
curling eaves was a reminder that, for fifty-five days, this had
been the command post for the defenders of the Legations. The
Chancellery on the other side of the courtyard still bore scars of
shellfire, revealing through a gaping hole in the wall not a neat
array of desks but beds and mattresses from when it had been used
as a barracks, dormitory and hospital.

The courtyard was littered with mementoes of the strange days
when the diplomatic community, their wives and dependants, had
huddled there for safety at the height of battle. They had sweltered
in the heat, stinking like animals, revolted by the dwindling diet
of mule, and often frightened when the firing from the walls
intensified; yet for all that – except on days when the gunfire
had been exceptionally heavy – they had conducted themselves
as if they had gathered for a picnic, gossiping maliciously over
their games of picquet, nibbling luxuries from the embassy larder,
organising concert recitals, and jealously guarding their respective
status and dignity, ready to snub, if necessary, any second secretary's
wife who sported a prettier sun hat or parasol. It had been that sort
of siege. The detritus in the courtyard told the story; on one side, by
the remains of the ginkgo tree, were piled ammunition boxes, and a
commissary cart leaning on one wheel; on the other side the redoubt

was made of the minister's stacked library books. Empty champagne bottles rolled in the sand among bully-beef tins; the ribbon of a lady's abandoned bonnet fluttered in the breeze, tangled with a stack of Lee Enfield rifles. On a small stool by the big embassy bell, which had rallied the defenders every morning for roll-call, and where Sir Claude MacDonald had made the direst public announcements when it looked as though all was lost, there rested an ancient gramophone and a pile of records, whose labels recalled the world of music-hall and opera.

It had been nearly a month now since that glorious mid-August day when an advance guard of Sikhs had penetrated the Water Gate of the old city walls thus signalling the end of the siege, but the Legation had remained as it was. It was as if those rescued were resisting a return to normality, basking still in reflections of their own heroism, relishing the *élan* and insouciance that they were sure they had each displayed when pitted against the might and terror of the imperial armies. Tidying the courtyard would have been tantamount to sweeping away their now glorious memories, cheapening their new image of themselves as warriors and survivors. Even those diplomats who had put on their old work suits wore them with a swagger these days, retaining pistols in their holsters and covering their heads with enormous bush hats as they chewed rough cheroots. It would be some time to come before Lady MacDonald would be entertaining the representatives of the powers again to a *Mikado*-esque ball in her once elegant garden.

For all that, the Legation was functioning. First and second secretaries moved purposefully between the tents they had converted to makeshift offices, carrying telegrams and memoranda for the minister to sign. From the direction of the small lawn behind the minister's residence could occasionally be heard the comforting click of croquet mallets or the murmur of ladies' conversation. Not even the aftermath of battle could quite take away the overlay of English calm.

The city outside the walls simmered with tension. Any visitor used to the noisy turbulence of a Chinese community would have been startled, first, by the unusual silence, and then by the singular absence of Chinese. The cowed population remained indoors. The few who ventured out scurried about their business with bowed heads and downcast eyes, as if seeking invisibility. They had reason to fear. Few homes had escaped the looting that had followed the lifting of the siege, and the occupying army, having tasted the spoils of victory, was by no means replete. Particularly to be feared were the spike-helmeted Germans and the fur-capped Russians, who had been known to stop and strip a man of his silk gown, leaving him like a naked coolie to crawl his way home. That is, if they did not press-gang him first into a work party, to rebuild a wall or to carry back to their lines the booty they had collected on their patrols. Not a woman dared venture into the street. Daughters and favourite concubines, those who had escaped molestation in the first house searches, hid in cellars or among the rafters.

The streets were left to the conquering armies. The tinny noise of their bands as they marched in their dress uniforms, hung hollowly in the air before it was swallowed again by the overwhelming silence. Each nation vied to outdo the others in martial pomp, as if by doing so they could lay claim to their own glorious role in the lifting of the siege; as usual, when Europeans contend together, they became caricatures of themselves. The superior British marched in spruce khaki to the growling bark of sergeant majors' unnecessary commands; the French *matelots* and Italian *bersaglieri* promenaded briskly, their elegant show somehow failing to disguise their underlying indiscipline, or to quench the humour that animated their faces; the Russians glowered; the Americans slouched; the Austrians paraded. The Germans – who had failed to arrive before the cessation of hostilities – were the most warlike of all: their caped *uhlans* clattered purposefully through the *hutongs*; their grenadiers growled with fixed bayonets at the slope, their heavy boots smashed down in unison as if beating the timing for a Wagnerian aria of revenge. Only the Japanese avoided these displays. Knots of their soldiers would observe these triumphant march-pasts with enigmatic passivity on their watchful faces, as they efficiently went about their tasks.

And in the heart of the Forbidden City where the generals had established their headquarters (the Empress Dowager had fled with all her court, pausing only to drown one of her nephew's concubines in a convenient well), Allied officers from every nation strolled among the looted palaces, smoking their pipes and wondering at the empty magnificence and the sterile symmetry of a heaven from which the godhead had departed.

It was a relief for the few British diplomats who still possessed any sensitivity or who believed in the essentially benevolent effect of the civilisation they thought they represented to return to their Legation and absorb themselves again in the comforting tedium of their work. For all that their Chancellery was now a tent, in the rattle of the telegraph they could hear the distant order of an *imperium* that they believed was above the tawdry triumphalism that hid the underlying reality of rapine, exemplary executions and greed which had consumed the city they had come to love, dishonouring the victors as much as it brought degradation to their victims. In their objective replies to the solemn queries from Westminster or Whitehall they could, for a while, sublimate their own sense of shame and failure as their fountain pens moved carefully through the measured phrases and Olympian platitudes of international diplomacy.

No amount of sensitivity or high ideals could protect Douglas Pritchett, however, from the darker reality. As the Legation's spymaster his business was to exploit the foibles of humanity. Sadly, he might have argued with himself that he was only compromising his ideals for the betterment of a noble cause, but his natural squeamishness had never prevented him doing his duty. He was, in any case, no longer the callow and bashful youth who had once sat next to Helen Frances Delamere at a garden party. The weeks with a rifle on the walls had hardened him. He had killed to avoid being killed, and not only in the heat of combat. More than one traitor had been discovered among the loyal Chinese staff who had remained behind in the Legation, and he had organised their despatch with quiet efficiency, after conducting the necessary interrogations first, again with a quiet efficiency. The memory of this sometimes disturbed his dreams, for no decent man, and Douglas Pritchett was a decent man, can ever entirely justify to his conscience all the demands of necessity. The puffiness round his eyes in the morning might have indicated to the observant the extent to which he was seeking oblivion in the bottle, but his work was not affected and there was no longer any trace of hesitancy in his manner. His kind smile and gentle demeanour he retained out of habit, but the cold, calculating eyes betokened nothing but ruthlessness. The Customs boys, who once had made him the butt of their teasing, had learned long ago to avoid him.

He was now seated at a table in the tent in the corner of the

compound that served as his office, observing patiently while a
man, whom he had once admired for being more ruthless than
he, leaned back in a canvas chair, his plastered leg stretched out
on a stool in front of him, absentmindedly smoking a cheroot as
he contemplated a document Douglas Pritchett had laid before him.
He could observe the progress of the man's reading from the darkly
ringed eyes that flickered sardonically over the page. Pritchett knew
the contents of the document by heart: he had written it himself.

*Your lordship will have received the Consul's report from Newchwang
with the minister's comments. We see as encouraging the steps taken
to restore commerce in the region. Representatives of our major
trading houses with operations in the coastal cities have by now
largely returned from their enforced exile in Japan and we expect
that it will shortly be considered safe for their operations in the
hinterland to reopen . . .*

'Do I really have to read all this stuff about tradesmen?' drawled
the man, looking up at him.

'You shouldn't be reading any of it,' murmured Pritchett. 'As you
can see it is marked "Secret". It's going to Salisbury.'

'The PM himself. I'm that important, am I?' The man smiled,
revealing a glint of white teeth in his sunburned face. He continued
to read.

*As to the general political situation, there is little of comfort to add to
the memorandum which I sent to your lordship at the end of August.
The three provinces that constitute the area known as Manchuria are
now firmly in Russian hands. A military commission has established
itself in the old palace in Mukden. General Saboitisch theoretically
liaises with the Chinese civil powers – but Governor General Tseng
Chi, though formally reinstated in the city Yamen, has no effective
authority. Construction of the Russian railway between Harbin and
Port Arthur has resumed, and the Chinese railway linking Tientsin
and Mukden, with its branch lines beyond, is now under Russian
control. This effectual annexation is justified by the continuing 'state
of emergency'. Russian troops have occupied all the key cities in the
provinces, and their patrols have even been reported over the border
in Mongolia.*

Our reports indicate that the suppression of the 'Boxers' – really any local power group that stands in their way – has been effected with ruthless brutality. Exemplary executions of 'rebels' or 'bandits' (there seems to be little distinction) are the norm. We have heard of mass decapitations and hangings, and there have been incidents where so-called rebels have been tied to the mouths of field guns. These punishments have been accompanied by looting on a major scale, particularly when Cossack regiments have been involved. The local inhabitants are miserable and cowed. Any initial relief at the eradication of the Boxer menace has long been replaced by a sullen resentment of the depredations they continue to suffer at the hands of their 'liberators'. We have heard that many look back to the short occupation by the Japanese at the end of the 1895 war as a civilised period in comparison.

'I would be interested to know your definition of "civilised",' said the man. 'Mind you, the Nips have behaved well enough in the recent show. It's about time we treated them as grown-ups.'

'I believe I go on to make just that point in the next passage,' murmured Pritchett.

From my conversations with counterparts in the Japanese Legation it appears that they are for the moment taking 'the long-term view'. It is unlikely that they will wish to do anything overtly to break the alliance formed between the powers at the beginning of the Boxer crisis, or to raise any form of diplomatic protest. The bravery displayed by the Japanese marines during the embassy siege and the efficient conduct of their contingents among the relieving forces has earned them a deserved respect internationally. As long as restraint will win them points on the negotiating table

'Ah, yes, reparations,' said the man. 'We all have our hands in that particular pot, don't we?'

they are unlikely to do anything to jeopardise their new reputation as a mature power. While the alliance persists, the Russians have not been able to prevent the dispatch of a Japanese military liaison mission to Mukden. These officers will no doubt be apprising their government of the situation in Manchuria, and forming their own relations with the Chinese authorities. The Japanese troops who were mobilised on the Korean border during the crisis have not stood down after the relief of the Legations. Clearly at some time in the future they will seek to challenge Russian supremacy in this vital sphere of their interest. For the moment they are watching, and waiting, as are we.

Your lordship has made an elliptical reference to events that may or may not have taken place in Shishan before the Boxer uprising, and you remarked how embarrassing it would be for Her Majesty's Government if it were to be implicated in any unauthorised dealings between British and Japanese agents of any kind.

'We're getting to the nub of it now, are we?' The blue eyes glanced up from the page.

'Yes, this is the passage I would like you to look at with close attention,' said Pritchett.

I am clearly given to understand that the Japanese Government would be equally embarrassed, if not more so, if such hypothetical proceedings were to come to light.

'I bet they would,' grunted the man.

I might mention that recently I was informed by my counterpart in the Japanese Legation that a report has been formally filed to their War Office stating that a quantity of field guns, machine-guns, howitzers, and other armaments from their arsenal in Tientsin disappeared during the recent hostilities; there is a convincing explanation attached of how these were captured when their position was temporarily overrun by Chinese forces; indeed, this is the version of events likely to appear in the official war histories. You may also be interested to know that one of their erstwhile military attachés, Colonel Taro Hideyoshi, after having received a medal from his Emperor for his courageous conduct during the siege, has since been reassigned to a post on the imperial staff in Tokyo. If any papers or promissory notes existed in his possession, they were utterly destroyed when his quarters in the Japanese Legation were consumed by fire during the fighting. I am confident that Her Majesty's Government faces no danger of embarrassing revelations from the Japanese.

Your lordship will already have heard Russian reports that the Mandarin of Shishan is dead, apparently murdered by one of his underlings as he attempted to escape the city after a disagreement with his Boxer confederates. It is presumed that the motive for his murder was robbery. He had apparently been fleeing with a large quantity of gold, which has since disappeared. Most of his militia were killed during an encounter with the Boxers as they took flight. Their commander, Major Lin, who might have been involved in any gun-running transaction, had one really been proposed, is missing, presumed killed with his men. Had these men survived they would no doubt have been tried and condemned for their involvement in the unspeakable atrocities that occurred in that town – as you know, the whole foreign community was beheaded at the Mandarin's order. It would certainly have been embarrassing had it been proved that any purported agent of ours had ever had dealings with such criminals, so it is perhaps providential that they received their just deserts without the necessity of a public trial.

That leaves the matter of our own supposed agent.

'You end it there,' said the man, letting the pages drop on the table. 'Pity, I would have liked to have read your comments on "our supposed agent". Is he in line for an imperial decoration too?'

'I think not,' said Pritchett. 'In the circumstances.'

'So I'm to be thrown to the wolves, am I? It wouldn't be for the first time,' said Henry Manners.

'I'm hoping that we can manage things so that there aren't any wolves,' said Pritchett. 'As far as Her Majesty's Government is concerned you were working for the China railways. There shouldn't be anything to connect you with us in any way.'

'There is the small matter of the arms cache and the Mandarin's gold,' said Manners. 'And my arrival in Tientsin did not exactly pass unnoticed.'

Pritchett managed a cold smile. The account of Henry Manners's escape from the notorious massacre in Shishan, driving a train with his Chinese concubines shovelling coal, was not only the stuff of legend but had become embroidered in every retelling.

'Yes, Sir Claude was not very pleased when he heard about that episode,' said Pritchett. 'Nor is he pleased, by the way, by the accounts of what you and your friend, B. L. Simpson of Customs, have been getting up to in the last few weeks. In our morning meeting he was discussing the reports of your "organised looting on a scale open only to those who can speak Chinese". I believe that those were his words. He was considering drawing up a warrant for your arrests. I persuaded him that in your case that may not be wise, but you might warn Simpson about it.'

'I'm obliged to you,' said Manners. 'Well, he's not changed, has he? Still the schoolmaster, I see.'

His eyes flickered towards a side table on which a large blue and white pot was standing. 'Bought that in the market, did you?' he asked. 'Or at one of the recent auctions? Looks very fine to me. Imperial quality, I would have said.'

Pritchett coughed, irritated by the red flush he felt on his cheeks. Quickly he changed the subject. 'How did you hurt your leg?'

'Bit of blazing building fell on it, actually. In a *hutong*. Don't worry, it wasn't in the British sector. May have a game leg for life, though.'

'I'm sorry to hear it. I hope that whatever you were doing when it happened was worth the while. You're quite healed from your other wound?'

'Pains me from time to time.'

'You're lucky to be alive.'

'If that bullet had gone an inch either way I'd be dead now. As it was, I bled rather a lot. Lucky that old muleteer of mine found me when I was unconscious and bound me up. Bloody good fellow, Lao Zhao. He deserves that pension I made you give him. If it hadn't been for him I couldn't possibly have got the train going.'

'It wasn't the women, then, who helped you?'

'The Mandarin's wives? You must be joking. They stayed at the back and wailed. No, it was Lao Zhao and Fan Yimei. They saved me. Amazing, really. They drove that train for two days, with me slipping in and out of unconsciousness on the tender.'

'Fan Yimei's the Major's concubine? Your – housekeeper now?'

'For the moment,' said Manners, looking him levelly in the eye.

'And she's to be trusted?'

'Without question,' said Manners, a hardness coming into his tone.

'I'm sorry. I had to ask. As you say, there is the matter of the gold, and the guns.'

'She knows nothing about the guns.'

'But she knows where the gold is?'

'Of course. She buried it. She and Lao Zhao. In fact, it was she who worked out what had to be done when she saw the first Russian patrol on the horizon. She got Lao Zhao to stop the train. They went off together and buried the boxes, and we steamed on again before the Russians could catch up with us. They left me sleeping all through this. Actually, I think I was delirious at the time.'

'So you don't know yourself where the gold is buried?'

'I didn't say that, Pritchett. I know exactly where the gold is buried. I also know where the guns are. And I can vouch for both Fan Yimei and Lao Zhao. They're entirely to be trusted.'

'I'm pleased to hear it,' said Pritchett, following a long pause. 'It's your problem now, after all, not mine.'

'Come again?' said Manners. 'Surely you're ultimately account-able for the return of the guns and gold.'

'Her Majesty's Government knows nothing of any guns or gold. I thought that would have been quite clear to you from that rather tortuous little memorandum of mine.' He paused, stroking the little moustache that he now sported. 'In fact,' he murmured, 'I'll go on to say that Her Majesty's Government does not really wish to know you, Manners, and would certainly not be interested to hear about any nefarious, and probably treasonous, activities you may or may not have been engaged in, entirely on your own account, while you were in Shishan. Sir Claude MacDonald himself may, in the past, have taken a personal interest in you in consideration of your titled father, but I fear that your notorious, not to say possibly criminal, activities have recently tried his patience, and I am formally warning you that your presence in our Legation is unlikely to be welcomed in the future.'

'Well, that was quite a speech,' murmured Manners. 'What *do* you want me to do with the guns and gold, then?'

'What guns? What gold?' There was a steely glint in Pritchett's eyes.

'I see,' said Manners. 'I'm being given my notice with a golden handshake? A very big handshake if I can find a way to retrieve it.'

Pritchett said nothing.

'I suppose that's very generous of you,' said Manners.

'There is a condition,' said Pritchett quietly.

'Silence?'

'Silence. Discretion. Nothing said now. Nothing said in the future. Nothing that might ever bring any embarrassment to Lord Salisbury or our government. I am proposing that my report will read that we did not have an agent in Shishan, and that we never at any time had dealings with the authorities there, either officially or unofficially, in any capacity whatsoever. Any actions of yours that may subsequently come to light were performed entirely in the spirit of free enterprise. Do you agree?'

'Do I agree to be bribed with a fortune to keep my silence? Of course I'll agree. You're giving me the means to become a very wealthy man.'

'I had assumed that you were already a wealthy man after your looting of the Forbidden City.'

Manners drummed the table with his fingers, his look abstracted. 'You realise,' he said, after a moment's thought, 'that Dr Airton suspected I was negotiating with the Mandarin?'

'Dr Airton's dead, isn't he?' said Pritchett icily. 'Did you not tell me that he and his family lost themselves in the Black Hills? We've made exhaustive enquiries with the Russians and nothing has been heard of them. If by a miracle they had survived I am sure that we would have known about it. It appears that no miracle happened.'

'You've – you've made such enquiries?' There was a sudden look of anxiety on Manners's face.

'Exhaustive enquiries,' said Pritchett. 'Why? Disappointed you can't get back at the old sawbones for going off and leaving you for dead?'

Manners ignored the jibe. 'You've heard nothing, you say?'

'I don't think that you have any need for worry in that quarter, Manners. Nobody could have survived in that wilderness. Your secret's quite . . .' He paused, noticing the haggard expression on Henry's face. 'I'm sorry,' he said. His voice had become extraordinarily gentle. 'I had forgotten. The Delamere girl. I had heard that you and she . . . I'm sorry. I quite misunderstood your concern. Forgive me . . . Yes, it's quite a shame . . .' He lapsed into silence. Then, 'Of course,' he added, 'we haven't given up all hope. Maybe in some outlying village, which the Russians have not yet reached . . . although, that said, there can't be many avenues that—'

'Write your damned memo,' said Henry, reaching for his crutches.

'Listen, if there's anything I can do . . .' said Pritchett, also rising.

Henry shook off his helping hand. He turned on his crutches by the door. 'Just keep searching. Find out what happened to them.'

He left.

Pritchett sat for a long while tapping his pen on the table. There was a thoughtful look on his face. That couldn't have been a tear in Manners's eye as he stood by the door? he asked himself. No, he must have been mistaken. Trick of the light. It would have been entirely out of character. Manners was a hard man, as he himself was learning to be. Emotionless. Practical. Corruptible – and therefore trustworthy. A man who understood and was bound by the rules of necessity.

He shook his head, and reached for the pages of his memorandum. After a moment of further thought, he began to write in his neat hand.

Summer passed into autumn. The officers had discovered the delights of the Western Hills, and their patrols threaded through the blazing red cover of the maples on the way to the temples they had commandeered.

More German forces arrived under the imposing General von Waldersee, who took over the high command from the avuncular General Chaffee. Denied any role in the actual destruction of the Yellow Peril, which the Kaiser had so thunderously denounced as he launched so publicly his latter-day crusade, his generals made sure that they were active after the event in punishing any Boxers on whom they could lay their hands – and since anyone on whom they did lay their hands was automatically considered to be a Boxer, the execution squads were kept busy for a good season. The inhabitants of Peking, who had decided it was safe again to come out of doors, returned to their homes, and waited for the furious flight of the Hohenzollern eagle to pass.

It did pass, as all things do.

The leaves began to fall. Autumn turned imperceptibly into winter. As cold winds blew through the strands of the willows drooping over the moat of the still occupied Forbidden City, embers of life revived among the frozen populace.

By the first snowfall in late November, the streets of Peking were back to their usual bustle. Haughty nobles being carried in their sedan chairs between their palaces thought it below their dignity to notice the foreign sentries who stood on the cold intersections of the Tatar City. Officials, who had returned to their offices in their various *yamens*, paused on their way home by the food stalls in Wangfujing or Hatamen to buy toffee apples for their concubines or children, and brushed shoulders with the red-faced corporals and sergeants from the occupying forces who were using their off-duty hours to explore the town. In the busy alleys of the Chinese City, which sprawled beyond the still ruined Qianmen gate, merchants discussed the price of silk in their now unboarded shops, and scholars might be seen peering over ancient scrolls in Liulichang, while others sought bargains among the many new curio shops that were suddenly flourishing and doing a roaring trade. In the chaos after the siege it had not only been the foreign soldiers who had indulged in looting: many Chinese fortunes had also been made. Few restaurant owners could remember a better season, and in the gambling halls and tea-houses sing-song girls were adapting themselves to a cruder, more exotic trade. There were, indeed, several new houses in the Chinese city that specialised in the entertainment of the 'lobsters', as the foreign soldiers were, not unaffectionately, called.

The Legation Quarter had not yet been restored to its former glory but gangs of coolies were toiling day and night to build even grander residences for the representatives of the foreign powers among the ruins of their old establishments. The litter of the siege had finally been removed from the British Legation and one night the windows of the Residence had blazed with light and music as Lady MacDonald launched her first ball. The only difference that anyone might have noticed between this ball and those that had preceded the siege was the greater preponderance of military uniforms on the glittering dance-floor. As usual, Monsieur and Madame Pichon from the French Legation had been the last to leave, and the American counsellor, Herbert Squiers, newly promoted from first secretary, and the journalist, George Morrison, had had a heated argument at the drinks table. Some things never changed.

The diplomats were, of course, very busy now. The acceptable old minister, Li Hung-chang, had returned to the *Tsungli Yamen* and was heading the interim government until terms could be agreed that might allow the Empress Dowager to return from exile in Shansi. The price for this, it was made clear, would be extremely high. Rumours were circulating that the indemnity, which would now certainly be imposed, would exceed a hundred million pounds sterling, not to mention further cessions of territory. The loud boys at the bar of the Hôtel de Pekin, headed by the now very wealthy B. L. Simpson, who had somehow managed to evade all warrants for his arrest, were vocal in their criticisms of the pusillanimity of the diplomatic representatives, declaring that if justice were to be done, the corrupt Ch'ing should be forced to pay out a sum ten times this amount. And the Empress Dowager, if she should be allowed to return at all, should be publicly horsewhipped in front of the Palace. B. L. Simpson had volunteered cheerfully to do the job himself.

Henry Manners hardly ever attended these gatherings. In fact, since his injury during the period of the lootings, he had hardly been seen out at all. At first the Customs boys had joked lewdly about his absence. It was well known that he had brought back with him a particularly beautiful sing-song girl from wherever he had escaped from in the north. He had been quite the hero of the hour then – but as time passed, as is the nature of these things, he had been forgotten.

It was believed that he lived in a house somewhere in the Chinese Quarter. Once B. L. Simpson and his gang, at the end of a drunken evening, had set off in rickshaws to find him. They had thrown stones over the wall and yelled insults, waking the whole neighbourhood, who feared that another round of looting might be beginning, but they had been greeted by an overwhelming silence from the courtyard of the house they had been told belonged to Henry Manners. The big wooden gate had remained closed, and after a while they had become bored and gone off to one of the new brothels.

Henry Manners kept himself to himself. If any of the Customs boys had managed to climb over that wall, they might have been surprised to find that their old comrade was not disporting himself lasciviously, as they thought, in the arms of his dusky beauty. He slept alone, and in the daytime he sat alone in a leather armchair, or on sunny days in a wheelchair in the courtyard, often with an unlit cheroot in his mouth and a vacant expression on his face. Occasionally Lao Zhao would come out and examine his leg. Sometimes he would say something to make Henry laugh, and then the tired blue eyes would flash with some of their old sardonic humour. Usually the two friends would sit in the yard in silence. Fan Yimei would bring them tea. In the evening she would sometimes prepare an opium pipe. The household would retire to bed early, and Henry would invariably rise late.

Lao Zhao and Fan Yimei would often discuss Ma Na Si Xiansheng's strange malaise – or, rather, Lao Zhao would proffer various explanations: Ma Na Si's wounds were not completely healed; he was waiting for something to happen; he was lying low, biding his time until the coast was clear for them to go back to Manchuria and collect the gold; he was hiding from the spies of the British Legation who would surely wish to follow him there; he was holding on until the Russian soldiers who roamed those parts should leave . . . Fan Yimei would listen in silence, watching him with her sad eyes. When he asked her for her opinion, she would silently shake her head. After a while, Lao Zhao would light his pipe, declaring: 'Well, to be sure. Ma Na Si knows what he's doing. You wait. You'll see.'

Fan Yimei never told him about the long conversations she had with Ma Na Si on those nights when he could not sleep, when he would walk across the courtyard to her room and sit softly on her bed, waiting for her to wake. The first time he had done this she had turned back the bedclothes and invited him to lie beside her, but he had only smiled and taken her hand. What he told her she kept to herself, never revealing her pain, pretending that she had never seen his tears. In the morning she would greet him with her usual sad smile.

On rare occasions, the Englishman, Pritchett, from the Legation, would call. He and Ma Na Si would sit together, talking quietly. He never stayed for very long. Fan Yimei hated him, she could not tell why: he always treated her with elaborate politeness, but his cold eyes never looked her directly in the face, and he seemed eager to get away. Usually, on the evenings after his visits, Ma Na Si would ask for the opium pipe.

One evening, towards the end of December, Pritchett visited at a much later time than his usual calls. He did not stay long with Ma Na Si, and left hurriedly to his waiting rickshaw. When she looked into Ma Na Si's room afterwards, she saw him sitting stiffly in his chair, looking intently but unseeingly at the wall. In his hand was a crumpled piece of paper, which appeared to be a telegram.

That night he visited her room and told her that Dr and Mrs Airton, their children and Helen Frances had been discovered by Russian soldiers in Mongolia. Helen Frances had given birth to a child. They had been brought by rail to Tientsin, and were expected to arrive in Peking any day.

By coincidence, on that very afternoon, the Airtons, with Helen Frances and baby Catherine, had called at the offices of the British vice consul in Tientsin. A waggish, insensitive man, with a good lunch inside him, he had remarked, in his arch manner, how pleased he was to meet a respectable family from Shishan; they were a marked improvement, he told them, on the last fugitive he had met from there. The Airtons had expressed some puzzlement at this remark, and he, laughing uproariously, had recounted the tale – one of the best in his repertoire – of how Henry Manners had arrived on the train. Or, rather, he started to tell the story – but he had to break off in mid-flow because the young widow, Mrs Cabot, suddenly turned deathly pale, rose to her feet, exclaimed loudly, staggered, and sat down again, pressing her fist to her mouth. Unfortunately in doing so her elbow brushed against a vase stand and one of the vice consul's best pieces, a rather fine statuette of Guanyin, shattered on the floor. It had all been very embarrassing, and extremely irritating, the official told his friends in the club that evening, but what could one expect from hysterical missionaries – female ones at that? He supposed that she had been shocked by his impropriety in mentioning Manners's concubines.

Chapter Twenty-two

I don't want to be a bandit. It's winter and the old people
need me.
Let the New Year bring rain.

Henry was leaning on his stick, half obscured by the potted plants that grew in profusion at the entrance to the tearoom of the Hôtel de Pekin. Inside, a *thé dansant* was in progress. A mournful-looking Hungarian violinist was playing a Strauss waltz. Accompanying him on the piano was a bejewelled matron whose eyes were closed in ecstasy as her fat fingers moved over the keys. Nobody was dancing. The deferential waiters in their long brown gowns moved softly between the tables, bearing silver teapots on trays or holding aloft pagodas with teacakes, sandwiches and scones. A swell of loud conversation, punctuated by brittle bursts of affected laughter, would occasionally drown the sound of the music altogether. The ladies were sporting fur hats and boas in the Petersburg fashion that was all the rage this winter season. It had been a long time since their men had assumed bush hats and khaki. The elegance of their frock-coats and tweeds would not have been out of place in any salon in Paris or Vienna.

Henry looked down at his shining oxfords – Lao Zhao had spent the whole morning polishing them to perfection. The creases of his trousers were immaculate, and the jacket of his recently tailored Harris suit hugged his trim waist, rising in neat lines to encase his broad shoulders. The rose, which Fan Yimei had placed in his lapel as he left his house, still emitted a faint scent, or perhaps that was the eau-de-Cologne, which he had patted self-consciously onto his chest and neck. In the gilded mirrors, that hung on either side of this *fin-de-sìecle* lobby, he could see his slightly elongated reflection. He was no less elegant than any of the other cosmopolitans who thronged this hall, but he observed critically the grey hairs that bordered his temples, the shadowy patches under his eyes, and the lines that had become ever more noticeably furrowed on his forehead.

A Belgian woman of the *demi-monde*, leaving the tearoom, glanced at him with approval, noticing as she passed how distinguished was this handsome man loitering like a tiger among the aspidistras. There was something that excited her imagination: the unmistakable look of experience on his face, the element of mystery, even danger, in his cool, cruel eyes; the presence of waiting energy ready to uncoil. She observed how he leaned upon a stick and wondered what adventure might have caused the injury to his leg.

Henry, however, was not aware of either her or her admiring glance. In his preoccupied, censorious state, he saw in the mirror's reflection only an ageing, haggard ruin of what he had once been. The pain in his leg, which forced him to hobble like an old man, diminished him in his present frame of mind to the status of a cripple. For the first time that he could ever recall, he lacked confidence in himself, and as he peered timidly through the pot plants into the tearoom, he suddenly knew that he had not the faintest idea of what he intended to do. Inching down his spine, like a trickle of cold water, was an entirely new sensation. It might have been fear.

He had seen them immediately when he first looked into the room. They were seated at a table in the furthest corner away from the piano, having tea with a couple to whom he had once been introduced long ago. He even remembered their names: Mr and Mrs Dawson. Horace and Euphemia Dawson; they were the Babbit and Brenner representatives in Peking. They worked for the company that had employed Helen Frances's father and Tom Cabot. They looked comfortable and prosperous, like all the other Peking swells who were gathered in the room. Horace Dawson sported three chins and a large gold watch-chain, and Euphemia was wearing a veiled hat decorated with a peacock's feather.

Dr Airton, Nellie and Helen Frances were sitting in a submissive row on the sofa, like country clients before a city bank manager; their clothes were as subdued as their countenances and they were listening intently to Mr Dawson, who seemed to be the only one speaking, although his wife would interject smiling remarks as she poured the tea, glancing with superior smugness at her husband, who would nod in approval and continue his flow. Occasionally he would wave his pudgy hand in the air to make a point. It was obvious to Henry that he was talking about money.

Not that he cared. He had eyes only for Helen Frances. She

was dressed in a sober green gown with a neat white collar, which modestly matched her pile of auburn hair. Her skin was darker than he remembered, and there was something different about her expression, a cool contemplativeness, a watchfulness, a sophistication, even, that he did not associate with the spontaneous girl of whom he had been dreaming these last weeks and months. For a moment he thought he was looking at a stranger. It was only when she smiled, at some inconsequential remark of Mr Dawson's, and he saw her green eyes flash with momentary humour – or might it have been scorn? – that his heart beat with an almost agonising pang of recognition. He leaned his head against the pillar, and closed his eyes while a kaleidoscope of memories tumbled in his mind, like a pack of cards spilling on a table. He was too far away from her to distinguish any sound, but he seemed to hear her peal of laughter, and he had a sudden clear vision of her turning her head, her red hair flying as she spurred on her horse, daring him to pursue. For a moment he was back in Shishan, and it was with a sense of dislocation that he returned to the reality of the Hôtel de Pekin, the hubbub of conversation and the strain of the violin.

When he looked back she was no longer a stranger to him. There was Helen Frances as he remembered her, only she had grown in stature since he last saw her. She had acquired the grace and maturity of a full-grown woman; and the image of her that flickered before his eyes – which, to his surprise and alarm, had blurred with tears – was more beautiful than he had ever seen before.

Ashamed of his weakness, he tore his gaze away from her. He focused on the quiet, white-haired man beside her, and felt a shock of sympathy. Airton had aged. There was an unfamiliar stillness about him, and he appeared to have shrunk in size. The eyes, which had always twinkled before, were rheumy and sad. He sat pathetically holding his teacup, which jittered slightly in his shaking hands.

Nellie was little altered, however. She sat erect on the sofa, dignified, composed, impressive as he had always remembered her. There were lines on her face, which had not been there before, a stretched quality to her skin, perhaps, and her hair had become distinctly grey – but her swan neck rose from her black dress, and her calm eyes observed the Dawsons with patience. She still looked magnificent, her integrity and serenity shining in this roomful of chattering people.

Henry tried to imagine the hardships they had undergone. Douglas Pritchett had told him something of what they had been through. He had a vision of Helen Frances, in hungry, pregnant state, staggering through the mountains and deserts. It was too painful to contemplate. Again, he closed his eyes. When he opened them, he saw the composed young woman who had once, unbelievably, been his lover, raise a teacup elegantly to her lips. He marvelled, awed by her poise, sensing the strength and courage that lay within her.

It was gradual, like the coming of night, but he became aware of his own unworthiness in comparison; and deep inside him he felt the fires of hope, which had impelled him to come here, begin to fade.

A terrible paralysis overcame him. The coward in him told him to slip away, to avoid the confrontation, but something fixed him to the spot. Like moths to a consuming fire, Henry's burning eyes were drawn to Helen Frances's beauty, yet it did not inflame him; instead, he felt a numbing chill in his veins. The more intensely he looked, the more inaccessible she seemed to become. He peered through the aspidistras in a sort of creeping terror. He felt like a drowning man sinking into fathomless depths, the light of everything for which he yearned fading in a murk of despair and self-contempt. The room captain, an imposing Chinese in a black gown, approached him to ask whether he wanted a table, but there was something in Henry's expression that obviously made him think better of it and, muttering an apology, he backed away.

As he watched, the party at the table made their preparations to move. Mr Dawson signed the chitty. Mrs Dawson leaned her face forward to be pecked. In a rustle of silk and platitude, they said their goodbyes. Henry backed deeper into the pot plants and they did not see him when, like two proud frigates, they passed him imperiously by. He remained hidden when the Airtons followed, Nellie and Helen Frances supporting the doctor by his arms.

She was passing only a few feet away from him. He could see the mole on her neck. He could even smell her scent. He felt an overpowering desire to throw himself forward, to embrace her and kiss her, or to prostrate himself at her feet begging her forgiveness – but he held back, hardly daring to breathe, his frantic eyes following her as she moved with the doctor towards the staircase. He heard her speak, that husky voice he remembered: 'I'm sure you'll be fine in the morning, Doctor. It can only be a chill.' He wanted to cry out after her, but he remained frozen where he was. In despair he saw the green hem of her dress sliding up the stairs. In a moment she would turn the corner and disappear.

It might have been only the habit of action – or, more likely a last stirring of pride, the inability of the gambler not to make one last throw – but whatever it was it impelled him forward. He leaned on his stick in the centre of the hall, staring after her wildly. Almost involuntarily he found himself calling out her name: 'Miss Delamere. Helen Frances.' His voice sounded unnaturally loud.

The trio on the staircase turned. The doctor's eyes widened in shock, and he slumped backwards, emitting what sounded like a whimper of fear. Nellie was quick to catch him, a severe expression on her face as she glanced down at Henry. Helen Frances let go of the doctor completely. She stood rigidly on the steps, her hands hanging by her side, frowning as she stared directly into Henry's imploring face. Her lips twitched as if she was about to say something. Her breast seemed to heave – then she hurriedly picked up her skirt, and turned back to the doctor. Taking him by the arm again she helped Nellie bring him to his feet, and in a moment they had all disappeared round the corner of the stairs.

Henry slumped against a pillar, the strength draining from his limbs.

'Mr Manners?' It was a questioning voice in a light Scottish brogue.

As if ascending from a well, he managed to focus, and saw Nellie looking at him with concern. She took him by the arm, steadying him. 'Oh dear, I fear you're not well,' she said. 'I'm sorry if we appeared rude just now, but my husband was not expecting to . . . Mr Manners, we have so much to discuss. Will you not have a cup of tea with me, for old time's sake?'

Like a patient under sedation he followed her into the tearoom, and sat where she told him to, in a leather armchair. Nellie ordered a pot of tea from the hovering waiter, before turning her clear eyes to face him directly. 'Mr Manners,' she said, 'I cannot tell you how thankful I am to see that you are alive and well. A man from the Legation, Mr Pritchett, came to see us this morning, and he told us a little – well, quite a lot, actually, more than he should have done perhaps – about the heroic, and . . . and patriotic work you were doing in Shishan. Do not worry. None of us will ever breathe a word about it to a soul – but I have to thank you, on behalf of all of us, for the sacrifices you have made on our behalf and for, well, saving our lives—'

She was interrupted by the waiter bringing the tea. By the time he left and the cups were poured, Nellie had become embarrassed, though Henry had said nothing.

'There I go,' she said, 'pouring it all out in a rush. You probably think I prepared this speech long beforehand. Well, I didn't, but I mean it sincerely. We owe you our lives, Mr Manners.' She paused, her expression a little agitated, but she forced herself to continue. Behind her, the violinist launched into a merry polka. Raising her voice only a fraction, she persevered: 'We also owe you something else, Mr Manners, though it shames me to say it. We owe you an apology. We – we misunderstood your motives, and then when you were wounded – on our behalf – my husb – we . . . we left you for dead.' Her voice cracked slightly on the last word, but she quickly controlled herself. 'It was a crime that will haunt us for the rest of our lives. We will have to live with that guilt, Mr Manners. Yes, it was unpardonable. I – I understand why at first you avoided us just now at the entrance to this tearoom . . . I saw you among the aspidistras – but even if you never choose to speak to any of us again, I would like you to hear just once how truly, truly sorry we are, and if, if you can ever find it in your heart to forgive . . .'

She stopped in astonishment, her cheeks flushed in confusion. Henry Manners had leaned back in the armchair and was laughing. 'I'm – I'm sorry, Mrs Airton,' Henry recovered himself, catching his breath. 'But – excuse me – it's just very, very funny. Ironic, really. You see . . .' There was a bitter look in his eyes. 'Don't you see? The reason I came here today was to ask for your forgiveness, for handling things so – so very badly.'

The polka finished and there was a polite round of clapping.

Nellie's face was still flushed. 'I – I'm not sure I understand you, Mr Manners.'

'Oh, Mrs Airton . . .' Henry took a deep breath. A waiter passed. Henry caught his arm and told him to bring him a brandy, a double brandy, and be quick about it. 'I'm sorry,' he muttered. 'I need something stronger than Darjeeling if I am to say this. I lack your inner strength,' he added, a trace of his old sarcasm returning to his voice.

Nellie stared at him in some perplexity.

'Before you honour me with any more apologies,' he continued, 'it might be better if you knew the end of my grubby little story.'

'Mr Manners, I—'

'Indulge me. I'm sure you've heard how we managed to get the train going again. You should have stayed with us, by the way. It would have spared you the terrible trials you underwent in the wilderness . . .' He raised his hand to stop Nellie interjecting. 'No, don't apologise again. You did what you thought was best in the circumstances. I understand – believe me, I do. I don't blame you, or Dr Airton. You had the children and Helen Frances to think about, and I looked done for. I *was* done for. You have nothing with which to reproach yourselves. Anyway, I deserved it.

'No, please don't interrupt, let me have my say. Your people talk about miracles. You might say it was a miracle that saved me. No, not one of your divine kinds of miracle. A very human miracle, consisting of courage, generosity, resourcefulness, and sheer grit on the part of two rather unlikely Chinese – Lao Zhao the muleteer and Fan Yimei the prostitute – who bound me up and somehow, God knows how, drove the train to safety.'

'A miracle can be a miracle for all that the agent is a human one,' murmured Nellie.

Henry's hard eyes rested momentarily on her face. 'You may be right at that,' he said. 'Anyway, I survived, though I shouldn't have. I didn't deserve to after everything I had done in Shishan. I hadn't really thought about it up to then. Those last few weeks in Shishan I'd been too busy being practical.' He repeated the word bitterly. 'Practical.'

'You were practical, Mr Manners. You were faced with some terrible decisions, but you did what had to be done to save our lives.' Nellie spoke gently.

'Oh, yes, I did what had to be done all right.' Henry laughed, draining the brandy that had been brought to him. 'Didn't I just? But you do have a rather overblown estimate of my character if you think I was there nobly saving lives. Didn't you say that Pritchett had told you? I was doing my bit for the greater glory of the British Empire, Mrs Airton.'

'Your duty, Mr Manners, you did your duty.'

'My duty! I should drink to that. Boy, bring me another brandy.

Yes, Mrs Airton, my duty. I thought a lot about my duty as I bounced on that coal tender, and lay strapped up in the bed of the military hospital afterwards. And it had a comforting ring. It certainly did. All those people killed – I didn't save everyone, did I, Mrs Airton? At that time I thought you and Helen Frances were dead as well. Failed there as well. Never mind. As you say, I'd done my duty. The guns were safe, and so was the gold. I could comfort myself that Her Majesty's Government would be proud of me.'

'This cynicism doesn't become you, Mr Manners.' She had to speak loudly above the polonaise.

'Ah,' said Henry, sipping his brandy. 'So Pritchett didn't tell you about the thirty pieces of silver I got for my pains, then? Well, he wouldn't, would he? That's top, top secret. Belongs in the cupboard with all of the rest of the Queen's dirty underwear.'

'Mr Manners!'

'Forgive me, Mrs Airton. I've become unused to polite company. Please forgive me. Sometimes my passion gets the better of me.'

'I still do not see why you are reproaching yourself. Terrible, terrible things happened – but you were not to blame.'

'Well, that's very generous of you to say so. I, on the other hand, think that I should have handled things much better. All those innocents executed. The nun. The Millwards. Tom. What happened to Helen Frances – oh, God, what happened to Helen Frances . . . I should never have . . . never have . . .'

'You're not God, Mr Manners,' said Nellie, reaching for his hand, but he pulled it away violently.

'On the contrary, Mrs Airton,' said Henry, in the quiet after the polonaise, 'I believe that I sold my soul to the Devil.'

'You poor, poor man,' breathed Nellie, and, slightly flustered, drank down her tea, which had gone cold on the table.

'You know, when I left the hospital,' continued Henry quietly, 'I became a madman. Yes, I think quite truly that I was mad. All I wanted was vengeance, to hit back. I should have allowed myself time to recuperate, but I didn't. I didn't mind the pain of my wound, which hadn't properly healed. Some other power was driving me. The Allied forces were marching on Peking then. God knows why they waited so long in Tientsin, but I was glad because I had my opportunity for revenge. I joined a company of scouts – well, free-enterprise marauders, to be more exact. We rode ahead of the troops and we killed, Mrs Airton, that's what we did, we killed. Probably quite indiscriminately, although we justified it at the time.'

'Mr Manners, you don't have to tell me this,' said Nellie.

'No, it wasn't very nice, and don't think I'm proud of myself. I'll spare you the details, except one. Every Boxer, every Chinese who came into my sights, or was pitted on the point of my sabre, had the same face. Do you know whose it was? It was Major Lin's, Mrs Airton.'

'That's horrific,' muttered Nellie, a chill running down her spine.

'Do you know? Even after the Legations were relieved I saw him, every time I went out. He was the beggar on the street corner. He was the merchant in a shop. He would have been that waiter over there,' he said.

Nellie gazed at him in alarm.

'I told you I was mad – or half mad. It didn't stop after we ended the siege. I came over the city walls with the American marines. There was quite a bit of fighting still to do. Yes, quite a lot more blood was spilled after that. Then I looted. I had some companions who were quite as mad as I was – and we were thorough, Mrs Airton, but you must understand that I was not interested in the loot. I wanted to destroy. I took a delight in the fear I saw on people's faces, Major Lin's face.'

'You poor, pathetic man,' said Nellie. 'Please don't go on.'

It was as if Manners had not heard her. 'One day, in one of the back *hutong*s, we burned a merchant's house. For no good reason, really. My companions were irritated because they hadn't found any gold or jade there. The merchant had been clever and hidden it, I suppose. Or he never had any. Anyway, we burned his house. I did my bit. We'd retired to the street, and were watching the flames through the mansion gate. We thought we'd cleared everyone out. We weren't murdering at that time, you see, although we did do other things. Yes, we did many other things ... Anyway, I was surprised to see a little girl come running out of one of the buildings, screaming in pain because her robe had caught fire. I don't for the life of me know why I did it, but I ran in and snuffed out the flames on her back with my jacket. It was as I was carrying her out – she was scared, but not badly hurt – that the burning gatehouse collapsed on me. The child was all right, but I – well, as you see, I've lost the use of this leg. Serves me right, I suppose you'll say. A few days after that, Pritchett called me into the Legation, paid me my thirty pieces of silver, and told me that my services would no longer be required. I've kept to myself since then. I don't believe I'm mad any more. It's rather worse, actually. I don't think I really like the prospect of going on living. Call it remorse, if you like. You missionary types should be quite pleased. Seems I've belatedly discovered a conscience. A rather full one, as it happens.'

'Oh, Mr Manners – can I call you Henry? I feel I know you that well. Oh, Henry, how my heart goes out to you.'

'I thank you, Mrs Airton. Nellie. Sincerely. I've always respected you. You don't judge people, as some do – but please don't feel sorry for me. I'm not one to be saved. There's no road to Damascus for the likes of me. I've rather dug my own pit, haven't I?'

'I won't insult you with a Christian platitude, but I don't believe you, Henry. I've seen the good in you, and the courage. Don't throw your life away. Vengeance is certainly not the answer.'

'No, it isn't. I think I've learned that. I – I did have a hope. One hope. No, never mind.' He reached for his brandy glass and saw it was empty. The *thé dansant* had ended. Although the afternoon crowd had by no means departed, waiters were already beginning to clear the emptied tables in preparation for the evening drinks session.

'A hope? You said you had a hope. Please tell me.'

Henry laughed bitterly. 'I suppose I've told you everything else. Why not? Although it's academic. I saw the look she gave me on the stairs. I thought that Helen Frances . . . I rather hoped Helen Frances might still . . .'

'Oh, Henry.' Nellie sighed.

'*Inshallah*,' said Henry. 'Well, I deserve no less.'

He reached into his breast pocket and, from behind his folded handkerchief, he pulled out a long cheroot. Nellie watched as he tried to disguise his agitation in the business of lighting the cigar.

'The baby?' he asked, blowing out a cloud of smoke. 'Rude of me not to ask earlier. The baby's fine, is she? I heard it was a girl. Does she have a name?'

'She *is* fine, Henry. A bonny wee lass. She's called Catherine.' Nellie paused. 'Catherine Cabot.'

'Cabot?' Henry's hand holding the cheroot froze momentarily.

His face smouldered with sudden anger. It took three furious puffs of his cheroot before he regained his composure, but his blue eyes glittered like ice. 'Cabot,' he repeated. 'Perhaps you'll be good enough to explain.'

'I suppose that I'm initially to blame,' said Nellie sadly. 'It was I who introduced Helen Frances to the Russian officer who rescued us as Mrs Cabot. Oh, I meant well. I was worried about the shame she might have to endure if it became known that she was an unmarried mother. So – so we invented a marriage.'

'How delicate of you,' said Henry, coldly. 'I see that you have the same capacity to be practical as I have. And Helen Frances was happy to go along with this lie?'

'I persuaded her. Edward and I persuaded her that it would be for her own good and that of the child. Yes, she agreed.' Weariness had crept over Nellie's face. 'At first it was a temporary subterfuge. We had no idea that the Russians would wire the British Legation, and that the British Legation would inform Mr Dawson at Babbit and Brenner, and that he in turn would inform Tom's parents in England. That's the problem with a lie. It takes on a life of its own. When we arrived in Peking it was already a—'

'A *fait accompli*,' said Henry. Suddenly he began to laugh – harshly at first, but Nellie was amazed to hear it turn into what sounded like genuine merriment. 'Well, well,' he said. 'Good old Tom. Scoring sixes from the grave!'

'Oh, Henry, how we've managed to hurt you,' murmured Nellie.

'I understand, Nellie. Believe me, I understand. You had two dead contenders to choose from – one of them certainly dead, the other, well, it would have been logical to assume that I'd succumbed to my wounds or been strung up by Major Lin, whichever happened first. No, I quite understand. You had a dead hero on one hand, a Christian gentleman, a martyr, and on the other, well, a dubious commodity at best. Call me a black sheep and leave it at that. Hardly a choice. I'm sure that the prospect of a Babbit and Brenner pension, and Tom's fat inheritance in Lincolnshire, never even occurred to you.'

'I suppose I deserve that,' said Nellie, dropping her head.

'Don't give it a moment's thought,' said Henry. 'You should be considering it now, even if you didn't at the time. It's good for

Catherine. She'll be a proper little heiress. And, by the way, how did your meeting with the Dawsons go this afternoon?'

'They were very generous,' muttered Nellie. 'Very kind.'

'Well, there you go,' said Henry. 'And so should I be going. You've done your duty, Nellie. Put me in the picture. With great tact, I might add. It must have been extremely painful for you. You won't see me again, but give my love to Mrs Cabot.' He ran a hand over his eyes. He might have been wiping away the emotion on his face, for when he moved the hand back to the armrest, Nellie saw that it was composed. When he spoke again, his voice had even lost its sarcasm. 'Know this, Nellie Airton, I bear no grudge against you or your husband. You behaved with nobility throughout, and Airton acted on the best of motives. As for me, I've reaped what I'd sown, and that's an end of it, but tell Helen Frances for me – tell Helen Frances . . .'

'Tell me what, Henry?' He heard the husky voice behind him. It was as if the paralysis that had struck him earlier among the aspidistras had returned with overpowering force. He could not move a muscle in his body. His heart was thumping, and his blood burned hot in his veins. He felt, coursing through his body simultaneously, conflicting emotions of elation, despair, hope, fear – above all, fear.

With a rustle of her skirt, Helen Frances sat down next to Nellie on the sofa. Nellie made a move to stand up, but Helen Frances put a hand on her knee. 'Don't feel that you have to go,' she said. Though her eyes were shining and her cheeks were a little flushed, her voice was calm, controlled.

'I'd better go, dear. Edward. The children,' murmured Nellie.

'Yes, the doctor is a little poorly,' said Helen Frances. 'It's only a cold, but he's feeling sorry for himself. He probably would like to see you. The children are fine, playing with the *amah*.'

'Mr Manners. Henry. I very much hope that we may meet again,' said Nellie, proffering her hand. 'You will visit us one day before we leave?'

Henry nodded automatically, his eyes still fixed on Helen Frances. He rose, shook the extended hand, and slumped back into his chair.

'Tell the *amah* I won't be long,' said Helen Frances. She watched Nellie thread her way gracefully through the tables. A waiter came up to where they were sitting. 'A chilled glass of muscatel, please,' she ordered, 'and another brandy for Mr Manners.'

'Well, Henry,' she asked softly, when the waiter had left, 'what were you going to ask Nellie to tell me?'

Henry felt that his tongue was frozen in his mouth.

'Was it perhaps that you loved me?' asked Helen Frances, her green eyes watching him solemnly. 'At one time I would have been overjoyed to hear those words from you.'

'And now?' It came out as a croak.

'Well, of course I'm still very pleased. Thank you,' she said to the waiter, as he put the glasses on the table.

'Pleased?' Henry managed.

'Yes, I'm flattered that you still remember me fondly,' said Helen Frances. 'Should I not be? I realise the expected response from a girl when a man says those words to her is to repeat them back to him – but I'm not sure that I can do that now.'

'I see,' said Henry.

'I certainly did love you,' she said, sipping her wine. 'I do still love the memory of our days together, and I regret nothing. No, nothing. And I'll always be grateful to you. You were – you once meant the whole of life to me.'

Did he imagine that small quiver of her brow as she said this? But her green eyes continued to observe him steadily.

'But not any more, apparently?'

'No,' she said. Again he saw the slight furrow of her brows. 'I – I think I'm over you now. Too much has happened. I'm sorry, Henry. This is difficult for me.'

Henry sighed. Helen Frances looked uncomfortable.

'I heard a little from Pritchett of the hardships you underwent,' he said, after a pause. 'It must have been a frightening experience.'

'Yes, it was terrible for a while,' she said, 'but – but there were good things too. The shepherd we stayed with. He was kind.'

'Pritchett said he was some kind of shaman.'

'He was a healer. Yes,' said Helen Frances. 'He – he helped us.'

'Yes, I've heard that some of these aboriginal types have the ability to tap into deep wells of wisdom,' said Henry. 'There's a lot that our clever scientists can't begin to understand.'

'Yes,' said Helen Frances. 'You're quite right.'

'Are we to sit here exchanging banalities?' asked Henry, after a

short silence. 'If it helps, I would like to tell you that I understand.
And I appreciate that you came downstairs to see me, and to tell
me to my face. You – you don't lack courage, Helen Frances.
Or generosity. I would have understood if you had avoided me
altogether after the terrible trials I inflicted on you. If I could have
found any other way, I would have sought to spare you. Please
believe that I did what I did only because I could think of no other
way. That you despise me now I accept . . .'

Helen Frances started. 'But I don't despise you, Henry,' she said.
'Why should I?'

'I treated you abominably,' he said.

'You were never anything but gentle with me. You honoured me
in the only way in which a man can honour a woman,' she said.
'And you saved my life, and that of my child – our child.'

'Honoured you, you say? I – I whored you,' whispered Henry. 'I
can never forgive myself.'

'Yes, you were even prepared to make that sacrifice,' she said.
'You were nobility throughout. I mean it.' She put the half-full
wine glass back on the table. 'Don't ever think of – the other,' she
continued, a look of pain pinching her features. She turned her head
away. 'It never happened,' she whispered. She closed her eyes. 'No,
it did happen. Of course it happened. It must have been terrible for
you who watched. Oh, Henry, how I feel for you – but for me, for
me . . .' She picked up the glass again and put it down untouched.
Her face twisted in perplexity as she tried to form her words. 'It
was a dream, Henry, a bad, bad dream. Like the opium dreams.
Not real. It didn't hurt me. At the end of the day, they didn't hurt
me. They couldn't hurt me. Not the real me. I've learned that now.
Oh, Henry,' she reached across and grasped his hands, 'you must
put that memory behind you too. It doesn't matter. Forgive them,
for only then will you be able to live with yourself.'

Henry slowly pulled his hands away from hers. 'What are you
saying? That I should forgive Major Lin?'

'Yes, yes, Major Lin, all of them,' she said urgently. 'I have.' She
reached for his hands again. 'Goodness, what a conversation to be
having in the tearoom of the Hôtel de Pekin.' She smiled.

Henry observed her coldly. 'I see that the Airtons' Christianity
has got to you,' he said.

Helen Frances laughed. 'You don't know how wrong you could

possibly be,' she said. 'Well,' she considered, 'maybe you're right in one way. I – I don't think I'm a Christian, not as they would like me to be, but maybe it all comes to the same thing.'

'I see,' said Henry. 'It's all dreams, then. Was I a bad dream too, one that you've managed to put behind you now?'

'There was never anything bad about you,' she said. 'Oh, God,' she cried suddenly, throwing herself back against the sofa, her self-control breaking down momentarily. The waiters' heads turned. 'I don't know, Henry. I don't know.' Her voice was shrill, piercing. Heads turned at other tables. 'What do you expect? You'll have to give me some time. I'm – I'm different now. I'm not the girl you knew.'

'I think that I can see that,' said Henry. He wanted to tell her that, in her passionate outburst, she was more beautiful than he had ever seen her, but the logic of this strange conversation somehow prevented him and the opportunity passed.

Helen Frances had recovered from her lapse into hysteria, but she spoke angrily. 'You can't just come back from the dead like this and expect to – expect to carry on where you left off. What was I to you, anyway, but a silly schoolgirl conquest? A diversion while you did whatever important things you were doing.'

'Is that what you really believe?'

'Yes.' Helen Frances glared at him defiantly, but immediately her shoulders slumped. 'No. Of course I don't believe that,' she whispered, 'but perhaps that's all I should have been to you. Why, Henry, why did you love me? What could you possibly have seen in me? Why did you give me so much?'

A look came into Henry's face, half smile, half surprise. His eyebrows lifted as his blue eyes observed her quizzically – and this appeared to infuriate her the more.

'Oh, come on, Henry, how much more stupidly or irresponsibly could I have behaved?' she demanded. 'I was like a child in a sweetshop, so greedy was I for you. Greedy for everything about you. The freedoms you opened up for me. The secret assignations. The love-making. The opium – even the opium. What a holiday I was having. Helen Frances goes to China and experiences it all – but that's all I was. A tourist, a silly tourist. I don't belong in your world. I never did. You intoxicated me, that's all – but I've sobered up now. By God, how I've sobered up. Talk about the School of Hard

Knocks. Anyway, I think I know who I am now. What I want. What I should have wanted all along.'

'And what's that?' asked Henry.

Helen Frances bowed her head. 'To be no one,' she said woodenly. 'To be ordinary. Just to be me. Ordinary, provincial me. Believe me, Henry, I wouldn't be a wife who could make you happy. You'd tire of me, I'd be a slow drain on your spirit, I'd pull you down into the depths – and I couldn't bear that.'

'I'd been rather counting on you to pull me up out of the depths,' murmured Henry. 'I'm not the hero and paragon you and Nellie make me out to be. I'm not much of anything, if truth be told. The idea of an ordinary life rather appeals.'

'There's nothing ordinary about you, Henry Manners. Nothing. Let me tell you something. When you died, and the doctor told us you did die, I felt nothing but relief. Relief, do you hear me? Because I knew I wouldn't have to go on loving you any more. Dr Airton thought he'd poisoned me against you with a whole lot of lies about how you had organised my rape, and that was why I didn't show any shock or horror when I heard you were dead – but that wasn't the reason. I never believed Airton. He just hated you because he envied you and you always showed him up – no, Airton's lies weren't the reason I didn't mourn you. It was relief for myself, Henry, sheer, sheer relief. With you gone, with that great, shining presence out of the sky, I felt that in my dim, dreary way, I might, just might, be able to get my life back again. And I had your child inside me, and that was enough. It would be my memory of you but it wouldn't be you. I felt I could manage loving the child, the baby. It wouldn't make any demands on me as you did—'

'You know you're talking rot, Helen Frances. Demands? What demands did I ever make on you?'

'None,' she said. 'None. That was the problem. You didn't need me. You kept saving my life every five minutes. How can a girl possibly be a wife to a man who keeps saving her life, in the most noble, noble way? Old Tom. He just went off and got himself martyred. You were so perfect you just martyred everyone else around you. Do you know? When I was on the floor being raped and you were tied to the bedpost, do you know what I thought you looked like? Christ, Henry. Christ on the Cross. I could see my own suffering in your eyes. And I hated you then,

I hated you. I hated you . . .' Her shoulders were shaking and she began to sob.

Henry reached into his pocket and passed her his handkerchief. 'Come on, old girl,' he said. 'Take this. You're – you're making a scene.'

The shaking subsided at last. She blew her nose noisily. This time he reached for her hands, and she allowed him to hold them.

'I got over you,' she whispered. 'I got over you. In the grasslands I had a dream about you. It was a beautiful dream. We made love and we said our farewells, and I was at peace.'

'Dreams again,' said Henry.

'Yes, Henry, dreams. Wasn't it – wasn't it somehow always a dream?'

'Not to me,' he said.

'I'm a mother now,' she said. 'I have somebody else to look after. Oh you should see Catherine, Henry. She's so, so beautiful, and little, and vulnerable.'

'I'd like to see her,' said Henry, and something perverse made him add, 'Tom Cabot's daughter.'

'That hurts you, doesn't it?' she said. 'But I should always have married Tom. It's his world I come from. The counties. That's the real me. I'm not decent and honourable and good like Tom was, but I could be. I want to be. Well, now I have the chance. I can at least pretend, and it won't really be acting. Deep down, deep down, that really is me. Dull. Provincial. It'd be an honest life – even though I'm getting there by a deception. But I know it would have been what Tom wanted. It won't be an exciting existence, not like yours – but I don't want excitement any more. I've had my holiday. My dream.'

'Catherine is not a dream, Helen Frances. I'm her father. For God's sake, I've never heard such madness in my life. You love me, so therefore you hate me – and you're going to be Tom's widow, because that's the real you. What is this, Helen Frances? I can't even follow you.'

Helen Frances frowned. 'Don't you think we owe something to Tom, Henry? We hurt him so badly.'

'To be frank, I don't. No, we don't owe him anything. To be crude, my dear, you made your bed with me. I'm living. He's dead. We love each other, for God's sake. Why can't we just accept that? Never mind the past. All right, call it a dream if you have to. But let's live the future together – because we can, you know.'

Helen Frances let go of Henry's hands, which she had been holding all this while. 'Oh, Henry,' she said. 'How I've hurt you. How bitter you've become.'

'Oh, I don't know,' he drawled, 'I think I've taken it rather well, all in all. It's not every man who would accept that his child has been given another man's name.' And as he said this, a voice inside him cried out at his own stupidity and wilfulness.

Helen Frances was shaking her head sadly. 'It's done now, Henry,' she said. 'Tom's parents are waiting to see their granddaughter. We're taking the train next week to Shanghai from where we'll catch the boat home. I've already agreed to accompany the Airtons, who are planning a long furlough in Scotland. You know they've got two children there. They say they'll come back to China. I – I don't know if I will.'

'But it's all a lie, Helen Frances. A damned lie. You never married Tom. It's not his child.'

'He said he would marry me. He said he would do the right thing. He would have married me, and become father to Catherine. Would you, Henry? Would you have married me?'

'Look at me,' he said, 'all fopped out in my best clothes. I came here today to propose to you. I still would, if you wanted me.'

'If only you had done so then,' she whispered. Her eyes had welled with tears. 'But it's all different now.'

'Why?' Henry's fists drummed the table and the glasses rattled. The waiters looked away. 'Why is it different?'

'Oh, Henry, I'm crying again and I wanted to be so brave. But it is. It just is.'

'That's not good enough,' said Henry. 'Why is it different?'

'Because I can't bear to be near anything any more that reminds me of that dreadful time in Shishan,' Helen Frances screamed. 'And you're part of it. You're all of it,' she sobbed. 'Oh, I loved you. I still do love you. You don't know how I sometimes long for you – but I'm different now. I'm different. I'm not that silly convent girl you once seduced. Not any more. Not any more.' She picked up a napkin and started fiercely dabbing her eyes. 'Look at me,' she said. 'I'm making a scene. There goes the reputation I've been so careful to cultivate as the respectable widow, Mrs Cabot.'

'Is that what it's all about?' said Henry softly. 'Reputation?'

'Yes,' she said. 'Partly.' She giggled through her tears. 'I wouldn't find any respectability married to you, would I?'

'No,' said Henry. 'I suppose you wouldn't.'

'Oh, come on, Henry. You're living with that prostitute, Fan Yimei. Not that I hold anything against her. I admire her. She's fine, and brave. But the whole town gossips about you two.'

'I suppose they do,' said Henry sadly.

'I don't care if you're sleeping with her. That's got nothing to do with my decision.'

'So it's a decision?' he asked gently. 'An irrevocable one?'

'I don't know. I don't know. Why are you pushing me? Oh, Henry, don't you see I need time? Away from you. Away from China. This terrible place. I've the means to be free now. I can be my own woman. Isn't that the modern thing to want to be? To be one's own woman. I have an adorable child. I'm a respectable widow. Yes, with money. More money than I could possibly need. God, Henry, I want air to breathe. Don't you understand that? You of all people?'

'Pick up your glass,' said Henry. 'Here. Here's to your freedom.' He clinked her wine glass with his brandy tumbler. 'I won't drink to your respectability, however, Mrs Cabot.'

'So you accept it?' she breathed. 'My going, I mean?'

'No,' he said. 'I think it's mad.'

'You could – you could come and woo me in Lincolnshire,' she said.

'Somehow I don't think that would work,' he said. 'I've rather outgrown England.'

'Oh, Henry, how I love you,' she whispered.

'And I love you too, my darling,' he replied. 'But that's not quite good enough any more, is it?'

For a long time they sat facing each other, saying nothing.

'Henry, I don't want us to end up this way. Can we not be friends? Please take up Nellie's invitation and visit us before we go. See Catherine. At least come and see Catherine.'

He promised. It was the easiest course. Henry was not a man to stay at the gambling table once he knew he had lost his winnings.

Quietly they finished their drinks. Henry smoked his cheroot. Suddenly he stabbed it into the ashtray. He contemplated Helen

Frances coolly. There was a hint of a smile on his face. 'I don't think I've told you tonight how beautiful you look,' he said. 'Lincolnshire's in for a bit of a shock. Come on, my darling, let me escort you out of here. Hold your head high, 'he added, taking her arm. 'After all, we both have our reputations to consider, don't we?'

They left the tearoom arm in arm. The heads of the few remaining guests turned away as they passed, but the room buzzed with animated chatter in their wake. Henry winked conspiratorially. 'I don't think they'll forget Widow Cabot for a time,' he smiled – and after a moment she smiled back.

Henry escorted her to the foot of the stairs.

'You'll come to see me again before you go?' she asked urgently. 'You'll come to see the baby?'

'Try to keep me away,' he said.

He leaned forward to kiss her cheek. She grabbed his head and pulled his mouth to hers. In full view of the doyens of the Hôtel de Pekin, they made a last, passionate kiss. It was Helen Frances who broke away, running up the stairs as fast as her dress would allow her. The gossipmongers afterwards could not agree whether they were pants or sobs they heard, as she turned the corner and disappeared down the corridor.

Somehow he managed to keep the smile on his face until she was gone, but when he turned he had the face of a dead man.

Henry made his way slowly to the door, leaning heavily on his stick.

He did not immediately call a rickshaw. He hobbled slowly down Legation Street in the direction of the canal. Night had fallen and the sky was glittering with stars. He smoked a cheroot. Its smoke coiled into the cold air. After a while the pain in his leg tired him, and he hailed a passing rickshaw.

He did not notice the beggar who had been sitting on the corner by the Japanese Legation, who got up after he passed and followed the rickshaw at a loping run.

Airton kept to his room, nursing his mild fever. There were some uncharitable types who construed that there was something diplomatic about this cold. Many of his colleagues among the missionary community, for example, would have liked to be told a lot more about the Shishan massacre. Some of the journalists, who had descended on Peking in the wake of the relieving forces, sensed a story. There were so many questions still to be answered, not least about the remarkable way in which the Airton family had escaped the general slaughter. At first there had been some sympathy for the survivors of an atrocity of this magnitude – especially in view of the hardships that everyone knew the Airtons had suffered during their escape. Airton's continuing silence, however, had its inevitable effect, and after a while old friends like the Gillespies found themselves taking a defensive attitude when the subject of Shishan was mentioned. Nobody said it outright, but there was a general feeling that it might have been more respectable for the head of one of God's missions, like the captain of a sinking ship, to have stayed at his post. Older missionaries shook their heads over their cups of tea. Young curates, about to start on a missionary life, were given patronising little lectures about the selfless fortitude required in their work, and how they must be wary of all too human frailty when faced with temptation or trial. The American missionaries were understandably smug. One of the Protestant foundations produced an inspiring little pamphlet bordered by a black wreath, profusely illustrated with drawings of hands folded in the attitude of prayer, kneeling figures holding candles, and not a few angels outstretching welcoming arms among the clouds – all these touching details surrounding a centrepiece consisting of daguerreotypes of Burton Fielding and Septimus Millward. The Airtons were not mentioned in the accompanying text. Nor were the Roman Catholic nuns.

It did not help that the Airtons were in the company of the young, attractive, and rather too composed widow, Mrs Cabot. As the bereaved wife of one of the martyrs – Tom might not have been a missionary, but he had been a gentleman, and came from a good public school, which included muscular Christianity among its traditions – it might have been expected that Mrs Cabot and her child would also have been deserving of sympathy, and even some of the reflected glow of martyrdom, but besides the equally imponderable question of how she, too, had managed to survive, the friendship that was apparent between her and the unsavoury Mr Manners, another dubious survivor, also set respectable tongues a-wagging.

In fact, there was something smelly about the whole affair, and after a while, despite the unquestioned saintliness shown by the likes of Millward and Fielding, it became the habit, when memorialising the martyrs of the Boxer madness, to focus on the demonstrably nobler sufferings of victims in such places as Taiyuanfu and Baoding, where there had been no embarrassing survivors, and to leave Shishan to a minor mention, if it was recalled at all.

If Nellie and Helen Frances were aware of these undercurrents, they did not show it. They spent the ten days that they were in Peking shopping in the silk markets, pushing a rented perambulator through the Ritan Temple Park, and taking the children to see the Forbidden City, the Temple of Heaven and all the other imperial sites, which, under the protection of sentries from the Allied armies, had been opened up since the siege, to the general public – or, rather, to any European civilian who applied to visit.

On most days Henry Manners would accompany them on these walks, keeping pace as he could with his game leg. A perceptive observer might have noticed a certain melancholy in his expression, except when he cast his eyes, as he frequently did, to the perambulator in which a well-wrapped little Catherine gazed up at the strange world passing over her head. Then a doting, almost wistful, quality would briefly animate his features, to be replaced, if anything, by an even greater melancholy when he looked away. George and Jenny would run and play with the scampering excitement of puppies off a leash, and sometimes Henry would join in their games, lifting – it took him an effort, these days – a giggling Jenny on to his broad shoulders as he had once done in that vanished world of Shishan, or reaching into his pockets to give George a daily souvenir, a carved seal, or an interesting stone and, once, a tile in the shape of a dragon's head. He appeared easier in the company of the children than the adults. When the latter walked together – the children off ahead – there was little conversation. What there was was inconsequential, remarks about the weather, admiring comments about the architecture, plans for the next day's sightseeing, but there was no animosity or tension either. The silence was comforting. Everything there was to say had been said, and they were relieved to be able to walk together in subdued familiarity, like old friends.

Sometimes Henry would have tea in the Hôtel de Pekin with them afterwards. Usually he made his excuses and returned to his house in the Chinese Quarter, where Fan Yimei would already have prepared his opium pipe. His expression when he was alone in his room was not of restrained melancholy but open and agonised despair.

On the penultimate day before their departure – all the shopping had been done, the packing finished, the arrangements made – they went for a stroll by the frozen lakes in the Hou Hai. The children skated. Nellie, Helen Frances and Henry sat on a bench and watched. Surreptitiously, so that Nellie would not notice, Helen Frances put her gloved hand into Henry's. He turned in surprise and saw the tears blurring her green eyes. She managed a smile. Tactfully, he turned away his head, looking rigidly to his front. They held hands until it was time to leave.

When they reached the Hôtel de Pekin, Helen Frances asked him if she could come back to his house. 'Just for a short while, a cup of tea, perhaps. I'd like to take farewell of Lao Zhao and Fan Yimei. To thank them,' she said. Henry looked questioningly at Nellie.

Nellie smiled and pecked him on the cheek. 'You two go ahead,' she said. 'Henry, we'll say our goodbyes tomorrow when you come to see us off at the station.'

'I won't be long, Nellie,' said Helen Frances.

'You take just as long as you like,' she replied, bustling the children through the door.

Henry hailed a rickshaw. They sat stiffly together in the narrow seat, covered by a blanket against the cold. When they reached the uneven paving stones of Great Eastern Street, the rickshaw wobbled, and Helen Frances was bounced against Henry's chest. He put an arm round her to steady her, and kept it there. She nestled her head against his chest. He kissed her forehead. She lifted her face to look into his. Her mouth was slightly open and there was a soft, yearning look in her eyes. He kissed her gently, then more passionately. She responded, urgently. They passed under the ruins of the Hatamen Gate in full, desperate embrace.

Under the blanket, inside her fur coat, his hand rounded her waist, his fingers slipped into her waistband, and up, under her blouse, to fold around her breast. Her hand was inside his shirt, stroking his chest. Their lips were burning, their tongues entwined. They were oblivious of the amused stares from the passers-by in the crowded streets of the Chinese city, as they jostled and peered with their usual curiosity inside the leather curtains. Their rickshaw coolie began to shout at a mule cart, which was blocking his way. Languorously,

Helen Frances moved her head to rest on his shoulder. 'This is mad, Henry,' she whispered. 'It won't change anything,' but her hand was softly moving across his stomach. She sighed as she felt his finger knead her nipple. They kissed again.

They reached the gate of his house. Henry paid off the coolie who trotted away, grinning. Helen Frances was smiling at him. 'Well, kind sir, and what plans do you have for this poor young widow-woman who's fallen under your spell again?' she whispered, resting her arms on his shoulders. He kissed her forehead, her nose and her lips. They hugged in the empty street. He took her hand, and pulled her after him. Playfully, she resisted, laughing. Suddenly he paused, in the act of reaching for the door-knocker. 'That's odd,' he said. 'The gate's been left open.'

She giggled, squeezing against him. 'Maybe they knew we were coming,' she whispered.

The courtyard was empty. 'Where is everyone?' he muttered, closing the creaking wooden door.

'Don't call them. Not yet,' whispered Helen Frances, running her hand up his arm. She reached for his chin and pulled his mouth on to hers. They embraced tenderly, their bodies moving slowly against each other. Henry gently disengaged himself. 'No, Helen Frances, something is wrong. Lao Zhao should be here.' His face was showing concern. 'He should be over there in the kitchen cooking the supper. He always does at this hour.'

Helen Frances watched, impatiently at first, as he limped over to the kitchen and looked inside, but she showed alarm at the grim set of his face when he returned. He crossed the courtyard to the room that led off perpendicularly from the main hall and peered through the darkened windows. 'Fan Yimei's not here either,' he said. 'Come, you'd better wait in my sitting room while I search the rest of the house.' She took his arm and they climbed the three steps to the main hall, which had been divided into Henry's sitting room and bedroom. He held open the door for her. 'At least they've turned on the lamps,' he said, and noticed that she was standing stock still in the doorway, staring at something inside. Her body was quivering, and her wide-eyed expression registered severe shock. At the same moment he heard a familiar voice: cold, reedy, sardonic. 'I think that you had better come in too, Ma Na Si. Quietly, behind the fox woman.' Over Helen Frances's shoulder he could see into the room. Major Lin – it was clearly Major Lin, although he was dressed in rags – was reclining in his armchair. He was relaxed, as he could afford to be, because in his hands was a Luger, the barrel of which was pointing at their heads.

'Please, Ma Na Si, come inside and sit on the sofa with your hands where I can see them. And you too,' he added, turning the gun on Helen Frances.

'It's all right. I won't let him hurt you,' whispered Henry, brushing the back of Helen Frances's hair with his lips. She nodded, moved jerkily into the room; he followed her, steadying her arm. Keeping their eyes on Lin, they went to the sofa to which he was gesturing, and sat down. Opposite them, on the other sofa, he saw Lao Zhao and Fan Yimei, on whom Lin had been training his gun earlier. Lao Zhao was looking angry and truculent. He pointed his finger at Lin's revolver and shrugged as if trying silently to say to Henry, 'What could I do?' Henry was gazing intently, however, at Fan Yimei, whose face was bruised and bleeding, and she was clutching one shoulder, which seemed to be giving her pain. Lin observed him carefully, an amused smile on his lips.

Fan Yimei noticed the anger that had burned in Henry's eyes. 'No, Ma Na Si,' she said urgently. 'Please don't do anything. I'm not hurt. Please be calm, Ma Na Si. Remember the wisdom of the night.'

'The wisdom of the night?' said Lin, raising his eyebrows superciliously. 'This whore of mine has a great gift for poetry, does she not? Is that why you stole her from me, Ma Na Si? Or do you consider her a fair exchange for that whore of yours I enjoyed? I see that the fox woman still remembers me. She can't keep her eyes off me.'

Henry squeezed Helen Frances's hand. 'Ignore him,' he whispered. 'He's only trying to scare you, but he can't hurt you. That's what you told me. He can't hurt you. He doesn't exist.'

'What are you saying to her, Ma Na Si? Are you asking her which one of us she enjoyed more between her thin thighs? Oh, she wriggled nicely under me. But you were there. You saw. Would you like to see me give it to her again?'

'I was under the impression that you were the type who preferred taking it to giving it, Major,' said Henry softly. 'Or, at least, that's what Colonel Taro told me.'

Lin's smile disappeared. For a moment his eyes spat venom,

but when he spoke again, his features had resumed their cold sneer.

'You're very bold, Ma Na Si. That is one thing I admire about you. You and I, we share some things in common – besides our women. Let us talk no more about whores. I have done with them. They are not important. I give them to you. Both of them. This is not a time for petty matters of revenge.'

'I assumed it was revenge that brought you here, Major.'

'You are wrong, then. I have come because you still possess something that belongs to me.'

'Fan Yimei doesn't belong to either of us, Major,' said Henry.

'I told you, I am no longer interested in whores. Even that one. Although I did take the opportunity to punish her for her ingratitude earlier while I was waiting for you. She, too, will remember me.'

'You know, I've noticed something about you, Major. You can be rather pompous,' said Henry. 'Like your old master, the Mandarin, who you murdered.'

'Do you think that by provoking me you will make me drop my guard? I will not react to such simplicity, Ma Na Si. I will use this gun if you force me to, but I will shoot one of the others, not you. I would rather that you and I got on with our business without these delays.'

'There's only one sort of business I have with you, and I'd rather do that man to man outside.'

'Please, Ma Na Si, you tire me. I have come for the guns. You will tell me where they are and then I will go. You made an agreement. You took the payment. It is now for you to deliver to me the secret of where the guns are hidden. If I am satisfied I will leave. You see, I am not even asking you to return the Mandarin's gold, which you stole without honouring your side of the bargain.'

'Any bargain I made was with the Mandarin.'

'You are wrong. You made a bargain with China. The guns belong to China. Now the Mandarin is gone I will act for him, as he himself acted for China.'

'You *are* pompous. You haven't noticed, perhaps, that China has recently been soundly defeated?'

'The Court and the forces of superstition have been defeated. These guns will be used to build a new China, after all your foreign armies have departed. A better China.'

Henry was about to retort sarcastically. He saw Fan Yimei's soft eyes pleading with him. He looked at Helen Frances who was sitting rigidly beside him, her mouth half open, staring at Major Lin, like a rabbit hypnotised by a snake.

'You say you'll go if I honour my side of the bargain?'

'If you satisfy me with the truth, as a gentleman to a gentleman.' Lin's cold eyes were almost expressionless.

'And if you should find out that I've deceived you?'

'Then I will be disappointed to have found out that you are not a gentleman, Ma Na Si, and I will return for my revenge – on you, but first on your whores. You will not be able to protect yourselves against me, however hard you try.'

'All right,' said Henry. 'I agree.'

'Is this another trick?'

'No, I will give you the map on which the arms cache is clearly marked. It's in that desk behind you. In a locked drawer at the back. The key's in there. Why don't you get up and take it?'

Lin smiled.

'Because when my back is turned you will attempt something foolish. No, you get the map.' He turned the gun to point directly at Helen Frances. 'If I suspect any trickery, I will shoot your whore between the eyes.'

Keeping the gun pointed at Helen Frances, he sprang to his feet with surprising agility, moving backwards slowly until he was standing at a point where he could observe both the desk and the hostages in the room. 'Now,' he said to Henry, 'you may get the map, if it really is there.'

Henry squeezed Helen Frances's hand one last time. 'It'll be all right,' he said. 'Just stay very calm. He can't hurt you.' She nodded. 'There's my girl,' he said. He reached for his walking stick and pulled himself to his feet. Slowly he limped to the desk and opened its lid. He pulled open a drawer on the left and retrieved a small key, leaving the drawer open. Leaning forward, he inserted the key into a lock on the right, and turned it twice. He pulled open the drawer. It was a long one, which reached right to the back of the desk. He inserted his arm and appeared to grope for something. Slowly he pulled out a canvas package, tied with string. As Lin watched suspiciously, he untied it, then unfolded the canvas. It was, indeed, a map. He spread it out on the front of the desk. 'Come and see,' he said. 'X marks the spot.'

Lin hesitated. 'Do you want me to bring it to you?' asked Henry. 'It'll be easier for me to show you if you come here.'

'No tricks,' warned Lin, edging towards him. The Luger was still aimed at Helen Frances.

'Here, where my finger is,' said Henry. 'You see where the railway branches to Mukden. A little to the left. You see the contour lines that mark the hills. There's a small gully here where there is a cave . . .'

As Henry spoke, Lin bent his head down to see. As he did so, Henry reached into the drawer he had first opened and snatched out his service revolver. In the same flashing movement, he pressed the muzzle against Lin's head, cocking the revolver as he did so. Lin froze, but his own gun was still pointing unerringly at Helen Frances. For a long moment nobody moved. Then Lin's twisted mouth curved into a smile.

'Very clever, Ma Na Si. You fooled me by showing me the actual map. I take it, it is the real one? Yes, of course it is. What happens now? Do I shoot the fox woman and do you shoot me? Or do we finish this matter in some other way?'

'I'm giving you three seconds to drop your gun,' hissed Henry. His eyes were burning.

'And what if I were to shoot your lady first?'

'I'll risk that,' said Henry. 'I'm firing in three seconds. One . . . two . . .'

With a strange laugh, Lin dropped his Luger on to the floor. Lao Zhao was on his feet before it had fallen and scooped it up. With a roar of pent-up rage, Henry struck Lin's face with his gun barrel. Lin staggered backwards, and Henry struck him again. Blood jetting from his broken nose, Lin stumbled forward and fell on his knees. Berserk with fury, Henry pistol whipped him until he fell. He knelt down and pulled Lin's face up by the hair. He thrust the barrel into Lin's mouth.

'Henry!' From far, far away he heard Helen Frances's voice calling him. 'Stop it. That's enough.' He felt soft arms pulling at his shoulders. Wildly, he turned his head, and saw Helen Frances and Fan Yimei, their imploring faces. He groaned, and threw the gun aside. Wearily, he allowed the women to pull him to his feet.

He staggered forward, and fell into the armchair, panting, spent. Helen Frances was kneeling beside him, pressing her head to his breast. Tears were running down her cheeks. 'It's over,' she kept repeating. 'It's over, Henry, it's over.' After a while, he nodded.

He looked to where Lin was groaning on the floor. Lao Zhao stood over him covering him with the Luger. 'Fan Yimei,' he whispered, 'pick up that map. Give it to him. Tell him to get out of here, and never come back.'

He leaned his head on the back of the chair and closed his eyes. Helen Frances kissed his face, his lips.

'You can't just let him go, Ma Na Si,' Lao Zhao was protesting. 'Let me take him out to the well. No, a simple drowning's too good for him. Let me beat him up a bit more first and then drown him,' he pleaded.

'No, Lao Zhao.' Henry smiled. 'Just give him the map. It's over now. Finished.'

Grumbling, Lao Zhao pulled the recumbent man to his feet. Lin swayed unsteadily, clutching his broken jaw. In his other hand he held the map. Lao Zhao kicked him towards the door. He stumbled forward, his rags flapping.

Fan Yimei was standing by the sofa, her eyes downcast. As he passed her, Lin paused. He was incapable even of a crooked grin now, but he could spit, which he did, in her face. His lips spattered blood. 'Whore,' he snarled.

Lao Zhao raised the gun. 'Don't tempt me,' he shouted. 'Be gone, you bag of toad piss!'

Lin hovered for a final moment by the door. His eyes surveyed the room and rested on Manners. He lifted the map. 'China thanks you,' he said, with some difficulty through his broken teeth. 'That whore,' he added, pointing to Fan Yimei, 'I give her to you.' They saw his other hand move quickly into the folds of his shirt. He appeared to pull something out and throw it. And with that he disappeared through the door.

It all happened so quickly that at first they did not understand why Fan Yimei was staggering. She seemed to be peering curiously at an object that protruded from her chest. With a low moan, she sank to her knees.

'*Ta made!*' shouted Lao Zhao. 'He's knifed her.' He ran out of the door in pursuit.

Henry and Helen Frances were by her side, supporting her. She was coughing, delicately, although blood was dribbling down her chin. She looked in some bewilderment at the two concerned faces beside her. Gently they laid her on the floor. Henry put a pillow under her head. 'Helen Frances, can you do anything?' Henry muttered. 'When you were with the doctor, did you . . . ?'

Silently, Helen Frances shook her head.

Fan Yimei lifted her hand to touch Henry's cheek, but it was too much of an effort. It fell, and she began painfully to cough. After a moment her sad eyes focused again. 'Ma Na Si,' she whispered, and smiled when she said the name. She frowned. She was making a great effort. 'Ma Na Si, will you promise . . . ?'

'Yes,' choked Henry. 'Anything.'

'Ma Na Si, will you promise . . . promise me . . . that you will forgive Lin Fubo? You will not . . . you will not . . . seek revenge?' The last word came out as a sigh.

'What's she saying? What's she saying?' Helen Frances asked urgently.

'She's asked me to promise not to take revenge on Major Lin,' said Henry, dully.

Fan Yimei could no longer speak, but her eyes begged him.

'Promise her, Henry.' Helen Frances's wide eyes bored fiercely into his. Her voice was shrill. 'For God's sake, if you love me. For everything I mean to you. Promise her, Henry.'

Henry looked at her wildly. He turned frantically to Fan Yimei, whose mouth was moving, although she could not speak. He grabbed her hands. Tears ran down his face. 'I promise,' he said. 'I promise.'

Fan Yimei smiled. The taut muscles in her cheeks relaxed. Her eyes lingered on Henry's face, moving slowly over his features, as if she was storing a last impression to keep with her for eternity. The soft brown irises examined his forehead, his nose, his lips, and moved upwards to take in his eyes again, and there they stopped moving, and remained fixed, slowly losing focus, glazing.

Lao Zhao came in quietly. He took in what had happened, the two kneeling figures with bowed heads by Fan Yimei's body. 'I lost him,' he muttered. 'I lost him in the side streets.' He threw the Luger on to the floor.

'Henry,' wailed Helen Frances, 'I can't take any more. I can't, you know. I want to go home.'

It was a hurried farewell. The Airtons arrived late at the platform, and then there was all the business of getting their luggage on board. The engine was steaming and the guard's whistle was blowing.

The doctor and Henry shook hands. Airton still found it difficult to look Henry in the face. He stumbled over his words. 'Mr Manners, I don't know how to ... I've not yet ...'

'You don't have to say anything, Doctor,' said Henry. 'We're parting as friends – and don't worry, you haven't seen the last of me. I'll come one day and drink some of your whisky and you can tell me all about Scotland the Brave.'

Nellie embraced him, unable to hold back her tears. 'You will visit us in Shishan?' she asked him urgently.

'You've really decided to come back, then?' he asked.

'Oh, yes, we'll be back,' she said. 'Someone had better try to undo all of that damage. I'll be expecting you,' she said, as she climbed into the carriage.

He gave his last presents to the children. 'Chinese kites,' he said. 'I want you to think of me when you're flying these from the top of Edinburgh Castle.'

'Coo, it's a dragon,' squealed George.

'And mine's an eagle. Thank you, Mr Manners.' Jenny was growing up now and conscious that she had to be polite.

He kissed Catherine, and watched as the *amah* carried her into the train – and found that he was left alone on the platform with Helen Frances. 'Are you all right?' he asked her softly.

'I thought nothing could hurt me again,' she answered. 'I was wrong. Why, Henry? Why? She was so good. So fine.'

'Pritchett says he'll alert the military police. They won't find him, though.'

'You'll remember your promise,' she said.

'I will,' he said.

'You must, you know. You owe her that.'

'I owe her a lot more than that,' he said.

'Funny,' she said. 'Us parting like this – and all we can think about is another woman.'

'Will you write to me?' he asked. 'You can always get a letter forwarded to me via my club.'

'Do you want me to?'

'Yes,' he said, 'to hear about Catherine. And you, of course. How you get on.'

'There won't be much to write about me. I intend to do nothing for a very long time.'

'Somehow I doubt that.'

'And you, Henry? What are you going to do?'

'I'll find something. Always have. I'll keep myself amused, somehow.'

'Oh, Henry,' she whispered.

The guard blew his whistle again.

'Goodbye, Helen Frances,' he said, kissing her on the cheek. 'I'm going now. I don't like staying to the very end.'

Abruptly he turned away. She watched him limp down the platform, his back erect. The engine driver pressed the lever to blow steam out of the cylinder cocks, and Henry became insubstantial, finally disappearing altogether in a cloud of smoke.

Chapter Twenty-three

Green shoots burst from a rich, wet soil. My wife scolds,
but one day
I will tell my son of his father's brave deeds.

10 April 1902

As the train arrived, Arthur Topps stuck his head out of the window and excitedly took in the first impressions of his new posting. The large sign above the wooden platform read 'Shishan' in three languages: Russian, English and Chinese. The neat white fences, the flower-beds, the smiling faces of the porters reminded him of a rural station in his own native Lancashire. He saw a large bird alight among the daffodils. Could it be a cuckoo shrike? He would have liked to look then and there in the beautifully illustrated book on birds he had bought in Liulichang on a shopping excursion with the Dawsons, but it was out of reach at the bottom of his bag.

Arthur had only a small trunk with him: the rest of his luggage had been sent on ahead. The black-bearded Russian stationmaster arranged for some porters to put it on to a trolley, and asked about his journey in broken English as they walked side by side along the platform. 'Train early,' he said, showing Arthur his fob watch. 'Wait with me in office. Have samovar,' he offered. 'Have nice tea cup. Mr Brown come soon.'

'Mr Brown?' asked Arthur, a little perplexed. 'I'm expecting to be met by a Mr Lu, our partner,' he said.

'Come. Have samovar,' boomed the stationmaster cheerily, patting him on the back.

At that moment two figures could be seen hurrying down the platform towards them: a young Englishman with wavy blond hair and an almost invisible moustache was calling, 'I say, are you Topps? I'm Brown. Sorry we're late.' Behind him Arthur saw a serious-looking Chinese, neatly dressed in a merchant's grey gown with a black silk waistcoat.

He bowed gravely as he came up to Arthur. 'Tuopasi Xiansheng,' he said, formally. '*Jiu yang. Jiu yang.* You are warmly welcome to Shishan. I am Lu Jincai. I have had the honour of working with your esteemed company for many years.'

'Mr Lu? Of course,' said Arthur, trying to remember the proper response. 'It's – it's I who should be saying *jiu yang*, Mr Lu. What you've done for Babbit and Brenner these last two years is much appreciated, even among the directors in London. You're – well, famous,' he added, a little flustered.

The man who had called himself Brown laughed. 'Come on, Mr Topps, there'll be time for all this later. Let's get you and your kit into the cart – no fancy traps here, I'm afraid. We'll talk on the way to town. I should introduce myself. I work with Dr Airton at the medical mission.'

Soon the pony-cart with them all aboard was climbing the hill. Arthur took in the breathtaking view – the little station and beyond it the rolling plains, the wide river and the train that was now steaming across an impressive railway bridge. The railtrack gleamed in the sunshine as it disappeared off north, towards a horizon of blue sky.

'Ah, you're admiring the Russians' great pride and joy, the Nicholas Bridge,' said Brown, lighting his pipe. 'Actually, they only finished it, they didn't build it. It was begun by the British, well, a German actually. He, poor fellow, was one of the victims of the Boxer madness. Before my time.'

'Oh, yes, I've heard all about that,' said Arthur. 'We lost two of our chaps in the massacre. In fact, I'm coming out to replace them, now that Mr Lu's got our business up and running again.' He smiled at the Chinese gentleman, who was driving the cart.

'You're referring to Delamere and Cabot, aren't you?' asked Brown. 'Airton won't talk much about those times. In fact, everyone here just wants to forget all about it. Even Nellie – that's Mrs Airton. You'll meet her – even Nellie's a bit closed-mouth about those days. Didn't Cabot's wife have a child in Mongolia or somewhere?'

'She did,' said Arthur. 'I met her in England before I came out. Oh, I quite forgot,' he said, turning to Mr Lu, who had been gazing ahead as the two young Englishmen spoke in their own language. Arthur switched to Chinese. 'I bear you the greetings of Mrs Cabot,' he said. 'She asked particularly that I pass on to you her warmest regards.'

Lu smiled. 'The fox lady,' he said. 'I remember her very well. Her father was a great man and a good friend of mine. De Falang was extremely proud of his beautiful daughter and so happy when she came to Shishan. I have often wondered what became of her.'

'Well, she's still very beautiful,' said Arthur. 'Lovely, actually, and her little girl's adorable. She was about to get married again when I met her.'

'Ah, yes,' smiled Lu. 'To Ma Na Si Xiansheng perhaps?'

Arthur looked puzzled.

'No, Mr Lu, to a Mr Belvedere, actually. He works for an insurance firm in the City. But just before I left I heard that the whole thing was off – there was a bit of a scandal apparently – and she was packing up to go on holiday to Japan or somewhere.'

Lu Jincai nodded silently. He smiled, and whisked the reins as they passed over a pot-hole.

'Ah, then perhaps she has gone to find Ma Na Si, after all,' he said, with a touch of smugness in his tone.

'If you say so, Mr Lu,' said Topps, now very bewildered indeed.

'Don't mind him,' said Brown confidentially. 'He's talking about a chap called Manners. Friend of the Airtons. He came here once, about three months ago, on a hunting trip. Stayed a couple of days. Odd, supercilious sort of character. Didn't like him, to tell the truth. He was also here before and during the Boxer madness. There were – how does one put it? – rumours that he and Mrs Cabot . . . It's all nonsense, of course, but the Chinese believe there was something going on between them. You'll find that these people, lovable though they are, are the most dreadful gossipmongers. Always getting the wrong end of the stick. I wouldn't think very much of it, if I were you. Don't, for Heaven's sake, raise this topic with the Airtons. They get very upset. My goodness, they do.'

'No, no, I certainly won't,' said Arthur, looking a little alarmed.

They drove on for a while in silence. The willows on either side of the road rustled in clouds of fresh green leaves.

'How long have you been in Shishan, Mr Brown?' he asked.

'Dr Brown, actually. I'm a medical missionary and a minister, but just call me Brown. I'm sure we'll be friends. I've been here just under a year. Arrived in June of 1901, a couple of months before the Airtons returned from home leave. The society thought they could do with a bit of help in rebuilding the mission. A pair of younger hands, you know. They'd had quite a terrible ordeal one way and another.'

'Was there – was there much to rebuild?' asked Arthur.

'I'll say. Place was a shambles. For a start the mission and the hospital had been burned to the ground. Pretty tense, too, with all the Russian soldiery about. There were executions, and the poor Chinese, most of whom had nothing to do with any Boxers, were scared for their lives. What do you expect with brute Cossacks allowed to run amok? Everyone was a Boxer in their eyes, and most of the time all they wanted to do was plunder. It was all rather shameful. One of those occasions when we white men did *not* set a good example.' He switched to Chinese. 'Mr Lu, we're talking about the period after the Boxers, when I first arrived in Shishan. Didn't the Russians give you some trouble too?'

'They were not happy times,' said Lu. 'It is better not to think about those days.'

'Cossacks went into Lu's home,' said Brown, in English again. 'He doesn't like to talk about what they did. They executed – well, murdered, actually – one of his best friends, another merchant called Jin. The man was entirely innocent. Oh, yes, you'll hear plenty of stories of that kind round here.'

'But what the Boxers did here was unforgivable,' said Arthur. 'Surely some justice was in order after the massacre?'

'Of course you're right,' said Brown. 'But who do you punish? Apparently they got some ringleaders. A few days after I arrived, they executed one notorious brute in the public square, some bandit with the rather quaint name of Iron Man Wang, whom they'd just captured after a big battle in the hills. They hung his body on the city gates in a cage where it rotted for months. Apparently he really had had something to do with all the atrocities. Even the Chinese say so – but the others? Well, who was a Boxer? Nobody will ever admit to being party to all of that, you know. Most of them, anyway, were just peasant boys. They emerged out of the fields, and now they've disappeared back into them. These days, it's fashionable to be a Christian, of course.' He laughed.

'Really?' said Arthur in surprise.

'No, I'm exaggerating,' smiled Brown. 'But it has been heart-warming to see the steady increase in conversions in recent months. Tell you the truth, I'm kept rather busy, though I'm helped by some very good Chinese lay pastors who I've trained. You must come to our next service – we have a proper church now on the site where the Airtons' old house used to be. The Catholics are here in force, of course. They're becoming a bit of a threat, to tell the truth, with quite a following. They've taken over an orphanage that used to be run by some Americans who were killed in the massacre. Dr Airton goes there quite often to help out on the medical side.'

'I heard a little about Dr Airton when I was in Peking,' said Arthur carefully.

'You probably heard a whole lot of rot,' laughed Brown. 'Oh, yes, I know the stories – but it's all malicious tripe. I've got to know him over the last year, and I can tell you there's nobody more courageous or downright decent on this earth. He's something of a saint, in his way. It's all one to him what denomination anyone is. He doesn't get too much involved in the missionary side of the work at all any more. As a matter of fact, he leaves that to me. He concentrates on what he's good at, which is healing people – but I'll tell you, more people have come to my door to ask about Jesus after being healed by him, or just having met him and been impressed by him, than any I could convert on my own account. He's exceptionally modest, selfless, unsparing of his time, doesn't live for anything except his healing work, and some of the cures he's made, why, if I didn't have the scientific basis to understand what he's doing, well, actually, I might think they were miraculous.'

'He sounds a marvellous man,' said Arthur.

'Oh, he is, he is,' said Brown. 'He's a saint, a living saint, as I've said. Not an ounce of bitterness in him, which you might have expected considering he was here right through the madness, and saw many of his friends put to death. In fact, you'd think it might never have happened the way he treats everyone – anyone – just the same. There's one man in our hospital, Zhang Erhao, who helps with the administration. He really was a Boxer, and by all accounts betrayed the Airtons. Well, this man came on bended knees shortly after the Airtons arrived back here, weeping and saying he was a Christian now, and Airton just raised him up, tears running down his own cheeks, and gave him his old job back. Oh, yes, Airton's a saint all right. The local people think so too. That's good for us. The Catholics haven't got anyone like him, you see. I say,' he said, a look of concern on his face, 'you're not Roman Catholic by any chance, are you?'

'No, I'm Church of England,' said Arthur.

'Well, that's a relief,' laughed Brown. 'Thought I might have put my foot in it, for a moment. Not that I've anything against the Catholics, of course, but it's good to have another member of the home team on board.'

'I'll – I'd be delighted to come to your service,' said Arthur, thinking that that was what was expected of him.

'Excellent. Excellent,' said Brown, puffing on his pipe.

'Are the Russian soldiers still here?' asked Arthur.

'Not in such numbers as before,' said Brown. 'There's a troop of cavalry in the barracks – not Cossacks any more, thank goodness. Their colonel, Tubaichev, sometimes comes round to dine with Dr Airton. Officially the Chinese are back in power. A new mandarin arrived at the end of last year and is ensconced in the *yamen*, but I don't know what he does. It's Tubaichev who calls the shots. Effectively he rules the place. He's not a bad sort – unlike his officers.'

'What's wrong with them?'

'Bunch of godless reprobates,' said Brown. 'Spend their time whoring and carousing in the Palace of Heavenly Pleasure.'

'What's that?' asked Arthur.

'The Palace of Heavenly Pleasure?' He laughed. 'You'd better ask old Lu here. It's not a place I've been near, I can tell you. Den of sin, run by a fearsome madam who might have stepped out of the pages of a penny dreadful. But Lu loves the place, the old rogue. He's probably itching to take you there. Mr Lu,' he said, switching to Chinese, 'do you plan to corrupt the morals of Mr Topps by taking him to the Palace of Heavenly Pleasure?'

Lu Jincai laughed politely. 'If Topasi Xiansheng wishes,' he said. 'The baked crab is excellent, and it is a place where we merchants gather from time to time.'

'Well, you make sure you stick to the baked crab, is my advice,' said Brown. 'Leave the after-dinner entertainments to the Russian officers.'

Arthur looked from one smiling face to another. He was not sure how to respond. 'Well, it sounds as if an interesting experience is in store for me,' he said.

Brown laughed. 'Well done, Topps,' he said. 'You experience everything. It's the only way. And remember, our church is always open to you if you find yourself tempted to stray off the straight and narrow. Seriously,' he added, 'you have to be broad-minded to get on here. China is still seething with every sin under the sun. We're doing our bit, quite a lot now, as I've said, to introduce these pagans to the True Path, but Airton – yes, it was actually Airton, one of the only times that I recall he spoke about the Boxer episode – said something to me that I've never forgotten. "We brought the madness down on our own heads," he told me, "because we had forgotten how to be humble." I spent a long time racking my brains to understand what he meant. And I think it's this. You're not going to change anyone by trying to make them into you. We know that the Christian path is the right one, but a Chinaman has his own way of looking at the world. We've got to find a means to cut our cloth to fit his. You won't get anywhere by judging too harshly, or forcing our superior knowledge down his throat. Best way to convert someone in fact is by not converting them at all. There's a conundrum for you, isn't it? Airton used a Chinese expression, which he said he'd got from the old Mandarin who lived here: "*wu wei.*"'

'Yes, it's from Lao Tse. The *Tao Te Ching*,' murmured Arthur.

'Oh, you know it, then?' said Brown, looking slightly disgruntled. 'Well, you probably understand what Airton was on about, then. Confess it's a bit deep for me, but I think it means something like "Everything good will happen in its own good time if you let it, and don't worry yourself in the meanwhile."'

'Yes, it's something like that,' said Arthur, blushing in case Brown felt he had been showing off.

The pony-cart trundled on in silence. Brown puffed on his pipe, his chatter interrupted – perhaps because Topps's knowledge of the Chinese classics had taken the wind out of his sails – but his was not a temperament to remain abashed for long. 'Well, Topps, what's the news from the big wide world?' he asked cheerily. 'What are they saying in Peking?'

'About politics, you mean?' asked Arthur. 'The Empress Dowager returned from exile in January. Most of the foreign troops are returning home. The Chinese government is working out how they are ever to pay the enormous indemnity that has been agreed. I – I think it's going to be difficult for them.'

'Serves them right,' muttered Brown, chewing his pipe. 'Hope some of the money comes our way. We've done well out of donations, and have rebuilt the hospital and put up a church, but there's a lot more we could be doing. Airton's set his heart on building a medical training school here. What else is going on?'

'There was a lot of talk about the deteriorating situation between Russia and Japan over this part of the world, Manchuria,' said Arthur. 'Rumours that one day there might be war between them.'

'Stuff and nonsense,' snorted Brown.

'I hope you're right. I had a conversation with a strange man in the British Legation who wanted to see me when he heard I was coming up here. A Mr Pritchett. Have you heard of him?'

'Can't say I have.'

'Well, he was anxious for me to write and tell him if I should ever come across any signs of the Japanese doing anything suspicious up here.'

'That's the trouble with diplomats,' said Brown. 'They live in a fantasy world. See conspiracies in the most innocent things. I'd forget about them if I were you.'

'There – there aren't any signs of Japanese here, then?' asked Arthur.

'Japanese? No, I've not heard of anything they're doing here. Well, there's a Japanese barber's shop in the high street. Funny little fellow who gives a good haircut. The Russian officers use him. And there was a Japanese officer who came through here on his way to a hunting trip in the Black Hills some while ago. Most sophisticated sort of cove for an Oriental. Dressed in tweeds. It was about the same time as that Manners fellow I was telling you about was here. In fact, I'm not sure if they didn't know each other. Yes, I think they did know each other, come to think of it. They both went to dinner with Colonel Tubaichev. Might have arranged to hunt together too. But that just goes to show you, doesn't it? Your Pritchard, or whatever you said his name was, would have woven a fantastic piece of skulduggery out of all that. And what could be more innocent than an officer taking his leave and hunting in the Black Hills? There are bears and even tigers up there. Some of the best hunting in Asia. And if Tubaichev thought there was anything odd in it, he wouldn't have invited them to supper, would he?'

'I daresay you're right,' said Arthur.

'No, it's not the Japanese,' continued Brown. 'It's the home-grown brew of bandits we have to worry about. There's one particular gang of disaffected Chinese army officers who were giving the garrison some bother in the Black Hills last Christmas. Preyed on the merchant caravans going up to Tsitsihar. Very well armed by all accounts, with modern rifles and howitzers and field guns and you name it. Tubaichev had to call for reinforcements and he himself led an expedition into the Black Hills. But they didn't find them. They'd dribbled off through the woods and are probably in Mongolia now. It's been quieter lately.'

As he was speaking he was peering ahead of him. He turned to Arthur with a happy smile on his face. 'There, ahead of us. Do you see it?'

Through the trees, Arthur saw a small hill, and on top of it green-tiled roofs gleaming in the sunshine. There was a square steeple on the crest, which looked as out of place in the Chinese countryside as a pagoda in an English village.

'That's our mission,' said Brown proudly. 'See the church? Gothic. Designed it myself. It's lovely, isn't it? We'll stop off at the hospital if Mr Lu doesn't mind and I'll introduce you to the Airtons. Don't worry. I'll come with you into town afterwards and see you settled into your hotel.'

The Airtons were not in the hospital. Zhang Erhao, the man whom Brown had said had been a Boxer, met them at the gate of the neat brick complex of two-storey buildings – the roof tiles might have been Chinese but the squat, purpose-built houses reminded Arthur of tenements he had known in Bradford. Arthur was a little nervous of this grey-pigtailed man who smiled ingratiatingly. He wondered what he had done to betray the Airtons – but Brown treated him casually enough. They were told that Ai Dun Daifu had gone to Shishan to visit the Catholic orphanage, and that Ai Dun Taitai was in the church at the top of the hill.

'Come on, let's go up there,' said Brown. 'She'll be tending the cemetery. She likes doing that. She's made a sort of martyrs' memorial out of it.'

'Martyrs' memorial?'

'Yes, didn't I tell you? That's where all the victims of the Shishan massacre are buried, what we found of them. Come on. I'll show you. You'll find your lot are up there as well – Delamere and Cabot, I mean.'

Nervously, Arthur followed Brown up the stone path that led to the top of the hill.

'Oh, I should warn you about Mrs Airton – Nellie, I mean,' said Brown, over his shoulder. 'On first acquaintance she might appear a bit fierce. It's her manner – but don't take any notice of it. Heart of gold, really. Heart of gold. We're great friends, Nellie and I,' he added. 'Great friends.'

Next to the church, behind a metal fence, was a little garden surrounded by newly planted yew trees. Inside, Arthur could see neat lines of gravestones to either side of a trim path. Daffodils were growing in profusion on the turf between the graves. The flower-beds, which bordered the path, still consisted of bare earth. Spring, he realised, came later in these northern parts. There was an atmosphere of calm and repose, as one might find in an English country churchyard.

The garden seemed to be empty, but after a moment he saw a tall, grey-haired woman wearing a straw sun-hat, stand up from where she had been kneeling behind one of the gravestones. In one hand she held some gardening scissors and in the other a bunch of freshly cut weeds.

'Well, well, Dr Brown,' she said, in a severe Scottish accent. 'So there you are. And where have you been all morning, may I ask? The wards in the hospital have been crying out for you.'

'Ah,' said Brown, a little taken aback. 'I've – I've been to the station to collect Mr Topps.'

'I see,' said Mrs Airton. 'And is Mr Topps – this young fellow here, I take it – incapable of getting here from the station by himself? I thought that it was arranged for Mr Lu Jincai to go there to meet him.'

'Well, to be sure, Mrs Airton,' muttered Brown, 'but I – I thought it might be hospitable, if I – if I . . .'

'Temporarily abandoned your duties to your patients, Dr Brown?'

'N-no, certainly not, Mrs Airton,' stuttered Brown. 'I – I . . .'

'Intended to return to your duties immediately? Was that what you were going to say?'

'Yes, of course. I – I'll go immediately, Mrs Airton. Um, Topps, I'm, er, sorry. I can't come into town with you now. We're rather busy here. I – I'll leave you. Yes. I'll call on you at your hotel – later.'

He backed out of the garden, his cheeks flushed with embarrassment. A moment later they heard the click of his boots as he descended the steps with some speed.

The grey-haired woman threw back her head, letting out a tinkling, rather attractive laugh. She walked forward with her hand outstretched to Arthur. 'I'm Nellie Airton,' she said. 'Welcome to Shishan, Mr Topps. Our young Dr Brown has no doubt been warning you about the dragon lady you would find here.'

'Not in so many words, Mrs Airton,' said Arthur, also smiling.

'He's a good boy,' she said. 'Very conscientious, but rather absent-minded and, goodness, what a chatterbox, as you've no doubt already discovered. From time to time the dragon lady has to take him in hand.'

'I'm sure he's very fond of you,' said Arthur, immediately comfortable in her warm presence. 'He spoke to me kindly of you, and of your husband.'

Nellie laughed again. 'Fond of me?' she said. 'He's scared to death of me. Well, never mind him. I am extremely pleased to meet you. Mr Dawson wrote to me about you, singing your praises. Now, let's take first things first. Have you eaten? Are you hungry? Have you a place to stay?'

'I believe that Mr Lu has booked me into a hotel in the town. Mrs Airton, I have a letter for you from Mrs Cabot.'

'Ah, yes, it'll be in answer to mine. Thank you,' she said, taking the envelope, and putting it into the pocket of her apron. 'Kind of you to carry it all this way. I'll read it when I have my spectacles. You know, Mr Topps, we would welcome you to stay with us here until you are settled. No? I understand. You wish to go ahead and explore this new world around you all on your own. You do remind me of young Tom when he first came to Shishan. You young things, you're all the same.'

'Tom?' asked Arthur. 'You mean . . . ?'

'Yes, I mean Tom Cabot.' She pointed at one of the graves. 'He's lying over there, poor boy. In peace, I hope.'

Arthur's glance followed her pointing finger to a small, square stone on which were inscribed the simple words, Thomas Charles Edgar Cabot, 1876–1900.

'I didn't put any mottoes on the gravestones,' said Nellie. 'I thought that the names alone would speak for themselves. They are remembered in the hearts of those who loved them.'

'May I? May I . . . ?'

'Walk around? Of course, take your time,' said Nellie. 'I have one or two things to finish off here. Then we'll give you and Mr Lu a bite to eat and see you on your way.'

As Nellie went back to her weeding, Arthur walked slowly down the path looking at the graves. Many of the names he did not recognise: Frederick John Bowers, 1867–1900, Emil Hermann Fischer, 1850–1900, the Reverend Burton Elijah Fielding, 1852–1900, Sister Caterina Pozzi, 1873–1900, Sister Elena Giubilani, 1874–1900. There were innumerable Millwards, most of whom had been so young, just babes. Babes! 1894–1900, 1895–1900, 1897–1900. That final, emphatic 1900, the year in which all those young lives had been extinguished – in the most brutal, brutal way. A sensitive man, he felt tears rising behind his eyes. He had, of course, read the accounts of what had happened in Shishan, but the reality of these graves was shocking in the extreme.

He felt Nellie's presence beside him.

'The youngest was only three years old,' she said quietly. 'Come, let me show you Frank's grave,' she said, 'and then we'll go down to lunch.'

He followed her along the path. On one of the two end stones was engraved simply 'Ah Lee', and the other 'Ah Sun'.

'They were our servants,' said Nellie. 'We couldn't find their bodies, but we wanted to remember them. They were very dear to us.'

He stood for a long time in front of the stone cross that marked Frank Delamere's grave, slightly separated from the others, next to a much older stone, which was the grave of Nellie's own infant son, who had died in childbirth in 1897.

'How – how could you bear to come back here?' he asked, after a while. 'With these memories?'

'Life must go on,' said Nellie simply. 'We must believe in better times to come. That there is purpose in the madness that humankind inflicts on itself. Otherwise, Mr Topps, there would be little point in going on living, would there?'

They had a simple lunch together in the hospital refectory. Towards the end of the meal the door opened and a bowed, white-haired man entered the room, supporting himself on a stick. Nellie introduced him to Arthur Topps as her husband. Dr Airton smiled kindly at Topps, but did not attempt to enter into conversation, quietly sitting down to his bowl of soup.

'Mr Topps has brought a letter to us from Helen Frances, dear,' said Nellie, speaking rather loudly. Apparently the doctor was a little deaf.

'Ah,' said the doctor.

'Yes, she's decided not to marry that man after all.'

'Oh. What a shame,' said Dr Airton.

Nellie chuckled. 'Well, my dear, can you imagine Helen Frances in the home counties? Playing croquet with the bank manager's wife and having the vicar to tea to discuss the next village fête?'

'No, it's difficult to envisage,' said Airton, finishing his soup. His pale eyes looked up at her over his spectacles; there was a hint of a smile on his red cheeks. 'I thought that I was supposed to be the busybody in the family, my dear,' he said quietly, glancing over the letter Nellie had passed to him.

Nellie's expression was one of pure innocence. 'I only wrote to tell her that a mutual friend had been to see us, and I may have mentioned that he was going on to Japan. I don't see what in the world is so busybody about that.'

'Well, you know what you're doing,' said the doctor, handing Nellie back the letter. 'I hope the poor girl doesn't have a wasted journey, and that she finds what she is looking for.'

'Oh, Edward,' said Nellie, seriously, 'let us pray she does. Do let us pray so.'

She noticed that Arthur Topps was looking at her with wide-eyed curiosity.

'Yes, Mr Topps,' she said brightly, 'my husband and I were talking about Helen Frances – Mrs Cabot. Did you have a chance to spend much time with her in England?'

'Alas, not very long. She gave me lunch when I called at her aunt's cottage in Sussex, and I met her daughter too. It was a marvellous afternoon. We talked about so many things. Her father and his work here. The sights I should see. And – and so much else. She was very kind to me.' He paused. 'She's – she's a lovely person, isn't she?' He blushed.

Nellie smiled. 'Aye, she is lovely. A rare bloom. Rather too exotic, perhaps, for an ordinary suburban garden. But I see that you sensed that for yourself, didn't you, Mr Topps?' She laughed at his confusion. 'Oh, Mr Topps. How I am embarrassing you! You don't know what I'm talking about, do you, and why should you? But you have brought us very happy news today, from a dear friend.'

'Mrs Airton, may I ask you a question? Who is Mr Manners?'

Nellie exchanged a quick glance with her husband, who raised an eyebrow and quietly spooned some vegetables into his bowl. For a moment she looked at Arthur severely, but her eyes had a smile in them when she replied, 'Ah, Mr Topps, what a question! Who indeed is Mr Manners? I think that is something we would all like to know, perhaps he himself most of all, poor dear. We'll find a time to sit down together, I promise you, and I'll tell you all the old stories, but not on your first day in Shishan. You have many other more exciting things to do and see, and Mr Lu sitting over there so quietly is itching to take you away. Now, would you like some more rice before you go? Or some vegetables? Or some tea? No? Then I'll ask only one thing of you. I want your word that you'll come back and visit us – often, do you hear? Good luck in Shishan, young man,' she said, offering him her hand.

Dr Airton also stretched out a hand to him as he passed. For such a frail-looking man the handshake was strong and firm. 'Good luck, my boy,' he said. 'Godspeed.'

Lu Jincai and Arthur Topps continued their journey. They spoke about the alkali plant, which Lu Jincai had rebuilt with his own money after the Boxers had sacked it. He brought Arthur up to date on their growing business with Tsitsihar and other towns in the region. Arthur told him about the new processes that Babbit and Brenner would like to introduce.

They turned a corner of the road and there before him were the walls of the city, rising like a fairy-story castle out of the plain and topped by a great turreted gate that might have come out of a medieval romance.

'Shishan,' said Lu Jincai, unnecessarily.

'It's – it's beautiful,' murmured Arthur.

They had to dismount from the cart for it to be inspected by the Russian soldiers. Arthur gazed above him at the swallows that were flying about their nests on the battlements.

He heard a strange mewing sound from his left and, looking down, saw a beggar sitting with his back to the city wall. It was a blind man, with a shaved head. He wore the robes of a Buddhist priest. The white, sightless eyes seemed to be contemplating him eerily. A little boy, accompanying the priest, held out a wooden bowl. Embarrassed, Arthur patted his pockets for a coin.

As it clicked into the bowl, he heard Lu Jincai calling him. The inspection was over. Forgetting the beggar, he climbed back on to the cart, and next minute he was looking up at the great portcullis that hung over his head.

With growing excitement, Arthur Topps entered Shishan. He felt that he was starting a new chapter in his life – the beginning of a great adventure.

Afterword

When I began to write this romance about the Boxer Rebellion I had very much in mind my own family antecedents in China. I would not be alive today if my great-grandfather, a Scottish medical missionary, had not managed to flee through the northern gate of the city of Changchun while the Boxers were coming in through the southern gate. If the Boxers had caught him in the city, he would almost certainly have been killed, and my grandmother would never have been born.

Since those days one or other member of my family has always been involved with China, either as doctors, railwaymen or businessmen. I was born in Hong Kong, my mother in Qinhuangdao, her mother in Changchun. I grew up on the Peak among the *taipans* in Hong Kong. For the last eighteen years I have been living and working in Peking (Beijing) employed by one of the oldest China trading houses.

This is not a family history. Far from it. My beloved grandmother would be rolling over in her grave at the suggestion that any of the dreadful characters I have created bear any resemblance to her own dear mama and papa – although I have taken the liberty of giving my central missionary character a passion for Wild West shockers, which, in our family lore was my Presbyterian great-grandfather's one indulgence, and I have awarded him a medal for his work in the plague. I have had handed down to me just such a medal – the Order of the Golden Dragon – awarded to my own great-grandfather in the closing years of the Qing Dynasty. It is the size of a saucer with glistening yellow scales, and holding it in one's hand, one feels a strange affinity with a vanished world: cruel and corrupt, magnificent and mysterious.

My city of Shishan is invented, but the type of things that happen there did occur in other parts of China. In 1900 there was a massacre of more than seventy missionaries in the city of Taiyuanfu in Shanxi Province. My former classics teacher, Hamish Aird, gave me letters from his great uncle, one of the victims, written from confinement in the uneasy days before the mass beheading. They are extraordinarily moving testaments of human courage and Christian acceptance of martyrdom. I have drawn on these to colour my own story, and one day last summer Hamish and I made a pilgrimage to the ground in front of the *yamen* in Taiyuan where his great-uncle died. By an extraordinary irony, we discovered that my Chinese wife's great-grandfather had been an official in Taiyuanfu at the time, and probably attended the executions. While Hamish was still staying with us, we had a dramatic game of Murder in the Dark with my children, when my wife, Fumei, became convinced that Hamish would use the opportunity of the darkness to wreak his revenge on her for the crime her family had committed against his a hundred years before!

When western people talk about the Boxer Rebellion most people think of the siege of the Legations. Anyone who has seen the movie *Fifty-five Days at Peking* will remember the aplomb with which David Niven, Charlton Heston and Ava Gardner held off the devil hordes. There have been some excellent histories of the siege, the best in my view still being Peter Fleming's *The Siege At Peking* published in 1959, although a number of new works came out to coincide with the anniversary year of 2000, including Diana Preston's *The Boxer Rebellion*, Henry Keown-Boyd's *The Fists of Righteous Harmony*, a collection of contemporary accounts *China 1900: The Eyewitnesses Speak* and, most interesting of all, the publishing of Sir Claude MacDonald's own report of the siege and other Foreign Office papers and telegrams of the time in the collection *The Siege of the Peking Embassy in 1900*, edited by Tim Coates. The contemporary accounts that occasionally find their way into print are well worth reading. I particularly recommend Polly Condit Smith's *Behind the Scenes in Peking* (written under the pseudonym Mary Hooker) and B. L. Simpson's *Indiscreet Letters From Peking* (again written under a pseudonym, B. L. Putnam Weale). The latter book is so scurrilous and the author so odious that I have been unable to resist making B. L. Simpson a character in this novel.

Yet all these accounts relate primarily to the siege and foreigners' heroics, which play a relatively small part in my story. I was more interested in the Boxers themselves. How could such a bizarre movement come about? And what was happening in the vast

Chinese countryside? After all, anyone who has lived in such an inward-looking country as China knows that the occasional bouts of anti-foreign xenophobia are usually impelled by internal dynamics that often only incidentally have anything to do with the foreigners who are the ostensible cause, and that in any violent eruption here the main victims are usually Chinese persecuted by other Chinese. The official view of the Chinese Communist Party is that the Boxers were proto-revolutionaries who were motivated by patriotic fervour and a nationalistic desire to protect the motherland. This has not always been the Chinese judgement, as Paul A. Cohen shows in his magnificent study of the historiography of the rebellion, *A History in Three Keys*. In the years just after the rebellion, Chinese writings about the events expressed horror at the superstition and the darker, animist side of their psyche that had been unleashed with such violent results. Some modern Chinese historians (and even senior Communist Party officials, if one talks to them privately) are now studying how this fundamentalist peasant movement, which in its origins was actually apolitical (as Joseph W. Esherick reveals in his brilliant study *The Origins of the Boxer Uprising*) were manipulated and subverted for the interests of factions in the Imperial Court. Is there any relevance in the Boxer explosion to the Chinese politics of today? Well, the serious reaction by the Chinese government to what many people in the West would see as a harmless mystical cult, the Falonggong, surely shows some fear of the animistic fundamentalism that many centuries of Confucian civilisation have not yet managed to eliminate, and which, if manipulated, might be turned to political ends. It was fundamentalist movements such as these that in historical times, destroyed dynasties (the White Lotus, the Yellow Turbans, the Taipings). Perhaps in 1900 the manipulators in the Imperial Court were right to turn the powerful forces unleashed in the countryside against the foreigners: the anger of these martial artists could just have easily been turned on them. As it was, the decrepit, corrupt Qing dynasty lasted only another eleven years before it was overthrown in the Nationalist revolution of Sun Yat-sen. The Mandate of Heaven was already being removed from their weakening grasp.

For the background of missionaries in China and their sufferings far away from Peking when the Boxer madness overwhelmed them I have drawn on contemporary books such as *Fire and Sword in*

Shansi, which, published in 1902, is an exhaustive account of the many 'martyrdoms' that took place two years before; Dougald Christie's *Thirty Years in Moukden* is a fascinating memoir of a medical missionary's life in north China. (Another family link is there as well: Dr Christie and my great-grandfather set up the Moukden Medical School together in 1912); the Christian epic *A Thousand Miles of Miracle* by A. E. Glover, and many others. I have dug deep into Nat Brandt's moving history of the Oberlin missionaries, *Massacre in Shansi*. For the details of Frank Delamere's alkali-making processes I have drawn on Patrick Brodie's history of ICI's early years in China, *Crescent over Cathay*. Frank's company, Babbit and Brenner, is a thinly disguised version of ICI's Brunner Monde (and again there are family links: my grandmother's second husband, R. D. L. Gordon, worked in China for ICI for thirty years.) For the activities within the Palace of Heavenly Pleasure I have read with much entertainment the extraordinary sex manuals that date back two thousand years and which Robert van Gulik introduced to the world in his magnum opus, *Sexual Life in Ancient China*.

Most of the events that take place in this novel, however, despite the historical context, in which they happen are pure fiction. In the balance between fact versus adventure and romance I have come down firmly on the side of the latter, hopefully for the enjoyment of the reader, certainly for my own.

I have many people to thank: my wife and children for allowing me to hide away in my study on weekends and public holidays, thus forgoing many enjoyable jaunts and picnics to the Great Wall. I fear that I have been an inattentive father these last five years. I would like to thank Humphrey Hawksley, Philip Snow and David Mahon for their constant encouragement and advice, and Peter Batey, who has sat patiently through readings of each chapter, giving me valuable advice on, for example, how to control a Mongolian horse or what would be on the menu at the Legation picnic, or how to decorate a Chinese railway carriage. I would like to thank Clinton Dines and Patrick Holt for their expert advice on how to drive a steam train, and Section Chief Yang of the Camel Camp section of the Liaoning Railways for allowing me to stand on the footplates. Thanks to Dr Simon Helan for letting me know how I might go about saving a shot Mandarin. I am grateful to Professor Wang Yi for his insights into the animism of the Boxers. My thanks to T. C. Tang for first teaching me Chinese and to His Holiness Professor Thomas Lin Yun for enlivening Chinese lessons with red herrings about the art of *feng shui* and Chinese mysticism. Finally I would like to thank Araminta Whitley, my agent, and Peta Nightingale, my editor, for their firm advice, and Carolyn Mays and Hodder and Stoughton, my publishers.

Adam Charles Newmarch Williams, Beijing, May 2002

About the author

Adam Williams, whose family has lived in China since the late nineteenth century, was born and raised in Hong Kong. For the last eighteen years he has been representative in Beijing of a Far East trading conglomerate. In 1999 he received an OBE for services to Sino-British trade. Adam is married to Fumei and has two children.